SHAUN HUTSON OMNIBUS

Captives
Breeding Ground

D1584570

SHAUN HUTSON OMNIBUS

Captives
Breeding Ground

SHAUN HUTSON

timewarner
paperbacks

A *Time Warner* Paperback

This omnibus edition first published in Great Britain by
Time Warner Paperbacks in 2003
Shaun Hutson Omnibus Copyright © Shaun Hutson 2003

Previously published separately:
Captives first published in Great Britain in 1991 by
Macdonald & Co (Publishers) Ltd
Published by Warner Books in 1992
Reprinted 1997, 1998, 1999, 2001
Reprinted by Time Warner Paperbacks in 2002
Copyright © Shaun Hutson 1991

Breeding Ground first published in Great Britain in 1985 by
Star Books, a Division of W.H. Allen & Co plc
Published by Sphere Books Ltd in 1990
Reprinted 1990
Published by Warner Books in 1998
Reprinted 2000
Reprinted by Time Warner Paperbacks in 2002
Copyright © Shaun Hutson 1985

The moral right of the author has been asserted.

*All characters in this publication are fictitious and any
resemblance to real persons, living or dead, is purely coincidental.*

All rights reserved.
No part of this publication may be reproduced, stored in a retrieval
system, or transmitted, in any form or by any means, without the prior
permission in writing of the publisher, nor be otherwise circulated in any
form of binding or cover other than that in which it is published and
without a similar condition including this condition being imposed on
the subsequent purchaser.

A CIP catalogue record for this book
is available from the British Library.

ISBN 0 7515 3499 4

Printed and bound in Great Britain by Clays Ltd, St Ives plc

Time Warner Paperbacks
An imprint of
Time Warner Books UK
Brettenham House
Lancaster Place
London WC2E 7EN

www.TimeWarnerBooks.co.uk

Captives

Dedicated to Mr Wally Grove.
My most valued friend.
From one unsociable bastard
to another.

Acknowledgements

As with all my books, there now follows a list of everyone or everything that contributed to the writing and beyond. Even if it was only to try and keep yours truly something approaching sane. To everyone mentioned you have either my thanks or my admiration (some even have both).

Extra special thanks to Gary Farrow, my manager, for his continuing efforts to ensure that anyone but *us* pays for expenses (and, no, I'm still not wearing a bloody suit). Thanks, mate. Thanks also to Chris Page at 'the office' (despite his taste in football teams). Many thanks to Mr Damian Pulle, the Houdini of the VAT returns.

Very special thanks to Nick Webb for his faith and his matchless ability to find gut-busting restaurants. To John O'Connor, Don Hughes, Bob Macdonald, Terry Jackson and Dave Kent and, especially, *all* my sales team for hammering everyone into submission. You don't release this lot, you *unleash* them. Thanks also to everyone in publicity and marketing. Extra special thanks to Caroline Bishop who put up with me 'on the road' (I promise to wear a vest next time, C.B. . . .). But to everyone who contributed to a superb campaign, I thank you. To Barbara Boote and to John 'I know that one' Jarrold, many thanks. In fact, to everyone at Little Brown/Warner I extend my thanks.

Special thanks, as ever, to Peter Williams and Ray Mudie. To Tom Jones (no, not *that* one) and UCI. To Steve Hobbs at Bletchley Library for his help and interest.

Very special thanks to Mr James 'this is how this one is going to end' Hale, editor *par excellence* (have I spelt that right, James?).

To Brian 'I've got two tickets here and by the way there's another one arriving soon' Pithers. To Graham Rogers at 'Late Night Late' (I always wanted to be on TV, Graham). Thanks also to 'Mad' Malcolm Dome and Phil Alexandar at *RAW*, to Jerry Ewing at *METAL FORCES* and to Krusher at *KERRANG*! (and GLR of course . . .) Thanks to Gareth James, John Gullidge, Nick Cairns and John Martin. To John Phillips, or should I say Rikki . . .

Massive, immeasurable thanks to David Galbraith (and to *ROCK POWER*) for the meat pie and the day of a lifetime and also to Dave 'can I have your autograph Mr Gilliam' Evans.

Extra Special thanks to the phenomenal Margaret Daly who tried to kill me in Dublin, but in the nicest possible way. Thank you for your amazing work.

Many thanks, as ever, to Broomhills Pistol Club, particularly to Bert and Anita. To Dave Holmes who sat and talked to me without giving a toss I'd only end up with three hours sleep. Thanks, mate . . . Keep the sick jokes coming.

Special thanks to all the staff and Management at The Holiday Inn, Mayfair, for their continued friendliness and kindness. Thanks also to everyone at Dromoland Castle in Ireland, to the Mandarin Oriental in Hong Kong, the Barbados Hilton and to Bertorelli's in Notting Hill Gate.

Thanks are due, as ever, to Steve, Bruce, Dave, Nicko and Janick for allowing me to share their stage and re-live more dreams. I am eternally grateful. Thanks also to Rod Smallwood, Andy Taylor, everyone at Sanctuary Music and to Mr Merck 'sliced into fifteen pieces by lunchtime' Mercuriadis.

Many thanks to Mr Jack Taylor, Mr Amin Saleh and Mr Lewis Bloch for all their help and advice. Thanks also to Mr Brian Howard at Russells for removing a rather annoying stone from my boot.

Thanks, for different reasons, to Alison at EMI, Shonadh at Polydor, Georgie and Zena.

Many thanks to Ian Austin who deserves a line on his own and who, in fact, deserves much more. The man whose ability to talk is surpassed only by his value as a friend. Thanks.

Indirect thanks to Queensrÿche, Nevada Beach, Thunder, Harlow, Black Sabbath and Great White. Also to Oliver Stone, Martin Scorsese, Walter Hill and Michael Mann.

This novel was, as ever, written on Croxley Typing Paper, wearing Wrangler Jeans and Puma Trainers (I don't give up easily you know . . .) Also many thanks to Yamaha Drums, Zildjian cymbals and Pro-Mark sticks for helping me clear numerous mental blocks . . . (come on, if I can try for some jeans I can try for a cymbal or two . . .)

My greatest thanks, as always, go to my Mum and Dad for everything they've done and continue to do and for my long suffering, ever-patient wife, Belinda. For putting up with me through this and other novels and for enduring the ups and downs of yet another season of me worshipping Liverpool FC, you have, and always will have, my thanks and my love.

And to you, my readers, for still being there, for sticking with me, thanks. To those of you joining the ride for the first time, welcome. Thank you all.

Shaun Hutson

Revenge is a kind of wild justice . . .
Francis Bacon

PART ONE

What is good? All that heightens the feeling of power, the will to power, power itself in man

Nietzsche

I don't believe in Love,
I never have, I never will.
I don't believe in Love.
It's never worth the pain that you feel.

Queensrÿche

One

He knew he was going to die.

Knew it.

He didn't *think* he might. Didn't *wonder* if he would.

Brian Ellis *knew* he was going to die.

The barrel of the shotgun was less than a foot from his face. It poked through the shattered remains of the safety glass partition, so close he could smell the oil and cordite from the yawning muzzle.

From that muzzle seconds earlier had come a thunderous blast which had ripped through the toughened glass as if it had been spun sugar.

It had been at that point that Brian Ellis had filled his pants. He stood there now, reeking. Standing there with a dark stain spreading across the front and back of his trousers. He couldn't think, couldn't move. All he was aware of was the sickening warmth around his lower body
coated in his own excreta.

And he was aware that he would die.

He wanted to scream. Wanted to be sick. Wanted to pray. Wanted to bellow at the top of his lungs that he was
only twenty-three and he didn't want to die. *Please don't kill me. Please, Jesus Christ, God Almighty for fuck's sake
don't make me die.*

The barrel of the Spas wavered closer to him and he began shaking uncontrollably.

Alarm bells were ringing; somewhere else in the bank

3

a child was crying. A baby. Someone was sobbing. Someone was moaning.

Brian heard the sounds but none registered in his mind.

All that registered was the sure and certain conviction that he would soon be dead.

The alarm had gone off automatically as soon as the safety glass had been blasted away. There had been no furtive attempts by one of the other cashiers to find the alarm button that linked the bank directly with Vine Street police station. There'd been no need. Besides, this wasn't a film where the cashiers and customers stood around calmly (if somewhat worried) while tills were rifled, lives were threatened and then masked men ran from the bank into the arms of the law, who had arrived in the nick of time after being alerted by that single, secret alarm. *How comforting was fiction.*

The man who stood in front of Brian Ellis wasn't wearing a mask; he hadn't warned everyone to be quiet, hadn't told them that if they did as they were told no one would be hurt.

He had walked straight through the door of the Midland Bank in the Haymarket, pulled a Spas automatic shotgun from inside his coat and opened fire. First he shot a woman who had been standing close to the door counting money before she pushed it into her purse. She now lay in a bloodied heap, her limbs tangled like those of a puppet with cut strings. Her handbag and its contents were strewn across the marbled floor, some five pound notes having come to rest in a puddle of her blood.

Scarcely had the sound of the first shot died away than the gunman had fired again, into the counter glass. It had exploded inwards, showering those behind it with fragments of needle sharp crystal. One of the other cashiers had suffered a badly cut face. It was her moans

4

that Brian could hear as she tried to pull a thin fragment of glass from one corner of her eye.

The child he could hear crying was in a pram at the other end of the counter. The mother was crying softly too.

Don't make me die.

His mind shrieked it again.

The gunman was looking at him, as if he had recognised him. A vague recollection of a face seen in a crowd. *His* face was calm, his eyes narrowed. These were not the staring eyes of a madman. There was deliberation in his movements. He appeared unfazed by the strident ringing of the alarm bells that continued to fill the bank.

'Give me the money,' the man said calmly, his eyes never leaving Brian's.

But Brian couldn't move.

'Now,' the man snapped, pushing the barrel of the shotgun closer to the cashier's face.

Despite its earlier lapse, his bladder managed to bring forth more. Brian felt more fluid running down his leg, soaking into his trousers.

Please don't kill me.

He could feel the tears welling up in his eyes.

Dear merciful Christ, not now.

'The money,' rasped the gunman through clenched teeth.

The child was still crying.

'Shut that fucking kid up,' snarled the man without turning his head. He actually poked the barrel of the Spas against Brian's cheek.

Sirens.

Oh sweet fucking Jesus. Lord God in Heaven please . . .

The sirens were blaring from the direction of Piccadilly. They would be here in a matter of moments.

Please, make him go. Please God, make him go now.

5

The alarms continued to screech. The baby was still crying. And the sirens came closer.

A look of mild annoyance passed fleetingly across the gunman's face. He took a step back.

Not now. Don't make me die now, Please God don't . . .

He fired once, the barrel only six inches away from Brian's face. The report was massive, drowning out all the other sounds for a moment as the discharge tore most of the cashier's head off. He remained upright for a second, blood spouting from what remained of his cranium, then he pitched forward, sprawling over the counter.

If God had heard Brian's prayers he had chosen to ignore them.

The gunman turned and headed for the door. As he reached it he paused and looked at the woman with the pram.

The child was still crying.

He looked at her, then at the pram, then he fired twice.

Both blasts struck the pram, ripping through it.

He pushed the door and walked out into the street.

Those passing saw the shotgun; some screamed, some ran. Some just froze.

A police car, blue lights spinning madly, sirens screaming, came roaring around the corner into the Haymarket. The gunman gritted his teeth and looked behind him. The traffic lights were on red.

The traffic was at a halt.

He tossed the Spas to one side, digging inside his jacket for a pistol. Pulling the Smith and Wesson 9mm automatic free, he ran towards a motorcyclist who was idly revving his engine, watching the lights, waiting for them to change. Exhaust fumes poured from the pipe of the 850cc Bonneville.

6

The lights were still on red.

The police car drew closer.

The gunman shot the motorcyclist once in the back of the neck, pushing his body from the bike, gripping the powerful machine by the handlebars to prevent it toppling over. He swung himself onto the seat, twisted the throttle and roared off, the back wheel spinning madly on the slippery road before gaining purchase.

He swung left into Panton Street.

The police car followed.

Two

As the Bonneville rounded the corner into Panton Street its rider found himself faced with an oncoming car.

The driver of the car blasted on his hooter as much in surprise as annoyance, looking on in bewilderment as the bike shot up onto the pavement and sped off.

A second later the police car skidded round in pursuit, slamming into the front of the car as it passed, shattering one headlamp.

Inside the police car Constable Norman Davies was speaking rapidly into the two-way radio, giving the location of the unit and also attempting a description of the man they were pursuing. He gave the number plate, forced to squint to read it as the bike hurtled back and forth from pavement to road, swerving past both parked and moving cars alike. Davies also called for assistance and for an ambulance to go to the bank in the Haymarket; although he had not seen the carnage inside, it was standard procedure.

Besides, he and his companion, Ralph Foster, now hunched over the wheel in concentration, had seen the motorcyclist shot. Davies winced as he remembered the police car inadvertently running over one of the dying man's outstretched legs.

He was informed that other mobile units were in the area and closing in on the bike, and that routes were being shut off. The man, he was assured, wouldn't get far.

Foster spun the wheel to avoid an oncoming car, jolting the Rover up onto the kerb. The driver of the other car also struggled to guide his vehicle out of the way. The blue lights and the wailing sirens were remarkably effective in clearing a path through even the most densely packed traffic, thought Davies, still gripping the handset, one eye on the fleeing gunman.

'Heading for Leicester Square,' Davies observed as the bike roared on.

Fragmented phrases floated to him across the airwaves as the Rover hurtled on in pursuit.

'. . . closing in from Coventry Street . . .'

'. . . three dead . . . Haymarket . . .'

'. . . in pursuit . . . identity unknown . . .'

'. . . armed . . . dangerous . . .'

Davies couldn't agree more with the assessment of their quarry.

The bike was heading towards the junction of Panton Street and Whitcomb Street. Leicester Square lay just beyond.

From an underground car park ahead a van emerged, reversing in front of the bike. The rider didn't hesitate, merely gunned the engine and sent the Bonneville rocketing up onto the pavement once more, ignoring the two people who had just emerged from the Pizzaland on

8

the corner. He struck one. The other managed to jump back but hit the window of the restaurant and the glass gave way. There was a loud crash as he fell backwards through the clear partition, sprawling across a table as glass rained down on him.

'Oh Christ,' murmured Davies.

The bike spun to the left again, up Whitcomb Street, still against the traffic.

Foster twisted the wheel and the rear of the Rover skidded on the wet ground, spinning round to slam into the side of the van. A jarring thud seemed to run the length of the vehicle, and both policemen winced, but Foster floored the accelerator and sped after the bike.

The rider did not once afford them even the most cursory glance. He was hunched over the handlebars, gripping the throttle, seemingly oblivious to the cars he sped past in the wrong direction. The wind streamed into his face, sending his shoulder-length hair flapping out behind him as he rode.

The street seemed to be filled with a cacophony of blaring hooters and shouts or screams as pedestrians found themselves forced to leap from the pavements as the Bonneville surged along, its rider oblivious to those he struck.

Ahead he saw a man snatch a child up into his arms and duck down beside a parked car, shaking as the police car also passed within a whisker of them.

Another police car was approaching from the left, lights and sirens joining its companion in a discordant melody.

The motorcyclist paused for a moment then sped off up Wardour Street, past the Swiss Centre, pursued now by two police cars.

'Units covering from Shaftesbury Avenue,' a metallic voice informed Davies. 'Give your position.'

9

He did just that, almost dropping the handset as Foster sent the car slamming into the side of a passing transit, sparks spraying into the air as metal grated on metal. A hub-cap came free, Davies didn't know from which vehicle, and went spinning across the road.

Many pedestrians had now stopped on the roadside and were watching the chase. Others walked on, ignoring it. More than one tourist hurried to take photos.

The Bonneville was speeding towards the traffic lights at the top of the street, leading into Shaftesbury Avenue.

They were on red.

'Right, you bastard,' snarled Davies.

The rider worked the throttle and gathered speed.

Still red.

The needle on the speedo of the motorbike touched sixty. The bike shot across the lights as if fired from a cannon.

'Keep going,' yelled Davies, watching the bike speed past an oncoming Sierra, causing the driver to brake suddenly. There was a loud crash as a Cortina close behind slammed into the back of the other car. The Sierra was shunted forward, rolling towards the onrushing police car.

Foster swung the car round and paint ripped from the rear of the vehicle as it scraped the front bumper of the Sierra. But they were clear of the crossroads, heading up Wardour Street now, the motorbike still trailing exhaust fumes, the police sirens still wailing. Behind them the second car had narrowly missed the pile up in Shaftesbury Avenue and it, too, was in pursuit. From a side street Foster glimpsed another motorbike, a white one.

A police bike.

One second was all it took.

One second of broken concentration, then he heard Davies screaming a warning.

As he looked back through the windscreen he saw a man step in front of him.

Three

The police car was doing fifty when it hit the pedestrian.

The impact catapulted the man into the air where he seemed to hang, as if magically supported, for several seconds before crashing back to earth, bones splintered and blood pouring from several ragged gashes. He rolled over in the gutter and lay still.

Davies looked back over his shoulder to see that the second police car had pulled up and one of the officers was getting out to look at the luckless soul.

'Jesus, Jesus fucking Christ,' shouted Foster, his face a mask of horror and revulsion. 'I couldn't stop. I couldn't . . .' He was breathing heavily, his face as white as milk. Davies said nothing; he merely gripped the handset and watched as the motorcycle policeman cruised up closer to the fleeing Bonneville.

He was almost level with his quarry when the rider reached inside his jacket and pulled out the automatic.

'No,' shouted Davies, as if in warning.

He saw the pistol being raised, pointed at the head of the motorcycle policeman.

The rider of the Bonneville fired once.

The high velocity round powered into the face of the other rider, blasting through the right cheek, pulverising the zygoma. At such close range the lethal bullet exploded from the policeman's skull through the left occipital bone, even blasting through his helmet, which

11

filled with blood. Portions of bone and smashed helmet flew into the air, carried on a geyser of crimson.

The bike merely flopped hopelessly to one side, colliding with a stationary car. The policeman was hurled from the seat, sprawling across the bonnet, blood spattering the windscreen.

The Rover sped past the body.

'Lima Six come in.'

The voice on the two-way, startled Davies and he jerked in his seat, hesitating a moment before answering.

'Lima Six, go ahead, over,' he said breathlessly, still watching the escaping motorcyclist up ahead.

'Lima Six, be advised that Oxford Street and all roads leading off it are now closed by other units,' the voice told him.

Now there's nowhere for him to go, Davies thought triumphantly. *Nowhere else to run, you bastard*.

'Lima Six, do you read? Over.'

'Understood, we will continue pursuit. Over and out.' He jammed the handset back onto its clip on the dashboard and leant forward slightly. 'Let's get this fucker,' he hissed.

The rider had still not looked behind him. Only when he reached Oxford Street did he glance over his shoulder, to see that the Rover was gaining on him. He looked right and left and noticed that there were two police cars moving towards him from the direction of Charing Cross Road. Ahead of him Berners Street was blocked; he could see police cars and uniformed men moving about on the pavement. Half a dozen of them moved towards him.

He turned the bike to the left, revved the engine and sped off down Oxford Street towards Oxford Circus.

The Rover came hurtling out of Wardour Street, wheels squealing on the tarmac as Foster struggled to keep it under control. He succeeded and the car roared off after its prey like a predatory animal in search of its next meal.

Traffic on both sides of the road had been halted; the only vehicles moving were the motorbike and the pursuing Rover.

Pedestrians stood, immobilised by shock, staring. From the safety of their own vehicles other drivers watched the chase, some with amusement, some with irritation. Always bloody traffic hold-ups in Central London.

A thought suddenly struck Davies.

He snatched up the two-way.

Ahead of them the Bonneville was slowing down, the rider swinging it round so that it was facing the shops. Onlookers scattered in terror as he revved up, looking towards the oncoming Rover.

'Is Ramillies Place sealed off?' Davies asked urgently.

'Negative. It isn't possible to get a car . . .'

The voice trailed off.

No, not a car.

The narrow walkway that led from Oxford Street to Ramillies Place wasn't wide enough to get a car through, but it *would* accommodate a bike.

Just wide enough for a bike.

The bike appeared to be aimed at the narrow alley next to Marks and Spencer but, as the police car drew nearer, Davies saw that it was not.

'What the hell is he playing at?' muttered Foster.

The motorcyclist revved his engine for what seemed like an eternity, the back wheel spinning, leaving great rubber slicks on the road as he held the power in check. He might have been daring the uniformed men to come closer.

The car was within fifty yards.

13

Exhaust fumes poured into the air around the bike, so thick that it appeared the machine was on fire.

Thirty yards.

He looked to his left and right and saw cars converging from both sides.

Fifteen yards.

He released the throttle and the bike rocketed forward.

The gap that would take him to freedom beckoned.

He was less than twenty feet from it when he turned the bike towards the window of Next.

The Bonneville hit it doing sixty, erupting through the thick glass, which exploded in a dense shower. Several shop window dummies were carried into the store by the impact, one trailing along, tangled in the front wheel of the bike by the garments it was dressed in.

The bike cartwheeled but the rider held on, like a rodeo rider anxious not to lose his mount, his face hideously cut by the glass.

Even when the bike exploded.

The blast shook the building, blowing out what remained of the front window, a searing ball of flame enveloping the machine and the rider. As he hit the ground his skull seemed to fold in on itself, the bone crumbling as he struck the floor with incredible force, sticky portions of brain bursting through the riven skull.

He lay beneath the remains of the bike, the flames devouring his flesh, stripping skin from his bones. Blisters rose, burst and then blackened as the fire engulfed him, turning him into a human torch.

Those who'd been in the store when he crashed through the window fought to escape the scene of devastation. Members of staff fled past fire extinguishers in their haste to flee what could rapidly become an inferno.

14

Uniformed men now forced their way in, held back by the flames that had engulfed the Bonneville and its rider, who now lay beside two blazing mannequins. As the fire destroyed them they dissolved, their false limbs melting in the ferocity of the inferno. One, still wearing the remains of a silk camisole and knickers, its false hair scorched off, seemed to roll over onto him, the heat twisting its plastic limbs into grotesque shapes, bending and moulding its arms so that they seemed to close around the dead man in a final fiery embrace.

Four: 29 December 1976

They had pulled three bodies from the wreckage.

The fourth they had found at the roadside, obviously thrown clear when the Metro first crashed.

The car was on its roof, a tangled mass of metal that looked as if it had been attacked by a gang of thugs wielding sledgehammers. The field in which it had finally come to rest was strewn with pieces of metal that had been torn from the chassis as the car had cartwheeled into oblivion. Other objects were also scattered around.

A high heeled shoe.

A handbag.

A couple of cassette tapes.

A watch.

A severed hand.

Wally Hughes gathered them all up, moving slowly round the wreckage, dropping the personal effects into a plastic bag. They might help with identification when the time came. The occupants of the car certainly couldn't. So bad were their injuries it was even difficult, at first glance, to tell which were male and which female. The driver had been impaled on the steering column. It had taken Wally and two of his companions over twenty minutes to remove the corpse, one of them vomiting when the body came in half at the waist as the torso was finally freed. Whoever had been in the passenger seat had fared no better. The head had been practically severed by broken glass when the windscreen had shattered. Portions of skin still hung from the obliterated screen like bizarre decorations.

Christmas decorations?

Wally shook his head and sighed, stooping to pick up a blood-flecked wallet. Death at any time of the year was a terrible thing, but at Christmas it seemed even more intrusive. In his twelve years as an ambulanceman he had noticed how the public seemed to take on an almost lemming-like mentality. Despite warnings every year not to drink and drive, to take more care in dangerous road conditions, men and women (sometimes children too) were pulled or cut or lifted piece by piece from car smashes. Huge pile-ups or single-vehicle accidents. What did it matter? Death was death, whether it happened to one or twenty at a time.

This time there had been four.

The car had come off the road at speed, obviously, hit a grassy bank, ploughed through a low stone wall, cartwheeled and ended up on its roof. How had it happened?

That was always the first question that came into Wally's mind as he approached the scene of an accident. He didn't even consider things such as, 'Will the victim be alive? If so, how bad will the injuries be?' Besides, it was usually simple to tell, on first glance at the scene

16

of carnage, how likely it was that there would be any survivors. In this particular case he had taken one look at the wreck and decided that the ambulance would be driving straight to the morgue, not the emergency wing of the hospital.

He picked up a glove, dropped it into his plastic bag and straightened up, wincing slightly at the pain from his lower back. Rheumatism. The cold weather always exacerbated it and tonight was cold. There was a thick coating of frost on the grass and the road was icy, especially on the bend.

Perhaps that was what had happened. The driver had lost control on the slippery road. Perhaps he'd been going too fast. Perhaps he'd been drunk. Perhaps he'd been showing off.

Perhaps. Perhaps.

None of that seemed to matter now. They wouldn't know why it had happened, not for a few days. In the intervening period, Wally and his companions would have countless other accidents to deal with. At Christmas time the ambulance service in Greater London alone dealt with upwards of 3000 emergency calls a day.

Merry Christmas.

By the roadside two ambulances stood with their rear doors open, the blue lights turning silently. The glare of their headlamps cut through the blackness of the night, one set pointing at the wrecked Metro. In the gloom Wally continued with his task of recovering personal effects. He noticed that blood had sprayed over a wide area around the car; it glistened on the frosted grass, appearing quite black in the blinding whiteness of the headlights. There was little talk among the other men as they went about their tasks. There was a weary familiarity about the whole thing. It wasn't the first time they'd seen it and Christ alone knew it wouldn't be the last.

The head of one of the passengers in the rear of the car had hit the back of the driver's seat so hard they had found three teeth embedded in the upholstery. Now, as he flicked on his torch and shone it over the ground, Wally found two more teeth. He picked them up and dropped them into the bag.

A police car was also parked close to the bend, and one of the officers was making notes. As soon as identification of the victims was made it would be the job of the police to notify the next of kin. Wally was glad he didn't have to do *that* job. It was one thing to pull a man from a car, a man who was still screaming despite the fact that he had no face, but it was something else to sit calmly opposite a mother and inform her that her son was dead. To tell a father his daughter had been crushed beneath a lorry, that it had taken twenty minutes to scrape her brains up off the road.

Wally shone the torch over the ground once more, then headed back towards the wall, stepping through the gap the car had made on its fateful passage.

He was heading towards the closest ambulance, glancing across at two of his companions lifting the fourth body on a stretcher, when he heard the shout.

'This one's still alive.'

Five

'We drew the short straw again.'

Detective Sergeant Stuart Finn fumbled in his jacket pocket for his Zippo, flipped the lighter open and lit the Marlboro jammed between his lips.

As the lift slowly descended he glanced across at his companion who was gazing distractedly at the far wall.

'I said . . .'

'I heard you,' Detective Inspector Frank Gregson told him, his eyes still fixed on a point on the wall.

Finn looked at his companion then across to where his gaze seemed fixed. He noticed a fly on the wall, sitting there cleaning its wings.

The lift bumped to a halt and Gregson glanced up to reassure himself that they were at the right floor. As he stepped towards the door he swung the manila file he held, squashing the fly against the wall, where it left a red smudge.

'I know how he feels,' murmured Finn as he stepped from the lift. The doors slid shut behind him. 'Flies eat shit, don't they?'

Gregson didn't answer.

'I *certainly* know how he feels,' the DS added wearily. 'Well, come on, Frank. Any ideas who this joker might have been?'

'How the hell am I supposed to know?' Gregson said. 'They drag the bloke out of a fire after he's been chased halfway across the West End. By the time they get him out he's so badly burned his fucking mother wouldn't even know him. If he's got one.'

Their footsteps echoed dully in the long corridor as they approached New Scotland Yard's forensic labs. Signs proclaimed: PATHOLOGY. Gregson looked down at the file again, glancing at the number in the top right-hand corner. That was all the man was to them at the moment. A number. No name and *certainly* no face. That had been burned away along with most of the rest of him. But he had to be identified and that job was to be done by the Yard's forensic pathologists.

Once identification had been made it was the task of Gregson and Finn to find out why the man had run amok.

Finn took a drag on his cigarette and swept a hand through his thinning hair. He was twenty-nine, a year younger than his superior but his bald patch (which worried him) made him look older. Gregson was greying at the temples but, he told himself, the light hairs were the result of stress and not the onset of more mature years. Both men were thick-set, Finn perhaps a little slimmer, although his belly strained unattractively against his shirt. He'd put the weight on a few months ago when he first tried to give up smoking.

Gregson opened the door of the pathology lab. The two men walked in.

'Where's Barclay?' the DI asked a man in a lab coat who was fiddling with a microscope slide.

The man nodded in the direction of a door marked PRIVATE: NO ENTRY BY UNAUTHORISED PERSONNEL.

Both policemen made for the door. Gregson knocked and walked in without waiting for an invitation.

It was cold inside the pathology lab.

The cold and the smell were two of the things that always struck him. The acrid stench of death and sometimes decay. He had seen things inside this room that others only saw in nightmares. *Call it an occupational hazard.*

The chief pathologist, Phillip Barclay, had his back to the men as they entered. He glanced over his shoulder and nodded a greeting. Behind him banks of cold cabinets stood like huge filing drawers. A storehouse for sightless eyes. Freezers containing bodies or awaiting them. On one of six dissecting tables lay a body covered by a sheet. It was towards this table that the two

20

policemen walked, their footsteps echoing even more loudly in the high-ceilinged room.

'If you've come looking for answers I'm going to have to disappoint you,' said Barclay, turning to face them.

Gregson looked challengingly at him, watching as the pathologist swung himself off the stool on which he'd been sitting. He walked across to the dissection tables and pulled the sheet back.

'Shit,' murmured Finn.

The shape beneath the sheet was little more than a blackened skeleton. Flesh, crisped and blackened by the fire, still clung to the bones but it looked more like a coating of thick ash ready to fall off at the slightest touch. A few teeth gleamed whitely through the blackened mess, but much of the skull had been pulverised on initial impact. Finn could see tiny fragments of brain, also blackened, welded to the inside of the shattered skull.

'I've examined what there is of him, obviously,' said Barclay, pulling the sheet further back and stepping back, arms folded. 'But it's going to be a long job identifying him.'

'What about dental records?' Gregson wanted to know, his eyes never leaving the corpse.

'As you can see, most of the head is gone. Obliterated. He hit the window head first when he went through it. Actually, that's the strange thing. From the extent of the damage to the head and upper body I'd say he was leaning forward when he hit that window.'

'Meaning?' Gregson wanted to know.

'He intended to do it. He was making *sure* he killed himself.'

'Looks like he did a pretty good job,' Finn remarked, sucking on his cigarette.

Barclay looked disdainfully at him.

'Don't smoke in here, please,' he said.

Finn looked aggrieved.

'Why? It's not going to bother *him*,' he said, nodding towards the corpse.

'It bothers *me*,' the pathologist said, watching as Finn nipped out the cigarette, burning his fingers in the process. He dropped the butt into his jacket pocket.

'You *could* identify him from dental records, though,' said Gregson.

'Like I said, it won't be easy. It'll take time but it's not impossible.' There was a long silence broken again by Barclay. 'How many did he kill?'

'Including the baby, five. Six more are in hospital, one on the critical list. It doesn't make sense,' Gregson observed, shaking his head. 'The whole thing was clumsy. He robbed a bank, but he left with no money and in a way which almost guaranteed he'd be caught. Then, when he *could* have escaped, he killed himself.'

'Bit elaborate for a suicide, isn't it?' Finn mused.

'Couldn't you take any prints from the guns?' Gregson asked.

Barclay shook his head.

'He was wearing gloves.'

The DI chuckled sardonically.

'Gloves but no mask. He didn't care if we got a look at his face but he didn't want us identifying him by his fingerprints.'

Again the silence.

'Can you get a report to me as soon as possible, Phil?' Gregson asked.

'I told you, it will take time.'

'Just do it,' the DI snapped.

'If he isn't in our records it's going to take even longer,' Barclay reminded the policeman.

'You're the expert,' Gregson remarked and headed for the door, followed by Finn.

As soon as they'd left the lab, the DS lit up another Marlboro. They headed back towards the lift.

'Why did he kill himself?' Finn muttered, sucking on the cigarette.

Gregson could only shake his head.

'Perhaps when we know who he is, we might know *why*?'

'You don't sound too hopeful.'

Gregson jabbed the 'Call' button on the lift.

'You saw the body. Would *you* be?'

It was probably part of the motorbike.

Perhaps even a fragment of the shop floor. The dead man had certainly hit the floor hard enough. Barclay didn't rule out the possibility that part of it had been embedded in the pulped skull upon impact.

The pathologist held in his tweezers the small piece of melted matter he had taken from the pulverised remnants of the killer's head. He gazed at the tiny melted fragment gripped between the prongs.

The intense heat had melted it, leading him to believe that part of it was some kind of plastic – incredibly hard plastic.

Barclay considered the fragment a moment longer, then dropped it into a petrie dish.

It would need closer analysis.

He reached for the phone on his desk.

Six: 14 March 1977

The room was small.

Less than fifteen feet square, its full extent was slowly revealed as lights were turned on one by one. Puddles of light filled the gloom, each one scarcely strong enough to fight off the blackness that shrouded the six occupants.

Doctor Robert Dexter stroked his chin thoughtfully as the light above him came on, bathing him in its cold white glow. He scanned the faces of the others in the room, listening to the soft click as each successive spot lamp was illuminated.

He was joined a moment later by a slightly older man who cleared his throat self-consciously, aware of the silence and apparently anxious not to disturb it. He pulled a chair closer to Dexter, wincing when it scraped the wooden floor noisily. He sat down and pulled nervously at the sleeve of his jacket.

The room was windowless, the only brightness inside provided by the spotlamps set in the high ceiling. Each one was aimed at the four other occupants of the room who sat in a line facing Dexter and his companion.

He looked along the line, pausing for a moment on each face as if trying to commit it to memory. In fact he knew each one well. Like a painter trying to decide on a subject, he moved his glance carefully from face to face, met only once by eyes that held his gaze.

And it was always those eyes.

Every day during the session they would begin the same way, in darkness. Then Doctor Andrew Colston

24

would switch the lights on one by one and Dexter would look at those same four faces.

And, always, he would be met by *those* eyes.

Dexter held the gaze for a moment longer, then glanced down at the clipboard on his lap. He matched each name to the four faces before him.

Colston shuffled his feet, as if anxious to begin. He too was eyeing the other occupants of the room but it wasn't their faces he was looking at.

It was the stout leather restraining straps that kept each of them firmly secured to the heavy wooden chairs.

Dexter glanced once more at the line of faces, aware, again, of the last of them and the incessant stare that seemed to bore into him. Once more he met those eyes and found himself unable to hold the stare.

Was that a sign of weakness?

Or fear?

'Who's going to start today?' he asked, his voice muted and flat inside the small room.

Silence.

There was no response from any of them.

Just that unflinching stare.

Dexter shuffled in his seat and smiled. His practised smile. His comforting smile. His reassuring smile.

'I'm sure one of you has something to say,' he continued, looking at the first of the four seated before him. 'Charles. Will you start today?'

The man looked at him, his eyes rheumy and red-rimmed. He looked as if he'd been crying. He held Dexter's gaze for a moment, then shook his head crisply.

The doctor sighed with exaggerated weariness. He raised his hands as if in surrender then looked at each face once more.

Those eyes still watched him.

Leave me alone. I don't want to talk.

25

'If you won't speak to me voluntarily then I'll have to ask you questions,' he told them all.

There was a thud and Colston looked across in alarm.

One of them had brought a fist thudding down on the arm of the chair.

Colston was grateful for the restraining straps.

'Silence is bad,' Dexter said. 'You shouldn't bottle up your feelings. Let them out. Imagine they're a river. Let your thoughts flow out. Speak.'

The rivers have dried up, thought Colston, using one hand to hide the slight smile which flickered on his lips. It vanished as he saw *those* eyes gazing momentarily at *him*.

'Very well,' said Dexter, turning over a sheet on the clipboard. 'We'll begin with Jonathan.' He sat forward in his chair. 'Tell us why you cut off your mother's head.'

Seven

It looked like a puddle of vomit.

James Scott looked at the remains of the pizza, now cold in the bottom of the box, and shook his head. His stomach rumbled noisily. He'd managed to force down half the pizza but that was all he'd eaten since eight o'clock in the morning. He glanced at his watch and saw that the time was nearly nine-thirty p.m.

Beyond the confines of his office Scott could hear music thudding away and the occasional shout. He sighed and ran a hand through his brown hair, pausing to stretch his shoulders, hearing the joints pop. He muttered something under his breath and peered round the office.

Framed photos of girls, some of them performers at

the club, stared back at him, pouting, smiling, licking their lips. Scott regarded them indifferently, his gaze flickering around the room to the calendar. That also featured girls, naked and half-naked. All shapes, all sizes, he thought, smiling humourlessly. Beneath the calendar, tacked to a bright red notice-board, was the rota. On it he had written, in his neatest script, the working hours for the barmen, the doormen and the hostesses. He had eleven people working for him, although one of the girls was only part-time. They were pretty reliable, most of his staff. They did their work, did what they were paid for and didn't cause him much trouble.

He'd been manager of 'Loveshow' for over three years now. The club was in Great Windmill Street, almost opposite the old Raymond Revue Bar. From his office window Scott could see into the street below, out onto the flashing neon and the rubbish that littered the road, some of it stacked up in large plastic bags and dumped on the pavements. He watched as pedestrians walked round it as if it were some massive dog turd. Others wandered in and out of the other clubs and bookshops that clogged the thoroughfare, each of them peddling the same merchandise. Books, magazines. Live shows. Scott remained at the window for a moment longer, then returned to his desk. He glanced at the portable TV set perched on one corner of it, thought about turning it on, then realised there was still work to be done.

He reached into his desk drawer for the drinks inventory. Time to re-order. Scott pulled off his jacket and hung it carefully on the back of his chair, rolling up the sleeves of his shirt to reveal thick, hairy forearms. Despite a life spent behind desks (or at least the last six years) Scott was stocky and bore only the smallest of unwanted podges. He looked down for a moment at the flesh straining just that little bit too tightly

27

against his shirt and shook his head. He sucked in a deep breath and held it, watching his stomach retract, smiling briefly before he released the breath and his belly flopped back into place. *Flopped*. He was hardly obese, he told himself. A few weeks working out in a gym would turn that irritating flab into muscle again. It wasn't too late. It was too early for middle-age spread. He was only thirty-two, for Christ's sake.

Forget your figure and get on with your fucking work, a voice inside his head told him. He nodded as if in answer to the silent beration and picked up his pen.

The office door opened and he looked up in surprise.

The girl was naked apart from a pair of stockings, a tiny pair of G-string knickers and a black basque.

'Fucking bastard,' hissed the girl, striding towards Scott's desk and lifting one leg onto it. 'Look,' she snapped.

'What's the matter, Zena?' he said wearily, inspecting her leg but seeing nothing untoward.

'Useless bastard shot his load all over my new stockings,' Zena Murray told him angrily. 'Look.' She jabbed a false fingernail towards a slick of slippery fluid on her thigh. 'Now he won't pay,' she continued.

'What happened?' asked Scott, getting to his feet.

'He bought a drink, bought *me* a drink. We talked, well, *I* talked for a few minutes then he pulled it out and asked me to wank him. I told him it'd cost him extra but he said that was okay.' She shook her head indignantly. 'So, what happens, I put one finger on it and he shoots, doesn't he? All over my . . .'

'New stockings,' Scott said, completing the sentence. 'So what's the problem?'

'They were new,' she yelled at him.

'Jesus Christ, take some money out of petty cash for

another pair. They're only fucking stockings,' Scott said, exasperated.

'It's not just that. He says he won't pay now.'

'So what are you bothering *me* for? Get Rick to throw him out,' Scott told her.

'Rick's not here,' she told him scornfully.

'All right, come on,' Scott said, pushing her in front of him.

They left his office and walked along a short corridor, passing two doors marked 'Private' and another which bore the word LADIES in white plastic letters. Beneath that someone had blue-tacked a piece of paper which bore the legend: NO PISSING ON THE TOILET SEATS.

The corridor smelt of stale urine and cheap perfume. It was a smell Scott had come to know well in the last few years.

'Where the fuck is Rick, anyway?' Scott wanted to know. 'This is the second time this week he hasn't come in. I've got better things to do than argue the toss with punters.' He smiled at his unintentional joke. Zena didn't see the humour in the remark. She raised her eyebrows indignantly and pushed open the door which led into the main area of 'Loveshow' and stalked in, Scott following.

The music that had been a dull thud in his office now enveloped him, roaring from the speakers mounted on the wall.

'. . . Our love is a bed of nails.
Love hurts good on a bed of nails.
I'll lay you down and when all else fails,
I'll drive you like a hammer on a bed of nails . . .'

Zena grabbed Scott's arm and pointed with one long

29

finger towards a balding man sitting in a corner, hidden for the most part by shadows.

'That's him,' she snarled.

'Okay,' murmured Scott, nodding. 'I'll handle it now.'

'Don't forget about my stockings,' Zena bellowed after him, shouting to make herself heard above the roar of the music.

What are you going to do, sunshine? thought Scott as he approached the balding man. *Get mouthy? Get scared?*

Let's see.

Eight

The floor show in the club couldn't have been more aptly named.

It consisted of a large double bed raised up slightly on a platform no more than six inches high. On two sides of the bed were nine or ten armchairs, each one faded and, in places, threadbare on the arms. Facing the bed, three sofas had been placed end to end. One was leather but the material was so cracked and worn it might as well have been draylon like the others. There were low coffee tables in front of each seat. The carpet, also worn, was dark brown to hide stains more easily. The walls were only slightly lighter and these were decorated with more framed pictures of girls, older than the ones in Scott's office. One or two were yellowed at the corners; one had even come free of the frame and a corner was turning up slowly. Customers were presumably supposed to be excited by the prospect that the girls in the pictures would actually be performing for them but, as one of the pictures featured Marilyn Monroe, that wish was at least a little vain.

The balding man was sitting in an armchair beneath a photograph of a girl holding a kitten. He didn't seem to notice Scott approaching him; he was too busy looking around.

There were about six other customers dotted around the place, drinking the warm beer and the grossly overpriced shorts. One man was in conversation with a hostess; she talked animatedly to him while sipping a Coke cradled in one hand and, with her other hand, trying to free the material of her knickers from the cleft of her backside.

On the bed in the centre of the room two young women writhed in the throes of practised pleasure, chatting to each other as they rubbed vibrators across each other's breasts, their voices drowned by the music.

A man in his early twenties, a cigarette dangling from one corner of his mouth, sat staring raptly at the two girls on the bed, his right hand, jammed into the pocket of his jeans, moving beneath the material.

Scott glanced across at the goings-on for a second then turned his full attention to the balding man, who had finally spotted him. Zena sat down beside the man and glared at him.

'You owe the lady some money,' said Scott, his face expressionless.

'Why?' said the man, looking first at Zena then at Scott.

'Because you bought me a drink, then you did *that*,' she rasped, jabbing her nail in the direction of the semen.

'I paid for the drink,' the man protested.

'You didn't pay for my conversation, or for anything else,' Zena told him.

31

'*Conversation*? What are you talking about?' the man said indignantly.

Scott snatched up one of the menus that lay on the coffee table and flipped it open.

'Buying the hostess a drink signifies agreement to pay the hostess fee,' he quoted, as if he were reading some point of law. Then he dropped the menu back on the table. 'You owe her sixty pounds.'

'Sixty pounds?' the man said, getting to his feet. 'Forget it.'

He tried to step around Scott but Zena pushed the table with her foot, blocking his way.

'Come on, pay up,' Scott demanded sharply.

The man raised a hand to push past him. Scott grabbed him by the wrist and shoved him away.

'Sixty,' he hissed, a glint in his eye visible even in the dull light of the room.

'I haven't got it,' said the man, swallowing hard.

Scared, eh?

'Well, fucking find it,' hissed Scott through clenched teeth.

The man tried to push past him again.

Scott pressed a large hand into the man's chest and shoved him back.

'You find that fucking money now. Sixty quid.'

He could see the fear on the man's face. Flabby white face, glasses. Suit, tie. *A respectable type.*

'You think you can walk in here and do what you fucking like.' Scott was breathing heavily now, the knot of muscles at the side of his jaw throbbing angrily. 'Get your money out.'

'Don't hurt me. Please.'

Scott almost smiled.

There was the fear again. Christ, he was beginning to enjoy this.

The balding man tried once more to get past.

'I told you not to push me,' Scott snapped.

'I didn't push you.'

His voice was wavering. He looked as if he was ready to burst into tears.

'Sixty quid or I'll push your fucking teeth so far down your throat you'll have to eat through your arsehole.'

The man fumbled for his wallet, pulled out three twenties and shoved them into Scott's hand. This time, when he tried to pass, the younger man let him. The man made for the narrow flight of stairs that would take him up out of the viewing area. As he was leaving another man was about to take a seat. The balding man muttered something to him and glared at Zena. She immediately scurried across and aimed a kick at the back of his legs.

'Fuck off,' she yelled at him as he disappeared up the steps.

Scott shoved the sixty into his pocket and headed back to the door marked STAFF ONLY.

'What about my stockings?' Zena said. He dug in his trousers and found a couple of pound coins. He tossed them to her. She caught them and smiled at him.

'You're a real charmer, Scotty,' she said.

He made his way back to the office, his breathing gradually slowing down. The sort of incident with the balding man wasn't unusual in clip joints like 'Loveshow' but Scott didn't think it was his job to deal with them. He'd done enough of that when he worked as a bouncer. Eight years ago. Ten. It seemed like an eternity. The scar on his left forearm was a reminder of it. At a disco one night he'd been ejecting a couple of piss-heads when one of them had cut him with a sharpened steel comb, opening his arm almost to the bone with the razor-sharp prongs. Scott had broken his jaw and three of his ribs before tossing him into the street.

Now he closed the door of his office, relegating the music behind him once again to nothing but a dull thud. He walked across to the window and peered out again into the street. It was raining heavily now; the street and pavements were wet. The sparkling neon reflected up off the slick concrete. It looked as if someone had spilled fluorescent paint on the thoroughfare. Across the street, in the doorway of an empty shop, a man was sitting, wrapped in a dirty coat, sipping from a bottle of spirits. When it was empty he hurled it into the street, where it shattered in front of a passing car. The driver slammed on the brakes, leapt out and ran across to the man, kicking him twice as he shouted his annoyance.

Scott returned to his desk and sat down, pulling the drinks inventory towards him, scanning the columns of figures.

They bought in bottles of whisky and vodka for about three pounds each. They sold them for seventy. He had one of the menus on his desk and he flipped it open, looking at the prices.

Five pounds for a coke. Ten pounds for a pint of lager. Then there was the list of cocktails. A screwdriver was thirty pounds. It went as high as eighty for a Tequila Sunrise.

Beneath the list was a line which read: ALL COCK-TAILS ARE DE-ALCOHOLISED.

You didn't get drunk but you pissed a lot.

If you chose to have the company of a hostess it cost you thirty pounds for a conversation with her. Anything beyond conversation was negotiable, but Scott knew the girls had their own price list for their services. Thirty for a hand job. Fifty for a straight fuck. Eighty for one without a rubber. One hundred quid could even get you a blow job without a rubber. Risky, these days, but then money was money, wasn't it? The entrepreneur always had to take a few risks.

He would take a trip down to the cash-and-carry in the morning, after he'd checked his stock of drink. He'd give Don, the barman, a call in a minute. He doubted if they needed much. The vodka was three parts water, as were most of the spirits. Scott sat back in his seat for a moment, his hands clasped on his lap. At least Don was reliable; he always turned in, no matter what. Not like that fucker Rick. He should have been there tonight.

I shouldn't have to throw punters out. It's not good for my image. The manager is here to manage, not get mixed up in rough stuff.

When and if Rick ever came back he'd find his cards waiting for him. Cunt.

Scott returned his attention to the inventory.

He was about to start work when there was a knock on the office door.

'Who is it? I'm trying to bloody work,' he called.

The frown on his face rapidly disappeared as the door opened.

Nine

'Sorry if I'm disturbing you, Jim,' Carol Jackson said apologetically.

Scott got to his feet.

'You're not,' he told her. 'Come in.' He smiled at her, relieved to see the gesture reciprocated.

She closed the door behind her and moved towards him, pausing as she looked down at the remains of the pizza. She wrinkled her nose and smiled again.

'Dinner,' he announced almost ashamedly. Then he took her in his arms and kissed her. Carol draped one arm around his shoulders perfunctorily and broke the kiss first. She perched on a corner of his desk and Scott looked at her appraisingly.

She was about three years younger than him. About five-two but slim. Blonde hair framed her face and cascaded just past her shoulder blades. As she stood close to him she toyed distractedly with the ring on her right middle finger. It was gold and held a small onyx.

One of Scott's gifts to her.

The metal was going black in places.

They had been seeing each other for almost fourteen months; the relationship could be called erratic. She worked at the club. Scott worked at the club. They saw each other almost every day during work. They had been seeing each other *out* of work for nearly as long.

She was wearing jeans and a baggy sweatshirt, a red one. Another gift from Scott. He liked to see her wearing things he had bought her. Now he looked at her and smiled.

You're beautiful.

He didn't even attempt to *say* it.

'I heard that Zena had a bit of trouble earlier on,' she said.

'It was nothing,' he told her. 'I sorted it out.'

'Manager's duty?'

He nodded.

'Do you want a drink?' Scott asked.

'I should go and get changed, I . . .'

'A quick one,' he insisted, smiling.

She agreed and he reached into the bottom drawer of his desk and pulled out a bottle of Southern Comfort and two glasses. She watched as he poured.

'Don't you ever get sick of this job, Jim?' she wanted to know.

Scott handed her the drink, looking bemused.

'It's a living,' he told her.

'I hate it,' she said, venomously. 'I hate what I do. I hate the people who come in here to watch me.' She took a long swallow of the drink and closed her eyes.

'Are you all right?'

'I'm okay. I'm just pissed off. Everyone has the right to be pissed off with their job don't they? It just surprises me you don't get pissed off with *yours*.'

'Like I said, it's a living. I don't hate it.'

It sounded like an apology. As if he should hate it and himself for doing it.

'You never used to be like this about it,' Scott said.

'I didn't think it would go on as long as this,' she snapped. 'I've been working clip joints since I was nineteen. That's nearly ten years, Jim. It's a long time. I wanted more out of life. I *want* more. More than being stared at by men with nowhere else to go. Fucking perverts. You know some of the ones we get in here. I hate them. And I'm beginning to hate myself for *performing* for them.' She took another long swallow and gazed across the room at the wall.

Scott got to his feet and moved closer to her, putting his arm around her, pulling her close.

'Do you want to talk about it later?' he asked, kissing the top of her head.

'What good is talking going to do?'

'I didn't know you felt the way you did. Perhaps if you spoke to me about it . . .'

'You don't understand,' she interrupted.

'*Make* me understand,' Scott asked.

She drained what was left in her glass and handed him the empty receptacle.

'Can I see you after work?' he asked.

She shrugged.

'Walk out and watch the show,' she said bitterly. 'You can see as much of me as you want.'

'You know what I mean,' Scott said, irritably.

Why do you make it so hard for me?

'Can I see you later?'

She kissed his cheek and turned to pull away but he caught her by the wrist and pulled her close to him. This time she responded with a little more passion, actually allowing his tongue to probe past the hard white edges of her teeth and into the moistness beyond. She touched his cheek as they parted in a gesture that was almost maternal. It wasn't the touch of a lover. He held on to her other hand, to the hand that bore the onyx ring.

The metal was turning black in places.

They were still holding hands when the office door opened.

'Can't you fucking knock?' Scott called.

The newcomer stuck his head around the door and looked first at Scott, then at Carol.

'Very cosy,' he said, noticing that they were holding hands. 'Sorry if I'm disturbing you.' He entered.

Scott swallowed hard as the door was pushed shut.

Ten

In all the years he had worked for Ray Plummer, Scott had never been sure whether or not to believe the rumours that his boss wore a wig. If it was a hairpiece, whoever had made it was to be complimented. There

38

was even a patch of thinning hair at the crown to add authenticity.

Now, as the older man entered the room, pulling a cigarette from the gold monogrammed case he'd removed from his pocket, Scott glanced quickly at the lustrous black hair that covered Plummer's head.

Toupee or not toupee, that was the question.

Scott smiled a greeting, hoping it would mask his amusement at his quip.

Watch it.

Carol stepped away from him slightly and also smiled at Plummer, who walked across the room and peered out of the window into the street below, puffing slowly on his Menthol cigarette. He hated the taste of the bloody things but his doctor had told him that if he didn't cut down from his usual forty Rothmans a day he'd be in line for lung and heart trouble before he was forty-five. And, with just seven years to go to that deadline, Plummer was taking no chances. He'd cut down on his intake of cholesterol, too. He'd even started jogging. He hadn't quite got to the stage of popping sunflower seeds but, if it made him healthier, he'd be quite prepared to start on all the organic shit, maybe even become a vegetarian. Although the thought of doing his weekly shop at a fucking garden centre instead of a supermarket made him wonder if he wanted to be *that* healthy.

He turned and smiled, a crooked smile exaggerated by the scar on his left cheek that reached from the corner of his mouth to the ridge of the bone.

'I was passing by,' he said. 'Thought I'd drop in and see how business was.'

Scott offered him a drink but Plummer declined.

'Got to watch the old liver, James,' he said, holding up his hands. *And the heart. And the lungs.*

'I'd better go,' said Carol. 'I'm due on in ten minutes.'
She smiled thinly at Plummer then at Scott.

'I'll see you later,' he said softly, but she had already
gone.

'Nice girl,' Plummer said. 'Lovely arse.' He blew out
a stream of smoke.

'Is this a social call?' Scott said, changing the subject.

'You sound suspicious, Jim. Think I'm checking up
on you?'

'I only asked.'

'Like I said, I was in the area, thought I'd pop in and
see how business was.'

'It's good. We took over two grand last night. Mostly
on drink, of course.'

Plummer smiled.

'Of course,' he echoed. 'I wish all my bloody joints
were doing as well as this one. Old Benny, you know
Benny Fox runs one of my places over in Dean Street,
he's lucky if he sees two grand in a fucking *week*.'
Plummer shook his head. 'It's the quality of the girls,
you know. I mean, some of them in the other places,
they're not top quality, if you know what I mean. There's
one bird over at Benny's I swear to Christ he got her from
Smithfield. Arse like a fifty-dollar cow. Face to match.'
He shook his head. 'We need more girls like that Carol.
She's tasty.'

Scott eyed his boss warily for a moment, anxious to
change the subject again.

Plummer sat down at Scott's desk and glanced at the
remains of the pizza.

'Not exactly *haute cuisine*, is it?' he said, wrinkling
his nose.

'If I had as much money as you, Ray, I'd eat better,'
Scott told his boss.

'Perhaps you could do with a raise. I can afford it.

Most of the shops and clubs turned a profit last year and my other *business* concerns are ticking over nicely.' He took a final puff on the cigarette, then ground it out in the middle of the pizza. He smiled that crooked smile again.

Plummer owned six clubs in Soho, most of them providing live sex shows. Four also showed imported films and sold a range of soft and hardcore magazines. The shop upstairs at 'Loveshow' dealt in that kind of literature. It came in on containers three times a month, carried in by lorry drivers paid to smuggle the banned material in the cabs of their trucks. He also owned a couple of gaming clubs in Kensington (the more respectable side of his business) and he had just bought into a syndicate responsible for opening a large outdoor sports arena in Fulham. With an annual profit of over ten million pounds, Plummer was one of the underworld's wealthier barons. He disliked being compared to a criminal gang boss, though. He had men working for him, some of them armed, but he wouldn't have called them a gang. Associates was a word he preferred. He didn't own clip joints, he operated adult entertainment emporia. To Plummer this wasn't a lie. He saw himself as a businessman, not a crook. There were those on the other side of the law who would disagree.

He had a criminal record, but the most he'd ever been charged with was possession of cannabis. That had been ten years ago. Now he made sure he went nowhere near the cocaine and heroin that had formed the bedrock of his little 'empire'. The passage of time had made him wiser, more cautious. More manipulative. Ray Plummer, in his own eyes, was an upstanding member of the community. For Christ's sake, he even had a firearms certificate for the Beretta automatic he carried in his car. It wasn't wise to cross the law.

Besides, it cost too much to pay the bastards off.

He ran a hand over his hair, smoothing down a piece that was sticking up.

Be careful or you'll have the whole lot in your lap, thought Scott.

Plummer got to his feet.

'I've got to go, Jim,' he said. 'Other calls to make.' He shook hands with the younger man. A firm grip.

'I'll walk out with you,' Scott said.

'No problem; you stay here, finish your work. I might have a look at the show on the way out.' He smiled. 'Maybe that Carol, or whatever her name is, will be on.' He winked and was gone.

Scott glared at the closed door, then pulled the bottle of Southern Comfort towards him and poured a large measure. He downed it in one, bringing the glass down so hard on the table it almost cracked.

Beyond the closed door the thud of the music continued.

Eleven

Zena Murray pulled off her stockings and balled them up, tossing them into the waste bin nearby. Then she took off her basque and G-string and sat naked in front of the mirror, taking her make-up off. Beside her, Carol Jackson was busy applying hers. The two women sat in front of the mirror which stretched the length of the wall in the dressing room. The term was rather grand for what was little more than an enlarged cupboard with lights and a mirror. Clothes were hung on hangers and suspended from hooks on the peeling walls. The light

42

bulbs which surrounded the mirror were flickering in places; some had blown completely. A drawer beneath the dressing table contained the girls' props, a selection of vibrators and dildos. There was a pay phone on the wall. One of the other girls had stuck a postcard of Mel Gibson on the side of it. There were other pictures sellotaped to the wall by the phone, cut from magazines. One of Jon Bon Jovi, another of Mickey Rourke.

'I'll be glad to get home tonight,' said Zena, wiping eyeshadow from her top lid with a cotton ball. 'Did you hear what happened with that bastard earlier on? Ruined my stockings, then didn't want to pay.'

'I heard,' I Carol affirmed.

'Scotty gave me the money for another pair. He's a nice bloke.'

Carol smiled into the mirror. The gesture looked strained, artificial.

'Are you still seeing him?' Zena wanted to know.

'Sort of,' Carol said, applying the thick red lipstick she always wore when she worked.

'Either you are or you aren't. You've been going out with him for a while now, haven't you?'

Too long.

'It's not like it used to be between us, but I don't think Jim realises that,' said Carol.

'Then don't you think you ought to tell him?' Zena said, looking at her companion in the mirror.

'Tell him what? That I don't want to see him any more? It's going to be a bit difficult while we're working together.'

'So you're going to keep the poor bastard hanging on? Thinking that you still feel something for him, just because it's not convenient for you to split up with him. Is that it?'

43

'It's not as simple as that, Zena. I like him. He's a nice guy. But he's going nowhere and he doesn't even realise it.'

'And where are *you* going, Carol?' She looked at her companion. 'Out in front of another audience, just like you do most nights. Just like you *will* be doing until your tits sag and your bum drops and you get fat and no one wants to come and see you any more. Then you'll probably start working the hotels and the streets full-time. Just like the rest of us.'

'Are you telling me I'm wrong to want more out of life?' Carol snapped. 'Do you honestly *enjoy* what you do here, Zena?'

'No, but it pays the rent, and that's all that matters to me at the moment. Look, Carol, it might not be much of a life but it's all we've got.'

'That's shit, there's more to it than that. There has to be.'

Zena wiped some foundation from her cheeks with a moist tissue.

'So, Scotty's only crime is that he's going nowhere. Is that it?' she said.

'I don't know how to tell him it's over. I don't know how he'll react. I know he thinks a lot of me. He's told me he loves me. I don't want to hurt him, Zena.'

'Well, you're going to hurt him a fucking sight more the longer you leave it,' Zena snapped. She got to her feet and started to dress, pulling on jeans and a T-shirt, stepping into a pair of ankle boots.

'Am I wrong to want more out of life?' Carol asked the other girl again.

'No, but I think you're dreaming, Carol. I'm not sure there *is* that much more. And if there is, it wasn't meant for the likes of you and me.' She smiled thinly, then

44

opened the door of the dressing room. The sound of the music was suddenly louder as Zena paused there.

'. . . skin tight leather on satin sheets . . .'

'Don't hurt him, Carol. He doesn't deserve it,' Zena said, smiling.

'. . . Now she's got me surrounded . . .'

Zena said goodbye and closed the door, shutting out the music once more.

Carol turned back to the mirror and studied her own reflection. She ran both hands over her breasts.

Starting to sag yet?

She reached for a cigarette and lit it, sucking hard, allowing the smoke to burn its way to her lungs.

There is more. There has to be.

The clock on the wall ticked soundlessly, the hands crawling around inexorably. *Showtime.*

She would tell Scott it was over. Zena was right. She shouldn't hurt him. She would tell him.

Eventually.

The phone rang.

For a moment Carol was startled by the ringing, then she turned and picked up the receiver.

She recognised the voice immediately.

'Hi. I'm just about to go on,' she said.

'I know,' the caller said. 'Where shall I pick you up tonight?'

'Same place as before.'

'Same time?'

'Yes. Look, I'd better go.'

'See you later.'

She hung up.

In the back of his Mercedes Ray Plummer was smiling as he replaced the car phone.

Twelve

Scott was still in his office when 'Loveshow' closed. He had some paperwork to finish but decided it could wait until tomorrow. He glanced at his watch, saw it was just after 11.30 and rubbed his eyes. He had to take the money from the bar and the hostesses round to the night safe and deposit it before he went home. The money taken at the door and that collected from the sale of books and videos upstairs in the shop was kept in the building until the next morning. Best not to bank the whole lot at once.

The bar takings were laid out before him, as was the money taken by the hostesses. Over eight hundred pounds in cash, all neatly arranged in piles according to denomination. Scott wound the piles securely with elastic bands and put them into the bag intended for the night safe.

Don Lloyd, the barman, stuck his head around the door and said goodnight. Scott waved and smiled, then looked at his watch again. After a moment or two he got to his feet and wandered down the corridor from his office towards the dressing room.

He knocked and waited.

'Come in,' a voice from the other side called and he poked his head in.

One of the other girls, a tall dark-haired young woman he knew as Lynn Fraser, smiled at him. She was completely naked, unconcerned by his presence. Scott was similarly uninterested in her state of undress; his attention, was drawn towards Carol, who was removing her make-up.

'How did it go tonight?' he asked.

Carol shrugged. 'Same as usual,' she said flatly.

'Well, my Rob's going to be overjoyed when *I* get home,' said Lynn, reaching for a tissue from the box nearby. 'I'm as horny as hell.' She wiped some of the moisture from her vagina with the tissue. 'Gets you like that some nights, doesn't it?' she continued, looking at Carol.

'I suppose so,' she replied unenthusiastically.

'Half an hour with a vibrator stuck up you,' Lynn cooed. 'I can think of worse ways to pass the time.' She giggled and began to dress. 'I hope Rob isn't banking on a good night's sleep.'

'Can I have a word with you when you're ready, Carol, please?' said Scott. 'In my office.' He smiled at Lynn and retreated from the dressing room before Carol could answer him. Behind him he could hear the dark-haired girl still giggling.

Scott went around flicking off lights. He waved goodnight to Lynn as she left hurriedly, chuckling. Then he made his way back to his office.

He sat down on the edge of his desk and waited.

Come on. Come on.

Carol finally appeared looking a little pale.

Scott smiled broadly at her.

'Ready?' he said happily.

'For what?' she said, somewhat bemused.

'I thought we could get something to eat. You said we could talk . . .'

She cut him short.

'I didn't say that, Jim,' Carol sighed. 'I don't feel too good. Maybe it's the time of the month.'

47

'Are you coming back to my place tonight? If it is the time of the month we don't have to . . .'

'I just want to get home.'

Tell him. For Christ's sake, put him out of his misery.

'I'm very tired, Jim.'

He clasped his hands together and nodded, the smile fading but still flickering on his lips.

'Maybe another night,' he said. 'Tomorrow, perhaps?'

She nodded.

That's it, just keep him dangling.

'I'm sorry,' she said. 'I just feel a bit rough.'

Lying bitch.

'You go home and get some rest. I'll see you tomorrow,' he said. 'You'll feel better then and we can talk.'

About what? About how it's all over?

She turned to leave but he crossed to her, put one hand on her shoulder and made her turn around. He bent forward and kissed her, aware once again that she was keeping her arms by her sides. He took one arm and draped it over his shoulder, then repeated the action with her other.

'Not too painful, is it?' he smiled.

She smiled back.

Don't hurt him.

They finally parted and she said goodnight. He told her he would see her tomorrow, he had some things to do before he left.

Carol closed the office door and made her way down the corridor. As she drew level with the dressing room the payphone inside began to ring. She opened the door, walked in and picked up the receiver.

'Hello,' she said wearily.

Silence. Only the odd pop and hiss of static.

'Hello,' she said again. 'Can I help you?'

'Carol Jackson.' It was a statement rather than a question.

'Yes,' she said after a short pause. 'Who's this?'

'I'm watching you.'

She held the receiver away from her ear for a moment and glared at it, as if her anger could somehow be transmitted down the line to the caller. When she pressed the receiver to her ear again she could hear soft breathing.

'If you're going to do it then do it properly, you useless bastard,' she hissed. '*Heavy* breathing, it's supposed to be.'

'I'm watching you.'

'Then what am I doing?' she asked.

'You're about to leave and I'll be waiting for you.'

This time her response wasn't quite so swift.

Other girls had received calls like this. It was almost an occupational hazard. She was about to speak again but the caller got there first.

'I'm waiting.'

There was a click as the phone was hung up and she was left with just the buzz of a dead line in her ear. Slowly she replaced the receiver. Then, wrapping her coat around her, she climbed the steps to street level and stepped out onto the pavement.

It was still raining, a thin, miserable mist of drizzle.

High up in his office, Scott watched her scuttle off towards Shaftesbury Avenue.

But his were not the only eyes that watched her.

Thirteen

It was almost 1.30 a.m. by the time Scott finally got home.

He trudged into the main entrance of the block of flats where he lived, heading towards the lifts. Behind him he left wet footprints on the tiled floor. As he reached the lifts he noticed that a sign had been affixed to the door: OUT OF ORDER. Beneath it, in biro, someone had scribbled: THEY ALWAYS FUCKING ARE.

Scott sighed and made for the stairs. Fortunately his flat was on the sixth floor; it wasn't too much of a trek. He wondered, briefly, how those on the fifteenth and sixteenth floors were managing. The block where he lived, like many others in Brent, was home to a wide variety of people. One-parent families, those in temporary accommodation, the usual ethnic mixture and, of course, long-term residents like himself. As he climbed the stairs he glanced at some of the graffiti sprayed or drawn on the green painted walls.

TORIES OUT
ARSENAL FC ARE CUNTS

As he reached each landing he glanced out of the large glass windows looking across to the other blocks that thrust upwards into the sodden night sky like pointing fingers. He saw the anti-collision lights of a plane high above in the blackness. It was leaving London, heading north. Scott wondered where its passengers were bound for.

He finally reached the sixth floor and rummaged in his jacket pocket for his key. As he stood in the corridor trying to find it he heard shouting from the flat next door. A man's voice, then a woman's, swapping obscenities and insults. Further down the corridor behind him a baby was crying.

Scott finally found the key and let himself in, shutting the door behind him, slipping the bolts across. There had been a spate of burglaries in the block lately. He didn't want to take any chances. He was, however, better prepared for intruders than most of the residents of the block. Locked away in the cabinet beside his bed was a 9mm Beretta automatic 92S.

He pulled off his jacket and trousers and hung them on a hanger over a radiator to dry off, then stripped down to his underpants and padded through into the kitchen to make a cup of tea.

From next door he could hear the couple still rowing. Scott didn't know their names, despite the fact that they'd lived next to him for more than five years. He'd never taken the trouble to get to know them or any of the other residents. He didn't *want* to know them, he wasn't interested in their lives and he was damn sure they weren't interested in *his*. He filled the electric kettle and pressed the 'play' button on the radio-cassette that stood beside it, adjusting the volume so that he could no longer hear the rantings from next door. *Noisy fuckers*.

> '. . . All alone now, except for the memories.
> Of what we had and what we knew.
> Everytime I try to leave it behind me,
> I see something that reminds me of you . . .'

He stood staring at the kettle as if willing it to boil. Then he pulled open a cupboard and searched for the tea bags, dropping one into his mug.

He thought about Carol.

The image of her floated into his mind unbidden. He savoured it for a moment, his thoughts interrupted by the clouds of steam that began to billow from the kettle.

Carol.

He wished she was with him now. She seemed to be on his mind constantly, whether he wanted it that way or not.

Couldn't he do anything without thinking about her?

That's what it's like when you're in love.

He grunted.

Love. What the fuck did he know about love?

His father had told him that many times.

His father . . .

He pushed the thoughts to the back of his mind and wandered through into the sitting room, switching off the cassette first. He drank his tea then decided to have a shower before retiring. He was tired and his body ached; he wouldn't need much coaxing to sleep but he felt as if he needed to cleanse himself.

He passed through the sitting room, through another door past his own bedroom. Past the other bedroom.

The one he kept locked now.

The one where his father . . .

Fuck it.

The memories were there; they always would be. No amount of time was going to make them disappear. Perhaps the years would make them less potent but they would not easily be excised from his consciousness. He paused by the door to his father's room, or what had once been his father's room. Then he twisted the key and walked in.

It was bare, completely empty but for the single bed,

now stripped, which stood beneath the window. His father had lived with him for three years prior to his death ten months ago. A stroke and then a gradual decline into senility, followed by a second devastating brain haemorrhage, had seen the old man off. It was the time after the first stroke that Scott had found so trying. His father, then seventy-two, had been rendered more or less helpless, housebound and unable to do anything but sit and stare at the television or out of the window all day. Scott's mother had left home when he was fourteen; he had no brothers or sisters to help him care for his father. The burden had fallen squarely on his shoulders. At first it hadn't been too bad. The old man could feed himself at least, but then he began to suspect that Scott was trying to poison him. He refused to eat. His weight dropped from twelve to seven stone. Scott had felt pity for him but, as the old man refused to eat, pity had given way to anger and then to hatred. He had seen his father wasting away but Scott had known that it could have been avoided. He lowered his head as he thought of the hatred he had felt for the man sometimes.

Was this shame?

Scott had brought him food only to see it hurled across the kitchen.

More than once he'd come close to hitting the old man.

Old bastard.

Now, now; he couldn't help himself.

Scott had wanted to believe that but it didn't alleviate the frustration he felt.

Don't you mean hatred?

At times it had become almost impossible for him to distinguish where he drew the line between his loathing of his father or his hatred of the illness that had transformed him.

'You bloody fool,' his father would repeat, glaring at him venomously. 'I can't eat that.' Then the tray or the plate would be hurled across the kitchen once again.

Just die, you old fucker. Do us both a favour and fucking die.

How easy it would have been to place the Beretta against the old man's head and blast what was left of his brains all over the wall.

And when the second stroke had taken him Scott had felt something akin to relief, until he visited him in hospital only hours before he died. He had walked into the room at the side of the ward and found his father's shrivelled form in an oxygen tent, tubes attached to his arms and nose. Scott had sat beside him, his mind blank, as if he had no pity, no hatred, no emotion of any kind left inside him. It was unsettling. His own indifference towards his father's impending death was infinitely more disturbing than any emotional outburst he may have been prone to.

Should have been prone to?

The hospital staff had told him it was just a matter of time; all he could do now was wait for the end. He might as well sit outside. But Scott had remained at the bedside, watching his father's sunken features, still unable to feel anything, still frightened by his own lack of emotion.

Why hang on? Just let go.

The father Scott had known and (*had he loved him? Truly loved him, ever?*) lived with for so many years had been dead long before this second stroke. The man he had (*loved?*) known had ceased to exist after the first haemorrhage. The soul was gone, he was watching the decay of the husk now. Scott had been preparing to leave when his father's eyes had flickered open and, instead of a glassy stare, Scott had seen recognition. It had shocked him, brought all his feelings flooding back. In

54

a moment of horrible clarity, it was as if his father knew and understood that he was going to die, and in his eyes that realisation was reflected. He knew he was going to die and he wept at the inevitability of it.

Then, just as quickly, the glazed look had returned and he had slipped back into coma and then beyond to death.

Scott stepped back and slammed the door, as if shutting out the sight of the room would close away the memories.

It didn't.

He couldn't sleep.

Scott had lain awake for over an hour listening to the wind whistling outside the window. Thinking.

He thought about his father.

He thought about Carol.

Finally he swung himself out of bed and crossed to the window.

Rain spattered against it like wind-blown tears.

He felt very alone and he didn't like the feeling. Not much frightened him but loneliness scared the hell out of him.

I don't want to die alone.

He thought of Carol.

His hope. His salvation.

She would be with him; he wouldn't be alone.

He glanced at the phone beside the bed, thought about calling her. He just wanted to hear her voice.

Maybe in a little while.

The wind continued to howl.

Fourteen: 3 April 1977

The man came hurtling across the room, mouth open, arms outstretched, his eyes bulging wide with rage.

Dr Robert Dexter took a step back from the observation slit in the door, relieved that three inches of solid steel separated him from the patient beyond. Inside the room, the man continued to fling himself at the door, banging his head against the metal partition, finally spitting on the glass of the observation window, the thick mucus obscuring Dexter's view of him.

'Increase his medication,' Dexter said, glancing down at the clipboard the held.

'He's on 50mg of Thorazine twice a day already,' Andrew Colston told him.

'Well, it doesn't seem to be working, does it? Up the dosage.'

Their footsteps echoed through the high ceilinged corridor as they approached the next door. Dexter slid back the observation panel and looked in.

The occupant of the cell was sitting cross-legged on his bed in a meditative pose, his head bowed. He was naked.

Dexter fumbled with the bunch of keys that dangled from his belt, inserted one in the lock and walked in. Colston followed.

The man looked up and smiled, then lowered his head once more.

'How are you this morning, Roger?' asked Dexter, sitting on one end of the bed. Colston stayed behind him.

Roger Lacey looked up and smiled broadly, revealing

a row of off-white teeth. His hair was cropped short, so short in fact that it was little more than stubble at his temples and the nape of his neck. His body was slender, heavily muscled, his hands resting one on each of his knees. As the two men watched he gently lifted his right hand and gripped the massive erection he sported. He began moving his hand up and down his shaft.

'It's time,' he said quietly.

'Roger, stop that for a moment,' said Dexter, his eyes fixed on the man's face.

Colston found his own gaze rivetted to Lacey's busy right hand.

'Where are they, Roger?' Dexter asked.

'Under the bed.'

Dexter nodded and Colston knelt down and reached beneath the bed. His hand closed over a thin plastic tray. He slid it out into view and passed it to his colleague who set it down on the bed in front of Lacey who had slowed the pace of his masturbating now.

On the tray were twelve watches, not one of which was working. The hands were frozen, all stopped at different times. Dexter lifted one and turned it over. The back had been clumsily but effectively opened then wedged back into position again.

With his breath coming in gasps, Lacey watched as Dexter pulled a pair of surgical gloves from the pocket of his jacket, lifted one of the time pieces and, after slipping the gloves on, flipped the back of the watch off.

The inner workings of the mechanism were coated and clogged by a thick, congealed substance Colston recognised as semen.

The other eleven time-pieces carried a similar cargo within them.

'You're not going to take them, are you?' asked Lacey, his face losing its colour, his hand now slack on his penis.

57

'What do you think would happen if we did?' Dexter asked.

Lacey shook his head agitatedly looking first at one doctor then the other. He licked his lips and tried to swallow but his throat was too dry.

'Roger,' Dexter repeated. 'What do you think would happen if we took the watches away? Do you *know*?'

Lacey shook his head even more vigorously.

'Did your wife take the watches away from you?' the doctor asked.

'Yes.'

'Is that why you killed her?'

'Yes.'

'So what do you think is going to happen if we take them away now? Can you tell me?'

'There have to be some survivors,' said Lacey falteringly.

'Survivors from what?' Dexter wanted to know.

'The war. When the war comes, everyone will die except those who are prepared.'

'Like you?'

'Yes.' He smiled.

'Why do you keep semen in the back of these watches, Roger?'

'They will be the survivors. They will grow. When the time comes.' He chuckled at his own pun. 'The time will come.' He began masturbating again. 'Every male discharge contains approximately two hundred million sperm. I have created enough to re-populate the world after the war. From each of them a person will grow.'

Dexter replaced the watch and got to his feet. Followed by Colston he headed for the door.

Behind them Lacey quickened the speed of his strokes, his breathing now harsher.

On the other side of the locked door Dexter pulled off the surgical gloves and shoved them into his pocket.

'How did he kill his wife? Stabbed her, didn't he?' the doctor mused.

Colston nodded.

'Apparently the police found traces of semen in every wound. All twenty-eight of them.' Colston looked through the observation slit to see Lacey reach his climax, thick white fluid pumping from his penis onto his hand. The doctor watched as the patient tried to scoop it up, desperate not to waste any of the precious ejaculate. He snapped the slide across and looked at Dexter.

'Do you think he's ready to be moved?' he asked.

'Not yet,' the other man proclaimed. 'Even though he killed his wife he didn't and still doesn't display any latent homicidal or psychopathic tendencies.' Dexter shook his head. 'He's not right for us.'

They moved further down the corridor, past other cells.

Past a young woman who had systematically torn out every finger and toe-nail to prevent dirt settling unseen on her body. (The interns called her Lady Macbeth.) Past a man in his early thirties who had killed both his mother and father with a garden fork because they refused to attend the baptism of his half-caste daughter. He had covered their bodies in axle grease to 'blacken' them, anxious that they should know what it felt like to be 'coloured'.

Dexter looked in on the man, checking his name. Colin Wells.

'Does he have any family?' the doctor wanted to know.

'A sister,' Colston informed him.

'What about his wife?'

'She ran away after the killing of his parents, took the baby with her.'

'Where's the sister?'

'She lives nearby. She still visits occasionally.'

'Damn,' murmured Dexter under his breath.

There were two doors left.

Dexter crossed to the first of them and peered inside.

The occupant was kneeling in the centre of the room wearing only a pair of boxer shorts. His body was thin and wasted, his face pallid. He was bald except for some snow-white hair over his ears. Even the hair on his chest and the thick strands that curled from his nostrils were as white as milk.

Thomas Walsh had been institutionalised for nearly thirty of his seventy-three years.

As he heard the key turn in the lock he turned, still kneeling, to face his visitors.

Dexter and Colston watched as he rose imperiously then pressed his palms together, touched his fingertips to his chin and bowed.

'Good morning, Tom,' said Dexter, peering around the room.

Hardly an inch of the wall was untouched, barely a fraction of the white paint showing through the mass of scribblings which had been completed with crayon, marker pen. Even blood.

The pattern was uniform, duplicated hundreds, thousands of times over and over again on the walls.

It looked like two musical notes joined together but the lines were harsher, drawn with quick flourishes.

It meant power.

Tom Walsh had been captured by the Japanese in Burma in 1940, forced for five years to work on the infamous Burma Railway, subject to the whims of brutal guards, starved and tortured. He had returned to England after the war a broken man both physically and mentally. Ten years in and out of hospital being treated for diseases he had picked up in the Malaysian jungles had seen his mental state deteriorate even further, his hatred of the Japanese grow ever stronger.

He'd been working in a car factory when a Japanese delegation had visited one day back in 1958.

Tom had managed to kill two of them and blind another with a soldering iron before he was stopped.

He'd been committed. He was the asylum's oldest patient.

Dexter exchanged a few words with him, then watched as he bowed ceremoniously when the two doctors left.

That left the last cell.

'*I* can check it if you like,' Colston said quietly.

Dexter thought a moment and shook his head. He took a step towards the final door, fumbling with his keys, his mouth dry. He didn't look through the observation slot first.

As he lifted the key to the lock, his hand was shaking.

Fifteen

The lift doors slid open with a muted whirr and DI Frank Gregson stepped out into the corridor.

He moved quickly but unhurriedly, his footsteps rattling out a tempo in the quiet corridor. At such a late hour every noise seemed amplified, too. Not that New Scotland Yard was run by the clock. Crime and criminals didn't hold regular hours, murderers didn't clock on and off.

By God, my dear Holmes, I should say not.

Gregson found the door to the pathology labs locked,

as he'd expected, but he had a key and let himself in, walking through the outer lab into the autopsy room itself. He paused in the doorway, recoiling slightly from the pungent odour of chemicals and death that greeted him like a long-lost friend. Reaching round he slapped at the panel of switches. Seconds later, the room was bathed in cold white light as the banks of fluorescents in the ceiling cast their luminosity over the dissecting tables. The light was reflected in their polished, stainless steel surfaces and Gregson caught a glimpse of his own distorted image in one as he passed.

The tables were empty, their occupants removed and stored in the cabinets that lined the walls. So many puzzles lay within those boxes. So many unanswered questions.

Gregson stood looking at them for a moment, the silence inside the lab quite overpowering. It was like a living organism, so complete it was almost palpable. It surrounded him. He felt as if it were penetrating his very pores, seeping into his bloodstream and circulating around his body.

He could hear the thud of his own heart in the solitude and its pace quickened as he found the locker he sought. He slid it out.

The body was covered by the familiar plastic sheet and the DI pulled it back to reveal the charred corpse beneath.

He stood gazing, for what seemed like an eternity, at the crushed skull, the wisps of hair that still clung to the blackened remains of the scalp. The scorched bones still covered, in places, by burned flesh.

He reached out and touched what was left of the face.

A piece of black flesh came away on his finger-tip. He looked at it for a moment then rubbed it away between his index finger and thumb. It crumbled like ash.

He looked at the body once more, his forehead deeply lined.

When he spoke, his gaze never leaving the charred body, his words echoed around the silent laboratory:

'Who *are* you?'

Sixteen: 15 April 1977

The new patient was due to arrive in a week.

At present he was still under guard inside Wandsworth, but according to the letters Dexter held in his hand – one from the Governor of that prison, the other rubber-stamped by the Home Secretary – he was to be receiving into his care a man by the name of Howard Townly.

Townly had, over a period of two months, kidnapped, tortured and finally murdered two men and three women, all of whom he had picked up while they were hitching lifts. He had made home movies of their deaths, replaying the videos over and over again for his enjoyment.

Townly was thirty-six.

About the right age.

Dexter checked through his notes on the man and saw that he had been unmarried. He was an only child.

This looked hopeful.

His mother had given evidence on his behalf during the trial.

Dexter shook his head.

No good.

Dexter sat back in his seat, massaging the bridge of

his nose between thumb and forefinger. He had the psychological evaluation of Townly before him, too. The police psychiatrist who had interviewed him had noted that the man had tendencies towards schizophrenia, paranoid delusions and sociopathic leanings. A hopeless case? That was probably the reason he was being sent to Bishopsgate. The institution, which Dexter had been in charge of for the past eleven years, had over three hundred patients within its antiquated walls. They ranged from those who visited on a daily basis through to the voluntarily committed, graduating to the criminally insane. In fact almost a third of the inmates were of that latter category. Prisons, unable to cope with them, shunted them off to Bishopsgate, Broadmoor or Rampton. Dexter often wondered if this was a genuine attempt to put them in the hands of those better equipped to deal with their mental instability or merely a way of relieving the pressure on an already overcrowded prison system which sometimes packed men three to a cell.

Perhaps the very fact that these men were insane had ensured they at least enjoyed a little more privacy for the period of their incarceration.

Insane.

It was a word he heard nearly every working day. One which he had been hearing for as long as he could remember in connection with the wildly aberrant behaviour and attitudes of some of his wards. What the hell was insanity? And who had the right to define it as such?

Dexter had come to see, with some individuals he'd treated, that insanity was not a disintegration of the mind but rather a re-building. Madness was sometimes displayed in a startling clarity of thought which apparently 'normal' mortals could never hope to understand. There was a relentless logicality to the way a madman thought. That madness sometimes proved to be so single-minded, so obsessively consuming, that Dexter found himself not fearing or hating these murderers he had charge of but admiring them.

Ted Bundy, an American mass-murderer convicted of killing more than twenty young women, was once quoted as saying 'What's one less person on the face of the earth, anyway?' When war, usually started and controlled by supposedly sane men, took the lives of millions, Dexter found it easy to subscribe to Bundy's observation. Who was madder, the solitary individual who killed a dozen for his *own* reasons? Or the soldier, trained to kill hundreds in the name of a cause he could not even understand?

His philosophical musings were interrupted by a knock on his office door.

'Come in,' he called.

Colston practically stumbled in, his face drained of colour.

'What's wrong?' Dexter asked, noticing his colleague's expression.

'One of the patients,' Colston said agitatedly. 'You must come now.'

'Is it *that* important?'

'It's in Ward 5.'

Dexter was on his feet in a second. He and Colston moved with great haste along the corridors, Dexter almost breaking into a run as they drew closer. His mind was in turmoil, ideas and visions flooding through it like a raging torrent through a broken dam. He didn't even think to ask Colston what had happened.

Ward 5.

He swallowed hard.

They turned a corner and came upon two interns standing beside a heavy steel door. It was firmly locked and secured.

The entrance to Ward 5.

The ward was in the East Wing of the institution and accessible only to half a dozen interns, Colston and Dexter himself. The two doctors watched as one of the interns, Baker, unlocked the door and stepped back to allow them through. He and another man called Bradley followed.

'Where?' Dexter said. 'Which cell?'

Colston led him past four doors, grey-painted and nondescript but for an observation slot and a small square hatch for pushing food through. Colston paused at the fifth and nodded towards Bradley, who unlocked the door and stepped back, allowing Dexter to enter the room.

The smell of excrement hit him immediately, but he was able to ignore the stench; his attention was rivetted to the body of the man slumped against the far wall of the cell.

He was in his thirties, Dexter knew, but a stranger would have found it impossible to guess at his age.

His face looked as though someone had been across it in all directions with a cheese-grater. His skin hung in bloodied ribbons from bones which were visible in places through the crimson mess. The front of the grey overall he wore was soaked with gore and, as Dexter moved closer to kneel beside the man, he noticed a thick, reddish-pink piece of matter lying in the man's lap. A glance at his open mouth revealed that the reddish-pink lump was the end of his tongue. He'd bitten through it, severing it. His teeth, visible because what remained of his shredded lips were stretched back in a rictus, were also coated with crimson. It looked as if he'd been using scarlet mouthwash. One eye, torn from its socket, dangled by the slender thread of the optic nerve. It rested neatly on his mangled cheek, the orb fixing Dexter in a sightless stare.

The doctor looked down at the man's hands and saw that the fingers were drenched with blood, strips of flesh, some two inches long, stuck beneath the nails. He had used his fingernails like claws on his own face, gouged his own eye from its socket.

Colston, standing in the doorway, was aware almost for the first time of the uncanny silence that reigned over the rest of the ward. It was as if the other occupants were in silent mourning.

'The same as the others,' he said quietly.

Dexter nodded and got to his feet, the expression on his face one not of sadness but of anger. He looked at Colston.

'I want a report on my desk by the morning,' he said. Then he looked back at the shredded features of the man, blood beginning to congeal in the wounds. 'We have to know.'

Seventeen

He gripped the headboard and thrust harder into her, each motion of his hips accompanied by a grunt.

Ray Plummer smiled down at her as he penetrated her, gritting his teeth in concentration, his efforts enlivened when he saw the look of pleasure on Carol Jackson's face.

She gasped and raised her legs, hooking them around the small of his back, raising her buttocks to allow him deeper penetration. She began to rotate her hips gently, coaxing him towards the climax she knew was close.

Come on, for Christ's sake get it over with.

She moaned loudly, knowing that the sounds she made,

67

coupled with the clenching of her vaginal muscles around his penis, would, as ever, bring him to climax quickly.

He was sweating profusely; as she ran her fingers up and down his back she felt their tips sliding through a sheen of perspiration.

Come on, Ray. You can't hold out much longer.

'That feels so good,' she cooed expertly. 'Do it faster.'

'Faster, slower,' he panted, trying to keep up his rhythm. 'Harder, softer. How do you want it?'

'All those ways,' she breathed.

Only just get a bloody move on and finish, will you?

She reached over and began to squeeze his testicles, stroking them gently, breathing ever more deeply, her exaggerated show of pleasure becoming more pronounced.

She felt him stiffen, felt his body tense.

'Oh yes,' she gasped with relief, knowing the time had arrived.

He thrust into her with one final, deep lunge and she felt his hot seed filling her, seeping from her vagina as he continued to pound away, his breath rasping in his throat.

She reached up to stroke his hair but he pushed her hand away, content that she should run her fingers up and down his back.

Get off me for Christ's sake.

He remained on top of her, his breathing gradually slowing.

'Jesus, that was good,' she gasped, her own breath coming in practised gasps.

He touched her cheek with his fingers and smiled a smile of accomplishment before finally rolling off her and lying exhausted on the bed, wiping perspiration from his forehead. Immediately she reached for the tissues beside

68

the bed and began mopping up the warm fluid seeping from between her legs.

'Leave it,' he said breathlessly, watching as his semen trickled through her pubic hair.

She rolled onto her side and began stroking his chest.

'It's all right for you,' she said. 'You don't have to sleep in the wet patch.'

He laughed humourlessly.

'You should be used to it by now,' he muttered, holding her chin between his thumb and forefinger.

I've done it to you enough times.

She moved away from him slightly and laid her head on his chest, listening to his heart pounding, closing her eyes in relief that it was over for another night.

'Felt good, didn't it?' he said, his tone self-congratulatory.

'Yes,' she lied.

She could feel his semen oozing uncomfortably over her thighs but she tried to ignore it, knowing that he would be asleep soon. Then, as she usually did, she would slip out of bed while he was snoring like a fog-horn and take a shower. Wash it all away. For now she lay where she was, aware that he was twisting her long hair around his fingers. Occasionally he would tug a little too hard and she would wince but she said nothing, content to let him play his little games.

It was warm inside the flat. In contrast, her own place was like a fridge. All she had to keep her warm was a two-bar electric fire close to the bed. Plummer's penthouse apartment was fully central-heated. In the large sitting room he even had an open fireplace full of mock logs. She would often sit gazing into the gas flames late at night while he slept, tracing shapes in them, wondering if some of those shapes were the shape of her future.

The flat itself was one of a group of four in Kensington, not too far from Kensington High Street. She knew that the other people who lived as Plummer's neighbours were well off. One was a lawyer, another a judge. She wasn't sure what the woman who owned the bottom flat did. Something in the City, she thought. It was ironic that a man of Plummer's means should be sharing the building with two people who, effectively, worked on the opposite side of the law to him. The apartment was worth, Plummer had told her (repeatedly), around three quarters of a million. He owned two houses in Belgravia as well, both of which were in the process of being converted into flats. He fancied himself as a landlord.

He reached across and picked up his glass of Jack Daniels, tiring of his game with Carol's hair. She heard the sound of his expensive ring clinking against expensive crystal as he picked the glass up. He took a sip and then swung himself out of bed.

'Where are you going?' she wanted to know.

'Don't be so nosey,' he told her, disappearing into the en suite bathroom. He emerged a moment later carrying a small rectangular box which he held out to her. As she took it from him she noticed that the lid of the box bore the legend: GARRARDS JEWELLERS.

He sat down on the edge of the bed and watched her open it.

The pendant was solid gold, twice the size of a thumbnail. The light from the bedside lamp caught it and sent golden beams radiating from it.

Carol opened her mouth in awe as much as surprise.

'It's beautiful,' she said, not taking her eyes from the velvet lined box and its costly contents.

'Put it on,' said Plummer, watching as she took it

from the box and fastened it around her neck. It hung invitingly between her breasts. 'Do you like it?'

'Thank you, Ray. It's gorgeous,' she told him, touching his cheek with her fingertips. She stroked his hair, but again Plummer pushed her hand away.

'I got it today,' he said, reclining on the bed, not bothering to cover his flaccid penis. 'Probably cost more than you earn in a year.' He smiled.

'You pay me,' she reminded him. 'You could do something about that.'

'I don't pay you. Scott does.'

'He pays me what you *tell* him to pay me.'

Plummer brushed a hand across the front of his hair.

'You still seeing him?' he wanted to know. 'Or should I say are you still fucking him?'

'I see him occasionally,' she confessed. 'It's all over between us, though; it's just that I can't seem to get around to telling him.'

'Does he know about you and me?' Plummer wanted to know. For a moment she saw a flicker of uncertainty on the older man's face.

'Would it matter if he did?' she asked.

It would make it easier for me, splitting up with him if he did.

'I suppose not,' Plummer said. 'It's just that he's a bit unpredictable. Flies off the handle a bit quick, sometimes.'

You're scared of him.

The realisation brought a slight smile to her lips and she touched the locket almost unconsciously. It wasn't the first gift he'd bought her. She had a solid gold Cartier watch at home, endless amounts of silk underwear. He'd even taken her to Paris for a weekend about six weeks ago (she'd told Scott she'd been visiting relatives in the

North). Of course she couldn't wear any of the things to work, Scott would want to know where they had come from.

'You shouldn't spend your money on me, Ray,' she said, looking at the pendant again.

'It's only money,' he said. Plummer enjoyed spending, enjoyed buying her things. He enjoyed impressing her with his wealth. Besides, she was a very good-looking young woman; he liked being seen with her. A number of his friends had remarked on her good looks, good figure. They envied him and he liked that. It was a good enough reason to hang on to her.

For the time being.

'Someone's got to look after you,' he said, stroking her hair.

'You're going to look after me?' she asked, smiling.

You're going to help me escape the life I hate?

He smiled.

'Who else is going to do it?' he wanted to know.

No one. She knew that. He was her only way out and she didn't intend to let him go. Whatever she had to do to keep him happy, she would do it.

Happy, was that the word? Perhaps satisfied was more apt.

'Take care of me, Ray,' she said softly, her eyes filling with tears. She leant forward and put her head on his chest.

Be careful, the mask is slipping.

He put his arm around her shoulders and pulled her closer.

'Don't worry, darling,' he said, his face impassive. 'I'm here.'

So make the most of it while you can.

The phone rang.

'What the fuck . . .' Plummer hissed, looking at his watch and then across at the bedside clock, as if to reassure himself of the time.

2.36 a.m.

The ringing continued.

'Shit,' he grunted and reached for the phone, picking up the receiver. 'Hello.'

'Ray Plummer.'

He didn't recognise the voice.

'Yeah. Do you know what fucking time it is?' he snapped.

'Shut up.'

'Who the fuck are you talking to . . .'

'Shut up and listen.'

'Who are you? Give me one good reason why I shouldn't hang up.'

'Because I've got something to tell you, you cunt. Something to your advantage. Now shut the fuck up and listen.'

Eighteen

Plummer sat up, the receiver pressed tightly to his ear, his eyes narrowed.

'Listening?' the voice chided.

'Yeah, go on,' he rasped.

Carol looked at him and mouthed 'Who is it?' but he raised a hand to keep her quiet.

He concentrated on the voice, listening to every syllable in an effort to work out his caller's identity. If it was somebody pissing about he'd have their fucking head.

73

'You're probably wondering why I called,' said the voice.

'Just get on with it. What do you want?'

'Patience is a virtue, Plummer. Now, do you want to hear what I've got to say, or shall we stop now?'

'You couldn't tell me anything I wanted to know anyway.'

'Oh ye of little faith.'

'Are you going to get to the fucking point, or what?' Plummer's initial bewilderment had turned to anger. He felt tempted to slam the receiver down.

'The point is you are about to be shat on from a great height,' the voice told him.

'By who?'

'Ah, now that's why I called. Interested *now*?'

He was about to shout something down the phone when the caller continued.

'Whoever has the most money controls London, right? Whether it's you or one of your . . . associates. You all own property, clubs, gambling places. You own people. I'm right, aren't I? The one with most money stays in control.'

'Yeah,' Plummer said slowly.

'Ralph Connelly is about to receive a shipment.'

'Of what?'

'Cocaine.'

'That's bollocks. Connelly doesn't deal in drugs. He makes all his cash by laundering other people's money. He does some of mine, for fuck's sake. I knew you were full of shit. Get off the fucking line . . .'

'Cocaine worth twenty million pounds. The shipment's coming in six days from now.'

Plummer hesitated.

Twenty million.

'Why should I believe you?' he asked.

'*Don't*. It makes no odds to me but twenty million, you'll agree, is a lot of money. By my reckoning that should make Connelly top dog.'

'How did you find out about this cocaine?'

'That's my business.'

'Then why make it mine too?'

'Just call it personal reasons.'

'You want a cut,' Plummer said, smiling thinly.

'I said it was personal.'

'Look, any arsehole could ring me and tell me something like this. There's still no reason why I should believe you.'

'Connelly bought a warehouse in Tilbury about a week ago, didn't he?'

Plummer paused for a moment.

'Yeah, he did.'

'What would he want with a fucking warehouse? Like you said, laundering is his business.'

'And business is good. Why would he want to start up with drugs?'

'Like I said, twenty million is a lot of money. Would *you* turn it down? He was offered the shipment by some people in France.'

Plummer stroked his chin thoughtfully.

'How do you know all this?' he asked, even his anger receding now.

'That's not important. What I *do* need to know is, are you interested in the cocaine?'

'Yeah, I am. Twenty million . . .'

The caller cut him short.

'I'll be in touch soon.'

He hung up.

'Wait,' snarled Plummer. Then, hearing the buzz of a dead line, he slammed the receiver down. 'Cunt,' he hissed. Watched by Carol he clambered out of bed and

75

padded through into the sitting room to pour himself another drink. Who the fuck had called him? he wondered. His interest had been aroused. Twenty million notes. Jesus. That *was* interesting. He smiled.

He might not have smiled so broadly had he realised his flat was being watched.

Nineteen

Scott replaced the receiver and sat staring at it for a moment.

He would ring again in five or ten minutes.

Outside, the wind had dropped slightly but the rain had intensified. It slapped against his window, the constant spattering like a thousand birds pecking at the glass.

Try again now.

He reached towards the phone.

No. Leave it.

Instead he hauled himself out of bed, angry that he'd been denied the welcome oblivion of sleep. He crossed the small bedroom to the dressing table, which bore a motley selection of after-shave bottles and deodorant cans, some empty. There were wage slips, too, piled up in order and weighed down with an ashtray still full of dog-ends.

There was a framed photo of himself and Carol.

He picked it up and ran his glance over it, his eyes pausing every so often to look at her face.

The picture had been taken about eight months earlier. They had managed to get out of London one night and spent two days in Brighton. The weather had been good and the picture showed Carol in a bikini, her arm around his shoulder. He'd asked some bloke sitting near them to take the picture, relieved when it had come out so well.

Christ, she was lovely.

He touched the photo with one index finger, as if to feel the smoothness of her skin. The warmth of that day seemed a million years ago as he stood listening to the rain hammering against the windows. He put the photo back and wandered through into the kitchen, where he retrieved a bottle of vodka from one of the kitchen cupboards. He took a glass from the draining board, then returned to the bedroom, sat on the edge of the bed and poured himself a large measure.

He used to give his father a drink. After the first stroke, a couple of shots seemed to put the old bastard in a better frame of mind. After the second one, dropping him in a vat of the stuff wouldn't have helped.

Fuck him. Forget about him.

He'd tried, but it had proved surprisingly difficult. When he remembered his father it wasn't as the wasted, comatose figure he'd watched over in hospital or the cantankerous sod he'd been forced to put up with for ten months. He remembered him as the sometimes abrupt, sometimes lonely but often funny man he'd shared his flat with for two years and eight months *before* the first stroke. Prior to that the old boy had lived in a flat of his own in Muswell Hill. He'd been forced to move out when it had been taken over by a new landlord.

Why the fuck had this particular spectre returned to haunt him, he wondered? Why was he thinking about his old man when the only person he truly cared for was Carol?

Perhaps it was the loneliness that made him think.

He felt lonely now, sitting on the edge of his bed, the drink cradled in his hand, listening to the rain. He thought how his father had once confided to him what *he* felt. And it was fear of that feeling which remained firmly embedded in his mind. Scott needed someone. No, not *someone*; he needed Carol.

He reached for the phone and jabbed out the digits of her number, just as he'd been doing for the past half-hour.

He just wanted to hear her voice.

The phone went on ringing.

Just let me hear her.

Perhaps she'd pulled the connection from the socket so she wouldn't be disturbed.

Pick it up.

Maybe she'd put the phone under a stack of pillows to muffle the ringing so it didn't wake her up.

Come on. Come on.

The ringing continued until he slammed the receiver down in frustration.

Perhaps she was ill.

Perhaps she wasn't there. She might have been hurt on her way home. She could be in hospital now.

What if . . .?

He downed what was left in the glass and poured himself another, gulping half of it down in one swallow.

She was not there. He knew it. *Felt it.*

Then where?

He gritted his teeth, his breath coming in short gasps.

Where was she?

He looked across at the photo on the dressing table. She smiled back at him.

Scott shouted and hurled the glass across the room. It hit the wall and shattered, spraying shards of crystal in all directions. Vodka dripped from the wet patch on the paper.

He wondered how long it took for loneliness to become despair.

Twenty: 16 April 1977

The tumour was as large as a man's fist.

Dexter looked at it lying in the metal dish, a huge collection of dead cells, darkish brown in colour, tinged a rusty red from the congealed blood which coated it. It had been taken that morning, from the skull of the dead man they had found in Ward 5 the previous day.

Now Dexter observed the tumour and tapped a pen gently against his chin, his thoughts running pell-mell through his mind.

'What about the others?' he asked.

Colston sighed and shrugged his shoulders, pulling up a chair beside the desk.

'Four out of the five are exhibiting similar symptoms to those of Baker,' he said. 'I checked them over this morning before I did the autopsy.'

'Damn,' snapped Dexter, getting to his feet. He crossed to the window of his office and looked out over the well-manicured lawns and the tall trees that swayed in the wind.

'Is there anything we can do?' he asked, without looking at his companion.

'If the tumours are developing at the same rate then I could operate, try to remove them. We'd at least save their lives,' Colston told him.

Dexter watched as an intern led two patients across the lawn, one of them kicking a football ahead of him like an excited child.

'You said four out of the five were exhibiting similar

symptoms,' he said quietly. He turned to face Colston. 'What about . . .'

The other doctor shook his head, cutting him short.

'So far no change,' he said.

A slight smile creased Dexter's lips.

'Then we're doing *something* right,' he said, clutching this small piece of optimism as a drowning man clutches the proverbial straw.

Colston sucked in a deep breath.

'And we're also doing something very *wrong*,' he said. 'That's the third death in as many months. If the tumours in the other four continue to develop . . .' He allowed the sentence to trail off.

Dexter returned to his desk and tapped the five files stacked in front of him.

Each one bore the note: WARD 5 in its top right hand corner. Below that was the name of the patient.

'What do we do?' Colston wanted to know. 'Stop?'

'Certainly not,' said the other man indignantly. 'It *will* work, Andrew. I'm *sure* of it.'

'Then at least modify the process until we see the progress of the other five.'

Dexter shook his head again.

'The other *four*,' he interjected. 'You said one of them was still all right.'

'It might just be a matter of time before a tumour develops there too . . .'

Dexter interrupted again.

'No,' he said with conviction. 'It *won't*. I just believe it won't.'

'Because it's what you *want* to believe.'

'Do you blame me?' he snapped.

There was a long silence, finally broken by Colston.

'No, I don't blame you,' he murmured. 'And don't worry, I'm not going to back out on you. Not now.'

80

Dexter smiled appreciatively and picked up the files marked Ward 5.

He flicked through the first four relatively quickly.

It was the last of them that interested him.

Twenty-one

The needle, almost six inches long, had been pushed through the girl's nipple, inserted with clinical efficiency through the fleshy bud.

George Kinsellar turned the page of the magazine and proudly displayed another double spread, this time of a young girl with several metal rings through her vaginal lips.

'What about that?' Kinsellar said. 'Be like shagging a scrap-metal yard, wouldn't it?' He chuckled his throaty laugh which ended as usual, with him hawking loudly, chewing thoughtfully on the mucus for a moment and then swallowing it again.

Kinsellar was a thick-set man in his early fifties, his face pitted, his hair thinning.

'How can anybody get their rocks off to something like that?' said Scott, shaking his head, taking the magazine from the older man and flipping through it. He finally dropped it into the supermarket trolley he was pushing and continued walking up the long aisle between the high shelves.

The warehouse was in Holloway and Kinsellar had owned it for the last six years. The bulk of his business was done with Ray Plummer's organisation, although he supplied a number of the other firms in the capital with videos, books, 8mm films and appliances. Fifty per cent of what he sold was illegal but business was booming. He followed Scott around, making notes on his pad of what the younger man was ordering.

The magazines were stacked up to three feet high on shelves that reached almost to the tall ceiling of the warehouse. Light struggled to penetrate a skylight which was so filthy it was nearly opaque. Inside, the place smelt of newsprint. As he pushed the trolley, Scott couldn't help but smile to himself. Whenever he visited this place (usually once a month to check up on new stock and place his order) he couldn't shake the feeling that, pushing his trolley around amidst shelves piled high with books featuring every kind of sexual perversion, he was like a shopper in some depraved branch of Sainsbury's.

'Some of this new stuff that's been coming in is fucking ace, I tell you,' Kinsellar said, making another note. 'Especially the German stuff. The krauts certainly know what they're doing when it comes to porn.' He chuckled, hawked and swallowed. 'I got a load of videos in the other day. You've never seen anything like it. Birds eating each other's shit. I was fucking amazed.' He smiled. 'I just kept thinking, "I hope they got it right on the first take". I mean, it's difficult enough getting an actress to cry on cue, isn't it? But to shit on cue.' The sentence disappeared beneath that mucoid chuckle.

Scott continued pushing the trolley, his mind elsewhere.

Carol wouldn't be in until eight that night.

He had another nine hours before he could ask her where she'd been last night when he was trying to call her.

They rounded a corner and began down another aisle.

'You're quiet today, Jim,' Kinsellar noticed at last.

They don't call you flash for nothing, George, do they? thought the younger man.

82

'Business bad, is it?'

'Business is fine.'

It's me that's fucked up.

'You still seeing that bird that works at the club?' Kinsellar wanted to know. 'Whatsername . . .'

'Carol,' Scott said, reaching for another magazine and flipping it open. He studied the first few pages, looking at the girls lying on a bed, their fingers thrust deep into their vaginas, their labia spread wide for the prying camera. He dropped the magazine into the trolley and walked on.

'Yeah, I'm still seeing her,' Scott said wearily.

'You don't sound very enthusiastic.'

Scott rounded on him.

'What do you want, a fucking blow-by-blow of the last two months?' he snapped.

'All right,' Kinsellar said, taking a step back. 'No need to bite my fucking head off. I just wondered if I could help. If you wanted to talk about it.'

'Stick to selling the mags, George. Being an agony aunt doesn't suit you,' Scott rasped.

'You young blokes are all the same. Think you know it all when it comes to women, don't you?'

'I wish I knew something. *Anything.* I don't understand them.'

'You and every other bloke around, my son,' Kinsellar told him. 'I've been married twice, lived with two other birds, the last one for fifteen years, and I'm still none the wiser. But I've seen more of them than most.'

'Are we talking crotches now, George?' Scott said acidly. 'Well, come on, let me have it. Let's hear some advice from the world's number one cunt expert.'

'Somebody really did rattle your cage this morning, didn't they?' Kinsellar said. 'You had a row with her, is that it?'

Scott shook his head.

'No, I haven't had a row with her,' he said. 'That's the trouble. We've hardly spoken in the last couple of weeks.' He suddenly became aware that he was opening up to Kinsellar. 'Fuck it, why am I telling you?'

'A trouble shared . . .'

'Fucks up two people instead of one. I know,' snapped Scott. 'Now can you stop asking me questions about Carol?' He glared at the older man.

Kinsellar shrugged and followed him in silence for a few paces.

'You still shagging her?' he asked at last.

Scott spun round, his eyes blazing. He grabbed the older man by the lapels of his jacket and hurled him up against one of the bookshelves, his face only inches away from Kinsellar's.

'No more questions,' he hissed through clenched teeth.

Kinsellar tried to nod but Scott's fists beneath his chin prevented that gesture.

'All right,' he croaked.

Scott held him a moment longer then pushed him away.

A large figure appeared at the end of the aisle. Six-four and over sixteen stone, he was Kinsellar's nephew, biceps and chest hardly covered by the T-shirt he wore, muscles pumped up by years of loading and unloading lorries and generally helping with the older man's business. He looked at his uncle then at Scott.

'It's all right,' Kinsellar called to him. 'Go back to work, Bernie. There's no bother.'

Bernie hesitated a moment, his gaze held by Scott.

You want some, too? Come on then, you big fucker.

Scott could feel the vein at his temple pulsing angrily.

The big man disappeared again.

Scott pushed the trolley on.

'You're bloody crazy,' Kinsellar said, catching up to him. 'I was only asking a question.'

'You ask too many questions, George. It's my problem, so *I'll* sort it out, right?' He looked unblinking at the older man, who nodded.

'You ought to watch that temper of yours, son. It's going to get you into bother one day.'

Scott looked at him impassively.

'What about the videos?' he asked.

The ordering took less than half an hour. Scott sat in Kinsellar's office gazing into space, a mug of tea gripped in one hand. He didn't seem to notice that it was burning his fingers. He finally looked across at the older man and got to his feet.

'I'd better go,' he said, glancing at his watch.

Another eight hours before he could see Carol.

'I've got some good stuff coming in next week,' Kinsellar told him. 'German again. Some bird in a video having toothpicks shoved through her cunt lips.'

'Just send some over, eh?' He headed towards the door.

'Are you seeing Carol tonight?' the older man asked.

Scott turned slowly to look at him, his face darkening.

'I told you not to ask me any more questions about her, George,' he rasped.

'Just curious,' he said, a slight grin on his face. 'Maybe it comes with age.' He cackled his mucoid giggle.

'And I told you, you ask too many questions.'

'I've got one more,' Kinsellar said, reaching for a magazine that lay on his desk. He flipped it open to the centre spread where a girl with her legs spread wide and fingers parting her moist vagina was smiling into the camera.

'What is it?' asked Scott.

Kinsellar held up the centrespread.

'Where do you reckon *she* lives?'

Twenty-two

Detective Inspector Frank Gregson leaned back on the two rear legs of his chair and began rocking gently, his gaze rivetted to the sheets of paper on his desk.

They were statements taken from witnesses to the shooting in the Haymarket two days ago. Jesus, it seemed longer than two days. It seemed like a fucking eternity. Maybe it *would* be an eternity before they identified the mysterious killer. Once that was done they might at least have a chance of figuring out why, when escape had been possible he had chosen to kill himself.

No word had come up from the pathology labs from Barclay as yet. He was still working on the remains of the corpse, trying to find some clue in the twisted, blackened remnants of humanity that might give them a lead on the individual who had, for no apparent reason, taken six lives (one of the victims on the critical list had died late the previous night) and then killed himself, all in the space of about five minutes.

Where did he come from?

Where did he get hold of the weapons?

Why did he chose to strike where he did?

Fuck it, thought Gregson, it was all questions and no answers so far.

The statements didn't help much, either.

'One says he was blond, another says he was ginger,' the DI muttered, flipping through the neatly typed sheets. 'One says short hair, another says tied in a pony-tail. It's a wonder they all managed to agree he was the same fucking colour.'

On the other side of the desk, DS Stuart Finn pulled a Marlboro from the packet and jammed it between his lips. He lit up, blowing a long stream of blue smoke into the air.

The DS was holding a photo-fit picture on his lap. It was held firmly in place by a bulldog clip at the top and bottom.

'That's the artist's impression,' he said, handing the sketch to Gregson. 'Based on the witnesses' statements.'

Gregson ran his gaze over the picture, his face expressionless. He tossed it onto his desk contemptuously.

'Does it match up with anything in our files?' he asked, clasping his hands clasped across his stomach. He was staring down at his desk as if trying to see through the wood, through the floors to the pathology labs below.

'There's only one way to find out and that's to go through every one. One by one.' Finn shrugged. 'Want to toss for it?' He smiled thinly.

'If there were two bloody statements which said the same thing about him then we might have a chance. As it is . . .' Gregson stopped in mid-sentence and flipped open the first file of statements. He leafed through them, pulling one out. It had been made by a cashier in the bank the man had entered. He looked hurriedly through the others until he found what he sought. The other statement was that of a motorist who had nearly collided with the killer when he'd been escaping on the motorbike.

87

'Staring eyes,' said Gregson, running his index finger over the words in both statements. 'Two of them *do* agree on *one* thing,' he said. 'The killer had staring eyes.'

Finn shrugged.

'Have I missed something?' he said. 'Perhaps he had thyroid. I'm not with you.'

'We nicked a guy about six years ago, he'd done a series of bank blags, never got away with much; he seemed more interested in hurting people than the money. He hit four banks all in Central London, same method every time. He walked in, blew out the cashier's window and took the dosh. He always carried a shotgun and an automatic.'

Finn nodded slowly, the recollection gradually coming to him.

'The most striking thing about him, most of the witnesses at the time said,' Gregson continued, 'were his eyes. His staring eyes.' He tapped the two newest statements. 'Staring eyes.'

'Lawton,' the DS said, a faint smile on his lips. 'Peter Lawton. Shit, I remember him now.' The smile faded rapidly. 'It's a coincidence, though, Frank; somebody imitating Lawton's methods, that's all. He's been inside for six years, still got another five to do before he even comes up for parole.'

Gregson nodded slowly.

'Weird, though, isn't it?' he muttered. 'Copy-cat killers, maybe, but copy-cat bank robbers?'

'What are you saying?'

The DI shrugged.

'I don't know what the fuck I'm saying,' he snapped. 'We know Lawton couldn't have done it because he's inside. So what do we make of these statements? The man had staring eyes,' he read aloud.

'Twin brother?' Finn offered somewhat lamely.

'Do me a favour,' said Gregson getting to his feet. 'At the moment, though, I'm willing to consider anything. Let's check his file.'

Finn looked at his watch.

Seven-twenty p.m.

He stubbed out his cigarette in the ashtray which was already overflowing with butts. A couple spilled over onto Gregson's desk and he swept them into his hand hastily before his superior noticed.

'Another fucking blank,' said Gregson, looking at the file on Peter Lawton. 'No family, no living relatives.' He looked at Finn. 'No twin brothers.'

'So what do we do next?' the DS wanted to know.

'You tell me.'

'Well, I fancy a drink. Join me?' Finn said, getting to his feet.

'No, I'm going to stay here for a while, try and think this through.'

'Frank, we're banging our heads on a fucking wall until pathology comes up with something concrete to identify the bloke. What's the point?' Finn asked, exasperated.

'You go, I'll see you in the morning,' the DI said, flipping open Lawton's file once again.

Finn hesitated, then said goodnight and left. Gregson heard his footsteps receding down the corridor.

Peter Lawton, sentenced to fifteen years for armed robbery and murder. Term being served in Whitely Maximum Security Prison, Derbyshire.

Term being served.

Gregson rubbed both hands over his face, exhaling deeply.

Another ten or fifteen minutes and he would leave. It was time to go home.

But first there was something he had to do.

Twenty-three

The wound was big enough to push two fists through. Portions of ribcage, shattered by the shotgun blast, protruded through the mess of pulped flesh gleaming whitely amidst the crimson.

Gregson looked long and hard at the photo, then slipped it carefully, almost reverently, on top of the others.

The baby had been practically cut in two by the blasts that had ripped through its pram.

Gregson looked at the tiny form, his face expressionless. There was another shot of it from a different angle. The angle made no difference to the massive damage that had been inflicted on the tiny child.

The DI took a swig from the glass of whisky he held in his other hand and pulled another photo from the pile on the table.

Before leaving New Scotland Yard he had collected the files on all of the victims of the gunman whose identity still remained a mystery.

There was a picture of the head of the motorcyclist the man had shot outside the bank.

The wound in the base of the skull looked relatively small, no larger than a ten pence coin. It was the other photo that showed the exit wound which caused Gregson to drain, a little more quickly than he would normally, the last dregs in his glass.

The bullet had exited just below the motorcyclist's right eye, shattering the cheekbone and dislodging the eye from its socket.

Although, Gregson reasoned, it hadn't been the shell itself that had blasted the orb free but the gases, released from the high velocity round as it had powered through the man's head. The eye was intact, still attached to the skull by the optic nerve.

Gregson dropped the picture down with the others and got to his feet, crossing the room to the sideboard. He opened it and took out the bottle of Teacher's. He poured himself a large measure, thought about adding some soda then decided against it. For long moments he stood by the sideboard, his breath coming in low, deep gasps, as if he'd just run a great distance. He rolled the glass across his forehead, his back still to the sitting room door.

He heard the door open but did not turn as his wife entered the room.

Julie Gregson was wiping her hands on a dishcloth. She muttered something about the diamond in her engagement ring coming loose and gazed across the room at her husband.

'Dinner's ready,' she said.

'I'm not hungry,' Gregson said flatly, his back still to her. He took a swig from his glass.

'Did you have any lunch?' she wanted to know.

He shook his head.

She moved towards him, passing the table where the photos were spread out.

'Jesus Christ,' she muttered, noticing the topmost of them. She moved a step away, her eyes still fixed on it mesmerised for a moment.

Gregson finally turned to look at her.

No. Not at her. At the table. The photos.

'What are they?' she said, the colour draining from her face.

'Isn't that obvious?' he said acidly, sitting down and looking at the photos again.

'*Who* are they?' Julie enquired, still keeping away from the table.

'Is it important?'

She moved the dishcloth from one hand to another, gazing at her husband then looking swiftly at the pictures once more.

She was a couple of years younger than him, her face etched with lines a little deeper than a woman in her late twenties would expect. She was slim, almost thin, her small breasts hardly visible even beneath the tight T-shirt she wore. Her jeans were faded, one knee threadbare, her skin showing through the narrow rent in the material.

'Why did you bring those home?' she wanted to know.

'It's part of my job,' he told her without looking up.

She balled up the dishcloth and dropped it onto the table beside the pictures. Then she sat down on the edge of the chair opposite him.

'Your bloody job,' she said quietly, but with anger. 'Everything is part of your bloody job, isn't it?'

'It pays the mortgage. Perhaps you should remember that.' He looked at her impassively.

'I work, too, Frank, in case you hadn't noticed. I do my bit towards the running of this house.'

'But it's my *bloody* job,' he said contemptuously, 'that pays the bills, isn't it? Perhaps you should think about that before you start moaning. What do you want me to do, give it up? Find something else to do?'

'When you're like this I wish you'd never joined the force,' she told him. 'Especially not the murder squad.'

'When I'm like what?' he said, that note of contempt still in his voice.

'You know what I'm talking about. *This* case, the last *few* cases, they've been getting you down *badly*.'

'Bullshit,' he sneered.

'It's *not* bullshit,' she rasped. 'It's true.' She glanced down at the photos briefly, revolted by them. 'Look at yourself, Frank, dwelling on what this man's done even when you're at home.'

'Do you think I can just wipe it clean when I leave my office?' he said, with scathing contempt. 'Do you think my mind is like a fucking blackboard? You scratch things on it, words, sights, you scratch those on it during the day, then at night I just forget about them? Is that what you think?' He picked up the next picture. It showed what was left of the skull of the cashier who had taken a blast from the Spas in the face. Gregson shoved the picture towards Julie angrily. 'Can you expect me to wipe something like that from my mind so easily?'

She looked away from the picture, feeling her stomach churn.

'I see things like that every day and every night,' he continued vehemently. 'And you expect me to forget them? Have you any idea what goes through my mind? What thoughts are in here?' He prodded his temple with his index finger. 'No, you haven't. You could never understand.'

'Then *make* me understand,' she said, tears welling in her eyes.

'You really want to know? You really want to hear about my work?' His eyes were blazing now, fixing her in an unflinching stare.

'You should talk about it more often. You bottle things up too much, Frank.'

'Okay, where would you like me to start?' he said,

93

glaring at her. 'Would you like me to tell you what the inside of that bank looked like after that fucking maniac had finished using the shotgun? How there were brains spread over the road when he shot the motorcyclist? Or perhaps you'd be more interested in another case. The one where the woman killed her husband with a carving knife because she'd found out he was having an affair. There were so many knife wounds in him it took us over an hour to count them all. And blood. You want to hear how much blood there was? She severed both his carotid arteries, you see. The ones in the neck. Nearly cut his fucking head off, in fact. She said later that all the time she was stabbing him he kept saying he was sorry. He kept saying he didn't want to die.'

Gregson was sucking in breath through clenched teeth now.

'What else would you like to hear?' he taunted. 'About the four-year-old who'd been sexually abused by her stepfather? He'd used a bottle on her. A beer bottle. Shoved it up her arse. The only problem was he didn't expect it to break. He didn't expect her to scream quite so loudly, so he jammed the rest of the bottle into her face until she shut up. That would have been bad enough but she'd been dead for three days when we found her. He'd put her in the attic. She was blue where she'd lost so much blood, apart from the bits of her that had turned gangrenous. Jesus, it stank in that fucking attic.'

Tears were rolling down Julie's cheeks now as she looked at her husband, the words pouring forth from him with a kind of monstrous glee.

'Is this what you want to hear?' he chided. 'Is this what you want to know about my job? What about the drunk that was mugged in Piccadilly the other night? I mean, there was nothing for them to take so they just beat him to death. They used his head like a football, took runs at him. Two would hold him down while the other one kicked him. Kicked him so hard that three of his front teeth were driven up into the roof of his mouth.'

She got to her feet.

'That's enough,' she sobbed, wiping her eyes.

'I've hardly started,' he said, looking at her. 'I thought you wanted to hear all about my work.' He smiled humourlessly.

'I wanted to help you,' she told him, sniffing.

'How can *you* help?'

'You should talk to me more.'

'I've just been talking to you and you can't fucking take it. You ask me what I do, you ask me to tell you what goes through my mind, and when I do you can't take it.'

She wiped more tears from her face.

'Can't you see what it's doing to you, Frank?' she asked.

'That's *my* problem, not yours.'

'It's not just *yours*. I can't stand to see what this job is doing to you.'

'Why?'

'Because I love you,' she snapped, a note of anger joining the despair in her voice. 'Christ knows why, but I do. Let me help.'

He shrugged.

'You want to help me? Leave me alone. That would be a great help. Get off my fucking back.' The words were spoken without a flicker of emotion.

She turned and headed for the door, turning as she reached it to look angrily at him.

'I tried. Don't ever say I didn't try to help you,' she said tearfully.

'Who asked you to help? *Me*? No.' He shook his head.

95

'Frank, please . . .'

He cut her short.

'You want to help? Then leave me alone.' He looked away from her. He didn't see her leave the room, only heard the door slam.

Gregson took another swallow from the glass. Then he picked the photos up and carefully began to go through them again, one by one.

Twenty-four

He watched her writhing on the bed, hardly aware of the music that roared out of the speaker above his head.

'. . . Lady Red light, rock me tonight . . .'

James Scott leant against the doorframe, peering through the gloom towards the bed where Carol Jackson was naked, a vibrator clutched in one hand. She was running the gleaming phallus up and down her body, pausing occasionally to look at the members of the audience.

There were two men dressed in suits sitting in chairs on one side of the bed, both of them chuckling as they watched Carol's rehearsed gyrations. Every few moments one of them would rub the erection he sported. They continued laughing, nodding towards Carol as she turned to face them, the vibrator between her legs.

Scott sighed as he watched the display.

He'd tried to talk to her when she arrived but she'd been late and she'd had to hurry off and change. She said she'd talk to him later. It offered some ray of hope, at least. He had so much to ask her. Before she'd arrived he had been angry, had told himself he would be firmer with her; but as soon as he'd seen her the anger had evaporated. She was here, that was all that mattered. She was near him.

He watched the display for a moment longer, glaring at one of the customers who whistled appreciatively when she took the vibrator from her vagina and kissed the tip.

As Zena joined her on the bed, Scott turned and headed back towards his office.

He wanted to ask her if she was all right, wanted to know why she hadn't answered the phone when he'd tried her number the previous night. And yet, strong as his curiosity was, something told him that he should *not* ask. He didn't own her. She wasn't accountable to him.

Yet he felt he had a right to know. After all, they had been seeing one another for over a year.

He sat in his office listening to the dull thud of the music, thinking about Carol and Zena lying on the bed together, performing their usual act.

Where had she been last night?

He sat forward in his seat, angry with himself for dwelling on the matter. He pulled the bottle of Southern Comfort from the drawer in his desk and poured himself a measure, swallowing half in one gulp.

Don't ask her, it's not important now.

He turned the glass in his hand, gazing into the dark fluid for a second before downing more of it. He refilled his glass, the thud of the music diminishing slightly. They must have finished.

Scott got to his feet and headed for the office door, the drink still in his hand. He walked down the corridor which led to the changing room, knocked and walked in.

Zena sat on one of the stools in front of the mirror, peering at her reflection. She smiled as she saw Scott standing there.

'It's a good job I'm not shy, isn't it?' she laughed, allowing the silk basque she wore to hang open, revealing her breasts. She noticed his drink.

'Whatever it is I'll have a swig, Scotty,' she said. 'I'm parched.'

He handed her the glass and she sipped from it as she slipped off first the basque then her panties. Naked, she sat on the stool.

'Where's Carol?' he asked.

'One of the punters called her over, I think she's having a drink with him.' Zena shrugged. 'It's another thirty quid, isn't it?'

Scott nodded and turned to leave.

'I'll nip back later,' he said.

'Scotty, wait a minute.'

She swivelled round on the stool to face him, completely unconcerned by her nakedness. It seemed not to bother Scott either.

'What is it?' he asked.

'You think a lot of her, don't you?' Zena said, cradling the drink.

'Is it that obvious?' he said, smiling humourlessly.

She nodded.

If only you knew, you poor sod.

Zena smiled at him, wondering if she should drop a hint of some kind, let him know that his feelings for Carol weren't reciprocated. But she decided it wasn't her business. They had to sort their own lives out. As she sat there, naked, Zena realised for the first time that she found Scott attractive. She enjoyed the thought of him looking at her and reddened slightly as she felt her nipples begin to stiffen.

Forget it.

'I'm sure she won't be long,' she told him, swallowing what was left in the glass. 'Do you want me to tell her you were looking for her?'

98

He shook his head.

'I'll come back later,' he said. Then he was gone, the door closing behind him.

Zena turned back to the mirror, studying her reflection for a moment longer. Then she began to take off her make-up. The dressing room door opened and Carol entered, still carrying the vibrator. She put it down on the dressing table, and exhaled wearily.

'What did that bloke want?' Zena enquired.

'A blow job,' Carol said. 'I told him to piss off.'

'You can afford to turn down a hundred quid, can you, Carol? You're lucky.'

Carol didn't answer; she just looked at Zena as the two women faced the mirror.

'Scotty was looking for you,' Zena said.

'What did he want?' Carol enquired.

'He didn't say. Are you going to tell him tonight?'

'Tell him what?'

'That's it's all over between you. How much longer are you going to keep him hanging on, Carol?'

'Look, Zena, it isn't really your business, is it?' Carol snapped.

'He's a nice bloke. I like him and I don't like to see him get hurt.'

'Then *you* go out with him.'

'Maybe I should. Maybe he's more my type than yours. I mean, according to you he's going nowhere. Well, I'm happy the way I am, too. Perhaps you get used to being a nobody after a while. We're not all like you, Carol. Some of us make do with our lives, make the best of what we've got instead of moaning about what we *haven't* got.'

'Thanks for the lecture,' Carol said, acidly.

'Why don't you stop being such a bitch and tell the poor bastard?'

Carol got to her feet, pulling a towelling robe around her.

'Drop it, will you?' she snapped.

'You're seeing someone else, aren't you?' Zena said, flatly.

Carol looked anxious for a moment.

'What makes you say that?'

She raised her eyebrows in mock surprise.

'I've done it myself, Carol, I know the signs,' she said. 'Want to tell me who he is?' She smiled. 'He must be well off if you can afford to turn down hundred-quid tricks.'

Carol didn't answer.

Well off. He was rolling in it.

'Is he going to be the one who's going to take you away from all this?' There was a note of scorn in Zena's voice.

'I told you, Zena, just drop it, will you?' Carol said irritably. 'It's my business, not yours.'

Their argument was interrupted by the ringing of the phone.

While Carol went to answer it Zena finished dressing, checking that she had all her bits and pieces before picking up her handbag. She paused to light a cigarette, watching Carol cradling the phone between her ear and shoulder.

On the other end of the line Ray Plummer was apologetic.

He couldn't pick her up tonight.

'It's Okay,' said Carol. 'What's wrong?'

Nothing, he assured her. He just had some business to attend to.

'Will I see you tomorrow?' she wanted to know.

He said she could bank on it. He'd take her out for a meal.

'Great,' she said, her tone not exactly jubilant.

Zena waved goodbye and slipped out. Carol raised a

hand in farewell and then she was alone in the dressing room with just Plummer's voice for company.

'Where are you ringing from?' she asked him.

He said he was at one of his gaming clubs in Kensington. He said he was sorry she was going to be alone tonight. He told her he wanted her.

'I want you, too,' she lied.

He said goodbye.

'See you tomorrow.'

He'd already hung up.

She put down the phone, stood gazing at it for a moment and banged the receiver.

'Damn,' she hissed. When she turned back to look in the mirror there were tears in her eyes.

Twenty-five

They didn't speak all evening.

Julie Gregson had sat looking at the television not really comprehending what she saw, while Gregson himself had continued drinking, flicking through the photos.

She'd looked over at him a couple of times, the expression on her face a combination of sorrow and anger.

Only when the hands of the clock crawled round to midnight did she speak. She asked him if he wanted a hot drink, tea or coffee, before she went to bed.

He shook his head and finished off the Teacher's instead.

'Are you coming to bed?' she asked.

'Soon,' he murmured, without looking up.

She paused in the doorway and ran a hand through her hair, watching as he flicked through the photos again.

'What do you think you're going to find, Frank?' she asked him. 'You've been looking at those damned things all night.'

'Just call it homework,' he said flatly.

'What are you trying to find?'

'Answers. It's my job.' He finally afforded her a glance she would have preferred he'd kept to himself. It was icy as he glared at her. 'But you didn't want to hear too much about my job, did you?'

'Don't start again, Frank,' she said wearily. 'Are you coming to bed? Yes or no?'

'You go,' he told her. 'I'll be up in a while.'

'How many whiskies later?'

He smiled thinly.

'Just go to bed, Julie. I'll handle it.'

'That's just the trouble, Frank,' she told him. 'I'm beginning to wonder if you *can* handle it any more.'

She left him alone. Gregson heard her footfalls on the stairs, heard her moving about in the bedroom above him. He listened to the sounds for a moment longer then got up and crossed to the sideboard where he retrieved another bottle of whisky. He poured himself a measure and sat down on the sofa once more.

He returned his attention to the photos.

Twenty-six

A thin film of condensation covered everything in the small bathroom, even the clock on the wall. Behind the veil of dewy moisture the hands had reached 1.15 a.m.

Water dripped from one of the taps. Carol Jackson watched the droplets falling for a moment, occasionally raising her toe to prevent the constant *plink*.

She ran both hands through her hair and put her head back, closing her eyes, enjoying the feel of the water lapping around her neck. The flesh on her fingertips was already beginning to prune but she felt as if she needed to stay in the water to wash away more than just the grime of the day and the evening. If only it could wash away her problems as easily.

Before she left 'Loveshow' that night Scott had spoken to her, asked her if she was okay, told her how nice she looked.

Christ, his attempts at small-talk had been so clumsy she almost felt sorry for him. It had taken him a seemingly endless time and a barrage of aimless chatter before he finally asked her why he couldn't reach her the previous night when he'd called. She had the lie ready and told him she'd unplugged the phone from the wall because she didn't want to be disturbed. As if she was regularly pestered in the early hours of the morning by social calls.

But Scott had merely smiled, nodded and said he understood. He'd been worried about her. She'd felt like telling him not to worry about her, that she didn't *want* him to worry about her. But she had not been able to find the words.

Lies were simpler.

He'd asked her to come for a meal with him when the club shut, but she'd found that another lie had been preferable. She'd told him she had to get home. Her sister was going to call her from America. She hadn't spoken to her for months. She would see him another night.

Maybe.

Carol dipped her hands into the water again and rubbed her face, catching a distorted view of herself in the mist-shrouded bathroom mirror opposite. She wondered what had made her think of the excuse she had used to Scott. Her sister was going to ring her? They hadn't spoken for months. That part at least was true. Carol hadn't spoken to any of her family for some time. She wrote occasionally, when she could be bothered, and her mother sometimes replied.

Sometimes.

The last time she had spoken to her sister, Fiona, had been on her birthday. Fiona was five years younger and worked for a record company in the West End. It was a well-paid job and she had her own flat in Hammersmith. Carol had never even seen the place but she knew that it must be an improvement on her own humble dwelling in the basement flat of a large house in Dollis Hill. There were four other flats above her and she was on nodding terms with the other resident. She even spoke to one of the women who lived on the top floor.

Carol should have hated Fiona. She had often thought that. Fiona had everything she didn't: a good job, a nice place. More than that, she had a future.

There were times, many times, when Carol could see herself this same way in ten years' time, lying in the bath regretting her wasted life. *And yet how was she to change it*? She sighed, knowing that it was not in her own power to do so. Her fate lay, to a large degree, with men like Plummer. He had wealth, power and influence. He commanded respect. He was her escape route.

And then there was Scott.

She closed her eyes more tightly, as if trying to blot him out of her thoughts. If only it were so easy to remove him from her life. She knew deep down she was afraid to tell him their relationship was over, not because she couldn't bear to speak those words but because she genuinely feared how he would react.

Feared? A little melodramatic, wasn't it?

He'd be hurt for a while but he'd get over it.

Wouldn't he?

Perhaps Zena had been right. She *was* a bitch.

She pulled herself out of the water and reached for a towel, wrapping it around herself, using another to dry her hair. She padded through into the sitting room and switched on the television. There was a black and white film on one channel, a discussion programme on another. She switched the set off and started drying herself, standing close to the two-bar electric fire that was the only form of heating in the room. She had an electric fire in her bedroom but the radiators on each wall were merely eyesores; they didn't provide the central heating she craved on cold nights like this.

As she was drying her hands she looked at the gold ring Scott had given her, the metal black in places. She ought to clean it.

It could wait.

She finished drying herself and pulled on a long sweater to cover her nakedness, then wandered into the kitchen to make herself a warm drink before she went to bed.

At first she didn't hear the phone ring.

The water was gushing from the tap into the kettle, obliterating all other sounds.

Then she heard it and turned towards the sound coming from the sitting room.

Who the hell was calling her at 1.30 in the morning?

She sighed. Scott. Checking that she was okay.

Why can't you leave me alone?

She put down the kettle and walked back into the sitting room, picking up the receiver.

'Hello,' she said resignedly.

Silence.

'Hello.'

Still no sound.

She felt her heart beat faster.

'I'm watching you.'

The voice cut through her as surely as if it had been cold steel.

She gripped the receiver until her knuckles turned white.

'How did you get this number?' she said quietly, trying to control the fear in her voice.

Silence.

'I know your sort,' she said, her show of bravado fooling neither herself nor the caller.

Only silence greeted her remark.

Slam the phone down.

'I know all about you,' the caller said, and now Carol was certain that it was the same voice as the other night. Not that she'd had much doubt in the first place.

Now she *did* slam the phone down.

For long seconds she stood looking at it, her eyes fixed to it as if it were some kind of venomous reptile that was about to bite her.

Take it off the hook.

She actually had her hand on the receiver when the phone rang again.

She snatched it up and pressed it to her ear but this time she didn't speak.

She heard a sound at the other end. A wet sound. Like someone licking their lips.

'I'm still watching you,' said the caller. Then he hung up.

Carol stared at the receiver, but all she heard was the dull monotone of a disconnected line.

She didn't put it back on its cradle.

She simply dropped it.

Twenty-seven: 10 May 1977

The explosion had been massive.

It had torn away the roof of the kitchen area, sending slates and lumps of stone hurtling skyward like shrapnel. The remains of the structure had simply collapsed in upon itself as if the walls had been made of paper. Tongues of flames thirty feet high had erupted from the wreckage, the pieces of burning debris showering down on the roof of the asylum like fragments of comet, some actually tearing through, others bursting again, causing more havoc, spreading the fire more rapidly than anyone could have imagined.

It took less than six minutes from the initial blast to transform Bishopsgate Institution into a blazing inferno.

The whisper was gas leak, the result was devastation.

The fire brigade had been called and ambulances were outside the building ready to ferry the dead and injured away. The air was alive with a cacophony of sirens and the roaring of flames. Firemen directed jets of water at the flames while their companions struggled to help the staff of the institution evacuate patients.

Smoke, belching from the burning building, hung like a thick black shroud over the blazing asylum. The air was filled with millions of tiny cinders, as if a plague of small flies had infested the air.

Inside his office Doctor Robert Dexter pulled on his jacket and ran out into the corridor. An intern hurtled past him, his white jacket smoke-stained, his hair singed. Dexter could hear screams of rage and fear as he started along the corridor, aware of the acrid stench of burning.

He saw two more interns running towards him, both sweating profusely, their faces dark, their uniforms dirty.

'The West Wing is clear,' said one of them. 'We managed to get everyone out.'

'The firemen are evacuating the rest of the building,' said his companion.

Dexter nodded.

It was then that he saw Colston round the corner.

Dexter ran towards his colleague, his face pale.

'We've got to get out,' said Colston, his breathing rapid. 'The whole place is coming down around us.'

As if to emphasise his words there was a loud creaking noise, a wrenching timber. A shower of sparks burst from the ceiling and covered the two men, who both ducked down. The smell of smoke was stronger now and Dexter could actually see the first wisps of it curling round into the corridor.

'We've got to get to Ward 5,' said Dexter.

'Let the fire brigade take care of it,' Colston said agitatedly, coughing now as more smoke filled the corridor.

Dexter grabbed him by the shoulders.

'And let them find what's in there?' he hissed, his gaze firmly on his colleague.

The realisation seemed to hit Colston and he nodded. Together they hurried up the corridor, relieved that the smoke wasn't too dense as yet. Even so, both men found that the acrid fumes stung their throats as they ran on through the clouds of smoke.

They passed a window and Dexter glanced sideways to see the firemen outside spraying the building with water. A number of people were being helped into ambulances, some supported by uniformed men.

The two doctors ran on, reaching a closed door. It led through into another corridor and Dexter snatched at the handle. He cursed at the heat of the metal in his grip but he pulled the door open, standing back as he did so.

A searing blast of flame swept through the open door and as Colston pushed himself back against the wall the fire scorched his sleeve. Dexter waited a moment then ran on.

The smoke was dense inside the corridor, tongues of flame flaring from both sides.

Doors of cells stood open, some of them blazing infernos. The incessant clanging of fire bells, curiously redundant in the blaze, filled their ears. Colston hesitated, but when Dexter bellowed at him he followed, shielding his face from the heat with one smoking arm. He could smell the burned hair on his arm. His eyes were watering, the back of his throat felt as if someone had turned a blow-torch on it. Dexter seemed unconcerned by the blistering heat; his only desire was to reach Ward 5.

They had two more corridors to pass through.

The first was clear.

The second was an inferno.

The roof had been holed by a lump of falling debris and the grey sky was visible through the clouds of smoke spewing through it. To the right Dexter saw something twisted and blackened, still ablaze, lying in the doorway of a cell.

It took him a second or two to realise it was a body.

'Leave them,' shouted Colston, forced to shout to make himself heard above the roaring of flames and the clanging of firebells.

Dexter turned to look at his companion, his watery eyes narrowed.

'We can't,' he roared back, ducking as a piece of the ceiling crashed down only feet from him. 'If the fire brigade reach Ward 5 before us . . .' He allowed the sentence to trail off, then shook his head.

Both men sucked in deep breaths and ran on. Colston thought his lungs were on fire too.

Another door and they would reach their goal.

It was ahead of them at the end of the corridor and, as he ran, Dexter pulled a bunch of keys from his pocket. As he reached the door he could feel an incredible heat from beyond, even through the thick steel.

He turned the key and wrestled with the handle, ignoring the blisters that rose on his hands. He tugged the door open. The two of them dashed in.

The ceiling was ablaze.

From one end of the corridor to the other the area above them was one writhing, twisting mass of fire. Lumps of blackened plaster and wood fell around them, some striking them.

Dexter moved towards the first door and selected a key.

From inside there were screams. Wild, almost animalistic yells of fear and rage.

'We can't' shouted Colston, shielding his head as more of the burning masonry showered down.

'We have no choice,' Dexter told him. Another piece of the ceiling fell inwards, driving them back, the flames rearing up, snatching at them like venomous reptiles. Colston shielded his face, raising his voice again to make it heard above the raging inferno that now threatened to engulf them.

'We can't get them all out,' he shouted, staring wide-eyed at Dexter.

The older man realised he was right.

He headed for the last cell.

'No,' shouted Colston in horror. 'You can't.' He tried to prevent Dexter opening the door but the other man already had the key in the lock. He pushed Colston away.

The door swung open.

Dexter thrust the bunch of keys into his colleague's hand.

'Open that door,' he bellowed, the heat now almost unbearable. He nodded to the door at the end of the corridor and Colston did as he was told, pushing the key in, straining to turn it, to release the lock.

More sparks showered him; the ceiling seemed to hover, as if suspended on invisible wires.

It was a matter of moments before the entire thing caved in.

Colston twisted the key helplessly in the lock, afraid that the heat might have warped it out of shape.

Inside the cell Dexter took a cautious step towards the occupant. As ever he found that he was shaking slightly as he drew nearer.

'We have to go,' he said, his voice calm and measured, his eyes never leaving the inhabitant of the room. He could feel how dry his throat was. Not all of it, he realised, was due to the fire. When he tried to swallow it felt as if somebody had filled his mouth with chalk.

'Come on,' screamed Colston.

'We must go now,' Dexter said, his tone more forceful.

'Dexter, for God's sake,' Colston bellowed, looking up at the ceiling.

Inside the cell the single occupant moved towards Dexter.

It was then that the ceiling collapsed.

Twenty-eight: Exile

The figure moved slowly in the darkness, treading carefully in the gloom, cursing the lack of light but welcoming the cover the blackness brought.

The only sound was the crunch of footsteps on the gravel of the driveway.

An owl sat in the lower branches of a nearby tree, unable to hunt as efficiently without the presence of the moon. It watched the figure that moved from the house to the car repeatedly.

More than once the figure would stand still beside the car as if listening to the stillness of the night, ears attuned to the slightest sound or movement. Then, satisfied that no one else was around, the dark shape would move stealthily about its business once again.

There was rain in the air, the odd gust of wind bringing with it the first droplets that threatened a storm. Banks of cloud were gathering to the west, blown ever closer by the rising wind. It rattled the branches of the trees and ruffled the feathers of the owl, which finally tired of watching the furtive movement and flew off, its wings beating quietly in the darkness.

The figure looked up, following the bird as it soared high into the night sky in search of prey.

After a moment longer spent listening to the stillness the shape returned to the house.

There were no lights burning within the building; the darkness inside was as total as that of the tenebrous gloom without. But the figure moved more assuredly within the confines of the house, scurrying back and forth from room *to room, sometimes pausing in one room, glancing around as if to check that everything was in place.*

Finally, the figure ascended the stairs, slowly but purposefully.

The rain began to fall more rapidly now, the wind propelling the droplets like handfuls of cold gravel.

When the figure emerged from the house again it turned its face to the rain as if in welcome, standing there for a moment before turning to another dark shape which accompanied it.

Had the owl still been perched in the tree it would have seen a second figure join the first in the blackness.

The first of them opened the passenger side door and ensured that the second was comfortably seated, then closed the door and locked it from the outside.

That task completed, the first figure walked unhurriedly around to the other side of the car and slid behind the wheel.

The silence was broken by the noise of the engine, which idled for a moment. Then the car was driven away from the front of the house, the wheels crushing gravel as the tyres rolled.

It began to pick up speed along the short driveway then turned into the road.

There was no traffic about at such a late hour. The occupants of the car may as well have been the last two people on earth.

The car disappeared into the night.

Twenty-nine

He'd stolen the car an hour earlier.

The automatic transmission on the Datsun had taken a bit of getting used to and when he'd first slipped behind the steering wheel he'd cursed his luck. But, fuck it, he needed a car. He'd manage. Now Mathew Bryce slowed up as he approached the traffic lights in Shaftesbury Avenue, his eyes scanning the hordes of people that filled the bustling thoroughfare. So intently was he studying the throng that he didn't notice the lights slip onto green. The blast of a hooter behind alerted him to the situation.

Bryce swung the car right, peering round at the driver behind, raising two fingers. The man mouthed his own insult back and drove past.

'Cunt,' muttered Bryce, his eyes still flicking back and forth. He saw couples. Old, young. Girls in groups. Sometimes alone. Some people hurried along, others strolled through the night. A young man was running along, trying to stop a taxi before it pulled away, but he was unsuccessful and stood, hands on hips, glaring at the vehicle as it moved off. Bryce passed him and grinned out at the man.

All around the neon signs from clubs, pubs and restaurants filled the night, creating a kind of artificial twilight. With the window wound down, Bryce could hear the crackle of so much static electricity. He slowed down as he saw a woman crossing the road ahead of him, watching her breasts bouncing in her tight fitting top. Her silver-coloured hair trailed over her shoulders,

114

blown by the wind that whipped through the narrow streets. It also disturbed the litter that lay in the gutters and on the pavements. An empty can was sent rattling across the concrete like a kind of bizarre tumbleweed. A youth passing by took a kick at it and sent it skittering into the road. Further along an old man, bundled up in a thick overcoat, was sorting through one of the overflowing dustbins, picking out portions of half-eaten food and carefully dropping them into the plastic bag he carried, making his choice as fastidiously as any gourmet at a buffet table.

Bryce swung the car right again, then sharp left into Rupert Street. Again he slowed down, peering at a young woman standing in a doorway talking to a tall man in a suit. Bryce stared at her with interest. She couldn't have been more than twenty, her shapely legs revealed by the short mini-skirt she wore. She was puffing contentedly on a cigarette as she spoke. Bryce stopped the car, the engine idling.

It was a couple of minutes before the man finally noticed and looked questioningly across at Bryce, who was now leaning on the windowframe, looking more closely at the girl.

'You lost, mate?' the man in the faded suit called.

Bryce didn't answer.

The girl also turned to face him now, brushing a stray hair from her mouth.

He looked at her features, his own face expressionless.

'What do you want?' the man called.

A car turned into the road behind Bryce, the driver braking to avoid a collision.

The man in the faded suit moved towards the car.

'You got a fucking problem, or what?' he said, irritably.

Bryce pressed down on the accelerator and the car moved off, leaving the girl to stare after him. He turned another corner and saw a car pulling out of a parking space. Bryce guided the Datsun into it, cursing when it juddered slightly. He switched off the engine and sat there for a moment, his window down, the noises of the night filling his ears. He leant forward, his forehead resting on the steering wheel. From across the street he could hear music and, all around him, voices and the ever-present crackle of neon. He put both hands over his ears as if to shut out the noise. Then, slowly, he sat up again, looking around him, catching a glimpse of his own reflection in the rear view mirror. It stared back at him accusingly. His face was pale, the dark rings beneath his eyes all the more prominent because of his pallor. His hair was thick but combed back severely from his prominent forehead. As he ran a hand over his chin he heard the rasp of his bristles against his fingertips.

Bryce grunted, gripped the rear-view mirror and tore it off.

He hurled it onto the back seat and sat there, panting. Then he turned slowly and looked at the blanket that lay across the rear seat.

The blanket had belonged to the owner of the car.

The can of petrol and the hunting knife it concealed belonged to Bryce.

Thirty

For a moment she thought he was going to fall over. Paula Wilson stood rigid as she watched Mark Eaton lurch from the doorway of the pub in Cambridge Circus. He shot out

116

a hand and steadied himself, smiling stupidly at her.

The gesture only made her more angry.

'You never know when to stop, do you?' she snapped angrily, looking first at him then at the night sky. The first drops of rain were beginning to fall. Paula pulled up the collar of her suede jacket. A large droplet of rain fell onto it and she sighed. Grey suede. It would be ruined in the downpour.

'I'll be okay,' said Eaton, stumbling towards her, bumping into a dustbin. Some of its contents spilled out onto the pavement and he stooped to pick them up as if he were tidying his own house. Passers-by looked quickly at the young couple, particularly at the young woman in the grey suede suit who was shouting so vehemently.

'You probably can't even remember where you left the car, can you?' she rasped.

'I just need some fresh air, that's all,' he told her, none too convincingly. 'I'll be fine.' He sucked in several deep lungfuls of the night air. The odour of burning hot-dogs came wafting to him and he noticed a street vendor cooking the blackened frankfurters a few yards away. The smell made him want to vomit. He saw Paula turn away and made a grab for her arm. 'Where are you going?' he wanted to know.

'I'm going home,' she told him, shaking free of his grip and setting off towards Romilly Street.

Eaton followed her.

'I'll drive you,' he said.

'I'm not getting in a car with *you* in *that* state,' she said angrily. 'I'll get a taxi.' She continued walking, Eaton now almost running to keep up with her. Her high heels clicked on the pavement, beating out a furious tattoo.

As she reached the side of the Prince Charles Theatre he grabbed her again and pushed her into one of the sheltered doorways marked 'Exit'. The theatre had been

117

closed for more than forty minutes now; they weren't likely to be disturbed.

'I'm not letting you go,' he told her, standing in front of her to block her way.

'Get out of my way, Mark,' she said, glaring at him.

'I told you, just let me clear my head and I'll drive you.'

'It's going to take more than fresh air to clear your head tonight. Maybe you should try dynamite.' She thought about pushing past him again, but as she saw the rain beginning to fall more swiftly she realised that perhaps, for the time being, sheltering in this doorway was more prudent. She looked up at him, her eyes still full of anger. 'Why did you have to spoil it, Mark?' she said, her voice quieter.

'I don't know what you're talking about,' he told her. 'Look, I had more to drink than I should have done. I'm sorry about that.'

'Well, it's too bloody late now, isn't it? You can't drive in your condition.'

He smiled that stupid grin again. It only served to make her more irritable.

'It's always the same when you get together with Dean and Richard, isn't it? They keep drinking and you have to keep up with them, don't you?'

'Don't speak to me as if I'm a child, Paula,' he said, wiping his mouth with the back of his hand.

'When you're with *them* you act like one,' she chided. 'Why did you tell them we were going to be in that pub tonight, anyway?'

'I didn't *tell* them,' he protested. 'That's where they usually go for a drink. It wasn't *my* fault they happened to come in while we were there. It's a free country, you know. What was I supposed to say? "Sorry, lads, but it's Paula's birthday, we're out celebrating, so would you mind pissing off and leaving us alone?" I work with them, for Christ's sake. They're mates.'

'Well, then, get one of them to drive you home,' she said bitterly.

'We were supposed to be spending the night together,' he said, touching her cheek with one hand. He grinned again.

'A celebratory fuck, is that what you mean?'

'I wouldn't have put it quite like that,' he chuckled, and the chuckle soon became a fully-fledged laugh.

Paula decided she'd rather get her grey suede suit wet than endure any more of his drunken ramblings. She pushed past him and out into the downpour. He tried to stop her but she pushed him away.

'I'm sorry, Paula,' he called after her.

'So am I!' she yelled back, pushing past a couple of young men who eyed her approvingly, one of them whistling as she swept along the road.

The bastard, she thought. The stupid, unfeeling, child-ish bastard. For a bloke of twenty-six he acted like a twelve-year-old sometimes, she thought, trying to ignore the rain. If his two idiot friends hadn't turned up then everything would have been all right. She *would* have gone back to his flat, she *would* have spent the night. A celebratory fuck had been high on her list of priorities to mark her twenty-third birthday. But now there would be none of that. Perhaps this was the excuse she had been looking for to stop seeing him. Over the past four months she had come to realise more and more that Mark Eaton wasn't the type of man she wanted a relationship with. She wasn't sure if she wanted a relationship with any man yet. Not a long term one, anyway. She was twenty-three, for Christ's sake. Her whole life was in front of her; the last thing she wanted was to be tied to one man.

The rain was easing up slightly, she noted with relief,

but it had still fallen with sufficient ferocity to soak her jacket and skirt. She cursed to herself, looking up the street for a taxi. One was just dropping off at Wheeler's restaurant ahead of her. She hurried towards it but the driver pulled away, switching his light off as he did so.

She turned and watched him go then trudged on, passing a club called Maxims. There were two men standing in the doorway, both of them foreign, she guessed, from a quick glance at them.

'You want to come inside, darling?' asked one, smiling at her, revealing a mouthful of yellowed teeth.

She ignored him and walked on.

'You've got a nice arse,' the other one shouted after her and she heard their laughter. She felt her cheeks burning but she also afforded herself a brief smile.

Yes, you bastards, she told herself, I have got a nice arse. It's for sure you'll never see it.

You or Mark Eaton.

She'd ring him at work tomorrow, tell him she didn't want to see him again, she decided. Time to be decisive, she told herself. Ahead of her was Dean Street, the lights from the McDonald's at the Shaftesbury Avenue end bathing the street round about. She'd be able to get a taxi outside there without any trouble. They were often dropping off at the hotel round the corner.

Ahead of her some construction work was being done behind the Shaftesbury Hotel. Even in the darkness she could see the outline of a crane nudging upwards towards the rain-sodden sky. The yellow shape of a JCB was also unmistakeable, even in the gloom. Safety lights had been placed at the entrance to the small site as a warning to motorists. She passed by the high boards that separated the site from the pavement, muttering to herself as she stepped in something soft. She hoped it was mud.

Balancing on one foot she reached into her handbag

and took out a tissue, wiping the mess from her shoe.

She noticed a taxi pass and saw, with relief, that it was dropping off at the end of the street. She slipped her shoe back on and prepared to sprint after the vehicle.

'Don't pull away,' she murmured to herself, almost slipping over in more of the mud, her eyes fixed on the cab.

From behind her, from the darkness of the site, one hand clamped around her mouth, another tugged at her hair.

She was pulled off her feet.

Swallowed by the blackness.

There wasn't even time to scream.

Thirty-one

Her mind went blank.

There were no thoughts at all, only emptiness. No flood of fearful imaginings as she was pulled to the ground. No terror at what fate befell her.

Paula Wilson's mind had been wiped clean as surely as if it had been a blackboard swept clear of chalk. All she was aware of was the pressure on her face and hair, which suddenly slackened as she was thrown down into the mud. The glutinous muck seemed to close around her, holding her motionless; but what stopped her moving was the absolute terror of her situation. The only thing that seemed to respond was her bladder. She wet herself, urine running warmly down the inside of her thigh.

She felt those hands on her again, tugging at her hair, clamping her jaw shut. She was being pulled behind the partition that separated the street from the construction site, out of sight of any passers-by.

Out of sight, out of mind.

A handful of her hair was torn from her scalp and she felt searing pain. Blood ran in a thin trickle down the side of her face, but even the pain wasn't sufficient to galvanise her into action. Her body and her mind remained as frozen as if they'd been injected with Novocaine.

She felt a great weight pressing down on her chest and stomach and realised that her attacker had knelt on her midriff, driving one knee into her solar plexus. The air in her lungs was expelled rapidly. She felt light-headed, as if she were about to faint, but the coldness of the mud on her face and legs kept her conscious.

Then she saw the knife.

The desire to survive suddenly became uppermost in her mind. Her muscles unlocked and she struck out at her assailant.

Mathew Bryce kept his weight on her torso and slashed at her hand as she struck him.

The blade sliced effortlessly through her palm, opening it in a wide and bloody wound, the edges of which slid back like an open mouth. Blood splashed him, its warmth a marked contrast to the chill of the night.

With one hand still fixed over her mouth he drove the blade forward again.

It punctured Paula's left cheek, grating against teeth as he pulled it free, ripping a molar away with it. The tooth, still fixed to a portion of gum, fell into the mud. She raised her hands to protect herself once more and his next thrust cut through the fleshy part of her thumb. He felt her breath against his hand as she tried to scream in pain and terror. He sliced through the fingers of her right hand, severing the tendons.

She was writhing beneath him now, finding reserves of strength he had not anticipated. He turned the knife in his hand and brought it down in a stabbing action, the blade shearing through her left breast and cracking two ribs. He tugged it free and brought it down again, this time breaking her left collarbone. Blood was pumping from the wounds, some of it spraying onto his face as she waved her hands about in a vain attempt to ward off the killing strikes.

Bryce finally rolled off her, grunting as she lashed out with her foot and kicked him in the side. She tried to scream but the gash in the side of her cheek had caused blood to run back into her throat and all she could do was to retch as the coppery liquid clogged her windpipe. She tried to raise herself up, mud sticking to her clothes and hair.

Bryce stabbed her again, just above the right kidney, and she pitched forward, trying to crawl now through the mud, tears of pain and fear streaming down her cheeks. He got to his feet and drove a powerful kick into her side, smiling as he heard a rib crack. He kicked again. And again. He stamped on the back of her head as hard as he could, twisting on his shoe to grind her face further into the mud.

Further into the mud.

He put all his weight on that foot, pressing with all his strength and weight, watching her trying to wriggle free, trying to raise her face from the mud which was suffocating her. Her movements gradually became less frantic, her bloodied hands clutching backwards ever more feebly at his leg.

She wasn't quite dead when he dropped to his knees in the mud beside her, grabbed her matted hair and tugged her face up so that he could look at her.

The initial impact with the ground, despite its softness,

had broken her nose. Her face was a mask of blood and sticky mud. Both her lips were split, crimson fluid running over her chin. Bryce rolled her onto her back and began tugging her clothes off, hurling them aside as he reached her underwear, tearing frenziedly at her bra, exposing her breasts, ripping her flimsy knickers off to expose her pubic bush.

He spread her legs wide, using his stained finger tips to part her vaginal lips. For long moments he knelt there gazing at her genitalia, then he reached behind him towards some crumpled, mud-soaked cellophane.

Balling it up he pushed it into her vagina, using his first two fingers to shove it deeper inside her. He found an empty crisp packet, the wrapper from a bar of chocolate. These he also pushed into the swollen orifice, jamming it with such force that he tore one of her vaginal lips. Fresh blood spurted onto the mud.

The ring pull from a can. He drove that into her as well, the metal tearing more of the delicate flesh.

She was still moving, still trying to scream with this fresh pain, this unbearable perversion he was committing. Her jaw was broken; she could not open it to vent her cry of agony.

He used the tip of the knife to force a piece of stone into her riven orifice, the razor-sharp edge gashing her badly.

Mercifully, Paula Wilson passed out.

Bryce crawled over her and looked into her face, pulling open her eyelids as if suspecting she was merely pretending to be unconscious. He stabbed her again, this time in the throat, leaving the knife there, driven with incredible force through her until the tip actually punctured the wet earth and left her pinned there like some exhibit in a museum.

He got to his feet and walked towards the partition, his

hands reaching assuredly in the blackness for the can of petrol. He unscrewed the cap and walked back towards Paula. The powerful smell of the fuel filled his nostrils as he tossed the cap away, raising the can into the air.

He tipped it up, feeling the thick fluid cascading down over him, soaking through his clothes, some of it trickling into his mouth. It made him retch, but he stood there until the can was empty and the golden cascade had finished. Then he tossed it to one side and stood there, hands by his sides, looking down at her corpse.

He reached into the pocket of his jacket and pulled out a lighter, holding it before him for long seconds, petrol dripping from his hand. He flicked it, looking at the flame which glowed dully before him, fluttering in the breeze.

Bryce smiled, feeling the petrol soaking through his clothes, feeling the cold clamminess on his skin. The smell was almost overpowering.

He lit the lighter once more, then, with a slow deliberate movement, he pressed the flame to his petrol-sodden clothes.

It ignited immediately.

Thirty-two

'What is this? Guy Fawkes week?'

Detective Sergeant Stuart Finn took a drag on his cigarette and looked down at the body of Mathew Bryce.

The corpse had been burned beyond recognition, the flesh stripped from the bones, his clothes simply vaporised by the ferocity of the fire. Finn noticed that the stud on Bryce's jeans had melted in the heat, the molten

125

metal having dribbled into the dead man's navel. The air reeked of the sickly-sweet smell of burned flesh.

Detective Inspector Frank Gregson knelt beside the body, his eyes fixed on the face. The mouth was open, stretched wide in an incinerated rictus. A couple of white teeth gleamed in the smoking hole that passed for a mouth but, as Gregson himself looked more closely, he saw that some fillings in the man's mouth had also melted. He prodded the remains with the end of his pen, watching as a sizeable chunk of burned flesh fell away. He got to his feet and motioned for the ambulanceman to replace the blanket over the body, hiding it from view once more.

About a yard from the remains of Bryce lay another blanket-shrouded shape.

The remains of Paula Wilson.

Gregson and Finn wandered across to the second body, both men looking around them.

The building site was a hive of activity now, despite the lateness of the hour. Both uniformed and plain-clothes officers were moving about. Men from forensics were picking their way slowly and carefully over the site, their search aided by several powerful arc lights that had been set up around the perimeter. The cold white glow of the lamps illuminated the murder scene.

Elsewhere on the site men moved around taking photos of the place and of the bodies. Outside in the street, would-be onlookers were kept away by uniformed men. A couple of ambulances stood at the entrance to the site, along with a police car. Unmarked cars were parked opposite. The officers who'd arrived in them were taking statements from those who had seen or heard anything, hoping that there would be some lead to the case, some clue as to why Paula Wilson had been murdered. Perhaps some clue as well to who had killed her.

126

The bodies had been found by the owner of a record shop in Dean Street. He'd been working late in the office above his shop and had caught sight of the flames coming from behind the partition as he'd been walking down the street towards Shaftesbury Avenue. The man had been taken to hospital suffering from shock. He was now under sedation. He'd managed to burble something about a burned body to a uniformed man who'd been on foot patrol nearby. The uniformed man had called through to New Scotland Yard.

Gregson and Finn had been there within fifteen minutes.

By 12.36 a.m. the area had been sealed off and was swarming with policemen.

'Where the hell is Barclay?' said Gregson as the two men approached the second body.

'He's been called, he's on his way,' Finn said, taking another drag on his cigarette.

Gregson dropped to his haunches and pulled back the blanket that covered Paula Wilson.

His face was expressionless as he studied the body, pulling the cover further down until he revealed the full extent of her injuries. He stroked his chin, his gaze focused on the rubbish stuffed into her vagina. Finn noticed it too and raised his eyebrows.

'Keep Britain tidy, eh?' he murmured quietly.

Gregson ignored his remark, his gaze fixed on the girl's torn and mutilated genital area.

He stuffed her full of rubbish.

Gregson looked at her other injuries, at the wounds in her chest and throat. The cuts on her face and hands. He pointed to the bad gash across her palm and the lesser ones on her fingers.

'Defence cuts,' he noted. 'She was trying to fight him off.'

127

'I'll tell you what puzzles me,' said Finn, looking down at the body. 'Why didn't he burn *her* as well as himself?'

Gregson could only shrug.

'Why did he burn *himself*?' the DI mused.

'Was there any ID on him?' Finn wanted to know.

'If there was, it went up in smoke with him. What about the girl?'

'Paula Wilson, twenty-three years old. Single. She lived with her parents.'

'Have they been told yet?'

Finn nodded.

'They've got to come in and identify the body, poor sods,' he said.

'What was she carrying when he attacked her?' Gregson wanted to know.

'Just a handbag.'

'Anything taken?'

'She had credit cards and fifty-seven quid on her. As far as I can tell he didn't even *look* in the bag.'

'Because he didn't intend stealing anything,' Gregson said flatly, pulling the cover back over the body and getting to his feet. His knees cracked loudly as he straightened up. 'He got what he wanted.'

'And then torched himself? It doesn't make much sense, does it?' said Finn.

'Just like the other one didn't,' the DI reminded his partner. Both men looked at each other. 'Hell of a coincidence, isn't it? One man robs a bank, doesn't take any money, kills six people then burns himself up. A few days later another man mugs a young woman, but he doesn't want her money; all he wants to do is kill her then, when he's finished, he sets fire to himself. Like you said, perhaps Guy Fawkes night has come a bit early this year.'

'You think they're linked?'

'What the fuck do *you* think?' snapped Gregson irritably. 'Two murderers commit motiveless crimes then burn themselves to death within one mile of each other in the space of a week. You're telling me there's no connection?' He shook his head. 'What we've got to find out is who they were and what the hell that connection *is*, because I've got a bad feeling about this.'

'Like what?'

'Like, they might not be the only two.'

Thirty-three

He paused before the mirror and adjusted the knot in his tie, finally satisfied that it was straight. Then Jim Scott took a last look around the room, checking that everything was tidy.

He'd been up since seven-thirty that morning, dusting, picking up any stray pieces of paper from the floor. He even managed to force himself into doing the washing-up, which had been lying in the sink for a couple of days.

Scott polished the handle of the door to the room which used to be his father's. He didn't go inside. There was no need. There was nothing to tidy up in there.

He had rung Carol at 8.30 that morning and asked her if she would see him after work. Would she come back to his flat? They could get a take-away and eat it when they got back. He had found himself gripping the receiver tightly.

Please say yes.

She had agreed without her customary reticence. Scott had put the phone down and shouted triumphantly, punching the air as if he'd just been informed he'd won the pools or come into a vast inheritance. All the anger and disappointment of the past few days was forgotten. She was going to spend the night with him. That was all that mattered.

She'd been to the flat on a number of occasions before, usually staying the night. When they'd first started seeing each other it had been almost every night. He studied his reflection in the mirror again, noticing that his smile had faded slightly. He wished that things could be as they were in the beginning. There had been passion between them then. There had never been any excuses about not being able to see him then.

Not like now.

Scott crossed the bedroom to the cabinet beside the bed.

So much they had to talk about.

He slid open the top drawer.

The Beretta 92S automatic lay beside a pile of hand-kerchiefs.

He looked at the weapon for long moments.

So much they had to talk about.

Scott slid the drawer shut once more.

Carol rolled over in bed and sighed, gazing at the poster of James Dean on her bedroom wall.

Beneath the picture of the film idol were the words: BOULEVARD OF BROKEN DREAMS.

They were the only kind of dreams she knew.

Broken. Wrecked.

Ray Plummer had rung about twenty minutes before Scott to apologise that, again, he couldn't see her. He'd make it up to her, though, he had said. He'd get her something nice. Something expensive.

130

When Scott had rung she'd said yes to him almost without thinking. Now she began to realise what she had agreed to do. To spend the night with him. By agreeing to spend the night, had she also agreed to sleep with him? They had been lovers, after all, still were occasionally; although the term lovers was redundant as far as Carol was concerned. *They had sex occasionally.* That was it. In her mind, there was no involvement, nothing other than physical contact.

She knew it was different for Scott.

But she knew that there were other reasons why she must see him tonight. She had no doubt that he was becoming suspicious of her. Of her excuses. She needed to spend time with him to allay those suspicions for a while.

Until when?

Until it was time to tell him that it was all over between them?

Until it was time to move in with Plummer?

Time for the final escape.

Carol rubbed her face with both hands and thought about getting out of bed.

For some reason she looked across at the phone, perhaps expecting it to ring again.

Only this time it might not be either Scott or Plummer.

When it had rung earlier that morning she had hesitated for interminable seconds before picking it up, remembering the call of the previous night. It had taken a monumental effort of will and courage finally to snatch up the receiver. Even in the light of day she felt the fear pricking her as she pressed it to her ear and spoke into it. She had been hugely relieved to hear Plummer's voice.

Should she tell *him* about the calls?

Perhaps she should tell Scott.

Tell someone, for God's sake. Don't keep it to yourself.

131

And if she did tell them? What could they do? She herself had no idea who was making them. Or why.

Carol swung herself out of bed and headed towards the toilet, glancing at the phone as she passed. She paused in the doorway, looking down apprehensively at the phone.

He wouldn't ring, she told herself. Whoever he was, he wouldn't ring now. Not so early. He seemed to prefer the hours of darkness.

Whoever he was.

She suddenly reached for the jack plug and pulled it from the socket in the wall.

She was safe from his calls now.

At least for the time being.

Thirty-four

The stench was appalling.

DS Finn pulled his handkerchief from his pocket and held it close to his nose as he peered down at the body.

'He's not as badly burned as the first one,' said Phillip Barclay, prodding the remains of the dead man's face with a probe. A piece of blackened skin came away from the cheek, exposing the bone beneath.

'Will that make identification easier?' Gregson wanted to know, his eyes never leaving the corpse.

'Theoretically,' the coroner told him. 'But his hands are very badly burned; that rules out finding him by his prints. It looks like it's going to be dental records again.'

'Provided he's in the files,' Finn added, his voice muffled through the handkerchief.

Gregson looked at his companion as if contemptuous of the fact that he found the stench of burned flesh so repellent. Then he returned his attention to the body.

'Any further progress on the first one?' he asked.

Barclay could only shake his head. He seemed more interested in his new subject. He used a probe to force the jaws open a little wider, peering into the black maw that was Bryce's mouth. Even the tongue was burned, black and swollen by the ferocity of the heat. Two fillings in the dead man's rear teeth had indeed melted and Barclay chipped away at the molten matter with one end of the probe, cursing when a whole tooth came free of the scorched gums. He retrieved it from the back of Bryce's throat with a pair of tweezers, dropping it with a dull clink into a small kidney dish.

'See the hands,' he said, lifting the first two digits of the dead man's left hand, indicating how the fire had stripped away the flesh and bone as far as the first knuckle. What remained resembled ash and Gregson feared it would simply blow away should a strong breeze fill the room.

All around them the steady hum of the air conditioning, keeping the room at an even sixty-five degrees, was the only sound apart from their voices.

'What about the girl?' said Gregson, moving to the metal table next to Bryce.

Laid out on it, her nakedness exposed for all to see, was Paula Wilson. Her skin was already tinged blue in places from loss of blood. The savage gashes made by Bryce's blade stood out even more vividly against the paleness of her flesh. Gregson stared down at the corpse, into the open eyes. He allowed his gaze to wander over the slashed throat, past the punctured chest. He looked briefly at the cuts on her hands, at the dark bruises which covered her torso and upper thighs like ink stains on blotting paper. The flesh of her vagina was torn and

133

swollen. Her pubic hair had been shaved off during the course of the autopsy. The Y-shaped incision from pelvis to throat had also been made by Barclay in his quest to discover more about the nature of the girl's death. It may have seemed obvious from the state of the wounds in her throat and chest, but he had to follow procedure.

Gregson saw that her entire body was a mass of cuts and bruises, some small, some huge. The fatal cuts.

'Cause of death, as you can see, was stabbing,' said Barclay. 'Although I found petechiae which would seem to indicate he . . .'

'What the hell is that?' snapped Gregson.

'Small haemorrhages in the blood vessels of the eyes, usually associated with strangulation or suffocation.' He pointed to her battered face. 'That would have happened when he pushed her face into the mud.'

'The wound in the throat was the death wound,' the pathologist continued. 'She lost an enormous amount of blood.'

'What about the things he stuffed inside her?' Finn wanted to know, glancing at the ravaged vaginal area, the flesh around it blackened with bruises.

Barclay shrugged his shoulders and turned to the work-top behind him. He picked up a small plastic bag and laid it beside the dead girl's body.

'I took eight separate articles from inside her vagina,' he said, indicating the contents of the bag. The stone. The ring pull.

'Sick fucker,' hissed Finn. 'What the hell would he want to do that for?'

'Was she raped?' Gregson asked.

Barclay shook his head.

'The vaginal swabs showed evidence of urine, but that was hers. The killer left no bodily secretions of any kind. Rape wasn't his motive. He just wanted to kill her.'

'Well, he made a fucking good job of it,' Finn said flatly. He nodded towards the defence cuts on her hands. 'Looks like she put up quite a fight.'

Barclay nodded slowly.

Gregson, one hand cupping his chin, stood staring down at the body.

Vagina stuffed with rubbish.

He had seen something like this before.

Coincidence?

'Was she dead when he did it?' Finn asked. 'When he shoved those things inside her?'

'No,' Barclay said matter of factly. 'The amount of bleeding from the vagina would indicate she was still alive. Aware of what he was doing. My guess is, if she'd been dead he wouldn't have bothered.'

'Like I said to you earlier,' Finn began. 'Why not torch *her* as well as himself?' He looked at Gregson, who had wandered back to look at the incinerated corpse of Bryce.

The DI stood as if mesmerised by the body before him.

The stillness of the pathology lab was beginning to make Finn uneasy and the infernal stench of burned flesh was repulsive. He waved a hand as if to dispel the odour. He thought about lighting up a cigarette, even reached for the packet, but Barclay's disapproving glance finally dissuaded him.

'Is your report finished?' Gregson asked the pathologist.

'Almost.'

'I want it as soon as it is.'

He turned and headed for the door, followed by Finn.

'I want to know who those two fucking blokes are,' he said sharply. 'And I want to know fast. There's two

135

now. There might be three soon.' He opened the door and walked out.

Finn scuttled after him.

'Frank, do you know something I *don't*?' he said irritably as they walked towards the lift, their footsteps echoing through the corridor. 'You said something back at the murder site about the two suicides being linked.'

Gregson nodded.

'What makes you say that?' Finn demanded.

'I just think it's a hell of a coincidence that two killers should both burn themselves up after committing a crime, especially when both could have escaped.'

They reached the lift and Gregson jabbed the button to call it.

Finn lit up a cigarette and puffed on it, glancing up at the numbers that lit up in turn as the lift descended towards them.

'So what do you make of it?' the DS wanted to know. 'The way you're talking, you make it sound like some kind of fucking conspiracy.'

'Look, I don't know what the hell is going on, right?' snapped Gregson as the lift bumped to a halt at their floor. He stepped inside. 'All I know is there's something fucking weird happening.'

'Ten out of ten for observation, Frank,' said Finn, smiling thinly. 'I think I'd have to agree with you there.'

Gregson glared at his companion.

'If you've got something on your mind you should tell me,' the DS said irritably.

'I'll tell you what's on my mind. That you should go home now and leave me to check a few things out. Got it?'

'Like what?'

'Go home, Stuart. Leave it to me. If it checks out then I'll tell you. If it doesn't, it's only *my* time that's been wasted, right?'

'We're supposed to be working *together* on this,' Finn reminded him.

The lift came to a halt and the doors slid open but Finn shot out a hand and closed them once more, his finger pressed on the 'DOOR CLOSE' button.

'What the fuck are you doing?' snapped Gregson.

'Level with me, Frank. Tell me what you're thinking,' the DS said, looking his partner in the eye.

Gregson looked down at Finn's hand, his finger still on the button.

'I'm thinking that if you don't move your fucking arm I'm going to break it,' he hissed.

Finn released the button and the doors slid open. Gregson stepped out, looking back at his partner.

'Leave this to me for the time being,' he said. Then, as the doors slid shut, he turned and walked away.

The MO was the same.

Gregson had known it from the first time he'd seen Paula Wilson's body.

Now he was sure.

Multiple stab wounds, no rape, but the vagina of the victim stuffed with rubbish.

He flipped through the file before him, checking the photos, comparing them to those he had of Paula Wilson. The photos in the file were eighteen months old.

Three different girls, but each one had been killed the same way. Each one had been mutilated, each one had been defiled.

137

Gregson ran a hand through his hair and sat back in his chair. He reached for his mug of coffee and took a sip, wincing when it was cold on his lips and tongue. He put the mug down, his gaze skipping over the pictures laid out before him.

Three girls, murdered eighteen months ago. Stabbed and beaten, their vaginas stuffed with rubbish.

And now, four hours ago, Paula Wilson, stabbed and beaten, her vagina stuffed with rubbish.

The DI reached for his phone, picked it up and jabbed the extension number for the Records Office. He waited as the phone rang.

Waited.

Finally it was picked up and he heard Steve Houghton's voice.

Gregson didn't bother to announce himself.

Steve, have you got a file down there on a bloke called Mathew Bryce?' he said, drumming his fingertips on his desk.

Houghton said that he had.

'When you've got a minute, I'd like to see it,' the DI told him.

It was there again.

He'd found it in more or less the same place as before. Removed it from the shattered, burned remains of the second killer's head.

Barclay looked at the blackened piece of matter in the dish; it was smaller than his thumb nail. Next to it was the portion of the mysterious substance he'd taken from the first body.

Both were blackened by the fire, both melted.

He frowned as he prodded first one, then the other with the end of his pen.

Analysis of the two pieces had shown that they were indeed composed of plastic and a number of other elements. Silicon had been found in both.

He exhaled deeply, wondering if he should include this piece of knowledge in his report, wondering if he should mention his findings to Gregson. He decided to withhold the information for the time being. Until he knew more. Until he had some idea, however vague, what these strange, melted objects were.

So far, he was clueless. And that worried him.

Thirty-five

'I think we've got trouble.'

The door to Jim Scott's office had been flung open without a knock and Zena Murray was standing before him, her face pale.

'What sort of trouble?' he asked, getting to his feet and following her out of the office.

'Two fucking drunks,' she said, her tone a mixture of annoyance and anxiety.

'Where the fuck is Rick?' Scott demanded. 'He's paid to keep things running smoothly. What kind of bouncer is he?'

'Rick's watching them but they've got some friends with them, too.'

Scott nodded and followed Zena out into the main floorshow area of 'Loveshow'.

He glanced across at the bed and saw Carol lying on it, her basque open to reveal her breasts, her tiny G-string barely concealing the tight curls of her pubic bush. On either side of the bed the seats were full.

He counted five men, all in their thirties, watching the tableau before them.

Close by him Rick Calder leant against the wall, hands dug in the pockets of his jeans.

Scott jerked his head towards the bouncer, a gesture designed to bring him closer. When Scott spoke he had to raise his voice to make himself heard above the loud music accompanying Carol's act.

> '. . . *I see you walking by,*
> *You got that faraway look in your eye . . .*'

Calder, a couple of years younger than Scott, kept his eyes on the five men as he listened.

'What's going on?' Scott shouted.

'Those fuckers over there,' Calder said, nodding in their direction. 'A couple of them are pissed.'

'Then why the hell did you let them in in the first place?' Scott demanded.

'I was having a squirt. I didn't see them come in,' Calder said defensively.

One of the men was on his feet, swaying in time to the music and also to Carol's gyrations on the bed. He took a stumbling step towards her, then seemed to sway and fall backwards into his chair. The other men laughed.

Scott looked on, his eyes blazing.

Carol continued with her act, trying to ignore the men close by.

'Show us everything,' shouted one of the men, his voice audible even above the thunderous music.

'Show us your cunt,' another called.

Carol ignored his remarks, her eyes closed momentarily as if she were concentrating on some complex choreographed movement. She slipped the silk from her

140

shoulders and pulled the flimsy garment off, rubbing it against her breasts.

'Do it, you fucking whore,' shouted one of the men, laughing. His companions laughed too.

The music roared on.

> '. . . I don't need your dirty love.
> I don't want you touching me . . .'

Scott stood still, his breath coming in gasps.

Carol ran her index finger over the slinky material of her G-string.

One of the men got to his feet again and lurched towards the bed.

Keep away from her.

Scott also took a step forward but halted as the first man's companion pulled him back.

'Get on with it,' another shouted, holding up his glass in salute.

Carol stood up on the bed, hooking her fingers into the top of the G-string. The five men began clapping in unison as she started to ease it over her hips, gradually revealing her pubic hair.

> '. . . There's a name for girls like you.
> You belong in the gutter I know you do . . .'

She finally pulled it free, allowing it to drop to her feet. Naked she stood before them, caressing her body with both hands as the music roared on around her and the shouts of the men grew louder. She tried not to look into their eyes, tried to concentrate on the dark outline of Scott, who stood close to the bottom of the steps to her left.

'Suck this,' shouted another of the men, fumbling with the zip of his trousers. Another moment and he had pulled his penis free. He staggered drunkenly towards Carol, his throbbing organ protruding from his zip.

'That's it,' snapped Scott and both he and Calder moved forward.

The man actually had his foot on the edge of the bed when Scott grabbed him by the shoulder.

'Sit down,' he rasped, and threw the man backwards. He landed squarely in his seat, his penis still sticking through his flies.

'What the fuck is this?' another of the men shouted, glaring at Scott.

'I think it's time you gentlemen left,' said Scott.

The first man was busy doing up his flies, yelping in pain as he caught a pubic hair in his zip.

'We paid our fucking money, we want to see the show,' another protested.

'Go and find another show,' Scott told them. He turned towards Carol. 'Get dressed.'

She nodded and moved away from the bed.

As she did, the youngest of the five men grabbed her around the waist and lifted her into the air, laughing as he did.

'We only came in for some fun,' he said, chuckling.

Scott turned furiously on the man, his body shaking as he saw the other man holding Carol.

Get your hands off her.

'At least let us have our money's worth,' said the man holding Carol.

'Let go of her,' snarled Scott through clenched teeth.

'You charge enough in here,' the man protested.

Let go of her.

Scott grabbed the man's hand and prized open his grip,

142

squeezing his wrist in a vice-like hold that threatened to break the bones.

Don't you dare put your hands on her.

Scott pulled the man close to him, his eyes blazing.

'What the fuck is wrong with you?' the man said, trying to shake free.

Scott glared at him a second longer then drove his head forward sharply, slamming his forehead into the bridge of the man's nose, hearing the sharp crack of bone with satisfaction. The man fell backwards, blood spurting from the shattered cartilage.

Immediately the other four men were on their feet. Two turned and ran for the stairs, but the others flung themselves at Scott.

He parried a clumsy blow and struck out with his left foot, driving it hard into the man's groin. As he crumpled up, Scott grabbed his hair to pull his head upright then he sent a powerful punch into his face, splitting the top lip.

Carol, still naked, stood close by, her arms around Zena, watching the fight.

The music roared on as an accompaniment.

> '. . . *You've been outta my life so long,*
> *There's no way I'll stay . . .*'

Calder struck another of the men in the stomach, hurling him over one of the sofas, aiming a kick at him as he scrambled to his feet and ran for the stairs.

The first man, blood streaming from his broken nose, struggled to his feet, his hand closing around a glass. He hurled it at Scott but missed. Scott turned to face him, dragging him upright by his lapels. He looked into the man's eyes, then across at Carol.

Scott brought his knee up into the man's groin so hard he felt it connect with his pelvis.

143

The man uttered a strangled cry and tried to clutch at his injured testicles.

Scott looked across at Carol again, still not releasing his grip on the man.

He drove his head forward again.

And again.

His own forehead was red now as he slammed it against the man's face. He opened a gash above his eye, another on his cheek. Blood from the injured man had spilled onto Scott's face and speckled his shirt. Scott hardly noticed that his adversary's eyes were closed. Instead he smiled across crookedly at Carol, holding him as if he were some kind of limp, blood-spattered rag doll. He grabbed a handful of the man's hair and yanked his head back hard, finally throwing him against the wall, watching with satisfaction as he slid down to the floor, his shirt a mass of blood, his face cut and bruised by the onslaught. The man's companion stumbled across and helped him to his feet.

'Get out,' hissed Scott. 'Next time I'll kill you.'

The men made their way up the stairs, one of them slipping half-way, almost falling.

Scott felt something warm and wet on his face and realised it was blood. He wiped it away with the back of his hand then looked at Calder.

'Make sure they don't come back in here,' he snarled.

The bouncer nodded and followed the men upstairs.

The music roared on.

'. . . I don't need your dirty love . . .'

Scott looked at Carol, who met his gaze impassively.

'You all right?' he asked.

She nodded.

'Go and get dressed,' he told her, smiling thinly. He

144

looked down and noticed that there was blood on his hands too. He pulled a handkerchief from his trouser pocket and slowly wiped the crimson stains away.

Carol and Zena disappeared through the door marked 'Private'. Scott finished wiping the blood from his hands then stuffed the stained cloth back into his pocket.

There was more blood on the carpet.

He smiled.

Thirty-six

Before he switched off the engine he glanced at the clock on the dashboard.

12.36 a.m.

Frank Gregson swung himself out of the Escort and slammed the door, fumbling in his pocket for his front door key. He finally found it and let himself in, careful not to drop the thick manila file he had cradled under one arm. As he moved through the house he switched on lights, finally ending up in the sitting room. There he dropped the file onto the coffee table, crossed to the drinks cabinet, took out a bottle of Teacher's and poured himself a large measure. As he stood drinking the fiery liquid he heard movement from above him, soft padding footfalls on the stairs.

He sighed and finished his drink, filling the glass again.

'I couldn't wait up any longer.'

The voice came from behind him as Julie moved into the room. He didn't bother to turn; he knew where she was. He heard the creak of springs as she perched on the edge of the armchair.

'You could have phoned,' she said. 'I was worried.'

'If anything had happened to me you'd have heard about it soon enough.'

'I'd cooked you some dinner; I had to throw it out.'

'My loss is the dustbin's gain,' he said, finally turning to face her.

She wore just a short housecoat. He knew she was naked beneath it.

Naked, like Paula Wilson had been on that slab.

'Do you want me to get you something?' she asked, curling her legs under her.

'I'll manage with this,' he said, raising the glass. He crossed to his seat and sat down, gazing at the file before him. 'Sorry I disturbed you,' he added, as an afterthought.

'I wasn't asleep. I was waiting for you to get in,' she told him.

He smiled thinly.

'Well, something came up at the office, dear,' he said acidly, taking a sip of his drink. 'That's why I'm late.'

'If you mean that girl, I saw it on the news.'

'Yes, I *do* mean that girl. Paula Wilson, aged twenty-three.' He raised the glass in salute. 'Rest in peace.'

'They said the man who killed her committed suicide.'

Gregson nodded.

'Went out in a blaze of glory, you could say,' he added.

'Do you want to talk about it?' she asked.

He shook his head and chuckled softly.

'We tried talking about it last time, if you remember rightly. It wasn't a raging success, was it?' he said flatly.

'Frank, don't start.'

'Well, what exactly do you want to know? What details interest you about *this* case?'

146

She pulled her housecoat tightly around her and met his gaze.

'Do you want to know how many times he stabbed her? Or how many pieces of rubbish he'd shoved inside her?'

'What do you mean?'

'He stuffed pieces of rubbish between her legs. Inside her vagina. He filled her cunt with garbage.' Gregson hissed the last sentence through clenched teeth. Julie swallowed hard and lowered her head slightly.

'Have you any idea who he was?' she said finally.

Gregson shrugged, got to his feet and poured himself another drink. He turned and looked at his wife for a moment before returning to his seat.

'Strangely enough I have,' he said. 'The only problem is, it doesn't make sense. My theory holds water about as well as a fucking colander.'

She looked at him questioningly, relieved at least that he was talking to her.

'The MO he used matches one of a murderer we put away eighteen months ago,' said Gregson.

'I'm not with you, Frank,' she said.

'No, you're not, are you?' he said cryptically. 'You're not with me.' He downed a large measure of the whisky. 'Perhaps it's better that you're not. I told you before that it isn't your problem.'

'And I told you that it was,' she snapped. 'You think I enjoy seeing you like this? Wrapped up in yourself, punishing yourself? There's no need for it, Frank. Not when *I'm* here, you don't have to keep your problems or your thoughts to yourself. I *want* to help. I'm worried about you.' Her tone softened slightly. 'It's you I want to help because it's you I love. Please don't shut me out, Frank.'

'You want to be a part of *my* world?' he asked sardonically. 'And everything in it?'

147

'Yes.'

He opened the file and pulled out one of the photos of Paula Wilson, holding it up for Julie to see, ensuring she had a good view of the knife wounds and the pulped face.

'Say hello to reality,' he said.

Julie glanced at the picture and lowered her head again.

'You wanted to look, then look,' he snapped, throwing the photo towards her. It floated to the floor. 'Perhaps you like this one better.' He flicked a picture of Bryce's burned body in her direction. 'How many more do you want to see?' He picked up the file and dumped it on the table in front of her, standing over her challengingly. 'Go on, look at them. Look at the fucking photos.'

He knelt down beside her and pulled another from the file, holding it up against her face as she tried to pull away from him.

Paula Wilson just before the autopsy.

'Look at it,' he shouted.

Bryce after they found him on the building site.

'Come on, I want to know what you think.'

She finally shook loose of his grip and struggled to her feet.

'I think you're crazy,' she said, fighting back the tears. 'I think this job is dragging you down and you don't even know it. Either that or you don't even *care.*'

'It isn't a nine-to-five job, Julie. You don't clock in and out. At least you don't clock your *mind* in and out,' he said. 'You carry it with you every fucking hour of the day and night. I carry those images and those sounds and smells in my mind, all the time.'

He took another gulp of whisky, wiping his mouth with the back of his hand.

Julie bent down and picked up one of the photos. She held it for a moment then dropped it in front of her husband.

When she spoke, her voice was low, strained.

'I'll leave you alone with your work,' she said.

Thirty-seven

'Something on your mind?'

Jim Scott looked down at Carol Jackson, raising himself up on one elbow.

She was gazing at the ceiling, tracing the outline of a crack in the plaster, holding his hand lightly as they lay naked side by side.

Tell the truth, shame the devil.

It had been one of her mother's sayings. Now she wondered if she should put it into practice.

Tell him. Put him out of his misery.

She glanced up at him and smiled.

No. Now wasn't the time.

He squeezed her hand and asked again what was on her mind.

'Nothing,' she told him. 'Why?'

'It looks as if there is,' he said, his own smile broader.

'So you're a mind-reader now, are you?' She looked into his eyes.

I'd be in trouble if you were.

He swung himself out of bed and wandered through into the kitchen, returning with two glasses and a bottle of Southern Comfort. He poured them both measures then got back into bed, watching as Carol shifted position, sitting up slightly to avoid spilling the drink. She looked at Scott as he drank, his eyes fixed on something across the dark bedroom.

Their lovemaking hadn't exactly been of the wild abandoned variety. Scott had barely been able to sustain his erection, due to Carol's relative passivity; it was as if his own ardour had been dampened by her perfunctory attempts to please him. But she had faked it enough times before with him and with Plummer. As far as she knew, neither man was aware of her disinterest.

Scott was just glad that she was with him. She was *his* tonight. They hadn't spoken about the incident in the club earlier when he'd fought to protect her. Scott smiled to himself as he remembered the sight of the man's bloodied face. It had been so easy to hurt him, to break his nose. To split his face open. He'd bled a lot. Scott downed his drink and poured himself another. A celebration, perhaps? He lay down beside her again, the drink resting on his chest.

'I've been thinking about getting a bigger place,' he told her finally.

'Why? This is enough for you, isn't it?' she said.

'Well, I won't be on my own forever, will I?'

It could have been a plea.

Carol didn't look at him.

'I mean,' he continued, 'if someone was to move in with me, it wouldn't be big enough.'

She smiled thinly.

'I'd worry about that when the time comes, Jim,' she said, sipping her drink.

'Have you thought of moving?' he wanted to know.

'I'm happy where I am, I suppose,' she lied. 'Although perhaps happy is the wrong word. It's just that I'm stuck with it.' She turned her head away from him for a moment.

150

No way out. Except perhaps through Plummer.

'I miss you when I can't see you at nights,' he confessed.

'You see me every night.'

'You know what I mean.' He took a long swallow of liquor. 'Seeing you at work, that doesn't count. Any bastard who pays can see you like that.' He began running his finger around the rim of the glass.

'If it's any consolation, I hate earning my money that way too,' she told him.

'I don't blame you for what you do. You've got a good body, why not use it to your advantage?'

'I don't do it out of choice, Jim,' she said, her tone hardening. 'I do it because I've got no bloody option. Do you realise how much I hate that job? Do you know what I'd do to get out of there? What I'd do to change my lifestyle?'

He shook his head.

'Anything,' she said. 'And I mean *anything*.'

'I didn't realise. I'm sorry.'

She took a swig of her drink.

'I've been doing it for over ten years now,' she told him. 'I've had enough.'

'But what else could you do? There isn't any way out.' He smiled. 'I'll probably still be working there in ten years' time.'

'Yes,' she said, with scarcely disguised contempt. 'You probably will.'

They regarded each other impassively for a moment.

'Maybe a rich Arab would walk in one night and whisk me off to a life of luxury,' she said bitterly.

'I hope not,' said Scott, his face set in hard lines. 'I wouldn't want to see you with anyone else.'

She swallowed hard.

Did he know?

151

'Why not? Things change, Jim. People change,' she said.

'Not people like you and me,' he said adamantly.

They lay in silence for long moments before she looked at him again.

'You said you wouldn't want to see me with anyone else,' she murmured. 'What would you do if there *was* someone else?'

He looked at her, his eyes blazing.

'I'm curious,' she said, qualifying the statement.

Christ, if only he knew.

Scott swung himself out of bed once more and pulled open the drawer of the cabinet. He took out the Beretta 92S and grasped it, pulling back the slide. The metallic click filled the room. Carol moved away inches involuntarily at the sight of the pistol.

'I'd kill him,' said Scott flatly.

He squeezed the trigger and the hammer slammed down on an empty chamber, the click amplified by the silence in the room.

'And what about me?' she asked.

Scott smiled, the pistol still gripped in his fist.

'I'd probably kill you too.'

Thirty-eight

He was gone when she awoke.

Carol rolled over sleepily and felt for Scott but found that she was alone in bed. She blinked myopically, trying to clear her vision. There was a piece of paper lying on his pillow; she reached for it, running one hand through her hair.

SEE YOU TONIGHT. LOVE, JIM.

Love.

She sighed and lay down on her stomach, the note resting on the pillow in front of her.

She knew now that it was going to be difficult, if not impossible, to break from Scott. Especially after what he'd said the previous night. He obviously felt more deeply for her than she had even imagined. That not only troubled her, it frightened her. Carol pulled herself across the bed to the cabinet and slid open the top drawer.

The Beretta was inside, underneath some notepads.

She took the pistol out and hefted it.

Would he really kill her if he found out she was seeing Plummer?

Common sense told her it had been a somewhat theatrical threat, but her knowledge of Scott told her otherwise. She had little doubt he would use the gun if he had to. Carol pulled back the slide, the weapon feeling heavy in her hand. She sat up in bed, the sheet falling away from her body to reveal her nakedness. Lifting the pistol she gripped it in both hands and aimed it at the mirror on the dressing table across the room, drawing a bead on her own reflection. She squeezed the trigger and the hammer slammed down.

She lowered the gun again and sat back against the headboard. Scott would never let her go. No matter how she told him, no matter how gently she broke it to him, no matter what explanation she gave.

She was trapped.

She should tell Plummer. But what good would that do? For a moment she gazed at her reflection, feeling as lost and alone as she ever had in her life. The mirror-image gazed back impassively. Carol put the gun back in the drawer and caught sight of a small box with a green lid. She took off the lid and found fifty 9mm rounds, all neatly arranged in rows of five. She lifted out one of the brass-jacketed rounds and held it between her thumb and forefinger, feeling the sleek lines, looking with bewilderment at the hollow tip of the bullet. Finally she put it back, closed the lid of the box and slammed the drawer shut.

Was she being unfair to Scott?

It was a question she had asked a dozen times in the past week.

She was seeing another man behind his back. She was giving him the impression she still cared for him, if somewhat guardedly. Yet all the time she knew she had to get away from him – not that she disliked him or hated him. Their relationship had run its course. It was as simple as that.

Simple?

She almost smiled.

It was anything *but* simple.

She realised that the longer she played out the charade the more damage it would do to Scott when the game finally ended. But after what he had said the previous night, how could she end it? Carol rubbed her face with both hands and shook her head.

No way out.

She glanced at the drawer and its lethal contents.

Perhaps there *was* a way.

Perhaps.

The journey back to her own flat seemed to take an eternity.

She sat on the tube staring absently at her fellow passengers, who either returned her gaze uncomfortably or gazed around, reading the advertisements over the seats. When there was no one opposite her Carol found herself confronted by her own image again. At one station a couple of youths got in and sat opposite her, the taller of the two eyeing her constantly as she crossed and uncrossed her legs. As they got out, the tall one leant close to her and muttered something about a blow job. They disappeared along the platform as the train moved off.

Carol walked from the station to her home, fumbling in her handbag for the key, finally letting herself in.

The room smelled of yesterday's food and she went around opening windows to dispel the odour. She'd taken a bath at Scott's place so, with a few hours left before she had to get ready for work, she made herself a cup of tea and sat down in front of the television.

It was then that the phone rang.

'Hello,' she said, putting down her mug, hissing as she burned her fingers on the hot china.

'Welcome home.'

She recognised the voice immediately.

'What do you want?' she said, her voice catching.

'Just to let you know I'm still watching.'

'What do you want?' she shouted, fear and anger now rearing up within her.

'You'll find out.'

The line went dead.

Carol slammed the receiver down and sat staring at it for interminable seconds, as if expecting it to ring again. Her hands were shaking so violently that she slopped hot tea onto her skin. The pain made her drop the cup which promptly sent the warm fluid soaking into the carpet. Carol watched as it spilled, unable or unwilling to do anything about it.

She lowered her head, cradling it in her hands.

Tears trickled down her cheeks as she began to cry softly.

Thirty-nine

The man had vomited, a reaction neither Gregson nor Barclay had observed before.

When relatives came to identify the bodies of their loved ones they usually fainted, burst into tears or just silently acknowledged the fact that it was their kin lying on the slab. Clive Wilson had taken one look at the pulped features of his daughter and doubled over, vomiting copiously on the floor of the pathology lab.

'Do we take that as a positive identification?' Gregson said as the man was helped from the room by two uniformed men.

Barclay was unamused by the DI's quip.

He merely pulled the plastic sheet back over the dead girl's face and motioned for two of his assistants to replace the body in its cold locker.

'Wait,' Gregson said. He took hold of the cover and pulled it down again, studying the cuts, bruises and patchwork of contusions that had disfigured the girl.

'Shouldn't you be taking care of Mr Wilson?' said Barclay.

'Finn's up there. He'll deal with it. Besides, I'm a policeman, not a fucking social worker,' Gregson said flatly, his eyes never leaving the body. Finally he pulled the sheet back and motioned for Barclay's assistants to continue. They lifted the body and slid it back into the locker, where it would be kept for the next two days until funeral arrangements had been made. Those final forty-eight hours would also give Barclay the opportunity to check the corpse once more for anything he may have missed, such as fibres, prints or anything else that might give a clue to the identity of her murderer. After that the body would be handed over to an undertaker and New Scotland Yard's responsibility would be discharged.

Paula Wilson's clothes had been put into a plastic bag, each item removed from the sealed forensic bags, along with what little jewellery she'd been wearing at the time of her death. These would be returned to her family.

Gregson stood beside one of the slabs, glancing down at the puddle of vomit left by Clive Wilson. The acrid smell permeated the air.

'You'd better get that cleaned up,' he said to the pathologist, who regarded him irritably, as if the thought hadn't occured to him.

'Have you finished in here now?' Barclay wanted to know.

'No. I want to see the two bodies. The killers,' the DI told him.

'Why, for Christ's sake?'

'Humour me, will you?'

Barclay crossed to one of the lockers and slid it open. Encased in a rubber bag like some kind of monstrous pupal life-form, the body appeared. Barclay undid the zip far enough to reveal the blackened remains of the features. Gregson stared at the charred corpse then glanced at Barclay and nodded, indicating that he wanted to look at the second corpse. The pathologist repeated the procedure so that both incinerated bodies were in view.

'Still no progress with identifying them?' the DI asked.

'Not with the first one; he was burned as badly as anything I've ever seen,' Barclay confessed. 'The second one, though . . .' He allowed the sentence to hang in the

157

chill air. 'I found part of a thumb print on the inside of Paula Franklin's left thigh.'

'Why the hell didn't you say something earlier?'

'Because I wasn't sure.' He sighed. 'I'm still not one hundred per cent sure but I thought that ninety-five was better than nothing. I sent the print down to photographic, they're going to work it up.'

The pathologist stood looking at his companion, watching how intently he gazed at the scorched remains of the two dead men.

'What is it about them, Frank?' he said, finally. 'Why the fascination?'

'Because they're mysteries to me, and I don't like mysteries or unanswered questions. But there's something else, too. I've got something nagging away at the back of my mind. Something to do with these two men. They both used MO's I've seen before.'

'That's not so unusual, is it? Copy-cat killings are nothing new,' Barclay said.

Gregson didn't shift his gaze.

'Does Finn know your theory?' the pathologist asked.

Gregson shook his head.

'It's best he doesn't.'

'Why?'

'Because if he knew what I was thinking, he'd probably suggest I was locked up.'

Forty

'. . . Police stated that there were anywhere between five hundred and a thousand protesters but that the march was peaceful . . .'

Jim Scott sat in his office, feet propped up on the desk, his eyes fixed on the TV screen. It flickered every now and then but not enough to bother him or to break his concentration. The black and white images were of a large group of people moving through central London, most of them carrying placards that the cameras managed to pick out.

STOP OVERCROWDING
PRISONS NOT ZOOS

Scott looked on impassively.

'. . . *The march was led by the Right Honorable Bernard Clinton, MP for Buxton, whose constituency houses Whitely Prison . . .*'

There was a close-up of a man in his late forties, dressed in a grey jacket and a large overcoat. The fur of the hood matched the white of his own hair. The man was chatting to people on either side of him and looking at the cameras every now and then. Reporters stepped in front of him, thrusting microphones forward.

'What do you hope this march will achieve, Mr Clinton?' asked one.

'Prisons in this country have been overcrowded for too long,' the MP replied. 'Whitely is probably the worst example. It just so happens that it is in my power to do something about it, or at least to make the Government aware of the problem.'

'What is your main complaint with the system as it is at present?' another reporter asked.

'In Whitely, as in many other gaols, remand prisoners are kept in the same sections of the prison, in some cases in the same *cells*, as convicted men, occasionally even murderers. This is intolerable.'

159

Scott sipped his drink and continued gazing at the screen.

'. . . *The movement for prison reform has gained momentum in the last three months, ever since the murder of a remand prisoner in Whitely by a convicted killer. Mr Clinton took up the case after relatives of the dead man approached him . . .*'

There was a shot of the Trafalgar Square and Scott could see the protesters milling around the fountains. Clinton stood at the top of the steps and was addressing them but the camera panned across to the reporter standing in the foreground who was addressing his remarks direct to camera.

'. . . *Officials from the Home Office are expected to visit Whitely Prison and a number of other maximum security gaols throughout the country in the next few weeks, to see at close hand how bad overcrowding has become. Mr Clinton himself will lead a delegation to Whitely before the end of the week and a motion to discuss the possible reform of the penal system has been tabled in the Commons.*'

The reporter signed off and the pictures of the rally were replaced by the newsreader in the studio. Scott listened for a moment to a story about yet another famine in Africa, to someone appealing for people to send money for food, and then switched off.

Send them money for food, next thing they'll be wanting money for clothes, he chuckled to himself. He pulled the phone towards him and jabbed the digits of Carol's number.

It rang.

And rang.

He glanced at his watch, sure that she wouldn't have left yet. He allowed the phone to ring another five times then tried his own flat, wondering if she

160

might have stayed there until it was time to come in.

There was no answer there either.

He tried her flat once more, and still all he heard was the insistent ringing tone. He pressed down on the cradle and replaced the receiver.

She should be at work soon, anyway.

Ask her where she was.

He decided against that. He just hoped she was all right. Perhaps she'd slipped out for something. Or to see someone.

To see someone? Like who?

Why had she asked him the previous night about what he'd do if he found out she was seeing someone else?

He dismissed the thought. There was no need to be suspicious, she was merely asking out of curiosity. He suspected she'd been surprised by his answer. Scott smiled. Perhaps it would make her realise just how much he felt for her.

He crossed to the window of his office and looked out. It was raining again; the pavements and road were slick with water. The neon signs all around were reflected in the moisture, as if they themselves lit the concrete from the inside.

Scott always thought of London as existing in two different times. There were those who lived and worked by day and those who did so by night. Worlds apart.

The time of darkness had come again.

He smiled.

PART TWO

Now hatred is by far the longest pleasure; Men love in haste but they detest at leisure . . .

Lord Byron

They have the morals of alley cats and minds like sewers . . .

Neville Heath, convicted murderer, on women.

Forty-one

The door crashed open and slammed back against the wall with such force it seemed it would come off the hinges.

Michael Robinson blinked and sat up, staring blearily in the direction of the noise. He rubbed his eyes and peered down from the top bunk.

The uniformed figure stood in the doorway, eyeing the occupants of the cell impassively.

'Move it,' said the figure. 'Slop out.'

Robinson yawned and swung his feet over the side of the bunk.

'I think this is our alarm call, Rod,' he said, stretching.

From the bunk below him Rod Porter grunted and turned over, as if to resume the peaceful sleep from which he'd just been disturbed.

'Move yourself, Porter,' said the uniformed figure brusquely.

'Fuck you,' murmured Porter under his breath.

Robinson jumped down from the top bunk.

'You interrupted my dream, Mr Swain,' said Porter, hauling himself out of bed. 'I was just getting a blow job from Michelle Pfeiffer.'

'The only blow job you're likely to get is a bike pump up your arse. Now move yourselves, both of you,' snapped the uniformed man.

Robinson and Porter both retrieved the small plastic

buckets from one corner of the cell and wandered out onto the landing. Robinson smiled as he lifted the plastic cover from the slop bucket to reveal a lump of excrement. He shoved it at the uniformed man's face, watching with pleasure as he recoiled from the stench.

'I think mine is a little bit underdone. Perhaps you ought to have a word with the kitchen staff,' he said, smiling.

In front of him, Porter grinned. The uniformed officer didn't appreciate the joke and pushed Robinson out onto the landing where, already, a steady file of men were spilling from their cells, joining the long line on either side of the landing as they made their way to the toilets.

Whitely Prison was coming to life.

On landings above and below them the same routine was in practice. They had followed it every morning and would continue to follow it until their sentences were up. Man shuffled along over the cold floors, some dressed in grey prison-issue pyjamas, others bare-chested or in boxer shorts. Each of them held a small bucket. Most were filled with excrement. Slopping out was as much a part of prison life as exercise, work and, for the fortunate ones, visits. Robinson and Porter knew it well enough. They'd been sharing a cell for the last two years. Robinson was in for ten years for armed robbery, while his companion was half-way through a twelve-year stretch for a similar crime. His extra two years had come about because he'd shot a security guard in the leg with a twelve-bore.

Both men were in their mid-thirties, and both had spent most of their lives in and out of institutions. Porter had been raised in a children's home from the time he was two years old. He'd run away repeatedly as he'd got older, never with anywhere to go but just anxious to be

166

free of the confining walls and restrictive atmosphere. As the years had progressed a series of petty crimes had seen him in remand homes, borstals and finally prison. It was usually robbery.

Robinson had experienced a more stable upbringing. He was married with a couple of kids. Stealing had come more as a necessity than anything else. His wife had expensive tastes and the kids always wanted new clothes or bikes or games. Both men had come to Whitely from other prisons, Robinson from Strangeways, Porter from Wandsworth.

A large proportion of Whitely's inmates had also come via other gaols throughout the country; prisons where they couldn't be handled adequately. In many cases Whitely was a last resort. Or a dumping ground, whichever way you chose to look at it. It was like a drain where the dregs and filth exuded from all the other prisons in the land had been gathered together; the human refuse brushed aside and locked up in an institution that was a dustbin for the unwanted and unmanageable.

Located in the heart of the Derbyshire countryside, surrounded on four sides by hills, it was a monument to the backwardness of penal reform. A massive, grey stone Victorian building, it housed over 1600 inmates, twice its allotted amount. Remand and convicted prisoners lived side by side.

Robinson nudged the man in front of him and nodded a greeting as the man turned.

The uniformed man noticed the movement and stepped close to Robinson.

'No talking,' he said.

Robinson shrugged and smiled innocently.

'Cunt,' he whispered, stifling the word with a yawn.

Across the landing an identical procession was filing

towards their own latrine. Men who had emptied their slop buckets were returning to their cells. There were the odd murmurings, the sounds echoing throughout the large building, but they were quickly quelled by warders anxious to maintain silence.

Porter peered over the landing rail, through the steel netting that was strung from one side to the other, and noticed that, on the landing below, prisoners who had finished slopping out had not in fact returned to their cells but were standing outside, their attempts at entry barred by warders. He frowned, wondering what was going on. His musings were interrupted as he reached the latrine. He and Robinson emptied their slop buckets into the waste chutes provided, rinsed them with boiling water and then made their way back to their cell.

The door was closed, the entrance blocked by another warder, Raymond Douglas. He was a red-faced man with a pitted complexion who always looked exhausted, as if he'd just completed a marathon.

'Stay there,' he said, toying with his key chain, holding up his free hand to add weight to his instructions.

Further down the landing, other prisoners also stood outside their cells. Irritated mutterings grew louder.

'. . . What's going on? . . .'

'. . . Why are we being kept outside? . . .'

'What's the deal, Mr Douglas?' Porter asked.

'You'll find out,' said the warder. 'For now, just shut it.'

Porter eyed the uniformed man malevolently, then exchanged puzzled glances with his cell-mate.

'Cell search?' Robinson murmured. 'Someone been smoking whacky baccy again?'

'I said shut it,' Douglas snapped.

'Just curious,' said Robinson, gazing around him.

On all the landings men now stood outside their cells,

increasingly frustrated and increasingly cold. It wasn't exactly warm inside Whitely and many of them were dressed only in shorts. The babble of discontent grew more insistent, to the point where even the warders couldn't quell it.

'What the hell is going on?' Porter wanted to know.

'SHUT UP.'

The voice boomed around the inside of the building, bouncing off the walls with its ferocity and power.

All heads turned in one direction, peering upwards to find its source.

'Shut up and listen,' the voice continued, and now the inmates could see where the thunderous exhortation came from.

On the uppermost landing, flanked by warders, stood a tall, powerfully-built figure in a dark blue suit, his greying hair slicked back so severely it appeared that he was bald. He gripped the landing rail with hands as large as ham-hocks. He regarded the men beneath him impassively, his eyes flicking back and forth as they looked up at him.

Peter Nicholson, the Governor of Whitely Prison, began to speak.

Forty-two

You could have been forgiven for imagining, that Peter Nicholson had undergone surgery to replace his vocal chords with a megaphone. His words boomed out, spoken with clarity and in a tone that suggested that he was keeping his words simple for the less intelligent inmates of the prison. On either side of him the warders looked down onto the other landings, watching for any signs of unrest amongst those below. Warders on each of the individual landings also ensured that silence prevailed as he spoke.

'As you may have heard,' the Governor said, smoothing his hair back with one hand, 'Whitely has been in the news lately. The media are obviously hard up for stories because they seem interested in what they refer to as our overcrowding problems here. Also, the local MP has taken it upon himself to look personally into what goes on in this prison.'

Robinson looked at Porter and raised his eyebrows quizzically.

'To that end,' Nicholson continued, 'a Home Office delegation will be visiting this prison tomorrow to see how it runs and to see how well you're all cared for.' He smiled sardonically.

A murmur rose that was quickly silenced.

Nicholson paused for a moment theatrically.

'The members of this delegation will be speaking to a number of prisoners. Asking about conditions, etcetera.' He looked around the upturned faces. 'You may speak to them if you wish. Help them with their questions. You may have some questions for *them*. If you have any problems or grievances, you're quite free to tell them.'

'Yeah,' murmured Porter. 'And get our fucking heads busted by the screws when they've gone.'

Swain took a step towards him, shooting him a warning glance.

'If any of you have any problems, at any time, you know you are free to speak to the officers in charge of your landing or to me personally,' Nicholson continued.

There was another babble of chatter, and this time it took longer to quieten.

Nicholson looked around once more. His green eyes,

like chips of emerald, caught the light and reflected it coldly. He brushed a speck of dust from his sleeve as he waited for the silence he required. Finally satisfied, he continued.

'I want this prison running perfectly for these visitors,' he said. 'I want co-operation between you and the officers. I want the cells spotless. I want them to be impressed by what they see. I don't like people meddling in the way I run this prison and that's what they're doing. Meddling. I want them to leave here, knowing that this prison is well run and that its inmates are being adequately dealt with. I don't expect them to leave here with a catalogue of stories about what a terrible place Whitely is. As I said, you may speak to them if you wish. That is your prerogative. But bear in mind that if they hear too many bad reports, they'll disrupt the way I run this prison. And I don't like disruptions. I hope that's understood.' He looked around him, then smoothed his hair back once more. 'That's all.'

Nicholson and his officers turned and moved away from the landing rail, out of sight of the other prisoners.

On all the landings the inmates were allowed back inside their cells.

'Breakfast in twenty minutes, get a move on,' said Warder Swain, slamming the door shut behind Robinson and Porter.

'Suck this,' rasped Porter, holding his penis in one fist. 'Fucking cunt.'

Both men started to dress, taking it in turns to wash as best they could in the small sink perched on the cell wall.

'I wonder if anyone will be stupid enough to tell this bunch of do-gooders the truth?' Robinson mused, drying his face.

'Are you joking?' Porter muttered, fastening his grey

171

overall. 'Even the screws wouldn't tell them anything. They're more frightened of Nicholson than most of the cons in here.'

Robinson nodded in agreement.

'A tour of the prison, eh?' he said, smiling. 'I wonder what they'll make of our humble little home.'

'Probably want to move in with us,' Porter quipped. He crossed to his locker and took out a comb, running it through his short black hair. The inside of the locker was a mosaic of photos: naked women, a team picture of Liverpool FC and a couple of postcards all vied for attention. He blew a kiss to one of the women, then closed the locker again.

Robinson was sitting on the edge of the upper bunk.

'I'll tell you one thing, Rod,' he said, 'and I'll bet money on it. There's at least *one* part of this nick they won't see. Nicholson will make sure of that.'

Forty-three

The office was large, functional rather than welcoming. Efficiency was the keyword. It was a place of work, after all, thought Peter Nicholson, and it had been *his* place of work for the last sixteen years. He'd seen many changes in the penal system as a whole and Whitely in particular during his days as Governor at the prison. The changes since he first began working in the service had been radical, to say the least. He'd begun back in the fifties as a prison officer. He'd served his early years in Wandsworth. In fact, he'd been one of two warders who had escorted Derek Bentley from the condemned cell to the hangman on January 28 1953. Bentley had been

172

sentenced to hang because his accomplice, Christopher Craig, despite having fired the shot that killed a policeman, had been too young for the rope.

After Wandsworth Nicholson had moved around from prison to prison, serving his time as surely as any of the inmates in those institutions. The difference was that he could go home at the end of every shift. He had an increasingly long key chain to show for his years of service.

His enthusiasm for his work and his intelligence had led to him being appointed Assistant Governor at Wormwood Scrubs. From there it had been only a matter of time until he was given his own prison.

Whitely was all he knew and had known for the last sixteen years.

The penal system he worked in was not the only thing that had changed during Nicholson's time. His own attitude had hardened, too. He'd originally joined the service after his mother had been attacked and beaten almost to death in 1950. He felt that he was acting, by proxy, for her and all victims of crime like her in his role as gaoler. And that was exactly how he viewed his job. He didn't see his task as correcting the ways of men who had strayed into crime and needed help; he and his warders existed to protect society from the kind of human garbage locked within the walls of Whitely.

He stood up, glancing across at the photograph of his wife on the desk. The image smiled back at him as he straightened the frame. He moved over to the window of his office and looked out.

He could see into the empty exercise yard. Beyond it, protected by a high stone wall, was a small chapel in the grounds of which were a number of graves, each one marked by a simple marble marker; some were actually decorated by headstones or crosses. They bore the names

173

of prisoners who had died at Whitely. Men who, with no family on the outside, had nowhere else to rest. Even in death they were confined within the walls of the prison.

A couple of inmates were picking up leaves from around the graves, sweeping them into a large black sack. The skeletal trees that grew close to the chapel rattled their branches in the wind, which whipped across the open ground.

The closest town of any size to the prison was over twelve miles away, across barren land now unfit even for farming. The remains of an open-caste mine, shut down over a decade earlier, lay to the west.

A single road, holed and pockmarked, connected the prison's main gates to a small tarmac road which wound through the hills and moors like a dry tongue in search of water.

The wind rattled the window in its frame but Nicholson remained where he was, keeping vigil, gazing out over his empire.

The buzzer on his intercom interrupted his thoughts.

He turned and flipped a switch.

'The warders you asked to see are here, Mr Nicholson,' his secretary told him.

'Send them in,' he instructed her.

A moment later the door opened and five men in uniforms trooped in. Nicholson motioned to them to take a seat. He leant on his desk top, waiting until the last of them was seated, then stood upright again, pulling himself up to his full six feet. He looked an imposing figure.

'You know what this is about,' he said curtly. 'I want to be sure that everything runs smoothly when this blasted delegation gets here tomorrow. Any hint of trouble, I want it stamped on.' He looked at each man in turn.

'Will you be showing them round yourself, sir?' asked John Niles.

Nicholson nodded.

'How many are there?' Raymond Douglas wanted to know.

'Four. One woman.'

'That should please the men,' said Niles, smiling. The other officers chuckled but Nicholson didn't see the joke.

'If any of those bastards finds out that one of them is going to be a woman, there could be trouble,' Nicholson said flatly. 'Take care of it.' He smoothed his hair back with one hand. 'I want them in and out of here as quickly as possible. I don't like the idea of people investigating my prison.'

'Why are they coming to Whitely, anyway?' Paul Swain enquired. 'We're not the only prison in the country that's overcrowded.'

'That's perfectly correct. Unfortunately, however, we *are* the only prison where a remand prisoner was murdered by a lifer recently.' He held up his hands in a dismissive gesture.

'I hope they're not too disappointed by what they see,' said Gareth Warton.

Nicholson looked at him unblinkingly.

'Meaning what?' he said irritably.

'You have to agree, sir, conditions *are* below standard.'

'Standard for what? This is a prison, in case you'd forgotten. The men here are here because they broke the law. Most of those in Whitely are here because they're too unruly or dangerous even for other jails to cope with.' He fixed Warton in his gaze. 'We, Mr Warton, have the scum of the earth under this roof.'

'They still deserve better conditions,' Warton persisted.

175

'They deserve nothing,' Nicholson hissed. 'They're here to be punished. We're here to ensure that punishment is carried out.'

'Isn't it our job to help them too, sir?' Warton said.

'*Yours*, perhaps, if that's how you feel. I don't see it as my job to help them. It's my job to help the people on the *outside* and I do that by making sure the scum in here *stay* in here.' He fixed Warton in the unrelenting stare of his cold green eyes. 'Do you know what we are, Mr Warton? We're zoo keepers, paid to keep animals behind bars.'

Warton coloured and lowered his gaze.

Nicholson sucked in an angry breath and turned back to look out of his office window.

'When the delegation arrives I want them brought here,' he said. 'I'll show them round the prison, round the recreation rooms and cells. If they want to speak to any of the prisoners they can. But I want at least two men present at all times.'

'Will you be taking them to the maximum security wing, sir?' Swain asked.

'Yes, and the solitary cells,' the warden told them.

'What about the hospital wing?' asked Niles.

'No,' snapped Nicholson, turning to face the officer. 'The infirmary, perhaps, but there's no need to show them anything else.' He looked up and down the line of faces. 'Are there any questions?'

There weren't. Nicholson dismissed the warders, returning to the window for a moment as if searching for something out in the windswept yard.

From where he stood he couldn't see the hospital wing.

The thought suddenly spurred him into action.

He turned back to his desk, picked up the phone and jabbed an extension number.

As he waited for it to be answered he drummed lightly on the desk top. The phone was finally answered.

'We have to talk,' said Nicholson. 'Come over to my office. It's important.'

Forty-four

Ray Plummer filled the Waterford crystal tumbler with soda and ice and handed it to John Hitch, and then repeated the procedure, passing the other brandy and soda to Terry Morton.

Morton thanked him, interrupted in his appraisal of a pair of Armani statues.

'And this stuff is worth money, is it, Ray?' Morton said, motioning towards the figurines.

'Of course it's worth money, you prat. Why do you think I bought it?' Plummer said. 'Fuck me, I'm surrounded by Philistines.'

He took a sip of his own drink and sat down in the leather chair closest to the fireplace, looking into the authentic fake gas flames as he sipped his drink. He touched his hair self-consciously, worried that the high wind outside might have disturbed it.

Morton remained on his feet, swaying backwards and forwards from the balls to the heels of his shoes. The delicate tumbler was out of place in his heavy hand; he looked as if he would have been more comfortable carrying a bottle of beer. Or a cosh.

'Sit down, Terry, you make the place look untidy,' Plummer told him, smiling at Hitch, who grinned back as his companion sat down hurriedly.

Both Hitch and Morton had worked for Plummer

for more than ten years and he trusted them as much as anyone in his organisation. Hence their privileged presence in his penthouse flat. They were two of only a handful of his employees allowed to enter this most private of havens.

Hitch was a couple of years younger than his boss but his long blond hair and perpetual sun tan (the product of a solarium) made him look closer to thirty than thirty-six. Morton was the opposite, dark-haired, squat, almost brutish in appearance. He'd been a successful amateur boxer before he joined Plummer's organisation. The flat nose was a testament to his habit of fighting with his guard down. Hitch maintained he could stop buses with his head (and frequently did).

'So, tell me what you found out about Connelly,' said Plummer. 'Is it right he's moving into drugs?'

'As far as we could find out, he's got no plans to expand in that area, Ray,' Hitch said, sipping his drink.

'He's making bundles out of the money business, isn't he?' Morton added. 'Why should he try that other shit?'

'Because *that other shit* is worth a damned sight more,' Plummer said scornfully.

'Well, we spoke to at least half a dozen members of his firm and none of them knows anything about a shipment of cocaine,' Hitch announced. 'That call must have been someone winding you up.'

'But why?' Plummer wanted to know.

Hitch could only shrug.

'The bit about the warehouse was right,' Plummer continued. 'Connelly's just bought himself a warehouse down by the docks.'

'Maybe his boats unload there, the ones that bring his mags in,' Hitch offered.

Plummer remained unconvinced.

'You spoke to members of his firm,' he said. 'They're

178

hardly likely to tell you what the cunt's planning, are they? Especially if he's planning to take over London with the money he makes from selling that fucking cocaine.' Plummer got to his feet and walked across to the fireplace, staring into the flames.

'There's no reason why he should want to try and "take over",' Hitch said. 'It doesn't make sense, Ray. There's been peace for over three years now. Connelly's not going to fuck it up by starting a drugs war, is he?'

'He might,' Morton offered.

'Oh, shut it, Terry, for fuck's sake,' Hitch said wearily.

'So what are you saying?' Plummer demanded. 'That the call was bollocks? A wind-up? If it was, I'd like to get my hands on the bastard that made it.'

'Forget about it,' Hitch advised, sipping his drink.

The phone rang.

Plummer crossed to it and picked up the receiver.

'Yeah,' he said.

'Ray Plummer.'

'Yeah, who's this?'

'We spoke a few days ago,' said the voice. 'Well, I spoke, you listened.'

Plummer, the receiver still pressed to his ear, turned to look at Hitch.

'You're calling about the cocaine shipment,' he said.

Hitch was on his feet in seconds.

'Well done,' said the voice.

Plummer put his hand over the mouthpiece and jabbed a finger towards the door to his right.

'The phone in the bedroom,' he hissed quietly.

Hitch understood and bolted for the door, picking the receiver up with infinite care so that he too could hear the voice on the other end of the line.

'Are you still interested in the shipment?' the caller wanted to know.

179

'Maybe,' Plummer said warily.

'What kind of fucking answer is that?'

'I'm interested if it actually exists,' he said.

'It exists all right. Ralph Connelly is going to be spending the money he earns from it pretty soon. Unless you decided you wanted it.'

'What do you get out of this?' Plummer wanted to know.

'That's *my* business. Now, if you're still interested, be here at this time tomorrow. I'll call then.'

The caller put down the phone.

'Fuck,' roared Plummer.

Hitch emerged from the bedroom.

'Recognise the voice?' Plummer wanted to know.

The younger man shook his head.

'If I was you, Ray,' he said. 'I'd wait for that call.'

Forty-five

'They're here, Mr Nicholson.'

The Governor of Whitely heard his secretary's voice over the intercom and glanced up at his wall clock. The delegation was punctual, if nothing else. It was exactly 10.00 a.m.

'Show them in, please,' he said, adjusting his tie and rising to his feet as the door was opened.

The first of the four visitors entered and Nicholson recognised him immediately as Bernard Clinton, the MP. He was followed by his companions. The Governor's secretary left them alone in the room, promising to return in a moment with tea and coffee.

Nicholson emerged from behind his desk slowly,

almost reluctantly. He extended a hand and shook that offered by Clinton, who introduced himself then presented his colleagues.

'This is Mr Reginald Fairham,' Clinton said, motioning towards a mousy-looking man in an ill-fitting suit. He was tall and pale and when Nicholson shook his hand he found it was icy cold. 'Mr Fairham is the Chairman of the National Committee for Prison Reform,' Clinton explained.

Nicholson said how glad he was to meet him.

A second man, chubby and losing his hair, was presented by Clinton as Paul Merrick.

'Mr Merrick serves in my office in Parliament. He's been active with me in this issue for the last few years,' the MP announced.

Nicholson looked squarely into the chubby man's eyes, scarcely able to disguise the contempt he felt for such a soft, weak handshake. Merrick needed to lose a couple of stone. His hands felt smooth, like those of a woman or someone who's never done a hard day's work in their life. Nicholson gripped Merrick's hand hard and squeezed with unnecessary force, watching the flicker of pain cross the man's face.

The fourth member of the group was a woman, in her mid-thirties, Nicholson guessed. She was smartly dressed in a grey two-piece suit and posed elegantly on a pair of high heels. Her face was rather pinched, tapering to a pointed chin that gave her features a look of severity not mirrored in her voice.

'Good morning, Mr Nicholson,' she said as she shook hands.

'Miss Anne Hopper is a leading member of the Council for Civil Liberties,' Clinton said, smiling obsequiously.

Introductions over, Nicholson motioned for his guests to sit down.

'We appreciate the chance to come to Whitely, Mr Nicholson,' Clinton said. 'Thank you for your co-operation.'

'Why did you choose Whitely?' the Governor asked.

'It is one of the worst examples of overcrowding in any prison in Britain,' Fairham said. 'And it does have one of the worst disciplinary records, too.' He clasped his hands on his knees. 'My organisation has been monitoring it for some time now.'

'Monitoring?' said Nicholson. 'In what way?' He spoke slowly, his gaze never leaving Fairham, who found he could only hold that gaze for a couple of seconds at a time.

'As I said, it has a very bad disciplinary record,' he offered.

'When you have over sixteen hundred violent and dangerous men in one place twenty-four hours a day, three hundred and sixty-five days a year, then the occasional problem *does* arise,' Nicholson said, leaning back in his seat and pressing his fingertips together.

'But the disciplinary record here is worse than at any other prison in the country. How can you explain that?' Fairham persisted.

'Because the class of prisoner is lower,' the Governor said scornfully. 'Perhaps your monitoring system didn't tell you that.'

'I think Mr Fairham means that we all share a concern over the incident that happened here not so long ago,' Clinton said.

'The death of the remand prisoner,' Fairham interjected, as if reminding Nicholson of something he might have forgotten.

'It was unfortunate, I agree,' the Governor said.

'It wouldn't have happened if the prison had been run more efficiently,' Fairham snapped.

182

'This prison is run *more* efficiently than most,' Nicholson rumbled, his eyes blazing. 'My staff are more highly trained than the majority of officers at other prisons in this country. But no matter how well-trained or well-organised warders are, they can't always anticipate the actions of these . . . men you represent. That killing would have happened in *any* gaol, not only Whitely. My men are trained to *control* prisoners, not to read their minds.'

Fairham swallowed hard and began drumming his fingers distractedly on his knees.

'I don't think anyone is casting aspersions on you or your officers, Mr Nicholson,' Clinton offered. 'What happened was unfortunate, we're all agreed on that.'

'It was also inevitable,' Nicholson said sharply. 'The men in here are unpredictable, violent and dangerous. To some, killing is a way of life, whether you want to face that fact or not. Mr Fairham obviously chooses to ignore it.'

'Do you feel that the killing would not have taken place had overcrowding been less intense?' asked Merrick, pulling a pair of spectacles from his top pocket. He began cleaning then with a handkerchief which, Nicholson noticed, bore his initials.

'The killing would have happened whatever the population of the prison. As I said to you, for some of the men in here it's all they understand.' Nicholson looked at Fairham. 'Most criminals are of low intelligence, as you're probably aware. The difference between right and wrong seems to escape them. Presumably you are aware of the dead man's background?'

'He'd been remanded to appear in court for a driving offence,' Fairham said.

'A driving offence which included being drunk in charge of a vehicle,' Nicholson said. 'A vehicle he

183

lost control of, which ran into a bus queue, killing a six-year-old girl in the process. A little more serious than an expired tax disc, I think you'll agree.'

Fairham didn't speak.

'You sound as if you feel his killing was a kind of justice in itself,' said Anne Hopper.

'They say God pays back in other ways, Miss Hopper,' Nicholson said flatly.

A knock on the door broke the heavy silence and a moment later Nicholson's secretary entered with a tray of tea and coffee, which she distributed before leaving once more.

'What attempts are there at segregation between remand prisoners and convicted men here?' Clinton finally asked.

Nicholson sipped his tea thoughtfully.

'Very little,' he said flatly. 'We simply don't have the facilities to cope with the number of remand prisoners sent here.'

'Does that *bother* you, Mr Nicholson?' Fairham wanted to know.

'They're all criminals,' the Governor said.

'No, they're not,' Fairham protested, putting down his cup. 'The men on remand are *awaiting* trial. Some may be acquitted. Yet you insist on placing them with men who have already been convicted of far worse crimes.'

'I don't insist on it,' snapped Nicholson. 'I have no choice. What would be *your* answer to overcrowding?' he said, challengingly.

'Build more prisons,' Fairham answered.

'If you empty a rubbish bin onto the ground, it doesn't mean the rubbish will disappear,' Nicholson said, smiling. 'All you do is re-distribute the rubbish over a wider area.'

'And what is that supposed to mean?' Fairham snorted indignantly.

'If you build more prisons you're doing the same thing,' the Governor said. 'You're not removing the problem, you're just re-distributing the rubbish.'

'I'm not sure I like your analogy,' Fairham said. 'We're speaking about men, not garbage.'

'You have your own view,' Nicholson said icily.

'Is that how you view the men in Whitely, Mr Nicholson? As garbage?' Anne Hopper wanted to know. She held his gaze as he looked at her.

'As I said, we all have our own views. Perhaps I'm the wrong one to ask about that.'

'I would have thought you were exactly the one to ask,' Fairham interrupted vehemently. 'You are, after all, in charge of over a thousand men. You are responsible for their welfare.'

'Perhaps you'd be better off asking the families of their victims how *they* feel,' hissed Nicholson, turning his full fury on Fairham. 'There's a man in here who kidnapped and murdered two babies. One of them was less than six months old. He beat them so badly there was hardly a bone left unbroken in either of their bodies. Why don't you speak to the mothers of those babies? Or perhaps Miss Hopper should speak to the women who've been raped by some of the men in here. Or to the husbands of those women. Speak to *them*.' He looked at the woman. 'Do you have any children?'

She shook her head.

'No,' he echoed. 'Then perhaps the prisoners in here who have sexually abused children won't seem quite so odious to you.'

Clinton held up a hand to silence the Governor.

'All right, Mr Nicholson,' he said, smiling ingratiatingly. 'I think we understand your point.'

'Don't patronise me,' he snarled. 'This is *my* prison. Run *my* way. I understand the mentality of the men in here. I see them every day and familiarity doesn't breed contempt so much as disgust in me. When you've lived around men like that for as long as I have, when you've seen at first hand what they're capable of, then you can come here and tell me how to handle my affairs. But for now this is the way things will continue.'

'Mr Nicholson, we didn't come here for a battle,' said Clinton. 'And I'm sure no one doubts your knowledge and ability in this job. We came to see how the prison is run. Perhaps now might be a good time to do that.'

He got to his feet and looked first at his companions and then at Nicholson, who nodded, a slight smile creasing his lips.

'If Mr Fairham will allow me to say one more thing,' he offered, the tone of his voice even, 'we also find overcrowding a problem here but the answer isn't to build more gaols. Before you leave here today, I'll show you how overcrowding can be dealt with once and for all. Not just at Whitely, but at every prison in the country.'

Forty-six

The rumbling of conversation gradually died down as DI Frank Gregson got to his feet.

'All right, keep it down,' he said, raising his voice, looking out at the twenty or so uniformed and plain clothes men seated in the room. The air was thick with cigarette smoke. Beside him, his colleague DS Finn was adding to the pollution, blowing out long streams from his Marlboro.

The babble gradually subsided into near-silence.

Gregson walked across to a blackboard that had a map of the West End stuck to it. There were several red-tipped pins protruding from it and an area of Soho had been ringed in red marker pen. To the left of the map pictures of Paula Wilson, plus the remains of the two dead murderers, were tacked. On the other side of the map there were several pictures which, from a distance, looked like ink blots. They were in fact the blow-ups of the print taken from Paula Wilson's thigh.

'Nine deaths, including two suicides,' Gregson began. 'All within the space of a week. The murders, as far as we can tell, are motiveless; the killers are now dead, burned to a crisp both of them. By their own choice. Nine bodies and no leads. That is the state of play at the moment.' He prodded a picture of Paula Wilson. 'You all know about this woman, how she was killed and where. What we don't know is why and by who. Now Dean Street, where he killed her, isn't exactly a quiet area; someone somewhere must have seen or heard something. And, seeing as no one has come forward with any information about this killing, I supposed we're meant to think that no one saw anything.' He smiled humourlessly. 'That's a load of bollocks.' The smile faded rapidly. 'If they won't come to us then we'll have to go to them. I want you to talk to people.' He looked slowly around the other faces in the room. 'I want pubs, clubs, clip-joints, restaurants and anything else you can think of, checked out. Talk to the staff. Two men have committed suicide within a one-mile radius of each other within a week. We've had a fucking chase through Soho and now a woman's been murdered. Somebody has seen something. Somebody *knows* something. I want that somebody found and I want them talking.'

'Who exactly are we looking for?' asked a plain clothes man in the front row. 'A suspicious character?'

A ripple of laughter ran around the room.

'In fucking Soho?' grunted Gregson. 'You might as well pull in every bastard who works there.'

More laughter.

'Just talk to them, find out what they've seen and heard over the last couple of weeks,' the DI said.

'Do you think there's a link between the two killers?' a tall ginger-haired officer asked from near the back of the room.

'It's possible,' the DI said quietly, his gaze still roving around the other men in the room. 'We know it isn't a gang-related thing. Not unless London's been invaded by a bunch of fucking fireaters who haven't quite mastered the trick yet.'

Another ripple of laughter greeted this remark.

'Maybe it's the Irish Fire Brigade,' a voice added and the men laughed even louder.

'All right, all right, enough of the joviality,' said Gregson. He turned towards the map and jabbed at the red-ringed area. 'This area is to be gone over with a fine tooth-comb. You'll each be designated one particular area. We don't want to be tripping over each other. As it is, there'll be more policemen than punters on that patch.' He looked round the room. 'You'll report back to me on a daily basis. I don't care if you think you've got nothing, I want to hear what you know, what you found out.'

'Have either of the dead men been identified yet?' another man asked, puffing on his cigarette.

Gregson shook his head.

'We got a print off the second one from Paula Wilson's body, though.' He pointed to the photo of the print. 'It would seem to be just a matter of time before the man's identified.'

'You seem very sure, Frank,' Finn observed.

'Humour me, eh?' Gregson said wearily.

Should he mention the possible copy-cat overtones of the killings? He decided not to.

'Right,' he continued. 'Let's go. If you move through into the next room you'll find the area you're to work. And, like I said, I want to know everything you hear, what anyone's got to say, from the pimps to the tarts through to the doormen at the clip-joints and the managers of restaurants. Got it?'

The men got to their feet and began filing through the door on Gregson's left, muttering to themselves and each other as they went.

'What are you expecting us to find, Frank?' Finn wanted to know.

'Some answers?' he mused, none too convincingly.

'The way you talk, Frank, I'm beginning to wonder if you know something I *don't*,' Finn said.

Gregson didn't answer.

Forty-seven

'What are the nets for?'

Anne Hopper paused beside the rail of landing three and looked over, running her gaze over the wire mesh strung from one catwalk to the other.

189

'To prevent suicides,' Nicholson explained, standing beside her.

'Are there many attempts at suicide, Mr Nicholson?' Paul Merrick asked.

'No more than usual in a prison this size,' the Governor answered without looking at the other man.

'And how many would be *usual?*' Reginald Fairham wanted to know.

'There are three or four attempted suicides every week,' Nicholson said, his tone emotionless.

'And how many are successful?' Merrick wanted to know.

'Two or three. It's a good ratio for a gaol with a population this size.' Nicholson began walking again, satisfied that his visitors were following him. Behind them Warders Niles and Swain walked slowly and purposefully, occasionally stopping to peer through the observation slots in the cell doors.

The small procession moved on towards a set of metal stairs that led them down to the second landing. Their footsteps echoed on the metal catwalks.

'The nets aren't that successful, then?' Fairham said. 'If you have three suicides a week.'

Nicholson caught the note of sarcasm in the other man's voice but he did not turn, did not look at the visitor.

'It wouldn't matter if we welded steel sheets across the landings,' he said. 'They'd still try and kill themselves. There are plenty of other ways than throwing yourself from a walkway.'

The tone of his voice hardened slightly. 'You might be interested to know, Mr Fairham, that the last prisoner who committed suicide by jumping from a landing also took a prison officer with him.'

Fairham didn't answer.

They continued along the walkway, the members of the delegation peering towards the cells or over the rails every so often.

'How many hours a day are the men locked in?' Clinton asked.

'Twenty-two, sometimes twenty-three. It depends on the circumstances,' Nicholson said.

'One hour outside their cells every day,' snapped Fairham. 'That's hardly sufficient, is it?'

'I said it depended on the circumstances,' Nicholson repeated irritably. 'The higher risk prisoners are locked up for longer. Some of the other men are allowed to work outside in the grounds of the prison, as you will see. Others perform duties in the kitchens, the infirmary or the laundry rooms. Every man is allowed a certain amount of time in the recreation room, too.'

'How many are there in each cell?' Clinton wanted to know.

'Usually three,' Nicholson said.

'Would it be possible to have a look inside one?' asked Anne Hopper.

Nicholson stopped his slow strides and turned to look at her.

'If you wish,' he said and nodded to Swain to unlock the nearest cell.

The warder peered through the observation slot then selected a key from the long chain that dangled from his belt. He opened the door and walked in.

'On your feet,' he snapped, glancing at the two occupants. They were both lying on their bunks, one reading, one scribbling a letter on a notepad.

Mike Robinson looked down from the top bunk and saw Swain standing there.

'Mr Swain, what a pleasure,' he said. 'What can we do for you?'

'You can shut your mouth and get on your bloody feet,' snapped Swain.

'Leave them, warder,' said Anne Hopper, moving past him into the cell.

Both men eyed her approvingly as she entered.

'Sorry to disturb you,' she said, smiling.

'No bother, darling,' Robinson told her, grinning. He swung his legs around so that he was perched on the edge of the bunk. He put his pencil and pad aside. Rod Porter peered at her over the top of his book, glancing at the other visitors.

'Less of your lip, Robinson,' hissed Swain. 'Show a bit of respect.'

Robinson caught sight of Nicholson standing on the landing and his smile faded rapidly. He nodded a greeting to the other three visitors, who crowded into the cell as if they were playing some bizarre game of sardines.

There was a table and two wooden chairs at the far end by the slop buckets. Clinton sat down beside the slop bucket and smiled at the two men. Robinson smiled back. Porter merely regarded the man indifferently, his gaze straying back to the woman.

'These are the visitors you were told about yesterday,' Nicholson informed the two men.

'You said there were usually three to a cell,' Clinton observed.

'That's right,' Nicholson repeated.

'There *were* three of us in here,' said Porter slowly, his gaze flicking from one visitor to the other, but always returning to Anne Hopper. 'Our cell-mate had an accident.'

'Shut it, Porter,' Swain said under his breath.

'No,' said Fairham, raising a hand. 'Let him speak.' He looked at the prisoner. 'What kind of accident?'

192

'He forgot to test the temperature of his bath water,' Porter said cryptically.

Robinson laughed, looked at Nicholson and then fell silent again.

'I'm not with you,' said Fairham.

'Neither is *he*, any more,' Porter said.

'What was this man's name?' Fairham wanted to know.

'Marsden,' Nicholson said. 'He was in here for sexual crimes against children.'

'He was a fucking ponce,' Porter said venomously.

'Watch your language,' snarled Swain.

'He *was*. We all knew it, the screws knew it too. That's why they didn't interfere when he . . . *hurt* himself.' The vaguest hint of a smile creased Porter's lips.

'You called him a ponce,' Clinton said. 'What *is* that?'

Robinson chuckled again.

'You must have got a few in the Houses of Parliament,' he said, smiling.

Porter looked directly at the MP.

'A ponce. A pimp. He lived off little kids,' the prisoner said contemptuously. 'Made them sell themselves. Girls *and* boys. He had kids as young as twelve in his stable when they lifted him. A ponce.' He emphasised the word with disgust.

'I still don't understand what you mean about him having an accident,' Fairham said.

'I told you,' Porter said. 'He didn't test his bath water. He got a bit hot.'

'Where is this man now?' Fairham wanted to know.

'He was taken to the hospital wing, then removed to Buxton General Hospital,' Nicholson said. 'He had been scalded. We found him at least two of my officers did, in a bath full of boiling water in the shower rooms. When

193

they got to him ninety-eight per cent of his body had been burned. There was nothing we could do for him here, so we had him transferred.'

'How did he get in that state?' Fairham asked, perplexed, his gaze shifting back and forth from Nicholson to Porter.

'He slipped on the soap,' Porter said.

Robinson laughed.

'He always *was* careless,' the other man added.

The realisation finally seemed to hit Fairham. The colour drained from his cheeks.

'You mean someone tried to kill him?' he said, his voice low.

'No,' Porter told him, flatly. 'He just had an accident.' He raised his book and continued reading.

The visitors turned and filed out of the room, realising that the conversation had come to an end.

Swain threw the two convicts an angry glance before slamming the door and locking it.

On the landing Nicholson was leaning on the rail.

'A man is nearly murdered in here and your officers knew about it?' snapped Fairham.

Nicholson rounded on him, his eyes blazing.

'My men knew nothing about what was going on,' he hissed.

'But that man said . . .'

'Are you going to take the word of a prisoner over mine?' snarled Nicholson. 'My men knew nothing about it.'

'But you don't deny that it could have been deliberate?' Anne Hopper added.

'Miss Hopper, the man who was injured ran a child prostitution ring,' Nicholson said, his tone a little calmer now. 'He set the children targets every day. If they didn't bring back the amount of money he'd told them to, he beat them with a baseball bat.' The Governor paused, for effect. 'A baseball bat studded with carpet tacks.'

'Oh God,' murmured Merrick.

'God had very little to do with it, Mr Merrick,' Nicholson added. He looked at the visitors. 'What you must understand is that even convicts have a twisted code of ethics that they live by. They have their own rules and their own hierachy. The gang members, the hit men in here are at the top of their tree. Child molesters are the lowest of the low, even to other criminals.'

'Why?' Anne Hopper asked.

Nicholson smiled thinly.

'Even scum have to have *someone* to look down on.'

Forty-eight

The figures moved furtively in the darkness, glad of the protection of night.

As they worked the sound of water slapping against the canal walls was a ceaseless accompaniment to their labours. The wind whipped down the narrow side-streets and alleys, whistling in the wide estuaries. The breezes seemed to skim off the water like stones. The surface was constantly moving, as if some unseen force were continually hurling large rocks into the water at the quayside.

The small boat moored there rocked with each wave. The men on board looked up towards their companions on the quayside, muttering to them to be quicker.

A pile of wooden boxes as tall as a man stood on the quay. Piles just like it had already been loaded onto the boat, carefully stowed in its hold, covered by heavy sheeting and secured.

The last of the boxes were being transferred from the back of the truck now, carried by men who sweated under the effort despite the chill wind that had come with the onset of the night.

Further up the quay, larger boats were anchored. Most of the crews or owners had gone ashore. Only the odd light burned, a warning to any other craft travelling the canals on the coal-black night. The churning water looked as impenetrably gloomy as the night, as if it were a liquid extension of the umbra. Pieces of rotting wood drifted past on the flow. The odd tree branch, too. Even a torn jacket.

When a car passed by the men gave it a cursory glance.

The lorry was unloaded. The last two boxes were lifted on to the small boat, the men who strained under their weight cursing as they completed their task.

One of them paused for a moment, inspecting the lid of the last box. It was loose. Several of the nails had come free. The man drew it to the attention of a companion and, together, they lifted the strut of wood clear. He reached inside, pushing his hand through the layers of packing and into something dark and pungent.

Coffee beans.

The aroma was strong in the chill night air but he dug deeper, finally allowing his hand to close on what he really sought.

He pulled the small plastic box free and laid it on top of the crate, fumbling in his jacket pocket for something.

The plastic box was about seven inches long and five across.

He opened it and looked at the video tape cassette inside.

In his pocket he found a screwdriver and inspected the narrow end as if he were a surgeon about to perform a delicate operation. Then, working swiftly, he undid the six screws that held the cassette together and gently eased the back off.

Nestling between the two spools was a tiny plastic packet, smaller than a thumbnail.

He inspected the plastic bag, satisfied that its contents had not been touched.

The cocaine looked like talcum powder, luminescent in the darkness.

The man quickly replaced the back of the cassette, screwed it in place and shoved it back into its box. This he returned to its position beneath the layer of coffee grounds. The grounds acted as a kind of olfactory barrier should the boat be searched and sniffer dogs be brought on. They couldn't detect the smell of cocaine through the more pungent odour of coffee.

The crate was re-sealed and loaded. The boat was ready to leave now and two members of its small crew began casting off, one of them pushing the boat away from the quayside with a long boat-hook. The current gradually took hold. The Captain decided not to switch on his engines until they were further away; he was content to let the vessel be carried by the tide.

The men watching from the quayside waited only a moment. Their duty was done now, their responsibility discharged. The shipment was someone else's concern. Not theirs.

They, at least, had ensured that the cocaine shipment was safely on its way.

The first leg of the operation was underway.

Forty-nine

The cleaver swung down with incredible power and accuracy, severing the leg with one clean cut.

It sheared through bone and muscle alike, the strident snapping of the femur reverberating inside the room.

Anne Hopper winced as she looked at the remains of the bullock lying on the large wooden worktop in the prison kitchen. As she watched, the tall thin man in the butcher's apron raised the cleaver once again and lopped off another part of the leg.

There were other men in the chill room, all dressed in white overalls. Some of them were spattered with blood from the carcasses that hung on a row of meat-hooks nearby.

'The man with the cleaver,' said Reginald Fairham quietly, cupping his hand conspiratorially around his mouth. 'He isn't a prisoner, is he?'

Nicholson turned and looked at the other man contemptuously.

'You maintain that the prisoners here are worthy of trust, don't you, Mr Fairham?' Nicholson said. 'Some of them have to work in the kitchens.'

Fairham swallowed hard as he saw another portion of the carcass cut away by a powerful blow.

'As a matter of fact the man with the cleaver is one of the warders here. He was a master butcher before he joined the service,' Nicholson explained.

Fairham visibly relaxed.

The procession moved through the kitchen, through clouds of steam from several large metal vats of food.

Clinton inspected the contents of one of the vats, smiling amiably at the man who was stirring the mass of baked beans. The man looked at Clinton indifferently and peered down into the vat. The MP moved on, rejoining his colleagues.

The procession moved through the prison at a leisurely pace, Nicholson answering the visitors' questions with the minimum of elaboration, constantly struggling to hide his contempt for some of the more idiotic queries they presented him with.

What did he think the effects of overcrowding were?

How many men took advantage of the educational courses?

How were prisoner and warder relationships? Nicholson remained slightly ahead of his group so that they could never quite see the expression of disdain of his face. He led them along corridors and walkways until they came to a double set of metal-barred gates.

The warder on the other side, at a signal from the Governor, pressed a button and the doors slid open with a faint electronic burr.

Nicholson led them through to another solid steel gate. This one was unlocked by a warder with a key. As he pushed it open a powerful gust of wind swept in from outside. Led by the Governor, they stepped out into the exercise yard. It stretched around them in all four directions, empty, enclosed by high wire mesh fences.

'How much exercise do the prisoners get?' Clinton wanted to know.

'An hour a day,' Nicholson said, leading them across the yard.

'It isn't long enough,' Fairham observed, looking round the empty expanse of concrete.

Anne Hopper noticed the chapel.

She pointed towards the graveyard beside it and the markers on the handful of graves.

Nicholson explained what they were. How the men buried there had no families, no other place to lie.

'It's a wonder there aren't more of them,' Fairham said.

'It's a *pity* there aren't more of them,' Nicholson rasped under his breath.

'Mr Nicholson,' Paul Merrick said, brushing loose strands of whispy hair from his face, 'you said you were going to show us some kind of answer to the problems of overcrowding. May I ask when?'

Nicholson glared at him.

'Now, Mr Merrick,' he said, the knot of muscles at the side of his jaw throbbing angrily.

The hospital block was ahead of them.

Nicholson looked up at the grey stone building. It was as dull as the overcast sky. The gaunt edifice appeared to have dropped from the heavens, a lump of the bleak sky fallen to earth inside the prison grounds.

'What's that?' asked Fairham, pointing at a rusted grille set in the concrete close by the wall of the hospital wing. The grille was about a foot square.

'It's one of the vents over the sewer shaft,' Nicholson explained.

'Hardly hygienic, is it?' Fairham noted. 'So close to the hospital.'

'This prison, as you know, is very old,' the Governor explained. 'The whole place is dotted with vents like that. A network of sewer tunnels runs under the prison. It isn't used now and most of it is blocked off. There's no danger to health from the outlets.'

As they neared the entrance to the wing, Nicholson slowed his pace imperceptibly. He looked up one last time at the grey edifice, licking dry lips.

Those inside had been given their instructions.
He just hoped to God they had followed them.

Fifty

It was smaller than a man's thumb nail and Nicholson held it between the thumb and finger of his right hand with surprising delicacy.

The microchip was square and the entire complex structure was encased in smooth plastic. Nicholson laid it on a piece of black velvet that lay on the work top, allowing his visitors to get a better look at the tiny object.

'Is this some kind of joke?' Fairham asked.

'Why should it be?' the Governor asked irritably.

'You promised to show us a way of relieving over-crowding. Is this meant to be *it*?'

'The idea was first perfected in America. A number of states are already using it,' Nicholson declared.

'But that didn't work,' said Fairham.

'Ours is a different system. The microchip is inserted into the gastrocnemius muscle of the prisoner's leg.' He looked at Fairham with scorn. 'The calf muscle, to keep it simple.' He held the other's gaze for a moment then continued. 'The operation takes less than fifteen minutes. It's carried out under local anaesthetic, there is no pain to the prisoner. No side effects.'

'What does it do?' Clinton asked, his eyes fixed on the tiny square.

'Once inside the prisoner's leg it gives off something called a Synch-pulse,' Nicholson said. 'A tiny electrical charge which in turn produces a signal that can be picked up by monitoring equipment here at the prison. It's like a tracking device.'

'What range has it got?' Merrick asked.

'Fifteen miles at the moment,' the Governor told him. 'The modifications that are being made to it will probably increase that range by anything up to thirty miles.'

'And what is the object exactly, Mr Nicholson?' Anne Hopper enquired, looking at the Governor.

'An end to overcrowding, Miss Hopper,' he said. 'The thing you all seem so concerned about.'

'How the hell can that,' Fairham jabbed a finger towards the microchip, 'help with overcrowding?'

'The device is placed in the leg of certain remand prisoners,' Nicholson explained. 'They can then be released from Whitely and monitored on our electronic equipment here. We know where they are twenty-four hours a day.'

'And what if they move outside the range of the tracking device?' Clinton murmured, his eyes still fixed on the device.

'We don't allow that to happen,' Nicholson said. 'The prisoners are picked for the operation according to the severity of their crime. Everything is explained to them, including the fact that if they do travel beyond the range of the device they'll be re-arrested and prosecuted for attempted escape. They usually co-operate. It's in their own interests to do so. Many of them prefer this to being stuck inside for twenty-three hours a day. Some are even working while they're on the outside waiting for their trials.'

'Do I detect a note of compassion in your attitude, Mr Nicholson?' said Fairham, contemptuously. 'You actually sound as if you care about what happens to the men who undergo this operation.'

'It gets them out of *my* hair, Mr Fairham,' the Governor said. 'It means that my officers have fewer prisoners to deal with.'

'How many men has this been tried on so far?' Clinton enquired.

'Ten,' Nicholson said. 'And all of them have been successful.'

'And what is your definition of success, Mr Nicholson?' Anne Hopper wanted to know.

He looked at her impassively.

'Not one of them tried to escape,' he said. 'They all reported to the police station they'd been assigned to and they all went on to stand trial.'

'When is the device removed?' Clinton asked.

'As soon as the trial is over.'

Clinton stood back and nodded, looking at the microchip then at Nicholson.

'Well, I must say I'm impressed, Mr Nicholson,' said the MP.

'Me too,' Merrick echoed. 'It seems a great step forward.'

Fairham merely prodded the device with one index finger.

'Who does the operations?' he wanted to know.

'There are a number of doctors involved,' Nicholson told him. 'None resident at the prison.'

'That's a pity,' Anne Hopper intoned. 'It would have been interesting to meet them.'

'The work is still in its infancy, Miss Hopper. They're not too anxious to be put in the limelight just yet,' Nicholson told her.

'Why? In case something goes wrong?' Fairham said, challengingly.

'As I said, the work is still relatively new. Until it's completely perfected we'd rather keep it quiet,'

203

the Governor said, glaring once again at the other man.

'I can understand that,' Clinton said, smiling. 'It seems to be successful though, Mr Nicholson. Full marks to you. We'll be reporting this as very satisfactory progress when we return to Whitehall.'

'Satisfactory?' Fairham snapped. 'This man is using remand prisoners as human guinea pigs and you call that satisfactory?'

'I think you're being a little over-dramatic, Mr Fairham,' Clinton said, smiling patronisingly.

'It is preferable to the alternative of being locked up twenty-three hours out of twenty-four,' Merrick echoed.

Nicholson smiled triumphantly at Fairham.

'What is your view, Miss Hopper?' the Governor wanted to know.

The woman shrugged slightly.

'I suppose I would have to agree with Mr Clinton and Mr Merrick,' she said. 'As long as the patients are volunteers and the risks are explained to them before the operation, I can see no objection myself.'

'You appear to be out-voted again, Mr Fairham,' Nicholson said, smiling.

'I'd like to know a little more about the actual mech–anics of the project,' Clinton said. 'How the tracking devices are built, what the operation entails, how the prisoners are monitored. That kind of thing. I will have to make a report to the House, you understand?'

Nicholson nodded, his ingratiating smile spreading.

'Certainly. If you'd like to come back to my office we can discuss it there,' he said, looking at Fairham.

The other man was flushed with anger.

The Governor turned to lead the small procession out.

'We've only seen a small part of the hospital wing,'

Fairham observed. 'I'd like to inspect the facilities here before we leave.'

Nicholson retained his air of calm.

'Of course,' he said, leading them towards a door at one end of the room. It opened out into the infirmary. There were half a dozen prisoners in the beds; other men in white overalls moved among them, performing their duties. One was mopping the floor, another dispensing pills. A third man was pushing a trolley, collecting dirty laundry. Patients and workers alike gave the Governor and his visitors only cursory glances. More lingering looks were reserved for Anne Hopper.

A warder stood at one end of the infirmary, standing by a thick metal door.

Nicholson looked towards him, hoping that none of the visitors noticed the look of apprehension on his face.

He stood back as the visitors moved among the men, speaking to them where possible, usually meeting with only perfunctory grunts in answer to their questions. The Governor caught the eye of the warder at the far end of the infirmary and the man nodded almost imperceptibly. A silent answer to an unasked question. The Governor licked his lips, aware that they were once more dry.

Come on, hurry up and get out of here.

One by one the visitors returned to join him.

They're not going to ask.

Fairham looked to the far end of the infirmary.

'What's through there?' he asked, pointing at the door.

'The morgue,' Nicholson said quickly. 'It's where we keep any prisoners who dic until they've been identified, or until arrangements can be made for their burial.'

Fairham nodded slowly.

Come on, come on.

'I think we've seen enough now, Mr Nicholson,' Clinton said.

Fairham was still gazing at the door.

The Governor licked his lips again.

'We'll go back to my office, then,' he said.

At last Fairham tore his gaze away and filed out in front of Nicholson. The Governor glanced back at the solitary warder and nodded.

As he walked out he let out a sigh of relief.

He would return here as soon as the delegation was gone. For now, at least, it was still safe.

Fifty-one

Coffee dripped from the bottom of the cup as DI Frank Gregson lifted it to his mouth and took a sip. It was strong. He pulled the lid from one of the other milk cartons and poured in the contents, stirring until the dark colour lightened.

Opposite him DS Stuart Finn was smoking a Marlboro, blowing out streams of smoke, alternately gazing into the depths of his tea cup and glancing out of the window.

The neon lights outside were barely visible through the sheen of condensation coating the inside of the café window. The film of steam combined with the patina of dirt on the glass made them almost opaque. Inside the café there were half a dozen other people. At a table in the corner three young girls sat, smoking and chatting quietly, occasionally glancing across at the two policemen.

Two men sat at a table near the counter, one of them

pushing huge forkfuls of food into his mouth, the other sipping at a cup of tea.

Another man sat alone at the table next to them, peering at a magazine. Finn noted that he was tracing a column of names and addresses with the tip of his pen, occasionally ringing one with the biro.

The place smelled of fried food and damp.

Finn stubbed out a cigarette in an already overflowing ash-tray and immediately lit another. He noticed that he was almost out of them and fumbled in his jacket pocket for some change to feed into the cigarette machine. On the radio in the background, a voice announced that it was nine-thirty.

'It's weird, isn't it?' said Finn. 'How all these places start to look alike after a while.'

Gregson shrugged.

'The cafés, the bars, the clip-joints,' Finn continued. 'In the bookshops, too, there's something familiar about them, every one of them. Even the same punters, it seems.' He chuckled. 'I was flicking through a couple of magazines at that last place.' He smiled. 'More cunts than a meeting of the Arsenal supporters' club.' The DS shook his head, still grinning.

Gregson didn't return the smile. He merely sipped at his strong coffee and ran a hand through his hair.

'Yeah, the places look familiar and the answers are starting to *sound* familiar, too,' he said wearily. 'No, never seen him. Never *heard* anything. Didn't *see* anything.'

'I wonder if any of the other blokes are having better luck.'

'Are you serious? This whole fucking area is sewn up tighter than a nun's crotch,' Gregson grunted.

'Then why are we here?'

'Because it's our job.'

Finn sucked gently on his cigarette and looked across the table at Gregson, who was peering through the window into the street beyond.

'You knew it was going to be like this, Frank,' he said. 'You knew that no one around here was going to help us. Why call a search in the first place?'

'Procedure,' Gregson told him.

'Bullshit,' Finn said, smiling thinly. 'What do you know?'

'I know that we should be asking questions instead of sitting on our arses drinking cups of tea,' the DI told him, pushing his half-empty cup away.

'Come on, tell me the truth,' Finn persisted. 'You owe me that. We've been working together long enough. If I had a hunch or an idea about these killings *I'd* tell *you*.'

Gregson smiled thinly.

'The idea I had was crazy,' he said slowly. 'Illogical. Impossible, even. I checked it out. You remember I said to you that the only thing any witnesses could agree on about the first bloke who killed himself was his staring eyes?'

Finn nodded.

'I checked the files, because that rung a bell somewhere. We arrested a bloke called Peter Lawton for a series of armed robberies. Remember me telling you?'

'Yes, I do,' said the DS 'He's banged up, though, isn't he?'

'In Whitely Prison in Derbyshire. Yeah. He has been for the last six years.'

Finn looked vague.

'The second killer, the one who murdered the girl, I checked out his MO because that sounded familiar, too.'

'And?'

'It matched with the MO of a guy called Mathew Bryce who was also arrested over eighteen months ago. He's doing time in Whitely as well. What conclusions can you draw from that?'

Finn shrugged.

'That someone copied them,' he said.

'Or that they both escaped and duplicated the crimes they were originally arrested for.' Gregson smiled when he saw the look on Finn's face. 'See why I didn't mention it before? It's fucking crazy. We know they didn't escape because we would have heard, the whole country would have heard. They're still inside Whitely.' The phrase on both the files he'd read re-surfaced in his mind. *Term being served.* 'But if someone imitated the crimes committed by Lawton and Bryce, what's to stop somebody *else* imitating murders committed by *any* killer locked up in *any* jail in the country?'

'That still doesn't explain why they torched themselves,' Finn observed.

Gregson shrugged.

'On that point,' he said, 'your guess is as good as mine.' The DI got to his feet and headed for the door. The other occupants of the café watched him go. Finn left some money for the tea and coffee on the table, then fed change into the cigarette machine and pulled a packet out. He joined his superior at the door, pulling up the collar of his jacket as they stepped out into the street.

'Where to next?' he said, cupping his hand around the Marlboro he was trying to light.

'Over there,' said Gregson, nodding in the direction of the neon-shrouded building opposite.

The lights formed the word 'Loveshow'.

209

Fifty-two

'Scotty. Police.'

Zena Murray emphasised the last word with distaste, stepping back to allow the two plain clothes men into Jim Scott's office. Gregson was the first in and he looked across at Scott indifferently as Finn entered, smiling thinly by way of a greeting.

'What can I do for you?' Scott wanted to know. 'The licence is in order, we haven't had any trouble on the premises and, as far as I know, my boss is bunging the back-handers in the right places. So, what can I help you with?'

'A comedian, eh?' said Gregson, flatly. 'Everyone's a fucking comic when the law arrive, aren't they?' The two men locked stares for a moment. 'You're Jim Scott, right? Manager of this . . . place?'

Scott nodded.

'Ray Plummer owns it, doesn't he?' Finn added, looking around the office.

'Actually it's a tax dodge for the Prime Minister,' Scott said smugly. 'What does it matter?'

'Look, Scott, we don't want to *be* here any more than you *want* us to be here,' Gregson told him. 'If I wanted to wade around in shit I'd go for a walk down a sewer. We just want to ask you a few questions and get out. We've already spoken to your staff. The quicker you answer our questions the quicker we'll be out of your hair.'

Scott glanced at each of the policemen in turn, then motioned to the chairs close to his desk.

'Have a seat,' he offered.

'No thanks,' said Gregson, wrinkling his nose.

'It's no problem, I can get it disinfected afterwards,' Scott told him.

Gregson met the other man's gaze and pulled a small photograph from the inside pocket of his jacket. He dropped it on to the desk in front of Scott who picked it up, studying the outlines of Paula Wilson's face.

'That girl was killed a couple of streets away from here the night before last. Have you seen her around here before?' the DI wanted to know.

'We don't get many girls coming in here as spectators,' Scott said, tossing the photo back across the desk.

'She might have come in with a boyfriend. This is supposed to be a show for *couples* to watch too, isn't it?' Gregson observed.

'Never seen her. I'm usually in here. I don't go out front much.'

'This is the nerve centre, is it?' Gregson said, smiling, scornfully. 'Where all the big decisions are taken?'

'I told you, I don't know the girl. I can't help you. Why don't you piss off? And don't forget to shut the door on your way out.' Scott sat down at his desk and turned his attention to the ledger he had before him.

'How many staff have you got here?' Finn asked.

'It varies. Between six and eight,' Scott told him.

'And you're in charge of all of them?' Gregson said with mock respect. 'What it must be to have responsibility, eh?'

Scott glared at the DI.

'I don't remember you showing me any fucking ID.' he snapped.

Both men flipped open the thin leather wallets they carried. Scott gazed at the photos, then at their faces.

'Satisfied?' said Gregson.

Scott nodded.

'Yours is a better likeness,' he said to the DI, a smile flickering on his lips. 'You look a miserable cunt in the picture, too.'

Gregson held his stare for a moment, a smile forming at the corners of his own mouth.

'I'm surprised I don't know you,' he said quietly. 'Geezers like you usually have form, or has Plummer been recruiting *up-market*?'

Scott merely glared at the DI. The heavy atmosphere was finally interrupted by Finn, heading towards the door.

'Come on, Frank,' he said wearily. 'Let's get out of here. He doesn't know anything and we've got other places to check.'

The DS actually had his hand on the door handle when it was turned.

He stepped back a pace, smiling broadly as he saw the young woman who stood before him, looking slightly surprised. She returned his smile as she stepped inside the office, glancing across at Scott's desk. Gregson eyed her disinterestedly.

'They're coppers, Carol,' Scott told her. 'Here to ask some questions,' he sneered.

'Another member of your staff?' Finn enquired. He showed Carol his ID as he spoke. She looked at him again but this time there was no smile on her face.

'Questions about what?' she wanted to know.

Never taking his eyes from her, Gregson slipped out the photo of Paula Wilson and quickly explained the reason for his and Finn's presence, enquiring whether or not the face in the monochrome picture rang any bells.

It didn't.

'Happy now?' Scott asked, noticing that Gregson was still gazing at Carol.

Stop staring, you bastard.

'Well, well,' said the DI, smiling thinly. 'Long time no see, eh, Carol?'

Scott glared at the policeman then at Carol.

What the fuck is this?

'How long's it been now?' Gregson continued. 'Two years?'

She looked at him through narrowed eyes.

'How the hell do you know him?' Scott wanted to know, unable to contain his anger.

'We met on a professional basis,' said Gregson, his smile broadening. 'I arrested her for soliciting.' He allowed his gaze to travel slowly up and down her shapely body. 'No wonder you were doing such good business,' he said. 'You still look good.'

Scott clenched his fists until his nails dug into the palms of his hands.

Carol didn't answer. Like some naughty child who's been caught playing a prank she just kept her head low, staring at the floor.

'Maybe I'll see you again,' the DI said as he and Finn reached the door.

'Just get out,' hissed Scott.

They closed the door and were gone.

Scott brought his hand crashing down on the desk top, his face pale with rage, the vein at his temple throbbing.

'Did you recognise him when you walked in?' he demanded.

'Jim, that was in the past,' she said. 'Besides, it's nothing to do with you. It was my problem.'

'How did he catch you? Had you fucked him before he lifted you?' There was a stinging vehemence in Scott's words.

Carol looked angrily at him, turned and headed for the door.

213

Scott shot out a hand and grabbed her by the shoulder, spinning her round.

'Had he?' he roared.

She struck him hard across the left cheek with the flat of her hand.

'Get off me,' she shouted.

Scott moved a pace towards her, his face stinging from the blow, his eyes bulging wide.

'You don't own me, Jim,' she hissed, her voice faltering slightly as she saw the look of pure rage etched across his features. She opened the office door. 'You don't own me.' She slammed it behind her and walked away hurriedly, her heart beating madly against her ribs.

Inside the office Scott touched the cheek she had slapped, his breath still coming in gasps.

'Bitch,' he hissed, turning back to his desk. He found the bottle of Southern Comfort and poured himself a large measure. His breathing gradually slowed as he propped himself against one edge of the desk, drinking. Again he touched his cheek, but this time he felt no anger, merely a deep sorrow.

One thought surfaced in his mind.

Would she forgive him?

Outside in the street Finn lit up another cigarette and looked at his watch.

'Where to next?' he said, pulling up the collar of his jacket.

Gregson didn't answer; he was staring at the doorway of 'Loveshow'.

'Frank. I said, where next?' the DS repeated, blowing out a stream of smoke and looking at his companion. 'Hello, is there anyone in there?'

Gregson looked impassively at his colleague.

214

'Something on your mind?' Finn asked.

'You could say that,' Gregson told him vaguely. He started walking and Finn followed.

'You're fucking weird sometimes, Frank, you know that?' he said. 'Who was that tart, anyway?'

'I said, I arrested her a couple of years ago,' Gregson muttered.

'You were right, she's good-looking. I'm not surprised you remember her.' The DS chuckled.

Gregson merely continued walking.

He remembered her all right.

Fifty-three

Ray Plummer looked at his watch, checking the time against the clock on the marble mantelpiece.

11.24 p.m.

He crossed to his drinks cabinet and poured himself another large measure of whisky, glancing at the phone every few seconds as if willing it to ring.

Perhaps it was a wind-up, he thought. There would be no phone call from the mysterious informant. The whole fucking scheme was somebody pissing him about.

Wasn't it?

He downed what was left in his glass and thought about pouring himself another. He looked at the phone again. What if the caller rang and couldn't be bothered to hold on?

Someone pissing about.

It was a hell of an elaborate plan just for a wind-up.

Could it be true about the twenty million?

He crossed to the drinks cabinet once more and tipped the bottle.

The phone rang.

Plummer spun round, almost dropping the bottle and his glass. Whisky slopped onto his hand as he hurried to pick up the receiver.

'Hello,' he said.

Cool it. Don't let the bastard think you're too interested.

'Ray?' said the voice.

First name terms, now, eh?

'Yes. What have you got for me?'

'Ray, are you okay?'

Plummer frowned.

There was something wrong here.

'Who *is* this?' he said, some of the tension leaving his voice.

'It's Jim Scott. What's wrong?'

Plummer exhaled deeply and gripped the receiver tightly in his hand.

'What the fuck do you want?' he snapped.

'We've had the law round here tonight,' Scott told him. 'That girl who was killed the other night, they've been checking the area.'

'Some girl was killed, was she?' Plummer muttered irritably. 'Jim, I couldn't give a toss if the Queen Mum has been gang banged.' The anger returned to his voice. 'I'm waiting for a very important call. Get off the line, will you?'

'I just thought you should know,' Scott said. 'They spoke to all the staff here. I know everything is covered with the running of the club, but I didn't think you'd be too happy about the Old Bill sticking its nose in.'

'I couldn't care less, get off the fucking line,' shouted Plummer and slammed the receiver down.

He stepped away from the phone, angry with Scott for disturbing him but also angry with himself for being so jumpy. He'd been in the penthouse flat since about nine that evening, trying to watch TV, trying to listen to music but with no success. All he could think about was the impending phone call. *If* it came. John Hitch had seemed convinced that it would and Plummer trusted the instincts of his colleague almost as he trusted his own. And yet.

11.36.

Fuck it. No one was calling, he thought.

He's six minutes late. That's all. Six lousy minutes.

He turned his back on the phone.

The strident ringing startled him again, but this time he turned slowly, gazing at the phone.

Plummer finally plucked up the receiver.

'Where the fuck were you?' the voice rasped. 'I said I'd ring at half past. Your phone was engaged.'

'What am I supposed to do, apologise?' Plummer snapped. 'Say what you've got to say.'

'It's on.'

'What's on?'

'The shipment is on its way, you stupid cunt. What do you think I mean?' the voice hissed.

Plummer gripped the receiver tightly.

'Listen . . .'

The caller cut him short.

'No, *you* listen. Perhaps you have a pen and paper with you, or will you be able to remember what I'm going to tell you?'

'Get on with it.'

'The shipment of cocaine will arrive two days from now. It's going to be on board a small boat called *The Sandhopper*. The coke will be in among a load of porn mags and videos, right?'

217

'Where is it being unloaded?' Plummer wanted to know.

'Chelsea Bridge.'

'What about that warehouse in Tilbury that Connelly bought? You said it was going to be there.'

'I never said that. I told you Connelly had bought a warehouse. I never said for sure that's where the stuff would arrive.'

'Chelsea Bridge,' Plummer murmured, more to himself than the caller.

'Yeah. The drop is scheduled for two in the morning. There'll be a lorry waiting to pick the stuff up. It'll look like a refrigerated lorry carrying beer.'

'How many of Connelly's men are involved?' Plummer wanted to know.

'I'm not sure.'

'How the fuck are they going to get the stuff up the Thames without the river police tumbling them?'

'What am I, an information service? That's your problem. That's all I've got to say now. I won't call again. Things are starting to get dangerous now.'

He hung up.

Plummer replaced the receiver slowly, massaging his chin thoughtfully with his other hand.

He was about to phone John Hitch when there was a knock on the door.

Plummer swallowed hard and froze for long seconds.

The knock came again, harder, more insistent.

He moved stealthily to the bedroom, to the wardrobe close to his bed. There was a small safe in the bottom which he hurriedly opened.

Plummer pulled the Delta Elite 10mm automatic from inside the safe and slid one magazine into the butt. He worked the slide as quietly as he could, chambering a

218

round, then he moved back out into the sitting room towards the door.

The knock came again.

'Yeah, all right, I'm coming,' he called, unlocking the door with infinite slowness. He left the chain on, the words of the caller flashing into his mind:

Things are starting to get dangerous.

Precisely *how* dangerous, Plummer was about to find out.

He turned the door handle slowly, the automatic gripped in his fist, held high so that he could swing it down into a firing position if necessary.

He opened the door, allowing it to reach only the length of the chain.

The Delta Elite was ready as he peered through the gap.

His voice was coloured with surprise as he gazed at the newcomer.

'What are *you* doing here?'

Fifty-four

Plummer slid the chain free, allowing the door to open wider.

Carol Jackson stepped inside.

'What's wrong?' Plummer wanted to know, closing the door behind her and slipping the bolts once more. He saw her expression of surprise as she noticed the automatic gripped in his hand. Plummer lowered the weapon, easing the hammer forward and slipping on the safety catch. He laid the pistol down and crossed to the drinks cabinet, pouring glasses of whisky for himself and

219

for Carol. He thought how tired she looked. She took the glass from him and drank.

'Why the gun?' she wanted to know.

'It doesn't matter,' he said. 'Just tell me why you're here.'

'Do I need a reason?' she asked, slipping off her coat and sitting down. She perched on the edge of the sofa, gazing into the mock flames from the gas fire.

Plummer ran a hand over his hair then stood beside her, touching her cheek with the back of his hand. It was an aberrant gesture but she reached up and touched his hand all the same.

'The law were in tonight, then?' he said.

'How do you know?' she asked.

'Scott told me.'

She looked up at him, her eyes filled with surprise and something more.

Fear?

'Scott's been here?'

Plummer explained about the phone call.

'He's going to kill us, Ray,' she said flatly.

It was Plummer's turn to look surprised.

'What the fuck are you talking about?' he gaped.

'I was with him the other night and some of the things he was saying, I know that if he found out about us . . .' She allowed the sentence to trail off.

'I thought you weren't seeing him any more.'

'I was going to finish it, but it's not that easy, Ray.' She recounted the conversation she'd had with Scott, telling Plummer about the gun. 'He'd do it, I know he would.'

'You're overreacting,' Plummer told her.

'I'm scared of him,' she blurted. 'And I think *you* should be, too.'

Plummer took a sip of his drink and wandered across to the window, peering out into the night.

'Mind you, he always was a bit unpredictable,' he murmured. 'You didn't tell him you were seeing me, did you?'

'I'm not stupid, Ray,' she said.

Plummer smiled thinly and rolled the glass between his hands.

'So what do you want me to do about it?' he asked. 'If we stopped seeing each other that would solve the problem, wouldn't it?'

'It's Scott I want to stop seeing, not you,' she told him.

It's your money I want.

'So stop seeing him.'

'I told you, it's not that easy,' she said irritably. 'He won't take no for an answer, I know he won't.'

'Why the fuck did you get involved with him in the first place?' Plummer wanted to know. 'You knew what he was like, didn't you?'

'I knew he thought a lot of me. I didn't think he was so obsessed.'

Plummer laughed.

'That's a bit strong, isn't it?' he chuckled.

'You don't know him, Ray,' she said. 'What I've told you is true. He's dangerous.'

Plummer peered into the bottom of his glass, as if seeking inspiration there.

'If he's dead he's no threat,' Plummer said, looking at her with cold eyes.

Carol looked puzzled.

'Do you want him taken care of? Put to sleep?' Plummer enquired.

'Killed?'

He shrugged.

'Jesus Christ, is that your only answer, Ray? Have him killed? That isn't what I want.'

'It sounds like you think more of him than you're letting on. You either want him out of your life or you don't.'

'I don't want him *killed*.'

'Still feel something for him?' Plummer enquired. 'Or won't your conscience allow it?' He smiled thinly. 'What do you want to do for the rest of your life, Carol? Hang around with a nobody like Scott, knowing you never dare leave him in case the mad fucker tries to kill you? From the sound of it he'd blow you away without a second thought. And he's supposed to love you.'

Carol could feel the tears welling up in her eyes. She wiped them away with the back of one trembling hand.

'What *do* you want?' Plummer continued.

'I want to get away,' she said, her voice cracking. 'From Scott, from that fucking club, from that whole lifestyle.'

'And how do you expect to do that?' he said flatly. 'It's all you know. It's all you *have* known.'

'What about you and me?' she said tearfully. 'Isn't there anything between us?'

Plummer smiled a predatory smile and crossed to the sofa, seating himself beside her. He put down his drink then took her in his arms, holding her tight. He could feel her tears staining his shirt.

'It's okay, sweetheart,' he said quietly. 'We'll take care of it. I said I'd look after you, didn't I?'

She snaked her arms around his neck, pulling him closer. Her body was racked by sobs, muffled as she pressed her head against his chest.

'Don't worry about Scott,' he said, glancing across at the Delta Elite lying on the table. 'I'll take care of everything.'

Before he comes after me.

'I don't want him hurt, Ray. Please,' she insisted, her cheeks tear-stained.

'Don't let him think there's anything wrong,' Plummer told her. 'Carry on seeing him for the time being. Until the time's right.' He looked into her face. 'All right?'

She nodded slowly.

'I don't want him hurt,' she repeated.

Plummer smiled.

'Trust me,' he whispered, pulling her close. His eyes settled on the automatic once again.

The night sky was full of rain clouds, swollen and ready to spill their load on the city below. Clouds which made the blackness all the more impenetrable. A tenebrous gloom which had prevented Plummer from seeing anything except the lights from other buildings nearby and his own reflection in the window of the flat.

Even if he had been aware of the presence, the darkness would have prevented him seeing the man who watched his flat.

Fifty-five

There were rumours of snow on the way and, as Governor Peter Nicholson made his way across the exercise yard of Whitely Prison, he could believe them. The wind was cutting across the open space at great speed, so cold it seemed to penetrate his bones. As he turned a corner it was like being hit in the face by a handful of razor blades.

If it snowed, as was threatened, there was every possibility that Whitely would be cut off. It had happened twice before in his time as Governor. Once, in the winter

223

of 1983, the snow had drifted up to ten feet around the prison walls; teams of prisoners working virtually round the clock had been unable to keep open the single road that linked Whitely with the outside world. No food had got through and the men had been put on half-rations. There had been rumblings about a riot, but Nicholson had received the warnings with little fear. His men were well equipped to deal with any such eventualities. There were small stock-piles of tear gas in the prison to be used in the event of riots or large scale disturbances and Nicholson would have had no compunction about using them.

It transpired that the snow went as quickly as it had come, the road was opened and supplies began getting through regularly again. Possible chaos had been averted.

Two years ago the same thing had happened, but for a shorter time. If anything, though, the more recent incident had proved more damaging. Prisoners, unable to exercise outside in sub-zero temperatures, had been allowed longer in the recreation rooms. Inevitably, men pushed together for long periods of time became edgy and, by the time the prison was freed from the grip of the snow, three men had been knifed (one of whom had lost a kidney) and another had been beaten severely with a pool cue.

Nicholson wondered, if the snow came, what he could expect *this* time.

He glanced to his left and saw the prison chapel, the weather-vane spinning madly in the powerful breeze. The skeletal trees in the graveyard rattled their branches in the wind, bowing almost to touch the ground as the breeze battered them.

Ahead of him was the hospital wing, the familiar grey of the stonework matching the colour of the sky.

224

Nicholson entered, feeling the warmth immediately. He paused by one of the radiators to warm his hands before approaching the doors that led into the infirmary.

Inside, the wind rattled windows in their frames. One or two heads turned to look at him as he strode through, glancing at the occupants of the place.

A man who'd been scalded in the kitchens by cooking oil. Another, who'd been injured in a brawl during exercise, sported fifty-eight stitches from the point of his chin to the corner of his left eye. When he left the infirmary he was due to spend two weeks in solitary. His assailant was already there.

Another man had his leg in plaster, recovering from a broken ankle. He regarded Nicholson coldly as the Governor passed by.

A man in white overalls was busy collecting dirty bed sheets and towels, pushing the excrement- and blood-stained linen into a trolley he was pushing up and down the ward. He stepped to one side as Nicholson approached him but made sure that he left a sheet soaked with urine dangling from the trolley, hoping that Nicholson would brush against it.

He didn't.

Ahead of him, the guard at the locked door stood up as Nicholson nodded. The warder found the key he sought, unlocked the door and allowed Nicholson through.

The ward beyond was empty but for ten beds, only one of which was occupied.

There were no windows in the walls, the only light being provided by the banks of fluorescents set high in the ceiling. Walls and floors were of the same uniform grey.

The one bed that was occupied was at the far end of the ward. As Nicholson headed towards it his shoes beat out a tattoo on the polished floor.

There was a man standing over the patient looking down at the face completely encased in bandages. The man held a clipboard he was scribbling on. He was tall, his hair grey, his features wrinkled. His cheeks were sunken and the onset of years had given him heavy jowls.

He turned to face Nicholson as the Governor drew closer. Nicholson thought that he looked vaguely pleased to see him; a small smile hovered on his dry lips.

'Can you spare me some time?' said Nicholson.

Doctor Robert Dexter nodded.

Fifty-six

The years had not been kind to Robert Dexter. The lines in his face had deepened into clearly defined wrinkles. The flesh of his forehead looked like pastry after someone has drawn a fork across it. He sighed and looked at Nicholson.

'Any progress?' the Governor said, nodding towards the man in the bed.

'I was just about to look,' Dexter said, his voice low and guttural.

With that he reached into the pocket of his white overall and took out a small pair of scissors. He cut the bandages close to the man's chin and began slowly unravelling them, pausing every now and then to lift the man's head. All that was visible was a small gap for his nose; the rest of his head was completely encased in gauze. Dexter continued with his task.

'If that delegation had got inside here the other day, you and *I* would be locked up in here,' said Nicholson.

'Does that bother you?' Dexter said.

'It's a change we were both prepared to take. We both knew the risks,' Nicholson said.

'What did they think of the electronic tagging idea?' Dexter wanted to know, still unwinding bandages.

'They liked it. Needless to say, I didn't mention our other little venture.'

'You won't be able to keep it secret forever,' Dexter exclaimed. 'Besides, secrecy wasn't my aim. Once the technique has been perfected there'll be no need to hide the truth.'

'And how do you propose to announce your findings, Dexter? By showing the world an example of your work?' He nodded in the direction of the man in the bed. The first layer of bandages was off. Dexter began on the next one.

'When it works, it'll be nothing to be ashamed of. It's what I've been working towards for most of my professional life,' the doctor said defensively.

'The world might applaud your achievement but I doubt if it will condone your methods,' Nicholson said, taking his eyes from the bandaged man to look momentarily at Dexter. 'Brain operations on convicted murderers.' He smiled. 'It'll be interesting to see how the Home Office reacts to that.'

'It was you who allowed me to work here; why do you ridicule me?'

Nicholson held up his hands.

'No offence meant.' He smiled again. 'I'm happy for you to do your work here.'

'It doesn't seem to bother you that it hasn't been altogether successful so far.'

Nicholson shrugged.

'I sometimes wonder if you realise what this work actually means, Nicholson. And end to man's violent

227

tendencies . . . An end by the insertion of a device constructed and perfected by me.'

'Don't lecture me, Dexter.'

'If this work is successful it could mean an end to places like Whitely. An end to violence.'

'You're starting to sound like a refugee from a bad horror film. The role of mad scientist doesn't suit you.'

'What the hell is mad about wanting to stop violence?'

'Because it's a wasted dream,' hissed Nicholson. 'If you believe you can stop violence by your surgery, *you're* crazy. You've seen some of the men in here; you know what they're capable of. How can you hope to stop that with technology? I find the twisted nobility of your scheme rather amusing, all the same.' he added sardonically.

'You don't care whether it works or not, do you?' Dexter said. 'You never have. If the men die as a result of the surgery you don't care.'

'They're murderers. If we still had the death penalty they'd be hanged, anyway. *You've* become the executioner, Dexter. All you're doing is carrying out a sentence that the courts no longer have the power to impose. *That's* what I agree with. Not the ethics behind your work.'

'And what about the ones who've survived? It was you who allowed me to release them. If they'd been traced back to here, it would have been your responsibility.'

'We've been fortunate, so far,' the Governor said, looking down at the man lying in the bed.

Dexter was pulling the last layer of bandages away, using the scissors to snip off any loose pieces, exposing the face beneath. Only the bandages around his scalp remained. Slowly Dexter began to loosen those, too.

'What makes you think you can succeed now, when

228

you couldn't all those years before?' Nicholson wanted to know. 'You were using surgery on your patients in the asylum.'

'When I was working in Bishopsgate I was using a different method,' Dexter explained. 'My colleague and I thought we could stop patients' psychotic tendencies by *removing* the parts of the brain responsible for triggering violence. I now know that was wrong.' He pulled more bandages away. 'Inserting the device inside the brain, actually placing it *in* the lateral ventricle ensures that the chemical is evenly spread around the brain.'

He pulled the last piece of bandage away, revealing the bald dome of his subject.

There was a thin cut running around the skull, stitched in several places but held, in others, by several aluminium clips fixed to the skull like large staples holding the cranium shut.

'Good morning, Doctor Frankenstein,' said Nicholson, smiling.

Dexter didn't appreciate the joke.

He took a scalpel from the pocket of his jacket and slipped the plastic sheath off its sharp blade. Then with infinite care, he loosened two of the clips, sliding the tip of the scalpel into the incision in the scalp.

As he applied pressure to the blade, a portion of the skull about the size of a ten pence piece came free. Beneath, the greyish-white brain was clearly visible, criss-crossed by countless tiny blood vessels. The brain was throbbing rhythmically, looking as if it was trying to well up out of the hole in the scalp. In the centre of the pulsing greyness was a gleaming object only millimetres square.

'When hormone levels in the blood rise, due to anger or aggression, the device releases an artificial chemical which neutralizes other bodily fluids like adrenalin,'

229

Dexter explained. 'It's like a warning system. As soon as the patient feels anger, the device releases the chemical, calming him down again.'

'Why is it placed there?' Nicholson wanted to know. 'I thought the mid-brain controlled sight and hearing.'

'It does, but no area of the brain has yet been identified as controlling reactions like reason. Violent men don't usually stop to reason first. The device is located centrally because the chemical can be distributed more quickly through the brain that way. It also makes the operation easier.' He kept his eyes on the pulsing grey matter.

'You said you used to cut away portions of the brain,' Nicholson said.

'That was useless,' Dexter said. 'I might as well have lobotomised the patients. It stopped them reacting violently because it stopped them reacting *at all*.'

Nicholson raised his eyebrows.

'I don't want to create mindless idiots, that's not my goal. It doesn't benefit them *or* me.'

Nicholson was unimpressed. He stepped away from the bed.

'Is he going to die?' he asked, nodding towards the patient, the brain still throbbing gently through the hole in the skull.

'Does it bother you?'

'Not really. No.'

'He's got as much chance as the others had.'

'If it works, Dexter, if he survives, this time we have to be sure before we go any further. We can't afford any more mistakes. *Either* of us.'

Fifty-seven

Pick it up.

Come on, for Christ's sake. Answer the bloody phone.

Jim Scott drummed his fingers on the table and held the receiver to his ear, irritated by the insistent ringing tone that throbbed inside his head.

He pressed down on the cradle, waited a moment then dialled again.

He listened to the hisses and pops of static as the number connected and the phone rang again.

'Come on,' he murmured under his breath, glancing at his watch, wondering where the hell Carol had got to at nine-forty in the morning. Perhaps she'd gone out to get some shopping, he thought. Perhaps she was in the bath.

Perhaps . . .

Perhaps she knew it was him and she deliberately wasn't answering.

How could she know? He rebuked himself for his stupidity. Anger that she wasn't answering now combined with concern and something approaching desperation in his mind. If only she would pick up the receiver. He needed to hear her voice, needed to speak and to hear *her* speak. Most of all he needed to apologise. In his clumsy, fumbling way he needed to say sorry for what had happened at the club the night before. He shouldn't have grabbed her, shouldn't have shouted at her. She was right, he had no hold over her. He didn't own her.

Pick up the fucking phone.

She had left the previous night without speaking to

him, without giving him the chance to say how sorry he was. He'd sat up for most of the night brooding about it, wondering what her reaction to him would be, finally deciding that he couldn't wait until the evening to find out.

He put down the phone, sat staring at it for a moment and then dialled once more.

The ringing tone greeted him.

'Shit,' hissed Scott and slammed it down. He got to his feet and pulled on his jacket, heading for the front door.

He *would* speak to her, no matter what.

The journey took him the better part of an hour, due to delays on the Tube, but now, as he walked from the station, he felt a curious mixture of elation and anxiety.

He was going to see Carol. Not just speak to her, but *see* her. He could tell her face to face how sorry he was for the incident of the previous night. As he walked he wondered if he should have bought her flowers. No. It was enough that he should have taken the trouble to visit her and offer his apologies.

What if she wasn't home?

He would wait for her. If she was out he'd sit on her front step and wait until she returned, or he'd walk around and try again later. He would not leave until he'd seen her.

He rounded a corner, passing three children kicking a football back and forth across the road. The ball bounced near Scott and he trapped it with his left foot, then swivelled and hooked it to one of the young boys with his right, smiling to himself.

The boy, no more than ten, looked at Scott and frowned. 'Flash cunt,' he called as the man walked on.

232

The kids continued their game.

Scott finally reached the house he sought. He knew that Carol occupied the basement flat. A short flight of stone steps led down to the entrance. Scott paused for a moment, looking up at the house. The paintwork on some of its window frames was blistered and peeling like scabrous skin. A pane of glass in one of the ground floor flats had been broken, replaced hastily with just a sheet of newspaper held in place by masking tape. There were tiles missing from the roof. Scott wandered down the short set of steps to Carol's door, noticing that there was a pint of milk on the step.

He banged twice and waited.

No answer.

Perhaps she was still in bed.

He banged again. This time, when he received no answer, he moved across to the window and, cupping one hand over his eyes, endeavoured to see inside the flat. Net curtains prevented his attempted intrusion. He could see nothing.

'Can I help you?'

The voice startled him and he spun round, looking up to see a young woman standing there. She was in her early thirties, dressed in a worn leather jacket and faded jeans. She was carrying a bag of shopping that she kept moving from one hand to the other.

'I live upstairs,' she told him.

'I'm looking for Carol Jackson,' he said, noticing that the woman was running appraising eyes over him. 'I'm a friend of hers. I've been ringing all morning but I couldn't get any answer.'

The woman nodded.

'I should have taken her milk in,' she said. 'I usually do if she doesn't come home.'

Scott frowned.

233

'She's not here, then?' he exclaimed.

'She didn't come home last night,' the woman told him.

Scott gritted his teeth.

'Where is she?' he demanded.

The woman shrugged.

'I take her milk in, I don't ask her for reports,' she said as Scott started up the steps.

He brushed past her.

'Can I give her a message?' the woman asked. 'I'll probably see her later.'

Scott was already stalking off up the road.

'*I'll* see her later,' he called over his shoulder.

The woman shrugged and made her way into the house.

When he reached the end of the street, Scott turned and looked back towards the house.

Where the hell is she?

Could something have happened to her on the way home last night?

Perhaps she never got home.

The ball the three youngsters were kicking about landed near Scott once more.

If she didn't go home, where the fuck did she go?

'Oi, our ball,' shouted one of the kids.

Scott looked at the lad, then at the ball close to his feet. He lashed out at it and sent it flying down the road, away from the trio of kids.

'You bastard,' one of them shouted as he raced after it.

Scott ignored his insult and continued walking, his face set in hard lines.

Where the hell was she?

Fifty-eight

The shutters were still closed, the door firmly locked. It would be another two hours before Les Gourmets opened for business.

Inside the restaurant the tables were bare but for cloths, all immaculately clean. The staff wouldn't arrive to set them for a while yet. Out in the kitchen preparations were already taking place in readiness for the lunch-time trade. The restaurant always did well at lunchtimes, situated as it was in Shepherd Market. It was one of five such establishments owned by Ray Plummer.

Now he sat at one of the tables, cradling a glass of white wine in one hand. With the other he gently stroked his hair.

There were five other men with him. They too had drinks. Plummer put down his glass and reached into his inside pocket for the monogrammed cigarette case. He took one and lit it, looking round at his companions.

'Same voice as the other night, Ray?' said John Hitch, flicking his long blond hair over his shoulders.

Plummer nodded.

'And I still couldn't pin the bastard down,' he complained.

'He says the shipment's coming in by boat?' Terry Morton said.

'*The Sandhopper*, it's called,' Plummer told him. He repeated the other details about the shipment of cocaine, as relayed to him by the mysterious informant the previous night. He sat back when he'd finished and sipped his wine.

'Could it be a set up?' Joe Perry wanted to know. Perry was a thick-set, bull-necked man who looked as if he'd been eased into his suit with a shoe-horn. The material stretched so tightly across his shoulder blades it threatened to rip. His face was smooth, almost feminine; it looked as if it had never felt the touch of a razor.

Plummer shrugged.

'It could be,' he said.

'It could also be bollocks, couldn't it?' Morton interjected. 'I mean, there might not even *be* a shipment of coke.'

'Then why bother phoning?' asked Adrian McCann, rubbing a hand over his close-cropped hair. Over his ears it was completely shaved. 'It's a bit fucking elaborate, isn't it?'

'That's what *I* said,' Plummer agreed. He turned to Hitch. 'You heard the geezer the other night, John; he didn't sound like he was joking, did he?'

Hitch shook his head.

'I agree with Joe,' he added. 'It *could* be a set-up.'

'But by who?' Plummer wanted to know, a note of exasperation in his voice. 'We know it's not another organisation in London, especially not Ralph Connelly's firm.'

'Could it be somebody working for Connelly with an axe to grind?' asked Martin Bates, running his finger around the rim of his glass. Bates was in his early twenties, one of Plummer's youngest employees.

Plummer shrugged.

'Who knows? The point is, do we go with it or not? Do we assume there *is* a shipment? And, if there is, do we knock it over?'

'Are you asking for votes, boss?' Hitch said, laughing.

The other men laughed too. Plummer didn't see the

236

joke and glanced irritably at Hitch, waiting until they calmed down.

'Right, let's assume there *is* a shipment of coke,' he continued. 'Let's say that phone call was kosher. The day after next the shipment is meant to be arriving, *if* the information's right. If it *is* right then the coke is hidden among a load of coffee beans. Now the question is, if this is a set-up, we're going to get hit when we try to take the lorry they're transferring the shit to. How do we get round *that*?'

'Take out the lorry first?' offered Joe Perry.

'No,' Hitch said, smiling. 'We hit it before they even take it off the boat.'

Even Plummer smiled.

'Hijack the fucking boat,' Hitch continued. 'Unload it somewhere else down the river. We have our own lorry waiting. Unload it, pack it away and piss off.'

Plummer slapped him on the shoulder.

'That's what we'll do,' he said. 'Take the shipment while it's still on the river.'

'Like pirates,' chuckled Morton.

The other men laughed.

'Ray, there are some other things to consider,' offered McCann. 'Once we've hit Connelly's shipment, he ain't going to be too happy.'

'I wouldn't be if I'd just lost twenty million,' Plummer said humourlessly. 'What are you getting at? You reckon he might come looking for bother?'

'Wouldn't you?' McCann said.

'He's right, Ray,' Hitch interjected. 'A fucking gang war is the last thing we want.'

'What am I, stupid?' Plummer said. 'There's no need for Connelly to know who turned him over. If it's done properly, and I'm not talking about fucking balaclavas and funny accents, there's no reason why he should know

237

who hit him.' He looked at Hitch. 'I'm leaving that side of it to you, John. Like I said, you got about thirty-six hours.'

Hitch nodded.

'If the worst comes to the worst and he *does* find out, what then?' Perry wanted to know.

'A gang war would be as damaging to Connelly as it would to us. He won't want it,' Plummer said with assurance. 'But if he *does*, he can't win. We're stronger and, for twenty million, I'm bloody sure we're going to be better equipped. Connelly will realise that. He's not stupid.'

'So we go with it, then?' Hitch echoed.

Plummer nodded. He reached across and touched Hitch's arm.

'John, I want Jim Scott to drive one of the cars,' he said quietly.

Hitch looked puzzled.

'Scott? He runs one of your clubs, doesn't he? I wouldn't have thought he was the right bloke for this kind of operation,' Hitch said.

'I *want* him involved,' Plummer said, his eyes never leaving Hitch. 'He knows how to handle himself. He'll be all right.'

'I'm sure he will. I just don't know why you want him in on it.'

'I've got my reasons,' Plummer said.

Hitch shrugged.

'I'm sure you have,' he said. 'Okay, I'll tell him. If you want him in, that's fair enough, Ray. You're the boss.'

Plummer smiled.

'Yeah, I *am*.'

Fifty-nine

They were watching him. He was certain of it now.

As the tube pulled into Westminster station Trevor Magee looked directly across the compartment and saw his own reflection in the glass. He tried not to look either left or right. As the doors slid open he glanced at the middle-aged couple who got out but then stared straight ahead again.

The doors remained open for a moment but no other passengers got on.

Magee realised that he was alone apart from the other two.

And he knew they were watching him.

The two youths, both in their early twenties, one black, one white, had boarded the train at Gloucester Road station. At first they had sat directly opposite him, but as the train travelled through the subterranean tunnel one of them had moved three seats to his left. The other had moved to the right. Both sat on the opposite row of seats and Magee moved uncomfortably under their gaze. He looked up briefly and saw that the black youth was watching him. He was tall, taller than Magee's six feet, dressed in faded jeans and baseball boots which made his feet look enormous. He had one hand in the pocket of a baggy jacket. The other he was tapping on his right thigh, slapping out a rhythm, perhaps the accompaniment to the tuneless refrain he was humming.

His white companion was also staring at Magee. He too wore baggy jeans and baseball boots, and across his

T-shirt the words 'Ski-Club' could be clearly seen. His face was pitted and he needed a shave.

Magee was painfully aware that he was alone in the compartment with the youths. He glanced at the map of the Underground on the panel opposite and saw that they were approaching Embankment Station. He decided to get off.

Would they follow him?

Out of the corner of his eye he could see the white youth had draped one leg over a plastic seat arm and was reclining, his gaze never leaving Magee.

He began to consider the worst possible scenario. If they both came at him at once, from opposite sides, how would he deal with them?

He tried to tell himself he was being ridiculous. He was, after all, thirty-six years old, six feet tall and well-built. Should they try anything he should be more than capable of dealing with them. But the doubts persisted.

The black youth got to his feet, standing still for a moment, swaying with the motion of the train, gripping one of the rails overhead for support. Then he began walking towards Magee.

The train was slowing slightly; they must be close to the station.

The youth sat down opposite.

Magee clenched both fists in the pockets of his long leather overcoat. The knot of muscles at the side of his jaw pulsed.

He was ready.

The train eased into the station and he got to his feet, heading for the door, pressing the 'DOOR OPEN' button even before it was illuminated. The orange light flared and he jabbed at it. The door slid open and he stepped out onto the platform, walking quickly towards the exit. Once there he paused and glanced behind him.

There was no one following.

He smiled and hurried to the escalator, scuttling up the moving stairway towards street level, finally emerging into the ticket hall. As he passed through he cast one last glance behind him to assure himself he was free of pursuers. Satisfied that he was, he walked out into Villiers Street, into the arms of the night.

A chill wind had come with the onset of darkness and Magee pulled up the collar of his coat as protection against the breeze. Both hands dug firmly in his pockets, he walked along the narrow thoroughfare, the lights of the Strand up ahead of him. A young woman passed close and smiled. Magee returned the gesture, nodding a passing greeting, turning to look at her, appreciating the shapely legs visible below her short skirt.

She had not been the first woman to offer him a smile during the past few hour. Magee was a good-looking man, his shoulder-length black hair and chiselled features making him look at least five years younger than his actual age. He had helped one woman with a pushchair and screaming infant on to a bus earlier, and she had gripped his hand tightly in hers as she had said thank you. He had merely smiled and waved to her as the bus pulled away.

You either had it or you didn't, thought Trevor Magee, smiling broadly to himself.

He passed a pub on his right called *The Griffin*, the sound of loud music swelling from inside. For a moment he thought about going in and fumbled in one of his pockets for some change, but he decided against it. He walked on, climbing the flight of stone steps that brought him up into the Strand itself.

To his right there was a McDonalds; behind him the lights of the Charing Cross Hotel glowed in the darkness. To his left was Trafalgar Square.

Magee's smile broadened.

He looked around him, aware of the traffic speeding up and down, of the people who walked past him on the pavement, of people coming out of McDonalds laden with fast food. There was a dustbin outside and an elderly man dressed in a filthy jacket and torn trousers was shuffling towards it. There was a dark stain around the crotch of the trousers; Magee wrinkled his nose at the stench the old man was giving off.

He watched as the tramp sorted through the rubbish, finally pulling out a soft-drinks container. He took off the lid and sniffed the contents, satisfied the liquid was drinkable. He swallowed it down as if parched.

Magee's smile faded to a look of disgust.

The tramp tossed the empty cup away and shuffled off in the other direction.

Magee watched him go, pushing his way past pedestrians, finally disappearing down a side street.

The younger man swallowed hard, then turned and walked briskly in the direction of Trafalgar Square.

He had things to do.

Sixty

She rubbed a thin layer of Vaseline over her lips and smiled, satisfied with the extra lubrication. Zena Murray had seen on television that beauty queens used the trick so she figured it would work for her. After all, she had to do a lot of smiling in her business, too. Contestants in a beauty contest had only judges to impress with their looks and stance. Zena had many other, more trenchant critics to impress. The punters were always demanding.

Jim Scott watched as she finished applying the vaseline, pacing the dressing room as she stood naked before him, slipping on a G-string and a suspender belt.

'And you haven't seen or heard from Carol since last night?' he said agitatedly.

'Scotty, we work together, that's it,' Zena told him, rolling one stocking up her leg.

'She didn't stay with you?'

'There's hardly room in my place for *me*, let alone bloody guests,' Zena told him.

Scott sighed.

'She's okay, I bet you,' Zena said, trying to sound reassuring. She looked at Scott, something close to pity in her voice. 'Look, Scotty, you shouldn't worry about her so much. She's got her own life to lead, you know.' *And you won't be part of it for much longer*. 'You'd be better off looking for someone else,' she smiled, her attempts at light banter failing miserably. 'I'm unattached, you know.'

'I don't want anyone else, Zena,' he told her.

She shrugged.

'Just trying to help,' she said. *Help, or soften the blow*?

Scott opened the door.

'When she comes in, tell her I want to see her, will you?' he said, then he was gone.

Zena pulled on another stocking and heard his footsteps echoing away up the corridor.

Scott returned to his office and sat at his desk, glancing at the phone, wondering if he should try calling Carol's flat again. He resisted the temptation, leaning back in his seat, running a hand across his forehead. A confusion of emotions tumbled through his mind: anger, concern, fear. He couldn't seem to settle on one that suited him. It was not knowing where she was that was so unsettling.

243

Or who she was with?

He pushed the thought to the back of his mind.

She wouldn't do that to him.

Would she?

He got to his feet and crossed to the window of the office. Below the streets were alive with people, all of them bathed in the neon glow that seemed to fill the very air itself with multi-coloured energy.

Who was she with?

Scott gritted his teeth.

There couldn't be anyone else. He would know. There would be signs he'd have spotted. He sucked in a deep breath. No. There was a rational explanation for all this and, when Carol arrived, he'd discover what it was.

If she arrived.

He returned to his desk and sat down. Even as he did there was a knock on the door and he was on his feet again instantly. The door opened.

John Hitch walked in, smiling at Scott, who merely exhaled wearily.

'Hello, Jim, I'm glad to see you too,' Hitch said, still smiling.

'Sorry, John,' Scott said. 'I was expecting someone else.'

The two men shook hands and Scott offered the other man a seat which he accepted and a drink which he declined.

'Is Ray with you?' Scott wanted to know.

Hitch shook his head.

'I'm allowed out on my own tonight, Jimmy boy,' Hitch grinned.

'This isn't a social call, is it, mate?' Scott said.

'No. Ray sent me. I've got a job for you.'

Scott looked puzzled.

'Tomorrow night,' Hitch continued. 'We're going to

hit a shipment of coke that Ralph Connelly's bringing in.'
He laced his fingers on the desk top. 'You're supposed
to drive one of the getaway cars.'

'Are you fucking serious?' Scott exclaimed. 'That's not
my line of work.'

'I know that. I was as surprised as you, but Ray
Plummer wants you in on it.' He sat back in his seat.
'I'm just a messenger, Jim. I do as I'm told, and he told
me to include you in this job.'

'Why?'

Hitch shrugged.

'Fuck knows. Like I said, I'm just doing what I
was told.'

Scott ran a hand through his hair, bewilderment on
his face.

'You'll be picked up from here tomorrow night at
twelve,' Hitch told him. 'You'll be briefed on what
you've got to do. I don't know what else I can say.'
He looked almost apologetic.

'I don't like this, John,' Scott told him.

'Maybe not, mate, but you've got no choice.' Hitch
got to his feet and crossed to the door.

'You got a shooter?' he asked.

'Beretta 92S. Why?'

Hitch nodded.

'Bring it.'

Sixty-one

The beating of dozens of wings sounded like disembodied
applause, receding gradually into the darkness.

Trevor Magee stopped and looked up as the pigeons

245

took off, anxious to avoid him as he made his way across Trafalgar Square. To his right was a hot-dog stand with a number of people gathered around it. From where he stood the pungent smell of frying onion was easily detectable. To his left one of the massive bronze lions that guarded the square had become a meeting place for some teenagers grouped around a ghetto blaster. Music was roaring from it. Magee didn't recognise the tune. Ahead were the fountains and Nelson's Column, jabbing upwards towards the overcast heavens as if threatening to tear the low cloud and release the torrents of rain that seemed to be swelling in them.

Magee walked on, across the square, hands still dug firmly into his pockets. Every so often he would glance over his shoulder.

As far as he could tell no one was following him. His pace remained steady as he walked past the low wall surrounding the fountain.

A man was standing precariously on the wall urinating into the water.

Magee stopped to watch him, his face impassive.

'What the fucking hell are you looking at?' the man slurred, almost falling into the water.

Magee stood his ground a moment longer, then headed towards the stone steps. He took them two at a time, pausing at the top to look back across the square.

He scanned the dark figures moving about in the blackness, saw the odd flash-bulb explode as tourists took pictures of one of the capital's most famous landmarks. Then he crossed the street in front of the National Gallery, glancing up at the massive edifice of the building in the process. There was a man outside, close to one set of steps, selling hot chestnuts, the smell of burning coals and roasting nuts filling Magee's nostrils. The sights of London at night were something to behold but how many people, he wondered, ever noticed the variety of smells?

He continued walking, past a queue of people filing aboard a sight-seeing bus, jostling for the best positions as they reached the open upper deck. Finally he turned into St Martin's Place.

Across the street, on the steps of St Martin-in-the-Fields church, there was movement.

Magee could make out two figures crouched on the steps near the top, quite close to the door of the church.

They were passing a bottle back and forth between them.

As he looked more closely he saw what appeared to be a bundle of rags behind them. On closer inspection the bundle of rags rose and revealed itself to be a woman, filthy dirty, her skin so grimy she was almost invisible in the gloom.

As Magee watched she tottered down the steps and wandered off down Duncannon Street in the direction of the Strand.

He stood watching her, his face set, the muscles in his jaw pulsing angrily.

After what seemed an eternity he moved on, casting a cursory glance across at the two men sitting on the steps outside the church. As he reached Irving Street he paused again, looking behind him.

Still no sign.

Magee quickened his pace, walking up the centre of the wide road, passing restaurants on either side. The people inside them reminded him of goldfish, seated in the windows, bereft of any privacy from prying eyes as they ate. He emerged into Leicester Square slowing his pace again, glancing once over his shoulder before moving off to his right, past a line of people waiting

247

to enter the Odeon. Two buskers were playing banjos, walking up and down the line, while a dwarf scampered in and out of the waiting cinema-goers with an outstretched hand, cajoling money from the queue.

He was holding a flat cap full of coins. As each woman dropped money into the cap he would kiss her hand before skipping on to the next.

He even looked up at Magee, who merely ignored the little man and walked on, hands still dug deep into his pockets.

A drain had overflowed at the end of the road and water was running down the tarmac. Magee paid it little heed as he continued his nocturnal stroll, looking around him constantly, occasionally slowing down to look over his shoulder or perhaps changing direction quickly, ducking into a group of people.

Just in case.

He could hear shouting up ahead; and there was a large gathering of people around a man who was obviously standing on a box of some kind.

Magee pushed his way carefully through the crowd until he reached the front. The man was dressed in a combat jacket and jeans, and behind him stood two more men, their hair cropped short, dressed in a similar fashion but holding two flags, a Union Jack and a red flag with a cross on it. Another was handing out leaflets with 'THE JESUS ARMY' emblazoned on them. Magee took one, glanced at it and stuffed it into his pocket.

The man on the box was shouting about death and re-birth, Heaven and Hell.

Magee smiled.

He walked on, heading round the square towards the cinema.

To his right he saw another of them.

Man. Woman.

248

At first he couldn't be sure. As he drew closer he saw that it was a man huddled beneath a thick overcoat, sitting on the pavement watching the crowds go by. In front of him he had a piece of cardboard on which was scrawled: HOMELESS AND HUNGRY.

Magee looked at the cardboard and then at the man who, he guessed, was younger than himself.

Two girls passed by and tossed coins into his small plastic cup.

The man nodded his thanks and watched the girls walk away. Both of them wore short skirts. He smiled approvingly.

Magee glared at him, his hands still deep in his pockets.

He hardly felt the hand on his shoulder.

He spun round, his heart thumping against his ribs.

He had been careless.

'You got a light, please, mate?'

A man stood there with the cigarette held between his lips. When he repeated himself, the words seemed to sink in. Magee nodded and fumbled in his coat pocket for some matches he knew were there. He struck one and cupped his hand around the flame.

'Cheers,' said the man and disappeared back into the throng.

Magee nodded in silent acknowledgement and slipped the matches back into his pocket.

As he withdrew his hand he felt the coldness of the knife and corkscrew against his flesh. He patted them through the material of his overcoat and walked on.

Sixty-two

The light on the telephone was flashing. Someone was trying to reach him. Steve Houghton ignored the red bulb. He finally pushed the phone aside so that he couldn't see the distracting light. That task completed, he returned his attention to the work in front of him.

On his desk there were six files. One of his assistants had worked slowly and laboriously through the records and come up with half-a-dozen prints which looked at least similar to the ones taken from Paula Wilson. Now Houghton reached for the first file and took out the piece of card that bore the fingerprints of a possible match. He looked at the name on the file. George Purnell. Murderer. He'd strangled two children with his bare hands, then called the police to give himself up.

Houghton traced every curve and twist of the prints, comparing them beneath his microscope when he felt it necessary.

He shook his head. No match. Not close enough.

He reached for the second file. William Fisher. Killer of three elderly women he had robbed. Again Houghton began the comparisons.

He paused for a moment, increasing the magnification on the microscope. A number of loops seemed similar. The radial loops were definitely alike. He sat back from the microscope for a moment, then looked again.

Were his eyes playing tricks on him? Perhaps he was tired. They seemed totally different now. Houghton convinced himself he was searching so avidly for the match that he was almost willing himself to find it.

He discarded Fisher's file and reached for another.

Mathew Bryce.

Murderer of a number of young women in a particularly brutal manner.

He slipped Bryce's prints beneath the microscope.

He peered through the lens, frowning slightly.

Maybe . . .

He crossed to the VDU on his other desk and punched in a series of numbers, checking the number on Bryce's file. He pressed in the number, then Bryce's name, his face bathed in a green glow as first figures then images began to appear on the screen. From the two and a half million prints on file those of Mathew Bryce appeared on the screen. First those of the right thumb. Houghton pressed a button and the index finger patterns appeared. He paused and looked through the microscope again, this time at the print taken from Paula Wilson. Then back at the green image on the screen.

'Jesus,' he murmured, looking at the loops and composites on the VDU screen.

There was a hook on the crime print.

Matched by one on the suspect print.

A fork on the crime print, glowing on the screen.

Houghton checked against the one beneath the microscope.

Match.

He knew that he was searching for sixteen points of comparison before he could be sure of positive identification.

The clock on the wall ticked noisily in the silence as he continued his task. The red light on the phone console stopped flashing as whoever sought his attention tired of waiting.

Thirty minutes had passed from his initial inspection to the point where he now marked down another match.

He had fourteen marks of comparison.

It was enough to convince him.

Now it was *his* turn to reach for the phone.

He tried Gregson's office.

Nothing.

Then his home.

His wife said he wasn't back yet.

Houghton asked her to instruct Gregson to call him as soon as he could. Then he put down the phone and glanced once more at the fingerprints beneath the microscope.

Sixty-three

It was the smell that alerted him.

Trevor Magee had passed the small entryway to Long's Court when he noticed it.

The rank odour of sweat and urine made him wince.

Long's Court was silent, a curious contrast to the noisy hustle and bustle of the square just yards away. The smell, coming from the rear of a building, might easily have been the unpleasant odour given off by a dustbin in need of emptying. There were bins in the small yard behind the building, even a large wheeled skip which bore the name BIFFA. But it was, in fact, a bundle of dark clothing that looked as if it had been hurled against the far wall of the darkened yard. A bundle which, as he drew closer, he realised was a person.

From more than a few feet it was impossible to tell even the sex of the figure. Magee moved closer, inside the high stone walls of the yard, walls that effectively cut it off from anyone who might be passing.

He moved into the impenetrable gloom of the yard, one hand slipping inside his left hand pocket. He was standing over the reeking individual now, peering close to get a look at the face.

It was a man. He was yet to reach his thirtieth birthday, Magee thought, but ravaged beyond his years. How long he'd been sleeping rough no one could tell. Magee looked closely at him, trying to focus on the face in the darkness, to pick out his features beneath the grime that covered his face like a second, darker skin.

The smell was almost unbearable; Magee could feel it clogging his nostrils.

He reached into his pocket and slowly pulled the knife free.

It was about eight inches long, double edged and as sharp as a razor.

Magee leant forward and touched the man's shoulder, simultaneously pushing the knife gently up beneath his chin so that the point was just touching flesh.

There was no movement.

'Wake up,' Magee whispered, as if trying to rouse a lover from slumber. His voice was gentle, cajoling. 'Come on, wake up.'

He shook the man more firmly, the knife still poised.

Magee could feel the beginnings of an erection pushing against his trousers. His breath was starting to come in low gasps.

'Wake up.'

The man opened his eyes and blinked myopically, trying to focus. He was suddenly aware of the coldness beneath his chin and his eyes widened in shocked realisation.

Magee smiled.

He drove the blade upwards with one powerful thrust, feeling it puncture skin, rip through muscle and crash into teeth. Gums were cut open and the knife scythed through the man's tongue, momentarily pinning it to the roof of his mouth before severing it. As the man opened his mouth to scream, part of his tongue fell into his lap. Blood gushed from the open orifice. Magee smiled broadly. He struck again, this time bringing the knife down into the top of the man's head, using all his strength to force it through bone that splintered and cracked with a strident shriek.

As Magee tugged it free a large lump of bone came away on the end of the knife. For fleeting seconds, a sticky mass of brain matter welled up through the hole.

The tramp had fallen forward onto his face, his body twitching madly, blood spreading out around his head. Magee ignored the crimson puddles and knelt beside the dying man again, this time rolling him over onto his back. He felt inside his own coat pocket and pulled out the corkscrew.

The tramp's eyes were closed but Magee used his thumb and forefinger to push back the lids. He drove the corkscrew forward, burying it in the man's right eye, shoving down hard on it, twisting it in the socket, ignoring the spouting vitreous liquid that erupted from the riven orb. He felt the point scrape bone and pulled back hard.

Most of the eye came away, torn from the socket. But the corkscrew had burst it like a corpulent balloon and its fluid ran down the tramp's face, clear liquid mingling with blood. Enough of the eye came free to please Magee, though, and he watched as it dangled on the optic nerve.

He rammed the corkscrew into the left eye and pulled again. This time the curled metal merely came away with jellied lumps of vitreous humour sticking to it. He tried again, uncaring that the tramp was motionless by now, the stench of excrement already beginning to permeate the air.

The corkscrew tore the flesh at the side of the man's nose before skewing into his eye again, gouging the torn sphere badly and tearing the lower eyelid. Magee shoved two fingers into the socket, scooping the eye out until it fell onto the concrete. He looked at it for a second then got to his feet and stamped on the eye, hearing it pop beneath his foot. He slipped the knife and the corkscrew back into his pocket and walked away, turning out of the yard and into St Martin's Street again. He walked unhurriedly to the bottom of it and peered down Orange Street.

A taxi was approaching, its yellow light on. Magee raised an arm to stop it, walking round to the driver's side.

The driver looked at him aghast.

'What the fuck happened to you?' he wanted to know.

'I want your cab,' said Magee, tugging at the door.

'Fuck off, I'll . . .'

The driver got no further.

Magee pulled the knife from his pocket and, with a blow combining demonic strength with effortless expertise, slashed open the taxi driver's throat.

Gouts of blood erupted from the wound and hit the windscreen with a loud splash.

The cabby made a squealing noise and clutched at the ragged edges of the wound as if trying to hold it together, to prevent the blood pouring through his hands.

Magee tore open the driver's door, grabbing the man by the shoulder, hauling him from the cab. He fell heavily onto the road, his eyes bulging wide with fear as he felt his life-blood draining away. As he tried to breathe the

255

chill night air filled the gaping hole in his neck. His body began to spasm.

Magee leapt into the driver's seat and pressed down on the accelerator, heading away from the scene of carnage, his own brow furrowed. He glanced into the rear-view mirror to see if anyone was following.

All he saw was the body of the taxi driver lying in the road, blood spreading out rapidly around him. There was blood all over the windows, too, and Magee had to wipe it away with the sleeve of his coat in order to see through the windscreen. The car was like a mobile abattoir.

He put his foot on the accelerator and the taxi shot forward. He found himself struggling with the wheel, fighting to keep the vehicle under control. As he swung it into Charing Cross Road he nearly collided with another car. The driver sounded his horn furiously as the taxi sped on. Magee paid it little heed. Up ahead the traffic lights were on red but he didn't slow up. The taxi went hurtling across the junction with Cranbourn Street doing sixty.

Hunched over the wheel, Magee smiled.

He was relieved that no one was following him. He didn't want anyone trying to stop him.

Not yet.

Sixty-four

Detective Inspector Frank Gregson tapped agitatedly on the steering wheel as he looked up at the red light, waiting for it to change.

He revved his engine.

Come on. Come on.

He sped away with them still on amber, narrowly

avoiding a car coming the other way. The driver banged on his horn but Gregson drove on at speed, unconcerned by the accident he'd almost caused.

He'd spoken to Houghton less than ten minutes ago.

The DI had returned home and been greeted by Julie telling him that the Records Officer had called. Gregson had asked what it was about. Julie had only been able to tell him that it was urgent. Gregson had called immediately and Houghton had explained about the fingerprints and how he was sure he now had positive identification of at least one of the bodies. Gregson had hardly allowed him to finish speaking before telling him he'd be there as soon as he could.

Julie had asked him what was going on but he'd rushed out without telling her, mumbling only that it was important and that he didn't know when he'd be back.

Now he pressed his foot down harder on the accelerator and eased the Ford Scorpio past a car, cutting in ahead of the driver. Gregson glanced at the clock on the dashboard and estimated that he could be at New Scotland Yard in less than thirty minutes, traffic permitting.

Thirty minutes. It seemed like a fucking lifetime.

However, mingling with that frustration was a small feeling of triumph. He'd been right about Bryce. The copy-cat MO theory he'd come up with had born fruit. It should prove so for the first killer as well. He almost smiled to himself.

He had been proved right, but how could it be? The men he had suspected were in prison serving life sentences. No escapes had been reported.

What the fuck was going on?

'Lima 15, come in.'

The metallic voice that rattled out of his radio made him jump.

257

'Lima 15, do you read me? If you're there, pick it up, Frank.'

He recognised DI Finn's voice.

'Frank, for fuck's sake . . .'

Gregson snatched up the handset.

'Lima 15, I hear you,' he said. 'This better be good.'

'Where are you?' Finn wanted to know.

'On my way to see Houghton, he's identified one of the dead killers.'

'Jesus,' muttered Finn. There was a moment's silence, then the DI spoke again. 'Frank, you'd better tell Barclay to have one of his slabs ready.'

'Why?'

'We've got another one,' Finn told him flatly. 'A murder suicide. Just like the other two. The guy tried to torch himself.'

'What happened?' Gregson demanded, hardly slowing down as he drove.

Finn told him about the murders of the tramp and the taxi driver. 'He stole the cab, drove it up Charing Cross Road then aimed the fucking thing at the fountains outside Centre Point. The car blew up as soon as it hit the wall.'

'Shit,' hissed Gregson. 'What about the driver?'

'Well, like I said, he was obviously trying to kill himself. The thing is, when the car hit the wall, *he* went through the windscreen. He was thrown clear. They fished him out of the water. He's badly cut up from the broken glass but he's more or less in one piece.'

'Any ID on him?' Gregson wanted to know.

'Nothing. Not even a name tag in his fucking underwear. Just like the other two. The only difference is, this geezer doesn't look like burnt toast.'

'No ID at all?' Gregson repeated. 'Could he have dropped it in the car? You said he was thrown clear. He might have been carrying something, it might be lying around . . .'

Finn cut him short.

'The boys here have been over the area with a fine toothcomb, Frank. I'm telling you. There was no fucking ID. All he had on him was a couple of quid in small change.'

'Where are you now?' Gregson wanted to know.

'I'm still at the scene. We've closed the road off while the boys go over the area. The fire brigade have put out the blaze, thank Christ.'

'Meet me at the Yard in thirty minutes. Stuart, I want a full report on what happened, right?'

'Thirty minutes?'

'Yeah.'

'I'll see you there, over and out.'

The two-way went dead and Gregson replaced it, pressing his foot harder on the accelerator, coaxing more speed from the Scorpio.

Another twenty minutes, he thought, then perhaps at last they might have some answers.

Sixty-five

Why?

The word kept rolling around in his mind like a marble.

Why?

Jim Scott looked at his reflection in the mirror, studying his features.

Why did they need *him* for this job? He sighed. Plummer had insisted that he be involved.

Why? Why? Fucking why?

He slammed his hand down on the top of the dressing table, causing some of the bottles to topple over. An aftershave bottle spilled its contents and Scott inhaled the aroma momentarily before stepping back. He crossed to his bed and sat down. Outside the wind was blowing strongly again, wailing around the block of flats. He heard footsteps passing his door as someone made their way home. There was a thumping noise coming from above that was a record player. He got to his feet, staring up at the ceiling, wondering whether or not he should shout to the owner to turn the volume down.

Better still, go up there and *tell* him.

Scott finally decided to do neither. He wandered out into the kitchen and took a pint of milk from the fridge, supping straight from the bottle.

He wiped his mouth with the back of his hand and walked back into the bedroom.

Why?

Why did they want him on this particular job?

Why couldn't he get in touch with Carol?

Why hadn't she been in to work?

Why hadn't she called him?

Fucking why?

He slammed the milk bottle down on top of the bedside cabinet, pulling the drawer open.

He reached in and took out the Beretta, cradling it in his hand, working the slide. He held the piece up and sighted it, squeezing the trigger, allowing the hammer to fall on an empty chamber. Finally he lowered the weapon and dropped it onto the bed beside him, then fumbled in the drawer again for the box of ammunition.

He began feeding 9mm shells into the magazine.

* * *

She could hear him moving about in the sitting room. Carol Jackson rolled onto her back and gazed at the ceiling, aware of the movement from the adjacent room and also of the perspiration that sheathed her body. She ran a finger through the glistening moisture, allowing her hand to trail lower, through her pubic hairs. She felt the wetness of Plummer's semen as it trickled from her. Carol sighed and reached for a tissue from the bedside table.

Plummer called through and asked if she wanted a drink. She called back that she didn't.

For some reason her thoughts turned to Scott. He must be wondering where she was by now. She hadn't been to work for two nights. Carol could imagine his state of mind.

Had he finally realised there was someone else?

If so, what was going through his mind?

She closed her eyes and swallowed hard. If only she'd had the courage to tell him she wanted to end their relationship when the cracks had first started to appear. He would have been disappointed. Upset. Perhaps even angry. But now she feared what he might do.

Would he *really* try to kill her?

She wished she could convince herself that what he'd said had merely been an idle threat. But she knew him too well. There was no avoiding the issue any more. Either he would find out she was seeing Plummer or she would have to tell him.

It was only a matter of time before the truth emerged. *And then?*

She exhaled deeply.

Plummer would look after her, wouldn't he? After all, he was her lover.

Carol almost smiled.

Lover.

261

The word implied some kind of emotional bond and that, she knew, they didn't have. But he thought a lot of her; he seemed to want her around.

If she could move in with him.

The prospect of escaping her job and her flat suddenly seemed to lift her spirits and the threat of Scott was momentarily shrouded.

Move in.

He'd never mentioned it to her and she had not even thought about it until now, but therein lay her escape. Both from Scott and from her lifestyle. Carol sat up, resting her back against the padded headboard. She wasn't escaping. She was running, running from herself as much as her surroundings. She wanted to move in with Plummer, though. Even loveless comfort was preferable to what she had.

She called to Plummer to come back to bed but he didn't answer.

Twenty million pounds.

He concentrated on the figure, held it in his mind, savouring it as a wine expert savours a fine vintage.

Twenty million fucking pounds.

Hitch had arranged details of the job and Plummer felt safe enough with him dealing with it. He hated having to trust anyone, but Hitch was one of the few he did. Plummer poured himself another drink, pulled his monogrammed housecoat more tightly around him and paced the sitting room slowly, glancing around at the expensive furnishings and ornaments which filled the flat.

Carol called him again and he called back that he wouldn't be long. He told her to go to sleep.

Pain in the arse.

He smiled and sipped his drink, glancing across at the phone as he refilled his glass.

There had been no more calls since the informant had rung with the news of the cocaine shipment. Plummer licked his lips and frowned.

Who the hell *was* the informant?

He'd wondered countless times, ever since that first call it had played on his mind.

Set-up?

Wind-up?

They'd soon know.

If it was a member of Connelly's gang it made no sense, yet who else would know about the shipment?

It made no fucking sense at all, but Plummer had his reasons for believing the information. Twenty million reasons.

Carol called to him again.

He smiled and headed for the bedroom.

Sixty-six

'You were right about the killers being linked,' said Phillip Barclay.

Gregson smiled to himself.

'But not just in the way you said,' Barclay continued. 'The MO's they used may have been copies of earlier killings, even this latest one. And the fact that they all burned themselves, or tried to. But there's something else, something more conclusive to link them, but it's more puzzling, too. That device – whatever the hell it is – that I found in Magee was made of the same material I found melted in the other bodies.'

'And I checked his fingerprints against the files on screen at Hendon,' said Steve Houghton. 'There's no doubt about it, the man *is* Trevor Magee.'

'And number one?' asked Finn.

'Going almost solely on your files and his MO, I'd have to say it was Peter Lawton,' the Records Officer told him.

Finn looked at his colleague, then at Houghton.

'Which we know is impossible, right?' he said, almost laughing. 'Lawton and Bryce are banged up.'

'So is Magee,' Gregson told him, flipping open the file. 'According to this.' He jabbed the file with his index finger.

Houghton crossed to the wall behind him and flicked a switch. Panels lit up and he reached for a number of X-ray plates which he attached to the luminescent plastic. They were skull X-rays.

'Now look. These are of Magee,' he said. 'Taken when they brought his body in.'

Barclay pulled a pen from his pocket and prodded part of the first plate. It showed a dark mass close to the front of the skull. On other angles it was also present. 'See it?' he said.

'What is it?' Gregson wanted to know.

'Wait,' Barclay told him. Houghton reached for another set of plate. The shape was far less well defined. 'These are X-rays of Mathew Bryce's skull,' said Barclay, 'at least what was left of it. Unfortunately he'd been burned, but not badly enough for the bone structure to be altered as it was in Lawton's case.' He jabbed his pen at a dark area on Bryce's X-rays too.

'Come on, Phil, what the fuck is it?' Finn muttered, reaching for his cigarettes but deciding not to light one when he saw the look of disapproval on the pathologist's face.

264

'Both men were suffering from brain tumours,' Barclay said.

'How can you be sure?' Gregson demanded.

Barclay sighed.

'It's on the plates, you can see it,' he said, motioning to the X-rays again. 'And, if you'd care to look at Magee, I haven't replaced the cranial cap yet and you'll *see* the tumour. Come down to the morgue and I'll show you.'

'I'll take your word for it,' Finn said. 'What you're saying is, these three fucking murderers we've got in cold storage have all committed crimes identical to ones committed by Peter Lawton, Mathew Bryce and Trevor Magee, right? Three blokes we *know*, for *sure*, are locked up, doing time in Whitely nick, yeah? Now, you're trying to tell me that this is the *real* Trevor Magee lying downstairs? That the *real* Peter Lawton killed six people and then killed himself on a motorbike less than two weeks ago? That the *real* Mathew Bryce cut up a girl, then torched himself? And tonight the *real* Trevor Magee murdered a tramp and a cabbie and then smashed his car into the Centre Point fountains? You're telling me that blokes we arrested, blokes we stood in court and saw sentenced, blokes we saw driven away in fucking armoured vans, have committed the exact same crimes that they were put away for? *That's* what you're telling me?'

Houghton looked almost helplessly at Gregson.

'It's bollocks,' said Finn angrily. 'Absolute bollocks.' He looked at Gregson. 'You said yourself it was impossible. If *one* of them had escaped from Whitely we'd have known about it, but *three* of the cunts? Do me a favour.' This time he *did* reach for a cigarette and light it up.

Silence.

'Somebody say something, for Christ's sake,' snarled Finn in annoyance. 'Somebody tell me again what all this shit is supposed to mean.'

'Could there be a mistake with the identification?' Gregson said.

'It's possible with Bryce,' Houghton admitted. 'I found fourteen matching characteristics in the ridge patterns of his fingerprints. There should have been sixteen, but I think my figure is conclusive enough. But even if I was wrong about Bryce, it's impossible I could be wrong about Magee. His prints match those on file. His dental records match. His blood type. Everything. Unless he's got a twin identical in every way, then that man is the same one you arrested.'

Finn shook his head.

'I don't fucking believe this,' he said, an incredulous smile on his face. 'It's not possible.'

'Then what's your explanation?' Houghton challenged him.

'You're telling me that you believe three convicted killers just walked out of Whitely prison without anyone noticing and now they've come back here to duplicate their original crimes? Do you believe that? Really?'

'I believe what I see here, Stuart, and this man *is* Trevor Magee,' Houghton said quietly. 'If it helps I'm as sceptical as you, but the evidence is here.'

'Evidence for what?' Finn snarled. 'That we're all going fucking crazy? They're inside.' He shouted the last two words.

Gregson crossed to the phone and jabbed the button. He asked the switchboard operator to connect him with Whitely Prison and waited.

Finn turned to his colleague.

'Frank, for Christ's sake . . .' he began, but Gregson held up a hand to silence him.

266

'Hello,' he said finally into the phone. 'My name is Detective Inspector Gregson. I'm calling . . . Yes, Gregson.' He spelt it out. 'I'm calling from New Scotland Yard. I'd like to speak with the Governor please. It's very important.' He sucked in an angry breath. 'Yes, Gregson.' He spelled it out again. Then he waited. The other men watched as he tapped gently on the desk top.

'When will he back?' he said finally. 'Can you get him to call me as soon as possible? It's very urgent. It concerns three of the inmates there.' They saw Gregson's features harden. 'Who *are* you, anyway?' He sighed. 'All right, perhaps you can help me. Their names are Peter Lawton, Mathew Bryce and Trevor Magee. I need to speak to Governor Nicholson about them as soon as possible, do you understand?' The other three saw a flicker on the DI's face. 'Say that again?' He looked across Finn, a look of bewilderment on his face. He shook his head slowly. 'Can you tell me when?'

'What the fuck is this?' Finn whispered, still watching his superior.

'Thank you,' said Gregson. 'Tell Governor Nicholson to ring me on this number as soon as possible.'

Gregson put down the phone.

'Well?' said Finn.

The DI looked at Houghton.

'Are you *sure* that's Trevor Magee?' he said, the knot of muscles at the side of his jaw pulsing.

Houghton held up his hands.

'Frank, for God's sake,' he sighed. 'If I had children I'd swear on their graves. It *is* Magee. There's no question of it.'

'And you're sure about the others as well?'

Houghton nodded.

'According to that guy I just spoke to,' said Gregson

267

quietly, 'Trevor Magee died six months ago. As a matter of fact he's buried in the same piece of ground as Peter Lawton and Mathew Bryce. They never left Whitely. All three of them are buried there.'

Sixty-seven

There was an explosion of blood and the nose seemed to burst.

The coloured man fell backwards, his legs buckling under him, a look of pain on his face.

As he fell the spectators rose, a chorus of shouts and cheers ringing around the arena.

'Good punch,' Ray Plummer shouted approvingly. The coloured boxer looked into the referee's eyes, then watched his fingers; he was raising them one at a time as he counted. His opponent was dancing about in a neutral corner, one eye on his quarry. The other eye had been closed for most of the fight by a left hook that had caused a large amount of swelling both above and below the brow. He was older, pale-skinned and looked too thin to be a welterweight, but the right cross that had put his younger opponent down had belied his looks.

As the referee reached the mandatory eight the black fighter rose quickly to his feet.

'Come on, Robbie,' shouted Plummer, cupping one hand to his mouth.

Beside him Carol watched the modern-day gladiators as they came at each other. She was wearing a tight red dress which showed off her shapely legs. It clung to her so tightly that she wore no underwear beneath. Plummer liked that. He also liked it when he saw other men

268

around the ringside looking at her approvingly. Look all you want, he thought. She's with me. She ran a hand through her hair and glanced up at the fighters again, one arm linked through Plummer's.

She saw him look at his watch again. He'd been doing it all evening.

'Are you expecting someone?' she asked. 'You keep looking at your watch.'

He shook his head, smiled at her briefly then returned his attention to the fight.

The younger fighter seemed to have recovered from the knockdown. Despite the blood streaming from his nose, he was driving in a series of combinations which looked to have his opponent in trouble.

'Work the body!' one of his cornermen shouted.

'Cover up!' the other fighter's trainer responded.

'Get away from him!' Plummer bellowed, watching gloomily as a body punch brought down his fighter's guard and a thunderous uppercut lifted him off his feet and sent him crashing to the canvas. 'Oh, fuck it,' murmured Plummer, as the referee started counting.

'If he counts until tomorrow night your boy won't get up, Ray,' said the tubby man sitting on Plummer's left.

Plummer nodded and glanced at his watch again.

10.46 p.m.

The referee made a sweeping gesture with his arm over the prostrate figure of the white fighter. It might as well have been the last rites.

Some members of the crowd moved away towards the bar between contests. Others were content to sit and wait, reading their programmes or gazing around. Television cameras were covering the bill and a number of those opposite the prying lenses spent the time waving at the cameras. Two men passed by and looked down at

269

Carol, who crossed her legs, dangling one high-heeled shoe from her toes.

She noticed with disgust that there were several droplets of blood on the patent leather. One of the perils of sitting ringside.

Plummer looked at his watch again and sighed.

10.48.

There were still nearly three hours to go.

The other staff had gone home. Jim Scott had locked up. Now he stood in his office drinking from a paper cup, swilling the Southern Comfort around, staring into the liquid.

The knock on the door was at precisely one minute after midnight.

He went upstairs and opened it, allowing John Hitch inside.

'You set?' Hitch asked him.

Scott nodded.

'Show me,' Hitch insisted.

Scott pulled the Beretta from its shoulder holster and handed it to Hitch, who held the weapon for a minute before returning it to its rightful owner.

'You've got good taste, Jim,' he said, smiling, pulling his own pistol into view.

Like Scott's it was a 92S. He holstered it and motioned towards the door.

'Let's go,' he said. 'Car's waiting.'

Scott followed him out.

It was a small boat, less than thirty feet from stem to stern. It moved quietly up the River Thames, hidden by the darkness, only its warning lights visible on the black swirl of the water. *The Sandhopper* moved evenly and unhurriedly through the water.

The river was quiet. Many of the small boats which usually travelled its waters were moored for the night and *The Sandhopper* passed a number of them as it made its way up river. Lights from the banks reflected off the water like a black mirror. One of the crewmen of the small boat stood looking out at the city all around him, smoking a cigarette and gazing at the myriad lights.

'I can see one of them.'

Martin Bates adjusted the focus on the binoculars, trying to pull into sharper definition the man moving about on the deck.

'Where's the boat now?' John Hitch asked, his voice breaking up slightly on the two-way.

Bates picked up the radio, still holding the binoculars in one hand, following the progress of the boat.

'Just passing Hay's Wharf,' he said.

'Tell Wally to keep his eyes open and let me know when they pass him,' Hitch instructed.

'Will do,' said Bates. He put down the radio for a moment, taking one last look at the boat as it chugged slowly up river. He leant on the car and lit a cigarette, puffing at it before he picked up the radio again.

'Wally, come in, it's Martin. You awake or having a wank?' He smiled to himself.

'I'm awake, you cunt,' a deep Scots voice thundered back.

'They'll be with you in about ten or fifteen minutes, mate,' Bates told him.

'Right,' muttered Wally Connor.

From his own vantage point he moved forward, leaning on the parapet of Blackfriars Bridge, peering down into the murky blackness of the river. Waiting.

Waiting just like the other four men Hitch had positioned at various places along the Thames.

Scott looked at the clock on the dashboard of the Lancia and sighed.

'How much longer?' he said irritably, gazing through the windscreen, out across the Thames. It looked like a swollen black tongue licking its way through the city.

'Not long,' John Hitch told him, looking first at his own watch then at the dashboard clock.

'I'd just like to know why I'm here,' Scott murmured.

'I told you, Scotty, it wasn't my idea. I get paid for doing what I'm told. It's as simple as that.' He looked at his watch again. Then he pulled the Beretta from its holster and worked the slide.

It jammed.

'Shit,' muttered Hitch.

Scott seemed unconcerned by his companion's problem and looked to his right. The four giant chimneys of Battersea Power Station thrust upward into the night sky like the upended legs of a gigantic coffee table. Below them was a pier, accessible by a set of stone steps. The steps were green with mould where the rising tide lapped against them. At the end of the pier another small boat was moored. Scott couldn't see the name painted along one side of it but he'd already been told it was called *The Abbott*. Not that he really cared.

Hitch was still struggling with the Beretta.

'Bloody slide's stuck,' he grunted, pulling back hard on it.

'Why do you need a gun, anyway?' Scott wanted to know. 'You intending to use it?'

'Just call it insurance,' Hitch said, still tugging at the

pistol. 'Fuck it,' he snapped finally. 'Give me yours.' He held out one gloved hand.

Scott hesitated.

'Give me yours,' Hitch repeated. 'Come on, you're going to be up here in the car. If things get too complicated, just drive off.' He sat there with his hand still open. 'Let me have your gun, Jim.'

Scott reached slowly inside his jacket then pulled the Beretta free and handed it to Hitch, who gripped the automatic in his fist and checked that the magazine was full, slipping it from the butt. Satisfied that it was, he slammed it back into place and holstered the weapon, sticking his own pistol in the belt of his trousers.

On the dashboard in front of him the radio crackled and he picked it up.

'John, can you hear me?' a voice enquired.

'Yeah, Rob, go ahead,' Hitch replied.

'*The Sandhopper* just passed under the Vauxhall Bridge. Should be with you any time now.'

'Cheers,' said Hitch and snapped off the radio. He pushed open the passenger side door and clambered out, turning to look back at Scott. 'This shouldn't take long,' he said, smiling, the wind ruffling his long blond hair. 'Just sit tight.'

Scott nodded, watching as Hitch scuttled across the road and disappeared out of sight as he began to descend the embankment steps towards the pier.

Scott switched on the radio, heard pop music, twiddled the frequency dial past classical and reggae and finally found a discussion programme. He listened for a moment then switched off again, content with the silence inside the Lancia. He drummed his fingers on the steering wheel and waited.

*   *   *

He couldn't sleep.

He knew he wouldn't be able to and now, as he swung himself out of bed, Ray Plummer wondered why he hadn't just sat in front of the television until the time came.

He pulled on his dressing gown and padded through into the sitting room.

'What's wrong, Ray?' Carol asked, rolling over.

He ignored her enquiry so she hauled herself out, slipped on a long T-shirt and followed him into the other room. She found him standing in front of the fireplace, his eyes fixed on the clock.

'Are you all right?' she wanted to know. 'You've hardly spoken since we got back.'

'I've got something on my mind,' he said sharply, sipping at the drink he cradled in his hand.

'Anything I can help with?'

'No, it's all right,' he said. 'Thanks for asking, though. It's just a little bit of business that's got to be done.'

She knew better than to ask what *kind* of business.

Plummer turned to face her, running appraising eyes over her long slender legs, her nipples taut against the thin material of the T-shirt.

'Get yourself a drink,' he said, nodding towards the cabinet. As she did he glanced at his watch once more.

Nearly time.

Carol crossed to him and slipped one hand inside his dressing gown, stroking his stomach. 'Are you sure I can't help?' she said, smiling a practised smile.

Plummer allowed her to rake her fingernails across his stomach, feeling her probing lower, encircling his penis with her hand. Then he took a step back, a slight smile on his face.

'No,' he said flatly. 'You *can't* help. Not yet.'

Again he looked at his watch.

Sixty-eight

The engine of *The Abbott* sounded deafening in the silence, the loud spluttering replaced rapidly by a rumble as the boat moved away from the pier.

John Hitch wandered towards the cabin, where Terry Morton was steering the boat, peering out over the river.

'How come you know how to drive these fucking things?' Hitch asked, looking for the first sign of their quarry.

'You don't *drive* a boat, you ignorant cunt,' chuckled Morton. 'You pilot it.'

'Whatever,' Hitch shrugged.

'My old man worked the river all his life, doing deliveries, pick-ups. They used to use it like a canal; anything that couldn't be moved easily by land, they'd stick it on a boat. My old man worked the length of it. He had a pleasure boat for about ten years before he died, used to run fucking tourists down to Hampton Court, that sort of stuff.' Morton moved the wheel slightly, bringing the boat around. 'He made a ton of money ripping them off. I used to go along with him a lot of the time.'

'John, check it out, mate,' called Adrian McCann from the small foredeck. 'Coming up on our right.'

Both Hitch and Morton looked and saw the warning lights of a small boat approaching. As yet it was a little over two hundred yards away. Hitch reached for the binoculars and peered through them. He read the name on the side of the boat.

'*The Sandhopper*,' he said, smiling. 'Bingo.'

Morton guided the boat towards the centre of the river, then towards the oncoming *Sandhopper*.

Still peering through the binoculars he could see movement on the other boat: two men looking ahead, one of them pointing towards *The Abbott*.

'They'll signal us to turn aside,' Morton observed.

'How do you know?' Hitch asked.

'Rules of the river,' Morton told him. 'What do you want me to do?'

'Bring us up alongside them,' said Hitch, and glanced across at his companion. 'You set?'

Morton nodded and inclined his head in the direction of an Ithaca Model 37 shotgun on the bench beside him.

Red warning lights were flashing the bridge of *The Sandhopper* as the two boats drew closer, Morton now angling *The Abbott* so that it was heading directly towards the other craft. Hitch reached inside his jacket and touched the butt of the Beretta he'd taken from Scott.

The two boats were less than one hundred yards away from each other now.

Morton slowed the speed a little, preparing to bring the boat to a halt when he needed to.

Eighty yards.

Adrian McCann stood by the prow of the boat, one thumb hooked into the pocket of his jeans, his other hand gripping the butt of a Uzi sub-machine gun.

Sixty yards.

Hitch could hear shouting from the other boat, though most of the words were indistinct. He saw one man motioning animatedly with his arms, as if to deflect the other boat from its route.

Forty yards.

'Steady now,' Hitch said and Morton slowed up a little more.

Twenty yards.

They seemed to be the only two vessels moving on the dark water; *The Abbott* was almost invisible in the gloom. The red warning lights of *The Sandhopper* glowed like boiling blood in the blackness.

Ten yards.

Hitch could hear the men shouting now, see them gesticulating madly towards *The Abbott* in an effort to divert it from what appeared to be a collision course.

Morton cut the motor.

The boat floated the last few yards until it actually bumped the side of *The Sandhopper*. One of the crew immediately crossed to the side of the smaller boat and pointed a finger angrily at Hitch.

'What the fucking hell are you playing at?' he bellowed. 'You could have sunk us. You haven't even got your lights on . . .'

The sentence trailed off as Hitch pulled the Beretta free and aimed it at the crewman.

'Cut your engines,' shouted Morton, swinging the Ithaca up into view, working the pump action, chambering a round.

McCann stepped forward too, the Uzi held in both hands the stubby barrel pointed at the deck of *The Sandhopper*.

'All of you get out where I can see you,' shouted Hitch.

'What the fuck *is* this?' the first crewman said. 'Are you the law?'

'No,' said one of his companions, looking at the Uzi. 'They ain't the law.' He lifted his hands into the air in a gesture of surrender.

'All of you,' Hitch shouted, watching as the third man

277

joined his companions on the foredeck. He was the youngest of the trio, in his early twenties, with short black hair. His companions were both in their forties, one of them greying at the temples, a squat, powerfully built man; the other was a tall gangling individual with deep set eyes which remained fixed on Hitch the whole time.

'Who the fuck are you?' the second man asked as Hitch stepped aboard *The Sandhopper*.

Hitch ignored the question.

'Get the hold open,' he said sharply, pushing the barrel of the pistol towards the tall man's face. 'Do it,' he rasped when the man hesitated.

The younger of the trio looked at McCann and Morton and decided he would be better advised *not* to try and reach the .38 he had jammed into his belt.

The tall man opened the hold and Hitch peered down into it, glancing at dozens of crates all of roughly the same size.

'Bring one out,' he said, watching as the tall man struggled with it, finally dropping it on to the deck. 'Open it,' Hitch told him.

'You're making a mistake,' said the second man.

'You're the one making a fucking mistake,' Morton snapped, raising the Ithaca and pointing it at his head. 'If you open your mouth once more I'll blow your fucking head off. Got it?'

There was a creak of splintering wood as the tall man prized off the lid of the crate. Hitch told him to back off, then moved across. Beneath a layer of foam rubber there was a dark brown carpet of coffee beans. He dug his hand through the aromatic blanket and his fingers closed round an unmistakeable shape. He pulled the video-cassette free and gripped it in his free hand, the pistol still trained on the tall man.

Hitch slammed the cassette hard against the crate. Once. Twice. It cracked, then split open.

Yards of video tape spilled onto the deck, along with pieces of broken plastic.

And a small plastic bag full of white powder.

He tore it open, moistened the end of one gloved finger then dipped it in the substance and touched it to his tongue. It felt cold as the powder reached his tastebuds. He smiled thinly and motioned the tall man back.

Morton looked across expectantly.

'We've got it,' said Hitch, smiling. 'Now let's get it loaded and get out of here.'

Sixty-nine

He was beginning to get cramp in his right leg.

Jim Scott massaged his calf for a moment, then pushed open the driver's side door of the Lancia and clambered out. The chill night air hit him like a fist. He recoiled, but the iciness in the breeze freshened his skin and helped to dispel the lethargy he had been feeling sitting in the car. He walked around the vehicle a couple of times, stretching his legs, stopping by the bonnet to squat down on his knees. As he straightened up he heard the joints pop and winced.

The river was silent. From where he stood, Scott could see nothing but the curling black tongue of water cutting through the centre of the city. He crossed the road, pausing on the kerb and looking back towards the Lancia. The two-way radio Hitch had been using was still on the passenger seat. Perhaps Scott should take it with him in case someone tried to make contact.

Fuck it. They knew where he was if they wanted him.

He strode across the road and headed towards the quayside, leaning against the black metal fencing that ran along the embankment. He gazed down river but could see nothing.

Behind him a car passed and he turned to look at the occupants. It was a young couple, who both looked at him for a second before driving on.

The girl was blonde.

A little like Carol?

He rested one foot on the fence and leant forward, hawking loudly, sending a projectile of sputum into the river below.

Where the fuck was she?

Why hadn't she called him? All he wanted to know was if she was all right. Just a phone call would satisfy him.

Would it hell.

He needed to see her, speak to her, touch her. He felt anger and concern in equal measures. It was the uncertainty that was so infuriating, not knowing where she was. His whole life had become a series of unanswered questions in the past few days. First Carol and now this.

This? This fucking job?

He asked himself again why they needed him here. He still could not begin to imagine why, as Hitch had told him, Ray Plummer had specifically asked for *him* to be included. He kicked irritably at the metal fence and then turned and headed back towards the car, hands dug deep into the pockets of his jacket.

Behind him, the river flowed by.

It took just over forty-five minutes to unload the crates (sixteen in all) from *The Sandhopper* to *The Abbott*.

Hitch, Morton and McCann stood over the other three men while they transferred the precious cargo, guns trained on them at all times.

'And there's twenty million quid's worth in there?' Morton said quietly, watching as the tall man lowered the last crate into the hold.

'Twenty million quid's worth of coke,' Hitch said.

'That's all of it,' said the tall man, wiping perspiration from his forehead. Beside him, the youngest of the three was trying to pull a splinter from his palm.

Hitch motioned them back onto *The Sandhopper*.

'Thanks for your help, fellas,' he said, smiling. Then, looking across at Morton, 'Start the engine, Terry, we've finished.'

'You're making a fucking big mistake,' said the second man, his teeth clenched in anger. 'When Connelly finds out about this . . .'

The sentence was interrupted abruptly as Hitch fired.

The first bullet hit the man in the chest, staving in the sternum, cracking two ribs and ripping through a lung. Gobbets of pinkish-grey matter exploded from the exit wound below the right shoulder blade. The man pitched backwards, blood spouting from the wound.

'What the fuck . . .' shouted McCann as he saw Hitch turn on the other two men.

The younger of the two ran for the side of the boat, perhaps in an attempt to dive over the side. A last desperate attempt to escape into the murky waters.

The first bullet hit him in the back, severing his spine. He crumpled to the deck, his sphincter muscle giving out. The soft sound of voiding filled the air as he rolled over in agony like a fish out of water.

The tall man fared no better.

Hitch shot him in the face, watching as he toppled

281

backwards, most of his bottom jaw blown off by the close-range blast.

Hitch moved swiftly from one body to the other, firing another shot into the head of each man. Into the nape of the neck of the youngest, who was lying on his stomach with part of his spine exposed, the flesh and muscle ripped away by the 9mm bullet.

Hitch jumped back aboard *The Abbott* and slapped Morton on the shoulder.

'Get us away from here,' he said sharply, and the other man guided the smaller boat away, allowing it to pick up speed.

'What the hell did you kill them for?' shouted McCann.

'They saw our faces,' Hitch said flatly. 'They knew we were with Plummer.'

'That's bullshit,' snapped McCann.

'If word of this had got back to Connelly there'd be gang war,' Hitch told him. 'We couldn't have left them alive.'

'Bollocks,' McCann roared. 'You didn't have to kill them.'

Hitch grabbed him by the lapels, pulling him close.

'And what the fuck would *you* have done with them, hot shot? Invited them out for a drink?' Hitch snarled. He pushed his companion away. 'We leave the boat to float there now. By the time somebody finds them there'll be nothing to link us to the killings.'

McCann sighed and banged his fist against the side of the boat.

'Shit,' he murmured. 'Fucking shit.' He let out a long breath then turned to look at Hitch. 'I suppose you're right.'

Hitch nodded.

Morton was already guiding the boat in towards the quay.

Hitch moved closer to the prow.

'What now?' McCann wanted to know.

'I'm getting off here. I've got to let Plummer know it went okay. You carry on down to Putney Bridge, get this lot unloaded. You know what to do with the boat.' He looked at McCann then at Morton. 'Sink it.'

Morton nodded.

Hitch was about six feet from the edge of the pier when he jumped, landing with surprising agility. He brushed dust from his sleeve and headed towards the flight of stone steps that led up to the embankment. The boat was already chugging away towards Putney. Hitch smiled and crossed the road to the Lancia, pulling open the door and sliding into the passenger seat.

'Let's go,' he said.

'I heard some shooting,' Scott told him, starting the engine. 'What was it?'

'Nothing for you to worry about, Scotty,' Hitch told him. 'Just get me to a phone, will you?'

Scott started the engine and drove off.

Hitch fumbled inside his jacket and pulled the Beretta free. He passed it to Scott.

'Take it,' he said sharply.

The driver did as he was instructed, slipping it back inside the holster, feeling the slight warmth in the metal.

'Tell me what happened,' he demanded. 'This fucking gun has been fired.'

'I had to frighten one of them,' Hitch lied. 'Fired above his head.'

Scott looked across at his companion.

'You better be telling me the truth,' he said threateningly, 'or I'll use the fucking thing on you.'

Hitch looked at him and saw the anger in Scott's eyes. He had no doubt at all that Scott meant what he said. He persisted with the lie, nevertheless.

'I had to frighten them, Scotty, I told you,' he said quietly.

'I heard six fucking shots,' Scott said. 'Why so many?'

'Just drive,' Hitch said.

Scott pulled the car over to the kerb, his right hand slipping inside his jacket. He pulled the pistol free and shoved it against Hitch's cheek.

'How many shots did you fire?' he snarled. 'Tell me or I'll blow your fucking head off.' He thumbed back the hammer.

'Six,' Hitch said. He reached inside his jacket and pulled his own pistol free. 'Here, take the mag out of my gun, replace it with the one from yours.'

Scott seemed satisfied by this and slipped the magazine free from his own pistol, jamming in the full one he'd taken from Hitch's Beretta. The two men glared at each other for a moment.

'That temper of yours is going to get you into trouble one day, Scotty,' Hitch told him. 'You ever pull that on me again and I'll fucking kill you.'

'You'll have to be quicker than you were a minute ago, then,' Scott hissed and pulled the car away from the kerb.

'Just get me to a phone,' Hitch said irritably.

Scott drove on.

'There.'

Hitch pointed to the pay phone on the corner of the street and Scott brought the Lancia to a halt, watching as his companion walked across to the phone, picked it up and dialled, feeding more money in.

'Ray, it's me,' said Hitch. 'It's done. Yeah, everything. Well, *nearly* everything.' He smiled. 'Scott's going to drop me off. No, didn't need him.' He listened for a moment, glancing round at his companion in the car. 'Right. I'll call you tomorrow.' He replaced the receiver, scooped his change out of the slot and walked back towards the car, clambering into the passenger side.

Scott drove on.

Ten minutes later he dropped Hitch off close by Clapham Junction Station then drove away, heading home. The traffic was light at such an hour. He might make it back by four in the morning, once he'd dumped the car.

Hitch watched the tail lights of the Lancia disappear and headed for the public telephones nearby. He fed more money into the machine, smiling as he dialled.

Seventy

He fumbled with the key, trying to push it into the lock, cursing when it wouldn't turn. Finally the door opened and Scott stepped inside. He closed the door behind him, leaning against it for a moment, catching his breath.

He'd dumped the car a mile away and walked back to his flat, passing less than half a dozen other people along the way. He'd gone over the car with a cloth, wiping fingerprints from the steering wheel and the door handles, then he'd tossed that into the Lancia, locked it and hurled the keys away. Scott stood motionless for long moments, sucking in deep lungfuls of air. His body ached mainly through lack of sleep, he told himself, reluctant to admit he was so unfit that a mile walk had drained him of energy. Finally he wandered through into the kitchen, pulled off his jacket and draped it over the back of a chair. He hastily unfastened the shoulder holster, too, and laid it on the table, then crossed to the fridge, found a can of 7-Up and drank deeply. He carried the can with him into the bathroom where he stripped off his clothes and turned on the shower. He sat on the toilet, watching the spray, waiting for the water to warm up, sipping his drink.

His head was pounding. It had been ever since he'd dropped Hitch off. Scott reached up and massaged his own shoulders as best he could.

He needed someone to do this for him. Someone to soothe away the ache.

Like Carol?

For once he pushed the vision of her to the back of his mind, his thoughts focusing instead on the events of that night. Most particularly on the six shots that Hitch had fired. Six shots just to frighten the crew of *The Sandhopper*? Scott shook his head.

He got to his feet and thrust a hand into the spray, satisfied that it was warm enough. He stepped under it, enjoying the feel of the water on his skin, his eyes closed, still confused about what was going on. About Carol. About what had happened that night. Christ, things were becoming a mess and he could see no way of sorting them out. He *had* to speak to her. Even if it meant sitting on her doorstep until she either came out of her flat or came home from wherever she was.

For all he knew she could be dead.

He opened his eyes, rubbing his face with both hands, increasing the speed of the jets so that the water stung his skin when it struck him.

He didn't even hear the knocking on the door.

The rushing of water from the shower masked every other sound.

The knocking came again, more insistently this time.

Scott ran both hands through his hair, smoothing it back tight against his scalp.

The banging on the door had become more frenzied.

He reached for the soap and began to wash.

There was a thunderous crash as the door was smashed in. It flew back on its hinges and crashed against the wall with an almighty bang.

Scott heard it at last and looked around, fumbling for the taps, trying to turn off the shower.

There was movement in his sitting room, in his kitchen. He heard voices. Then, through a gap in the shower curtain, he saw a dark shape.

What the hell was happening?

The dark shape was coming closer.

Scott steadied himself, waiting until the shape was only a couple of feet from him, then leapt forward, crashing into the intruder.

Both men went hurtling backwards, Scott slamming the newcomer's head against the bathroom cabinet. The mirror shattered and pieces of glass cut into the intruder's neck. Scott grabbed him by the lapels and hauled him to his feet. But now there were others coming into the room.

He saw the uniforms.

The two policemen in the doorway stared in at him, one of them taking a step closer, anxious to rescue their plain clothes colleague from Scott's attack. The man was dazed but managed to shake loose of Scott's grip. He felt the back of his neck and brought his hand around covered in blood.

'Put some fucking clothes on, Scott,' he said angrily. 'You're under arrest.'

'You've got no right to come bursting in here like this,' Scott snarled. 'What's the fucking charge, anyway?'

287

The plain clothes man looked at him, his eyes narrowed.

'Murder.'

Seventy-one

'I'm here to help you. But I can't do that unless you help *yourself*.'

Brian Hall leant on the edge of the table and looked down at Scott.

Hall was about thirty-five, dressed immaculately in a charcoal-grey Armani suit. He was clean-shaven and his hair combed perfectly. The contrast between the lawyer and Scott was stark. Scott was dressed in jeans and a T-shirt which needed washing. He sported a thick growth of stubble and his eyes were sunken, with dark rings beneath them. He'd managed to grab a couple of hours' sleep in the cell since they'd brought him in, but it was scarcely enough to refresh him. He looked as bad as he felt. Now he cupped both hands around the plastic beaker full of luke-warm coffee and lowered his head, staring into the depths of the brown liquid as if seeking inspiration there.

Hall had arrived at Dalston police station about twenty minutes ago and announced that he was acting for Scott. He'd been shown to the interview room where Scott sat with a uniformed officer close by the door. The room smelt of stale sweat and strong coffee. All it contained were the table and two wooden chairs, one of which Hall now gripped the back of, looking first at the policeman then at Scott.

'Talk to me, Jim,' he said. 'That's what I'm here for.

I'm here to help you but I can't do that unless you talk to me. Tell me what happened.' There was a hint of exasperation in his voice.

Scott looked up at him and motioned towards the policeman.

'Could I have a few minutes alone with my client, please?' Hall said. The policeman nodded, got to his feet and walked out, closing the door behind him.

'*Now* will you talk to me?' Hall said.

'How did Plummer know I was here?' Scott wanted to know.

'I don't really see what that's got to do with it . . .'

'How?' snarled Scott.

'Word gets round, Jim. Once he heard you'd been arrested it was just a matter of finding out which police station you were being held at,' Hall said. 'He called me, asked me to help you.'

Scott was unimpressed. He lowered his head again, the knot of muscles at the side of his jaw pulsing angrily.

Plummer knew where he was.

'And are you supposed to get me out of here?' he asked, sardonically.

'I can't do that,' Hall said, flatly. 'You know that. They won't even post bail with the evidence against you.'

'I didn't kill those blokes,' Scott told him.

'I'm sure you didn't but . . .'

Scott interrupted him, angrily.

'I didn't fucking kill them,' he snarled.

'That's as maybe, but unfortunately the evidence points to the fact that you did.' Hall exhaled deeply. 'The three men were shot with *your* gun. *Your* fingerprints were found on the spent shell cases they found on

The Sandhopper's deck. On top of that you've got no alibi for the time of the murders.' Hall walked slowly up and down. 'They've got enough evidence to throw away the key, Jim. My only advice to you is to plead guilty.'

Scott smiled humourlessly.

'Well, thanks for that brilliant piece of help,' he sneered. 'Did Plummer send you here just to tell me that?'

'I don't know what else to say to you. The evidence against you is overwhelming.'

'I didn't kill them.'

'Then who did?'

'John Hitch,' Scott said flatly. 'Hitch killed them with my gun on Plummer's orders. I've been fitted up.'

'That's ridiculous,' Hall said. 'If Plummer was trying to frame you, why send me here to help you?'

'All part of the fucking act. He's done me up like a kipper and I fucking fell for it. That's what annoys me as much as anything. I walked straight into it.' He clenched his fists.

'You say Hitch killed them. You may believe that . . .'

'I *know* it,' Scott snarled.

'All right,' Hall said, raising his own voice. 'You *know* it. *You* know it, but on the evidence against you there isn't a jury in the world that's going to believe you.' He lowered his voice slightly. 'You'll go down for life.'

Seventy-two

She could hear their voices from the sitting room. As Carol Jackson moved about in the kitchen she could hear the steady burble of conversation, punctuated every so often by a laugh.

She cracked eggs into a frying pan and stood over them while they cooked, wincing as hot fat spat at her from the pan. It missed her skin and stained Plummer's monogrammed dressing gown. Beneath it, Carol was naked. She had hauled herself out of bed about twenty minutes ago when she'd heard the doorbell. Plummer had told her to make breakfast while he spoke to John Hitch. The blond man had nodded a greeting to her, and Carol had been aware of his appraising gaze. She retreated to the kitchen to cook breakfast but the odd sentence floated to her through the smells of frying bacon and toasting bread. Words and sentences, some of which she found unsettling.

'Scott was arrested . . .'

'Three killed . . .'

'The boat was sunk . . .'

Scott was arrested. She had almost dropped the frying pan when she'd heard that. She wanted to rush into the sitting room and ask why, ask where he'd been taken, but she knew she could not do that. And she wondered why she felt such a sense of despair.

Or was it loss?

Was it despair for Scott or for herself?

You wanted him out of your life; well, now he'll be gone for good.

But that wasn't how she wanted it. She didn't want him hurt.

He won't be hurt, just locked up. Locked away for the rest of his life.

Carol ran a hand through her tousled hair and sighed. *Out of sight, out of mind.*

She heard Hitch mention where he'd been taken.

The fat spat at her again and she jumped back in surprise and pain as, this time, it burned her hand. She ran it beneath the cold tap for a moment then dried it and returned to the pan, lowering the heat, scooping the eggs out and onto a plate. She called to Plummer that his breakfast was ready and a moment later he ambled in, followed by Hitch. Both men sat down and Plummer began eating immediately. Hitch accepted the cup of tea Carol offered him, looking at her as she turned her back on him. He gazed at her shapely legs, exposed as far as her thighs. Carol gave him his tea then sat down at the table next to Plummer, who carried on eating.

'When will it be unloaded?' he wanted to know.

'By the end of the day it'll be hidden. Safe. Then all we have to do is sit on it until the time's right,' Hitch told him. He glanced across at Carol. She self-consciously pulled her dressing-gown more tightly across her breasts.

'And there's no way Connelly can trace the job back to us?' Plummer said, shoving a piece of bacon into his mouth.

'Not without witnesses,' Hitch said, smiling thinly.

Plummer smiled and shook his head.

'Twenty million fucking quid,' he chuckled.

Carol looked at him. She couldn't even begin to imagine that amount of money. The figures were enough to make her head spin.

And Scott? She wanted to ask. Instead she glanced across at Hitch and found his gaze on her again.

'Nice cup of tea,' he said, smiling.

Carol smiled thinly in response and picked at the piece of toast on her plate.

The phone rang.

Plummer got to his feet immediately and walked through into the sitting room to answer it.

'Is that how you keep your figure?' Hitch asked, lowering his voice slightly. 'By not eating much?' He was gazing at her breasts again.

She shrugged.

'What do you mean?'

'You've got a good figure,' he told her, glancing quickly towards the door to make sure Plummer hadn't returned.

'More tea?' Carol asked in an effort to change the subject.

He shook his head, leaning back slightly, watching as she drew one shapely leg up beneath her on the chair.

From the sitting room he could still hear Plummer speaking.

'You used to go out with Jim Scott, didn't you?' Hitch asked.

She nodded slowly.

'I'll bet he'll miss you inside,' said Hitch. 'Only his right hand for company when he used to have *you* to get his rocks off.' Hitch smiled again. 'Are you moving in with Ray, then?'

'It's not really your business, is it?' she said, glaring at him.

He shrugged.

'I just wondered what was going to happen to your little flat if you *did* move out,' he said, his gaze never leaving her. 'Dollis Hill, isn't it?'

'How do *you* know?' she demanded.

'My business to know,' he told her. 'You're mixed up

293

with Ray, Ray's my boss, I have to look out for him. I just did some checking, that's all.' He took a swig from his mug, pushing the empty receptacle towards her. 'I think I *will* have that cup of tea.'

She took the mug and moved across to the worktop, aware of Hitch watching her every move.

'You must have done a thing or two working in that club,' Hitch said, still looking at her. 'I've seen some of the acts.'

She pushed the mug towards him and sat down again, trying to avoid his gaze.

He glanced towards the door, still able to hear Plummer on the phone.

'Did you used to get off on what you were doing?' he enquired. 'I mean, especially with other girls?' He smiled.

Carol looked directly at him.

'If all the blokes I knew were like you then I'd be better off with another girl, wouldn't I?' she said scornfully.

Hitch held her gaze until he heard Plummer heading back towards the kitchen. He sat down and prodded his breakfast.

Hitch finished his tea and got to his feet.

'I'd better go,' he said. 'I'll pick you up in an hour, Ray. I've got a couple of things to do.'

'All right, John,' Plummer said. 'Carol, see John out, will you?'

Hitch smiled thinly.

'It's okay, I can manage,' he said, looking again at Carol's breasts. 'See you later, Ray.' He held her stare this time. 'See you around, Carol.' His smile broadened and he walked out. She heard the door close behind him.

'Are you going to work tonight?' Plummer asked.

'I wasn't planning to,' she said, still uneasy about Hitch. 'I thought we could stay in and . . .'

'I've got business to take care of tonight,' he said.

Carol regarded him impassively.

'I'm going to have a bath before Hitch picks me up,' he told her. He waved an expansive hand around the kitchen. 'Tidy this place up a bit, will you?' Then he was gone.

Seventy-three

He'd been dozing in his sitting room when the noise from upstairs woke him.

Doctor Robert Dexter sat forward quickly, sucking in a deep breath as he regained his senses. He looked around the large sitting room, catching sight of the clock on the mantlepiece. The hands had crawled around to 1.26 a.m.

Again the noise from upstairs.

Footsteps.

Dexter got to his feet, glancing up at the ceiling. He swallowed hard and headed for the door that opened out into the hall. Outside the wind was blowing strongly. The house stood on top of a low hill, joined to the main road by a narrow driveway flanked on both sides by dwarf conifers. As he moved into the darkened hallway he could see those conifers bowing deferentially to the strong breeze.

Dexter stood at the bottom of the stairs, looking up into the gloom at their head. He reached across to the bank of switches at his right hand and flicked a couple. The darkness at the top of the stairs was dispelled swiftly by bright lights.

He put one foot on the bottom step and prepared to ascend.

The crack came from behind him.

A sharp slap of wood on glass. He spun round to see that a skeletal branch from one of the bushes beneath the hall window had been blown against the pane.

Dexter felt his heart beating a little faster as he began to climb the stairs.

From above him the sounds of movement had all but ceased; only the creak of a solitary floorboard broke the silence now. As he reached the landing he paused, looking around at the five closed doors that faced him.

He knew which one the sounds were coming from.

Dexter sighed and made his way across to the third door, halting outside it.

He found that he was shaking.

After all these years he was still afraid.

Afraid of the occupant of that room, afraid of what he might find, yet, simultaneously, knowing *exactly* what he would find. The same sight would confront him that had confronted him for the past fifteen years.

He stood by the door, listening for movement, and again heard the slow footsteps, pacing back and forth over the carpet. The creak of the one loose board.

Dexter closed his eyes for a moment. Perhaps it would just be best to walk away this time. Go to bed. Go back downstairs.

He heard breathing on the other side, close to the door. As ever, he was aware that the occupant was listening for him, was perhaps aware even now of his presence there. The time to turn back had passed. He knew he must enter.

Dexter unlocked the door, turned the knob and walked into the room.

His heart was thudding hard against his ribs and

he felt the first droplet of perspiration pop onto his forehead.

The occupant of the room was sitting in one corner. Dexter closed the door behind him.

PART THREE

'Vengeance is mine; I will repay,
saith the Lord'

Romans 12:19

'In this last and final hour,
You can't hide.
There's nowhere now that you can run . . .'

Black Sabbath.

Seventy-four

The door crashed shut, the loud clash of metal on metal reverberating inside the cell.

James Scott stood in the centre of the small room for a moment, looking round, then sat down on the edge of the bottom bunk.

He felt numb, as if his entire body had been pumped full of novocaine. There was a lead weight where his heart should have been. He felt as if every last drop of feeling had been sucked out of him. The past two days had passed quickly, so quickly in fact that the events of those four days were somewhat hazy. And yet still he retained memories of that time. Like splinters in his mind.

The journey to the court. The police had brought a suit he'd requested from his flat and he'd changed into that, shaved and smartened himself up.

The trial.

He had decided, as advised, to plead guilty and proceedings had moved with dizzying speed. The gun had been produced as evidence. Pictures of the dead men had been circulated around the jury. Scott could remember one of the jurors in particular. She had been in her mid-forties, a smart, efficient-looking woman who had hardly taken her eyes off him throughout the trial. And he had seen hatred in those eyes. When sentence had been passed he glanced at her and was sure he could see the trace of a smile on her lips.

Scott had heard little of the Judge's summing up or,

indeed, of his comments after the life sentence had been passed. Just the odd word here and there, like 'horrendous', 'brutal', 'cold-blooded' or 'dangerous', had filtered through the screen that seemed to have erected itself around him. He felt as if he'd been inside a cell ever since his arrest, imprisoned within his own mind.

He had spent much of the trial gazing around the court room particularly into the public gallery, but not once did he see Carol.

Bitch.

God, how he needed her now.

If only he could have spoken to her one last time before he'd been taken down. Touched her. Kissed her. But that was not to be. She was gone now, out of his life as surely as if she were dead.

After sentence had been passed he had been taken to the cells, then back to Dalston in a black van. From there he'd been taken in a police van to Whitely by two police officers.

The journey, despite the distance between London and the prison, had taken a surprisingly short time. Or so it seemed to Scott. It was as if time had lost all meaning, as if even that were conspiring to hasten him to this place where he would spend the rest of his life.

The rest of his life.

The finality of the words hit him once more; only now, within the confines of the cell, they had an almost deathly abruptness. He looked around the room, at the bunks, the other small bed on the other side of the cell. At the thick metal door, the wooden table and chairs. The slop buckets. There was one single window set about seven feet up the wall, covered by wire mesh as well as being barred. Freedom was now only something to be glimpsed through steel. Death must be similar to this feeling, he thought. The four walls of the cell might as well be the wooden sides of a coffin. There was no such thing as life within prisons, only day-to-day existence. Passing time. Waiting for the only real release, which would come in the form of death; the actual termination of life, not the living death of captivity.

He had been shown which locker in the room was his and told that one of his cell-mates was on work detail, the other in the exercise yard. Scott didn't really care. He unzipped his bag and took out what few possessions he'd been allowed to bring in to the cell: a small cassette-radio and a few tapes. The towels were prison issue, along with the roll of toilet paper and the clean white T-shirts and underwear. He crossed to his locker and opened it. From the pocket of his overalls he took a photo of Carol. She was smiling out at him, her long blond hair tousled. She was wearing jeans and a denim shirt (which he'd bought her). He looked at that smile.

A mocking smile?

He wanted her badly.

Bitch.

He needed her.

She had betrayed him.

Perhaps she would visit him. He wedged the picture inside the locker door and stood staring at it.

No, she wouldn't visit him.

Perhaps she'd write.

He looked at the photo.

His jaw was clenched tightly, his eyes narrowed.

Why did you betray me?

I love you.

'Fucking bitch,' he snarled and drove his fist against the door, against the photo.

When he looked at it, there was blood oozing from two split knuckles.

303

Red spots had splashed across the picture. Across her smile.

Fucking bitch.

'I love you,' he breathed softly.

The blood dripped from his gashed hand.

Seventy-five

John Hitch drained what was left in his wine glass and put it down, looking across the table at Carol Jackson, who held his gaze for a moment and then went on eating.

Beside her, Ray Plummer was struggling to wind spaghetti around his fork but it kept falling back into the dish. Cursing, he began cutting it up, pushing the shorter strands onto his spoon.

Les Gourmets was busy, to Plummer's relief. The trade in all his restaurants had been slack over the past couple of weeks, and he was glad to see so many lunchtime diners. The babble of conversation was punctuated by the chink of bottles against glasses. Hitch poured himself another glass of Chablis, raised his eyebrows at Carol expectantly and moved the bottle towards her, but she shook her head, covering her glass with one hand.

As she did he saw the ring on the third finger of her left hand; the large diamond sparkled brightly.

Fuck knows how much that cost, Hitch thought, glancing at the impressive stone.

He afforded himself a quick glance at Plummer, who was still struggling with his spaghetti.

The manager of the restaurant, a short Italian with sad eyes and a pinched face, emerged from the kitchen and chatted briefly with Plummer about the improvement of business.

Hitch kept his eyes on Carol; by this time, she was beginning to feel uneasy under his almost unwavering stare.

The manager disappeared a moment later, leaving them alone again to finish their meal.

'Dozy bloody wop,' muttered Plummer. 'He used to work for Ralph Connelly. Ran one of his clubs in Kensington.'

'If you don't like him, why did you employ him?' Carol wanted to know.

Plummer shrugged.

'When I took over the club from Connelly I agreed to give old Guiseppe there a job,' he explained. 'Just part of the process, sweetheart.' He smiled at Carol. 'It's called diplomacy. We shafted Connelly when we took his shipment of coke but a gang war wouldn't have been any use to either of us. He knew he couldn't win one; I had too much money behind me. So we agreed to compromise with him on certain things, in return for him keeping his nose out of my business.'

'I still don't trust that cunt,' said Hitch. 'He could still try something.'

Plummer shook his head.

'If he was going to do anything, he'd have done it months ago. You worry too much, John.'

'Maybe you're a little too settled, Ray,' Hitch said challengingly. 'You might get over-confident . . .'

Plummer glared at him.

'Are you trying to tell me I've lost my bottle?' he rasped.

'I didn't say that,' Hitch added hastily.

'Then what the fuck are you saying?'

Hitch looked at Carol, then at his colleague.

305

'Well, you and Carol, you're sort of settled now, aren't you?' he said. 'You've got enough money to keep you for the rest of your life. It must be easy to lose your grip. Without even realising it, that's all I'm saying. I'm thinking about *you*.'

'Your concern is touching, Johnny boy,' chuckled Plummer, 'But don't worry about me. Just because Carol's wearing that ring doesn't mean I'm ready to get out my fucking pipe and slippers, either.' He eyed Hitch malevolently. 'So if *you've* got any ideas . . .' He allowed the sentence to trail off.

'Leave it out, Ray,' Hitch said indignantly, reaching for his glass of wine. He looked round at the other diners. Mostly businessmen. A few couples, laughing and joking, talking animatedly. Fucking yuppies, all of them, thought Hitch, glancing back across the table.

She's got you where she wants you, you silly cunt, he thought, watching as Carol slipped one hand onto Plummer's thigh, stroking gently as he ate.

Horny little slag.

Carol looked at Hitch and smiled.

A smile of triumph?

He held her gaze, allowing his own eyes to drop to her breasts, which were pressing against the clinging material of her dress. He could see the outline of her nipples.

Got him right where you want him, haven't you?

She lifted her glass, the light striking the ring, reflecting off the diamond.

To Carol it was a symbol of victory. A hard-earned trophy fought for and suffered for.

She felt she deserved it.

Sometimes she even felt something for Plummer.

Sometimes.

It wasn't love, that much she was sure of.

Gratitude, perhaps. Appreciation that he had provided

306

her with the escape route she had so badly sought? She wasn't sure. What was more, she didn't care. She was here now. She was with him. She wore his ring. She shared his penthouse flat.

She looked at Hitch and smiled thinly, wetting her lips slightly with the tip of her tongue.

The gesture was provocative and he knew it.

Little slag.

Beneath the table, his fists were clenched.

Seventy-six

'We spoke on the phone a few days ago.'

Detective Inspector Frank Gregson shook hands with Governor Peter Nicholson, feeling his own strong grip matched. Nicholson motioned for him to sit down.

'I'm sorry I couldn't see you earlier, Inspector,' Nicholson said.

'*Detective* Inspector,' Gregson corrected him. The Governor smiled thinly.

He offered the policeman some tea but he declined.

'What exactly can I do for you, *Detective* Inspector?' Nicholson wanted to know. 'I must say, I was a little surprised by your enquiries.'

Gregson exhaled.

'Well, it's like this. I've been investigating a series of murders in London. In each case the killer imitated an MO used before and then killed himself, committed suicide. It took a while to identify the first two but we've finally managed to do that. The third one there was no mistake with.'

'I don't see what that has to do with this prison.'

'All the killings were committed by men incarcerated here.'

Nicholson smiled.

'That's impossible. Are you trying to tell me that some of my prisoners have escaped without me noticing?' He chuckled.

'Do the names Peter Lawton, Mathew Bryce and Trevor Magee mean anything to you? Because if they don't, let me refresh your memory. They were all in here doing life sentences for murder.'

'I appreciate the refresher course, Detective Inspector, but I was familiar with those three men. I'm also familiar with the fact that they are no longer with us. By that I don't mean they've left the prison; I mean they're dead. They died here in Whitely.'

'I'm aware of that,' Gregson said.

'Then why are we having this conversation?'

'Because the three men that I've got in the morgue back at New Scotland Yard are Peter Lawton, Mathew Bryce and Trevor Magee.'

'You realise what you're saying?' Nicholson murmured incredulously.

'I know bloody well what I'm saying,' Gregson snapped, 'and if it's any consolation it sounds as crazy to me as it probably does to you. But the fact is, those three men committed nine murders between them in London less than three weeks ago.'

'Men who looked like Lawton, Bryce and Magee perhaps?'

'No. Not their doubles. Not their fucking twin brothers, either. *Those* men,' rasped Gregson, exasperated.

'It's not possible.'

Gregson got to his feet.

'I know it's not possible but it's happened,' he said angrily. 'Look, we have more than enough forensic

308

evidence to back up their identity. What I'm asking is, could there have been some kind of mistake here, at your end?'

Nicholson pressed his finger-tips together.

'What you mean is, could we, by accident, on three occasions, have released murderers back into society? Could we have let the wrong men go?' His smile faded, to be replaced by a look of anger. 'We might make the odd administrative error, Detective Inspector, but releasing the wrong men doesn't usually fall into that category.'

'Then *you* explain what the hell is going on,' Gregson challenged him. 'Because I feel as if I'm running around in circles looking for answers.'

The two men regarded one another silently across the desk. The silence was finally broken by Nicholson. He got to his feet.

'There's a simple way to settle this,' he said. 'Come with me.'

Together they left the office, walking down the short corridor to a set of steps. Nicholson led the way. At the bottom of the steps was another corridor, a much longer one this time. They finally reached a door which opened into the courtyard at the rear of the building. A blast of cold wind hit them. Gregson pulled up the collar of his jacket.

'What did they supposedly die of?' Gregson wanted to know.

'I don't remember exactly, but if you'd like to check their medical files before you leave you're quite welcome to,' the Governor said.

'Thanks, I think I might,' the DI said, following his host towards the church. The weather-vane on top of the small steeple was spinning madly in the wind. A couple of inmates were collecting fallen leaves and stuffing them into black bags. Another man was trimming the grass in the churchyard with a pair of shears, raking the clippings into a sack.

'This way,' said Nicholson, heading up a short path by the church.

Gregson followed. The inmates watched them.

'There,' said Nicholson, pointing at a simple wooden cross.

Gregson peered at the name on it.

MATHEW BRYCE.

'And here,' said Nicholson, pointing at another of the markers.

PETER LAWTON.

Gregson felt the wind whipping around him, felt the chill grow more intense.

There was one more.

TREVOR MAGEE.

Gregson looked at the dates on each one, noting the year and month each man had died. All had expired within the last eighteen months.

'Satisfied?' Nicholson said. 'I don't know who you've got in your morgue back in London, but as you can see they're not the three men you thought they were.'

Gregson jabbed the nine on the phone to get an outside line and pressed the digits he wanted.

He sat on the edge of the bed in his hotel room and waited for the phone to be answered. When it finally was he recognised the voice immediately.

'Stuart, it's me,' he said.

'How's it going, Frank?' DS Finn wanted to know.

'I wish I knew,' Gregson said wearily, and repeated what he'd seen at Whitely. 'The fucking graves are there, no question, no mistakes.'

310

'The graves are there, fair enough, but there's no mistake about who the three geezers in cold storage *here* are either. What the fuck is going on?'

'I wish I knew. Listen, I need you to check something out for me. Go through some files. I want you to check on any murderers who've been convicted and sent to Whitely in the last three years, got it? I want a list on my desk by the time I get back.'

'When will that be?'

'Tomorrow. Early afternoon, if I can get a train.'

'Okay, Frank.'

'Stuart, just a minute,' Gregson said hurriedly. 'When you check those files there's something specific you should look for. Like I said, I want to know how many murderers have been sent to Whitely in the last three years. More importantly, I want to know how many of those men died there.'

'What have you got, Frank?' Finn asked, quietly.

'Maybe nothing. Just check those files. If you find anything, call me here at the hotel.' He gave him the name and the number of the hotel in Buxton. 'Otherwise I'll see you tomorrow.'

Gregson hung up and sat back on the bed, cradling a glass of whisky in his hand which he'd poured himself from the room's mini-bar.

He felt as if he needed it.

Outside it was beginning to get dark.

Seventy-seven

Scott looked up as he heard the key turn in the lock. The heavy iron door swung open and a man stepped into the

311

cell, the door hurriedly closing behind him. The sound of the turning lock seemed deafening.

'Scott, right?' said Mike Robinson, crossing to his own bunk. 'Jim Scott?'

He nodded.

'How do you know my name?' he wanted to know.

Robinson smiled.

'The same way we know what you're in for,' he said. 'There isn't much we *don't* know about in here. At least when it comes to other members of the population.' His smile faded. 'Besides, it pays to know a few things about a bloke you're going to be sharing with, especially when that bloke's topped three other geezers.'

Scott looked at him angrily.

'I didn't kill them,' he said. 'I was set up.'

Robinson crossed to the small washbasin in the corner of the cell and spun the taps.

'Yeah,' he muttered humourlessly. 'You and everybody else in here. We're all innocent, Scott. We were *all* fitted up.' The smile returned.

'It's the truth. I didn't kill those men,' Scott insisted.

'Look, I'm one of your cell mates, not a fucking jury, and it's a bit late to start pleading innocence, isn't it?' Robinson dried his hands on the towel. 'I don't care if you killed three or three hundred. The only thing I care about is that I've got to share a cell with you. So if you cut your toenails don't leave them lying around on the floor, don't make too much noise if you have to use the slop bucket at night and if you're a shit-stabber then I'll tell you now, my arsehole isn't for rent. Right? I don't care how much snout, cash or force you use, my ring-piece is out of fucking bounds and if you try anything I'll cut your heart out.'

Scott looked impassively at him, a slight grin on his face.

312

'You trying to say I'm queer?' he said quietly.

'No, I'm just telling you that if you *are* then you're going to have a long love affair with your right hand because *I'm* straight and so is Rod. But there's plenty in here who aren't. If you want to find them, good hunting.'

'Who's Rod?'

'Rod Porter. The other bloke in this cell. He's on work detail at the moment.' Robinson swung himself up onto his bunk and pulled a magazine from beneath his pillow.

Scott regarded him impassively for a moment.

'You know enough about *me*,' he said. 'Who are *you*?'

'Mike Robinson.'

Scott extended his hand in greeting.

Robinson regarded it cautiously for a moment, then shook it, feeling the power in the other man's grip. Scott squeezed more tightly, the muscles in his forearm standing out like chords. When he finally released his grip, Robinson's hand felt numb but he managed to hide the discomfort.

'You got life, didn't you?' he said.

Scott nodded.

Jesus, even the words made him shiver.

Life.

'What else do you know about me?' he asked.

'In the real world you worked for Ray Plummer,' Robinson told him. 'And just a word of warning on that score. There are a couple of Ralph Connelly's boys in here who weren't too happy when they heard you'd blown away three of their mates.'

'I didn't kill them,' Scott snapped.

'Sorry, I forgot. You're innocent,' Robinson said. 'Whatever the case, watch your back with Connelly's boys. I'll point them out to you when I get the chance.'

313

Scott nodded.

'You done time before?' Robinson asked.

Scott shook his head.

'What about you?' he wanted to know.

Robinson smiled.

'I've been in and out since I was ten,' he said with something bordering on pride. 'Remand homes, detention centres, borstals and nicks. They're all much the same. It's usually just the screws who are different. The ones here are okay, as far as screws go. It's the Governor who's the *real* cunt.' He described Nicholson briefly, and mentioned particularly his words before the visit of the prison delegation. Scott sat on the edge of his own bed listening intently, hands clasped on his knees.

Robinson was still giving him the low-down on life in Whitely when the key rattled in the door again and it opened to admit Rod Porter. He was wearing a white overall on top of his grey prison issue clothes and he pulled the overall off as soon as he was inside.

Scott noticed there were bloodstains on it.

'Hard day at the office, dear?' chuckled Robinson as Porter crossed to the sink and began splashing his face with water.

He finally turned and looked at Scott.

'Well,' he said. 'I suppose a murderer is better company than a ponce.' He extended his right hand. A token of greeting.

Scott shook it.

Brief introductions were made and Porter explained about their last cell-mate, just as he had to the prison delegation.

'There's just one thing, Rod,' Robinson said, still smiling. 'Old Jim here is innocent. He didn't kill those three blokes. He was framed.'

314

Porter smiled.

'How many fucking times do I have to tell you?' snarled Scott. 'It *wasn't* me who killed them.' There was fury in his eyes.

'The cheque's in the post, I love you and I promise not to come in your mouth,' Porter added. '*They're* the three most common lies, mate. Except inside and you just added the fourth. We're *all* fucking innocent. I don't know why they don't just open the gates and let us all out now.'

'Fuck you,' Scott rasped.

'You don't have to,' said Porter. 'A jury already did that. They fucked me, Mike and you and everyone else in this shithole. There's no virgins in here. The law fucked everybody.'

Robinson chuckled.

'Very philosophical,' he said.

Porter stretched out on his bunk, hands clasped behind his head.

'So what do you think of the hotel?' he said.

Scott shrugged. He felt cold, as if all the warmth had been sucked from his body. He sat down on his own bed, exhaling deeply.

Life.

He nodded in the direction of the balled-up overall Porter had been wearing.

'What's that for?' he wanted to know.

'Work detail,' Porter explained. 'Laundry. I collect it and deliver it. It's better than sitting in here every day. Apart from the hospital wing.' He grunted. 'That's where the blood came from. Blood, shit and Christ knows what else. It used to be used as a punishment: they'd make inmates clean up the hospital wing, that sort of thing. Even make them change sheets and empty fucking bedpans.'

315

'What did anybody do to get that punishment?' Scott wanted to know.

'It was usually if somebody tried to escape,' Porter said.

Escape.

'Has anyone ever managed it?' Scott wanted to know.

'Not since I've been here,' Porter told him. 'A couple of blokes tried to go over the wall about a year ago. Before that, some prat even managed to hide in the boot of one of the warders' cars.' The other two men laughed.

'Somebody did it a while back,' Robinson said. 'Actually got out. They didn't get far, of course, but they managed to get out of the prison itself . . .'

'How?' Scott demanded, cutting him short.

'This place is very old, as you know. Supposedly there's a network of sewer tunnels running under it,' Robinson explained. 'Most of them have probably caved in by now. But one old boy over in B Wing was telling me that it's like a fucking maze down there. Some geezer got down into the tunnels and found his way out.'

'Rather him than me,' Porter muttered. 'That was probably how they found him. Just followed the smell of shit.'

Robinson laughed.

Scott *didn't*.

He sat back on his bed, looking around at the confines of the cell.

Life.

He sucked in a deep breath, closing his eyes momentarily.

A vision of Carol filled his mind.

Then Plummer.

He gritted his teeth.

'You all right?' Porter asked.

Scott nodded slowly, opening his eyes.

When he spoke his words were almost inaudible.

'I was just thinking.'

LIFE.

The word screamed inside his brain.

No. *There had to be a way*.

Seventy-eight

The raindrops against the window sounded like a handful of gravel being hurled at the glass by the strong wind. Rivulets of water coursed down the panes, puddling on the sill.

Governor Peter Nicholson watched the rain, hands clasped behind his back, his office lit only by the desk lamp at one corner.

He was looking out over the prison courtyard, watching the sheets of rain falling, the brightness of the observation lights along the prison walls reflecting in his eyes.

The wall clock ticked somnolently in the silence, each movement of the minute hand magnified by the stillness in the office.

It was 10.56 p.m.

'As far as I can see, it's a perfect choice.'

The voice cut through the stillness like sunlight through night.

Nicholson didn't turn, hardly seemed to acknowledge the other voice. He merely shifted position slightly, knotted his fingers more tightly together and continued gazing out of the window.

'No living relatives. There's no family anywhere, as far

317

as I can tell,' said the other voice. 'There's a history of violence, at least that's what the psychological profile says. More recent events would appear to substantiate that supposition.'

Nicholson remained silent.

'I need to be one hundred per cent sure, though,' the voice added.

At last Nicholson turned to face the other occupant of the room.

Doctor Robert Dexter ran a hand through his hair and nodded slowly, as if answering his own unasked question.

'How soon do you want to start?' Nicholson asked.

'I think we should leave it a week,' the doctor told him. 'I need to observe. As I said, I have to be one hundred per cent sure.' He exhaled deeply. 'In fact, perhaps we ought to wait longer than that.' He looked questioningly at the Governor. 'You said that policeman had been here.'

'He suspects nothing,' Nicholson said dismissively. 'I showed him the graves.'

'Even so, it might be an idea to stop work for a while. Just until the fuss has blown over.'

'What fuss? I told you, I showed him the graves.'

'But you said they'd identified Lawton, Bryce and Magee. What if he *isn't* satisfied with your explanation? He might come back.'

'And find what?' Nicholson leant across the desk and looked closely into Dexter's eyes. 'We've gone too far to turn back now. There's no need to delay the work, let alone stop it altogether. Unless *you're* beginning to have second thoughts.' He smiled scornfully. 'One failure too many, perhaps?'

'They were not failures, Nicholson. It *can* work, I've proved that.'

'So you say, doctor. I'm yet to be convinced.'

318

'It doesn't matter to you if they die, anyway, does it?'

'Not really, no.'

'I sometimes wonder why you became involved in the first place.'

'You know why.'

'Medical executions,' said Dexter quietly. 'That's what you see them as, isn't it? The ones that don't work.'

'You know my views,' Nicholson said sharply. 'This current situation is all that concerns me at the moment. Will you do it or not?'

'I need a week to observe, as I said.'

Nicholson nodded thoughtfully.

'However, the choice is perfect,' the doctor continued. He picked up the file that lay on the desk and flipped it open. Amid the plethora of papers there was a photo. He picked it up and studied the contours of the face, a slight smile on his lips.

'He'll be a good subject,' Dexter murmured. 'I'll operate as soon as I'm ready.'

He slipped the picture back into the file and closed it, looking once more at the name on the cover:

JAMES SCOTT.

Seventy-nine

Detective Inspector Frank Gregson paced slowly back and forth from one side of his office to the other, his gaze occasionally shifting to the blackboard behind his desk. To the names written on it.

DS Stuart Finn took a long drag on his cigarette and nodded at the board.

'Six murderers have been sent to Whitely in the past three years,' he said. 'I checked it out, just like you asked. Four of them died in there, all in the last eighteen months.' He looked at the blackboard once again.

'Including *our* three men,' Gregson said, finally perching on the edge of his desk. He looked at the last name on the list.

GARY LUCAS.

'It's a hell of a coincidence,' the DI muttered. 'All died there, all buried there.'

'All except Lucas,' Finn told him.

Gregson turned to look at his companion.

'By terms of his will, Lucas asked if he could be buried near his home, instead of in prison grounds. This burial in unconsecrated ground crap hasn't been enforced since they stopped the death penalty,' Finn went on. 'It's just that none of the other three had any family to protest.'

'Nor had Lucas, had he?'

'No; but, like I said, the terms of his will specified he could be buried outside prison grounds. They planted him in a cemetery in Norwood about three weeks ago.'

Gregson stroked his chin thoughtfully.

'What did the coroner say was the cause of death?' he wanted to know.

Finn blew out another stream of smoke.

'It says cardiac arrest on the death certificate, but a proper autopsy was never carried out,' said the DS, 'The certificate was signed by some geezer called . . .' he consulted his notes, 'Doctor Robert Dexter. He's down as resident physician at Whitely. The body was *prepared* there too, you know. They even put him in the coffin and shipped him home instead of leaving it to a local undertaker. Thoughtful, eh?' He took another drag on his cigarette.

320

'Jesus Christ,' muttered Gregson, his eyes fixed on the name of Lucas.

'Lucas must have fitted in well with the other three there,' Finn observed. 'He killed four people, including an eighty-seven-year-old woman, with a claw hammer before he was caught. Apparently he kept the old girl's left hand in his wardrobe. After he killed her he tried taking her wedding ring and when he couldn't get it he hacked her whole fucking hand off.'

Gregson appeared not to hear this last piece of information. He was already reaching for his phone, jabbing an extension number.

It rang. And rang.

'Where the hell is the boss?' he hissed.

'I should think he's gone home, Frank,' Finn said. 'It is nearly midnight, after all. What do you want him for, anyway?'

Gregson slammed the phone down.

'If I want an exhumation order he'll need to go and see a magistrate. I want Lucas dug up.'

'Are you serious?' Finn murmured uncomprehendingly. 'You want to dig Gary Lucas up? Why, for Christ's sake? He's dead.'

'So, apparently, were Lawton, Bryce and Magee.'

'You know they're dead. You saw their graves.'

'Yeah, I did. I also saw the three bodies downstairs in pathology. The ones that were positively identified as those same three men.' Gregson pulled his jacket on.

'Frank, where the fuck are you going?' Finn demanded, standing up as his superior headed for the door.

'I'm going to find out once and for all what the hell is going on,' Gregson told him.

Finn gripped his colleague's arm but the DI shook loose.

321

'Get off me,' he snapped.

'This is fucking crazy,' Finn blurted.

'If you want to help me, that's great,' Gregson said quietly, his voice soft but his tone and expression full of menace. He pointed at Finn. 'If not, stay out of my way.' The vein at his temple throbbed angrily.

Finn stood there helplessly for a moment, his own breath coming in gasps as he looked into the wild eyes of his superior.

'Where the hell are you going?' he demanded.

'Norwood Cemetery.'

Eighty

The Ford Scorpio came to a screeching halt at the massive wrought-iron gates of the cemetery.

Gregson looked at the huge barriers and banged the wheel angrily.

'You didn't expect them to be open, did you, Frank?' Finn grunted. 'Perhaps you should have called ahead and warned them we were on a zombie hunt. They might have laid on some lights too *and* some fucking shovels.'

'We're going in there,' Gregson snapped, his face hidden by the gloom of the night. He hauled himself out of the car and walked towards the stone wall surrounding the necropolis. The DI looked up at it, estimating the height to be about six feet.

He could climb it easily.

Taking a few steps back he ran at it, gripped the top row of bricks and pulled himself up onto the rampart. Balanced there, he looked into the cemetery. To his right was the chapel of rest; a little to the left of that was a wooden hut he took to be the domain of the cemetery caretaker.

They would find tools in there.

'Come on,' he called to Finn.

'You're fucking mad,' the DS snarled, looking up at him.

In response Gregson merely leapt down from the wall, landing on the gravel drive of the cemetery and rolling over to cushion his fall. The pieces of stone crunched loudly beneath him.

Finn sucked in a deep breath and ran at the wall, springing up and swinging himself over. Cursing quietly, he lowered himself down, dropping the last foot or so to the ground. He set off after Gregson, hearing his own feet crunching gravel as he hurried to catch up with his superior.

A cold breeze whipped across the open space, stirring fresh flowers on a new grave close by. One of the blooms was lifted from its pot and sent tumbling across the grass.

Trees towered over both sides of the driveway, which snaked through the vast graveyard like a mottled tongue. Branches stirred by the wind clattered together like muted applause as Finn finally caught up with his companion.

'Frank . . .' he began.

'We've got to get this door open,' Gregson said, ignoring his colleague. He took a step back and kicked at the doorknob. It came loose. Another similar impact and it gave way, the door flying inwards to crash against the wall. Gregson walked in, squinting in the gloom. 'Give me your lighter,' he said to Finn, who fumbled in his pocket and pressed the Zippo into his superior's palm.

Gregson flicked it on and raised it above his head, the sickly yellow puddle of light spreading out to illuminate

323

the inside of the hut. There was dried mud on the floor and the place smelt damp. Ahead stood a wooden work-bench; to the right on the wall there were cupboards. To the left there were tools. Gregson smiled at the shovels, spades, picks and assorted other pieces of hardware.

'Try and find some lights,' he said to Finn, who shook his head and wandered towards the cupboards.

In the darkness he cracked his leg against a wheel-barrow, yelping in pain, then cursing as he rubbed his shin.

Gregson picked up a couple of spades and a pick-axe and turned to see that his companion had discovered a large torch in one of the cupboards.

'Bring that,' he snapped as Finn flicked it on. The beam was powerful and broad. 'We've got to find the grave.'

'I joined the force to uphold the law, not play at fucking Burke and Hare,' snapped Finn.

Gregson smiled thinly and motioned for his companion to lead the way.

'Take this,' he said, handing Finn a spade.

'There must be thousands of people buried in this fuck-ing place,' snarled the DS. 'How the hell are we supposed to find *one* grave? We don't even know where it is.'

They set off along the driveway, feet sinking into the loose chippings.

'If Lucas was only buried three weeks ago, I know which part of the cemetery he'll be in,' Gregson reassured his companion. 'A friend of my father's died about a month ago. He was buried here, too. I came along with my old man. All the new ones are put in the same place. It's not far.'

As they walked Finn shone the torch from side to side, the light picking out graves on either side. Headstones stuck up from the earth like accusatory fingers, many moulded with age. Larger, sepulchral edifices appeared occasionally out of the night; marble reflected the beam of the torch. Some graves had crosses, others were completely unmarked. In many places the grass was overgrown. Great long tufts of it encroached onto the graves, the blades stirred by the strengthening wind.

As the path sloped upwards slightly, both men spotted a secondary track that was little more than a well-worn path carved out by the passage of many weary feet.

'Over there,' Gregson said, indicating the muddy path.

They changed direction. Finn sucked in breath.

'Do you reckon they'll still pay us our police pensions when we're locked up in a nuthouse? Because that's what's going to happen when people find out what we're doing,' he said.

'This is no joke,' hissed Gregson.

'You're fucking right it's not,' snapped Finn. 'Traipsing round a graveyard at one o'clock in the morning isn't my idea of a fun way to pass the time.'

'Give me the torch,' Gregson snapped, taking the light from his companion. He shone it over the headstones, picking out names.

'It's around here somewhere,' he said. 'It has to be.'

'I hope to Christ you're right,' Finn said, pulling up the collar of his jacket against the wind. A tree nearby bowed mockingly, its skeletal branches clacking together.

Gregson noted that most of the graves had fresh flowers on them. He could smell violets as he moved from one plot to another, moving the torch beam steadily over the monuments, careful not to tread on any of the graves. He noted the names, the inscriptions. The ages.

VALERIE SUTTON
BELOVED WIFE – SLEEPING
MARK KELLER –
TAKEN BY GOD
JONATHAN PIKE –
THE LIGHT OF OUR LIFE –
DIED MARCH 8th AGED 11 MONTHS

'This could take all night,' said Finn. Every time he stepped on a grave he apologised to its occupant, feeling stupid but unable to stop himself.

Gregson kept the torch beam moving steadily.

LOUISE PATEMAN –
OUR DARLING DAUGHTER – AT REST.

A metal rosebowl, overturned by the wind, clattered off its plinth and rolled against a headstone.

'Shit,' hissed Finn, spinning round.

COLIN MORRIS –
A SPECIAL HUSBAND – SADLY MISSED

The roses from the bowl were quickly scattered by the wind. The bowl continued to roll back and forth.

Finn reached for his cigarettes.

'Stuart.'

The sound of the voice startled him and he spun round to look at Gregson who was holding the beam on a simple plinth set into the ground. It bore only the name.

'I've found it,' said the DI.

Eighty-one

Gregson propped the torch up on a nearby headstone, ensuring that the beam pointed towards the grave of Gary Lucas. Then he shrugged off his jacket, draped it over a marble cross and gripped one of the shovels, driving the blade into the earth.

'Come on, help me,' he snapped, looking, up at Finn.

'This is fucking crazy,' the DS said, shaking his head, watching as Gregson lifted huge clods with the spade. His own breath was coming in short gasps now. He wondered if Gregson had gone insane.

'Dig, for Christ's sake,' the DI snarled. Finally, Finn began to drive his own spade into the moist earth.

'This isn't *right*, Frank,' he said angrily.

Gregson didn't answer, but continued digging, perspiration already beading on his forehead despite the chill wind whipping around them.

The two men hardly spoke as they burrowed deeper into the earth, leaving mounds of dirt on either side of the hole. Finn paused for a moment to catch his breath but Gregson kept up his labours, digging deeper all the time. His shirt was sticking to him now and he was panting like a cart horse but still he persevered, driving the spade into the soil and hurling dark mud away behind him.

They were getting close now, he knew it.

Finn ran a hand through his hair, feeling the slickness of sweat on his face, but one look at Gregson's expression persuaded him to continue digging.

There was a loud scraping sound of metal on wood.

327

They had reached the coffin.

Gregson immediately scrambled down beside it, scraping earth from the top of the casket with his hands.

'Give me the torch,' he said, snatching it from his companion and shining it on the lid.

'What now?' Finn asked, breathlessly.

Gregson reached up over the side of the grave and found the pick axe.

'We open it,' he said flatly.

Finn grabbed him by the shoulders.

'Frank, you can't do this,' he said angrily.

'Why the fuck do you think I dug him up, to admire the craftsmanship of the bloody box? I want to *see* that body.' He pushed his companion away. 'Hold that fucking torch over here,' he rasped, sliding the end of the pick-axe beneath the first of the coffin screws.

Finn wiped sweat from his face and pointed the torch downwards watching as his colleague exerted all the force he could muster on the other end of the pick.

As the screw came loose, part of the coffin lid broke away.

Gregson drove the pick underneath the lid, prizing upwards until the casket snapped again.

One more screw loose and he'd be able to remove the lid.

He forced the pick between the two edges of wood and pressed down.

Finn's heart was thudding madly against his ribs as he held the light steady over the ghoulish tableau.

The screw came loose with a whine of snapping wood.

Gregson pulled the lid free and tossed it aside.

Finn shone the torch into the coffin.

'Jesus Christ,' he murmured slowly, the colour draining from his cheeks.

Gregson stood beside him, panting, his eyes riveted. He shook his head very slowly.

'What the hell is it?' Finn whispered, his voice cracking, almost lost in the blast of wind that swept across them.

The DI leant forward slightly, still gripping the pick in one hand.

In the bottom of the coffin was a black dustbin bag, its top secured by a piece of thick string.

Nothing else.

No body. No rotting corpse.

Nothing.

Gregson used the pick to tear the plastic open while Finn shone his torch at the bag.

The DI reached in and pulled something out, holding it up.

A brick.

There were a dozen more in the dustbin bag.

'What the fuck is going on?' murmured Finn. 'Where's Lucas?'

Gregson slumped back against the wall of the grave, his eyes closed. Then he dropped the brick back into the weighted coffin.

Finn looked at him, his face pale.

'Where's Lucas?' he asked.

Gregson shook his head.

'I wish I knew.'

Eighty-two

The huge refectory of Whitely Prison was filled with rows of long tables, each of which could seat over fifty men.

Above, warders patrolled the catwalks, looking down onto the seething mass of grey-clad men, while other uniformed officers stood on either side of the queue for food. More warders were positioned at every third table, eyes constantly flicking back and forth over the rows of faces as they ate.

The inmates were usually allowed in according to the number of their landing. Each landing would eat in turn, then the refectory would be emptied of mainstream prisoners while the occupants of D Wing were ushered in.

Those in D Wing were kept in permanent solitary for their own protection. They were men guilty of child molestation or abuse, who had either already been threatened or injured by other inmates. These men, twenty-six of them, would be closely guarded even as they ate before being ushered back to their cells to the jeers and threats of the prisoners who were now locked up again.

Jim Scott had come to know these men from D Wing and he felt the same disgust and anger towards them as so many other inmates of Whitely. Twice he had seen men from that wing have boiling water thrown over them by the kitchen workers, the last one just two days earlier. After that, Scott was offered a job on kitchen detail. He accepted mainly because it was preferable to the boredom of being locked inside the cell for twenty-three hours of the day.

He cleaned, peeled potatoes, even helped to cook the vast quantities of food necessary to feed the inmates. He stood at the counter to splash dollops of stew or thick wads of mashed potato onto their plastic trays as each presented it in turn, moving in a slow and well ordered line along the counter, gathering mugs of tea and plastic cutlery at the end before taking their seats.

Scott was ladling soup into the bowl of a prisoner when he looked up and saw a familiar face.

Mike Robinson nodded a greeting to him and held out his bowl. Scott scooped soup from the massive copper container.

'A woman's work is never done, eh?' Robinson chuckled, winking at his cell-mate.

He reached for a bread roll, allowing the man behind him to pass by, obviously not enticed by a bowl of soup that resembled bubbling vomit.

Robinson's smile faded rapidly. He looked first at Scott, then back down the line to where a red-haired man stood, hands thrust deep into the pockets of his overalls.

'Clock the geezer with the red hair,' Robinson said.

Scott looked.

'See him?' Robinson persisted.

Scott nodded.

'His name's Vince Draper. He's one of Ralph Connelly's boys. Remember I warned you there were two of them in here? Watch yourself.' He moved on, noticing one of the warders moving across towards him.

Scott glanced up and saw that the red-haired man was coming closer. He had the plastic tray in his hand now, about three places back.

'Fucking cunt,' the words came drifting towards Scott. It was Draper who had spoken them. He was looking directly at Scott.

The warder who had approached Robinson had retreated to a nearby table, out of earshot.

Scott ladled more soup and tried to ignore Draper.

'I knew those three guys you shot, you fucker,' the red-haired man said, drawing closer.

Robinson glanced back to see what was happening.

'Did your girlfriend know you killed them?' Draper said, smiling. 'Did you do it to impress her?'

Scott gritted his teeth.

'You didn't have to kill three blokes to impress her,' Draper continued. 'You could have waved a twenty-quid note in front of her. That would have impressed her. It's good enough to get anyone else a fucking blow job, isn't it?' He laughed quietly.

He was two places away now. Scott gripped the handle of the ladle until his knuckles turned white, pouring the boiling soup into the bowl of the man in front of him.

'I bet she's impressed with Ray Plummer,' Draper said.

Scott glared at him.

'Impressed with his money, his power and his cock,' the red-haired man said. 'She must have had it up her and in her mouth enough times.'

He was level with Scott now.

Scott could feel himself shaking with rage. He glared at Draper.

'Fill it up,' Draper said scornfully, pushing the bowl towards Scott. 'Fill it like Plummer fills your bird's cunt.' He smiled. 'Everyone knows about them. Everyone knows she's fucking him. Everyone knows they made a prick out of you.'

Scott's face darkened; the vein at his temple throbbed. His entire body was quivering.

'Come on, fill the fucking bowl, Scott,' Draper said. 'Just try not to think about your tart with Plummer's dick stuck down her throat. Carol Jackson, isn't it? Carol "I take it anywhere for a tenner" Jackson.' He leant towards Scott. 'Seems like the only dick she's not getting any more is yours.'

Scott struck out, bringing the ladle down with incredible force on the top of Draper's head. The blow split his scalp. Already warders were running towards them, but Scott moved quickly.

He grabbed Draper by the hair and shoved his face downwards into the boiling vat of soup.

The red-haired man struggled madly as the searing fluid stripped flesh from his face and neck.

Scott pushed his head deeper, ignoring the pain in his own hand as the boiling liquid lapped around his wrist.

Others had seen the struggle now and a chorus of shouts and cheers rose from the other prisoners.

Scott, his face contorted madly, drove down with even greater force, dragging Draper off his feet.

The entire vat of soup toppled backwards, spraying up in all directions as the copper container hit the floor, spilling its load over the tiles.

Scott still had hold of Draper's hair. As he pulled the other man upright, he looked into his face. The flesh was red-raw, large portions of it hanging off the muscles where the incredible heat had stripped it away. Slivers of flesh hung like leprous wet tendrils from the blistered mess that had once been Draper's features. The other man was burbling incoherently, his eyes rolling upwards in their sockets, but he remained on his feet, supported by Scott's hand, until finally he felt the thunderous blow from the metal ladle once again. This time it was across his swollen face. His nose was shattered by the impact, blood bursting outwards, spattering his overalls, mixing with the soup and the slivers of skin.

The first of the warders crashed into Scott, knocking him to the ground.

The new clash was greeted by a fresh wave of shouts from the other inmates.

Another warder pinned him down, forcing the ladle from his grip. A third man pulled Draper away, sickened by the hideous sight of his scalded features. Blisters that had already risen on the face were liquescent and close to bursting.

Scott struggled in vain as two more officers dragged him to his feet and hauled him away.

Away from the bloodied image of Draper. Away from the deafening shouts of the other inmates.

Scott found that he too was shouting, screaming his rage not just at his captors and at Draper but at someone else.

At Plummer.

At Carol.

Consumed by rage unlike anything he'd ever experienced, he was dragged bellowing from the refectory.

Up above, on one of the catwalks, Governor Peter Nicholson had seen the entire tableau. He watched as Scott was dragged away, his face impassive.

He stood there for a moment, listening to the cacophony of sound crashing all around him, then walked off.

Eighty-three

To Finn it was as if they'd been sitting there for hours.

The Detective Sergeant fidgeted uncomfortably, his hand moving habitually towards the pack of cigarettes in his jacket pocket, but each time he glanced across the outer office his eyes were met by the sign which proclaimed NO SMOKING in large red letters.

Beside him, DI Gregson kept crossing and uncrossing his legs, occasionally rubbing the palms of his hands over his thighs. Every now and then he would glance at his watch, wondering how much longer they were going to be kept waiting.

334

The outer office of Police Commissioner Lawrence Sullivan was large and brightly decorated. There was a desk behind which sat Lawrence's secretary, an officious woman in her early forties with long auburn hair and, Finn had noticed, a terrific pair of legs. Gazing constantly at her legs had just about made the wait worthwhile, taking his mind off the task to come. She had already offered the men coffee; the DS had accepted but Gregson had refused. Now Finn was considering whether or not to ask for another cup, even if only to watch her sashay out of the office. His request was interrupted when a buzzer on the intercom sounded and she leant forward to press a button. She answered and got to her feet, approaching the two policemen. They also rose and followed her as she beckoned them.

She showed them into the Commissioner's office, then left.

Sullivan was a powerful, bull-necked specimen of a man who looked more like a refugee from a bare-knuckle ring than Commissioner of Police. He was in his mid-forties, his complexion ruddy, his nose flat against his face. His normally piercing eyes were almost hidden by thick eyebrows.

On his desk Gregson saw a number of framed photos. His wife, his children and one that looked strangely incongruous, considering Sullivan's demeanour; it showed the Commissioner cradling his baby son in his arms, feeding him with a bottle. Gregson thought he might have looked more at home using one hand to choke a goat.

The big man was reading a report of some kind when the other two policemen entered and did not look up.

'Sit down,' he said sharply.

They obeyed.

Sullivan glared at them immediately.

'You're lucky I'm not suspending both of you,' he

snarled. 'What the bloody hell were you playing at last night? Digging up a man's grave? I should have you locked up.'

'There wasn't time to obtain an exhumation order, sir,' Gregson said.

'Why?' Sullivan roared. 'Was the man you dug up leaving? What was so important it couldn't have waited one more day?'

'If you'll just listen, sir, I'll tell you,' Gregson said, aware of the acid glance Sullivan shot him. The DI waited a moment, wondering if his superior was going to interrupt again. When he didn't, Gregson began, keeping it as brief as he could. He mentioned the three killers, their victims, the suicides. Sullivan didn't move a muscle as he listened, his eyes never leaving Gregson as he talked about his visit to Whitely. How he'd seen the graves of men who, he knew for a fact, were actually dead and in the pathology room at New Scotland Yard itself. About four men who had died in Whitely in three years and now . . .

Sullivan held up a hand to silence him.

'Enough,' he said, rubbing his forehead with one thumb and forefinger. There was a long silence finally broken by the Commissioner himself. 'You *are* aware of what you're saying, Gregson?' he asked. 'You're asking me to believe that three men returned from the dead to re-enact their crimes? You're talking to me about zombies?' He smiled menacingly. 'If you're not out of this office in five seconds I'm going to have you both suspended. You'll be pounding a bloody beat by the end of the month.' The anger had returned to his voice.

'They didn't return from the dead,' Gregson said defiantly. 'Lawton, Bryce and Magee never died in the first place. They each committed suicide after re-enacting their crimes.'

'They were all in prison, you said yourself you saw their graves,' Sullivan reminded him.

'The men who committed those murders recently *were* Lawton, Bryce and Magee. There is no mistake,' the DI insisted. 'As I said, they never died in prison. Their deaths were faked. Just like the death of Gary Lucas. Someone went to a lot of trouble to make out that Lucas died of a heart attack inside Whitely. A weighted coffin was buried in that cemetery at Norwood to make it look convincing.'

'So where's Lucas?' Sullivan asked.

'We don't know yet.'

'And, more importantly, why would anyone want to fake his death? Are you trying to tell me there's some kind of conspiracy going on?' Sullivan got to his feet. 'Four murderers are pronounced dead, headstones are erected for them, and they're still alive? Why would anyone want to do that?' he continued. 'But you're not just implying that their deaths were faked, you're trying to tell me they escaped from Whitely. Four killers over the last three years escape from one of Britain's biggest maximum security prisons and nobody hears about it.' He turned on Gregson angrily. 'For God's sake, man, do you *really* know how ridiculous that sounds?'

'Then *you* explain the weighted coffin, sir,' Gregson said defiantly.

'I don't have to explain it,' Sullivan told him. 'I'm not the one who dug it up. As I said, you're both lucky I'm not suspending you.' He looked at Finn, too, and the DS blenched and lowered his gaze.

'There was no corpse in that coffin,' Gregson said.

'Then it must be buried somewhere else,' Sullivan said dismissively. 'I suggest you find out where. I also suggest you keep these *revelations* to yourself until you have more evidence to back them up.'

'How much more fucking evidence do we need?' snapped the DI.

'More than a *fucking* weighted coffin,' Sullivan bellowed, the two men holding each other's gaze. 'Now get out of here.' He motioned towards the door.

Gregson and Finn rose. The DS was only too happy to leave. His companion hesitated a moment.

'Lucas will kill again, sir, I'm sure of it,' the DI announced.

'Gary Lucas is dead,' Sullivan pronounced with an air of finality.

'No, he isn't,' Gregson said. 'Lucas is alive and I'm going to find him.'

Eighty-four

He could feel his hand throbbing.

Scott sat on the floor of the cell looking at the raw flesh, wincing as he touched it. It was beginning to blister in places, large pustules rising on the pink skin. At the time he'd felt nothing. Even when he'd forced Draper's head into the boiling soup he'd felt no pain. All he'd felt was the furious pleasure of being able to inflict agony on his tormentor. For all he knew Draper could be dead. A slight smile touched Scott's lips. So what if he was? What could they do to him? What more could they threaten him with? He was destined to spend the rest of his life inside; how else could they punish him? *Fuck them.*

Fuck the law.

Fuck Draper.

Fuck Plummer.

Plummer.

He clenched his fists as he thought of his boss. The act of closing his hand causing him pain, but he seemed not to mind it. One of the blisters on his palm burst, spilling its clear fluid over his skin.

Fuck Carol.

That treacherous, lying, spineless little whore.

He closed his eyes and sucked in an angry breath through clenched teeth.

Carol.

He hated her.

The vision of her came into his mind.

He wanted her.

Just to see her would be enough. For a few fleeting seconds.

To touch her.

To kill her.

He whispered her name.

Fucking slag.

The sound of the key in the lock startled him. He looked up to see the door opening, a shape silhouetted in the doorway. The solitary cell was tiny, less than six feet square, containing just a mattress and a slop bucket. Scott banged against the bucket as he hauled himself onto the mattress, trying to see who his visitor was. It was dark inside the cell and the light from the corridor outside dazzled him momentarily, obscuring the features of his visitor. As the door closed the light inside the cell went on. Scott looked up at the man but was none the wiser.

'They'll stick another five years on your sentence for what you did to Draper,' Nicholson told him.

Scott sneered.

'What's five more years on top of life?' he grunted.

'You would have been out in fifteen with good behaviour. Now you'll be an old man when they let you out.'

'What difference does it make to you? Who are you, anyway?'

Nicholson introduced himself.

'And, by the way,' he added. 'It makes no difference to me at all when and *if* you get out. You can rot in here for all *I* care.'

'So why the visit?' Scott wanted to know.

'Do you want to spend the rest of your life in here?'

'That's a fucking stupid question. What do *you* think?'

'I think that you'd settle for another six months in here instead of another twenty years,' Nicholson said cryptically. 'But there are risks.'

Scott looked vague.

'If I told you there was a possibility you could be out of here in six months, would you be interested?'

Six months is too long.

Scott looked wary.

'How?' he demanded.

'Would you be interested?' Nicholson persisted.

'Tell me how.'

Nicholson banged on the door and a warder opened it. He turned to leave.

'Tell me,' snarled Scott, getting to his feet, moving towards the Governor.

'Remember, there are risks,' Nicholson said as he stepped out of the cell. The door was slammed and locked. Scott was left with his face pressed against the metal.

'I don't care about the risks,' he shouted, banging his fist against the steel door. He struck it again, ignoring the pain as more of the blisters burst. Blood began to dribble down his arm. He pounded for long moments.

'I don't care,' he whispered breathlessly, but there was no one to hear his words.

He sank slowly to the floor of the cell and lay there gazing at the ceiling.

Eighty-five

There was always one.

David Lane muttered to himself as he rang the bell and the bus pulled away, passing Kensington Market on the right.

Always one who wanted to sit upstairs. Always one who ensured that he, as conductor, would be forced to climb the bloody stairs. At the beginning of a shift he didn't mind; he'd happily bound up and down the stairs to collect fares. But today he could hardly manage to walk from one end of the bus to the other, let alone up to the top deck. He'd pulled a muscle in his thigh playing football the previous Sunday and it was giving him a lot of pain. He'd thought about calling in sick, but he had actually received a phone call asking if he'd work a double shift as someone *else* had called in to report an illness. Consequently Lane had been working for almost ten hours, with just a break for lunch, and his leg was killing him. He moved among the passengers on the lower deck, cursing the single passenger who had chosen to sit above.

The bus was moving slowly, picking up at nearly every stop as it moved down Kensington Road towards Hyde Park Corner. Just the odd one or two extra passengers but they all, luckily, chose to sit downstairs.

Except the one bloke who'd got on at the earlier stop.

Lane massaged the top of his thigh gently as he waited

for an elderly woman to find her bus pass. Perhaps he was getting too old to be dashing about every Sunday morning. He was approaching thirty-three and his wife had told him he should be taking it easier now. But what the hell, he enjoyed playing, despite the fact that he'd picked up half a dozen niggling little knocks since Christmas. And his pub team were doing well in the league; he didn't want to forsake them now. Anyway, thirty-three was hardly an age to think about 'taking things easy'. Plenty of time for that when he got old. He smiled as he thought of his wife's concern. Michelle was always worrying about him. The long hours he worked, how little sleep he sometimes got. His musings were interrupted as the old girl found her bus pass and presented it to him. He smiled and handed it back to her, steadying himself as the bus came to a halt and two passengers got off. He rang the bell and continued collecting fares, making his way to the back of the bus, pausing at the bottom of the stairs. As they passed Hyde Park Corner he began to climb.

The pulled muscle in his thigh stiffened as he moved higher and it was with something akin to relief that he finally reached the top deck.

The man was sitting at the front, gazing out at the lights of London, oblivious to Lane's presence. The conductor moved towards him, using the backs of seats as support as the bus lurched on into Piccadilly.

'Fares, please,' called Lane. But still the man didn't turn, didn't even move to reach for money.

He continued staring out of the front window as if mesmerised by the lights, glancing to his left as they passed The Hard Rock Cafe.

'Fares, please,' Lane repeated more loudly as he drew level with the man.

'Where to, mate?' he asked, shifting his weight onto his other leg.

The man didn't answer.

Perhaps he was deaf, Lane wondered. He was in his mid-thirties, his hair short, his face covered by a dark carpet of stubble. The collar of his jacket was pulled up around his neck and there were holes in the knees of his jeans. *Don't tell me you've got no fucking money.*

'Where do you want to go?' Lane said, more loudly.

The man looked at him, his eyes large, almost bulging in their sockets. Lane could smell the drink on him.

Piss-artist. Great, that was all he needed. He turned the wheel of his ticket machine and cranked out an eighty pence ticket. If this bloke was smashed then he wanted him off at the next stop.

'Eighty pence, please, mate,' Lane said.

The man nodded and reached into his pocket, fumbling beneath his jacket.

'Eighty pence,' he repeated.

He smiled and looked up at the conductor.

'If you've got no money . . .' Lane began.

'I've got no money,' the man said, grinning. 'I got this.'

He pulled the .357 Magnum free and pointed it at Lane.

'Have you got change?' asked Gary Lucas.

Then he fired.

Eighty-six

The roar of the pistol was deafening in such a confined space. The muzzle-flash briefly lit the interior of the bus upper deck as the Magnum spat out its deadly load.

Lucas fired from less than ten inches. The impact of

the heavy grain shell bent Lane double at the waist as the bullet tore easily through his abdominal muscles, destroying part of his lower intestine before erupting from his back, tearing away most of one kidney. A sticky flux of viscera spattered the shattered window behind him and he fell backwards. Lucas got to his feet and fired again at the fallen man, the second bullet powering into his face just below the left eye, punching in the cheekbone and staving in the entire left side of his head. The skull seemed to burst as the bullet exited, greyish-pink slops of brain carried in its wake.

Lucas turned and headed for the stairs, noticing that the bus had slowed down slightly.

He reached the running platform in time to see two of the other passengers rising, obviously having heard the shots from above. One of them, a woman in her early twenties, screamed as she saw Lucas raising the gun.

He fired, hitting her in the left shoulder, the bullet shattering her clavicle. Blood spurted into the air as he turned towards the other passengers. There were four of them.

He shot the older woman in the back of the head, watching gleefully as her grey hair turned red, her skull riven by the bullet. She pitched forward, slamming what was left of her head against the seat in front.

The bus veered to one side and Lucas cursed as his next shot missed its target. Instead it smashed through the window at the front, glass spraying in all directions. He fired again, his next shot hitting a man in the chest, caving in his sternum and bursting one lung.

Two passengers were left, a young couple at the front of the bus.

The youth was already advancing towards him, his face pale, while the girl screamed madly.

Lucas squeezed the trigger.

344

The hammer slammed down on an empty chamber.

Scarcely believing his luck, the youth ran at Lucas, crashing into him, knocking the gun from his hand. They both fell onto the running platform. However, despite his efforts, the youth was slightly built compared to Lucas and the older man fixed his hands around the younger man's neck, lifting his head up. He brought his knee up into the youth's groin and heard the grunt of pain.

His girlfriend was still screaming.

The bus lurched across the road and Lucas realised it was beginning to stop.

He rolled over, hurling the boy from him into the road, then scrambled to his feet, snatching up the .357. He flipped out the cylinder and pushed in fresh cartridges.

The bus had almost come to a halt now, the driver glancing behind him to see the madness on the bus.

The girl screamed once more, even as Lucas fired.

The bullet entered her open mouth, tore through the back of her throat and practically decapitated her as it pulverised sections of spinal cord. She dropped like a stone, blood spraying everywhere.

Lucas immediately turned to the driver and fired off three shots.

The first crashed through the glass partition and exploded from the front windscreen; the second hit the man in the back, squarely between the shoulder blades. The third took off most of the right side of his head. As his body went into spasm, the driver's right foot was forced down onto the accelerator, and suddenly the bus sped forward at incredible speed, crashing into a car and sending another spinning aside.

It flattened the traffic lights at the junction of Piccadilly and Berkeley Street, picking up speed as it roared towards the front of the Ritz Hotel. The blue-uniformed doormen ran fearfully from the oncoming juggernaut, which bore down on the hotel entrance with the dead driver slumped over the wheel.

Lucas shouted in triumph.

Guests and others outside ran in all directions. The sound of screams filled the air.

Then the bus hit concrete.

There was a massive explosion as the vehicle went up, bursting into flames, portions of it flying across the street like massive lumps of shrapnel. Other pieces, propelled by the force of the blast, stove in great sections of the hotel's front. The revolving doors, with two guests inside, disintegrated as the bus engine was sent flying into them. The sound of shattering glass mingled with the deafening roar as the explosion shook Piccadilly. A searing reddish-white ball of fire blossomed out from the riven bus, a thick mushroom cloud of smoke rising from the inferno. Windows not shattered by the impact were forced inwards by the sheer power of the concussion blast.

Immediately, cars parked outside the hotel, caught in the detonation, began to burn. A Mercedes exploded with incredible ferocity, part of its roof spinning across the street and smashing through the plate glass windows of a chemist's. It was as if the first blast had set off a chain of smaller eruptions as half a dozen cars disappeared beneath shrieking balls of flame. Those running for cover were lifted off their feet by the shock waves; some were hit by flying glass. There were people lying all over the road and pavements, cars immobile as their drivers scrambled to escape the inferno that had filled the road and engulfed the Ritz.

In the shattered, blazing wreckage of the bus lay Gary Lucas, flames slowly devouring his skin, blistering lips still frozen in what looked like a grin.

Eighty-seven

Scott was waiting when the cell door was opened. He dutifully followed the two warders, walking briskly between them, his eyes occasionally straying to right or left as he heard voices behind the thick steel of the doors.

The trio marched along one of the catwalks around landing C and descended the iron steps carefully.

It felt good to be able to move about again after the cramped conditions of solitary. As the three men reached the exercise yard, Scott sucked in deep breaths of air. The sky above was the colour of wet concrete but he didn't care. Anything was better than the cold, insipid yellow walls of his cell.

Life.

He sucked in another lungful of air, remembering his conversation with Nicholson.

Risks. What kind of risks?

He didn't care. There was a chance of escape, perhaps. A chance to get away from this place. To return to London.

To Plummer.

To Carol.

He marched faster as they drew near the hospital wing. Despite himself, Scott felt a shiver of fear run along his spine.

Was the means of release within that gaunt edifice? And, if so, what form did it take?

Release.

He clung to the word like a dying man clings to life.

The trio entered the building, Scott recoiling from the pungent odour of disinfectant. He was led down a long corridor. At an office door one of his escort knocked and was told to enter.

Scott waited, glancing at the other warder. He remained impassive. Finally Scott was ushered in, the first warder hesitating inside the door.

'You can leave,' said Dr Robert Dexter.

'He's dangerous,' the warder insisted.

'Wait outside,' Dexter said, and the uniformed man left reluctantly. He waited until the door was closed, then motioned for Scott to be seated.

'Do you know who I am?' Dexter asked.

'Should I?' Scott enquired.

Dexter smiled thinly.

'No, I suppose not.' He introduced himself quickly. 'And you are James Scott.' He had a file open before him. 'A convicted murderer.'

'I didn't kill those men . . .' Scott began.

'That's as maybe, but as far as the law is concerned you're guilty. You're going to spend the rest of your life inside.'

Life.

Dexter looked at the file, even though he already knew the contents well enough.

'You lived alone; you have no family. No wife. No children,' he said quietly. 'No one.'

Scott regarded him coldly.

'Nobody to miss you,' Dexter continued.

'Try telling me something I *don't* know,' Scott snapped. 'You seem to know such a lot about me. Who the hell are you? A doctor? Big deal. What's that got to do with me?'

'More than a doctor, Scott. A surgeon. I specialise in disorders of the mind. God alone knows there are

348

enough in this place.' He smiled thinly, but it faded quickly.

'I still don't understand what this has got to do with me,' Scott told him. 'I couldn't give a fuck if you're a brain surgeon or a gynaecologist. Perhaps you'd be better off if you were. There are plenty of cunts in here, most of them wearing uniforms. Why should it matter to me?'

'The same way it mattered to the five men before you. Four of them were released from here. Four convicted murderers, like you, allowed back into society. Most had only served a year or two of their sentence.'

Scott sat forward.

'They were *just* like you,' Dexter continued. 'Alone. They had no one. That's why we chose them. The same way we've chosen you. They knew of the risks and they accepted them.'

'Nicholson said something about risks. What did he mean?' Scott wanted to know.

'The operation always carries a risk . . .'

'What fucking operation?' Scott snapped.

'The insertion, into the forebrain, of a tiny electronic device. Once it's placed there, after a few months you'll be released.'

Scott sucked in a deep breath. His mouth felt dry, and when he tried to lick his lips he found that his tongue was also as dry as parchment.

'No one except the Governor, myself and my immediate staff know about this. It's up to you whether or not you decide to go through with the operation, but think about the possibility. Release.'

'What about the law? They'll know I'm gone, that I've escaped.'

'But you won't have escaped, you'll have been *released*. And there'll be no police interference. All the arrangements will be taken care of here.'

349

Scott stroked his chin thoughtfully.

'You said you experimented on five men, but you said *four* were released. What happened to the other one?'

'He died. There were complications, the risks that Nicholson mentioned.'

'What happened to him?'

'A massive brain tumour developed where the device was implanted. There was nothing I could do to save him, but he'd known about the possibility of failure from the beginning. It was a chance he was willing to take.' Dexter eyed the other man coldly. 'Are *you* willing to take that chance, Scott? Six months at the most and you'll be able to leave here. Six months. Not life.'

Life.

'If I agree, how soon can you operate?' he wanted to know.

'Tomorrow.'

Six months, Scott thought. Six fucking months and then out. Back to London. Back to Plummer.

Back to Carol. The bitch.

Six months.

Fuck it. He wouldn't wait that long.

He looked directly at Dexter, his eyes unblinking, his voice even.

'Do it,' he said quietly.

Eighty-eight

'Could there have been a mistake?'

Police Commissioner Lawrence Sullivan looked up from his desk at Phillip Barclay.

The pathologist shook his head.

'The body that was pulled out of the wreckage *was* Gary Lucas,' Barclay confirmed. 'The dental records matched and so did the fingerprints.' The pathologist sighed. 'And, like Lawton, Bryce and Magee, I found that Lucas had also been suffering from a massive brain tumour. There was enough left of the head to ascertain that.'

Sunshine was pouring through the windows of Sullivan's office. Gregson could feel the warming rays on his arms as he sat looking at his superior.

Now tell me I'm wrong, you smug bastard, he thought.

'What were the final figures on dead and injured?' Sullivan wanted to know.

DS Finn flipped open his notebook.

'Twelve dead – that includes Lucas – and twenty-four injured,' he announced.

'I suppose you think this supports *your* idea, Gregson?' said the Commissioner.

'It seems hard to argue with the facts now, sir, I would have thought,' he said triumphantly.

'The facts, according to you, being that Bryce, Lawton, Magee and Lucas didn't die inside Whitely. Their deaths were, for some unknown reason, faked. Correct?'

'How can you argue with the evidence in front of you, sir?' Gregson wanted to know.

'I can argue with it because *this*,' he held up a blue, bound file, 'is the report of a Government committee chaired by an MP called Bernard Clinton. It seems that he and three of his colleagues visited Whitely not long ago to investigate the overcrowding there. He doesn't mention anything unusual. In fact, he compliments the administration there for their work in trying to alleviate overcrowding.' Sullivan dropped the file onto his desk with a thud. 'No mention of anything like a conspiracy.

351

No mention of faking the deaths of murderers, then releasing them.'

'Well, I don't expect he was shown the process, sir,' snarled Gregson.

'What process, for Christ's sake?' Sullivan demanded. 'Four men died in Whitely. Their crimes were imitated . . .'

'The crimes were re-enacted by their original perpetrators,' Gregson interrupted angrily. 'What the fuck is it going to take to make you realise what's going on?'

Finn looked warily at his companion, then at their superior.

'What do you want, Gregson?' Sullivan asked.

'I want exhumation orders for those other three men,' the DI said flatly. 'I want to go into Whitely. I want those graves dug up. I want to see that Lawton, Bryce and Magee are in the coffins they're supposed to be in.'

'You're insane,' Sullivan hissed.

'Just like I was insane to dig up Lucas? If I'm crazy then so is Finn, because he saw that empty coffin. So is Barclay, because he's told you that it's Lucas we've got downstairs, just like it's the others we've got down there keeping him company. I'm beginning to think it's *you* who's crazy, sir. You refuse to believe what's right in front of your nose.'

'There'll be a dismissal notice in front of *your* nose if you ever speak to me like that again, Gregson. Do you understand?' Sullivan rasped. 'I've seen the evidence, I've heard the facts but I can't issue exhumation orders for those other three men.'

'Why *not*?' Gregson asked, exasperated.

'Because this isn't just police business, it's political,' Sullivan said. 'What the hell do you think the Press would make of it? Police officers, digging up graves in a prison to find out whether or not the men supposedly buried there are really dead? There's a Home Office report testifying to the efficiency of Whitely Prison and *you're* trying to tell me there's a conspiracy going on there with the full knowledge of the Governor.'

'At least consider the facts, sir,' Gregson said, leaning forward. 'We have irrefutable proof that the four men lying in the pathology lab supposedly died anything up to a year before they actually *did*. We know their identities. We know the death of at least one of them was faked. They all duplicated their original crimes, they all committed suicide. Every one of the four was suffering from a massive brain tumour at the time of his death, and every one had been an inmate at Whitely Prison.'

Sullivan exhaled deeply, sitting back in his chair, massaging the bridge of his nose between his thumb and forefinger. He looked at the pictures of his wife and kids on the corner of his desk, reaching across to straighten one of them slightly. When he spoke again his tone was softer.

'Gregson, I *have* considered the facts,' he said. 'But I've also considered something *you* obviously haven't. Namely, the consequences. Have you stopped to think, once, of the ramifications involved if you're right?' He looked at the DI whose gaze never faltered. 'Christ alone knows, there's enough public concern about what goes on in our prisons at the moment; can you imagine what would happen if you were proved to be right? A conspiracy of officials at one of the country's leading maximum security prisons? As I said, it isn't just a police matter. It's a question of politics, too. Politics and ethics.'

'I'm sure the people that Lucas and the others killed would be impressed if they were alive to hear you, sir,' Gregson said acidly.

'I can't sign those exhumation orders,' the Commissioner said wearily.

'Why not?' snapped Gregson. 'It's our only way of finding out once and for all what's going on. How many more times has this got to happen before you'll agree?'

'Appeals to my conscience won't work,' Sullivan told him.

'I'm not appealing to your conscience, I'm appealing to your common sense.'

There was a heavy silence, finally broken by Sullivan.

'You're so sure you're right,' he began.

'The evidence . . .'

Sullivan cut him short.

'I know all about the bloody evidence,' he interrupted, holding up a hand to silence the DI. 'But just suppose, for one second, that you're wrong.'

'Then I'll resign,' Gregson said flatly.

'You and all the rest of us, too,' Sullivan said, looking around the room. 'You still don't know *why* the murderers are being released again.'

'And the only way I'll do that is by getting inside Whitely and seeing inside those graves,' the DI said.

'You could be wrong,' Sullivan repeated.

'It's a chance I'm willing to take.'

The Commissioner rubbed both hands over his face.

'Well, I'm *not* willing to take that chance,' he said.

Gregson got to his feet angrily.

'That means you won't sign the papers for the magistrate's order?' he rasped.

'Not until I've thought about it more.'

'How much longer is that going to be?' Gregson wanted to know.

'As long as it takes,' Sullivan told him. 'Now get out.'

As the three men filed out of the office Sullivan called to the DI.

'You want an answer?' he said, reflectively. 'You can have one. In forty-eight hours.'

'Forty-eight hours could be too long,' Gregson snapped.

'You don't have a choice. I'll give you my answer then.'

Gregson nodded, closing the office door behind him.

Sullivan turned his chair to face the sun, looking out over London, the beginnings of a headache throbbing at his temples.

Outside, the sun had been obscured by a thick bank of dark clouds.

Sullivan closed his eyes, fingertips pressed together beneath his chin as if he were praying.

It seemed most appropriate.

Eighty-nine

Pain.

Pain like he'd never experienced before.

Jesus, it felt as if his head were going to explode. As if someone were filling it steadily with molten lead, his veins swelling inexorably.

Make it stop.

James Scott tried to open his eyes but even that simple act seemed beyond him. Whatever he did, it brought more pain.

For fuck's sake stop it.

He clenched his fists, the veins on his arms standing out like cords.

It was into one of these bulging veins that the needle had been pushed, puncturing the throbbing vessel as if it were some kind of bloated worm.

Scott hardly felt it. The massive agony that filled his head eclipsed everything else. He groaned softly, the sound muffled. Again he tried to open his eyes and, again, found it impossible. There was only darkness. Was he blind? Sightless and voiceless, only his pain for company? What was happening to him?

'Scott.'

He heard the voice close by. Whispered so close he could feel the breath on his ear.

'Scott. Can you hear me?'

He tried to speak but no sound would come; his throat felt as if it had been scoured with steel wool. He croaked something inaudible, wondering if his ability to speak had gone the way of his sight. *And all the time there was the pain*.

'If you can hear me, move the fingers of your right hand,' the voice said.

Scott tried but couldn't. Paralysis, blindness and an inability to speak. He only needed deafness and he had a full set.

'Move your fingers,' the voice urged.

Again he tried, this time managing it.

Christ, that pain was still there, screaming inside his head.

'Good,' said the voice.

Scott moved his lips but still no sound would come. He opened and closed his mouth like a goldfish.

'I've given you 50cc of morphine,' the voice told him. 'That should help the pain quickly.'

Scott was sure his head was going to explode. He was beginning to wish it *would*; at least it would mean an end to this pain.

This unbearable, fucking pain.

He clenched his fists, not realising at first that he'd managed to move his hands.

'That's good,' the voice assured him.

Scott lay still, his breath coming in shallow gasps. He

was aware of the pain subsiding slightly; perhaps the morphine was working. His skull still felt as if it were full of boiling steel, but the agony was diminishing by the second. He tried to swallow, but it felt as if someone had filled his mouth and throat with chalk. He could only make a strangled hissing sound.

'Drink,' the voice said and Scott felt the cold edge of a beaker against his lips. Drops of water splashed onto his tongue and down his throat. He gasped.

The pain was still there but it was easing off now.

He was still blind, though.

It took him a moment or two to realise that his eyes and, indeed, most of his head were covered by bandages. More water spilled into his mouth. Some of it ran down his chin, to be wiped away by a gentle hand.

'You can hear me?' the voice said. It was a statement rather than a question.

'Yes,' Scott croaked hoarsely.

'The operation is over. You've been unconscious for ten hours.'

It felt like ten years.

'Was it successful?' Scott asked, a renewed stab of pain jolting him.

'You're alive, aren't you?' Dexter said. 'I won't know *how* successful for a while yet.'

'How long is *a while*?'

'You must be patient. All I want you to do now is rest.'

'Take the bandages off my eyes,' Scott said quietly.

Dexter gently cut through the gauze until he revealed the two cotton wool pads covering Scott's eyes. He lifted each one away with a pair of small forceps, noticing how dark the lower lids were.

'Open them slowly,' he instructed.

Scott tried but couldn't.

The pain throbbed inside his head once more.

'I can't,' he hissed.

'Yes, you can,' Dexter insisted, reaching for a piece of cotton wool. He soaked it in liquid and gently rubbed Scott's lids. When he tried again he managed to open his eyes. The light caused the pain to intensify and he snapped them shut quickly. After a moment or two, however, he opened them again, the lids unfurling like ancient roller blinds. He could make out Dexter's blurred shape. He blinked to clear his vision, his eyes still narrowed.

The image sharpened.

'Can you see?' Dexter wanted to know.

'Yes,' said Scott, a note of relief in his voice.

'Rest now,' the doctor told him. 'I'll be back to check on you in a couple of hours.' He turned and walked away, his footsteps echoing inside the ward. He disappeared through a door at the end and Scott was left alone.

He looked slowly to his left and right, the movement of his eyes causing him pain but nothing as intolerable as that he'd experienced upon waking. He saw that the ward comprised just six beds; only his was occupied. The windows were large, arched and equipped with shutters that were pulled shut. It was difficult to tell whether it was night or day beyond them. A single light in the ceiling above provided the only source of illumination. Scott stared at it until his eyes hurt and the throbbing pain in his skull began again.

Stop the pain.

As he lay there with his eyes closed it lessened and he let out a sigh of relief.

He was tired; his eyelids felt as if they'd been weighted.

Sleep.

If he slept, though, he had no guarantee the pain would not creep over him again like some malignant invader.

There was always the morphine.
Sleep. Pain. Morphine.
A simple equation.
He closed his eyes.
He slept.

'Scott.'
He heard the voice, perhaps in a dream.
'Scott.'
More insistent now. A hand on his arm.
Get out of my dream.
He opened his eyes.
Pain. Not as bad as before.
He blinked hard, trying to make out the features so close to his own.
'It's me, Porter,' the other man said, his voice low.
Scott recognised his cell-mate.
'What are you doing here?' he said, his throat dry. He reached for the water on the table beside him but couldn't get it. Porter put the beaker in his hand and helped him drink. 'How did you get in here?' Scott persisted.
'Laundry, remember? I was told to bring in some clean sheets, leave them here.' He looked at his cell-mate. 'What the fuck have they done to you?'
'Listen to me.' Scott gripped the other man's wrist with almost unnatural strength for someone in his weakened state. 'I need your help. I've got to get out of here.'
'Out of where?' Porter said scornfully.
'Out of Whitely.'
'You couldn't get out of fucking bed.'
'With your help I can,' Scott hissed, wincing as he felt the stab of pain in his skull.
No, please, not that again.
'Help me, Porter.'

'How?' the other man asked. 'You look as if you're ready for the fucking morgue.'

'I'm not going to any morgue,' Scott snarled, his eyes blazing. 'I'm getting out and you're going to help me. Now listen to me. There isn't much time.'

Porter sat on the edge of the bed as Scott began to speak.

Rain clouds were filling the skies, hastening the onset of evening.

It would be dark in three hours.

Ninety

The needle slid easily into his vein and Scott looked down at it, welcoming the morphine as it was pumped into his system.

Anything to stop the pain.

Dexter swabbed the puncture and fixed a small plaster over it.

'You should be all right for the rest of the night now,' he assured Scott. 'One of the orderlies will be around if the pain gets too bad, but I've told them not to disturb you until the morning.'

Scott sucked in a deep breath.

Dexter reached into his pocket and pulled out a pen-light which he shone first into Scott's left eye then his right, watching the pupils react accordingly. He nodded to himself.

'You should be fine until the morning,' he said. He turned to leave, pausing at the door to take one final look at Scott. He walked out, leaving the patient alone.

Take it easy now. Take your time.

He glanced at the wall clock.

8.36 p.m.

The pain in his head was just a dull ache now, thanks to the morphine. He wondered how long it would stay like that.

Forget the pain.

He closed his eyes.

Silence.

Scott awoke in a stillness broken only by the spattering of rain against the windows. Through the gloom he could see the clock.

11.06 p.m.

He blinked hard, feeling a slight pain in the roof of his skull. He turned his head slowly from side to side; the pain was never very far away. Yellow light spilled beneath the door from the room beyond. He could hear no sounds of movement from the other side of the door.

Scott slowed his breathing and then, with infinite slowness, raised his head from the pillow.

The dull ache remained but did not develop suddenly into the searing pain he had come to know so well. For that, at least, he was grateful. He propped himself up on one elbow and rose a few more inches, swinging his feet out of bed, touching the cold floor with his toes.

He sat upright.

No pain.

Steadying himself, he prepared to stand, aware of the weakness in his legs.

He stood up.

A wave of dizziness hit him; for a moment he thought he was going to collapse. The room spun madly around. He shot out a hand to steady himself, almost knocking over the jug of water on the bedside table. It teetered precariously for a second but remained upright. He leant against the bed, closing his eyes, waiting for the dizziness to pass. He stood up more slowly this time, pressing each of his feet in turn hard onto the floor.

All right, hot-shot. Now let's see you walk.

He took a faltering step, afraid that the dizziness would return, or worse than that, the pain.

Neither happened.

He walked with relative ease towards the door, turned and walked back again. He repeated his movements, still aware of the silence beyond the closed door.

He had to know if there was anyone there.

From what Porter had told him, he knew he had to get into the adjacent room.

Porter.

Scott hoped he'd managed to fulfil *his* part of the plan. Not that it would matter if he had or not, if Scott couldn't get into the next room.

He reached down for the door-knob; his hand rested on it.

If the orderly was there he would want to know why Scott was out of bed.

If he wasn't, he couldn't be far away.

If . . .

Scott glanced down at the door-knob again.

He swallowed hard.

Still silence from the other side.

He hesitated, looking across at the bedside table. To the jug of water.

Scott turned and headed back, sitting on the edge of the bed. He waited a moment then pushed the metal jug. It landed with a loud clang on the floor.

No one came running to see what was happening.

The door didn't open.

Scott got to his feet and crossed to the door, this time turning the knob immediately. He peered out into the room beyond. It was empty but for a small desk and some cupboards round the walls.

On the corner of the desk was a steaming mug of tea.

Scott realised that the orderly who'd left it would be back to claim it.

He had to move fast.

The laundry chute was directly opposite him, a hole in the wall about three feet square.

Scott closed the door behind him and made for the chute, clambering in feet first, feeling the cold metal against his back when the surgical gown opened. He supported his weight against the frame of the chute, aware of the dull ache in his skull.

Please don't let it be a long drop.

He let go of the frame.

His weight carried him faster than he would have liked; in seconds, he found himself coming to the bottom of the chute. He went hurtling off the metal lip and sprawled on a pile of dirty sheets, rolling over once.

He grunted in pain as he hit the bottom and flopped over onto his back, the pain in his head intensifying for a moment.

It was almost pitch black in the laundry room, the only light coming from a furnace that stood in the centre. It was used to burn any linen too soiled to be used again. The small chamber was lit by a hellish red glow from the furnace's mouth.

Scott got to his feet, touching his head tentatively, aware of the stench around him.

The sheets he was lying on were smeared with excrement. Scott grunted and dragged himself upright, wiping the reeking mess from his hands with a clean portion of the sheet. Still, they had served their purpose to break his fall. As he looked around he could hear the low rumble of the furnace. The stone floor beneath his feet was warm.

Scott squinted in the gloom and finally found what he sought.

The laundry cart was there, just as Porter had promised.

Scott crossed quickly to it, rummaging through the dirty linen inside.

He found the prison overall.

Moving swiftly he pulled off the surgical gown and tossed it aside. Climbing into the overalls, he held on to the side of the cart momentarily as he felt a particularly violent stab of pain inside his head.

Not now.

It passed. He continued searching through the cart, ignoring the stench that rose from its contents.

His hand closed over the torch and he pulled it free. Ficking it on, he tested the beam in the gloom of the furnace room.

At the bottom of the cart he found the knife.

It was fully ten inches long; Porter must have taken it from the kitchen. Scott ran his thumb gently along the edge of the blade, feeling its razor sharpness. Satisfied, he slid it into his belt.

The door of the furnace room opened out onto one of the prison's two courtyards. As Scott peered into the night he could see search-lights moving slowly back and forth over the open, cobbled area.

A little to his left was the drain cover, two feet square and rusted. He knew he must remove it.

He stood there for moments, trying to estimate how long he had between the light passing. It was no more than ten seconds.

The beam swept by and Scott hurried across to the cover. He dug his fingers inside and pulled.

It wouldn't shift.

The light was turning, sweeping back towards him.

He pulled at the lid again.

Jesus, it was heavy.

Five seconds before the light returned.

He pulled.

Pain filled his head as he grunted with the effort.

Four seconds.

It moved a fraction.

Three.

Scott dropped the lid again and scurried back inside the furnace room as the light swept by.

He watched it disappear in a wide arc then tried the lid for the second time.

It moved a fraction more, the rusty metal scraping against the stone.

Come on. Come on.

The light was beginning its movement back towards him.

Scott lifted, his muscles screaming with the effort, the pain in his head intensifying.

Nine seconds away.

The drain lid was coming away.

Eight.

He lifted it free with a final triumphant grunt and shone the torch down into the black maw below.

Seven.

The powerful beam picked out a rusted metal ladder. Far below, the light reflected on the surface of a stream of filthy water.

Six.

Scott swung himself into the outlet, climbing down the first few steps. Gripping the metal grille in one hand, he hauled it back into place behind him.

Five.

Jesus, the pain.

Four.

The grille dropped into place above him.

Three.

He clambered down the next few rungs as the light swept over. Scott hugged the ladder, his breath coming in gasps. He shone the torch below surprised how far down the shaft went. The old sewers must be a good seventy or eighty feet below ground. Scott swallowed hard, then began to descend.

Ninety-one

The stench was almost unbearable in the tunnels but Scott pressed on, wading through filthy water that lapped as high as his knees. The walls on either side of him were crumbling, pieces of rotten stone falling away as he touched them. Occasionally his hand encountered patches of the green slime that coated the subterranean passages like putrid mucus. It was like walking through the gangrenous veins of some sleeping giant, paddling in stagnant blood.

Scott realised that the sewer tunnels were so full because of the rain that was still falling. The knowledge hardly made his journey any more palatable, all the same. He would stop every few hundred yards to catch his breath and try to get his bearings. The tunnels usually ran straight, but when he reached the junction of two he had to be sure he was travelling in the right direction; otherwise he would merely double back on himself and end up wandering these cavernous halls until he collapsed.

There was one such junction up ahead.

Scott leant against a wall, feeling the slippery slime soaking through his overall. He ignored the cold and pointed the beam ahead. It cut through the tenebrous blackness, picking out something that glinted dully in the luminosity.

About fifty yards ahead there was a grille, the steel not yet rusted and crumbling like most of the metalwork down there. It must have been recently fitted, he assumed. Behind the grille the tunnel was much narrower. At present Scott could walk without needing to stoop; if he'd been able to get past the grille he would have been forced to crawl, such was the narrowness of the outlet beyond.

He moved off to his right, grunting as he felt a renewed stab of pain inside his head.

He tried to quicken his pace, but the water rushing around his knees prevented that. He fought his way on through the reeking flow.

Again he paused, sucking in deep lungfuls of the vile air, coughing at its rankness. The spasm set off a dull and persistent ache in his skull. He closed his eyes for a moment, touching one hand tentatively to his bandaged head.

When he brought his hand away he noticed, with horror, that there was blood on his fingers.

'Oh God,' he whispered, the sound amplified by the confines of the tunnel.

He must have opened up the wound when he fell from the laundry chute, he guessed. He'd have to be careful to keep it clean. If any of the dirt down in the sewer got into it, God alone knew what would happen.

Scott pushed on, reaching another tunnel junction.

Left, right or straight on?

He shone the torch first one way, then the other.

The right hand tunnel was blocked about twenty feet on by a new stone wall.

He chose to go straight on, trying to get some kind of mental picture of where he was. He guessed he was below D Wing by now. He couldn't be that far from the wall, surely? It felt as if he'd been walking for hours. His body was quivering from the cold and the pain inside his skull was getting worse.

Perhaps it was the cold breeze blowing into his face which . . .

The realisation hit him like a thunderbolt.

Cold breeze blowing into his face.

The breeze had to be coming from up ahead.

He'd passed beneath many outlets above, but had felt no cold air coming through them because of the depth of the tunnels. But now the wind was blowing *into* him. He *must* be heading in the right direction. He pushed on, his throat dry, his head throbbing but the thought of escape now giving him added energy.

Escape.

It had a beautiful ring to it.

He even managed a smile.

Ahead of him there was a loud splash.

Then another.

Something had dropped into the water.

Scott shone the torch around and it picked out two pinpricks of yellow light.

Eyes.

Staring back at him.

There was another splash, closer this time.

He felt something nudge his leg.

There were rats in the water.

The knowledge brought with it a stark and quite irrational terror that he found difficult to shake off. He moved forward more slowly now.

Close by him a furry shape scuttled along the low ledge that ran alongside the flowing effluent.

Scott moved away, his hand sliding into more of the noxious slime that coated the walls.

He moved as quickly as he could, the cold breeze now strong in his face.

Ahead, less than twenty feet away, he saw the grille.

Beyond it he could smell grass.

He tried to run, to reach the barrier more quickly, gripping it with both hands when he finally did. He could see through, out into the darkness of the night. He could see trees swaying, silhouetted against the swollen clouds that filled the sky. The stream of filth was now hardly over his boot tops. He tugged at the grille.

It remained firmly in place.

He tried again.

Still no luck. It was stuck fast, secured by six heavy screws which fixed it to the wall.

Scott pulled the knife from his belt and placed the blunt edge in one of the grooves on the screw-head. He turned it, putting all his strength into it, his teeth clenched.

He closed his eyes as he felt that all-too-familiar pain inside his skull.

The screw began to come free.

He turned it, twisting it the last quarter of an inch with his fingers. He dropped it into the water and set about the second one. Then the third.

Despite the cold wind he could feel the perspiration on his face as he worked to remove the screws.

The last one came free and he tugged the grille away from the wall, hardly feeling the pain as the steel cut into the palm of his hand. He tossed it aside and blundered out into the fresh air, almost slipping on the muddy ground. He breathed in the air. Clean air. Untainted by the stench of captivity.

The air that came with freedom.

He wondered if revenge would smell the same.

A brief image of Plummer flashed into his mind.

Then Carol.

He set off across the open ground towards the trees. Beyond it there was a road.

He would be well away before first light.

Free.

He ignored the pain in his head as best he could, but as he ran across the muddy ground a thought occurred to him.

The effects of the morphine were beginning to wear off.

And when it did, the pain would return.

Pain unlike anything he'd ever felt before.

Scott looked back over his shoulder, as if fearing he was being followed.

The prison seemed to be a part of the night itself, the huge walls apparently hewn from the solid blackness.

He ran on.

He knew what he must do now.

Ninety-two

The pain was returning.

Unchecked by pain-killers, it filled his skull more intensely as each moment passed.

Scott fell against a tree and leant there, slumped and dishevelled, trying to get his breath, trying to think about something other than the excruciating agony that was lancing through his head. He put both hands to his temples and felt the bandages there. He fancied he could feel his cranium swelling with each beat of his heart.

He had reached the road now. Looking back in the direction of Whitely, he could see that the prison had all but disappeared in the tenebrous blackness of night. Rain was falling heavily now, the cold droplets beating onto his head. He stumbled onto the tarmac and began walking, not even sure which direction he was heading. Scott didn't know how far the nearest town was but, he surmised, there must be a house of some kind in the vicinity. It was farming land around the prison. Surely there would be somewhere for him to seek shelter. He flicked off the torch and jammed it into his belt along with the long bladed knife, using both hands to wipe the rain from his face as he walked. Every step seemed an effort. And, with each contact he made with the ground, that searing pain would spear through his skull, making him wince, once almost making him topple over.

Make it stop.

He leant against one of the trees at the roadside, hoping the pain would subside. Then he pressed on, turning a bend in the road.

To his left, across a dark field, he saw some lights.

A house.

Just ahead of him was a wooden gate that opened onto an unguarded dirt tract. Scott assumed it led to the house. He could see rain falling in the puddles that had formed in the ruts of the track. As he tried to edge his way forward, avoiding the worst of the mud, one foot slipped in the slimy ooze and he sank up to his ankle in the clinging muck.

Cursing, he shook himself loose and prepared to trudge on towards the beckoning lights.

The approach of car headlamps made him duck back into the bushes.

The car, he guessed, was about a hundred yards off, its lights cutting a swathe through the gloom as it drew nearer.

It was moving slowly, the driver obviously taking care in the treacherous conditions.

Scott, his head throbbing, remained hidden in the sodden bushes.

If only he could stop it . . .

He touched the hilt of the carving knife almost unconsciously.

The car was less than fifty yards away now; soon the headlamps would pick him out.

He moved quickly, walking out into the road, lying down on the wet tarmac. It was an old trick but it was all he could think of.

He lay on his side, facing away from the car whose engine was now audible. His left arm was stretched out beneath his head, his right resting on his hip, close to the knife.

The pain filled his head as he lay there, rain beating against his pale face.

The car rounded the corner, its lights picking out his immobile form. He heard the driver slam on the brakes, the slight squeal of rubber as the car came to a slippery halt on the greasy surface. He lay there, rain soaking through his overalls, waiting.

Waiting.

The car was still where it had stopped, its lights bathing Scott in a cold white glow.

This wasn't right. The driver should have leapt out of his car. Instead, Scott could only assume that the man was still sitting behind the wheel wondering what to do.

Come on. Come on.

He heard a door open, heard a woman's voice in the

372

background saying something about being careful. Then he heard a man's voice too.

There were two of them in the car, perhaps more; he couldn't see from the position he was in.

He heard footsteps coming closer, hesitant and unsure.

His right hand slipped a couple of inches so that it was touching the hilt of the knife.

The footsteps came nearer. A shadow fell over him, the driver silhouetted in the powerful headlamps.

'I think he's alive,' the man called, moving nearer.

He could hear the engine of the car idling.

The man could only be a few feet from him now.

Scott heard more footsteps. Drawing closer.

Closer.

The man knelt beside him; Scott could even hear him breathing. He felt a hand on his shoulder, turning him gently on to his back.

'Oh, Christ,' murmured the man, noticing Scott's prison uniform, spotted as it was with blood and excrement, reeking of filth.

Scott's eyes snapped open and he found himself gazing into the terrified features of a man roughly his own age.

Scott struck out with his left hand, catching the man full in the face with a punch that broke his nose. He fell backwards, cracking his head on the concrete of the road, opening a gash on the back of his skull that immediately began oozing blood.

Scott was up in a second, hurdling the prone man, heading for the car.

He saw and heard the woman scream as she locked the passenger side door, then leant over to secure the driver's side of the Renault.

Scott grabbed the handle and tugged, managing to beat her to it.

She screamed again and tried to back away from him,

but he grabbed her by the hair and pulled her across the driver's seat, hurling her from the car into the wet bushes at the roadside. One of her high heels came off and she scraped her face on the branches as she fell, blood running from a cut on her cheek.

Scott slid behind the wheel, jamming the car into gear.

The man was rising, coming towards the car again, blood streaming from his nose.

Scott floored the accelerator and the car roared forward like a bullet.

It slammed into the man, hurling him into the air and sideways into the bushes where he landed on his back close to his companion, who screamed again as Scott roared away, exhaust fumes filling the air, mingling with the acrid stench of burned rubber.

The Renault hurtled off down the road, leaving the woman to crawl over to her injured companion.

Scott could see her in his rear-view mirror, sobbing helplessly as she sought to revive the man who, for all Scott knew, could have been dead. Come to think of it, the speed the car had been travelling when it hit him probably *would* have killed him. Scott took one more look in the rear-view mirror but the former occupants of the car were nowhere to be seen.

He put his foot down.

He knew he had to get out of this prison uniform and into some normal clothes. The journey back to London was going to be difficult enough without advertising where he'd just come from.

Back to London.

He gripped the wheel tightly.

Back to London.

He guessed it would take him about five or six hours. He should be there before morning.

Back to Plummer.

His head was throbbing mightily now, but there was a fearful determination etched on his face.

Back to Carol.

He glanced at his own reflection in the rear-view mirror and saw the bandages that covered the top of his head and most of his forehead. He slowed, stopped and tore most of them off leaving just the one that covered the wound of his operation.

The dashboard clock said 2.06 a.m.

The pain seemed to be getting worse.

Scott gripped the wheel more tightly. He must get out of these overalls.

But before that, there was something else he must do.

Ninety-three

There were two Scania trucks parked in the car park of the petrol station. Apart from the two juggernauts, Scott could see no other vehicles.

He drove past them once, trying to see into the cabins, but there was no sign of their drivers. He winced as the pain struck him again, even more forcefully, like a physical blow. The Renault went out of control momentarily but he brought it into line and drove on, slowing down as he reached the covered area that formed a canopy leading up to the door of the service station entrance.

There was one figure in a red overall inside the building. A man in his early twenties. Scott could see that he was reading a newspaper.

Scott parked the Renault around the corner and sat behind the wheel for a moment, waiting for the pain inside his head to diminish.

It didn't.

On shaking legs he forced himself out of the car, ensuring that the knife was hidden as he approached the double doors that led into the service area. Like many along motorways it sold not just books, papers and magazines but also food, drink and even clothing. Scott could see several pairs of jeans hanging up inside, as well as some shirts.

He approached the double doors and pulled at one.

They were locked.

The young man in the red overalls looked up and ran appraising eyes over Scott.

'Use the night window,' he called, indicating the small hatch where he sat.

Cursing under his breath, Scott ambled along to the window, reaching behind him once to touch the hilt of the carving knife.

The young man was looking intently at him, or, more to the point, at his clothes. The grey, blood-flecked, reeking prison overalls made Scott ridiculously conspicuous. He may as well have worn a day-glo sign on his chest proclaiming 'Escaped Convict'.

'What do you want?' the young man asked, his eyes constantly drawn to Scott's overalls.

'I need to use your toilet,' he said.

'We lock it at night. I'll have to give you the key,' the young man told him.

Scott nodded, watching as he retrieved a bunch of keys from the counter.

'I need some things too,' Scott said. 'I want to come inside.'

'Sorry, but it's company policy. This place has been

robbed too often in the past year or so. You tell me what you want and I'll get it for you.'

Scott gritted his teeth, both in pain and also frustration. Even if he could get the jeans, the shirt and the pain-killers he wanted, how the hell was he going to pay for them?

'The keys for the toilet,' said the young man, extending his hand, the keys lying on his palm.

Scott stepped back slightly, forcing the young man to extend his hand through the narrow gap at the bottom of the cash window.

'Take them,' said the attendant warily.

Scott looked deeply into his eyes, those bloodshot orbs blazing with intent.

He moved so quickly the youth had no chance to pull away.

Scott grabbed his arm just above the wrist, simultaneously yanking the youth forward, slamming his face into the glass with such force that it dazed him. Then, with his free hand, he pulled the knife from his belt and brought it down with terrifying force onto the young man's outstretched wrist.

The blow severed the hand with one cut.

The appendage fell to the ground, blood spurting from the torn arteries, jetting onto the forecourt as Scott held his victim up against the glass, gripping on above the stump of the wrist that was spewing crimson violently into the air. He jerked the boy forward again and again, each time slamming his head against the thick glass, until he also opened up a hairline cut along his scalp. The glass was smeared with crimson.

Scott continued to hang on to the handless arm, tugging with such force that it seemed he must rip the youth's arm from its socket. He allowed him to lean back a few inches then pulled savagely on the arm forcing the young man's head against the glass with sickening and powerful force.

A crack appeared in the glass.

Then another.

The fingers of the severed hand at Scott's feet were jerking as if in time to the impacts of the boy's head against the glass, which had now spider-webbed. Crimson poured down the attendant's face; Scott fancied he could see bone gleaming whitely through the pulped and torn flesh on his face and forehead. He finally let go of his victim's arm, allowing the body to sag to the floor. Then he gripped the hilt of the knife in his fist and drove it hard against the splintered glass.

It broke immediately, pieces of glass flying inwards, showering the prone body of the attendant.

Scott looked around, then pulled himself up into the frame of the small window. It was a tight squeeze. He groaned as he tried to pull himself through, yelping in pain as he cut his calf on a chunk of broken glass. Blood began to soak through the overalls as he fell into the motorway shop, sprawling onto the unconscious attendant.

Scott struggled to his feet and hurried over to the rack of jeans and shirts. He pulled half a dozen pairs off the hangers, grabbed an armful of shirts. Then he hurried back behind the counter, picking up a large bottle of lemonade, his eyes scanning the shelves for pain-killers. He stuffed packets of aspirin, paracetamol and any other pill he could find into his pocket. He grabbed two tins of Elastoplast. Then, carrying his haul, he clambered back over the unconscious attendant and out of the broken window, dropping two pairs of the jeans in the process. One pair fell across the pulped face of the attendant, hiding his terrible injuries. Blood began to soak through the denim.

Scott fell onto the concrete of the forecourt and sprinted for the Renault, cursing as he looked down to see blood from his torn calf seeping through the material of his overalls. He tossed the jeans and shirts into the back of the car, slid behind the wheel and drove off, struggling one-handed to free some paracetamol from their container. He shook two out and pushed them into his mouth, chewing them dry, almost gagging at the bitter taste. Then he swallowed another two, washing them down with a swig from the lemonade bottle.

In a short while he would pull in somewhere and change into a pair of the jeans and a shirt. It would give him a little more camouflage for his journey.

He gripped the wheel tightly, closing his eyes momentarily against the pain.

On the opposite carriageway a police car hurtled past him, lights flashing.

Scott drove on, past a sign which proclaimed: LONDON 143 MILES.

He looked at his watch, wincing once again at the unbearable pain inside his head. He swallowed two more tablets, wondering how long they would take to work. *If* indeed they did.

He drove on.

Ninety-four

The cell door crashed open, slamming back against the wall, the impact reverberating round the small room.

Mike Robinson blinked hard, shocked from sleep by the sound and, now, by rough hands on him, pulling him from the top bunk.

Beneath him, Rod Porter was also being pulled from the warmth of his bunk, hurled across the room by the first of the warders who had barged into the cell.

'What the fuck is *this*?' snarled Porter but, as he turned, he was struck hard across the face with a baton. The hardwood split his cheek and he fell to the ground, blood pouring from the gash.

Robinson was thrown against the wall, a fist driven into his stomach, knocking the wind from him. Through pain-misted eyes he saw his locker torn open and its contents scattered, saw the bunks being overturned, saw the small cupboard that had housed James Scott's belongings ripped open. The photograph of the blonde woman Scott had spoken of (Robinson couldn't remember her name) fluttered to the floor where it was trodden on in the melée.

Then another blow to the stomach sent him crashing to the ground, where he was allowed to lie for only brief seconds before being dragged to his feet behind Porter. Both men were dragged on to the landing.

Other prisoners, woken by the noise, were shouting and banging against their doors, not knowing what the early morning disturbance was. As warders passed by cell doors they smashed their batons against them by way of warning, but this only served to inflame the inhabitants further. The cacophony of noise rose to deafening proportions as Robinson and Porter were dragged along the landing towards the stairs, almost hurled down them by their captors.

'What the fuck is going on?' shouted Robinson at one of the men pulling him.

'Shut it,' the warder hissed, driving a punch into his kidneys, almost throwing him down the metal steps behind Porter.

The noise from the other cells filled the prison.

'How could he have got away?'

Governor Peter Nicholson glared at Dexter, his eyes unblinking.

'I wish I knew,' Dexter said. 'He would have been weak from the operation. In pain. I can't understand how he managed it.'

'Well, he won't get far,' Nicholson said, an air of conviction in his voice.

'I can't see how he'll survive so soon after the operation,' Dexter added.

'I don't care if they bring him back dead but I want him back here.'

'You never *did* care, did you? It never bothered you whether the men who were operated on lived or died.'

'That isn't what's at stake here, Dexter,' Nicholson hissed. 'No one has ever escaped from a prison where I've been Governor and I don't intend to let Scott be the first.'

'Your pride doesn't matter any more, Nicholson. The man is already out. He got away, that's the point. He *did* escape.'

'We'll find him. He'll be brought back. I want to know how he did it.'

There was a knock on the office door and Nicholson called for the visitor to enter.

The door opened and Warder Paul Swain entered, supporting Porter. The other two men in the room saw the blood pouring down the convict's face.

Nicholson nodded and Swain threw the man down.

Robinson followed, landing heavily on his arm.

'Get up,' snapped Swain, kicking Robinson hard at the base of the spine.

The office door slammed shut behind them.

381

'Don't tell me I won't get away with this,' Nicholson said, a slight smile on his lips, his gaze flicking back and forth from one inmate to the other. 'You can report this to the prison authorities if you like, but you'll never prove it happened. No matter what we do to you.'

'What do you want from us?' Robinson said.

'You were cell-mates with Scott; I want to know how he got out. I want to know if he talked about escaping. I want to know if you helped him.'

Porter eyed the Governor coldly, a slight smile on his face.

Nicholson saw it, took a step forward and struck Porter hard across the face, splitting his bottom lip. He fell backwards into the arms of Swain, who drove a fist into his kidneys then let him drop to the ground.

'For God's sake, stop it,' Dexter said.

'You keep out of this,' Nicholson roared. 'This is *my* prison and this is *my* affair.'

'You've lost him, Nicholson,' Porter said, sucking in a painful breath. 'He's long gone by now and *you* won't find him.'

'Did you help him escape?' the Governor rasped.

Porter spat blood, then clambered to his feet.

'Yeah, I gave him a leg up over the fucking wall,' he said.

Swain hit him hard across the small of the back with his baton.

Porter doubled up, falling to the floor once more.

'This will put another five years on your sentences,' Nicholson snarled. 'Both of you.'

'We don't know where he's gone,' Robinson protested angrily.

'Five years,' Nicholson spat. 'And I'll make it five years of hell.'

'Fuck you,' rasped Robinson and hawked loudly, propelling a gob of mucus into the Governor's face.

It hung there like a tear, trickling slowly down his cheek until Nicholson wiped it away.

Swain struck Robinson across the shoulder with his baton, then the shoulder blades, both blows almost cracking bone. Then the warder turned and opened the office door. Two of his colleagues, jackets already removed and sleeves rolled up, walked in.

'Take these men to solitary,' Nicholson said. 'See if they feel more like talking there.' He nodded, watching as the two men were dragged away.

'You can't do this,' Dexter protested as the office door slammed shut behind them.

'I've told you before,' Nicholson snarled. 'This is *my* prison and I can do what I like. Now, if you're not a solution to this problem then you're a part of it, so get out of here.'

Dexter turned to leave.

'I'll find him, Dexter,' said the Governor. 'And if he's not dead when he's brought back, he will be by the time I've finished with him.'

Ninety-five

'I don't like having to trust other people, Gregson.' Police Commissioner Lawrence Sullivan held the pieces of paper in his large hands, shuffling them like playing cards. 'I warned you before, you'd better be right, otherwise I'll have you back pounding a beat quicker than you can imagine.'

DI Gregson looked on indifferently.

'I told you, if I'm wrong, I'll resign,' he said flatly.

Sullivan got to his feet, the three pieces of paper in his hand.

'These,' he said, brandishing the papers before him, could be the key to what's been going on, or they could mean an end to your career *and* mine. I hope you realise what a bloody risk I'm taking. Not only do I dislike having to trust other people, I also hate gambles. And this, to me, is a gamble.'

'There's too much evidence . . .'

Sullivan cut him short.

'I know, you've told me that before. Well, after considering it all, I tend to agree with your theory that things at Whitely are, shall we say, a little irregular. But while there's the slightest element of doubt I don't like it. A conspiracy is one hell of an accusation, Gregson. Like I said, you'd better be right.' He sat down at his desk, the exhumation orders laid out in front of him.

'Are you going to pass them, sir?' Gregson asked, looking at his superior.

'They're already signed,' said Sullivan. He handed them to Gregson.

'A helicopter will take you, Finn and two other men to Whitely. It'll pick you up in an hour. It shouldn't take more than about fifty minutes to get there.' He exhaled deeply. 'Gregson, I want a full report on what you do or don't find up there, do you understand? An investigation of this kind makes me accountable to the Government as well as to our own people and the prison authorities.'

Gregson nodded.

'Do *you* think I'm right, sir?' he finally asked, quietly.

'Would it matter one way or the other?'

'Not really. I'm just curious as to what made you decide to get these.' He held up the exhumation orders.

'You seemed to have a pretty strong case to support your argument and if there *is* some kind of conspiracy going on at Whitely, then it should be exposed. Or perhaps, for once in my life, I decided to gamble.' He looked at Gregson. 'But there's a lot on this bet. More than I think you either care or realise.' They exchanged glances once more then Gregson turned to leave.

'A full report,' Sullivan reminded him as he left. The door closed and the Commissioner was left alone in his office. He sat back in his seat, hands clasped together beneath his chin, gazing out of his window at the overcast sky.

'I got them,' Gregson said triumphantly, holding the exhumation orders in front of him.

'Now what?' Finn asked him.

Gregson explained about the helicopter, the impending journey to Whitely.

'I doubt if they're going to be very helpful up there,' the DS observed.

'I couldn't give a fuck,' rasped Gregson. 'They don't have to be helpful. The only thing that matters is, with these exhumation orders they can't stop us.'

Ninety-six

He'd slept in the back of the car on a side-road, the merciful oblivion he sought interrupted so often by the pain in his head. Finally, after two disturbed hours, Scott had decided to drive on. He'd discarded his prison overalls in favour of one of the shirts and a pair of the jeans but he still wore his prison boots. He'd washed his face and hands in the rain and he'd fixed a small bandage over the surgical dressing with Elastoplast. The wound in his calf had stopped bleeding, but it hurt; every time he pushed his foot down on the clutch, fresh blood seeped out.

The pain inside his head was less insistent. That was the handfuls of pain-killers he'd taken, he told himself. But it was still there, ever-present as he drove, glancing around him, wincing in the early morning sunlight that streamed through the windscreen.

He was well inside the outskirts of London now, heading for his own flat in Brent. If only he could reach it, the flat would provide a haven at least for a couple of precious hours. Providing the police hadn't already covered it, waiting for him to go there. No, surely they wouldn't expect him to head back to London so soon. *Would they?* He was convinced his escape must have been discovered by now, but he'd seen precious little in the way of police pursuit. Not as yet, anyway.

He decided to return to his flat; he would take the chance. Besides, there were things there he needed. A change of clothes, for one. And after that?

He gripped the wheel tightly, wincing at the pain that filled his head.

Plummer.

Scott ran one index finger tentatively over his forehead.

Carol.

She wouldn't be expecting him back, either.

The bitch.

How surprised they would be to see him.

Scott almost smiled. He glanced down at the passenger seat, at the pile of shirts and jeans there.

And the carving knife that lay hidden beneath.

This time he *did* smile.

As he glanced ahead once more he saw the police car.

It was travelling slowly up the other side of the road towards him; there was just one man in it.

Scott gripped the wheel, a reflex action brought about by a combination of pain and panic.

Should he pull in to the side of the road until the police car had gone?

It was getting closer. He knew he must make up his mind quickly.

He drove on, his eyes fixed firmly on the road as he by-passed the vehicle. Its driver offered him only a cursory glance. Scott watched the car in his rear-view mirror, saw it turn a corner and disappear from sight. He exhaled deeply, checking his mirror again to ensure that the police car hadn't turned to follow him. Satisfied that it hadn't he drove on, drawing nearer to his flat.

He saw no police cars parked outside; no officers waiting for him, at least none in uniform. They'd be plain clothes, he thought, angry with himself. The cars would be unmarked. There was an old Capri parked outside the block of flats where he lived, but it had no occupant. Scott looked around. A group of school-children were making their way noisily across the road in front of him, one of them slapping the bonnet of the Renault as he passed. Scott ignored the children, his eyes flicking back and forth as he drove past the block, satisfied that he was safe. He parked the car behind the Capri and climbed out, walking briskly across to the main doors, the knife tucked inside his jeans, covered by the folds of his shirt.

He would have to use the knife to get into his flat as he had no keys.

Wearily he began to climb the stairs. He felt the blade cold against his flesh.

The razor-sharp blade.
He thought of Carol.
The knife.
Plummer.
He continued to climb.

Ninety-seven

'Down there.'

The pilot tapped Gregson's shoulder and directed his attention towards the ground.

Through the cockpit windows of the helicopter the DI could see the shape of Whitely Prison standing darkly against the moorland that surrounded it.

He nodded as the pilot said something else, his voice metallic through the headset the policeman wore. The noise of the rotor blades filled the small cockpit as the twin-engined Lynx cruised smoothly towards its destination. Gregson checked his watch, noting that it had taken less than an hour to reach the prison from London. He glanced behind him to the rear seats, where Finn and two other plain clothes men sat. One of them, a tall man in his early forties called Clifford, was looking distinctly queasy. The other, Sherman, was looking out of the side window, watching the countryside rising up to meet them as the Lynx swept lower.

Finn was tapping his fingertips against his knees, waiting for the helicopter to land. He didn't like flying at the best of times and the Lynx, as far as he was concerned, offered even less protection in the air than an aircraft. He was looking forward to getting his feet back on firm ground. One glance at Clifford told him the tall man felt the same way.

'You okay?' Gregson said, raising his voice above the roar of the rotors.

Finn nodded.

'Where do you want me to drop her?' the pilot interrupted, tapping Gregson's arm once again.

The DI scanned the prison below and stroked his chin thoughtfully. From their present height the huge Victorian structure looked like a model. He could see figures moving about within the grounds, some doubtless able to see the approaching chopper and wondering about its presence.

'Land in the exercise yard,' Gregson answered, pointing. 'There.'

The pilot nodded and the Lynx went into a swift descent which caused Finn to hold his stomach. The uncomfortable feeling he always experienced upon landing, his ears popping, seemed to intensify in the small aerial vehicle. Clifford thought he was going to be sick. Sherman felt like an extra from *Apocalypse Now*. He smiled at his own joke.

Gregson looked down as the Lynx descended, scanning the prison, wondering if Nicholson had seen them coming, wondering what the Governor was thinking as he saw the helicopter dropping gently out of the sky. The DI almost unconsciously touched the exhumation orders inside his jacket pocket. He felt a curious kind of exhilaration as the Lynx went lower, an excitement at the thought of finally finding an answer to the riddle of the killers. If there were answers, they were here at Whitely. He was sure of it.

The helicopter wavered slightly as the pilot prepared to set down. A strong gust of wind caught it and one of the skids bumped the concrete of the exercise yard

389

but it re-adjusted and gently touched down. The pilot immediately switched off the rotors and Gregson and his companions hurriedly unstrapped themselves, the DI pushing open the passenger door.

'Keep your heads down,' the pilot yelled as the rotors continued to carve a pattern through the air. 'What do you want *me* to do?'

'Wait here for us,' Gregson told him, cupping one hand to his mouth to make himself heard over the dying engines.

The pilot raised one thumb in an attitude of acknowledgement, watching as the other three men clambered out and hurried away from the helicopter.

Two warders were approaching them, bewildered by the sudden, unannounced arrival of the Lynx. Before either of them could speak Gregson had taken his ID out and was holding it out in front of him for inspection.

'I want to see Governor Nicholson,' he snapped. '*Now*.'

Ninety-eight

What if they were waiting inside for him?

The corridor was deserted, just as the stairs had been during his tortuous climb. Maybe they were waiting in the flat itself.

Scott hesitated a few paces away, the thought turning over and over in his mind. He reached for the knife and pulled it from his belt, inserting it in the door frame close to the lock.

He had to take the chance.

Scott moved the knife gently but firmly and the lock finally slipped.

He stood close to the door, listening for any signs or sounds of movement. Satisfied that there were none, he pushed the door open and stepped inside the flat, closing the door quickly behind him.

The place smelt damp. Cupboards were open and furniture lay overturned, the way it had been the day they arrested him. Scott stood looking around for long moments, pressing one hand to his temple as a particularly vehement stab of pain lanced through his brain. He gritted his teeth, thought for a second he was going to pass out. When it cleared, he moved into the bedroom. There he pulled open his wardrobe. His clothes were still there, at least. He tried the bedside cabinet.

The Beretta was gone.

He slammed the drawer shut, realising that the police had obviously kept it. Bastards. He sat down on the edge of the bed, acutely aware not only of the pain from his head and his leg but of his weariness, of the stench he was giving off. He decided a shower would remedy both those problems and stumbled through into the bathroom, spinning the cold tap and scooping water to swallow two more aspirins. Then he turned on the shower and pulled off the shirt and jeans he'd been wearing, finally standing naked.

Scott turned to the bathroom mirror and looked at his reflection. His skin was pale, his eyes sunken through pain and lack of sleep but it was the bandage to which he addressed his attention. With infinite slowness he began to peel it off, finally dropping it onto the floor. There was a piece of gauze on his forehead, held in place by two pieces of surgical tape. Carefully, the noise of the shower filling the room now, Scott removed them, pulling the encrusted gauze pad free.

The wound in his skull was less than two inches long, running from just below his hairline, diagonally towards his right eyebrow. The wound was caked with congealed blood and the dark stitches stood out even more vividly against the paleness of his flesh. He looked more closely, the breath sticking in his throat.

The wound was pulsing gently.

As he put his forefinger to it, he noticed that his hand was shaking.

The wound throbbed rhythmically, like a small heart, but the steady beat was not that of his pulse.

It bumped gently to its own tempo.

Scott swallowed hard, closing his eyes as a fresh wave of pain hit him.

Make it stop.

He moistened a piece of cotton wool and cleaned some of the dried blood from around the wound. The pain was intense. He rubbed both hands across his face and stepped beneath the shower, allowing the streams of water to wash the accumulated filth from him. He closed his eyes briefly, then looked down at the cut on his calf. It was deep and had bled profusely but he could attend to it himself. Besides, it was only a dull ache compared to the excruciating agony inside his skull. He washed quickly, seeing blood swirl around the plug-hole as he stepped out, switched off the shower and began to dry himself.

He found some bandages in one of the bathroom cabinets and hastily wound one around his calf, securing it with a stout bow. The wound on his forehead, he discovered, could be covered by a large plaster. Careful not to press too hard on the wound, he affixed it, leaning on the sink for support. He swallowed more aspirin and found, to his joy, that the pain was subsiding. He splashed his face with cold water and dried it carefully, satisfied the plaster was in place. Then he wandered back into the bedroom and slipped on a shirt, a fresh pair of jeans and a pair of cowboy boots.

He slid the knife down the side of one boot.

He crossed to the phone, checking that it was still connected.

He dialled Carol's number and waited.

Waited.

Nothing.

Three times he tried it. Three times he was greeted by the ringing tone.

Finally he pressed down on the cradle, listening to the monotonous buzz of the dial tone for a moment before punching new digits.

Ray Plummer's phone rang.

And rang.

And was picked up.

'Hello.'

He recognised the voice immediately.

'Hello. Who is this?' Carol Jackson wanted to know.

Scott gripped the receiver in his fist then, with a loud roar, slammed it down the force of the impact shattering the plastic phone in two. He picked it up and hurled it across the room.

Fucking slag.

Dirty fucking slag.

He got to his feet, pulling on the leather jacket he'd taken from the wardrobe, and headed for the door.

The knife bumped against his leg as he walked.

The drive to Plummer's flat would take him less than an hour, he guessed.

But first, he had other tasks to perform.

Ninety-nine

He had seen the helicopter land, seen the four men disembark.

Now Governor Peter Nicholson heard the commotion outside his office, the raised voices of his secretary and of a man. A man who, seconds later, barged into the office, pushing Nicholson's secretary aside.

'What the hell is going on here?' the Governor asked.

'I might ask you the same thing,' Gregson snapped, followed into the room by Finn, Sherman and Clifford.

'I tried to stop them, Mr Nicholson,' the secretary protested. 'But they . . .'

'It's all right,' Nicholson said, waving her away. When the door was shut he turned on the invading policemen. 'How dare you come barging in here like this? I want to know what's going on.'

'So do we, that's why we're here,' Gregson said. 'In case you've forgotten, my name is Detective Inspector Gregson . . .'

'I remember your last visit,' Nicholson told him scornfully.

'Good, then you'll remember what it was about. Well, this time I'm not leaving until I get the answers I want.'

Nicholson smiled.

'And what answers are those?' he said.

'I'm going to find out what's going on in this bloody prison. I'm going to find out how four convicted murderers, supposedly locked up here, could re-appear in London and re-enact their crimes. I'm going to find out what your game is, Nicholson.'

'Get out of here now before I call your superiors,' the Governor said angrily, turning his back on the policemen.

'My superiors know I'm here and they know *why*,' Gregson announced.

The colour drained from Nicholson's face and he remained with his back to the DI, hiding his expression.

'Do they know what you're accusing myself and some of my staff of?' he said, some of the bravado gone from his voice.

'Cut the bullshit, Nicholson, we haven't got all day. We've got work to do,' Gregson hissed.

Nicholson turned to face him.

'Perhaps you should reconsider what you're doing before it's too late.'

'It's already too late, too late for *you*.'

'And what, exactly, are you proposing to do?'

'I'm going to open the graves of Peter Lawton, Mathew Bryce and Trevor Magee.'

'You can't do that,' Nicholson said quietly, the steel gone from his voice.

'Why not? We've already opened the grave of Gary Lucas,' Gregson told him, leaning forward on the desk. 'And do you know what we found? Nothing. Fuck all. No corpse. Just a bag of bricks. Lucas never died, did he? Just like Lawton, Bryce and Magee never died. You faked their deaths to cover up what you'd done to them here. Then you released them.'

Nicholson shook his head.

'You're insane,' he snarled.

'Maybe I am, but I'm also *right*.'

'You can't open the graves,' Nicholson said defiantly. 'I won't allow it.'

'You have no choice,' Gregson said triumphantly. He reached into his jacket pocket and pulled out the three exhumation orders, hurling them down in front of Nicholson. 'You can read them if you want to, but the most important thing is the signature at the bottom. Look at it.'

Nicholson picked up one of the documents with his thumb and forefinger, as if he were handling some kind of contagious material. He saw the sweeping hand of Commissioner Lawrence Sullivan on the order and the signature of a well-known Judge.

'Do you still want to argue with me?' Gregson said.

Nicholson merely glared at the policeman.

'The records we had on Lucas say that his body was *prepared* by your resident doctor,' the DI said. 'Someone called . . .'

'Dexter. Dr Robert Dexter,' Finn interjected.

'I want to speak to him, too,' Gregson insisted. 'No autopsy was carried out on Lucas, according to the records. Did Dexter *prepare* the other three, as well?'

Nicholson nodded.

'Was he the one who experimented on them?'

'What are you talking about?' Nicholson snapped.

'There's nowhere to run *now*, Nicholson. We know it all. We have the bodies back at New Scotland Yard. We know the men were all suffering from massive brain tumours, possibly triggered by some kind of brain surgery. Surgery performed by Dexter. Where is he?'

'In the hospital wing.'

'Get him. Now.'

Nicholson's hand hovered over the phone.

'And then?' he asked.

Gregson smiled thinly.

'We've got some digging to do.'

One hundred

Scott could see the 'CLOSED' sign on the door of Les Gourmets as he pulled up across the street from it. He parked the Renault and sat behind the wheel for a moment, his head resting against the steering wheel.

Stop this fucking pain.

He swallowed hard and opened his eyes, squinting at first to clear the mist of pain that seemed to have clouded his vision. A cobbled walkway ran alongside the restaurant and led to the back entrance. Scott swung himself out of the car and crossed the street. The walkway was wide enough for a small delivery truck and Scott noticed that there was a dark red Rover Sterling parked there.

He recognised the car; it belonged to Terry Morton.

As Scott moved towards the rear of the restaurant he saw two men in shirt-sleeves carrying large metal bins to a skip in the back yard of the eatery, emptying waste into the receptacle. He paused for a moment, his hand slipping down to touch the hilt of the knife. He pulled it free and slipped it into the back of his belt, hiding it beneath his jacket.

Scott moved closer as the men finished their task. He could hear the clanking of pots and pans inside the kitchen at the rear and there were several excitable voices being raised within. He peered around the corner and noticed that the door to the kitchen was open.

He assumed that Morton was inside.

He edged towards the back door, cursing as he slipped in a mess of spilled potato peelings. He walked on, into the kitchen of the restaurant. Several curious heads turned to look at him.

'Can I help you?' one of the staff asked, wiping his hands on a tea-towel.

'I work for Mr Plummer,' Scott said, regarding the man coldly. 'I noticed one of my friends is here. I saw his car parked round the side. Where is he?'

The man seemed to relax.

'Mr Morton is through there in the restaurant with Mr Perry,' he told Scott. 'Shall I tell them you're here?'

Scott shook his head.

'No, I'll surprise them,' he said, pushing past the man, who watched as he stepped through the macramé streamers that separated the kitchen from the dining area.

It was dull inside the restaurant, despite the daylight outside. The shutters were only half-open.

Morton and Perry were sitting at a table close to the window, a bottle of wine between them. Perry was glancing at a newspaper.

Scott took a couple of steps towards them.

It was Morton who saw him first.

Jesus Christ,' he murmured.

'Not quite,' said Scott softly, a thin smile on his face.

'You're supposed to be banged up,' Morton told him, as if imparting information only *he* was aware of.

'Yeah, well, there's been a change of plan,' Scott told him.

'You look like shit, Jim,' Perry said, putting down his paper. 'What happened?'

'It's a long story. Where's Plummer?'

The two men looked at each other, then back at Scott.

'Why?' Morton asked.

'I want to talk to him. We've got some business to discuss. About twenty years' worth.' Scott moved closer.

Perry's hand moved to the inside of his jacket.

'Back off, Jim,' he said, his hand touching the butt of the .357 inside his jacket.

'Fuck you,' rasped Scott and moved the last few paces towards them with lightning speed.

He pulled the knife free as Perry went for the pistol.

Scott brought the knife round in a wide arc, the powerful backhand swing catching Perry across the face, slicing through his cheek and shearing off bone. A flap of skin fluttered uselessly. Perry shrieked in pain, blood spouting from the wound. He fell backwards off the chair, the gun falling from his hand.

Scott kicked it away from him, driving his weight against the table at the same time, knocking Morton back against the window.

Perry made a grab for the pistol but Scott kicked him hard in the side of the face, shattering his left cheek bone. Then he himself snatched up the .357, aware of shouts from behind him as the terrified staff watched the struggle.

Scott swung round, bringing the pistol to bear on Morton, who was reaching for his own gun.

'You fucking . . .'

The words were drowned by the massive discharge of the .357, the sound amplified within the confines of the deserted restaurant. Scott was blinded momentarily by the searing muzzle-flashes as he fired three times.

The first bullet missed, shattering the window behind Morton, but the second two struck home. One tore through his chest to the left of the sternum, exploded a lung and erupted from his his back, carrying blood and portions of bone with it.

The other heavy-grain slug caught him in the stomach, doubling him up as it macerated a large portion of the duodenum and pulverised the liver on its deadly

399

course. Morton was hurled backwards by the impact, blood jetting from the wounds, his own pistol falling to the floor.

He pitched forward, crashing into the table, spilling the bottle of wine, sending it flying. Scott stepped back and looked down at Perry, who was still trying to crawl away.

Scott shot him once in the back of the head, the bullet blasting away a sizeable portion of his skull, exposing his brain. He lay in a spreading pool of blood, his body twitching spasmodically.

Moving quickly now, Scott snatched up the pistol Morton had dropped, jamming the Smith and Wesson 459 automatic into his belt. He then rifled through the dead man's pockets and found his car keys. These he dropped into his own pocket before straightening up and moving across to Perry.

Scott found two full quick-loaders in the man's jacket. Each one carried six hollow-point .357 rounds. He pocketed those, too, then hurried towards the rear of the restaurant, where the staff who hadn't bolted in panic at the sound of gunfire were standing paralysed with fear. At one of the stoves a gas flame leaped high beneath a large copper pot. Scott's eyes narrowed.

'Get out,' he shouted at the staff. 'All of you, get out of here, now.' The sight of the .357 and the tone of Scott's voice combined to accelerate the evacuation. He crossed to the gas flame and stuck a balled up tea towel in it, watching as the material ignited. He tossed it inside the dining area, then threw another after it, watching with delight as flames began to lick at chairs and tables, began to ignite table cloths. Fire spread rapidly, greedy tongues of it flaring wildly inside the room. Scott looked through the curtain of flames to the bodies of Morton and Perry, then turned and headed out into the yard and around the corner to the waiting Rover. He unlocked it and clambered in, sliding behind the wheel.

He stepped on the accelerator and the car sped away past the front of the restaurant.

Smoke and flame were already belching through the shattered front window.

Another few minutes and the entire building would be an inferno.

One hundred and one

All three of the coffins were empty.

They lay beside the graves, as if forced up from the dark earth, now discarded by it.

Empty.

Gregson moved slowly between them, not quite ready to believe the evidence of his own eyes but aware of the twinge of triumph deep within him.

The wind, blowing across the cemetery, ruffled his hair as he stood looking at the boxes. Beside him Sherman, Clifford, Finn and the two warders who had helped to disinter the caskets also looked on.

Nicholson and Dexter said nothing.

'There was a reason for it,' said Dexter finally.

Nicholson looked contemptuously at him.

'I'm not interested in your reasons,' Gregson told him.

'It was to *help* the men,' Dexter protested.

'What about the public, you bastard,' snapped the DI. 'You released murderers back into society, knowing they'd kill again.'

'No,' Dexter protested. 'The experiments would have

401

worked. Their violent tendencies *would* have been cured.'

'Well they *weren't*, were they? You're as guilty of murder as the men who actually pulled the triggers or used the knives.'

'They got what they deserved,' said Nicholson. 'They died. Died as they would have done thirty years ago. We did the country a favour by experimenting on men like Bryce and Magee. What else would they have done? Sat here for the rest of their miserable lives feeding on taxpayers' food, clothed by the state, protected.'

'Well, it's over now, Nicholson,' said the DI. 'You're both under arrest.'

'It isn't over,' the Governor told him flatly.

'What the hell do you mean?'

'A man escaped from here last night. Another man we'd experimented on.'

Gregson's expression changed to one of shock.

'Who was he?' he demanded.

'He can't have got far,' Dexter said, dejectedly. 'I only operated . . .'

'Who was he?' Gregson roared.

'His name was James Scott,' Nicholson said.

Finn and Gregson looked at each other.

'How long's he been gone?' the DI wanted to know.

'We can't be sure,' Dexter said. 'Probably since late last night.'

'Jesus Christ,' murmured Gregson. He looked at Finn. 'Stuart, you take care of things here. I've got to get back to London as quickly as possible.'

'You think Scott will head back there?' the DS said.

'It's the only place he knows,' Gregson said, stepping over an empty coffin. 'I'll put out an alert to all units to watch for him. If he got a car he's probably there by now.' He looked at Dexter. 'Have you any idea what you've done?' he snarled.

'All I wanted to do was help them,' Dexter said quietly.

Finn pushed him and Nicholson away, nodding in the direction of the graves.

'Fill those in,' he said.

Gregson ran off across the cemetery, almost slipping on the mud in his haste. He sprinted across the exercise yard towards the waiting helicopter, wrenching the passenger side door open. The pilot hurriedly stubbed out his cigarette and looked in surprise as the DI scrambled into the other seat.

'Get us back to London as fast as you can,' Gregson told him. 'Move.'

He was already strapping himself in as the pilot switched on the motor and the rotors began to turn, carving an arc through the air as they rotated with increasing speed. The power built up rapidly.

Gregson clenched his fists together, his emotions a curious mixture of elation and foreboding. Elation that his theory had been proved correct. And foreboding at what Scott might do or, indeed, might have already done.

As the Lynx rose into the air he found that his hands were shaking.

One hundred and two

'I don't want to kill you, Rick. But I will if I have to.'

Rick Calder froze when he heard the voice. He felt the colour drain from his face, felt his bowels

403

loosen as the barrel was prodded into the small of his back.

'Open it up,' James Scott told him, watching as Calder turned the key in the lock that secured one of the two metal grilles at the front entrance of 'Loveshow'. Calder hooked his fingers beneath the sliding screen of metal and pushed upwards.

'I thought you were inside,' he said quietly. His hands shook as he tried to find the key to open the door.

'Yeah, you and everybody else,' Scott told him, prodding him a little harder with the 459. 'Come on, get a fucking move on.' He looked to his right and left, satisfied that the gun he held was hidden from the view of any passers-by.

Calder finally found the right key and unlocked the door, stumbling inside as Scott pushed him through the entrance and slammed the door behind them. He winced as he felt that all-too familiar pain inside his head, throbbing and pulsing. His brain seemed to be swelling, trying to burst through his skull.

'How the fuck did you get here?' Calder wanted to know, turning to face the other man, seeing the automatic levelled at him.

'It doesn't matter,' Scott told him.

'Jim, I didn't have anything to do with this,' Calder blurted. 'I don't know what you want with me. I haven't done anything to you.'

Scott thought Calder was going to start weeping.

'I know you haven't,' he said flatly. 'It isn't you I want,' he continued.

'So what are you doing here? Did you escape? How did you get out?' Calder's words were almost incoherent, they were spoken so quickly.

'Rick, just shut it, will you?' snapped Scott, taking a pace towards him. 'Give me the keys.'

Calder handed them over without hesitation.

'Take them, do what you want. Just don't hurt me, please,' Calder babbled, his eyes flicking from Scott's face to the barrel of the Smith and Wesson. 'I'll help if you want, just don't hurt me.'

'Rick, shut up will you,' Scott said wearily.

'I'll shut up, I'll shut up. Whatever you want, Jim. I'll shut up. Don't hurt me, though. I won't say anything else but . . .'

'For fuck's sake,' hissed Scott, taking another step towards Calder, whose eyes widened in terror. 'Shut up,' he roared.

He struck Calder on the temple with the butt of the pistol, the sound of metal on bone making a sickening thud. Calder dropped like a stone and lay still. Scott leant back against the wall, his breath coming in gasps. There was an ugly cut on Calder's temple, and already the area around it was beginning to darken. A thin trickle of mucus dribbled from his mouth.

Scott gritted his teeth.

Stop this fucking pain.

He sucked in several deep breaths, his hands pressed to his temples, his eyes closed.

He stood there for several seconds, finally taking one last glance down at the prone figure of Calder. Then Scott made his way downstairs.

He slapped on lights as he reached the bottom of the flight. Everything was how he'd last seen it. The bed in the centre of the room, the old chairs and sofas. The fading pictures on the peeling walls. He walked through towards his office, past the changing room, selecting the key to his office. He walked in, looking round.

Scott exhaled wearily and walked across to his desk.

With a shout of anger he overturned it, then snatched up the chair, swinging it wildly around his head, smashing

405

the light bulb as he lashed out. The chair shattered and he was left holding just one of the legs. Brandishing it like a club, he headed back into the other room. There he smashed the nearest picture on the wall, overturned chairs and sofas. He picked up one of the small coffee tables and hurled it across the room, watching as if broke against the far wall. Scott's breath was coming in gasps now as he moved towards the small bar.

He stuck out his hand and, with one movement, swept the bottles from the shelves. They landed on the floor, glass shattering, contents spilling everywhere. He picked up one bottle and hurled it across the room, watching it smash against the far wall. Then another. And another. The place was filled with the sound of breaking glass. He hurled the bottles at the pictures, at the bed, at the walls. When there were no bottles left he ripped the shelves from their brackets, wielding one like a staff, breaking it across the bar top.

Scott picked up a handful of match books. He struck one match and held it close to the others, watching them ignite, then he dropped the flaming bundle to the floor.

The alcohol that had been spilled there ignited immediately, flames leaping up around his feet. He moved away from the bar and lit more matches, tossing them onto the bed, the sofas. All went up with a loud whump. Flames began to take hold now, scorching their way across the floor in the wake of the spilled drink. Like the tentacles of some fiery octopus the flames shot out in all directions, incinerating everything they touched.

Satisfied that the fire had taken hold, Scott headed for the stairs, thick smoke already swirling around him.

As he reached the top of the stairs he noticed that Calder had regained consciousness. He was sitting up, tentatively touching the spot where Scott had hit him.

As he saw the other man he cowered back against the wall.

'Jim, please . . .' he began.

'If I was you, I'd get out of here, Rick,' Scott told him and headed for the door.

Thick black smoke was already beginning to fill the stairwell behind him.

'Oh Jesus,' murmured Calder, seeing the noxious clouds coming from below.

Scott pushed the door and stepped out on to the pavement, striding across to the Rover which was parked across the street. He slid behind the wheel and started the engine, noticing that, as Calder bolted from the building, the smoke billowed out of the door after him.

The flames had taken a grip. They would work their way up the stairs, destroying everything.

Scott watched for a moment longer then started the engine. As he shifted position slightly he could feel the two pistols jammed into his belt. They had a reassuring bulkiness to them. In one pocket he had the two quick-loaders, in the other a couple of spare magazines for the automatic.

He took one last look at 'Loveshow', smoke now belching from its door, and drove off.

One hundred and three

'How much further?'

DI Frank Gregson looked at his watch then at the pilot, who adjusted his microphone before speaking.

'Another twenty or thirty miles,' the pilot told him.

Gregson muttered something under his breath and looked out of the side window, watching the cars on the motorway below speeding along. The journey had seemed to take an eternity, although he realised they had been in the air less than forty-five minutes. Already the outskirts of London were appearing below them; the areas of greenery they had passed over when first leaving Whitely were now giving way to more densely populated conurbations.

The steady drone of the rotor blades continued and the maddening sensation of little or no speed only served to exacerbate the policeman's impatience. Again he checked his watch.

He'd called through to New Scotland Yard within minutes of leaving Whitely, to tell them that Scott was loose and probably back in the capital. He had also said that the man was possibly armed and extremely dangerous. Gregson had asked for armed squads to aid in the hunt for the fugitive. The radio had been conspicuously quiet, apart from the pilot picking up flying instructions. Despite Gregson's insistence that someone get back to him with a progress report, nothing had disturbed the airwaves yet.

He glanced at the radio and thought about calling again.

Had Scott been caught yet?

Had he been cornered?

Gregson wondered if he might even have been shot?

But no information had been forthcoming. No pieces of knowledge for him. Christ, he felt helpless.

'Tango Zebra, come in.'

The metallic voice over the radio seemed to startle Gregson.

The pilot flicked a switch on his control panel.

'Tango Zebra, I hear you, over,' he said.

'I want to speak to Detective Inspector Gregson,' the voice said.

Gregson tapped his microphone and the pilot nodded.

'Gregson here. What have you got?' he said.

'James Scott has been sighted in two places.'

'Where? How long ago?'

'He killed two men at a restaurant called Les Gourmet about an hour ago. The men are believed to be Terry Morton and Joe Perry.'

'What do you mean, believed to be?' Gregson snapped.

'After he killed them he set fire to the place. The bodies were quite badly burned. He also wrecked and burned the place where he used to work, a clip joint called "Loveshow". Both places, as you probably know, were owned by Ray Plummer. Morton and Perry worked for Plummer. It seems like Scott's on a little crusade.'

'When was he last seen?' the DI demanded.

'About forty minutes ago. He's driving a stolen Rover Sterling which belonged to one of the men he killed.'

Gregson chewed his bottom lip thoughtfully for a moment.

'Tango Zebra, can you hear me?' the voice said, insistently.

'Don't try to take Scott alive, do you understand?' the DI said.

Silence from the other end.

'Did you hear what I said? *Don't* try to take him alive. Is that understood?'

'Understood.'

The Lynx was descending now, the shapes and outlines of the buildings below beconing more discernible.

'If you see Scott,' he said, 'Shoot to kill. Over and out.' He switched off his microphone.

The pilot looked across at him, saw the expression on his face and decided to say nothing.

Below them Gregson could see the Thames, winding through the city like a dirty ribbon.

It wouldn't be long now.

One hundred and four

The black police transit van stood with its back doors open, two uniformed men waiting.

DS Stuart Finn shielded the flame of his lighter as he tried to light the Marlboro he'd just taken from the pack. The wind was blowing strongly now; twice the lighter flame was extinguished. Cursing, Finn stuck to his task, drawing gratefully on the cigarette at last. He looked up to see Governor Nicholson being led out of the main building by two of his warders.

The irony of the situation was inescapable. The two men looked bewildered, embarrassed almost as they led the older man towards the waiting transit. He allowed Finn only a cursory glance as he passed, clambering up into the back of the van and sitting down on one of the benches. A uniformed policeman joined him.

Finn watched as Dexter was also led towards the van. He had taken off his lab coat and now wore just a pair of plain brown trousers and a brown jacket. His shirt was undone at the collar. Finn thought how weary he looked. His face was pale and drawn, his eyes sunken and lifeless.

He was scanning the exercise yard as she walked, noting that there were a couple of unmarked police cars nearby as well as an official one besides, of course, the transit in which he was about to take his place with Nicholson.

The plain clothes men who occupied the unmarked cars were standing around chatting, two with their hands dug in their pockets, collars turned up against the icy wind cutting across the open courtyard.

Inside the van, Nicholson looked out and saw Dexter approaching. So this was how it was to end, he thought. The irony of the situation was not lost on him. He glanced up at one of the windows of B Wing to see an inmate staring down.

The two men would be held at the nearest police station until charges could be formally brought against them. What exactly those charges were, Finn wasn't sure as yet.

Conspiracy. But conspiracy to do what?

Pervert the course of justice?

What did the rule book say about brain operations on convicted murderers? Where were the clauses on experimentation and release of those same murderers?

That, he was relieved to think, was not his problem. His only problem was getting these two men to the nearest police station. He took another drag on his cigarette and patted the side of the transit.

He'd ensured that the coffins had been reburied before they left. It was rather an empty gesture, considering they'd been without occupants, but Finn had a curious feeling of respect and dread for graves and he felt it only right that the cemetery be restored to its former state before he and his colleagues departed.

Dexter was slowing down, looking at the transit.

Perhaps the realisation was finally hitting him, Finn thought.

The doctor looked at the black vehicle and seemed to swoon. He took a step backwards.

Finn frowned, moved forward to help the older man.

Dexter ran at him and crashed into him, the power

411

of the impact unexpected enough to send Finn toppling. He spun round in time to see Dexter running towards the nearest of the unmarked cars.

The drivers were standing about twenty feet away. They hadn't seen what had happened.

Dexter was already behind the wheel of the black Sierra.

'Stop him,' Finn bellowed, now chasing after the doctor. Dexter had started the engine, oblivious to the plain clothes and uniformed men running at him from all direction.

The closest of the officers actually managed to get a hand inside the car through the open side window. His fist closed around Dexter's collar, but the doctor stepped on the accelerator and the car shot forward, dragging the policeman.

With one hand Dexter hammered at the vice-like grip, speeding up as he approached the open prison gates. He braked hard and the jolting impact caused the policeman to lose his hold. He somersaulted, landing heavily on the concrete.

Dexter drove on, glancing in the rear-view mirror, seeing that Finn had clambered into the blue Citroën and was following. The marked car was also in pursuit.

Dexter roared through the open gates and felt the car skid on the slippery track, but he regained control and drove on, flooring the accelerator, the needle on the speedometer touching ninety.

Behind him the Citroën and the police car followed, Finn hunched low over the wheel.

The Sierra reached the road and Dexter wrestled with the wheel, guiding the vehicle to the right. It skidded madly on the road but he kept it under control, noticing that Finn was closing the gap on him.

The police car had cut across in an attempt to head

him off but Dexter saw what was happening and sent the Sierra speeding towards a ridge ahead. A wire fence separated the road from the field beyond, the bank sloping up like a ramp.

Dexter gripped the wheel and drove straight at the fence, crashing through it, the Sierra hurtling up the low bank. It was moving at such a speed that all four wheels left the ground and the vehicle seemed to hang in mid-air, suspended as if on invisible wires, for long seconds before slamming down with a bone-jarring crash.

The car skidded again, great geezers of mud spraying up behind it, but Dexter, his face covered by a thin sheen of sweat, kept control and sped on across the field.

Finn, his face set in an attitude of concentration, followed. The Citroën hit the bank and hurtled through the air, banging down in the muddy field.

The police car wasn't so lucky.

The driver, either because of misjudgement or fear, eased up his speed and the car hit the bank. But instead of sailing through the air, it nose-dived into the mud, the rear end toppling over until the entire vehicle crashed onto its roof, metal buckling under the impact.

Finn saw in his rear-view mirror that the other car had come to grief but he was more concerned with the Sierra now, roaring away from him across the field.

Surely, he thought, Dexter would have had more chance of outrunning him on an ordinary road. The muddy field could only slow him down.

What the hell was he playing at?

The cars roared on.

One hundred and five

How easy it would be to turn the gun on himself. To push the barrel of the .357 into his mouth and squeeze the trigger.

End the pain forever.

So simple.

Scott sat behind the wheel of the Rover, his head spinning, his vision clouding. And all the time there was the pain, gnawing away at him like some parasite feeding off his brain.

Take the gun and bite down on the barrel, taste the gun oil and the metal, then fire.

He could picture his own head exploding as he fired. Could feel the blissful oblivion. Could see himself at peace.

Could . . .

Fuck it.

No. He would not die yet. He refused to give up now. He had come too far, gone through too much to get to where he was now.

He gazed across the road towards the block of luxury flats where Ray Plummer lived. The one at the top. The penthouse flat. The pinnacle.

What had Cagney said in that film? 'Made it, Ma, Top of the World'. And then . . .

Scott pulled the Smith and Wesson from his belt, worked the slide and chambered a round. Then he jammed the pistol back into his belt and reached for the .357, flipping out the cylinder, checking that every chamber was filled with its deadly hollow-tipped load.

He was satisfied.

So it had come to this. His quest was almost over. He felt like some kind of medieval adventurer, some searcher after a lost treasure who could see that prize just yards away.

His prize was revenge.

It had kept him alive so far. Now he needed to claim that prize.

Scott swung himself out of the car, leaning against it for a moment as a fresh wave of pain hit him.

Keep me alert.

Stop the pain. Just for a while.

If he'd believed in God he might well have whispered a prayer.

Stop the pain.

He began walking, heading towards the entrance to the small block of flats.

Just for a while.

Just until . . .

He walked with his head down, gazing at the floor, only looking up as he reached the opposite pavement.

Had he looked up he might well have seen Ray Plummer watching him from the top window.

Scott reached the main entrance and slipped inside, pausing as he looked first towards the lift, then the stairs.

Which way to approach the penthouse?

If he took the lift he would be a sitting target as soon as the doors slid open. At least the stairs offered a modicum of cover.

He began to ascend.

Scott moved slowly, to minimise the sound of his footsteps. As he reached the second landing he pulled the 459 from his belt.

The doors on the other landings were closed, shut

tightly like the eyes of onlookers at an accident who don't wish to see the carnage.

He reached the third landing.

One more left and he would have reached the penthouse.

He paused.

One floor above him, crouching at the top of the stairs, was John Hitch.

He had the Beretta 92S loaded and ready.

He listened as Scott ascended.

One hundred and six

'Get out of the fucking way.'

DI Frank Gregson banged the steering wheel furiously and roared at the car in front of him.

The learner who was driving the car had stalled at traffic lights and was now endeavouring to get the vehicle restarted as traffic built up behind.

Gregson glanced up and saw that the lights were about to change to red.

He would be stuck.

'Come on, come on,' he snarled.

The car in front remained stationary.

The lights were on amber.

Gregson reversed a few feet, almost bumping the radiator grille of an Audi behind him, whose driver now shouted at *him*. He then swung the Ford Scorpio around the back of the learner and, as the lights changed to red, shot across the junction, beating the oncoming stream of vehicles, ignoring the chorus of indignant hooter blasts that accompanied his move.

He floored the accelerator and drove on, swerving to avoid some pedestrians who had stepped out into the road.

The car sped on towards Kensington Road.

Gregson didn't know if he would be in time; he could only try and reach Ray Plummer's flat before Jim Scott.

The helicopter had landed back at New Scotland Yard less than twenty minutes ago. Gregson had gone straight to the armoury and checked out a Taurus PT-92 automatic and three magazines of 9mm ammunition. He'd been told that Commissioner Sullivan wanted to see him but he'd ignored the order, saying he must get to Plummer.

Scott, he already knew, had destroyed one of Plummer's restaurants and one of his clip joints. It seemed only logical that he should now go after the man himself.

Gregson tried to coax more speed from the Scorpio, but ahead of him, coming into Kensington High Street, the traffic was slowing down again.

He had called once already for armed back-up, given the address of Plummer's flat.

Would he be too late?

There had been no answer yet.

He snatched up the radio, banging the hooter with his free hand as a car turned left ahead of him without indicating, causing him to brake hard.

'This is Lima 15, do you read me?' he rasped.

'Lima 15, go ahead.'

'I asked for back-up, *armed* back-up to some flats in Kensington. Where the hell is it?'

Silence for a moment, just the hiss of static.

'What address was that, Lima 15?' he was asked.

Gregson gave the address again.

'What the fuck are you playing at there? I need those

417

men fast. Do you understand?' he added angrily.

'Affirmative, Lima 15. A unit is on its way . . .'

Gregson snapped off the handset and replaced it, speeding on, cursing again when the traffic came to a standstill. He glanced to his right and left, thought about guiding the car up onto the pavement. No, too many fucking pedestrians about.

He looked at his watch again.

Something told him he was too late.

One hundred and seven

The step creaked under this weight.

Scott paused a moment, thinking how loud the sound seemed in the silence of the stairway.

He was about five steps from the top now, ducked low, the Smith and Wesson automatic gripped in his fist.

He prepared to move again.

Another creak.

From ahead of him this time.

A sound not of *his* making.

Scott looked up, saw a shadow. A dark shape crouched there.

He moved down a step.

There was more movement ahead, above.

John Hitch took a couple of steps towards the head of the stairs, the Beretta gripped in his hands.

Scott raised his own pistol simultaneously. There was a thunderous roar as both men fired. The stairway was

418

lit by muzzle flashes so brilliant they could have blinded. The walls shook as the roar of the automatics bounced around, amplified in the stairwell.

Scott felt a bullet blast through his shoulder, blood and portions of bone spraying the wall behind as he fell backwards, but he managed to get off three shots of his own.

One blasted a huge chunk of plaster from the wall, another hit the step Hitch was standing on. The third caught the man in the right shin. The bullet shattered his tibia, the strident cracking of bone audible even above the monstrous discharges of the pistols. A part of the bone tore through the skin and also through the material of Hitch's trousers. He shrieked in pain and dropped to the ground as Scott tried to force his way back up the stairs. His left shoulder was already beginning to go numb but he forced himself to keep a grip on the 459, firing again.

Another bullet hit Hitch in the forearm, but it passed through the muscle without touching bone.

He shot Scott in the stomach.

Scott felt as if he'd been punched by a red-hot fist. The air was knocked from him and the impact almost lifted him from his feet but he remained upright, blood running freely from the wound. The bullet exited through his side, taking muscle with it, spraying the bannister and stairs with blood, but Scott was lucky. No vital organs had been touched by the 9mm slug.

Scott fired twice at his prone foe, who was now trying to drag himself away from the top of the stairs.

The first bullet caught him in the left side of the chest, smashing two ribs as it blasted its way through, punching an exit hole the size of a fist and almost throwing Hitch against the far wall, which was sprayed with crimson and gobbets of lung tissue.

The second shot hit him, more by luck than judgement, in the hollow of the throat, blasting two cervical vertebrae to powder as it exploded from the back of his neck.

His head flopped back uselessly, his eyes rolling upwards in their sockets.

Death was instantaneous and Scott heard the soft hiss as the sphincter muscle relaxed. He smelt the excrement, saw a dark stain spreading rapidly across the front of Hitch's trousers.

Scott stumbled to the top of the stairs, the stench of blood and cordite strong in his nostrils.

He had pain now, but it was everywhere.

His head. His shoulder. His stomach.

He coughed and tasted blood in his mouth. A thick crimson foam dribbled over his lips; streamers of bloodied mucus hung from his mouth. He spat, wiping his mouth with the back of his hand.

As he reached the top of the stairs, stepping over the body of Hitch, he could see the door to Plummer's apartment.

He moved slowly towards it, ejecting one magazine from the automatic. Scott rammed another in and worked the slide.

He moved closer to the door.

The fucking pain . . .

He thought he was going to faint.

Not yet.

He was outside the door now.

Not yet.

There was a spy-hole in the door.

He threw himself to one side as a fusillade of bullets tore through the wood, blasting huge holes in it.

Scott landed heavily on his injured side, more blood

420

filled his mouth. He swivelled round, hauling himself upright, and crawled towards the door.

Silence had descended again; only his own wheezing breath was audible in the desolate solitude. Curtains of smoke wafted around, grey-blue smoke flecked with tiny cinders and pieces of wood that settled like dirty snow on the carpet.

He dragged himself upright, smearing blood against the wall. Then he stood beside the bullet-blasted door, steadying himself.

He gritted his teeth.

Now. It was time.

Scott swung his foot at the door with incredible force and it flew open, slamming back against the wall.

He dashed in, firing wildly to cover his entrance.

Bullets raked the apartment; ornaments were hit, blasted into oblivion.

Scott kept his finger pumping the trigger, firing all fifteen of the bullets until the slide flew back, signalling the pistol was empty.

He saw Ray Plummer standing to his left, in the entrance to the bedroom.

Carol was behind him, her face blank, drained of colour.

Scott turned on Plummer, realising that his gun was empty.

Plummer held a 10mm Delta Elite on him.

Scott opened his mouth to roar his rage but the sound was lost beneath the thunderous blast of the Delta.

The bullet hit Scott in the chest, punctured a lung and exploded from his back, chipping the bottom of his left scapula, tearing an exit hole large enough to get two hands in. Portions of greyish-red lung tissue and pulverised bone erupted from the wound.

Scott was lifted, as if by some invisible hand, and

sent sprawling over the sofa, blood spraying out behind him.

He crashed into a coffee table, the impact almost making him black out. Then he rolled onto his stomach, his mouth open, his eyelids flickering.

He heard Carol call his name, heard Plummer tell her to shut up.

Footsteps came close.

Through pain-misted eyes he saw Plummer looking down at him, the 10mm levelled.

Scott was lying on his right hand, his fingers within reach of the .357. He felt his shaking digits touch the wood of the stock.

'You should have stayed away,' sneered Plummer. 'Stayed in prison. You came a long fucking way to die.' He aimed the pistol at Scott's head.

Scott rolled onto his back, the .357 now in his hand. The fired upwards, twice.

The first bullet blasted Plummer's nose off, obliterating the fleshy appendage, which dissolved in an explosion of blood.

He screamed in agony but the sound was cut short as the second hollow tip bullet hit him below the chin, tearing upwards into his head, through his brain and finally bursting from the top of his skull, lifting him off his feet.

His head looked as if someone had place an explosive charge inside it. The entire cranial cavity seemed to detonate, blood and brain spattering the ceiling, spraying everything within a foot or so.

His wig was blown clear, flying off to one side like a flattened cat.

Plummer tottered for interminable seconds, his bald dome open to the air, portions of his brain hanging from the riven cavity, blood jetting madly into the air. Then he fell forward across the sofa, his body sliding to the floor, crimson spreading in a pool around him.

Carol could only stand mesmerised. Her body shook, her nostrils were filled with the smell of cordite and death, her eyes had been blinded by the muzzle flashes, her ears rang from the thunderous discharges.

She looked at Scott, then at Plummer.

Scott. Plummer.

Scott.

She moved towards him, noticed that his chest was rising and falling slowly. She could hear a soft, wet sound. It was Scott's breath wheezing through the hole in his lung. The place was drenched with blood – floor, ceiling, walls.

She felt the warmth beneath her bare feet, felt a jellied lump of matter between her toes and almost vomited when she saw it was part of Plummer's brain. She stepped back and looked down at Scott once again.

He was lying on his back, his eyes half-open.

Carol swallowed hard as she saw the wounds, the one in his chest gaping, a portion of bone shining through the pulped flesh and the bright blood.

She knelt beside him, ignoring the blood that had soaked into the carpet around him.

'Jim,' she whispered, touching his cheek with the back of her hand.

He could see the tears in her eyes.

'Oh God, Jim, I'm sorry,' she breathed. 'I'm so sorry.'

He tried to breathe but couldn't.

Tried to speak. Couldn't.

Blood ran over his lips and down his chin.

'Jim,' she repeated, touching his face once more, stroking it as a lover might touch a partner.

His eyes narrowed too.

423

Fucking bitch.

'I'm sorry,' she said again.

You betrayed me.

His own eyes were moist now, both from pain and emotion.

And fear?

He could almost feel death touching him.

'I didn't want this to happen,' she told him, still stroking his face. 'I'm so sorry.'

Tears were coursing down her cheeks.

She lowered her head, as if in prayer, her hands resting on her thighs.

Scott raised the .357 and pointed it at her head.

Carol had her eyes closed now.

Bitch.

He thumbed back the hammer.

It was then that she looked up.

The roar of the single shot was deafening.

One hundred and eight

The sound of the discharge reverberated inside the apartment for what seemed like an eternity.

It mingled with Carol's scream.

She had seen Scott lift the gun and point it at her, their eyes locked for precious seconds, then she had seen his head burst as the 9mm bullet had hit it, pulverising his forehead.

Frank Gregson stood in the doorway, the Taurus automatic still aimed at Scott, as if he feared the man would move again.

Carol looked at Scott, then at the policeman.

Tears were still coursing down her cheeks.

'He would have killed you,' Gregson said, walking into the room, glancing at Plummer's body. 'Just like he killed the others.' He looked at Plummer once more. 'He was a madman. He wanted revenge.' Gregson nudged Plummer's body with the toe of his shoe. 'He did me a favour, though. Getting rid of Plummer.' The DI smiled. 'I just didn't want *you* to get hurt.'

'What difference would it have made to you?' she wanted to know.

'A lot of difference,' he said, his smile fading. 'I care what happens to you very much. I have done ever since I first arrested you.' He sat down on the edge of the chair, looking down at her. 'That's why I called you.'

Carol looked vague.

'What are you talking about?' she wanted to know.

'The phone calls,' he said. 'I called you at your home, at work, even here.'

'Oh God,' she murmured.

'I hated to think of you with men like Plummer and Scott,' he said. 'You deserved better than that. I wanted you to know I was watching you. I wouldn't have let anything happen to you.'

'You were the anonymous caller,' she blurted, everything now beginning to drop into place with appalling clarity.

'I didn't just ring you,' he said. 'Who do you think tipped Plummer off about that cocaine shipment?'

'But why?' she wanted to know.

'Plummer was too powerful. The gang's in London had taken over,' Gregson said angrily. 'They were running things. Men like Plummer and Connelly. Scum. Criminals and fucking murderers.' He spat out the words vehemently. 'I wanted a gang war, I wanted them to wipe each other out. To save *us* the trouble of trying

425

to arrest them. Getting them to court on charges we knew would never stick. That's what we've been doing for years. The police are fighting a losing battle against men like Plummer and Connelly. I knew the only way was to use force but *I* can't do that, my *responsibility to the community* says I can't. I couldn't stop them. So I realised I'd have to make *them* stop each other. Kill each other. Wipe each other off the face of the fucking earth. That's why I tipped Plummer off about Connelly's shipment; I knew he'd take it because he was greedy. I knew if he took it Connelly would never stand for it. I knew there would be war, and there would have been. *I* would have won. The fucking *law* would have won for a change.' He sucked in a deep breath. 'Well, now it's all over. Now you're not tied to him anymore. You're free.'

'Am I supposed to thank you?' she said softly.

'Perhaps,' he said, smiling thinly.

'Why did you have to do this to Jim?' she wanted to know.

'Plummer set him up, not me.'

'And if Plummer *hadn't*?'

Gregson shrugged.

'Then I'd have got rid of him some other way,' he said.

'You're insane,' she said quietly.

'The whole fucking world is insane,' he said wearily.

'What about me? What happens to me now? You've told me everything. I know about you and what you've done. You're the evil one. You would have let dozens of men kill each other. You let Scott die for no reason. And I know it all.'

'Who's going to believe you?' he said, smiling.

'No one,' she said quietly.

'You're mine when I want you now,' Gregson told her.

426

'And there isn't a thing you can do about it.' He smiled.

'No,' she said. 'I suppose you're right. No one's going to believe me, are they?'

'You're mine, Carol,' he said mockingly.

'I don't have a choice, do I?'

'No,' he told her.

She picked up the .357 lying nearby, steadied herself and fired twice.

Both bullets hit Gregson in the chest. As he fell she got to her feet and put two more into him.

The hammer finally slammed down on an empty chamber.

Carol continued to pull the trigger, looking down at the motionless, bloodied corpse of the policeman.

'All right, drop it.'

The voice boomed through the flat as the first of the armed policemen entered, pistols trained on Carol. She smiled thinly and dropped the gun.

'Jesus Christ,' one of the men murmured, looking round at the carnage.

Carol felt strong hands grab her. She felt lifeless, unable to move; only her eyes, it seemed, were functioning. She looked down at Gregson then at Scott.

Words drifted to her through a haze that seemed to have enveloped her brain. It was as if she were watching herself from outside, through other eyes. The words continued;

'. . . four dead . . .'

'. . . Maybe she killed them all . . .'

'. . . Tell his wife . . .' Two of the men were kneeling beside Gregson, checking for any signs of life.

One of them looked up at Carol. This time, the words did seem to penetrate the haze.

'Shooting a policeman,' he said angrily. 'You'll get life for this.'

Carol looked across at Scott's dead body.

'You'll get life for this,' she heard again as she was ushered out of the room.

'. . . life . . .'

She smiled thinly.

One hundred and nine

The needle on the petrol gauge was touching empty, Finn noticed with alarm. Nevertheless he kept his foot pressed down on the accelerator of the Citroën, glancing up ahead to see, to his relief, that Dexter too was slowing down.

There was a road of a kind up ahead, a badly tarmacked track that separated the fields from a large house built of dark stone.

Dexter was guiding the Sierra up the short driveway of this house.

Finn saw the doctor clamber out of the car and head for the front door, letting himself in, slamming the door behind him.

Finn screeched up the drive behind him and stood on the brakes. He ran to the front door and banged on it several times, shouting Dexter's name. When there was no answer he turned and looked into the Sierra, noticing that Dexter had left the keys hanging from the ignition. Finn pulled open the door and dropped the keys into his pocket, then made his way slowly to the side of the house.

He found a pathway leading down the side of the

building, its entrance guarded by a carefully cut arch of privet. Finn pushed open the gate and walked through, moving briskly around to the back.

The large house towered above the DS as he peered through windows into the kitchen then, moving along, into what he took to be a study of some kind. As he passed the kitchen door he tried the handle but found that it was locked. A long, immaculately kept garden stretched out behind the house.

He saw several objects lying on the lawn.

Toys.

There was a doll and a small yellow ball. A skipping rope.

Finn picked up the doll, looking into its lifeless eyes for a moment, then dropped it back onto the grass and headed back towards the kitchen door.

There were panels of glass in it.

He broke one with his elbow then reached through and turned the key in the lock, stepping inside.

He called Dexter's name as he moved through towards the sitting room.

'Give it up, Dexter,' he shouted. 'There's nowhere else to run now.' He moved through the sitting room. 'If it isn't me it'll be someone else. I've only got to make one call and this place will be swarming with uniforms in less than five minutes.'

He moved out into the hall.

'Don't make things any worse,' he called. 'Chuck it in, now.'

A sound above him.

Finn looked up towards the landing.

The stairs were directly ahead of him. To his left was the door of the study, to the right the front door.

Finn wondered why Dexter hadn't just continued driving in the first place, why . . .

429

Another noise from upstairs.

. . . Why not escape? Why come here?

He began to climb the stairs, one hand trailing along the bannister.

Why come here?

He was half-way up the stairs now, glancing around, his eyes always returning to the head of the flight.

Another ten steps and he'd be there.

He could hear the sound of his blood roaring in his ears.

'Dexter,' he called.

Silence.

'There's no way out,' he continued.

Movement.

As Finn reached the top of the stairs, Dexter appeared from one of the room.

He had a double-barrelled shotgun levelled at the policeman.

'That's no answer,' Finn said, his eyes drawn to the yawning barrels of the Purdey. 'If you kill me, you make it even worse for yourself.'

Besides which, I don't want to die, you fucking maniac.

'This gun has been in my family for three generations,' Dexter told him conversationally.

'Why don't you just put it down, then we'll talk,' Finn said, wondering if his skin looked as pale and cold as it felt.

'The experiments at the prison, they would have worked,' Dexter said. 'They *had* worked.'

'There's a lot of dead people who are lying around to contradict that argument, Dexter.'

'It *did* work. It *can* work,' he insisted. 'I *made* it work.'

He snapped his fingers, the barrel still aimed at Finn.

The DS heard movement from behind Dexter, from the room he had his back to.

'Come out,' Dexter said, turning his head slightly, his eyes never leaving Finn.

A figure moved onto the landing beside him.

'Oh, dear Christ,' murmured Finn, his eyes widening as he studied the features of the newcomer.

It was a woman; at least he thought it was. The short hair made it difficult to tell at first, and the voluminous nightdress managed to conceal any shape convincingly. Perhaps she had once been pretty. Finn could only guess. If she had, those days were long gone. The skin was the colour of rancid butter and hardly an inch of flesh on the face was not disfigured by scars, welts or stitches. The forehead had been worst affected, the hair shaved back almost to the top of the head, criss-crossed by stitching, bruises and half-healed wounds, some of which had scabbed over. Others were only purple knots where skin had begun to form but had been picked away.

Finn shook his head.

'Jesus Christ,' he muttered under his breath. 'What is it?'

'There was a car accident,' Dexter explained. 'In January 1976. At times it seems as if it was only yesterday, other times it seems like centuries ago. She was taken to hospital, but they couldn't do anything for her. The brain damage was massive. I worked in an asylum, then. They brought her there to see if I could help. I think they would have been happy if she'd just been locked away, but I didn't want that.'

Finn noticed that the figure next to Dexter was holding a doll like the one that lay on the lawn outside. She was prodding the glass eyes.

'I knew I could do something. They said she was violent. The brain damage had caused some kind of

431

psychosis. My colleague and I experimented on her. Her and a number of others. The others died, but she responded. I've looked after her ever since, here at this house.'

Finn was breathing deeply, his gaze moving from the figure then back to the shotgun.

'You would have been kinder letting her die,' he said, his voice a hoarse whisper.

'No,' Dexter said, shaking his head. 'I wouldn't let her die. Never.' There was a note of anger in his voice as he looked at the policeman. 'Not my own daughter.'

Finn swallowed hard.

The woman smiled at Dexter, streams of mucus running from her mouth, hanging from her lips like thick, elongated tears.

'*Daddy*,' she slurred.

Finn clenched his teeth together until his jaws ached.

'When I'm gone there'll be no one to care for her,' Dexter said. 'No one.'

'*Daddy*,' she whined in metallic voice.

'I won't leave her,' the doctor said.

With that he spun round, aiming the shotgun at his daughter's head.

'No,' roared Finn.

The sound was lost beneath the blast as Dexter fired.

She dropped like a stone, the doll falling from her grasp. Blood spattered the walls behind. Finn saw fragments of brain and bone dripping from the ceiling.

He lunged towards Dexter, who spun the shotgun in his grasp, bit down hard on the barrels he'd stuck in his mouth and pulled the other trigger.

The top of his head erupted like a bloody volcano as the blast carried most of his skull away.

He fell backwards, sprawled across the legs of his daughter, the Purdey falling with a thump.

'Oh Jesus,' Finn murmured, holding one hand to his mouth, gazing at each body in turn. The air smelt of death.

The DS picked up the doll the girl had dropped.

Girl? Woman? God alone knew how old she was. And God had long ago tired of watching over *this* particular wretch.

Finn held the doll in his hands, looking into its cold eyes, then dropped it.

As it hit the floor he heard a whirring sound followed by one word, a metallic whine:

'*Daddy.*'

He turned and walked away, heading for the stairs, for the phone.

The word echoed in his ears. In his mind.

'*Daddy.*'

'He who considers more deeply knows that, whatever his acts and judgements may be, he is always wrong . . .'

Nietzsche

You can't win. You can't break even and you can't even get out of the game.

Ginsberg's Law

Breeding Ground

To Bob Tanner the man who first lifted the stone and invited me to crawl out from under it. Thank you.

'Close the city and tell the people
that something is coming to call . . .'
– *Ronnie James Dio*

Acknowledgements

I would like to thank Mr Greg Teckover of the Metropolitan Water Authority for his help. Also, thankyou to Mr Paul Hayers. Special thanks, as ever, to everyone at W.H. Allen. Also, for different reasons, thankyou to Niki (the only lady I know who managed to turn watering house plants into a health hazard). To Chris and Kim at Ripple Records; to Dave Risby (it's a fair cop); to Belinda (who really ought to be careful where she stubs her cigarettes out) but, most of all thanks to YOU, the reader. To everyone who's ever parted with some of their cash to buy one of my books, I thank you.

Shaun Hutson

Prologue

The farmer watched impatiently as the crates of lettuce were unloaded from the back of his lorry. He chewed the end of his pipe, which, as ever, remained unlit.

All around him the place was alive with the sounds of crashing boxes, raised voices and laughter. The usual cacophony which accompanied the early-morning proceedings at Covent Garden.

The summer sun was already high in the sky above London, pouring its unrelenting heat down over the capital. The day promised to be another scorcher.

The farmer disliked the city. He'd lived in the country all his life and the frenzied hustle and bustle which characterized the sprawling metropolis unsettled him. He shifted the unlit pipe to the other side of his mouth, watching as his produce was inspected. The buyer moved from crate to crate, swiftly but expertly checking the contents. Occasionally he would remove one of the lettuces, tossing it onto a nearby pile of other discarded vegetables.

'Good crop again,' said the farmer.

'Yeah, only a few bad ones,' murmured the buyer, picking up another lettuce.

Noticing something inside the inner leaves, he threw it onto the pile with the other rejects.

After fifteen minutes he was finished. The deal was concluded and the farmer climbed thankfully back into the lorry. He waved farewell to the buyer and set off to battle his way through the traffic, anxious to get home to the relative peace of his farm.

As the day progressed, the pile of discarded vegetables grew higher until it was almost as tall as a man. The heat of the sun caused the green stuff to wilt and a powerful smell began to rise from it, but those nearby ignored the stench.

Stallholders shouted out their prices and bickered with their rivals. It was a normal day.

No one noticed the lettuce which lay near the bottom of the pile, rejected because of the strange cylindrical objects inside its inner leaves. The transparent mucoid tubes with the black centres.

Despite the searing heat of the sun the tiny shapes glistened as if perpetually wet and, slowly, as if triggered by some secret, silent alarm, they began to split open. One by one the liquescent tubes disgorged their contents.

The slugs were less than one centimetre long, almost transparent and already covered by a thin film of slime. Against the dark, rotting vegetation they were barely visible and they remained in one gently moving cluster no bigger than a matchbox.

They grew swiftly. Much more swiftly than normal, and with that growth came another change.

At first almost invisible, they began to darken in colour. A pale, pus coloured yellow first, then a light brown. They remained clotted together, hidden within the wrinkled folds of the lettuce.

And they grew.

Though still smaller than a finger nail, by noon they had doubled in size.

Tuesday – the 11th

One

The half-eaten hamburger was still warm and Tommy Price smiled to himself as he stuffed it into his mouth, oblivious to the revolted stares of a passing woman who had seen him plunge his hand into the waste-bin and retrieve the food. He chewed quickly, wiped his hands on his jacket and then peered into the bin once more, rummaging around in the rubbish in search of something else to satisfy his raging hunger. He found nothing, however. Muttering to himself, he moved on to the next bin and dug his hand in like a child at a lucky dip. The search yielded a half-full carton of milkshake, but when Tommy removed the plastic lid he saw that the thick liquid was covered by a rancid sheath of grey-green mould. Flies buzzed around him, one settling on the rim of the carton, savouring the sweet curdled fluid. Tommy dropped the milkshake back into the bin.

In the cloudless blue sky, the sun hung like a ball of fire, baking all below it with fierce rays. As Tommy walked, the pavement felt hot beneath his feet, the warmth having little difficulty reaching his bare soles through shoes which were nearly worn through. As he made his way along the Strand he paused at each waste-bin and performed his familiar ritual, hunting through the rubbish for anything vaguely edible. During the last four or five weeks he had discovered that the human digestive system was capable of absorbing almost anything. Especially if its owner was nearly starving.

Even though he had not eaten a good meal for nearly two months, Tommy did not seem to have lost much weight. He was a powerfully-built individual, standing around six feet,

11

the jacket he wore stretched almost to breaking point across his broad back and shoulders. The cuffs were frayed, the elbows shiny and it bore numerous stains. His trousers, once part of a suit, were too short and the unfashionably wide bottoms could not conceal his filthy socks which puckered round his ankles like surgical stockings.

Tommy Price walked on up the road, sometimes bumping into tourists and shoppers, although they did their best to avoid him. Tommy didn't smell very good, especially in such hot weather. He ran a hand through his hair which hadn't been washed for weeks, wincing as his fingers touched a large spot just below his hairline. He caught sight of his reflection in a shop window and paused for a moment, taken aback by the sight which greeted him. It was like looking at another person, someone alien to him. He wondered if the apparition would vanish if he blinked. He tried and it didn't. The same unkempt reflection continued to stare back at him.

He had been in London for the last two months since leaving Newcastle, and it had been eight weeks of misery. The pit where he had worked since he was sixteen had closed down over a year ago, and at the age of forty-seven he had found himself on the scrap heap, like so many of his generation. He remembered the stories his father had told him of the great march from Jarrow in 1926. Now he, like his father, had come to London but for different reasons.

Tommy did not, like many misinformed youngsters, believe that he would find a fortune in the country's capital, but he had at least expected some work. He didn't care what it was. Nothing had come his way, however. His savings had dwindled and, within two weeks of arriving, he had found himself seeking shelter in Salvation Army Hostels. And now he could not even find solace there any longer.

Tommy liked his drink. If he had to steal it then that was fair enough, but he needed it. He'd been caught trying to liberate a bottle of Haig from an off-licence, and owing to his circumstances the judge had dismissed the case. But Tommy had been desperate, and the sight of two five-pound notes in the pocket of another man at the hostel that night had been too much of a temptation. He'd been banned after being caught. Now he walked the streets every day, carrying his belongings in a battered hold-all and searching dustbins and hotel rubbish skips and pub yards for what meagre pickings there were.

He had thought once or twice of returning to Newcastle but there was nothing there for him any more. He was without a family. He had never married. Both his parents were dead, his younger brother had been killed in a pit accident at twenty-four, and his sister now lived in Canada with her husband and children. He pushed the thoughts of the past out of his mind, surprised at how easily they disappeared. It was as if he had been traipsing these London streets all his life, foraging like some kind of carrion crow, accepting anything and everything edible. He had suffered from a stomach upset at the beginning, but now his belly seemed immune to whatever vile garbage he chose to inflict upon it.

Tommy wiped the sweat from his face with one grime-encrusted hand and walked on. Another five minutes and he had reached his destination.

Covent Garden seemed unusually busy on this blistering summer's day but Tommy moved purposefully through the crowds, peering longingly at the fruit and vegetables laid out on stalls all around him. He paused to inspect a waste-bin and his face lit up as he found a bottle of Guinness. The neck was broken and jagged, but Tommy raised it to his lips and drank. The dark fluid was warm and sour but he swallowed most of it, wiping his mouth with the back of his hand before moving on. He belched loudly and his stomach rumbled protestingly. Tommy took another swig from the bottle, aware now of a particularly rank odour which assaulted his nostrils.

Just ahead of him he saw a pile of fruit and vegetables, discarded by the stallholders in the market. Without hesitation he crossed to it and began grabbing handfuls of the sub-standard produce. His fingers sank into a rotted tomato but he merely wiped the orange mush on his jacket and pushed some more food into his hold-all.

'What are you doing, mate?' a voice asked and Tommy

13

turned to see a broad man, stripped to the waist, standing before him.

'You don't want this, do you?' Tommy said, indicating the pile of discarded food.

'Help yourself,' the man told him and wandered away.

Tommy continued his little harvest, ignoring the hordes of flies which swarmed round the reeking mound. He picked up a handful of small potatoes and pushed them into his pocket.

The lettuce he dropped into his hold-all.

The leaves were wilting but it was moist, perhaps a little sticky, he thought. Tommy saw something glistening on the leaves, shining brightly in the sunshine, but he paid it no heed.

Inside the lettuce, the small slugs remained in their tight bundle, held firmly together by the thick coating of slime which surrounded them like some kind of gelatinous cocoon.

Finally, his pockets and hold-all stuffed with the discarded fruit and vegetables, Tommy left the remaining garbage to the flies and wasps which swarmed over it like an undulating cloud.

He left the traders and their customers behind, seeking out the nearest empty doorway in which to enjoy his feast. There was a shop close by, its windows boarded up. Paint had been sprayed all over the wood and Tommy glanced briefly at the grafitti:

IF THATCHER WAS THE ANSWER IT MUST HAVE BEEN A FUCKING STUPID QUESTION

99% IS SHIT

Why give the other 1% the benefit of the doubt? thought Tommy, seating himself in the darkened doorway amongst the yellowed newspaper and discarded cigarette packets. He rummaged through one and found a more or less intact Marlboro. This was his lucky day. Except for the fact that he had nothing to light it with. He put it in his breast pocket for future use and settled down with the food he'd scavenged just minutes before. He still had some Guinness left in the broken bottle, too.

He devoured the food ravenously, ignoring the sometimes

rancid flavours. It filled his stomach and that was all that mattered.

He pushed lumps of the lettuce into his mouth, swallowing large pieces of it whole.

A vile taste suddenly filled his mouth, and for a moment he thought he was going to vomit. His stomach contracted as something thick and slimy touched the back of his throat before sliding down. He licked his tongue around his mouth and lips, spitting out some viscous fluid which looked like mucus. He coughed and spat again, reaching for the bottle of Guinness, which he downed in one long swallow in an effort to wash away the foul taste. He threw away what remained of the lettuce, rubbing his stomach. After a moment or two the taste seemed to fade away and he got to his feet, belching loudly once again. It was more than he'd eaten for a week. Tommy fumbled in his pocket and found the cigarette, then wandered off in search of a light.

The sun had reached its zenith. The city sweltered beneath the merciless onslaught of heat.

Tommy took off his jacket as he walked, enjoying the feel of the sun on his skin.

It was another two hours before the pains began.

Almost reluctantly, as if loath to give up its domination of the heavens, the sun sank lower in the sky and darker skies signalled the onset of evening. The clouds above London were stained purple and crimson and layered one on top of another. The rich colours spread across the sky like ink soaking into blotting paper. Tall buildings became featureless black monoliths against the multi-hued backdrop.

In London's West End, however, the streets were bright. The glow of thousands of light bulbs and strands of neon created an artificial, many-coloured day which lit all but the darkest corners and alleyways. And the ceaseless activity, if anything, seemed to intensify as people went about their pleasure and, in some cases, business. The night people were out.

Some were buying, some were selling.

Tommy Price moved slowly down Regent Street, his face pale and expressionless, one hand clutched tightly to his stomach.

The pain had begun, he estimated, soon after three o'clock that afternoon. Slight nagging discomfort at first, centred around his navel, a griping annoyance which he had expected to leave him. But now, six hours later, the pain had grown to almost unbearable intensity, gnawing away at him relentlessly until it felt as if his entire torso, even his bowels, were filled with fire. He walked unsteadily, with a drunkard's gait, and more than once he attracted stares from passing policemen. But no one stopped him as he careered on down the street, past shops now closed, past the Rent boys who waited at the exit of Piccadilly Tube station. The buyers and sellers.

Tommy blundered across the road, narrowly avoiding a collision with a motor-cyclist, stumbling up the kerb on the other side, almost losing his footing. He stood still for long moments, aware only of the agonizing pain which gripped him like a steel fist, the fingers tightening by the second. He felt a wave of violent nausea wrack his body and it was all he could do to prevent himself from vomiting. He leant against the window of a nearby Wimpey Bar, gazing in at a group of young children, one of whom stuck his tongue out at the ghastly apparition looking through the glass at him. The other children laughed and pointed at Tommy, who whirled away, banging into a tall youth in a camouflage jacket.

The youth grunted and pushed Tommy, who staggered and fell.

Passers-by kept well away from him, although one or two stopped to look at him as he crouched helplessly on the pavement, clutching his stomach.

He groaned as a wave of pain so intense it almost caused him to scream aloud shook him and, this time, he could not contain himself. His stomach contracted and a foul-smelling stream of vomit gushed from his mouth and splattered on the pavement. Those standing nearby hurried on. Two young girls laughed disgustedly but Tommy did not hear what they

16

said because just then a second spasm shook him and another stream of hideously-coloured liquid flooded from him, puddling in thick clots on the pavement. He tried to rise, reeking streamers of thick vomit and mucus hanging from his lips and chin. Through eyes blurred with pain he saw that there were dark streaks in the puddle of vomit before him. And, along with the bitter taste, he also detected that of blood. He wiped his mouth, his breath catching in his throat as he saw the crimson liquid glistening on the back of his hand. The sight of it made him want to be sick again but he managed to control himself, rising with a monumental effort of will. He tried to straighten up but the pain dug white-hot knives into his belly, groin and chest. He struggled a few more yards then slumped against a wall, his breath coming in agonized gasps. A voice close by told him to move on and he saw that he was propped against the glass window of a cinema cash-desk. The cashier, a short thin woman with thick spectacles, shouted at him once more to move away and, as a burly-looking doorman approached, Tommy managed to do so.

As he crossed the road figures swam before him as if he were looking through a heat haze. He saw the expressions on their faces as they looked at him, his jacket and trousers stained with vomit and blood. He saw the disgust, the bewilderment. Even the amusement. He felt like crying out to one of these people for help but he knew it would be futile for, indeed, how *could* they help him? Could they stop the pain he was feeling? The screaming agony which made him feel as if his intestines were being knotted repeatedly by red hot fingers. Clutching his stomach with both hands, he lurched on towards Leicester Square, the lights from the Swiss Centre winking invitingly at him as he drew nearer. There were wooden benches outside the building. Perhaps if he could reach one of those and sit down . . .

Tommy practically ran towards the benches, almost falling onto the nearest one. He doubled up in pain again, tears of suffering running down his grimy cheeks. Behind him a small crowd had gathered around a man who was playing a saxophone in the street. Mellow, soothing notes floated up on

17

the warm evening air, but they did nothing to sooth the pain which Tommy felt. He sat a moment longer, then wrenched himself upright once more, passing a middle-aged couple who stood and watched as he stumbled away.

He made his way across Leicester Square, the lights which shone from the front of the Empire Cinema dazzling him. There were many youngsters there, seated on the walls which surrounded a variety of small trees and shrubs dotted around the concrete expanse. Some of the kids followed his stumbling progress indifferently as he headed for the entrance to the public lavatory.

At the top of the steps Tommy steadied himself, slowing his pace in case he should slip and fall. Step by step he descended, the pain now beyond belief. He felt as if his entire torso was contracting, then expanding, swelling as if ready to burst. He felt the nausea building once more, a tidal wave of pain which he knew was unstoppable. Tommy rolled the last few feet down the steps and sprawled on the wet floor, blood dribbling in a thin ribbon from one corner of his mouth.

A man standing at the urinal looked round in surprise and alarm. So anxious was he to be away from this frightful-looking apparition, he almost wet himself pushing his penis back into his trousers. He whipped up his zip, wincing as he caught a pubic hair in his haste, and sprinted up the stairs, leaving Tommy sprawled on the tiles.

Tommy began to crawl towards one of the cubicles, inch by agonizing .inch, his lower body and chest ablaze with pain, blood spilling onto the dirty tiles, spreading out like blossoming crimson flowers. He felt his stomach lurch again but he clenched his teeth, his mouth filling with vomit which forced his cheeks to bulge until, at last, he let it go in a fetid spray of blood flecked yellow ooze which spattered the cubicle and the toilet itself. Head bowed over the bowl, he emptied his stomach until blood began to colour the water. Thick crimson fluid coated the cracked porcelain and spilled down Tommy's chin and chest. He tried to scream but the blood and vomit clogged in his throat. He felt something warm and wet running from his anus but he didn't realize that

18

this was blood as well.

He couldn't breathe. His head felt as if it were being pumped full of air and, all the time, the pain in his stomach intensified until he prayed for death to come and release him from the insufferable torment.

That death seemed to be a long time coming.

The cubicle door swung shut behind him.

Two

'Look, I'm telling you, they lock this place up at twelve,' Paul Hilston said, looking around the deserted lavatory.

'Then we've got another hour, haven't we?' Howard Mallows chided him. 'Have you got the fucking stuff or what?'

Hilston nodded, clutching a large brown paper bag to his chest.

'The fucking police come down here at night you know,' he said, agitatedly. 'I ain't getting caught with this lot.' He held up the bag.

'Well, if you're scared, piss off now. Right?'

'I ain't scared.'

'Then get the fucking stuff out, before some nob-head walks in,' demanded Mallows. 'Let's go in one of the cubicles.'

They both stepped into the furthest one and slid the bolt. Mallows lowered the seat and planted himself on it, watching as Hilston opened the brown bag and took out two tubes of Bostik and two smaller, plastic bags. He handed a tube of glue and one of the bags to his companion, who unscrewed the top of the tube and began squeezing the thick fluid into the plastic bag.

Mallows was smiling broadly, revealing a set of teeth which hadn't encountered toothpaste for some time. He was twenty, his face pock-marked and deeply pitted. There were dark scabs around both his nostrils and he picked at one as he squeezed the glue into the bag. His hair cut short, accentuating the size of his ears, which stuck out prominently from a head which looked too small for his body. The jeans he wore were cut short to show off his long boots. The red laces matched his T-shirt.

Hilston was a year or so younger. A thin, foxy looking lad with smooth, almost feminine skin which had yet to feel a razor's edge. His hair, however, was even shorter than Mallows' and a little lighter, making him appear almost bald. He waited while his companion emptied the last of the Bostik into the bag, tossed the tube away and then scrunched up the plastic to form a nozzle. This he placed over his nose and mouth. He inhaled, then exhaled deeply, never allowing the bag to leave his face. Hilston watched for a moment longer then followed his example.

It was the first time he'd ever sniffed and the initial dose of fumes made him cough, but he tried again despite the fact that his eyes had begun to water. It felt as if someone had stuck a lighted match up each of his nostrils. The smell seemed to fill his head, and for a second he swayed and thought he was going to faint, but as he kept breathing he found that a pleasantly light-headed feeling was beginning to engulf him.

For his part, Mallows sat back on the toilet seat, his face still buried in the bag. When he lowered it, his nose and the skin around his mouth were bright red. He chuckled and looked at his companion.

'Fucking great, eh?' he said, his voice distant and slightly slurred.

Hilston nodded and dropped his own bag.

'It's better when you get out in the air,' Mallows added. 'Come on.' He got to his feet and slid back the bolt on the door, and they both walked out into the dimly-lit lavatory, which as far as they could see was still deserted. The glue tubes lay discarded in the cubicle.

'What if the filth are around?' asked Hilston. 'They'll smell it on us.'

'Fuck them,' said Mallows, kicking the door of the cubicle next to him. He went to each one in turn and repeated the mindless action, chuckling to himself. When he reached the last one the door swung back only a foot or so. He kicked it again, feeling resistance on the other side.

Both of them stood still for a moment as if taken aback by the temporary obstruction. Then Mallows kicked the door again, the impact of boot on wood echoing loudly in the silent cavern.

'There's somebody in there,' Hilston announced, dropping to one knee. He could see a dark form inside, hunched close to the lavatory bowl. In the gloom it was difficult to distinguish colours and the glue was further affecting his vision, but he could make out a pool of dark liquid around the base of the bowl, some of which had trickled beneath the door.

'Perhaps he's got diarrhoea,' Mallows chuckled. Then, kicking the door again, he shouted, 'Come on mate, it's time to go home.'

The thick wooden partition moved another couple of inches, enabling Mallows to squeeze his considerable bulk into the cubicle. He looked down at the man slumped before him. Now he could see the filthy, vomit-spattered jacket and trousers, the matted hair and the unearthly paleness of the skin made all the worse by the dull glare of the fluorescents in the lavatory.

'Leave him,' Hilston said. 'Let's go. Come on.'

'Had a few too many have you, mate?' Mallows chuckled, looking down at the ragged mess before him.

Tommy Price did not move.

'Howard, come on,' said Hilston again, peering over his friend's shoulder. 'He's pissed out of his fucking mind, you can see that.'

Mallows shot his companion an angry glance.

'He might have got some money, you prat,' snapped the

21

older youth. Then he returned his attention to Tommy once more, nudging him with the toe of his boot.

'Oi, wake up,' he said, prodding him again.

There was no response.

'Leave it out, Howard,' Hilston insisted. 'He's right out of it.' Then, for some reason, he began laughing. 'He don't look like he's got any fucking money, does he?'

Mallows seemed unconcerned about the dark liquid which surrounded Tommy, congealing on the dirty floor like drying paint. The big youth kicked at the motionless man's legs, the force of his blows increasing with each kick.

'Wake up, you cunt,' he hissed, transferring his attention to Tommy's upper body. He pushed him with the sole of his boot, watching as the body merely slid down onto the floor, the pale face tilted upwards, eyes closed. Mallows rubbed his eyes, his head swimming. He sniffed back some mucus and gritted his teeth, made a hawking noise and spat a thick green globule at Tommy. It hit his cheek and rolled down like a huge sticky tear.

Enraged by his failure to arouse any movement in the tramp, Mallows stepped back, preparing to strike harder.

'I'll wake you up, you bastard,' he snarled and drove his foot forward with as much force as he could muster.

The boot struck Tommy in the stomach.

The flesh and muscles seemed merely to burst and, as his shirt split open, so too did his lower torso. From pelvis to sternum, the body seemed to rupture, like some kind of pea pod. The entire cavity opened like a pair of obscene lips, sliding back to welcome the intruding boot of Mallows which disappeared into the seething mess inside. Flesh tore like fabric and the skinhead almost overbalanced as his foot sank into the tramp's body, forcing its way through to the spine, such was the force of the impact.

His eyes widened in horror as he looked down.

Hilston tried to scream but he could only stand riveted, wondering, for precious seconds, if he was hallucinating.

He wished that he had been.

Slugs filled the riven torso like maggots in an open wound,

slithering over one another, their thick slime mingling with blood and the spilled green bile which had oozed from Tommy's gall bladder. The hideous black creatures, some as long as six inches, looked as if they had been sealed together by the glutinous muck which covered them. Like a huge black carnivorous cancer which had grown inside the tramp, literally devouring his internal organs, eating him away from the inside. Until now, at last, aided by Mallows' boot, they had burst forth.

Tommy's lips moved soundlessly and Mallows watched, mesmerized, as a thick black shape nudged its way free of his mouth. The slug's eye stalks extended slowly, and as it slithered down the pale face of its host, another followed it, then another.

A smaller rent opened at the hollow of Tommy's throat and still another slug emerged, blood also running from the cut as it ate its way free. The writhing forms inside the torso seemed to move as one, spilling from the gaping hole with a sickening slurping sound which seemed all the louder because of the silence. Blood and fragments of uneaten intestine flowed forward with them, carried on the reeking carpet of black bodies which began to move towards the watching skinheads.

Mallows felt his bowels loosen, felt something soft and warm splatter his underpants. The stench of his own excrement mingled with the vile smell which rose from the slugs like a noxious cloud. Those that had emerged from the throat and mouth of Tommy Price were now busy devouring the wasted face, burrowing through the eyes and upwards into the brain. Others fastened themselves to the bloated lips and began feeding on the soft flesh and clotted fluid within.

Mallows turned and ran, knocking Hilston over in his efforts to escape this nightmare vision. Hilston got up and turned to follow, doubling up as he did, his stomach finally surrendering to the contractions which tore through him. He unleashed a stream of vomit as he ran, almost slipping over in it. His footsteps clattered frantically up the steps.

Finally the lavatory was in silence again, except for the obscene sucking sounds made by the horde of slugs as they continued to slither from the body of the tramp until only a huge cavity remained, the bones of the ribcage shining white through the blood and slime where internal organs had once been. Like the sloughed skin of a snake the body was now merely an empty shell, and the face had been decimated by those slugs as yet unsatiated. Both eye sockets were empty now and the mouth yawned open like a black chasm to reveal that even the tongue had been eaten.

The leading slugs, the larger ones, hauled their bloated forms across the soiled floor of the lavatory, followed by their smaller companions. An undulating slimy mass which left a glistening trail of mucus behind, they moved easily and surprisingly quickly across the floor and slipped into the trough at the base of the urinals. They crawled or floated in the yellow stream of urine, allowing themselves to be sucked down into the pipes which eventually deposited them in the sewers far below. The darkness seemed to welcome them, and in the blackness they were invisible.

Above, the last few slithered down the pipe and out of sight. There were perhaps a hundred of them.

There would soon be many more.

Three

The smell was almost overpowering. A fetid combination of urine, excrement and vomit but also something more powerful. More pungent. The smell of death.

It was a smell which Detective Inspector Ray Grogan knew only too well, and he recognized it as soon as he entered the lavatory in Leicester Square.

A flashbulb exploded, momentarily illuminating the

24

subterranean cavern with cold white light. Grogan winced slightly and slowed his pace as he reached the bottom of the stairs. He dug into his pocket, produced a breath freshener and aimed it at his mouth. The peppermint spray missed and went up his nose. Muttering to himself, Grogan tried again and succeeded, then dropped the spray back into his pocket. He looked around him at the two uniformed men and three plain-clothes policemen who were also present. A photographer was standing just ahead of him taking pictures of the tiled floor outside one cubicle. At the far end of the row, another plain-clothes man was collecting exhibits. The man was wearing a corduroy jacket worn at the elbows. His hair was long, almost reaching the collar of his blue shirt. He wore brown slacks which needed turning up an inch or two. When the man saw Grogan he turned and walked towards him.

The two men exchanged greetings and Grogan's colleague lit a cigarette. Detective Sergeant Martin Nicholson offered one to his superior.

'I've given up,' Grogan reminded him, trying to ignore the smell of smoke as it wafted towards him. He sighed. 'Well, what have we got? It'd better be worth dragging me out of bed at this hour.'

Grogan checked his watch again and saw that it was just after 1.00 a.m. Then he followed Nicholson to one of the cubicles and peered in.

'Oh Christ,' he murmured.

The photographer stepped aside to allow the DI a better look at the remains of Tommy Price.

Grogan ran a quick appraising eye over the corpse, or what remained of it, his stomach churning slightly as he gazed first at the empty eye sockets, then at the gaping hole in the torso. He turned to look at Nicholson.

'Who is he?' the DI wanted to know.

'We don't know. He wasn't carrying any ID. Or if he was it was taken.'

'It doesn't exactly look like a mugging, does it?' Grogan said, cryptically. 'What about fingerprints? Dental records?'

'They'll be checked as soon as Forensics get started.'

Grogan nodded, massaging the back of his neck with one broad, powerful-looking hand.

'Who found him?' he wanted to know.

'One of our uniformed blokes,' Nicholson said. 'He was checking down here around midnight...' He allowed the sentence to trail off. 'I've never seen anything like it before.'

'Join the club.' Grogan peered around the door of the cubicle once more, his eyes drawn to the gutted corpse. 'What's that stuff on his face?'

'It looks like mucus of some kind. It's everywhere. Look.' He motioned to the tiles beneath their feet and the sticky fluid which glittered with a vile lustre beneath the blinking fluorescent. 'We found this as well, in one of the other cubicles.' Nicholson held up the bag he'd been holding to reveal the empty tubes of Bostik. 'We should be able to get some prints off these. It might give us some kind of clue.'

Grogan nodded slowly, stroking his chin contemplatively.

'It could have been a couple of kids,' Nicholson offered. 'If they'd been sniffing, you never know. I'd just like to know what sort of weapon they used.'

Grogan entered the cubicle and crouched down beside the body of Tommy Price, his gaze travelling to the dead man's hands.

'There aren't any defence cuts on the hands,' said the DI. He looked at the dried vomit which had crusted on the tramp's jacket. 'It looks as though he could have been out when he was attacked. Drunk maybe.' The smell finally became too overwhelming and the DI stepped back out of the cubicle. However, he continued to study the carnage inside the small enclosure. 'There isn't much blood,' he observed. 'If he was stabbed it'd be everywhere. That wound in the throat would have cut his jugular vein. The whole place would be covered in blood.'

'Maybe he was killed somewhere else and dumped here,' Nicholson suggested.

'I think somebody would have noticed a person dragging a gutted body across Leicester Square. I mean, the place isn't exactly deserted at...' He paused a moment. 'What do you think was the time of death?'

'We won't know for sure until the lab boys have finished with him, but looking at the skin on the hands, it can't have been much later than eleven or so. Our bloke found him just after midnight and rigor mortis has only just started to set in.' Nicholson shrugged and took a long drag on his cigarette, blowing the smoke out in a long blue stream which momentarily masked the rank odours in the lavatory.

Grogan looked almost longingly at the haze of smoke and the cigarette, then stepped away from his colleague and gazed down at the glistening trail of slime across the floor. It was too thick to be saliva, he thought, and how come there was so much of it on the body, too? Grogan dug his hands into the pockets of his jacket and sighed. Usually upon reaching the scene of a crime he could glean at least two or three clues from what he saw. Possible murder weapon, sometimes even motive. But this body offered no such help. They didn't even know who the poor bastard was. The glamour of the police force, thought Grogan sardonically. Standing in a public toilet at one o'clock in the morning, surrounded by blood, piss and puke, staring into the trough of a urinal.

He brushed a hand through his tousled mop of greying hair and sighed heavily. Maybe the pieces would fit together better after the body had been examined by the lab boys. He certainly hoped so.

There was a flurry of movement from the top of the steps, and a moment later two ambulancemen descended, carrying a furled stretcher.

'In there,' said Grogan, hooking a thumb in the direction of the cubicle.

The stretcher was laid on the floor and one of the uniformed men entered the small enclosure. Grogan heard his low exclamation of revulsion as he saw the body. He turned to watch as the two men struggled to manoeuvre the corpse onto the waiting stretcher, one of them holding the spindly legs, the other hooking his arms beneath the shoulders of Tommy Price. They lifted carefully, but not carefully enough.

The body broke in half at the waist.

Grogan swallowed hard and turned to Nicholson as the two pieces were laid on the stretcher and covered with a blanket.

'Give me a cigarette,' said the DI as the ambulancemen passed close by with their grisly cargo.

'I thought you'd given up,' said Nicholson, as he watched his superior take an Embassy from the packet and light up.

'I had.'

Wednesday – the 12th

Four

The first thing which greeted Doctor Alan Finch as he entered the surgery was the strident ringing of the phone. He paused a moment, putting down his briefcase, but a second later the phone was answered by someone in reception. He heard a woman's voice and realized that the receptionist had already arrived. He should have realized it when he saw his mail and that of his two partners neatly laid out in separate piles. He smiled to himself as he reached for his own stack of white and brown envelopes.

There were a couple of circulars from drug companies, one offering a new tablet to aid in the relief of pre-menstrual tension, the other claiming that it had by far the most reliable new drug for controlling blood-pressure. Finch folded them both up and replaced them in their envelopes to read later. Then he opened the other mail. A blood test result confirmed his diagnosis that a particular patient was hypoglycaemic, and another told him that an exploratory operation to remove a growth from a middle-aged man's left lung had found the tumour to be benign. Finch smiled again.

He walked out into the reception, which was still empty of patients. A tall, heavily-built woman in her mid-thirties sat on the chair behind the reception desk, an appointment book open before her.

'Good morning, June,' Finch said, reaching for the pile of patients' notes which had been stacked carefully for him. 'Looks like being a busy day,' he added, indicating the notes.

'That's just for this morning, doctor,' June Webber told him. She stood up to retrieve a notepad which lay beside

31

another phone. June was a big woman, almost five-ten, only an inch shorter than Finch himself. She had jet-black hair and an embarrassingly noticeable profusion of facial hair, particularly on her upper lip. But despite her physical shortcomings, she was a first-class worker and she, perhaps more than anyone else, had helped Finch to settle into this new practice which he'd been part of for just three months.

The surgery was a three-man collaboration in Bloomsbury Square and Finch, at thirty-two, was not only the newest partner, he was also the youngest. His colleagues were both only in their early forties but the age gap was sufficient to allow them some good-natured fun at the expense of the younger man. He took this in good humour because it made him feel a part of the set-up. He was 'the new boy' but the label was one which he didn't mind. He had found it surprisingly easy to settle in following the departure of his predecessor through ill health. Even that doctor's regular patients seemed to have taken to the newcomer, warming to his sincerity and concern. Such was the number of patients that each doctor was allocated just five minutes per patient, but people seldom left Finch's room in less than fifteen.

'You've got one or two calls to make before you see your first patient, doctor,' June told him, checking the notepad. 'There's one at a house in Clerkenwell.' She gave him the name and address. 'A woman is worried about her little boy. And there's another one at a flat in Flaxman Court, a Mrs Molly Foster. The notes are here.' She handed him two files which he read quickly.

'When's my first appointment in the surgery?' he asked.

'Ten thirty,' she told him.

'OK, I'll get going then.' Clutching the files, he made his way towards the rear entrance of the building. He crossed to his car, waving to one of his colleagues who had just pulled up nearby. Finch didn't wait to exchange greetings, but slid behind the wheel of the Chevette and started the engine. As he did so, he leant across and wound down the passenger-side window as well as his own. Although it was only 8.38 a.m., the sun was already climbing high into a clear blue sky. It promised to be another scorcher. Finch couldn't remember the last time it had rained, and on the news that morning he had heard talk of water rationing if the blazing weather continued. Already, parts of Britain were completely without water because reservoirs had dried up.

As he drove, the smell of petrol and diesel fumes filled the car, but Finch decided this was preferable to the unbearable heat he'd have to endure with the windows shut. He drove on, having decided to make the Clerkenwell call first. He flicked on the radio. Theresa had bought the radio and cassette player for him four years ago . . . He allowed the thought to trail off, trying to push any images of his wife from his mind. He turned up the volume and concentrated on weaving his way along streets which were still busy with commuters who insisted on the daily confrontations which driving to work brought. Finch was relieved that he didn't have too far to go.

'. . . who said that talks had broken down once more.' The newsreader's voice filled the car. 'Police in London today are trying to identify the remains of a man found in a public convenience in Leicester Square. The man had been badly mutilated but, as yet, his identity remains a mystery. Scotland Yard would not say if the man was murdered or not but they are treating his death as such . . .'

Finch eased the volume down again, turning the radio off as he swung the car into the street he was searching for. He double-checked the address on the sheet of paper beside him and drove the Chevette into a handy parking space.

It was 9.02.

Finch double-checked that his doors were locked before leaving the car. The sun was pouring heat down mercilessly now. The doctor wiped a bead of perspiration from his forehead with the corner of his handkerchief as he walked across the street towards the three-storey block of flats in Flaxman Court. The trip from Clerkenwell had taken him just under twenty-five minutes, not bad allowing for traffic. The call, he decided, had been necessary. The child, a boy of six, had been suffering from severely inflamed tonsils and a

33

very bad cough. Finch had left a prescription and instructions that he was to be called again if there was no improvement within thirty-six hours. The boy's mother had been most grateful, the child himself a nice little chap. Not unlike his own son, Chris...

Finch gritted his teeth, as if the memory was a painful one. With effort he succeeded in driving away the thoughts of his child. Temporarily at least.

He walked up to the first floor and found the flat he sought. Number five. Finch pressed the bell lightly and heard the two-tone chime inside. A moment later the door was opened and the doctor found himself confronted by a young woman he guessed to be in her late twenties. He settled on twenty-nine although her drawn expression perhaps added unfairly to her years. The dark rings beneath her eyes, he imagined, were the result of tears shed rather than sleepless nights. Otherwise, she was extraordinarily attractive, her small face framed by thick brown hair, high-lighted in places as if the sun were permanently shining on it. She looked at him with deep blue eyes which were at once welcoming and apprehensive.

'Doctor Finch?' she said, before he could speak.

He nodded, allowing himself to be ushered inside the flat.

It was light and airy, populated by dozens of house plants which stood like green sentinels all around the room. A particularly large rubber plant towered over the television set in one corner, its leaves brushing against a photo of the young woman who now led Finch towards a door to another room. He glanced quickly at the photo, which apparently had been taken recently. It showed the girl in some kind of uniform, but he couldn't make out what it was. Quite a contrast, however, to the flowing cheesecloth dress she wore now, the flared bottom reaching as far as her knees, revealing evenly tanned calves.

She motioned him into the next room where there were more plants, but smaller ones this time. It was a bedroom and he frowned as he caught sight of the occupant of the single bed.

34

'Could you leave us for a moment, Miss...'

'Foster,' she told him. 'Lisa Foster.'

He smiled, waited until she had left the room and then moved to the bed.

Finch laid his bag on a nearby dressing table and turned his full attention to the woman in the bed.

Her greying hair was pushed back from a sweat-stained forehead to reveal two large boils, one above the right eye, the other slightly higher. Both of the boils were badly swollen and looked on the point of bursting. On her sunken cheek there was another of the pustules, but this one was cracked and a thick yellowish fluid was dribbling slowly from it. There was another boil on her chin. Thick folds of flesh hung around her neck like a collar, and nestling in the hollow of her throat was another of the oozing sores.

'Mrs Foster,' said Finch, shaking the woman gently. 'Can you hear me?'

Molly Foster opened her eyes and looked at him with surprising alertness. There was a sparkle in those eyes which seemed to have deserted the rest of her body. She even managed a smile but, as she did, the boil on her chin opened slightly, releasing a thick purulent ooze. The smile dissolved into a wince of pain.

Finch took a tissue from a container in his pocket and wiped away the pus, then reached for his bag and removed a thermometer and stethoscope. He slipped the thermometer under Molly's tongue before easing down the sheets to expose her chest.

There were more lesions on her shoulders and breasts, one bulging and throbbing angrily like an extra nipple. Finch listened for the rhythmic thudding of her heart. It was normal. He checked the thermometer.

It too was normal. The mercury had not risen above the designated mark.

'How long have you been like this, Mrs Foster?' he asked, taking his opthalmoscope to peer into her eyes.

'Since last night,' she told him. 'Well, this morning really. I couldn't sleep, my daughter will tell you. Ever since my husband passed away I've had trouble sleeping. I got up at about four this morning to make myself a cup of tea.'

'Are you in pain?'

'Well, these,' she indicated one of the sores. 'They're painful, but otherwise no.'

He took the sphygmomanometer from his case and fastened the velcro strip around Molly's arm and then, using the small rubber pump, he began inflating the arm band to the correct pressure. Finch shook his head almost imperceptibly.

Her blood pressure was perfectly normal too.

'What's wrong with me, doctor?' she asked him.

Finch felt momentarily useless as he put his equipment away.

'Something which *I* can't discover with my simple methods,' he said, smiling. 'Do you have a phone I could use? I think you'd be better off in hospital, at least until we can find out what's caused those lesions. I'll call an ambulance.'

Molly nodded and watched him silently as he walked out of the room. He found Lisa sitting tensely on the edge of a chair. She stood up as he entered the room, the anxiety still on her face.

'What is it, doctor?' she asked.

'I don't know,' he said, somewhat apologetically. 'Some tests will need to be done. I have to call an ambulance.'

She showed him the phone and stood by as he dialled.

'Could it be an allergic reaction?' Lisa offered hopefully.

Finch shook his head.

'It's too extreme for that,' he told her. The phone at the other end was picked up and he gave the necessary information. The ambulance, he was told, would be there in twenty minutes.

'Perhaps you could pack some things for your mother,' Finch said. 'They may well want to keep her overnight.'

Lisa nodded.

'Which hospital?' she wanted to know.

'The Middlesex,' he said as she turned back towards the bedroom. 'Could you tell me where the bathroom is, please? I'd like to wash my hands.'

Lisa directed him, then she herself retreated from the room.

Finch filled the basin with warm water, scrubbed his hands twice, then rinsed them thoroughly. That done, he emptied the basin, ran some cold water and splashed his face with it in an effort to cool himself down. Moisture ran in rivulets down his face until he found a towel and dried himself, studying his reflection in the mirror above the sink for a moment. Molly Foster's condition certainly had him puzzled. Her heartbeat, temperature and blood pressure were all perfectly normal. Everything seemed to be normal except for the boils.

What the hell had caused them?

He replaced the towel and turned to leave the bathroom, noticing that in this room too there was greenery. A small rubber plant stood near the toilet.

What he didn't notice was the thick, glistening slime which criss-crossed the lower leaves.

Five

Some days the smell seemed stronger than others, and today it was particularly rank.

John Bateson coughed and waved a hand in front of his face but the smell of excrement swirled thickly around him like a dense cloud in the darkness of the sewer tunnel. The tunnel itself was over ten feet in diameter, with a ceiling high enough for a six-foot man to walk comfortably without stooping. As Bateson moved through the stream of dark fluid, it reached as high as his calves, but the thigh-length waders which he wore protected his legs from the evil-smelling water.

Somewhere ahead he could hear the steady dripping of

more water, and as he shone his torch upwards he saw that part of the brickwork about half-way up the side of the tunnel was cracked, several lumps of masonry having fallen into the effluent. Dark mould clung to the walls and ceiling of the tunnel, adding its own damp odour to the smell of excrement. Bateson held up his safety lamp, one eye on the red light, which as yet remained unlit. If it should glow even slightly, he and his companions would be forced to leave the sewer as this signalled a pocket of gas.

The water in the storm relief sewer was lower than usual because of the hot weather. It never rose much above five feet, unlike that in the large interceptor sewers. There, the level could reach seven or eight feet, completely filling the tunnels, especially in wet weather, but at the moment levels all over the system were down.

'You'd better check further on,' Harold Oldfield said, aiming his own torch deeper into the blackness. 'I'll take care of this break.'

Bateson nodded and splashed on down the tunnel, his torch beam moving back and forth ahead of him.

The constant flow of water had cut a deep swathe into the stonework near the water level. Bateson knelt to examine this more closely and prodded some of the eroded bricks. A lump of stone came away in his hand.

'This wall is going too,' he called to his colleague, his voice echoing in the silence of the tunnel.

'I'm going up to fetch the tools,' Oldfield called back. He turned and headed for the metal ladder, clambering up towards the manhole through which they'd both descended minutes earlier. The silence suddenly seemed to overwhelm Bateson. Alone in the tunnel he felt hemmed in by the solitude and gloom. The beam of his torch was powerful but he could see nothing outside its narrow width. There was a hazy shaft of light pouring in from the manhole above like some kind of ethereal shape in the blackness, but it was too far away to offer any comforting light.

Bateson had been a sewer engineer for just over two years, since he had left school, but still he had not managed to adjust to the sometimes claustrophobic conditions in which he worked. The darkness, the smell and the silence combined to make his work both uncomfortable and, more often than not, a little frightening. He had thought about leaving on numerous occasions but now, with his wife Karen expecting their first baby within the month, that was out of the question. He'd been lucky to get this job, and it was hardly the time to start looking for another one. He kept telling himself that he'd get used to it, but besides the sheer discomfort of wading around in other people's waste, there was an element of danger attached to the work. The sewers could flood, particularly after a heavy storm, with very little warning. He'd heard of men being swept to their deaths in torrents of water, and of others who had become lost in the maze of tunnels and had finally suffocated, died of fright or been gassed by the many pockets of lethal methane which collected below ground. And then there had been the stories of the rats. Oldfield and the other older men in his maintenance group had sworn that they'd seen rats as big as dogs in the tunnels. Bateson had dismissed their stories – giant rats existed only in horror films.

He heard a low rumbling sound, growing steadily louder, and it took him a second or two to realize that it was a Tube train passing below. Some of the sewers ran above the lines, others below them. Many were less than forty feet underground. The rumbling passed and the silence returned.

Somewhere behind him he heard a faint splash and he spun round, aiming his torch beam in the direction of the sound.

He could see nothing.

There was another splash, louder this time. Then another. Then silence again.

Bateson exhaled deeply. What the hell was the matter with him today? He administered a swift mental self-rebuke, trying to quell his unusually shaky nerves. He told himself that it was because he was worrying about Karen. Despite his insistence that he should stay at home with her (in case the baby was premature, he had argued), she had pushed him out to work. There was no way she was going to have the child yet, she assured him.

The thought of the birth did bring a momentary smile to his face. When the lad grew old enough he'd take him along to Stamford Bridge to watch Chelsea, dressed in his little blue-and-white scarf and hat. He'd make sure the little fellow didn't get into any bother. Bateson had many friends among the fraternity in The Shed and, besides, he knew how to handle himself. But once his son was with him things would be different. His son. The thought sent a swell of pride through him.

What if it was a girl? Shit, he hadn't though of that. He'd look a bit of a prick taking a girl to watch football, wouldn't he? He dismissed the idea. No, it was going to be a boy. No sweat.

Bateson's train of thought was suddenly broken by another loud splash, closer this time, and a second later something bumped against his boot.

He shone his torch down and saw that it was a turd.

The large black slug floated past unnoticed.

From the direction of the manhole there were sounds of activity, and a moment later Oldfield returned carrying a couple of tool bags, one of which he handed to his younger companion. Then he splashed back up the tunnel to get on with his own work. Both men set about their business.

'When's your old lady going to drop the foal then?' Oldfield called out. His voice reverberated eerily around the tunnel.

'Anytime now,' Bateson replied, reaching into his tool bag for a chisel.

'You're nervous, aren't you? It's easy to see. I was the same with my first one. My old lady was in labour for twelve hours, they thought she was going to die. But with the second and third, well, that was like shelling peas.' He chuckled loudly.

Bateson laughed too, the sound drowning out another series of splashes, each one closer to him than the last.

Five large slugs, each more than six inches in length, glided through the water with a grace unbefitting their bloated, obscene forms. They moved toward Bateson. Above him, clinging to the roof of the tunnel, dozens more slithered

40

along, leaving their thick, reeking slime trails behind.

The first of those in the water reached Bateson's tool bag and crawled up onto it, hidden by the enveloping blackness.

'What are you going to call your youngster?' Oldfield enquired.

'I thought about Peter or David, maybe even Pat,' the younger man said, reaching into his bag for a hammer. He broke away some chipped brick and replaced the tool, his hand almost touching the second slug, which had now hauled itself inside.

Above, the other black abominations continued to draw closer.

'What if it's a girl?' Oldfield said, laughing.

Bateson thought for a moment then smiled broadly.

'Kerry,' he said, unhesitatingly. 'What do you reckon?'

Oldfield didn't answer.

'Harry, did you hear me?'

Still no answer.

'Harry, I . . .'

'I think we've got a problem,' Oldfield said, quietly, his eyes on the lights of his safety lamp.

The red warning light had begun to flicker rapidly, and now it glowed brilliant red.

'Gas,' he said hoarsely. 'Let's get out of here.'

Bateson was on his feet and starting to move when he felt something hit his back. He shuddered, wondering if a piece of mould had fallen from the roof of the tunnel.

Something else dropped onto him.

Something thick and wet. It was on his shoulder.

'Come on, move it, quick!' Oldfield called, already at the ladder which led up to the manhole.

Bateson brought his hand round and tried to brush the sticky lump from his overalls. In the darkness he was unable to see what it was. It felt cold and soft, like rancid faeces.

He grabbed his torch and swung it up, directing it at the roof above him, the light picking out the mass of slugs which seemed to be suspended there.

'Oh my God,' murmured Bateson, disgust in his voice.

41

As one, the slugs dropped from the roof.

Half a dozen latched onto his exposed face, fixing themselves to his flesh with their razor-sharp central teeth. Immediately the rasp-like radula teeth began slicing through skin and muscle as the slugs burrowed into Bateson's face. One of the monstrosities slipped into the welcoming wetness of his mouth, forcing its thick, swollen form down his throat and causing him to retch violently. But even the stream of vomit which spewed forth could not dislodge the slimy creature. Anchored by its central tooth, the slug remained where it was, eating into the back of its victim's throat.

Bateson clutched at the slugs on his face, tugging madly at one which was forcing its way into his left nostril.

Another slithered across his eye, driving its sickle-shaped main tooth into the tender tissue. Blood ran down his face in torrents, mingling with his vomit and the reeking slime exuded by the slugs.

Finally, close to unconsciousness, he toppled backwards into the stream of effluent, still tugging at the feeding beasts who were devouring his face. His groping fingers could not hold onto the slippery abominations and he writhed in helpless agony in the filthy water until, finally, one flailing hand touched something in the open toolbag.

He gripped the pliers and raised them to his face, fixing the jaws around the slug which had all but disappeared into his nostril. He only succeeded in snipping the tumescent form in half. A thick, reeking yellowish pus burst from the torn body, some of it spurting into his open mouth which was already filled with his own blood and the foul slime of the slug feeding inside his throat. He managed a loud gargling sound which echoed around the cavernous tunnel but then the slug detached itself, forcing its corpulent body even further until it blocked his windpipe.

Bateson thrashed about like an eel on a hot skillet, unable to breathe and wracked by agony such as he could never have imagined, yet still he fought back, using the pliers once more. He seized the head of another of the black creatures which was in the process of eating its way through his cheek. With a final defiant gesture, he snapped the pliers together, catching a large portion of his own skin between the blades. He pulled, his eyes bulging wide in unendurable pain. The slug came free but so did a sizeable strip of flesh. There was a sickening sound much like that of tearing material and the skin was ripped away like peeling wallpaper. A great, dripping flap of it hung from the pliers, which Bateson finally dropped. His body began to convulse madly, churning the filthy water around him into a froth.

Those slugs that had remained in the water moved swiftly towards the bloodied ruin which had once been his face, slithering and crawling over the bleeding lump.

Bateson felt as if his head were going to explode and now, as the slugs began eating into the flesh of his neck, he prayed for the end.

Moments before it came he felt more slugs dropping onto his body from the roof of the tunnel like a vile rain.

Then, mercifully, he felt nothing at all.

Harold Oldfield looked at his watch.

Over two minutes had passed since he had shouted his warning to Bateson, yet still the younger man had not emerged from the manhole. Finally, Oldfield fastened on his breathing apparatus and tested the flow of oxygen. He took another mask and cylinder from one of his colleagues and lowered himself back into the hole, climbing cautiously down the metal ladder. He paused halfway down and glanced at the warning beacon on his safety light.

As yet it had not lit up. Perhaps the pocket of gas had dispersed, Oldfield thought. He climbed the remaining few feet and lowered himself to the floor of the tunnel, glancing again at the warning light.

It flickered weakly but then went out completely.

Oldfield waited for long moments, then took his mask off.

'It's clear,' he shouted up at his colleagues who were peering down the shaft. Oldfield moved along the tunnel, his torch cutting a broad swath through the blackness.

'John,' he called.

43

Silence.

'John. Can you hear me?'

Still nothing.

Oldfield almost tripped over the tool bag.

He shone his torch down, over the area where Bateson had been working.

There was blood on the tool bag and something else too.

Something which glistened in the beam. A silvery fluid which dripped from the bag in thick globules. As he shone the torch around him he saw that the silvery secretion was on the walls and ceiling of the tunnel as well.

Of Bateson there was no sign.

Six

The clock in the reception area of the Middlesex Hospital showed that it was 7.21 p.m. Finch looked at his own watch and noticed that it had stopped. He decided to put it right later. He walked past the unattended desk near the main doors and strode towards a tall slim nurse who was helping a middle-aged man out of a wheelchair and onto a pair of crutches. Finch waited until she'd finished the delicate manoeuvre and then smiled warmly at her, happy to see the gesture returned.

'Could you check your record of admissions for today, please?' he asked. 'There's someone I'd like to see.'

The nurse made her way back to the reception desk, followed by the doctor.

'What was the name of the patient?' she asked, opening a large, bound tome on the desk.

'Foster. Molly Foster,' he told her. 'I'm her doctor. My

44

name is Finch.'

The girl ran one slender index finger down a column of names, jabbing at the one she sought.

'Mrs Foster is in Ward 5C, the lift is over there.' She pointed in the appropriate direction.

Finch thanked her, walked to the lift and punched the '5' button. The doors slid open promptly and he stepped in, leaning back against the rear wall of the car as it rose. His surgery had finished an hour earlier. He'd found the time to shower and drink a cup of tea before changing into an open-neck shirt and jeans. Then he'd driven to the hospital, determined to see if Molly Foster had made any progress, or at least to discover if the tests had yielded answers to the baffling questions he'd been confronted with earlier in the day. Finch couldn't help but wonder if he would always find time for individual patients, as he was doing now. In years to come, would he be unconcerned what became of them outside surgery hours? He knew that many doctors felt that way, but so far he had not been able to decide whether a detached attitude was unavoidable or essential, the product of over-work or of cynicism.

The lift bumped to a halt at the fifth floor and he stepped out.

There was a vending machine nearby, being fed coins by a youth in a leather jacket. A teenage girl, with her right leg in plaster, sat on the leather seat beside the machine and looked on as the lad pressed buttons and made a choice of drinks. The machine coughed out two cans of Coke and the couple talked animatedly as they drank.

The doctor glanced up at the sign above a set of swing doors which bore the legend 'Ward 5C'. He walked in, turning right, heading for the ward sister's desk. She was a small, slightly built woman in her thirties, a ladder in one stocking. Her face had a pinched look, made the worse by her long nose, but the harshness of her features was counter-balanced by the softness of her voice when she spoke.

'Can I help you, sir?' she said, in an accent with a slight Irish lilt.

Finch asked to see Molly Foster, told her why and waited to be shown to the appropriate bed. The duty sister accompanied him, indicating a set of screens which hid Molly from the view of the other patients. It was visiting time, so most patients had at least one friend or relative present and a low burble of conversation filled the ward. Finch approached the screens and moved them aside just enough to allow himself access.

Lisa Foster turned to look at him as she heard movement from behind her. She started to rise but Finch shook his head, looking first at her and then at her mother. Molly was asleep, her head turned to one side. The boils and sores had been dressed, and most of her face, neck and arms were now covered in bandages.

'I hope you don't mind me calling in,' Finch said. 'I thought I'd see how she was getting on.'

Lisa too had changed clothes since their first meeting. She now wore a light sweater, the baggy sleeves rolled up to her elbows. The folds of material largely concealed her small breasts but the tight jeans she wore accentuated the smoothe curve of her buttocks and the shapeliness of her thighs. Her hair looked as if it had been freshly washed for it gleamed beneath the lights. She wore only the merest hint of eye make-up.

'They gave her a sedative about an hour ago,' she told him. 'The ... boils were beginning to hurt her, she said.' Lisa looked away from Finch. 'I've been with her since they brought her in this morning.'

'You could do with a break,' he told her.

'I popped home for twenty minutes to change. I'm OK.'

Both of them turned as the screens were parted and a tall, raven-haired man in a white coat entered. He looked at Finch and Lisa over the top of his glasses, then picked up the board which hung from the bottom of Molly's bed.

Finch introduced himself and said, 'I'm the doctor who asked for Mrs Foster's admission.'

The other man nodded.

'Have you any idea what the problem might be?' Finch

asked.

'Not yet.' The man looked at Lisa and smiled thinly. 'Would you step outside for a moment, Miss Foster?'

Lisa looked concerned.

'Is anything wrong?' she said.

'You'll be told everything we know, but not until we know it,' the man in the white coat said, then remained quiet until Lisa was out of earshot. Then he looked at Finch. 'My name's Benton. Peter Benton. I'm in charge of the tests we're running on Mrs Foster.' He sighed. 'I'm afraid her condition has deteriorated since she was admitted.' He stepped to the bed and lifted one of Molly's arms, carefully unwrapping a dressing beneath her elbow. He removed the gauze pad which covered the affected area.

The boil looked on the point of bursting, a liquescent nodule seeping pus from its edges, but it was the area around the boil which Benton indicated. It looked yellow beneath the bright lights, the veins standing out darkly against the wasted skin.

'The infection's spreading,' Finch said flatly, recognizing the symptom.

'Her temperature has risen in the last two hours, and so has her blood pressure,' Benton informed him. 'She was in so much pain we had to sedate her.'

'What have the tests revealed?'

'We're still waiting for the results. We took blood samples, skin sections and tissue from the pustules themselves. We haven't tried any medication yet, not until we know what we're dealing with.' He carefully re-bandaged the sore. 'The next step is to remove one of the lesions and examine it.'

Finch nodded and turned to leave.

'I'll be in touch,' he said.

'Could you have a word with her daughter?' asked Benton. 'Try to persuade her there's nothing she can do? I've tried but...' He shrugged and let the sentence trail off. 'She'd be better off at home.'

'I'll see what I can do,' Finch promised and walked back up the ward.

He found Lisa sitting by the window looking out at the sun, which had finally lost its earlier intensity and was sinking slowly toward the tall buildings of London's skyline. Now reduced to a glowing orange disk in the gathering evening haze, its soft warmth was a welcome relief from the fierce mid-day heat.

Finch paused for a moment, studying Lisa's profile as she gazed out of the window, then he coughed loudly and theatrically. She turned, getting to her feet.

'Can I go back in now?' she asked him.

'Your mother will be out for quite a while yet,' he said. 'Sitting staring at her isn't going to do either of you any good.' He raised his eyebrows.

Lisa nodded.

'Can I buy you a cup of coffee?' he asked, smiling, moving towards the vending machine.

She nodded and followed him, standing nearby as he pushed the coins in and then jabbed the buttons. The machine dropped a cup obligingly, but proceeded to fill it with nothing more than hot water.

'Do you take sugar in your water?' he asked, with a grin.

Lisa looked at him blankly for a moment, and then, for the first time since he'd met her, she too smiled.

'Perhaps we'd be better off in the canteen,' Finch suggested.

They walked to the lift.

Seven

Lisa cradled the coffee cup in her hand, looking down into the swirling brown liquid which she had just stirred for the third time.

Finch sipped his own drink and looked at her as if waiting for some word or reaction.

The hospital canteen was filled with patients, visitors, doctors, nurses and other staff, all drinking coffee or eating sandwiches. A steady babble of conversation filled the room.

'To use a time-honoured medical cliché,' said Finch, his eyes never leaving Lisa, 'worrying about your mother won't help either of you. There's nothing you can do here at the moment.'

'That's what Doctor Benton told me,' she admitted. 'He suggested that I go home and wait until they contact me.'

'That's very good advice.'

'Doctors stick together, don't they?' she said sardonically.

'Listen, Miss Foster, no one's saying you don't have a right to be worried but if you carry on this way you'll be exhausted and no help to your mother when she needs you.'

'Are you persuading me or patronizing me, doctor?' There was a slight edge to her voice which Finch was not slow to pick up. He saw a momentary iciness in her blue eyes, but it rapidly melted. 'I'm sorry,' she sighed. 'I didn't mean that. I know you're considering *my* health as well.' She took a sip of her coffee. 'By the way, it was thoughtful of you to come and see my mother. Thank you.'

'A doctor's duties shouldn't end when his surgery closes, Miss Foster.'

'Lisa,' she told him. 'Please call me Lisa.'

Finch smiled, and was pleased to see her return the gesture.

'Have the rest of your family been told about this?' he enquired.

'I didn't see any reason, doctor,' she told him.

'Alan,' he said. 'My name is Alan. Doctors have first names too.'

She smiled again, the gesture lighting her face.

'Alan,' she repeated. 'No, I haven't told any of my family about what's happened because there wouldn't be much point. I'm the only one who sees Mother from one week to the next. If I hadn't called in today she'd have stayed the way she was. On her own with no one to help her.'

'I didn't mean to pry,' Finch said, almost apologetically. She dismissed his words.

'Why should I keep it a secret? I've got two sisters and two brothers and if Mother sees any of them more than twice in a year, then she's lucky. One of them will phone occasionally if they've got nothing else to do but apart from that I'm the only one who calls in on her. I sometimes stop there at weekends.'

Finch looked briefly at her hands and saw that there was no sign of a wedding or engagement ring.

'She's got two three-year old grandchildren that she's never even seen,' Lisa continued, as if anxious to relieve herself of some kind of burden. The bitterness in her voice was unsettling. 'That's the way it's been for as long as I can remember. I've always been the one who looked after her when she needed help, and God knows I owe it to her.'

'What about your father?' Finch enquired.

'He died when I was fifteen. My mother worshipped him. After his death she was never the same. She never stopped loving him, she never will. I often wonder what it must be like to feel that way about someone.' She took a sip of coffee, lowering her eyes momentarily as if she had opened up just a little more than she wanted to.

'Up until today, though, your mother's been a fit woman, hasn't she?' Finch said. 'I checked back through the records.'

Lisa nodded.

'And you've no idea at all what might have caused this . . .' He allowed the sentence to trail off.

'She phoned me this morning about six and asked me to call in on her. When I got there that was how I found her.'

'Where do you live?' he wanted to know.

'I'm a receptionist at the Strand Palace Hotel, I've got a room there. The wages aren't too great but at least the food and lodging are free.' She smiled humourlessly. 'But I'm staying at my mother's place until all this is sorted out. I was due a few days' holiday. The management are pretty good about things like that.' She finished her coffee and pushed the cup away. Finch watched as she ran both hands through her thick hair and shook her head, causing the silken cascade to shimmer beneath the lights.

'Well, you know the *interesting* things about me,' she said, mockingly, 'but I don't know anything about you. Can you tell me or is it breaking the Hippocratic Oath?' She smiled.

'What do you want to know?' he asked.

'How long have you been a doctor?'

'I studied medicine until I was twenty-eight. When I finished I joined a National Health practice in Camden Town for a year, then I moved to another in Notting Hill, full time, up until three months ago. I've been with this private practice since then.'

'Are you married?'

'Divorced,' he said, his tone softening.

'I'm sorry. Still, at least you've had your chance. I sometimes wonder if I'm going to end up on the shelf. Twenty-eight and still single. Even my mum has been telling me it was time I settled down.'

'I don't think there's much chance of *you* ending up on the shelf. You're a very attractive young woman.'

Lisa smiled self-consciously and attempted to change the subject.

'You obviously enjoy your work,' she said to him.

'Yes, I do. But it has its moments of pain too.' His voice took on a reflective note. 'Trying to tell a young couple that their ten-month-old son is dying of leukaemia isn't easy. I sometimes admire other doctors who are able to cut themselves off from their patients, at least on an emotional level. I'm afraid I haven't been able to do that. Not yet anyway.'

Lisa ran an appraising eye over him, studying his face. His hair was dark, almost black, and although he was clean shaven, the skin around his cheeks and chin also looked dark, as if his whiskers defied even the sharpest razor. His forehead was deeply lined, his eyes framed by thick eyebrows and high cheekbones. She looked at his hands, clasped on the table before him, and sensed a gentleness in them, despite their size. His forearms were thick and heavily muscled, clearly

51

visible as his sleeves were rolled up.

He noticed her looking at him. Their eyes met and they held each other's gaze for fleeting moments.

'You look tired,' Finch told her.

'I'm all right,' she reassured him. 'I think it's time I got back up to the ward.'

'Lisa, Doctor Benton was right. There's nothing you can do there.'

'I can't bear to think of my mother here, alone.'

'She's being well cared for. Now, will you let me drive you home? My car's outside.'

She hesitated and inhaled deeply, letting out the breath in a long sigh.

'All right. I suppose there *is* nothing I can do,' she admitted reluctantly. 'I'd appreciate it if you'd take me home.' They both rose and walked slowly from the canteen, through reception and out into the dusk. The sun had just sunk out of sight and a slight breeze had sprung up. Lisa rolled down the sleeves of her sweater while she waited for Finch to unlock the Chevette. She slid into the passenger seat and he settled himself behind the wheel a moment later, adjusting his rear view mirror before starting the car.

As he guided it out into the traffic an ambulance passed them, its lights spinning silently. Finch glanced behind him and saw two uniformed men hurrying from the vehicle carrying a stretcher and its load. They disappeared through the doors marked 'Casualty'.

Neither he nor Lisa spoke.

The doctor drove steadily, in no hurry to reach his destination, and Lisa seemed quite content to gaze abstractedly out of the window as the Chevette threaded its way through the cars and lorries, bikes and vans which dotted the streets leading away from the hospital.

'You said you were divorced,' she said, quite unexpectedly. 'How long had you been married? If you don't mind me asking?'

He shook his head.

'Six years,' he told her.

52

'Any children?'

Finch was silent for a moment and Lisa looked across at him, studying his profile. She was about to repeat her question when he answered.

'One. A boy. We had him soon after we were married.' He smiled but there was no warmth in it. 'Even doctors make mistakes occasionally, you know.'

Lisa realized that she had touched on a delicate point and she dropped the subject, her own problems now drifting back into her mind.

'Do you think my mother is going to die?' she asked him suddenly.

Finch frowned.

'No,' he said, softly, and once more their eyes briefly locked.

They drove the rest of the way in silence until he eventually pulled up outside the flats in Flaxman Court.

'Thank you,' said Lisa, reaching for the door handle. 'You've been very kind.' She flashed him that radiant smile once more. 'Perhaps I'll see you again.'

'I'm sure you will,' he replied. 'Though hopefully under happier circumstances.'

They exchanged brief farewells and she climbed out of the car. Finch watched as she walked quickly to the flats, not looking back. He exhaled deeply. Should he have told her that the infection was spreading?

No, leave it to the hospital, he told himself.

As he started the car he wondered about Lisa's question.

Was her mother going to die?

He wished he knew.

Finch drove off, the cool wind through the open window making him shiver.

Eight

In the growing darkness, the waters of the Thames looked black. The river curved through the city like a huge bloated tongue. The current heat wave had taken its toll even on the mighty river and the water level was down a good two feet. The banks on either side were clearly visible, sloping down at a sharp angle to the murky water. Normally hidden by the constant flow, they were now revealed as dirty stretches of shale and mud, baked hard in places by the day's unrelenting heat. A faintly rancid smell hung over the water, drifting ashore every so often when propelled by the gathering evening breezes.

Lights on the embankment high above, and on the parapets of Westminster Bridge, were reflected in the surface of the river like jewels in a dirty mirror.

'You know, we must want our bleeding heads tested,' said Ralph Patterson, trying to force a maggot onto his hook.

'I'm telling you, Ralph,' Trevor Doyle insisted. 'Some geezer told me he'd heard that there were trout in the Thames again.'

'All that's in the Thames is a few hundred tons of junk and some extra shit from these bleeding sewer outlets.' Patterson turned and looked at the yawning mouth of the pipe behind him. It emerged from the wall of the embankment like a hungry worm, a vile smell wafting from the black maw. Normally the pipes were covered but the drop in the water level had exposed them.

'Trout feed on human waste and that,' Doyle insisted. 'There's bound to be more of them around here. It stands to reason. I bet you we catch one.'

He cast his line into the black waters and stood contentedly.

'All we're going to catch is a roasting off the law,' Patterson told him. 'I'm sure this isn't legal.'

Doyle ignored him and re-adjusted his line.

Both men were in their late twenties, Patterson slightly older. He had the collar of his denim jacket pulled up to protect his neck from the cold breeze which was blowing along the embankment.

Doyle wore only a short-sleeved sweatshirt and the flesh on his arms had already risen into goose-pimples.

'I hope the tide doesn't come in,' he said, shivering.

Patterson looked at him and shook his head, but his frown dissolved into a look of surprise as he felt his rod buck in his hand.

'Sod me, I reckon I've got something,' he said in amazement. He began reeling in, tugging hard to coax his catch free of the water. The rod was bending from what was obviously a considerable weight on the other end and Doyle stood by, mesmerised, as his companion continued to wrestle with whatever he'd hooked.

'Well, don't just stand there,' Patterson said. 'Get hold of the bloody rod and help me pull.'

'I told you, didn't I?' Doyle said, grinning. 'You wouldn't believe me, would you?'

Both men gave a final mighty heave and an object cleared the water, flew through the air and landed with a thud close to them. They both spun round to look at it.

'And how do you suggest we cook *that*?' said Patterson, irritably.

He prodded the wooden toilet seat with the toe of his trainer and glared at his companion.

'Someone must have chucked it over the side of a ship,' Doyle said. 'Well, it would have been asking too much to get a fish straight off, wouldn't it?'

Patterson didn't answer. He was busy pushing another maggot onto his hook.

'You know, we'd have more chance of catching a trout in

Trafalgar Square fountains,' he said, casting his line once more into the murky river.

'All we've got to do is wait,' Doyle assured him.

'We could have been sitting in the pub, you know. I'm giving it half an hour, tops, then I'm off. You can stand here all night if you want to.'

'Ralph, you know your trouble? You've got no spirit of adventure,' said Doyle.

Five minutes passed.

Ten.

Doyle was starting to feel colder.

'Lend us your jacket for a minute,' he said, shivering.

'Piss off,' Patterson said. 'You wanted to come fishing, you put up with the weather.'

'Oh come on, Ralph, you've got a sweater on under there.'

'Keep fishing and shut up,' Patterson said, chuckling.

Another five minutes and Doyle put down his rod.

'Where the hell are you going?' his friend asked.

'I'm going to shelter inside that bloody pipe for a minute,' he said, motioning towards the sewer outlet. 'I'm freezing to death.' He walked the five or six yards to the mouth of the culvert and climbed in, glad to be out of the chill breeze for a moment. Perhaps Ralph was right. Maybe there weren't any trout in the Thames. He muttered to himself. He'd hammer the bastard who'd told him there were. Doyle rubbed his arms and stamped his feet in an attempt to restore some warmth to his limbs. He wrinkled his nose at a particularly vile stench which seemed to be coming from just inside the pipe. It was like bad meat. He recognized the smell because he'd once worked in the freezer room of a meat factory, humping the carcasses. One day the fridges had blown out and every single piece of meat had gone off. The stench had been unbelievable.

And now he was smelling it again.

Doyle turned, peering into the forbidding blackness of the tunnel. However, there was enough light to illuminate the first six or seven feet of the large pipe.

The body was sprawled in an unearthly position, one arm

56

stretched out in front of it, the other bent and twisted behind the back. Both legs were tucked up to what remained of the chest, as if the corpse were kneeling. Its face was pressed to the floor of the culvert, away from Doyle's view.

'Jesus Christ,' he murmured, crouching low, covering his nose against the choking stench. He reached out one shaking hand and touched the outstretched arm.

Even that was enough to cause the body to topple over and Doyle found himself staring into what had once been a face. The flesh had been stripped from it as cleanly as if someone had gone over it with a blow torch, removing every last shred of skin. There were several loose flaps around the neck, which was holed in numerous places as if it had been punctured. The mouth hung open in a silent scream.

'Ralph,' he shrieked, his eyes riveted to the body, staring in horror at gleaming bones and the tattered remains of skin which still clung to the outstretched hand. He shouted Patterson's name again.

'Come here, quick,' he bellowed.

Patterson dropped his rod and sprinted over to where his friend stood gaping at the corpse. The smell hit him like an invisible fist and he covered his face with one hand.

'Fucking hell,' he mumbled, trying not to vomit, but his stomach kept turning violent somersaults as he studied the body. It was clad in overalls, torn and holed in several places, especially around the chest. Those empty, sightless eye sockets fixed him in an unseeing stare, and finally he turned away, gulping down great lungfuls of air.

'We'd better get the law,' said Doyle, backing off. 'Come on.'

Patterson needed no prompting. Both men turned and ran, but as he moved away from the monstrous vision which lay in the pipe, Doyle noticed something.

On the third finger of the left hand, the digit now fleshless and broken, a wedding ring glinted.

Six or seven arc lamps had been set up around the entrance to the sewer outlet, their blinding iridescence causing Detective

Inspector Grogan to wince as he made his way towards the opening. Two or three forensics men were already on the scene, one on his hands and knees near the pipe scrabbling around in the muck and stones. There was another light hanging inside the pipe, illuminating the remains of the corpse. Grogan wrinkled his nose as he climbed in.

Detective Sergeant Nicholson and a uniformed man were standing over the twisted remains.

'Who is he?' asked Grogan, nodding down at the body.

'His name's John Bateson,' the DS said. 'He was reported missing this afternoon by a couple of his workmates. It seems they were working in a storm relief sewer just off the Haymarket. The others cleared out because there was a gas leak. When one of them went back down there was no sign of Bateson.'

'So his body was swept here by the water in the sewers?' Grogan asked.

Nicholson nodded.

'What the hell happened to his face?' the DI pondered aloud. 'It looks like the same kind of damage we found on that poor sod in Leicester Square.'

Nicholson stooped and unfastened the dead man's overalls, pulling them open.

The entire chest and stomach cavity had been removed. Only shreds of mottled flesh and cracked bone remained beneath the overalls.

Grogan sighed, looking down at the wedding ring on the finger of the corpse.

'Someone had better tell his wife,' he murmured. Then, turning to leave, he looked back at Nicholson.

'I want the pathologist's reports on both victims as soon as possible. Let's see what he makes of it.'

The smell of death hung heavily in he air.

Nine

Finch juggled the cartons of Chinese food in both arms as he entered the kitchen, nudging the light on with one elbow. He winced as he felt hot barbecue sauce dripping through a rent in one of the cardboard containers onto his hand. The doctor dumped his supper on the table and wiped his hands on a towel. Ironically for a man who spent a good deal of his working life extolling the values of a balanced diet, Finch was a junk-food fanatic. Chinese or Indian, Macdonalds or just plain fish and chips, he was never averse to a take-away meal even though it might be lacking in nutrition. He found himself a knife and fork, then went and retrieved the evening paper from the front-door letterbox before sitting down at the table to eat straight from the cartons.

The house seemed strangely unwelcoming and silent, and Finch felt as if he were intruding upon the solitude. He ate slowly, pushing each carton aside when it was empty. As usual, he managed to time his last mouthful perfectly to match his completion of the paper. Then he got to his feet and stuffed the food containers and newspaper into the waste bin. The doctor wandered into the sitting room and flicked on the standard lamp. Again the silence seemed to swallow him up and he switched on the television. It at least provided the illusion of company.

The house in Westbourne Terrace was large, too large for one person, Finch had decided, and he'd been toying with the idea of selling it and moving into something smaller. A flat, ideally. Now that he was on his own the extra space was unnecessary.

On his own.

The thought drifted around in his mind as he sat down facing the television, looking at the picture but not really seeing anything.

He had lived alone for almost two years, ever since the break-up of his marriage. The split between Theresa and himself had been an ugly one and, at least on her part, the hostility had not ended with the separation. Their relationship had always been stormy, due in part to their very definite views on how they each wanted their careers to progress. Both possessed a single mindedness which bordered on obsession. His to become a doctor. Hers to take over the position of editor on the fashion magazine she worked for. Theresa was impulsive, quick-tempered, and when the need arose, ruthless. She was also stunningly attractive. A tall, statuesque woman with flowing auburn hair and a voice pitched so low that the word husky might well have been invented to describe it. She smouldered with an understated sensuality which many men found irresistible. Unfortunately for Finch, Theresa was not noted for her fidelity. Twice while they were engaged she had indulged in petty affairs, on each occasion with someone from the magazine where she worked. Quite how they came to be married sometimes seemed a mystery to Finch. But, at the beginning, things had run smoothly enough. Until she had discovered she was pregnant.

At that time he had discovered a curious ambivalence in her character. She knew that the birth of a child would wreck her chances of becoming editor of the magazine and yet she refused an abortion. The full weight of her anger and disappointment was directed at Finch. She blamed him for her pregnancy. Despite the fact that she had been taking the contraceptive pill for four years it had still happened. Finch himself ascribed the mishap to the fact that she had been suffering from a virus around the time she fell pregnant. It would have been quite easy for her to have vomited up the pill.

He understood her anger and disappointment but something nagged at the back of his mind. It had done at the time and it still did. Theresa had been involved with an advertising executive at the magazine, and Finch harboured suspicions that the child was the secret offspring of the other man. This had never been proved, or even discussed by himself and Theresa, but the fact that since she had left Finch she'd been living with that same man seemed to substantiate his fears. Nevertheless, when the child, a boy, had been born, both he and Theresa had shown it more love than any child could have expected under the circumstances. Theresa was a wonderful mother, but she had still felt an antagonism towards Finch which as time progressed had fermented into open dislike and resentment. He had his career, after all. It was she who had sacrificed everything.

The divorce had been almost inevitable and Finch, despite the fact that he loved his son, did not contest custody. He knew that Theresa and her lover could provide a better home. The doctor had to be content with his twice-monthly visits. He reached for the letter which lay on the coffee table beside his chair and opened it, re-reading the brief note which had arrived that morning. It was written in Theresa's distinctive sweeping script:

Dear Alan,
You can pick Christopher up at noon this Sunday. I'll meet you outside the main entrance of Regents Park. If I'm not there then Richard will be. Have Christopher back at my place by seven.
Theresa.

He replaced the letter on the table and sat back in the chair, rubbing both hands over his face. The television flickered before him, a programme about the actress Meryl Streep. She was talking about her role in the film *Kramer Versus Kramer*, particularly the scene in which she was in court fighting for the custody of her son and...

Finch switched it off.

61

Thursday – the 13th

Ten

George Bennett stood gazing out of the window, enjoying the feel of the sun on his skin. The heatwave showed no sign of letting up and London, indeed the entire country, once more faced the prospect of baking in the unrelenting heat. The long-term forecast offered no respite. The air conditioning inside the office was turned on full but the room was still like a greenhouse.

Bennett took another sunflower seed from the small bag which he held and popped it into his mouth. He'd been up since six that morning. He'd reported in to Scotland Yard at eight-thirty, changed out of his track-suit into more suitable attire and set to work. Bennett had jogged to work from his home in Upper Norwood for the last eight months. That regular exercise combined with his carefully-prepared diet, he was convinced, had made him a healthier person. He had, over the last week or so, managed to persuade his wife to give up all red meat and other cholesterol-rich foods. The next step was to coax her into the programme of exercises which he'd devised for her. He himself visited the local leisure centre at least three times a week to work out with weights and tone up his body. After so long abusing it, Bennett was at last beginning to feel the benefits of his regime. Not only did it make him feel better physically, it also sharpened his mental abilities, and the meditative part of his work-out enabled him to blot out the sights and sounds of his day's labour.

He felt that this was essential, owing to the nature of that work.

He'd been a pathologist for nearly twenty-two years,

twelve of those at Scotland Yard. There wasn't much that escaped his keen eyes and mind, but at the moment he was worried. His face, perpetually round and flabby despite the exercises, did not carry its usual look of casual humour. Lines creased his forehead as he continued looking out onto the sun-drenched city.

Behind him, seated at his desk, Detective Inspector Ray Grogan scanned the two reports once more, then sat back in his chair, wiping a thin film of perspiration from his forehead. He hated the heat. The DI loosened his tie slightly and took a sip of his coffee, which he found to his distaste had gone cold.

'So the wounds on both bodies weren't made with knives?' he said.

Bennett walked around to the front of the desk, popping another sunflower seed into his mouth. He shook his head.

'X-rays on both Bateson and the tramp showed no evidence of metal fragments anywhere on the body. Besides, the edges of the wounds were ragged, especially those in the chest and abdomen. A blade would have left a cleaner cut. Also there was no scoring on any of the bones. I expected it on the faces, I mean, they'd been almost completely removed, if that's the right word. As if someone had peeled them off, piece by piece.'

Grogan nodded.

'I know, I saw them. Remember?' he said, sardonically. Then, referring to the reports once more, 'You've got Bateson's weight as five stone four pounds. He was over five feet ten, he should have weighed at least twelve stone.'

'There was so much tissue loss,' Bennett explained. 'Don't forget, in both cases, the thorax was empty of organs. The liver, intestines and lungs alone make up a large proportion of the body weight. And besides that, the flesh had been stripped to the bone from the legs and arms, in fact over most of the body.'

'So the manner of death in both cases is identical. And yet there's no conceivable link between the two victims. A tramp and a happily married man about to become a father.' Grogan tapped the desk agitatedly. 'What the hell do they have in common?' He sighed and reached for his cigarettes.

'You should smoke low-tar if you *have* to smoke,' Bennett told him.

'Yeah, I know,' Grogan said. 'I should also change my socks twice a day and not moan about my old lady's cooking.' He sucked hard on the fag, blowing out a long stream of blue smoke. 'I'll tell you what puzzles me. Bateson was down the sewer when he was killed and three of his mates were close by. How did the murderer get to him?'

The question went unanswered and silence descended for a moment, finally broken again by Grogan.

'If it wasn't a metal blade that inflicted the injuries,' he began, 'could it have been a synthetic weapon of some kind? Very hard plastic maybe?'

'No. Traces of any other substance would have showed up on the ultra-violet scan I did.'

'You're a great help, George,' Grogan told him, raising his eyebrows. 'Could it be two different murderers? We're only assuming the killings are linked.'

'With exactly the same MO? You know better than that, Ray.'

'Indulge me, you bastard, I was playing that much maligned game affectionately known as clutching at straws.' The smile faded rapidly from the DI's face, to be replaced by a look of angry bewilderment. 'In both cases the flesh was stripped away and the internal organs removed, so why haven't we found any trace of them? They weren't taken from the scene of the crime in the first place, or we'd have found fragments, or at least blood leading out of the toilet. What the bloody hell happened to them?'

Bennett continued munching his sunflower seeds, a thought flickering behind his eyes.

'It could be some kind of animal,' he ventured.

Grogan raised his eyebrows.

'Just an idea,' the pathologist said, almost apologetically.

'Well, that's all we've got, isn't it? Ideas?' Grogan said, wearily. 'Two corpses, a few ideas but not one fucking lead.' He ground out his cigarette angrily and watched the plume of smoke rise mournfully into the air.

Eleven

The dog was a cross-breed, part Alsatian, part Collie, retaining the elegance of the latter and the sleek build of the former. It padded slowly up the street, the pavement uncomfortably hot beneath its paws. Every now and then it would stop and prick up its ears as a car or motor-bike passed, sometimes barking at the offending machine. For the hot weather made the dog listless and irritable. It moved past people without a sound, however, for it had no hatred of man. The dog had always been treated well by its owners.

It paused for a moment to lap at the spilled contents of a Coke can which lay in the gutter, the fizzy liquid slaking its thirst at least for the moment. What the dog really sought was shade, somewhere to shelter from the merciless blanket of heat which lay over the city like a stifling shroud. High above, the vapour trails of aeroplanes criss-crossed the canopy of blue like chalk-marks on a blackboard.

The dog rounded a corner, tongue hanging from its mouth. Up ahead it saw what it sought. It moved on without increasing its pace, passing the odd parked car. It had tried crawling beneath one of the machines before but the smell of petrol had driven it away. Now it approached the empty building, the black gap in the boarded-up window beckoning it. The dog was barely able to squeeze through the opening between the planks but, panting heavily, it finally succeeded in hauling its sleek form into the murky, welcoming coolness.

The dog sniffed the stagnant air, detecting the smell of decay and filth, but also something more potent. A pungent odour which, simultaneously, both repelled and attracted it.

The building had once housed a small delicatessen. The empty shelves were now thick with dust and ancient cobwebs where large spiders lay in wait for the dozens of flies which buzzed lazily around the abandoned building.

To the rear was a small kitchen area, used by staff when the shop had been open, and it was towards this that the dog headed, drawn by the strange smell it had detected on entering the building.

The sink had been removed and only a hole in the ground remained where the pipe had once been.

Around this pipe were several trails of slime, thick and glutinous, cutting through the dust on the floor like tears down a dirt encrusted cheek.

The dog licked at one of the slime trails, shaking its head and growling as it tasted the vile substance. It tried to remove the sticky fluid from its tongue by scraping it with one dusty paw but this didn't seem to work. The dog made a retching sound, but seconds later it seemed to forget the foul taste. Its ears pricked up and it stood motionless, watching the top of the pipe.

The first slug, seven inches long and as thick as a man's index finger, slithered from the pipe.

It was followed by a second. And a third.

The dog didn't move.

Mark Franklin had been following the dog for nearly fifteen minutes, and more than once he thought he'd lost track of it. His mother had told him that Prince liked to roam the streets and Mark had decided to use his dog's habit for his own amusement. He'd let Prince out, given him thirty seconds start, then followed him just like they did in 'The Professionals'. They called it 'putting a tail on the suspect'. He chuckled to himself. Not hard to do as Prince already had a tail. Mark turned the corner just in time to see it disappearing as his dog slipped through the gap in the front of the empty shop.

He pulled the plastic radio from his belt, and without

taking his eyes off the shopfront, he spoke into it:

'This is Bodie calling Cowley. Suspect cornered. Will take action now. Over and out.'

He replaced the radio and took a model .45 automatic from the plastic shoulder holster which he wore, then made his way slowly down the street towards the building.

There was a sudden movement off to his right and he spun round.

Two children, younger than himself, were emerging from a small newsagents' clutching ice-creams. Mark decided that the suspect could wait until he'd bought himself a Mini Milk. He put his plastic gun away and rummaged in the pocket of his jeans for some money.

It was cool inside the shop and he stood beside the fridge, enjoying the cold air which wafted up from the freezer. Finally he reached in and selected a lolly, joining the small queue to pay for it.

Mark was eleven. He was happy playing on his own. Other children in the area didn't bother with him much, and even at school he had not yet found a group of friends who would share their time with him. His mother had worried at first, but Mark did not seem to care. He was more than able to amuse himself during the long summer holidays, something for which his mother was grateful because she had a cleaning job in a West End cinema and couldn't stay at home to keep Mark entertained.

He was a slightly built lad. His short hair gleamed in the sunlight, brushed back from a high forehead which already bore one or two small spots – a portent of the onslaught of acne which would no doubt plague him in his teenage years. He wore a brilliant white T-shirt with 'L.A. RAIDERS' on it in large red letters (a present brought back from the States by his grandparents), and a pair of brown cords which were a little too long and concertinaed around the tops of his trainers.

Mark leant against the wall of the newsagents' and slurped away at his Mini Milk. The suspect could wait until he'd finished.

The slugs oozed out of the pipe like a treacly river of oil, spilling onto the dusty floor of the abandoned shop. The largest ones moved towards the dog, which still sat motionless, watching intently. Finally, when the closest was less than a foot way, Prince ducked his head close to the slug and sniffed the black creature, which immediately retracted its eye stalks and stopped moving. Those around it, however, did not.

The dog licked one of the others, again growling at the vile taste of the mucus covering which sheathed its fat body.

The slug bit into the dog's tongue and hung there, suspended by its central tooth, as if attempting to pull the tender strip of muscle from its root.

Prince tried to yelp but only succeeded in making a high pitched whine deep in his throat. He shook his head, retracting his tongue and grinding the bloated slug between his powerful jaws. A mixture of blood and mucoid pus dripped to the floor in thick dollops.

Two more of the larger slugs fastened themselves to one of the dog's forepaws and began burrowing into the flesh. Prince snapped at them but could not dislodge them, and now more slugs were slithering up his other front leg, burrowing deep into skin and muscle.

He fell forward, and in that split second five or six more of the black monstrosities were able to grip his side. He snapped at another, pulping it between his teeth, heaving at the disgusting taste. Blood jetted from his wounds and sprayed across the dusty floor.

One of the largest slugs slithered up the dog's back, resisting all attempts to dislodge it until finally it reached the exposed ear. The monstrous creature fixed its mouth parts firmly inside Prince's ear and began feeding, boring deeper. Towards the brain.

The dog at last tried to run but the sheer weight of his attackers slowed his flight and he could only crawl as more and more slugs found their way onto his body and set to work with their teeth, sucking his warm blood which filled their bodies, pumping them up like leeches until it seemed they would burst.

And still the dog tried to crawl away, leaving a trail of blood and slime.

Even when his front legs had been eaten to the bone he kept trying to escape.

From the pipe in the floor yet more slugs emerged. A never-ending black torrent of death.

Mark finished the last mouthful of the lolly and read the joke on the stick:

What do you call a gorilla with ear muffs?
Call him what you like, he won't hear you.

The youngster tossed the stick away, his attention now directed once more towards his objective. He walked down the street purposefully, unhooking the plastic radio from his belt again.

'Bodie to Cowley. I'm going in. Over and out,' he said, with a degree of authority.

As he drew closer to the boarded-up shopfront Mark slowed his pace, wondering if he was going to be able to squeeze through the gap by which Prince had gained access. He knelt beside it and peered into the gloom beyond, wrinkling his nose as a particularly noxious stench drifted through the hole.

'Prince,' he called.

The dog usually came running at the sound of his name but Mark waited in vain.

He called again.

Silence greeted his call.

Perhaps the dog had fallen asleep somewhere inside, Mark reasoned. He knew he shouldn't go in, but what the heck, the shop was empty, and he wasn't going to steal anything. He got his head through, then his shoulders, with relative ease. He pulled himself the last few inches, rolling over in the dust which covered the floor. He brushed himself down but his T-shirt and cords were filthy. His mum would go mad when she saw them. He decided he'd better find Prince and return home as quickly as possible.

He straightened up, looking around him at the neglected shelves which formed aisles. It was humid inside the old shop, not as hot as outside but the air smelt stale...

No, it smelt revolting.

He coughed as the nauseating stench enveloped him, growing stronger as he moved cautiously down one aisle towards the rear of the shop. He ran his hand along the shelf as he walked, accidentally disturbing a large beetle. It scuttled away and Mark jumped back in surprise and horror.

'Prince,' he called again, wondering if the dog had perhaps found another way out of the building. He might well have passed straight through the shop and left via a rear exit. If so, Mark thought, he'd have a hard job to find him.

The appalling smell was growing stronger, combining with the cloying warmth to make him feel faint.

He rounded a bank of shelves, preparing to shout the dog's name again.

The sound caught in his throat.

Blood had spread out in a wide puddle, mingling with the dust and slime to form a reeking stain which covered much of the floor in front of Mark. In the centre of the crimson pool lay the twisted remains of the dog, its jaws hanging open, the skull gleaming whitely even in the gloom. Pieces of fur and torn flesh were strewn near the carcass which looked like a blood-soaked rag. One fleshless leg stuck up into the air at an impossible angle.

With morbid curiosity overcoming his initial revulsion, Mark moved towards the remains, almost slipping in the slicks of blood. He reached forward and touched the skull, finding that it was coated by a thick, jelly-like substance which dripped from the rest of the remains like glutinous tears.

Mark felt the stuff on his fingers. He rubbed it between his thumb and forefinger, finally wiping it on his cords.

'Prince,' he said softly, reaching for the dog's collar. He loosened it, pulling the circlet free of the ravaged neck. Blood and sticky fluid coloured his palms as he held the collar before him, eyes still riveted to the bloodied pile of bones and fur

73

which had once been a dog.

He suddenly felt very afraid. He wished he was home with his mum. He'd have to tell her about what happened, perhaps even show her.

Mark turned and ran, scrambling through the gap in the planks, the collar still gripped in one hand. He ran all the way home, holding back his tears.

He wondered why his fingers and hands were beginning to feel so painfully itchy.

Before he reached home, the unpleasant tingling sensation had crept up his arms as far as his elbows. It was as if someone were rubbing his flesh with sandpaper.

Twelve

'Mum, I'm telling you the truth, honest,' Mark Franklin protested. 'I think somebody killed Prince.' The youngster held out the bloodied collar for inspection but his mother didn't touch it.

'You said you saw him squeezing through some planks,' Denise Franklin said. 'He could have cut himself doing it, perhaps pulled his collar off at the same time.'

'There was blood everywhere. He looked like he'd been *eaten*,' Mark insisted.

'Look, Mark, you'd better not say anything about this when your dad gets home, you know how he feels about that sort of thing. He says you watch too much television as it is. You remember those nightmares you had a few months back?'

'I wasn't dreaming what I saw, Mum. I think Prince was eaten by something.'

She shook her head, watching her son over the rim of her teacup. They were both seated at the kitchen table having a bite to eat, but Mark was merely prodding at his food, taking small mouthfuls occasionally, as if he couldn't stomach what lay before him.

'Is there something wrong with that?' Denise asked, nodding in the direction of the plate.

'I'm not very hungry,' he said, wearily, putting down his fork to scratch his other arm. As he did so, Denise noticed how red the skin was. Blotchy in places, it looked as if it had been scalded. Even the palms of his hands were the same. She saw two or three small welts on the flesh of his forearm.

'Are you feeling all right, Mark?' she asked him, wondering if perhaps he'd been out in the sun too long. The temperature that day had hovered around ninety-one degrees and Denise wondered if the boy was suffering from some kind of heat rash. His face, however, looked distinctly pale.

He continued scratching himself.

'Mark,' she repeated. 'I asked if you were feeling all right.'

'I feel a bit sick, Mum,' he told her, finally pushing the plate away. 'I'm going to stay in my room for a while.' He clambered down from the table, swaying uncertainly for a second, then walked out of the room, heading towards his bedroom. Denise drained what was left in her cup, one eye on the dog collar which still lay on the table. She frowned at it, then took a knife and lifted the bloodied circlet and dropped it into the waste-bin, afterwards running the knife beneath the hot tap for a moment to clean it. Then, she put the plates, her own cup and Mark's 'Ghostbusters' mug into the sink and ran some more hot water onto them. That done, Denise strode into the sitting room and pulled a thick book down from the shelves.

'The Encyclopaedia of Family Health,' she read aloud. She flicked through the alphabetical listings, looking for 'Rash', then 'sunburn' (although she doubted if that was really the cause of the reddening on her son's arms). Neither entry offered much help so she flipped through to 'Skin Disorders'. However, there were more than four pages of entries and

Denise couldn't take the time to read the whole lot. She replaced the book and headed down the hall towards Mark's room.

No sounds came from inside and she wondered if he was lying down. Perhaps he'd dropped off to sleep.

She rapped gently on the door.

'Mark! Are you OK, love?' she called.

No answer.

Without waiting to knock again she opened the door and walked in.

Mark was sitting on the edge of the bed staring down at his outstretched arms. He did not lift his head as his mother entered the room.

From elbow to fingertips, on both arms, his skin was a deep crimson, the veins standing out darkly against the swollen flesh. But that wasn't what immediately struck Denise.

It was the liquescent pus-filled boils which caused her to gasp. There were more than half a dozen on each arm, and when he looked up at her, his face a pale mask of fear and pain, she saw that there were also three of the throbbing lesions on his cheeks and forehead.

Denise froze momentarily, not knowing what to do.

Mark didn't move, he merely looked down again at the large swellings which disfigured his arms.

Finally Denise turned and ran back into the sitting room, snatching up the phone. When she got through, the receptionist told her that the doctor was fully booked for the rest of the day and could see no one. Perhaps tomorrow...

'My son is very ill,' Denise protested, angrily. 'I have to see the doctor.'

The receptionist asked if she'd like to make an appointment for the following day.

Denise slammed the phone down and stood helplessly for a moment, then snatched up the receiver once more and called for a taxi to pick her and Mark up in ten minutes. Before the despatcher had even confirmed the pick-up, she put the phone down and headed back towards her son's bedroom.

When the time came, she had to practically carry him out to

the waiting cab.

Thirteen

Len Pearson watched the green Fiat pull away from the front door of 25 King Street. He strained his eyes to see if there was any movement inside the house across the street, but without his glasses he could see little. He'd left them on the table beside his armchair, and by the time he retrieved them and returned to his vantage point, the occupant of the house was locking the door and walking away.

She was a good-looking woman in her thirties, large-busted and narrow-waisted, though perhaps a little too broad in the hips.

'Bloody tart,' muttered Len, watching her as she disappeared from view. 'If only your husband knew.'

He was convinced that the woman across the road was having an affair. Every day around lunchtime a green Fiat was parked outside the house for approximately an hour, and then its owner, a man who always wore immaculately-cut suits, emerged from the house and drove away. Len saw these comings and goings, and much more, because he spent most of his time peering out of his sitting room window. But then there wasn't much else he *could* do to pass the time.

At the age of 58, Len Pearson was practically house-bound. He'd worked for British Rail for more than forty years prior to his accident. One winter's day, as he climbed into his engine, his foot had slipped off the cab steps and he'd crashed down between the train and platform. His left leg had been shattered in two places, and after two operations to re-set it, gangrene had set in and the limb had been amputated. Now, with the aid of an artificial leg and a walking frame, he was able to move around his flat with relative ease. But he also had a bad case of chronic bronchitis, and the two infirmities in combination kept him more or less confined to his home.

With that confinement had come bitterness. He had never married and now he lived an isolated existence except for the odd visit from the meals-on-wheels lady and, if he was lucky, the local home-help. She wasn't due again until the end of the week, and all she did anyway was run the hoover around and do a bit of polishing, and the stupid cow always put his ornaments back in the wrong places. Something which greatly annoyed him. Come to think of it, there wasn't much that *didn't* annoy him. He hated the hot weather because it made him sweat. He hated the cold because it played havoc with his arthritis. He disliked the home-help because she was always telling him not to complain, and the meals-on-wheels woman because she simply talked too much.

Len moved away from the window, taking one last look at the house across the street. There was no doubt about it, that bloody woman was up to no good. Little wonder she attracted the men, he thought, flouncing around with no bra, wearing skirts split up to the top of her bloody thigh. She might as well stick a red light over the door. Len grunted. He wouldn't put even *that* past her. For all he knew there might well be other men visitors who called there. He made a mental note to keep his eyes open for any others who might turn up in future.

The young couple in the flat next door to him weren't much better. Bloody newly-weds. They acted as if they'd just discovered sex. Many a night, Len had stood by the wall adjoining their bedroom listening to the laughter and moans coming from within. He was certain they'd break the bed one of these nights. They were away on holiday at the moment so he was getting a bit of peace and quiet until they returned. It was probably one of those 'Club' holidays, or whatever they called them. Len had read about them in the Sunday papers. People only went on them for one thing. If they didn't shag everything that moved then they hadn't had a good time. Getting pissed every night and screwing around at every

78

opportunity. Yes, he knew the type of thing.

The girl on the other side of him was oriental. She was hardly ever home and Len could only guess at what she did for a living. Probably a stripper or something. But he'd noticed that when she *was* home she never had any men in her flat. More than likely a bloody lesbian. Yes, he knew the type.

People nowadays, he thought, didn't seem to have any backbone. The kids were scum, all bloody glue-sniffers or drunks by the time they were twenty. The parents were no better. Marriages breaking up, blokes mucking around with other blokes' wives and the women, like that tart across the road, flaunting themselves for all to see.

Len shook his head in disgust. He knew what went on in this so-called enlightened society and it sickened him. The world was made up of hooligans, slags, con-men and degenerates.

He knew, he read *The News of the World*.

His stomach rumbled and he muttered to himself. He was sure the fish that the meals-on-wheels woman had given him had been off. Complaining about falling standards, he made his way to the bathroom. Balancing delicately on his good leg, supported by his frame, he unfastened his trousers, pulled them down and plonked himself on the toilet.

The slug slithered soundlessly up from the lavatory pan, its eye stalks extending as it broke the surface of the clear water. Half a dozen more followed it, their black shapes resembling animated faeces as they crawled up the white porcelain.

Len shifted position on the plastic seat and murmured something to himself about the meals-on-wheels woman. She'd given him a boiled egg the day before last, silly cow, he was probably constipated now.

More slugs spilled through the pipe, clogging the pan with their numbers, swarming over each other as they dragged their swollen bodies up the gleaming surface.

The closest of them had reached the plastic seat.

He'd tell her next time she called, Len decided. He'd tell the old bag what she'd done to him, how she'd buggered up his insides with her lousy food. He'd . . .

Pain, intense, excruciating pain suddenly tore through him and he cried out. A guttural, rasping groan.

Three of the largest slugs were eating their way into the meaty part of his buttocks while a fourth pushed its obscene form into Len's anus, the lubricating slime helping its passage as it found access to his bowels.

Blood burst from the wounds, spraying the white porcelain and the seething mass of slugs which oozed up the sides of the lavatory in search of food. More of them began digging into the tops of his thighs, and from the waist down he felt as if his body was on fire. Two of the black monstrosities glided up between his legs and Len shrieked with renewed ferocity as they chewed through the soft skin of his scrotum. The fleshy sac seemed to burst and one purple, egg-shaped object dropped into the pan. Blood was now flowing thickly and freely into the lavatory and it further incensed those slugs who had not yet reached the feast.

More and more poured up from the crimson depths seeking the flesh they needed to sustain them.

Len tried to rise but he overbalanced and sprawled helplessly on the floor of the bathroom, his frame clattering over in front of him.

Another slug penetrated his anus, joining its bloated companion in a murderous act of blood-stained sodomy. Fragments of excretion leeked from the riven lower bowel, mingling with the blood which was now spreading across the floor in a sticky pool.

More slugs came swarming over the rim of the lavatory, gliding down the other side, slithering onto Len to feast on his writhing body. He felt one last mind-numbing eruption of pain as the leading slug finally ate its way up into his belly, and then, mercifully, he blacked out.

Some of the creatures tried to chew into his false leg but they soon realized that this was not what they sought and they moved on up his ravaged form until they reached the small of his back, where they plunged their razor-sharp central teeth into the flesh and began feeding. Before long they had bored their way through to his kidneys.

Across the street, the woman from number 25 had returned.

There was another car parked outside the house now, and she smiled as she saw it. The woman glanced up towards the window of Len Pearson's flat, trying to catch a glimpse of the old bastard at the window. She'd seen him spying on her. Well, it didn't bother her. Sod him. Let him carry on looking, and if he didn't like what he saw then tough luck.

But as she entered her front door and glanced back once again at Len's window, she saw no sign of his hunched figure skulking behind the curtains.

Perhaps he'd found something better to occupy his time, she thought.

Fourteen

Finch glanced at his watch as he dried his hands. It was almost three in the afternoon. His last patient had been dealt with, and he now had two hours until the evening surgery. He decided to nip out for something to eat. He'd had nothing since breakfast. His two partners had already finished and departed. Finch closed his briefcase and was about to leave the room when he heard a commotion from outside.

Raised voices.

One of them he recognized as June, the receptionist.

'Surgery is not open again until five...'

'I have to see him *now*. My son can't be left like this all afternoon!'

'I'll ask the doctor...'

'You *must* let me in!'

Finch opened the door and looked out to see June barring it, as if protecting him from another, slightly older woman who was holding a young lad close to her.

'What's going on, June?' Finch asked.

'I must see you, doctor. It's my little boy,' Denise Franklin blurted.

'This lady has no appointment and...'

Finch took one look at the boy and barely managed to conceal his surprise.

Mark Franklin's face was almost completely covered in bulbous, festering sores.

'Come in,' Finch said, looking straight past his receptionist. He ushered Denise and Mark into his room, then turned to June. 'It's all right, June, I can manage.'

He stepped back into the room and closed the door behind him. Mark was sitting on one of the two leather-bound seats facing the doctor's desk and Finch crossed to him immediately, noting a glazed look in the boy's eyes as well as the all-too-obvious infection of the skin.

'What's his name?' Finch asked, without taking his eyes off the boy.

Denise told him.

'What's wrong with him, doctor?' she added.

Finch ignored the question. 'Is his condition recent?' he asked. 'Did it begin without warning? I mean, these lesions.'

'When he went out this morning he was fine,' Denise said.

'He's been in contact with nothing corrosive?'

'What's that?'

'Acid, strong solvent, anything like that?'

'No. Not that I know of.'

Finch placed a thermometer in the boy's mouth, then removed a wooden spatula from its sterilized plastic wrapping and prodded the edges of one of the sores as cautiously as he could.

The skin stretched and looked as if it was going to break. Mark whimpered softly, keeping the thermometer in his mouth.

Finch waited a moment longer, then removed the thin glass tube. The mercury was nudging 101. If the boy was suffering from the same illness as Molly Foster then it was in a far more advanced state, Finch thought. He asked Mark to remove his T-shirt which, with difficulty, he did.

His back and chest were also dotted with the suppurating sores.

'We'll need to get him to a hospital,' Finch said. 'I can't deal with this here.'

'But what is it?' Denise Franklin demanded.

He wondered whether he should mention Molly Foster and the frightening similarity of her disfigurement, but he decided to remain silent.

'Can't you give him anything?' Denise pleaded.

'Only pain killers if he needs them, Mrs Franklin. I'm dealing with something which even *I* don't understand. I've never encountered anything quite like this before.' He turned to Mark. 'Are you in pain, Mark?'

The boy looked at his mother as if waiting to be given the answer. Then he glanced at Finch and nodded almost imperceptibly. The doctor reached for his prescription pad.

'I don't want to go to hospital,' Mark said, swallowing with some difficulty. 'Please don't make me go.'

'If you don't go, Mark, you'll become even more ill,' Finch said. 'You don't want that, do you?'

'I don't want to go,' the boy said, tears welling in his eyes.

'What will happen to him if he stays at home?' Denise asked.

'If he does then *I* can't take any responsibility for his well-being,' Finch told her, bluntly.

'I want him with me,' Denise said.

Finch bit his lip and fixed the woman in an icy stare.

'You realize the risk you're taking?' he said. 'If it turns out to be a contagious disease of some kind then you and your husband are also at risk.'

'Please don't make me go to hospital,' Mark pleaded again, that glazed look returning to his eyes. Finch felt as if he were staring into two opaque marbles when he looked at the boy.

'All right,' he said finally, 'but take this.' He scribbled something on a piece of paper. 'It's my home phone number. If there's any deterioration in his condition let me know. It doesn't matter what time of the night it is.' He passed her the paper. 'I'll call in tomorrow and check on him.'

'I think he'll feel happier at home, doctor,' said Denise, getting to her feet.

'If he hasn't improved by tomorrow, Mrs Franklin, then you'd be foolish not to let him undergo hospital tests.'

'I don't trust hospitals,' she said sharply.

Finch didn't answer.

'May I have your address, please?' he said, wearily.

'Number five St Anne's Court,' Denise replied.

Finch frowned and slowed the speed of his writing for a moment. St Anne's Court. He knew that name from somewhere.

'We'd better go, doctor,' she told him. 'There's a taxi waiting outside for us.' She promised to ring if necessary.

Finch waited until he heard the footsteps recede down the corridor, then he sat back in his chair, staring at what he'd written, thinking about what he'd just seen. Could it be a contagious disease of some kind, he wondered? Then again, he knew of no disease which manifested symptoms as severe as those he'd seen on the boy and on Molly Foster. Besides, if it was that vehement, why hadn't Lisa been infected? Why not the boy's parents? Finch tapped his pen on top of his desk, glancing once more at the address before him. His eyes suddenly widened and he got to his feet, crossing the room to a map of central London which was pinned to the notice board on the far wall. He ran his finger over it until he found the area he sought.

'St Anne's Court,' he whispered.

Now he knew why the name rang a bell.

Mark Franklin lived just one street away from Molly Foster.

Finch massaged the bridge of his nose between thumb and forefinger, his forehead wrinkling into a frown.

With both victims living so close together, could it be coincidence?

He hoped, for reasons he was not yet sure of, that it was.

Fifteen

The boy lay in the darkness listening to the ticking of the clock.

Unable to sleep because of the steadily growing pain, he shifted from his back to his side, then onto his stomach but the position change only aggravated his discomfort, so finally Mark Franklin swung himself out of bed and flicked on his bedside light. He opened his pyjama jacket, gazing down at his body with eyes like glass.

The whole of his chest and abdomen was a festering mass of oozing sores. He could feel them on his back too, the swollen tips brushing against the light material of his pyjamas. But despite the pain he did not cry out, he merely got slowly to his feet and headed for the door of his room.

His mother had told him that, if he felt bad, he should call out and either she or his father would come to him. They would call the doctor if things got too unbearable.

Moving somewhat unsteadily on legs which by this time were also ulcerated, he padded down the hall to the bathroom and tugged at the long, dangling cord. The light flickered into life and Mark moved to the sink where he gazed at his reflection in the large mirror. One eye was nearly closed due to the discoloured sore which was forming on the lid, the other was bloodshot and glazed. He gripped the sides of the sink for a moment as the pain jabbed red hot knives into him. His head was throbbing madly, as if someone had set a steam-hammer going inside it. Waves of nausea swept through him but he retained his balance, reaching for the door of the medicine cabinet.

He took down his father's safety razor and slowly, painfully, unscrewed the blade, releasing it. The wickedly sharp edge glinted as Mark inspected it, hardly able to feel the thin sliver of steel between his bloated fingers.

After a moment or two he crossed to the door again, pulled the light cord and walked slowly down the hall.

The door to his parents room was open, as were the windows. The curtains, stirred by the light warm breeze, waved gently and Mark stood in the doorway watching them for a moment, as if hypnotized by the softly flowing material. However, his attention finally turned to the sleeping forms of his parents.

Both Roger and Denise Franklin were naked, only a sheet covering them. As Mark moved closer he saw the soft rise and fall of his father's broad chest, the single bead of perspiration glistening on his forehead.

He lifted the razor blade in swollen fingers, his entire body feeling as if it were on fire. The light from the hall glinted on the blade's vicious edge.

Mark steadied the blade in his hand, then swiftly drew it twice across his father's throat.

The sheer steel sliced effortlessly through skin and muscle, opening veins and arteries which immediately began spurting forth fountains of blood, some of which splattered Mark. But he stood by unperturbed as the two cuts seemed to widen and finally join, forming one massive rent. The edges quivered like lips around a blood-filled mouth. Crimson sprayed wildly from the deep slash, the blood from the severed carotid arteries rising a full three feet, propelled by the pumping of the heart. The crimson cascade hit the wall behind the bed and ran down like paint thrown at a canvas.

Roger Franklin's eyes jerked open, the whites standing out in stark contrast to the pupils as the orbs bulged in their sockets. The pain from the wound was minimal but he could feel the powerful jets of crimson bursting from his body with a force that caused him to convulse. He opened his mouth to scream but he could not. The bitter taste of his own life fluid filled his mouth before it ran down from both corners, bubbling over his lips to form a thick purple foam as it mixed with the saliva.

Mark moved away from his dying father, the razor blade still held in his fingers.

He walked quickly but unhurriedly around to the other side of the bed where his mother was now awake, hurtled into consciousness by the cascade of blood beside her. She saw her husband's body jerking wildly as he clawed at the huge gash in his neck, the blood jetting through his fingers. The walls, the bed, her own body were all covered in the warm red fluid. There were even spots of it on the ceiling. She shook her head in disbelief and horror as he turned towards her, his eyes rolling upwards in the sockets to reveal the whites. He made a liquid gurgling sound and then lay still, his hands falling to his sides. A soft rumbling, followed by a pungent smell, signalled that his sphincter muscle had relaxed.

Denise was barely aware of Mark standing beside her.

He brought the razor blade down in a swatting action and she screamed as the steel gashed her arm from shoulder to elbow. She tried to roll off the bed but her escape route was blocked by the body of her husband.

Mark struck again, slicing open the sole of one flailing foot, then, with another lightning blow, her calf.

Still screaming, she practically threw herself across Roger's body, landing with a thud on the carpet, the wind momentarily knocked from her. As she tried to stand a searing pain shot up her cut leg and she toppled over once more, blood soaking into the carpet as it pumped from the hideous gashes.

Mark followed, moving purposefully around the bed, his blank eyes fixing her in an emotionless stare. He watched her claw her way up onto her knees, tears now streaming down her cheeks as she saw him advancing on her. She called his name, a note of pleading in her voice along with sheer, uncomprehending terror.

He struck again, catching her across the right breast, puncturing the soft flesh, almost severing the nipple.

She screamed again and reached for something to ward him

off, her hand closing around the bedside lamp. As she reached for it he raked the razor blade down her back, feeling it scrape on bone as it carved across her right shoulder blade. Blood ran down her back but she turned and brought the lamp crashing down on his head, the impact knocking him backwards. He crashed to the floor, the razor blade slipping from his fingers.

As he hit the carpet he screamed in agony. The boils on his back burst in unison, gouts of evil-smelling pus pumping from the torn lesions.

Through tears of pain and desperation, Denise saw her son writhing before her as more and more of the running sores began to burst. Thick yellow fluid exploded from them until it seemed that his entire upper body was a liquescent mass. It was as if his entire torso and face had been transformed into one giant festering pustule. His skin seemed to peel away and now blood was mingling with the sticky discharge which oozed from the burst boils.

Mark shrieked, his limbs going rigid as new waves of pain tore through him, and Denise could only watch helplessly, the life draining rapidly from her own body. Her vision was dimming as she slipped towards unconsciousness, but she could still see the motionless form of her husband lying on the bed, some of his spilled blood beginning to congeal thickly, while beside her on the floor her son was undergoing the last involuntary spasms which signalled the end of his life.

The room smelt like a charnel house, the pungent odours of blood, pus and excrement mingling together to form one stomach-turning stench of death.

Denise Franklin felt the blood draining from her. She felt searing pain from the four wounds. With a last despairing moan she collapsed.

The banging on the front door began less than thirty seconds later.

Sixteen

At first he thought he was dreaming. That the strident ringing of the phone was inside his head. But as he forced his eyes open he realized it wasn't his imagination.

The ringing continued.

As Finch reached for the receiver he mumbled something about late nights. It seemed barely two or three hours since he'd climbed beneath the sheets. Now his regular alarm call was signalling the start of another day.

He blinked hard and checked his watch.

3.00 a.m.

He picked up the receiver, stifling a yawn.

'Hello,' he croaked, wondering why anyone should be calling at this ungodly hour of the morning.

The voice at the other end sounded sharp and alert and Finch shook himself, feeling at something of a disadvantage.

'Dr Alan Finch?' the voice asked.

'Yes. Who is this?' He could not prevent himself yawning this time.

'My name is Nicholson. Detective Sergeant Nicholson. Could you come to number five St Anne's Court? Now, please. We can send a car for you...'

Nicholson allowed the sentence to trail off.

Finch rubbed his eyes, still somewhat bemused.

'No, it's OK,' he said. 'I'll drive.' There was a moment's silence, finally broken by the doctor. 'What's happened?' he asked.

'You'll see when you get here,' he was told, then Nicholson hung up, leaving Finch to stare at the buzzing receiver. He replaced it slowly onto the cradle, stretched once, listening to his joints pop and crack, then he got to his feet and began dressing.

Within ten minutes he was behind the wheel of his Chevette, heading towards his appointed destination.

The streets were understandably deserted and he drove with ease, glimpsing just one other vehicle. The journey would normally have taken him close to forty-five minutes but he made it in under thirty. As he pulled the car into a parking space opposite the flats in St. Anne's Court, he saw two police cars and an ambulance parked in the road and on the pavement outside the building. The blue lights of the ambulance were turning silently, and as he climbed out of the car, it seemed to Finch as if he had entered a strange soundless world. He almost longed for the screech of sirens to break the oppressive silence. Lights were burning in some of the windows and he caught sight of a figure peering out at him as he approached the flats.

A uniformed policeman standing at the door asked him who he was. Finch took out an identity card and passed it to the policeman, who checked the unflattering photo against its owner's features for a second before returning it. Finch proceeded up the stairs.

He found more policemen outside the flat and had to repeat the identification procedure before being allowed inside.

There were at least half a dozen plain-clothes men moving about in the sitting room and hallway of the flat, occasionally disappearing into a room at the far end of the long hall. Then a man with long hair and a corduroy jacket emerged from the room. He looked at Finch and attempted a smile but decided against it, choosing instead to shake hands with the doctor.

'Doctor Finch?' he said. 'I'm Detective Sergeant Nicholson. Come this way, please.'

As he entered the room, Finch almost recoiled from the vile smell which hung in the air. He saw three other men in the room, one of whom was taking photographs of the carnage. Of the blood-drenched walls and bed and of the three bodies which lay sprawled like disfigured mannequins.

Finch had seen dead bodies many times before, road accident casualties and victims of muggings or industrial accidents, but nothing he had seen could compare with the horror of the sight which he now looked upon.

As he stared at the corpse of young Mark Franklin, the skin mottled red and blue, raw and bleeding, Finch suddenly felt a stab of guilt. Was it guilt? He lowered his head slightly. If only he had insisted that the boy be admitted to hospital instead of allowing the mother to talk him out of it. Perhaps the boy, at least, would not now be dead.

He glanced at the other two bodies and shook his head slowly. One of the men who had been in the room when he entered now approached him and introduced himself.

'Sorry to get you out of bed, Doctor Finch,' Detective Inspector Grogan added, lighting up a cigarette. 'Especially for this little lot.' He gestured towards the bodies.

'Why did you call *me*?' Finch wanted to know.

'You were the boy's doctor, weren't you?' the DI said.

Finch nodded.

'We found your phone number on a pad in the living room.' The policeman blew out a stream of smoke. 'What was wrong with the boy?'

Finch sighed.

'I wish I knew,' he faltered, then corrected himself. 'I wish I'd *known*.'

'How long had you been treating him?' Grogan wanted to know.

Finch told him about the visit that afternoon, about wanting to have the boy admitted to hospital. Grogan listened without taking his eyes from the doctor, merely nodding occasionally.

'Why is the boy's illness so much of a concern to you?' Finch asked finally.

'Because he murdered his parents,' said the DI in a matter-of-fact tone. He held out his hand and Nicholson handed him a plastic envelope.

It contained the bloodied razor blade.

'He used this,' Grogan continued.

Finch ran a hand through his hair, looking first at the razor blade then at the bodies.

'A neighbour heard screams. She gave us a call. All three of them were dead when we arrived. The father had been dead about twenty minutes, the mother had bled to death and the boy . . . we're not sure about.' There was a momentary silence while the policeman took another long drag on his cigarette. 'You were his doctor but you say you don't know what was wrong with him.'

'May I look at the body?' Finch asked and Grogan stepped aside.

Kneeling beside the corpse was George Bennett. He was taking skin samples with a small scalpel, dropping them into a series of thin glass test tubes which he then sealed and placed carefully in his pocket. The pathologist smiled thinly at Finch as he joined him. The doctor could clearly see the deep welts and craters in the skin where the boils had burst. Some of the pus had formed a sticky film on the skin, but in other places it had hardened into a scab-like coating.

'Have you ever seen anything like it before?' Bennett asked him.

Finch shuddered involuntarily as he thought of Molly Foster.

Was the same thing happening to her now? He wondered whether or not he should mention the other woman. He decided not to.

For the moment, anyway.

'When are the autopsies being carried out?' he asked.

'As soon as the bodies are taken back to Scotland Yard,' Bennett told him.

'Why do you want to know?' Grogan inquired.

'Well, the lad *was* my patient,' Finch said. 'I'd like to be there when it's done.'

'That's not the way we do things, I'm afraid, doctor. But you will be told as soon as we have anything worth telling you.'

'Is there some objection to me being present?' Finch asked.

Grogan looked at Bennett.

92

'It doesn't matter to me,' the pathologist said. 'And I'm sure it won't matter to those poor sods.' He hooked a thumb in the direction of the trio of corpses.

'What are you hoping to see, doctor?' the DI asked.

'I wish I knew,' Finch told him. 'Perhaps it'll help me find some answers.'

'Just lately,' Grogan sighed, 'answers seem to be in short supply.'

All three men turned once more to gaze at the dead bodies which littered the room.

Seventeen

The summer night was a warm and humid one, but in the pathology lab it was like autumn. The temperature was kept down to a steady fifty-eight degrees, although neither Finch nor Bennett noticed the chill in the air. The pathologist was washing his hands at a sink on one side of the room, while Finch sat close to the stainless steel slab which bore the body of Mark Franklin. He was looking down at the boy, almost mesmerized by the appalling appearance of the corpse. It looked as if someone had blasted the youngster with a flame-thrower. And if they had, Finch mused, his remains couldn't have smelt much worse than they did now.

On the other two slabs behind him lay the bodies of Denise and Roger Franklin, both covered by white plastic sheets, only the feet protruding from beneath the thin coverlets. Attached to the right big toe of each corpse was a tag bearing the name, weight, height and time of admittance.

Finch looked across to the trolley which stood beside the first slab. There was a thick rubber sheet laid on it, and spread out on that was an assortment of scalpels, saws and long bladed knives. He also saw what looked like a large pair of bolt-cutters, the implement he knew would be employed to open up the ribcage when the time came. There was also an appliance very much like a dentist's drill, except that it bore a small metal wheel, serrated around its edge. On the end of the trolley there was something which Finch did not expect to see.

A carton of yoghurt.

'My breakfast,' said Bennett apologetically, removing the carton from the trolley. 'At least it keeps cool down here.' His smile faded slowly and he looked at the body of Mark Franklin. 'You know, there's an old saying,' he began wearily. '"The psychiatrist knows all and does nothing. The surgeon knows nothing and does all. The dermatologist knows nothing and does nothing."' He paused. '"The pathologist knows everything, but a day too late."'

'Very philosophical,' said Finch, attempting a smile which didn't quite materialize.

Bennett raised his eyebrows matter-of-factly, then reached up and activated the tape-recorder. He pulled the microphone closer to him.

'The victim has been weighed, all items of clothing have been itemized and prepared for analysis. External examination follows. I shall omit anal smears and nail scrapings as these are not felt to be necessary. If requested they will be carried out. The same applies to any other rudimentary external tests.' He paused for a moment, picking up a small scalpel which he used to raise a flap of skin which had once formed the sheath of a reeking pustule. 'The entire body is covered by lesions the origin of which is not yet known.' Reaching back onto the trolley he picked up a syringe, ran it into one of the large pustules and drew off as much of the thick liquid as he could. He deposited it in a Petri dish which he then sealed.

Returning to the body, Bennett took another syringe and drew 25ml of blood from the boy's arm. Still nattering to the tape recorder as Finch looked on silently, the pathologist announced that he was going to begin the internal examination.

He took a large, long-bladed scalpel and made a Y-shaped incision which ran from throat to pubic region, curving slightly to avoid the navel. That done, he pulled the torso open with his hands as if he were unwrapping a present, folding back the flaps of skin to expose the glistening tangle of viscera within. An almost palpable blast of foul-smelling air rose from the cavity and both men wrinkled their noses. The pathologist prodded and poked the various organs curiously.

'There doesn't appear to be any damage to internal organs,' he said into the tape recorder. 'I will remove the thorax section now.'

Bennett picked up the large bolt-cutter-like instrument and cut quickly and efficiently through the ribcage. The sound of snapping bone filled the room and Finch watched as the lungs and oesophagus were exposed. The heart too, now still and greyish in colour, was visible amongst the other organs. All were slightly shrunken. The pathologist removed the lungs and the remainder of the section and carefully laid it in a large stainless steel dish. A dribble of dark fluid came from the lungs, followed by several large, almost black clots of blood.

He followed the same procedure with the stomach and intestines, holding the entrails as if they were bulging, slippery lengths of bloated spaghetti. These he placed in a separate dish for weighing and then more detailed scrutiny. The entire chest and abdominal cavity was now empty.

Wiping one hand on his apron, the pathologist switched off the tape recorder.

'I think we'll have a look at those samples before we open the skull,' he said. Picking up the Petri dish and the syringe full of blood, he carried them to one of the laboratory workbenches, followed by Finch. Using the end of a scalpel, Bennett took some of the pus from the dish and smeared it on a microscope slide. He repeated the procedure with a droplet of the blood, then slid the first slide beneath the powerful lens, adjusting a knob until the image swam into focus.

Finch saw him frown.

'Have a look at that,' he said, stepping back.

The doctor pressed close to the eyepiece and squinted through it at the slide. It was matter taken from one of the sores.

Thousands of tiny snake-like shapes writhed beneath his gaze.

'Pus is basically a combination of white blood cells and dead bacteria,' said Finch. 'If anything, these cells should be spherical.'

'Have a look at the blood sample,' Bennett suggested, pushing the slide towards him. Finch slid the second slide beneath the lens and adjusted the magnification.

The same snake-like entities were present.

'These bacteria should be dead,' he commented, a note of puzzlement in his voice. He continued gazing at the millions of writhing shapes before him, invisible but for the incredible enlarging powers of the microscope.

Bennett had already got to his feet and returned to the body of Mark Franklin, switching on the tape recorder again.

'I'm going to open the skull,' he said into the microphone. With that he picked up the slim object which resembled the dentist's drill, checked that it was plugged in and switched it on. The circular blade on the end spun with a high pitched whine and the pathologist seemed satisfied. He switched it off, took a scalpel and carefully cut a line through the skin of the boy's forehead, just below the hairline. Then, as Finch rejoined him, he activated the electric saw once again, lowering the spinning blade until it made contact with bone. There was a sound like fingernails on a blackboard as the skull was cut open.

Finch watched Bennett put down the cutting instrument and slowly pry the skull lid up, using the scalpel as a lever, revealing an inch or two of brain. Finally he pulled the encasing bone free as if he were removing a hat, exposing the greyish-pink meat inside the head. Using another scalpel, he cut a thin segment away and laid it on a third microscope slide.

The pathologist then studied his sample beneath the powerful lens. He sighed and stepped back, motioning Finch forward.

'What do you make of it?' Bennett asked.

Looking through the microscope, the doctor shook his head almost imperceptibly.

Even the portion of brain contained the black, writhing shapes.

They appeared to have no discernible features save for their reptilian shape. At first they reminded Finch a little of sperm cells, but he could see no head. There was just that writhing, whip-lash shape, tapering slightly at either end.

'Could it be a virus?' he wondered aloud.

'You're the doctor. What do you think?' Bennett asked him. 'Personally, I don't think it is,' he added.

'Well, I'll admit I've never seen cells like that before in a viral infection.' The doctor stroked his chin thoughtfully and looked at the pathologist. 'What do *you* think it is?'

'Those black shapes don't look like bacteria,' Bennett said. 'And also, the chances are that most of them would have died out by now if they had been. I think they're blood flukes of some kind.'

Finch looked back at the brain section, studying the wriggling shapes.

'Well,' he said, quietly. 'If they are, they're certainly not of human origin.'

Friday – the 14th

Eighteen

Dawn was hauling itself sluggishly across the sky as Finch brought the Chevette to a halt outside number five Flaxman Court. He had driven fast from Scotland Yard, perhaps a little too fast. On one occasion, in the Haymarket, he'd run a red light, but fortunately traffic was light and no one had been in his way. Now he almost sprinted from the car towards the steps which would take him up to the flat. His mind was in a turmoil over what he had seen both in the flat at St Anne's Court, around the corner, and at the police laboratory. If Mark Franklin, by some chance, had been suffering from the same disease as Molly Foster, then there was every reason to suspect that *she* would suffer the same fate. He felt it his duty to tell Lisa Foster, no matter how shocked she might be. There seemed every possibility that Molly was in grave danger, and if that was the case, Lisa had a right to know. As he climbed the steps he wondered how he was going to break it to her.

The door of the flat suddenly opened and Lisa stepped out.

Both of them froze for a moment, gazing at one another, shivering in the early-morning breeze. It was Lisa who broke the silence.

'Alan, what are you doing here?' she wanted to know.

He noticed, even in the subdued half-light, that her face looked pale and drawn. There were dark rings beneath her eyes, as if someone had smudged her lower lids with charcoal. She wore a voluminous black coat which hid her shapely figure, flapping around her like a cape when she walked.

Finch was struggling to decide if he should tell her the real

101

reason for his presence when they heard a car pull up across the street. Finch saw that it was a taxi, and the driver was peering across at the flats.

'I've got to go,' Lisa said. 'The hospital called. It's my mother.'

Finch clenched his teeth, sucking in an almost painful breath.

'Her condition's deteriorated.' Lisa tried to sidestep him. 'I've got to get to the hospital, Alan,' she insisted.

'I'll take you,' he said, taking her arm, almost pulling her towards his waiting car.

'But the taxi...' she protested.

'To hell with the taxi,' Finch snapped and slid behind the steering wheel of the Chevette. He twisted the key in the ignition and the engine roared into life.

The cab driver clambered out of his vehicle as the other car drove off, taking with it his prospective passenger. He watched until it disappeared, swearing to himself, then he got back in and drove off.

'When did the hospital get in touch?' Finch asked, not taking his eyes from the road.

'About ten minutes before you arrived,' Lisa told him. 'They told me I should get over there as quickly as possible.' She studied his profile for a moment. 'Alan, you remember me asking you if you thought she was going to die?'

He nodded.

'She is, isn't she? Otherwise they wouldn't have called me.'

Finch gripped the wheel tighter, trying to disguise the concern in his voice when he spoke.

'Your mother is in the best possible hands,' he said, none too convincingly. 'Did they tell you anything at all about her condition?'

'Only that it had deteriorated and that I should get to the hospital as soon as possible,' she informed him. There was a protracted silence during which her eyes never left him. 'You know something about what's going on, don't you?'

Finch didn't answer. He swung the car around a corner and

102

the hospital loomed before them.

'I have a right to know,' she persisted. 'Why were you calling at the flat at this time in the morning?'

He sucked in a deep breath.

'A boy died tonight,' he said. 'He murdered his parents first and then he died. He had the same symptoms as your mother.'

'Oh my God,' murmured Lisa, and she was out of the car almost before it had stopped moving, bolting for the main entrance of the hospital, followed closely by Finch. They both dashed into the reception area, past a bewildered night porter who shouted something after them. But they did not hear, and even if they had, they wouldn't have stopped running.

Finch caught up as Lisa reached the lift. As he spun her round he could already see the tears welling in her eyes.

'Lisa, if only I'd known what was wrong with her,' he said. 'But no one knew, they still don't...'

The sentence trailed off as the lift arrived, the doors sliding open to allow them access. Both stepped in and leant against the sides of the car as it rose, finally disgorging them on the fifth floor. Lisa ran from the lift, hearing shouts and screams coming from the direction of the ward. Finch ran after her and together they hurtled into the ward.

Lisa looked frantically to her right and left, trying to trace the source of the commotion. As she moved up the corridor she caught sight of Doctor Benton emerging from a side room. His face was covered in perspiration and he looked as if he'd just run ten miles, but when he saw Lisa moving towards him he seemed to recover his composure and attempted to intercept her.

Finch followed.

'Where's my mother?' she blurted, trying to push her way past Benton. 'I got a call saying she was worse and I should come as soon as I could.'

'Yes, I know, but we've had to transfer her to another room,' Benton said.

'I have to see her.'

'That's not a good idea at the moment, Miss Foster,' he told her.

A scream of pain and rage came from the room and the sound caused an icy tingle down Finch's spine.

'There's a nurse in there with her at the moment. We're going to sedate her,' Benton informed them.

'I must see her,' Lisa persisted, trying to manoeuvre herself around Benton, but he continued to bar her way.

There was another scream and Benton looked at Finch.

'Keep her here,' he said, indicating Lisa, then he retreated back into the side room, closing the door behind him. The cries and moans were momentarily muffled.

'Alan, please let me go,' she begged, attempting to pull away from him.

Finch shook his head, his own curiosity now roused, mixed with a terrible foreboding.

'Wait until she's sedated,' he said, his mind straying to the sight of that bedroom where he'd seen the bodies of Mark Franklin and his parents. Could Molly Foster be afflicted in the same way? The shouting, Finch assumed, was coming from Molly and he marvelled at how a woman who was supposedly so ill could muster such shattering roars of pain and anger.

Was it anger?

'You must let me see her,' Lisa pleaded, tears welling up once more in her wide eyes. 'Please, Alan.'

He loosened his grip slightly, and in that split second she managed to escape him, her hands reaching for the door of the room.

He tried to stop her but, together, they blundered inside.

Lisa froze, her eyes riveted to the tableau which met her, to the ... creature on the bed for, had she not known, she would never have guessed that it was her mother.

Every inch of Molly Foster's skin was swollen and bulging with thick, oozing sores which were continually bursting, weeping their viscous contents onto the sheets. Her eyes were almost closed because of the pustules which had formed around them, and as she tried to lift her arms, the bulk of the swollen flesh made the task look impossible. As the young nurse who was holding the hypodermic needle attempted to grip Molly's arm, she found that she was holding only the sticky discharge of half a dozen boils which burst as they were touched. It was as if someone had pumped the woman's body up with compressed air, filling it to bursting point with the thick yellow mess which was pumping from so many of the throbbing lesions.

'Get her out of here,' Benton yelled at Finch.

In that split second, Molly managed to pull loose from the nurse's grip. The hypodermic flew into the air as the nurse was knocked to the ground by a ferocious back-hand swipe. She crashed into a trolley, knocking it over, yelping in pain as scalpels and knives fell onto her, cutting her in half a dozen places.

Molly swung herself out of bed, her yellowed eyes fixed on Lisa.

Benton made a grab for the discarded hypodermic but Molly's bloated fingers closed around it first and she lashed out at the doctor, who just managed to avoid the thrust. The nurse, by this time, had struggled to her feet and she came at Molly from behind, trying to wrest the sharp hypo from her swollen hand. Molly spun round and thrust again.

The needle buried itself in the nurse's eye, snapping off half-way as she fell, blood running down her cheek like crimson tears. She screamed in agony and tried to pluck out the thin probe but her blood and spurting vitreous fluid made it impossible. She rolled onto her side and lay still.

With the remainder of the needle glinting evilly beneath the fluorescents, Molly moved towards her daughter, holding the syringe up like a knife.

Lisa could only shake her head in horrified disbelief until she felt strong arms pulling her away from the monstrous creature which had once been her mother, but now looked like something that had stepped straight from a nightmare. Molly opened her mouth as if to say something but all that came forth was a low wail of agony and she stopped in her tracks, her body jerking as if electricity were being pumped through it. She dropped the needle and clapped both hands to her face as the boils began to erupt, spewing thick yellow fluid everywhere. Her whole body was quivering madly now and she dropped to her knees, the pustules on her legs bursting with a series of obscene splattering sounds as she crushed them.

Finch tried to turn Lisa's head away but he too found himself mesmerized by the appalling sight before him. Benton had dashed out into the corridor to find help.

The nurse, her eye pierced by the snapped needle, still lay motionless.

Molly Foster raised a defiant hand towards her daughter and then, with an agonized moan, she fell forward and did not move again.

Finch moved away from Lisa and rushed to Molly's side. He turned her over carefully, anxious not to allow any of the thick yellow fluid to get on his hands, and looked closely at her face which was now cratered by dozens of deep holes, some of them spilling a thin stream of blood onto the floor. It appeared that almost all of the boils had burst, even those around her eyes, and the hardening pus had almost welded the lids together. The stench which rose from the body was frightful.

Lisa clutched her stomach, gagged and turned away, fighting back the urge to vomit, but as she caught a glimpse of the dead nurse she finally lost the struggle and retched violently.

Staggering out into the corridor, she saw Benton returning, accompanied by two interns and a nurse. The nurse stayed with Lisa until some of the colour came back into her cheeks, then she followed her companions into the room.

No one spoke for long moments until Benton finally broke the silence.

'Get the bodies out of here,' he said, wearily. 'Down to pathology immediately.'

One of the interns hurried off to fetch a gurney.

Finch pulled a blanket from the bed and covered both Molly and the dead nurse.

'I didn't expect anything like this to happen,' said Benton, quietly.

Finch seemed to ignore the comment.

'When will the autopsy be performed on Mrs Foster?' he asked.

'Not until the pathologist arrives in the morning. Why?'

Finch looked out into the corridor at Lisa, who was leaning against the far wall with her head bowed, crying softly.

'Get somebody to take care of her until I've finished,' he said, softly.

'Finished what?' Benton wanted to know.

'I want to look at Mrs Foster's body before the pathologist comes in. There's something I've got to find out.'

Finch looked on silently as the corpse of Molly Foster was pushed into the selected cold drawer. The array of doors reminded him of a large filing cabinet. There were enough compartments to hold fifteen bodies, but only those of Molly Foster and the dead nurse were stored there at the moment. They would rest in the coffin-sized compartments until the pathologist arrived.

Finch looked at the syringe in his hand, at the 25 ml of blood which he'd drawn from the body of Molly Foster only moments earlier. Then he went to the microscope which stood on a work-bench nearby and selected a slide, forcing a droplet of the blood from the syringe onto the thin glass section. He sandwiched it with another, then slipped it beneath the probing lens of the microscope.

The slide was alive with moving shapes and Finch swallowed hard.

The snake-like organisms which writhed furiously beneath his gaze were identical to those he'd seen earlier at the police lab.

Nineteen

As he drove, Finch looked across at Lisa who was gazing blankly out of the window, her hands knitted together in her lap. Her cheeks were tear-stained, her eyes red-rimmed. He wondered if she was going to start crying again. They had left the hospital ten minutes earlier, but only in the last few moments had she stopped sobbing. Finch had tried to persuade her to stay in hospital for a day or two or at least seek the comfort of a tranquilizer, but she had declined both suggestions. She sniffed and pulled a tissue from her handbag.

'I'm sorry,' she said, her words almost inaudible.

'I'm the one who should be sorry,' he said with genuine remorse. 'If I could have done something for your mother in the first place . . .' He allowed the words to trail off.

'You did everything you could,' she told him, her gaze still fixed outside the car. She felt a shiver run through her, and for a moment she thought the tears were going to flood once again, but she clenched her fists and managed to fight them back. There was another protracted silence, then Lisa spoke again. 'Why did she kill that nurse?'

Finch opened his mouth to speak but she did not give him time.

'Alan, she was trying to kill me too.'

She finally looked across at him and he saw a single tear trickle down her cheek. Lisa brushed it away with the tissue.

Finch felt angry with himself. Angry because he had been unable to help either Molly Foster or Mark Franklin but also because he felt so helpless. The disease (if that was the correct word) which had claimed their lives was completely unknown to him and he felt at a disadvantage. Mixed with his anger, though, was fear. If it was a disease of some kind then the two who had died so far might not be the only sufferers. He pondered on how many people were, at this moment, undergoing agonies similar to those suffered by his other two patients. It was too much to hope that they were isolated cases, wasn't it?

He brought the car to a halt outside the flats and Lisa reached for the door handle. As she did, he noticed that she was shaking. He leant across to open the door for her.

'Thank you for your help tonight,' she said to him, still clutching the balled-up tissue.

'If there's anything at all that I can do, promise you'll ring me,' Finch said.

She tried to smile but it wouldn't come.

'I promise,' she told him and pushed herself out of the car.

The doctor watched as she made her way across the road to the flats, climbing the stairs wearily until she reached the door of number five. He saw her disappear inside. Only then did he put the car in gear and pull away.

Lisa Foster stood in the gloom of the sitting room for a moment, her back pressed to the door. She closed her eyes and sucked in a deep breath, pausing briefly before she went through to the kitchen. As she filled the kettle she noticed that her hands were still shaking. Spooning sugar into her cup she spilled some on the table, but it didn't seem to bother her. She sat down and waited for the kettle to boil, running her index finger around the rim of the cup. If there was anything to be thankful for in this entire tragedy, it was that she would not be called to identify her mother's body. Lisa knew that she could not have tolerated standing over the ravaged corpse again. A vision of her dead mother swam briefly into her mind and she brushed away the tears once more, surprised that she had any left. But, as the kettle finally began to boil, she discovered that she had a more than ample reserve of tears. It was like opening the floodgates. She sank forward, head resting on her arms, her body racked by uncontrollable sobs.

In the background, almost eclipsed by Lisa's anguished crying, the kettle continued its banshee wail.

Twenty

The early-morning light had trouble penetrating the layers of dirt which coated the window of the old flat. The place smelt damp despite the incessant sunshine which had bathed London and the entire country for almost three months.

Situated in Dean Street, the flat was above a disused Chinese take-away, accessible only via a rusty fire-escape at the rear of the building, but that had presented no obstacle to Steve Pollack and his companion when they had first found the empty dwelling. They had been squatting there for over a week now. Pollack guessed that the place couldn't have been empty for more than a few weeks. There was still running water from the taps in the kitchen and the toilet still flushed. When that packed up it would be time to move on and find something else.

Pollack was approaching his twenty-fourth birthday. What little time he'd had outside of reform schools, borstals or prison had been spent squatting in a succession of London's many empty buildings. His father had thrown him out when he was fifteen after discovering that Steve had taken to dipping into the old man's pockets for a quid or two when he was short of fags. He'd left without a row. As he'd said at the time, he had nothing worth staying at home for anyway. Within a week of being out on the streets he'd been arrested joyriding in a stolen car and given six months at a borstal in Oxford.

It was during his stay there that he'd met Bill Lawrence. Lawrence was two years older than Pollack. The two of them had been inseparable since that first meeting, except for the occasions when they'd been banged up in different places. Now, with Lawrence's girlfriend Michelle in tow, they moved around together. Stealing, begging and anything else they could do to keep themselves in money. For a time Michelle had even gone on the game, bringing home anything up to fifty or sixty quid a night. This had been an easy time for Pollack and Lawrence, but after one punter beat her up in an effort to get his rocks off, Lawrence had decided that the three of them would find some other way to get cash. He'd managed to find a reliable fence who handled their stolen goods for them for a reasonable percentage. Some of the stuff they kept for themselves. Like the radio-cassette that Pollack now fiddled with, trying to find Radio One. He had knocked it off from an electrical store in Charing Cross Road only two days before. The manager of the shop had chased him but Pollack had bolted down the nearest subway and eluded the man in the crowds. He smiled at the recollection, turning the frequency knob until he found the station he sought, then he increased the volume slightly.

Moving to the window, he peered out through the film of grime, spitting on the glass and rubbing to make a clear spot. Perspiration glistened on his naked body, and from behind him he could hear the groans of pleasure from Michelle and Lawrence as they made love. Pollack turned to watch for a moment, his penis hardening as he enjoyed the spectacle of Michelle grinding herself hard onto Lawrence's own erection. She looked over to Pollack and smiled, her long hair, matted with sweat, swishing back and forth across her face as she bounced up and down. She was twenty-one but looked almost ten years older. Her body, though slim, was scarred in a number of places, her face pockmarked.

Pollack moved closer, his eyes fixed on her large breasts and swollen nipples.

'Come on Steve,' Lawrence said to him, reaching up to grab her bouncing breasts in his rough hands. 'There's plenty for both of us.' He smiled broadly.

'I'm going to have a piss,' Pollack informed him and padded across the bare floor towards the toilet. He passed through the kitchen with its cracked enamel sink, now scarred with mould. Past the small calor gas cooker which they used to heat up the tinned food. Cans both unopened and empty lay in an untidy pile on the floor nearby. There were a number of flies buzzing around the open ones, or crawling over the remnants of the food.

Pollack found some of the insects in the toilet as well, one of them crawling up the side of the pan. He stood there grinning, directing a stream of urine at the fly, which quickly flew off. With a grunt of annoyance, he looked down to see that water was seeping around his feet. The porcelain was cracked badly in a couple of places and moisture was dripping out. When he'd finished he didn't bother flushing for fear of causing the whole pan to give way. Drying his feet with a piece of toilet paper, he made his way back to the other room.

The first two slugs slithered up the side of the toilet, their forward tubercles extending as they broke the surface. Leaving a trail of thick slime behind them, the large black creatures moved upwards, followed by more of their companions, until finally the toilet was full of them and they started to overflow onto the floor, landing in a reeking pile, slithering over each other in their eagerness to reach the source of food which they knew was very close.

Michelle was on her knees, her pert bottom waving about invitingly, her slippery cleft exposed for the pleasure of the two men. Lawrence guided his throbbing member into her, gripping her hips, pulling her onto him. She squealed with pleasure as she felt the penetration.

Kneeling in front of her, Pollack nodded approvingly as she reached out and closed one hand around his penis, moving it up and down in time to Lawrence's deep thrusts. With her other hand she cupped Pollack's testicles, massaging them until she felt them tighten. Smiling, Michelle lowered her head and planted her lips around the bulbous head of his penis, moving her head up and down. Pollack felt her hair flicking over his groin and it added to his pleasure. He reached out and held her breasts, thumbing the erect nipples until they grew even stiffer. He looked up to see Lawrence pounding relentlessly into her, his own body now sheathed in perspiration.

The slithering carpet of slugs oozed beneath the toilet door like a spillage of oil, moving inexorably towards the three figures ahead of them.

Pollack closed his eyes as he felt the sensations of pleasure increasing. Michelle's head bobbed up and down more rapidly now, her tongue exploring every inch of his shaft, flicking at the moisture which oozed from the tip. He gripped her breasts tighter but the rough treatment seemed to inflame her passion and she sucked harder realizing that his climax was not far off. Nor was her own. She squirmed as she felt Lawrence slip one hand between her legs, his probing fingers searching out her swollen clitoris. He rubbed his index finger along her wet and puffy outer lips, lubricating the digit before he began rubbing in a circular motion on that most delicate spot.

The leading slugs, by now, were actually in the room, moving towards the entangled humans, sensing the warmth of their flesh and blood. As they approached, sliding over each other in their haste, they produced a vile sucking sound but their intended victims did not hear it.

More, many more, crawled up from the lavatory to join their companions.

Michelle was going to come and she closed her eyes as the enveloping feeling of warmth began to spread from her thighs and vagina to her breasts and stomach, wrapping her in what felt like a warm blanket. She pulled her mouth away from Pollack's erection long enough to gasp her pleasure, her hand now moving furiously up and down his glistening shaft until he thrust it forward towards her open mouth. She smiled as she watched the thick white fluid spurting forth, and immediately lowered her head again to catch and swallow the remaining liquid, twisting her tongue around the swollen head to lick it clean.

A second later she almost screamed with pleasure as she felt Lawrence climax inside her, his own organ filling her with ejaculate, some of which dribbled warmly down the inside of her thighs.

Pollack opened his eyes.

'Oh Jesus Christ!' he exclaimed almost falling backwards.

The room was half full of gigantic slugs. A black, glistening wall of them faced him as if they had risen from the very floorboards.

Lawrence, still trying to regain his senses after the intensity of his orgasm, was the first to feel pain as three of them bit into his calf. He pulled away from Michelle, his penis slipping out of her.

He overbalanced and rolled amongst the seething mass of slugs.

They moved with surprising speed, sliding up onto his chest and belly, digging deep into him with their sickle-like teeth, burrowing hungrily into flesh and muscle. Shrieking in pain and terror, Lawrence tried to rise but the weight of the black monstrosities held him down and all he could do was crawl, dozens of them covering him. Blood from numerous wounds mingled with the vile slime which the slugs exuded and it dripped from him like wax from a melting candle.

'Help me,' he shrieked. 'For fuck's sake help me.'

But Pollack could only stand and watch as his friend raised a hand which was itself already eaten almost to the bone by the slugs which clung to it.

Michelle was also screaming. She bolted for the door which led to the fire escape.

Their only way out.

As she ran she felt numerous slug bodies bursting beneath her feet, others bit into her toes. One particularly large creature, close to nine inches in length, managed to drive its central tooth into her ankle just below the bone. The sudden pain, coupled with the slippery floor, caused her to overbalance and she fell heavily, trying to tug the recalcitrant beast from her foot. Blood jetted onto her hands and she found that she could not get a grip on the black beast because of the foul-smelling slime which it exuded. Others now fastened themselves onto her thighs and buttocks and began eating. Michelle was screaming uncontrollably as the pain grew more intense and she felt the oblivion of unconsciousness beginning to drift over her. But she was denied that mercy when another of the larger beasts slithered up her belly and began eating her left nipple, digging deeper until it was feeding on the soft meat of her breast. The unbelievable pain prevented her from blacking out.

Blood soon covered the room as if sprayed from a hosepipe and Pollack sank almost resignedly to his haunches in one corner of the room, his eyes bulging wide with terror as he watched the remains of his two companions being devoured by the black horrors. Tears began to course down his cheeks. Tears, at first, of fear but then he began to laugh insanely. For that was all he could think to do. What he was witnessing was a dream, a vile corrupted nightmare. It had to be. Nothing like this could really happen.

He watched as the slugs seethed over the ruined bodies, sometimes emerging from *inside* the corpse, having eaten their way out. He saw the blood. He smelt the choking odour which they gave off, he sniffed the rancid smell of excrement.

Yes, this had to be a nightmare, he thought, still laughing.

The slugs drew closer, encircling him, filling the room until all he could see was an undulating black carpet of glistening bodies, bloated and yet still hungry.

He drew his knees up to his chest as the slugs moved in.

He didn't attempt to move.

A song played on the radio called 'Two Minutes to Midnight'.

It seemed most appropriate.

Pollack began to laugh even louder.

He was still laughing when the first of the slugs reached him.

Twenty-one

By the time Alan Finch reached his home in Westbourne
Terrace he could hardly keep his eyes open. He checked his
watch, then the clock on the mantlepiece, and saw to his
disappointment that it was almost 7.06 a.m. There seemed
little point in going to bed now. By the same token, there
seemed even less point in attending surgery. In his state of
exhaustion he would be a positive liability to his patients.
Although he knew his appointment book was full he decided
to ring in later and tell June that he wouldn't be in. His
colleagues could cope with the extra work-load for one day.

The armchair looked inviting and the thought of his bed
even more so, but instead he went to the kitchen and filled the
kettle for coffee. It would be another hour before he could
contact the surgery, and as tired as he felt, he dared not sit
down in case he nodded off. So instead he made his way
wearily up the stairs to the bathroom. There he splashed his
face with cold water in an effort to banish some of the dullness
from his mind. He leant on the edges of the sink studying his
reflection, looking at the dark rings beneath his eyes. Caused
by lack of sleep and also by the horrors he had witnessed that
night. Even the warm early-morning sunshine seemed
incapable of banishing the chill he felt as he thought about
Mark Franklin and his dead parents. Or Molly Foster and the
murdered nurse.

Or of how many others might be afflicted by this
mysterious disease.

He thought briefly of Lisa and then, pushing the thoughts
to the back of his mind, he splashed his face with more cold

water until his skin was almost numb.

The phone rang.

Snatching up a towel, Finch headed for the bedroom.

'Doctor Alan Finch,' he said, wedging the receiver between his ear and shoulder while he dabbed away the last of the water.

'Finch, I need to speak to you in person. Now.'

He recognized the voice immediately.

'Bennett. What is it?' the doctor asked.

'Can you get to my laboratory immediately?' the pathologist wanted to know.

Before Finch had a chance to protest the other man continued.

'It's important,' he urged. 'There's something you must see.'

The doctor exhaled deeply. He decided not to mention that he'd been up since three that morning, that he'd seen another victim of this strange and deadly plague, that...

'Finch, did you hear what I said?' Bennett asked, agitatedly.

'I'll be there as soon as I can.'

Bennett hung up.

'Something you must see,' Finch repeated, replacing the phone on its cradle. He left the towel in the bedroom, took the time to pull on a clean shirt and trousers, then hurried downstairs to switch the kettle off.

Another five minutes and he was on his way to New Scotland Yard.

When Finch entered the lab he found Bennett perched on a stool beside one of the work-benches eating a sandwich. He nodded a greeting to the young doctor, put his sandwich down and got off his stool. Finch noticed how pale and drawn the pathologist looked.

'You look like death warmed up,' Finch said.

'Coming from you that's quite a compliment,' the pathologist told him. '*You* don't exactly look ready to run a marathon.'

117

The doctor explained briefly what had happened after he had left Bennett earlier that morning.

The pathologist nodded intently as Finch spoke about the death of Molly Foster, then he guided the younger man to a microscope which had already been set up, the slide prepared. Finch peered through the lens.

'My God,' he whispered.

On the slide before him were more of the blood flukes he'd now come to recognize so well. But they were much larger.

'That's from the same section of brain we looked at earlier,' Bennett told him. 'They've more than doubled their size and numbers in less than six hours. But that's not all.' He turned away from the microscope, back towards the stainless steel slab where the body of Mark Franklin still lay, the feet and fingers now stiff with rigor mortis. Bennett pulled back the sheet to expose the head. He had replaced the top of the cranium, shielding the brain, but now he carefully removed it once more so that Finch was able to see the contents of the skull.

'What the hell are those?' he asked, softly, indicating several growths the size of a man's thumbnail which had appeared on the crinkly surface of the cerebral cortex.

'After you left,' Bennett told him. 'I tried to figure out how blood flukes from an animal could have got into a human being's bloodstream and, more to the point, how they could have caused the damage they did. Now I know. I also know the animal they belong to.'

Finch frowned, then stood back as the pathologist took a scalpel and carefully cut round one of the growths, pulling away a small portion of brain with it. The lumps looked like polyps – small bulges which sometimes occur in the vagina or the anus. Only these were darker, like clots of congealed blood. Bennett transferred the severed growth to a Petri dish, then placed the dish on the worktop.

'It looks like some form of cyst,' Finch observed.

'It is,' the pathologist told him, his eyes never leaving the dark lump. 'It appeared about two hours ago, growing inside the brain, like the others.'

'I don't see what this has to do with the blood flukes,' Finch said, noticing that Bennett's attention seemed riveted to the revolting object which lay in the dish before them.

'The flukes *formed* those cysts,' the pathologist told him, flatly. 'The easiest comparison I can quote you is that of an amoeba. When conditions are unfavourable for an amoeba or most other single-celled animals, they have the ability to encyst. To convert themselves into cysts by forming a tougher outer covering of tissue. That's what these blood flukes are doing except that, in this case, they also undergo a metamorphosis.'

'You're telling me they can change their cellular structure?' Finch said.

Bennett nodded, his eyes still fixed on the cyst in the dish.

'You said you knew which animals they came from,' the doctor persisted. '*How* do you know?'

As if in answer to his question, Finch saw that the lump in the dish was beginning to split open. Like some small, overripe bursting plum it spilled its contents into the dish. Finch saw several small shapes slithering about in the dark liquid.

'Slugs?' he gasped, incredulously.

The creatures were barely 5mm long, but their shape was unmistakable. As he and Bennett watched, the newly hatched slugs began feeding on the fragment of brain to which the cyst had been attached.

'The flukes get into the bloodstream by penetrating the skin,' Bennett explained. 'That's the usual form of transmission. Once inside they reach maturity, grow and form cysts like those in the boy's brain. The lesions and boils on the skin are also full of the blood flukes. Inside those cysts the metamorphosis takes place. The slugs hatch and use the host as a source of food, growing all the time.'

'My God, they use their victims like incubators,' said Finch, looking with distaste at the half a dozen or so slugs which had emerged from the crimson swelling and were devouring the portion of brain. 'Some spiders and wasps use the same method, don't they? The eggs are laid inside the host, then there's a ready-made food supply waiting for the young.'

'That's exactly what we've got here,' Bennett said.

'So the boy and Molly Franklin were in contact with slugs?' Finch said, his voice low.

'The flukes travel in the slime trails which the slugs leave behind. These two victims must have touched that slime. It permeated their skin.'

The doctor took a scalpel and carefully eased it under one of the pale creatures in the Petri dish. It was a sickly white, yet to attain its mature black colour. The small body was stained with crimson and, as Finch looked at it, he saw its eye stalks extending like twin aerials.

Bennett crossed the lab to a cupboard, retrieved a large glass jar and returned to join Finch. The pathologist held up the jar, revealing the contents.

Slithering around inside were a dozen or more slugs, slipping and sliding over each other, some nudging at the lid of the jar. Not one was less than two inches long. Thick and black, they looked like severed, re-animated fingers.

'These hatched four hours ago,' said Bennett, flatly. 'From the size of a thumbnail to two inches in such a short time. It's incredible.'

Finch didn't answer. He took one last look at the slugs in the jar, then pulled on his jacket.

'Where are you going?' Bennett wanted to know.

But Finch was already half-way out of the door.

The pathologist gazed in at the slithering black creatures, wondering where the hell Finch had dashed off to, also wondering how he was going to explain his findings to Detective Inspector Grogan. Then he looked again at the smaller slugs, which continued to feed on the portion of Mark Franklin's brain.

It took Finch some time to convince the morgue assistant at the Middlesex Hospital that he should be allowed to see the body of Molly Foster.

'You're not a relative, are you?' the man said, picking a

120

piece of food from between his dirty, protruding front teeth.

'No, I told you, I'm her doctor,' Finch said.

'You're a bit late to help her, aren't you?' the man chuckled humourlessly. 'She's been in the freezers for over two hours.' The man eyed Finch suspiciously for a moment and then finally relented, leading him down to the morgue.

'The coroner isn't arriving until later this morning,' he said. 'I don't think he's going to be too happy if he knows someone's been fiddling around with one of his stiffs. If you get my meaning?'

'Just let me see the body,' snapped Finch, irritably.

The man held up both hands in a gesture of placation, then he turned and found the appropriate door. Finch stood by expectantly as the drawer was pulled out.

He recoiled from the vile stench which rose from the metal coffin but it was the morgue attendant who spoke first.

'What the fuck is this?' he gasped.

Where the body of Molly Foster had been only a short time before, there now remained only a bloodied mess of bones and wasted flesh. The face, including the eyes, had been completely stripped of flesh as had the neck and most of the upper torso. Congealed blood coated the corpse, mingling with thick slime to form a sheath. Finch saw some of the oozing fluid dripping in heavy globules from one exposed rib. The cabinet itself was full of the slime too, gleaming with a vile lustre beneath the powerful fluorescents.

The attendant reached out towards the glistening mess but Finch grabbed his wrist.

'Don't touch it,' he snapped, unable to take his eyes from the remains of the body.

It was only when he stepped back that he noticed a number of mucus trails leading from the cabinet, across the floor to a drain which lay close to one of the stainless steel slabs. The silvery paths had hardened and crusted over, like a scab over a cut.

There was no sign of the slugs.

Saturday – the 15th

Twenty-two

It looked more like a blue-print for a computer than a map of London's sewer system.

The large piece of paper was laid out on the polished oak table and held down at each corner by the weight of an ashtray.

Donald Robertson stubbed out his cigarette in one of the crystal dishes and immediately lit another. He regarded the map warily, peering at the dozen or so red crosses marked on it. His left eye twitched for a moment, as it had a habit of doing when he was worried or annoyed. He'd been head of the Thames Water Central Division for the past eighteen months, but this was his first major problem. There'd been the incident about six months ago when one of the old sewers had caved in, trapping three maintenance men for a couple of hours, but nothing on the scale of what he was facing at the moment.

He peered at the map once again, his eye twitching almost in time to his pulse.

'Soho, St. Giles, Piccadilly and Bloomsbury,' he said, tapping the map with the end of his pen. 'All the complaints have come from that area.' He drew a circle around it. 'If this goes on much longer we'll have the Department of the Environment banging on the bloody door wanting to know what's going on.'

'It's pretty obvious, Don,' said the second man in the room. He had yet to reach forty, a year or so younger than Robertson. He wore a dark blue suit which was badly in need of pressing. The collar points of his shirt were curled upward

125

like dead leaves, looking as though they might poke his eyes out if he bent forward too quickly. 'One of the filters is blocked,' he continued.

'Well, that's your responsibility, Ed,' Robertson told him, his eye twitching madly. 'I thought the bloody things were checked out regularly.'

'They are,' Edward Dowd assured him. 'Every filter is inspected and cleaned at least three times a week.'

The third man in the room stepped forward and ran his finger over the map. Max Kelly was a tall, powerfully built man with arms like tree-trunks and hands the size of ham-hocks. His head, on the other hand, balding and bearing a pair of heavy-lensed glasses, looked as if it belonged to someone else, perhaps the unfortunate result of a misconceived transplant. He had the body of a lumberjack and the head of a cartoon boffin.

'It must be one hell of a blockage to cause the problems we've been notified of,' he said.

'Some of the sewers around that area are pretty old, it could be that there's been a collapse,' Dowd offered.

Robertson began pacing the floor agitatedly, drawing hard on his cigarette.

'Toilets won't flush,' he snapped. 'Effluent can't be disposed of and there's even been raw sewage coming up into the streets in a couple of places. I've got a letter here from some bloke who went down to his cellar for something and the poor sod nearly drowned in sh... in waste. It had come up through his floor.'

'I'll get a team of maintenance men down there straight away,' Kelly said.

'I can't understand why all this has started happening so suddenly,' Robertson said irritably. He looked at Dowd. 'And before you say anything, Ed, I don't think a collapse would cause this amount of damage. I'm sticking with the filters.'

'I'm not arguing with you, Don,' the other man said. 'I just *suggested* it might be a tunnel collapse.'

'Well, whatever it is, I want it cleared fast. I don't have to tell either of you about the health risks from something like

126

this.'

The three men looked at each other, then at the map with its profusion of red crosses.

'If we don't get something done quick,' added Robertson, taking a final puff on his cigarette, 'we'll have all kinds of diseases in the city. I think the first plague of London was enough, don't you?'

Whether his remark was intended to be humorous or not the other men didn't know.

Either way, no one laughed.

In two streets just off New Oxford Street, raw sewage oozed up from the drains and spilled into the road. The stench, intensified by the blistering heat, was unbelievable.

A number of office buildings had to be evacuated when toilets overflowed, spilling waste everywhere.

A hotel in Shaftesbury Avenue received complaints from a number of its guests when they found puddles of partially diluted human waste seeping beneath the doors of their rooms.

The courtyard of the British Museum was flooded by gallons of reeking water which bubbled from a drain.

A group of tourists visiting the waxwork display in The Palladium Cellars were shocked to find that they were rapidly being engulfed by stinking water which rose up to their ankles in only a minute or two.

A number of stations on the Central, Northern and Piccadilly lines found that sewage was beginning to form pools beneath the electrified tracks.

By 2.00 p.m. the situation was all but out of control.

Twenty-three

'Slugs?'

Detective Inspector Ray Grogan shook his head incredulously, then looked again at the jar, which now seemed to be full of twisting, writhing black shapes.

'You're trying to tell me that the tramp we found chewed up in Leicester Square and that sewer bloke we dragged out of the pipe near the Thames were killed by *slugs*?'

'I found it as hard to believe as you, Ray,' Bennett confessed.

'You mean slugs like you find in your garden?'

'Do these look like the type you'd find in your garden?' Bennett asked, holding up the jar. 'They're hybrids. Somewhere along the way they interbred, maybe with some carnivorous species, perhaps even with another gastropod like a leech. I don't know. What I do know is that we've got one hell of a problem on our hands.'

'Make that two problems,' Grogan said. 'There's been a foul-up in one or more of the sewer tunnels under central London. I just heard from the Water Board. The streets are going to be full of shit in a few hours and now you're trying to tell me I've got an army of man-eating slugs roaming around.' He lit up a cigarette. 'What the fuck do you take me for, George? Do I look like a twat? Slugs that eat people! Do me a favour.'

'We found no traces of a murder weapon having been used on either the tramp or the sewer man,' Bennett persisted. 'But I found secretions on both bodies which carry the same type of blood flukes that infected Mark Franklin and Molly

128

Foster.' The pathologist looked at Grogan's cigarette. 'By the way, don't smoke in here, please.'

The two men, along with Finch and DS Nicholson, were seated around one of the workbenches in the laboratory. Bennett had just finished his explanations of what he and Finch had discovered earlier that day.

'You reckon that both the lad and the old girl came into contact with these slugs,' Nicholson said to Finch. 'How come they weren't eaten?'

'They didn't come into direct contact with the slugs, only the slime trails they'd left behind,' Finch corrected him.

'Assuming that's true,' Grogan interjected, 'if this disease is passed on by touching the slime, why didn't Bennett catch it? He examined both victims who'd supposedly been "eaten".' The DI tried to disguise the scorn in his voice but couldn't quite manage it.

'I was wearing gloves on both occasions,' the pathologist explained. 'For the slime to have effect it must come into *direct* contact with the skin.'

'Also, there's every reason to believe that it loses its potency after a certain time,' Finch added.

'So anyone coming into contact with these bloody things has got two ways to go. They either get eaten or they catch this disease. Right?' said the DI.

'They end up as food eventually, anyway,' Finch said.

'Oh of course, I forgot about the eggs hatching out inside them,' Grogan said, disdainfully.

'Not eggs, cysts,' Bennett insisted. 'Look, Ray, you can be as sceptical as you like, the evidence is here in front of us. The two men that were found were devoured by slugs. Both Molly Foster *and* Mark Franklin contracted a disease transmitted by those same slugs.'

'Christ, and I had a salad for lunch,' said Nicholson, chuckling.

'It's not funny,' the pathologist snapped. 'If the slugs *are* using the sewers to move around in, then all that sewage that's flooding the streets will be contaminated with the same disease. God knows how many more people will be infected.'

An awkward silence descended, finally broken by Finch.

'Slugs give off what's called a repugnatorial secretion,' he began. 'It's formed by certain cells which they utilise to form the mucus trails. The sewers must be full of it, and now it's getting into people's homes as well.'

Grogan looked at the jar full of black slugs and chewed his lip contemplatively.

'Let's just say for a minute that I accept what you're both saying.' He exhaled. 'How in God's name can a man be eaten by slugs? It's not as if you can't outrun the bloody things, is it?' He smiled thinly.

'There must be thousands of them by now,' said Bennett. 'It wouldn't be a case of outrunning then. They'd overwhelm their prey by weight of numbers. And size too.' He raised his eyebrows.

'*Giant* slugs?' Grogan shook his head. 'No, sorry, George but I'm not swallowing that. You'll be asking me to believe in Father Christmas next.' He reached for another cigarette, stuck it in his mouth, but didn't light up.

'Not giants, just large ones,' Bennett said. 'It's like the goldfish-bowl theory. If you put a goldfish in a small bowl it'll stay small because there's no room for it to grow. The principle is the same with these slugs. If they're using the sewer tunnels to breed then that gives them much more room not only to multiply but also to increase in size. Maybe the heat wave makes a difference too. They've got a combination of the perfect breeding ground and heat like a tropical jungle.' He pointed to the monstrosities in the jar. 'These are twice the size of common slugs and they've got that way in a third of the normal time. They begin growing as soon as they emerge from the cysts; the growth rate is phenomenal.'

'So what do we do?' Nicholson asked, some of the lightness now gone from his tone. 'We have to warn people.'

Grogan held up a hand.

'We still don't have any concrete proof,' he said. 'If we announce your . . . *findings*, then people are going to panic.' Again Finch caught that slight hint of mockery in the policeman's voice, although this time, to a certain extent, it

130

was tempered by caution. 'And that's just for starters,' Grogan went on. 'The other thing that bothers me is, if you're wrong, I personally don't fancy trying to explain to the commissioner that we made a balls-up. If I mention man-eating slugs to him I'll be walking the beat again.' He sighed. 'Just let it rest for a day or two...'

Finch interrupted.

'We don't *have* a day or two,' he snapped. 'It's just one area of London at the moment, in two or three days it could be the whole city.'

'How do you know it's only one area?' Grogan demanded.

'Molly Foster and Mark Franklin lived close together. The tramp you found was discovered in Leicester Square, the sewer man was washed out of that pipe near Westminster bridge. The incidents have a pattern to them.'

The DI shifted the unlit cigarette from one side of his mouth to the other.

'Whereabouts is the sewage leaking? Which streets?' the doctor persisted.

'All over the bloody West End from what the Water Board told me,' Grogan admitted. 'It's worse in some places than others of course.'

'What is the Water Board doing about it?' Bennett enquired.

'They're sending teams of engineers down to find out what's causing the blockage and clear it.'

'Well, let's hope they find the answer quickly,' Finch said. 'Because if that sewage continues pouring into the streets we're going to have an epidemic on our hands.'

'With this heat too, there's a risk of more conventional diseases breaking out, like cholera or typhus,' the pathologist put in.

Grogan massaged the bridge of his nose between thumb and forefinger.

'Flesh-eating slugs, typhus, cholera and a disease that turns people into raving maniacs,' he sighed. 'Does someone want to give me some *good* news?'

131

Twenty-four

The traffic cones had been placed close together at either end of Bucknall Street and a number of policemen stood or walked back and forth in front of the cordons, ensuring that interested onlookers didn't begin to form a crowd, and also directing the diverted stream of cars, buses and lorries which found the thoroughfare closed.

As the afternoon sun continued to blaze relentlessly in the cloudless sky, more than one of the uniformed men found perspiration soaking through his shirt. The men were thankful that they had been allowed to remove their tunics, but that seemed to help little as the humid heat covered the city like a suffocating blanket.

The heat alone would have been bad enough, but they also had to contend with the stench which filled their nostrils at every turn.

The street was flooded to a depth of at least three inches with vile-smelling brown water which had poured out of the drains and spread across the tarmac like ink soaking into blotting paper. Some of the more solid matter amidst the liquid was beginning to bake hard beneath the merciless sun, and most of the policemen did their best not to look at the muck which had been spewed forth.

Parked inside the cordon was a large transit van which bore the legend THAMES WATER AUTHORITY on both sides.

It was from this van that the four engineers had emerged who now stood around the manhole in the centre of the road, looking down into the murky depths. One of them, holding a

132

plan of the sewer tunnels, pointed to the spot on the map which marked the manhole around which they were gathered.

'The water level's receded since we were first called,' Max Kelly said, shining his torch down into the hole. A long way down it glinted on the surface of the water. 'See if the others are down yet,' he told a man on his left.

The man plucked a two-way radio from his belt, fiddled with the controls and pressed the set to his ear, ignoring the violent hiss of static which erupted from the hand-set.

'Atkins, come in, please,' the man said. 'Can you hear me, Terry? This is Irvine.'

There was another crackle of static.

'Yeah, I hear you,' a metallic voice answered.

'Are you down yet?' Irvine wanted to know.

'We're on our way. What about you?'

'Likewise.'

Kelly held out his hand and took the two-way from Irvine.

'Atkins, it's Max Kelly. What are the conditions like where you are?'

There was a moment's silence, as if Atkins were considering his answer. Then he spoke again:

'Well, the street's flooded but I don't know about down below. I think the water level's dropped but we don't know for sure until we get down into the tunnels.'

Kelly signed off, reminding Atkins to get in touch if he discovered the problem. The second team of engineers were in Wardour Street, less than a mile away.

'This is a low-level intercepting sewer according to these plans,' Kelly said, pointing at the manhole. 'We should be able to move through without too much trouble.' He turned once more to the man on his left. 'Irvine, you stay up here. The rest of us will go down,' he motioned to the other two men with him. 'Keep in contact with us and with Atkins' crew, right?'

Irvine nodded, watching the first man swing himself down into the manhole and catch hold of the metal ladder which disappeared into the blackness below.

He began to descend, followed by the next engineer, then

133

finally by Kelly himself, who checked his safety lamp briefly before clambering down the ladder. With such an apparently large overflow all the men were aware that there was much more danger of gas pockets.

As they climbed deeper into the enveloping gloom the leading engineer, a tall, red-haired man named Hamilton, flicked on his torch and stuck it in his belt. He heard the sound of water slapping lazily against the walls of the tunnel, and a moment later his foot was immersed in the reeking brown fluid. He descended further, the river of effluent reaching his knees, then his thighs. With a shiver he felt it spill over the top of his waders, soaking into his overalls. Hamilton paused, his foot on the bottom rung of the ladder. The water should have been no higher than his thighs but it was already sloshing around his waist. He pulled the torch from his belt and shone it around the tunnel.

Even the walls and roof were dripping. The water had, at some time earlier, filled the tunnel completely. And, he thought with a shudder, there was no guarantee that it would not happen again. Gritting his teeth he stepped off the ladder and the water lapped at his chest.

'Jesus,' he called. 'It must be over five feet deep down here.'

Kelly heard the shout and steadied himself to join his two men in the chest-high muck. As he reached the bottom of the ladder he swayed uncertainly for a moment, almost slipping on the slimy ooze which clung to the tunnel floor. He relayed the information to Irvine then switched off the two-way.

The sewer tunnel curved away to the left and Kelly moved ahead, finding that it was difficult to move easily with the weight of water against him. He and the other two engineers forced their way onward through the vile discoloured liquid, trying as best they could to ignore the stench.

'Some of this lot should have run off into a storm relief outlet,' Kelly said, panting from the effort of wading through the effluent. Every so often a lump of solid waste would bump against him but he ignored it and pushed on, the torch beam cutting a swath through the gloom.

Kelly paused and held up his safety lamp, checking that there was no flicker from the red light.

So far they were still clear. The three men moved on, noticing that the tunnel was widening slightly as the curve became more pronounced.

Hamilton suddenly stopped.

'Listen,' he urged, holding up a hand.

His two companions both stopped in their tracks and cocked their ears in the direction he was pointing.

Kelly heard it too.

A series of loud splashes, and something even louder. A low sucking sound, like many feet being pulled from clinging mud.

It was coming from just ahead of them, around the curve in the tunnel.

All three men recoiled from a particularly powerful and nauseating odour. A smell so fetid that, for a second, Kelly felt as if he'd been struck physically. He coughed, trying to breathe through his mouth to minimize the effects of the choking stench. They all knew the smell of the sewers, they recognized the first tell-tale whiffs of methane and the stink of excrement and urine, but this was something else. A smell so putrid it stopped them in their tracks.

In the silence there was a sudden harsh crackle from the radio and Hamilton almost lost his footing.

Kelly grabbed the two-way and pressed it to his ear.

'What's happening?' Irvine wanted to know. 'Is everything OK?'

'We're just about to find out,' Kelly told him, rounding the corner. 'I think there could be a blockage...'

The words trailed off as he shone his torch around the tunnel bend, swinging the beam back and forth.

His lips moved but no sound would come forth. The radio quivered in his hand.

'Oh my God,' he whispered.

'I didn't get that,' Irvine said. 'Have you found the blockage?'

Hamilton too was standing, arms held limply at his sides,

135

gazing wide-eyed at the far end of the tunnel.

The third man, Turner, could only shake his head in disbelief.

'What's happening, Max?' Irvine's voice on the two-way sounded miles away.

'Oh Christ,' Kelly murmured, his mouth dropping open.

The tunnel was at least twelve feet wide, perhaps eight feet high. More like a railway tunnel than a sewer.

Every square inch of brick was covered by a seething mass of slugs.

They stretched across the tunnel and up it, their glistening black bodies catching the torch-light like obscene cat's-eyes. A wall of slimy, bloated shapes blocking the filter which Kelly knew was behind the reeking horde. It was these monstrous creatures which had caused the overflow, their hideous forms packed so tightly together that the water could find no way through.

As they slid up and over each other some fell into the filthy water and that, the men realized, was had made the splashing sound they'd heard.

Moving slowly, as if he feared that any sudden action might cause the black mass to move, Kelly raised the two-way to his mouth.

'Call Atkins,' he said, quietly, the words almost catching in his throat. 'Tell him and his men to get out of the sewer.'

'What's wrong?' Irvine wanted to know.

'Just do it,' rasped Kelly, his eyes never leaving the slugs as they crawled and slithered, heaving their bloated bodies over the bricks and over each other, occasionally dropping into the water.

Dropping into the water.

The realization hit him like a thunderbolt and he began backing off, moving with difficulty against the swell of effluent.

'Let's get out of here,' he said, and his two companions needed no second warning. Turner, in particular, tried to turn and run but the depth and volume of the viscous liquid made that impossible. Arms flailing, he tried to push past his companions, knowing that the ladder which led to safety was no more than twenty yards away.

It might as well have been twenty miles.

Hamilton, still watching the slugs, saw one particularly large creature fall into the water, and moments later he felt something nudge against his thigh.

Sudden agonizing pain tore through him and he roared in surprise as he felt a series of stabbing motions against his leg. He thrust one hand into the water, his fingers closing over the large slug that was burrowing into his flesh. With a shriek he tore it free, holding it before him for a second, noticing with a twinge of disgust that a long streamer of skin hung from its churning mouth parts.

His skin.

He was about to hurl the monstrosity away when it suddenly twisted in his grasp and drove its sickle-shaped central tooth into the back of his hand. Blood burst from the wound but the slug tore itself free and struck again, driving its hungry mouth at the meatier part of his forearm.

Hamilton screamed again and turned to run but he overbalanced.

Kelly saw what was going to happen and pressed himself against the nearest wall.

Hamilton disappeared beneath the surface of the water. His head appeared a second later with two slugs boring into his face. He tried to scream but a third slipped inside his mouth, pressing against the back of his throat until he gagged violently.

At the same time, Turner found that half a dozen of the creatures were clinging to his back, eating their way through his overalls in an effort to reach the flesh beneath. When they finally did so his shrieks filled the cavern, bouncing off the walls until Kelly thought he would go mad.

For his own part he pressed on, noticing that more and more slugs were now dropping from the walls into the water, all eager to reach this fresh prey. He shivered with horror as he saw Turner disappear beneath the water.

Were these things slugs? he thought, immediately

answering his own question. No, it was impossible, slugs didn't eat human flesh . . .

He realized how wrong he was.

Searing agony shot through him from crotch to brain as two of them began boring into his inner thigh. He tore one free, and the second he crushed in his hand, its body fluids oozing over his fingers. A fresh stench assailed his nostrils as the slug split in two, the half he still held pulping yellowish pus-like blood everywhere. He snatched at his radio, gritting his teeth as he felt new pain in his thighs and buttocks, then the small of his back.

One of the larger creatures was eating its way through to his kidneys.

'Irvine,' he gasped. 'Get help for God's sake . . .' The pleas dissolved into shouts of pain as he felt his lower body enveloped by red-hot pain. He could actually feel blood bursting from his back. He could sense the slug digging deeper inside him.

But he struggled on, now alone in the tunnel.

Both Turner and Hamilton were gone.

'I'm coming down,' Irvine told him.

'No! Just get help.'

Blood filled his mouth and he felt himself swaying but just ahead, visible in the semi-darkness beneath the manhole, was the ladder.

His head was spinning now and he knew that he was going to fall. There was nothing he could do to stop himself. He pitched forward into the stinking water.

When he finally dragged himself upright another slug was eating into his ear. Blood was pouring down the side of his face and he was moaning gutturally, but he found the strength to wrench the creature free, ripping most of his ear away with it. His nose was full of filthy liquid, his mouth was clogged with blood, but he fought his way on until at last his hand gripped one of the ladder rungs.

'What's happening down there?'

Irvine's voice rattled from the two-way.

Kelly didn't answer. He was trying to drag himself up the

metal ladder. One of his legs dangled uselessly, eaten to the bone. The other barely supported him. Calling on all his reserves of strength he began dragging himself up, one rung at a time, aware that two or three slugs were still clinging to his body.

One was slithering up his spine towards the hollow at the base of his skull.

'Help me,' Kelly screamed, desperation giving volume to the bellow of pain and frustration.

He was less than two feet from the manhole.

The slug on the back of his neck fixed its tooth into his flesh and attacked.

The pain was so sudden and unexpectedly excruciating that he lost his grip and fell several feet. One outstretched hand gripped a rung further down and he came to a jarring halt, blood gushing from the numerous wounds on his body.

Above him, Irvine peered down into the blackness, shining his torch down onto what could have been a picture plucked from some insane horror film.

Kelly was hanging by one arm, his face was white as milk, smeared with blood and excrement, his overalls in tatters, matted and crimson. And the engineer noticed something else.

The thick black shapes that glided so easily over his companion's skin.

Kelly looked up, sensing that his grip on consciousness was fading rapidly. He tried to call out but all that came forth was a thick gout of blood, spilling over his lips and chin. With every fibre of courage and endurance left, he began to climb once more.

Irvine straightened up and yelled to the nearby policemen.

'Help me, quick,' he shouted and two of the constables hurdled the cordon of cones and came sprinting across the flooded street towards the sewer man. Together, they hauled Kelly up the last couple of feet from the black mouth of the manhole.

The last slug fell from his body and disappeared beneath the water far below.

As Kelly rolled over on the filthy pavement the full extent of his injuries was clear for the three observers to see. His eyes were bulging wide in their sockets, as if something on the inside were trying to force them out and his lips fluttered soundlessly, blood spilling from his mouth.

'I'd better get an ambulance,' said one of the policemen, hurrying away.

Kelly's body underwent a violent muscular spasm, then was still. A soft hiss signalled the collapse of his sphincter muscle.

'No need to hurry,' the other constable sighed. 'It's not an ambulance he needs now.'

The fierce sun beat down relentlessly upon the little tableau.

Detective Inspector Ray Grogan lit a cigarette and looked one last time at the body of Max Kelly. Then he nodded and the blanket was pulled back over the mutilated mass which had once been a man.

'There was slime on the corpse,' said Bennett in a weary voice, wiping a bead of perspiration from his forehead.

'What about the other men who went down there with him?' Grogan asked Irvine.

'There's been no sign of them,' the sewer man told him.

The DI sucked hard on his Marlboro. He was aware of Bennett's gaze upon him.

'And neither of you saw anything?' Grogan asked the two constables.

'No, sir,' they said in unison.

'Tell me again what *you* saw,' the DI said to Irvine.

'Like I told you,' he began. 'There were ... *things* crawling on him. Black things.'

'*Things* is a vague word.'

'Animals of some kind, like worms only much bigger. Horrible fucking things whatever they were.'

'Slugs,' said Bennett.

'Yeah,' Irvine confirmed. 'They looked like slugs.'

Grogan took a last drag from his cigarette and dropped it to the ground, only half-smoked. It hissed angrily in the spilt water. He looked at Bennett, his face set in tight lines.

'Well, Ray,' the pathologist said. 'Do you want me to come with you when you go to see the Commissioner?'

Twenty-five

Finch couldn't remember how long he'd been sitting watching the house in Melbury Road.

He'd driven there immediately after leaving New Scotland Yard. The journey to Kensington had not been an unduly long one but it had been made more uncomfortable by the searing heat. In places, the tarmac was beginning to blister.

The street was quiet except for a couple of children squatting on the hot pavement near his car, who were amusing themselves by dropping small pebbles onto some ants which had made their nest between two paving stones. Finch sat back in his seat, feeling the perspiration soaking into his shirt. He watched the children for a moment longer, then clambered out of the car, wiping the palms of his hands on his trousers. He found that his hands were shaking slightly, but he remembered that they usually did when he stood before this particular house.

He walked swiftly up the short path and rapped three times on the front foor. There was no answer so he knocked again. After a moment or two he heard sounds of movement from inside and then the door was opened.

'Hello, Theresa,' he said, a vague smile on his face.

His ex-wife regarded him impassively. If she was surprised to see him then it certainly didn't register in her expression.

'Hello, Alan,' she said, that distinctively husky voice still as potent as ever but with no trace of emotion in it.

Finch cast her a rapid appraising glance, enough to realize that she was still as attractive as ever. Her long auburn hair was drawn up, held in position by slides. She was wearing a white T-shirt, her nipples straining darkly against the material. The faded denim skirt she wore clung tightly to her buttocks, the split in it revealing a good portion of her long, slender legs.

'What do you want?' she asked him. 'You're not supposed to pick Christopher up until tomorrow.'

'I know that.' There was an awkward silence as they looked at one another, then Finch spoke again. 'I need to talk to you. Could I come in for a minute, please?'

Theresa hesitated then stepped aside and ushered him in.

'Richard's not here at the moment anyway,' she said, closing the door behind him.

'It wasn't Richard I came to see,' Finch told her, a note of irritation in his voice. He walked through to the sitting room, welcoming its relative coolness.

'Would you like a drink?' she asked him, moving towards a cabinet on the other side of the room.

He declined at first, but when she poured herself a large scotch and soda he accepted an orange juice. Theresa handed it to him and seated herself in one of the large armchairs. Finch did likewise.

'Where's Christopher?' he asked, smiling as he saw his son's photo on the mantlepiece.

'He's at a birthday party. One of the kids he goes to school with is six today. It's over in Bloomsbury somewhere, I've got to pick him up later.'

A flicker of concern passed behind Finch's eyes but he said nothing.

'You look tired, Alan,' she told him, without the slightest hint of concern. 'Have you been overworking or is it a case of too much bed and not enough sleep?' She raised her eyebrows.

'You know better than that.'

'Of course. It might interfere with your career.' Her voice

142

was heavy with sarcasm.

'Theresa, I didn't come here to argue. I came here to ask you something.' He rolled the glass between his hands. 'I want you and Chris to leave London. Go today if you can, but just get out.'

Theresa paused, the glass almost touching her lips.

'I don't know what Richard will think of that,' she told him.

'I couldn't care less what Richard thinks,' Finch rasped. 'I'm asking you to do it for Christopher's sake. Isn't that enough?'

'Why do you want us to leave?'

Finch exhaled.

'I don't know all the details,' he began, wearily. 'Not yet, but I know that there's a virus of some kind spreading through the city. I've already seen a couple of cases personally and I know there'll be more.'

'What kind of virus?'

He wondered if he should mention the possible threat of the slugs but eventually decided against it.

'No one knows exactly,' he said. 'Listen, Theresa, can't you take my word for it? I wouldn't have come here if I didn't think it was important.'

'We're not married any more, Alan. I can make my own decisions.'

'I'm not telling you what to do, for Christ's sake.' His face darkened as he continued, barely able to keep his temper under control. 'Despite what's happened between us I still care about you. It might be possible for *you* to wipe out the memory of six years of marriage but I can't. I still care about you but I *love* Chris. I'm not asking you to do anything for me, I know you better than that. Do it for Chris.'

They regarded each other across the room, each one waiting for the next cutting barb. Theresa sipped her drink, watching her ex-husband over the rim of the glass.

'It's not as easy as that, Alan,' she said, her tone softening slightly. 'Despite what you may think of Richard he's still my . . .' She struggled to find the words.

'Lover,' Finch interjected. 'Don't be afraid of using the

143

term in front of me, Theresa. It's not as if you're telling me something I didn't already know.'

'I don't know what he'll say.'

'Well, if he won't go, then leave without him.' Now it was the doctor's turn to rely on sarcasm. 'Or if you can't bear to be without him, send Chris to me and *I'll* get him out.'

Theresa gazed into the bottom of her glass for a moment, lost in thought, then she looked Finch directly in the eye.

'What are you going to do?' she wanted to know. 'Assuming that I do take Chris out of the city. Are you leaving too?'

'I don't know,' he said. 'I think my talents would be better employed here if the virus does spread, as it seems it will.'

'The good doctor will always be on hand. Right?' The fire had returned to her voice.

Finch got to his feet.

'I've already said my piece,' he announced. 'Please do what I've asked. You owe it to Chris.'

Her eyes narrowed to tiny slits.

'I don't owe Chris anything,' she hissed. 'I've given him more love in the last six years than any child has a right to expect so don't tell me I *owe* it to him.'

'Then you'll take him out of London?' said Finch.

Theresa didn't answer, she merely swallowed what was left in her glass, then got to her feet, crossed to the drinks cabinet and poured another large measure of scotch.

From the direction of the hall they both heard a key being turned in the lock, and a moment later, Richard Crane entered the sitting room. He looked at Finch, then at Theresa, then back at Finch again.

'Hello, Alan,' he said.

'It's all right, Richard, I was just leaving,' the doctor told him, heading towards the hall. He turned as he reached it, his face focussing on his ex-wife.

'Remember what I've said,' he asked. Then he was gone. He closed the front door behind him and walked back down the path, past the two kids who were still bombarding ants with stones, back to his car. Finch slid behind the wheel and twisted the key in the ignition. He took a final look at the house, then drove off.

Twenty-six

Carol Mendham, turned away coughing, unable to take any more of the vile fumes rising from the blocked toilet. She pushed the bathroom window further open, stuck her head out and sucked in several lungfuls of clean air. There might not be any cooling breeze but it was better than bending over the reeking bowl. As the evening approached slowly, almost tentatively, the sun lost some of its potency. Sinking low in the sky it glowed brilliant blood red, like some kind of huge warning flare, giving notice that the next day would bring no respite from the soaring temperatures.

Carol pulled off her rubber gloves, took one last defiant look at the blocked lavatory, then threw the garments into the nearby waste-bin. She washed her hands thoroughly, muttering to herself when she saw a red mark on the back of her left hand. Peering more closely at it, she saw that it looked like a heat bump. No wonder in this weather, she thought, rinsing the soap off. The damn thing itched too.

There was another on her forearm and one, slightly larger, on her wrist. She dried her hands and reached into the medicine cabinet on the bathroom wall, searching through the contents for the calamine lotion. As she opened the door she caught sight of her own reflection and was surprised to see how pale she looked.

What was more, she noted with annoyance, there was another of those blasted bumps on her forehead.

Carol found the calamine and dabbed it on; she had to tilt

her head to get a proper look in the mirror. She smiled to herself. The cabinet was on a slant. She'd told Hugh when he'd put it up that it wasn't straight but he would hear none of it. He could learn anything from a book, he'd told her, so with the Do-It-Yourself manual open in front of him and his tools laid out like a surgeon's implements, he'd set to work. The lop-sided cabinet was only one of his 'triumphs'. She'd lived with Hugh Francis for over nine months now, and in that time she had learned that his attempts at DIY were positively lethal. The sort of bloke who changes plugs with a hammer, her father called him. The thought of plugs brought back memories of the time he'd tried to wire up the new video and managed to fuse the lights in the whole block.

Carol looked back at the toilet and wished that he really did have a knack for household repairs, particularly plumbing.

It had been blocked for nearly a day now. They'd emptied buckets of water into it to disperse some of the waste, but with only limited success. Carol had scrabbled around trying to locate the blockage, but she had not discovered one. Other flats in the block, she knew, were suffering similar problems with their water works, and she'd heard on the news that some streets nearby had been flooded.

She made her way along the hall, the smell of food greeting her as she entered the kitchen. Carol felt her stomach contract despite the appetizing aromas and, for one second, she thought she was going to be sick. But the feeling passed and she didn't say anything.

Hugh was standing by the oven door, a towel wrapped around each hand, pulling a deep dish from inside the oven. He wore only a pair of jeans, but perspiration was rolling off his back. As Carol entered the room he turned and placed the joint of beef on a plate.

'A roast on Saturday evenings,' she said. 'People will think we're rolling in it.'

'Well, if we can't celebrate my appointment to a Fleet Street newspaper in style then I think there's something wrong,' Hugh told her.

He'd been a free-lance journalist for the past four years but lately one of the Fleet Street tabloids had published his work on such a regular basis that they had decided to offer him a full-time position. Hence the celebration.

He stood over the joint, the electric carving knife in his hand, carefully and effortlessly slicing off portions of the meat. Carol sat back in the chair watching him, becoming aware of a dull ache building slowly at the back of her neck.

'Are you feeling OK, love?' he asked.

She nodded.

'If the toilet's still blocked on Monday I'll give the water authorities another call,' he said, carving the last of the meat and laying the knife down. He turned towards the fridge and pulled out a bottle of red wine.

'Mustn't forget the *vino*,' he said, chuckling. 'It's a pity it's not champagne ...'

He heard the loud clatter of the electric carving knife behind him, building to a muted roar as the blades moved back and forth with dizzying speed.

The smile on Hugh's face faded as he turned round and saw Carol holding it before her, her features twisted into a grimace.

She drove the knife forward, using both hands to push it further. The rapidly moving twin blades effortlessly slashed through the muscles of Hugh's stomach before churning on into his intestines. He screamed and dropped the wine bottle which shattered, the alcohol mingling with his own blood which was now gushing freely from the hideous rent in his belly.

He fell, trying to push Carol away, his eyes bulging wide in pain and terror as he saw severed lengths of intestine bulging through the massive cut.

Hugh raised his hand to ward her off but she sliced off two of his fingers with the lethal implement, sweeping it downwards so that the serrated blades powered into his neck at the point where it joined his shoulder. A huge fountain of crimson erupted from the cut, splattering Carol who kept both blood-drenched hands on the electric knife, moving it back and forth in a sawing motion which threatened to sever

Hugh's head. His head lolled backwards at an impossible angle as she cut through his windpipe, the blades grating against, then pulverising, his larynx. Pieces of skin flew into the air like grisly confetti and only when she was too exhausted to hold onto the knife any longer did Carol finally switch it off.

In the relative silence which followed, she slumped back, staring blankly at the mutilated corpse, feeling the blood soaking into her clothes.

As it dripped from the walls it sounded as if the kitchen had a faulty tap.

David Maguire sat on the edge of the bed and carefully put his weight on first his left foot then his right.

He hissed in pain each time.

The blisters on the soles of his feet made the act painful in the extreme. Walking was almost impossible. He couldn't believe that they'd come up so quickly. Earlier in the day, he and his wife, Jill, had been sitting on the grass in Golden Square enjoying the sunshine and he'd kicked off his sandals as he wandered around. Within two hours of their return home the first of the blisters had appeared and now, with the time approaching 10.46 p.m., the pain seemed to be intensifying. He wondered if he'd stepped in some dog shit at first but had been relieved to find he hadn't. Even if he had, he wouldn't have expected his feet to swell up like two pounds of unwrapped mince.

There was another blister on his shoulder and a smaller one on his stomach, both of which were throbbing mightily, but David did his best to ignore the pain. He stretched out on the bed, naked, listening to the sounds of running water from across the landing. He closed his eyes and tried to picture his wife beneath the spray of the shower, and as he did, his penis began to stir into life.

They had been married for almost seventeen years. She had been twenty then, three years his senior. During the intervening years Jill had presented him with two daughters, both of them as beautiful as their mother. He never ceased to marvel at how his wife had managed to retain her shape despite the onset of years. Although thirty-seven was by no means old, she worked hard to keep her figure and that hard work certainly paid off as far as David was concerned. They were a rarity in the world of quick divorces and unhappy relationships. They had managed to keep that spark of romance and excitement which even the closest couples eventually lose to some degree. David knew that the time would come sooner or later, but as yet, their love for each other and, more importantly to him, their passion, showed no signs of abating.

Saturday night was something special for them. The girls were packed off to their grandparents and David and Jill had the house to themselves for what they jokingly called 'depravity night'. It was one of the little rituals which made their lives more enjoyable. David knew, at this minute, that his wife was in the bathroom applying her make-up. Another minute or two and she would be with him.

He tried to forget the blisters and also the nagging pain which had settled like a clamp around the base of his skull.

He heard the sound of footsteps crossing the landing and he closed his eyes, aware now that she had entered the room.

'I thought you'd nodded off,' Jill said softly and he opened his eyes and looked at her, his face a combination of pride and longing.

She was wearing a white basque, the red lace across the front pulled tight to accentuate the curve of her waist and the full swell of her breasts. Her long blonde hair cascaded over her shoulders, attractively framing her youthful, sensual face. Her cheeks were rouged and her slightly parted lips were painted a brilliant red.

David felt his penis growing to full erection as she moved closer to the bed and his gaze roved lower, delighting in this vision of sexuality. She walked slowly and gracefully, her long legs encased in fine silk stockings, the red high-heeled ankle-strap shoes she wore making her look even taller. She stood beside the bed for a moment, hands on hips, allowing him a full view of her stunning form, then she raised one leg and placed her foot on the bed beside him. He swung himself around until he was sitting on the edge of the bed facing her, his eyes following her right hand as it moved slowly across her belly then down between her legs. There she used her index finger to open the gash of her crotchless knickers, allowing the digit to brush through her pubic hair. She rotated it gently, arousing herself.

David leant forward but she stopped him, that finger still working feverishly.

'You watch,' she whispered and began using two fingers. He caressed the inside of her thighs, the feel of the slinky material exciting him even more. He could feel her tensing every so often and her breathing was becoming heavier. David reached up and expertly unfastened the lace which secured the basque, working it free until he exposed Jill's breasts. Her nipples were already swollen and, as David flicked his tongue over them, paying careful attention to each in turn, he felt them harden.

Sensing that her husband's excitement was now reaching fever pitch, Jill lowered her leg and slowly knelt between his thighs, trapping his throbbing organ between her breasts. She rubbed it between the firm mounds, bending her head forward every so often to lick at the bulbous, purple glans which was already leaking clear fluid. He groaned with pleasure as the exquisite torment continued for what seemed like an eternity. She would bring him almost to the point of climax and then stop, repeating the action until she felt his already swollen testicles grow even firmer beneath the kneading action of her fingers.

Jill stood up once more, slipping her knickers off as she did so, standing before him again, only this time she allowed him to use his tongue on her, lapping at her distended vaginal lips. She gripped his shoulders, her red-painted nails digging into his flesh.

He winced as one of them almost touched the blister which was forming there but he fought back the cry of pain.

He planted a kiss on her lathered vagina, then leant back, retrieving something from beneath the pillow.

He held the vibrator before her for a second before flicking it on. Jill smiled as he brought the ten-inch cylinder close to her eager cleft, running it over her mound, teasing her clitoris until she felt like screaming her pleasure. He worked the appliance around her slippery valley, finally pushing it an inch or two into the hot wetness. At the same time his mouth fastened around her hardened bud, his tongue flicking over it. He pushed the vibrator further, increasing the speed as he inserted it.

She held him tighter as the feelings between her legs grew in intensity. David eased her down onto the bed beside him, the humming phallus still embedded in her, only now he began to work it in and out, occasionally rubbing the gleaming tip over her clitoris.

Jill bucked her hips up to meet the thrusts, realizing that the warmth which was spreading around her thighs and belly signalled the beginnings of her first orgasm. She sighed with mild disappointment when David withdrew the vibrator, replacing it with his fingers as he manoeuvred the dripping instrument over her mound to her breasts. Her nipples responded just as willingly to this new-found attention, however, and she reached for his penis, rubbing swiftly but gently, wanting the beautiful torment to continue but also needing the release of a climax.

He lifted the vibrator to her lips, switching it off as he did so. She licked at it, tasting her own juices on the mock phallus, aware of his churning fingers deep within her. He rested his thumb on her clitoris and rubber harder, still pushing the vibrator into her mouth, a slight smile on his face as she licked and sucked it as if it had been his own organ.

He pushed harder and Jill gagged as she felt its tip touch the back of her throat.

Her eyes jerked open and she looked at David, trying to shake her head, to tell him to stop. This part of the game was no longer comfortable.

He increased the pressure, clambering onto her as he did so, the weight of his body pinning her down. She felt a sudden twinge of fear as she looked into his blank eyes and her stomach contracted violently as she felt the sleek cylinder being forced deeper into the maw of her throat. He was using all his weight on it now, and Jill tasted blood as the tissue near her nostrils ripped under the assault. Vomit rushed up from her stomach, filling her mouth, causing her to shudder beneath him.

But still David forced the intruding object further down her throat, stretching her lips wide, until there was barely three inches of it left.

She writhed beneath him in a hideous parody of sexual ecstacy, her eyes rolling upward in the sockets. She tried to cry out but only a liquid gurgle issued forth, and finally her frenzied movements slowed. Then stopped completely.

David looked down at her body. The thick stream of yellowish-red fluid which was spilling from her mouth had stained the sheets and a rancid stench filled his nostrils, but he seemed to take no notice. He rolled off and lay on his back beside the corpse. The pain at the base of his skull was now almost unbearable.

The vibrator still protruded obscenely from his dead wife's mouth.

He could hear its low buzzing as it rattled against her teeth.

As he tried to rise he felt a fresh onslaught of pain, both from his head and also from the newest blister which was bulging from the flesh on the small of his back.

The ones on his shoulder and belly were already weeping pus.

That same night in an area less than a mile square, from Piccadilly to Bloomsbury, another twenty-seven people were killed.

Sunday – the 16th

Twenty-seven

It didn't seem like a Sunday morning.

Inside the large room with its maps and plans tacked to the walls, Alan Finch sat tapping his pen against the notepad before him.

He was seated at a large oval table with eight other men. Every one of them had a pitcher of water in front of him, most of which were already half-empty. Despite the air-conditioning in the room, the blazing early-morning sunshine contrived to turn the room into a hothouse. This was hardly surprising as two sides of the office consisted almost entirely of glass. Through the huge transparent walls the river Thames was clearly visible, licking its way through the city like a dirty parched tongue.

Apart from the occasional aeroplane vapour trail the sky was unblemished. The burning orb of the sun hung against a canopy of blue the colour of faded denim.

Smoke from half a dozen cigarettes eddied in the warm air and many of the ashtrays were already full of dog-ends.

George Bennett waved a hand in front of his face, trying to clear away some of the bluish-grey haze which had settled around him like a fog. It was a curious piece of logic which he'd formulated but which seemed to hold true, that smoke always reached a non-smoker no matter where he was in the room. It was probably only his imagination, but Bennett longed for a fan at this precise moment. Anything to clear the air. The pathologist was nibbling on a whole-wheat biscuit, looking impatiently around him.

Finch rubbed one hand across his stubbled cheeks and

wished that he'd had time to shave before arriving at New Scotland Yard but he'd received the call at eight o'clock and they'd told him it was urgent. He hadn't slept too well the previous night, his mind occupied with thoughts of Theresa and Chris. Would she follow his advice and leave London, he wondered? He could only pray that she would.

He cast quick appraising glances at the other men seated around the table and found that, apart from Bennett, he recognized only Detective Inspector Grogan and DS Nicholson. It had been Bennett who'd called him earlier that morning, asking for his presence at the meeting, though what its purpose was he still didn't know. The pathologist had told him about the incident with the slugs in the sewer the day before and the deaths of the maintenance men. That had been shock enough for Finch but, when he heard that more people had been murdered by victims of the hideous plague and that the crazed killers too had finally succumbed to the monstrous disease, he found his thoughts turning with even more insistence towards his ex-wife and his son. But he also found room in his troubled contemplations for Lisa Foster. He determined to get in touch with her and, if she hadn't already done so, urge her too to leave the capital.

His thoughts were interrupted by the tall, grey-haired man in the dark blue uniform who rose to his feet at the far end of the table.

Sir James Hughes was in his early fifties, a slightly built but nevertheless imposing figure. He had been Metropolitan Police Commissioner for the past eight years. His face was pockmarked, deeply pitted around the cheeks, and a nasty crescent-shaped scar curved from one corner of his mouth giving him the appearance of having a perpetual sneer. He coughed loudly and tapped the table.

'If we could get down to business, gentlemen,' he said, his voice low and rasping as if his throat were full of gravel.

All eyes turned in his direction and a relative hush replaced the muted babble of conversation of a moment before.

Hughes turned to face a large map of Central London which was fastened to a cork board. He stood before it for a moment, as if lost in his own private thoughts, then he jabbed a finger at the Soho area.

'If we take this as the hub of the wheel,' he began, 'for at least half a mile in all directions incidents were reported last night and there have been others over the past week.' He exhaled deeply. 'Now, I just about managed to believe that there was some kind of virus or disease in the city simply because there had been so many similar cases reported. What I did find hard to believe and, if it wasn't for so much evidence, I still wouldn't believe, is the presence of these . . . slugs in the sewers.'

'Surely the disease is the first priority to be dealt with,' said Bryant, an official from the Department of Health. He was dressed in a checked jacket, immaculately clean, and as he spoke he pulled at one end of a well-groomed moustache.

'The disease is *caused* by the slugs,' Bennett interrupted. 'The two problems are not independent of one another.'

'Do you honestly believe that there are flesh-eating slugs in the sewers of London?' the man with the moustache said, barely hiding a smile.

'I lost three of my men to the bloody things yesterday,' Donald Robertson barked.

'There is no disputing that the slugs exist and that their . . . feeding habits are as we feared,' Hughes said. 'The question is, how do we deal with the problem.' He looked at Bennett. 'Or should I say problems?'

'Why can't we just destroy them?' asked Bryant, tugging at his moustache again.

'I wish it were as easy as that, Mr Bryant,' Hughes said. 'There are reckoned to be hundreds of thousands of them by this time.'

'Well, how the hell did they get down there in the first place?' Bryant grunted indignantly.

'If we knew that, we wouldn't have this problem, would we?' snapped Robertson.

'That's not strictly true,' Finch interjected. 'Even if someone had known where these slugs came from, and how they got into the sewers, no one could have stopped them

from multiplying. The sewers are a perfect breeding ground
and they also make it easy for them to move around.'

Hughes picked up a manila file folder from the table and
flipped it open.

'Mr Dowd.' He looked at the other Water Board official.
'Your report says that the slugs are blocking a number of
filters in the sewer tunnels. That's what is causing the
overflows of effluent into the streets and homes in these
areas.' He hooked a thumb over his shoulder at the map.

Dowd nodded.

'But there's no way of clearing the filters,' he said. 'There
are too many slugs.'

'So, in other words, anyone living in the affected area will
have to contend with raw sewage pumping out of their drains
for as long as the slugs are down there?' Bob Archer said,
irritably.

Archer was a year or two younger than Bryant, a lean-faced
individual with darting blue eyes. He had been with the
Department of Health for over five years, but had never been
confronted with a problem of this magnitude before.

'Do you want *your* men to try unblocking the filters?'
Robertson snapped at him, challengingly.

Hughes raised a hand for silence, fully aware of the strain
which everyone in the room was under. Not least himself.

'We do have one option,' he said, slowly. 'Perhaps the only
one.'

The others looked at him expectantly.

'We can evacuate people from the affected area.'

There was a moment's silence, broken by Grogan. The DI
lit another cigarette and drew on it.

'We haven't got the men to supervise an operation as big as
that, sir,' he said.

'I realize that, Grogan,' Hughes told him. 'We'd need help.
From the army. It's the only way I can see of avoiding further
deaths.' He shrugged. 'Clear the entire area.'

'But that doesn't take care of the slugs,' said Bennett.

'Or the disease,' Finch added.

'We don't know how far they've spread through those

158

tunnels,' the pathologist continued. 'If we evacuate one area of the city then they'll simply move on to another area where the food supply is more plentiful.'

'And we can't clear the entire city, sir,' Grogan said.

'Well, at the moment, evacuating at least the critical area seems the best and *only* choice we have,' the commissioner insisted. 'The question is, how to begin.'

'What about broadcasting a warning over the TV and radio?' Archer suggested.

'No,' Hughes said flatly. 'That would cause a panic. We've got enough to contend with without people fleeing in their thousands from the city, clogging the roads and getting in each other's way. We'd have more deaths from road accidents than we would from the slugs or their disease.'

'I wouldn't bet on it,' Bennett commented cryptically.

'Well, I agree with the commissioner,' said Bryant. 'Evacuation seems to be the only solution.'

'The final solution,' murmured Finch, raising his eyebrows when Bennett looked at him. The doctor shrugged, almost apologetically.

'Will you call in the army then, sir?' Grogan asked.

'I'll have to speak to the Home Secretary first,' Hughes told him.

'And in the meantime?' Robertson wanted to know. 'The people in the affected areas are still at risk.'

'They should be warned,' Dowd echoed.

'I told you, I don't want a panic on my hands,' the commissioner snapped.

'You've already got one,' Finch protested in exasperation.

There was a heavy silence as the men looked at their empty notepads as if wanting to avoid eye contact with each other. Every one of them scanned the blank sheets as if they expected some miracle solution to appear magically on them. DS Nicholson was the only one who had used his paper. He'd drawn a cat on it. He looked at the comic sketch, then balled it up, feeling as helpless as the others in the room.

'The area must be sealed off and evacuated,' Hughes repeated. 'It's the only way. The army will have to assist.'

'What makes you think they're any better prepared for this than your own men, or anyone else for that matter?' Robertson said, chewing his nails.

'Have you got any better suggestions?' the commissioner snapped.

'So, assuming all the people can be cleared from the affected areas,' Bennett said, slowly, 'I repeat, what do you intend to do about the slugs?'

'I was hoping that you might have some answers on that score. You and the doctor,' Hughes said. 'You are supposed to be men of science. How would you suggest we kill them?'

'Salt kills slugs, doesn't it?' said Bryant, smiling. 'Let's just hope they decide to attack a Saxa factory.' He chuckled.

Bennett shot him an acid glance and the Health Officer coloured beneath the pathologist's glare.

'Have you *any* ideas?' Hughes said, hopefully.

'Poison of some kind,' Finch suggested. 'But there's no guarantee it would work.'

'What kind of poison?' Grogan asked.

Finch shrugged.

'Something non-combustible if possible,' he said. 'With the amount of methane in those tunnels any explosion down there would bring half of London down with it.'

'Cyanide,' Bennett offered. 'It would be absorbed on contact. It's a fast worker.'

'Have you any idea how many gallons would be needed to flood those tunnels?' said Robertson. 'And besides, where the hell do you think it would go afterwards? All effluent is eventually re-cycled into drinking water and you're talking about using cyanide in it.'

'Also,' Edward Dowd added, 'if the filters are blocked, which we know they are, the cyanide would bubble up into the streets.'

'All the more reason to evacuate those areas then,' the Commissioner said with an air of finality.

'If we can't use poison,' Grogan said, 'what the hell do we do? Go down there and shoot the fucking things one at a time?' He shrugged and swallowed hard, angry with himself

160

for swearing.

'What we all seem to be forgetting is those people infected by the disease,' Robertson said. 'If it turns them into raving maniacs like you said, then the army is going to have its hands full coping with them.'

'The disease works very quickly on the nervous system,' Finch said. 'It has a very short incubation period, perhaps six hours. After that, the victim is lucky to survive much longer than two hours, depending on the severity of the infection.'

'Two hours is plenty long enough to kill somebody,' said Grogan, crushing out his cigarette in the ashtray.

Commissioner Hughes drew a hand across his forehead and sighed.

'I don't think there's anything more we can do at the moment,' he said. 'I'll contact the Home Secretary immediately and get clearance. We'll start the evacuation as soon as possible.'

'And what about the people *not* being evacuated?' said Bennett. 'What do we tell them? That they'd better move just in case they're next on the bloody menu?' His voice carried a note of scorn.

Hughes ignored the question.

'We'll see what the army can do,' he said. Then, turning to Grogan, 'You and your men are to give them every support.' He paused for a moment, licking his dry lips. 'Grogan. Some of the people in the affected areas are likely to be homicidal, psychotic. See to it that at least three men in each unit are issued with sidearms.'

The words hung in the air, like the wreaths of cigarette smoke.

'Anyone dangerous, anyone infected is to be shot.'

Twenty-eight

As he and the other men left the room, Finch felt an almost crushing weariness descend upon him. While Bryant, Archer, Robertson and Dowd all hurriedly left the building, Grogan and Nicholson remained in the commissioner's office. The doctor himself, with Bennett, wandered across the corridor to the washrooms opposite.

While Bennett relieved himself, Finch filled a sink with cold water and splashed his face.

'Shoot on sight,' said Bennett, contemplatively. 'You know, that might have even sounded funny if Hughes hadn't meant it.'

'It's a bit drastic, isn't it?' Finch said, cupping more water in his hands and dousing his face. He blinked hard, as if trying to waken himself.

'What choice do they have?'

Finch studied his reflection in the mirror above the sink. His face looked pale, his eyes were red-rimmed, the whites criss-crossed by veins which stood out prominently. He wouldn't have thought it possible but he looked as rough as he felt.

'Could one of the infected victims be cured?' he pondered aloud.

'Only time will tell, my friend,' Bennett said, zipping up his flies and crossing to the other wash basin. 'But time is one thing we don't have.'

There was a moment's silence, then Finch looked at the pathologist.

'Are you married?' he wanted to know.

Bennett smiled and nodded.

'For almost twenty years.'

'Any children?'

'No.' His voice took on a note of sadness. 'We had a daughter but she died when she was eight. Some stupid bastard hit her with his car. The police never did find him.' He swallowed hard, then attempted a casual shrug, attempting to dismiss the memories.

'You never had any more children, then?' Finch said.

'We couldn't bear to risk that kind of pain again. Anyway, why the sudden interest in *my* domestic life?' He smiled.

'I was just curious.'

'Curiosity. The prerogative of doctors and pathologists. Quite an apt quote, don't you think?'

'Who said it?'

Bennett chuckled.

'I did, I just made it up.'

Finch let the water out of the bowl and dried his hands and face on the nearby towel-roll. Then he headed for the door.

'Where are you going?' Bennett wanted to know.

'I'll see you later,' was the doctor's only answer. Bennett found himself alone in the washroom.

Finch found two public phones on the ground floor, close to the main entrance of the building. He ducked inside the plastic canopy of the nearest one and fumbled in his trouser pocket for change. He dialled the number, then waited for what seemed like an eternity until the receiver was picked up at the other end. As the rapid pips sounded in his ear he pushed in some coins.

'Hello,' he said, one part of his mind wishing that the phone hadn't been answered.

There was a crackle of static then he heard an all-too-familiar voice.

'Hello. Who's calling?' Richard Crane asked.

Finch gripped the receiver until it seemed that it would break.

'Hello,' Crane repeated.

163

If Crane was still at the house, then so too were Chris and Theresa, Finch thought almost angrily. He glared at the receiver, hearing the other man's voice becoming more agitated.

'If this is someone playing silly buggers...' rasped Crane.

Finch knew that all he had to do was ask if his ex-wife and his son were there. Perhaps they *had* left without Crane.

'For the last time,' Crane snarled.

Ask if Theresa and Chris are there.

'OK, pal, have it your own way. Fuck you.'

There was a muted crack as the receiver was slammed down at the other end and Finch was left listening to the slow buzz of the dial tone. He dropped the phone gently back onto its cradle, then turned and headed for the main doors.

The sun was only an hour from reaching its zenith and the tarmac felt hot beneath the soles of his shoes as he walked across the car park, trying to locate his Chevette. The fact that it was a Sunday made no difference in the number of vehicles present. Marked and unmarked cars stretched away in profusion on either side of him. Just another working day. Criminals didn't take weekend breaks, thought Finch as he found his own car. The metal of the door handle was uncomfortably hot. He slid behind the wheel, immediately winding down both front windows in an effort to drive out some of the sickly, cloying heat.

As he pulled away he felt a slight breeze on his face. Even that was warm. Perspiration beaded on his face, but despite the unbearable temperatures Finch felt a peculiar coldness within himself.

He looked at his watch and saw that it was 11.36 a.m.

He swung the car in the direction of Kensington, hoping that the drive would not be too tortuous.

Twice during the journey he almost hit, or was hit by, another car. It was as if his concentration had evaporated as surely as rain beneath the scorching sun. Finch gripped the wheel tighter, trying to focus his mind on his driving. Visions of Chris and Theresa kept surfacing to torment him.

Perhaps he was a little disturbed by the depth of feeling which he found he still had for her. Despite their abrasive meetings he retained an affection for her which he sometimes wished he could discard. But at the moment all he could think of was the safety of his family.

He prayed that for once she had listened to reason and left the city as he'd asked, but as he turned the car into Melbury Road, he felt that icy coldness gripping him once more.

Finch parked the car two or three houses away and walked back. The street was relatively quiet apart from an elderly couple who were out for their pre-lunch stroll, and further down, a young lad who was busy cleaning his car. The doctor thought how peaceful everything looked.

It was hard to imagine that just a mile away, around Soho, Piccadilly and Bloomsbury, the streets were running with sewage and the police were probably already starting to move in to begin the evacuation operation.

Finch walked up the path to the front door and knocked three times.

There was no answer.

He tried again.

Still nothing.

Had they left between the time of his call and his arrival here? He hoped so.

He looked around but could see no sign of the car which Theresa drove. The red Renault which he'd bought her shortly after they'd married was nowhere to be seen. He'd knock once more, he decided, then leave.

He was about to turn away from the door when he heard sounds of movement inside and his heart sank.

Richard Crane opened the door, his face immediately darkening when he saw Finch.

'What the hell do you want?' Crane snapped.

'I want to see Theresa and Chris,' the doctor told him.

Crane snorted.

'Do you?' he rasped.

'If Theresa told you to send me away . . .'

Crane cut him short.

165

'She's not here,' he snarled. 'She left about two hours ago, took Christopher with her.'

'Where did she go?'

'She didn't say. All she did say was that *you'd* told her Christopher could be in danger if they stayed in London. Now I want to know what the fuck you've been telling her. I tried to get her to stay but she wouldn't listen to me.'

'Be thankful she didn't Richard,' Finch said calmly. 'Why didn't you go with her?'

'Leave the city because you think there's some disease wiping out the population? What do you take me for? You've always disliked me, haven't you? Because I took what was yours.' His voice was thick with sarcasm. 'Well, I *didn't* take her, she left because she'd had enough of you, but you couldn't let it rest, could you? Sticking your fucking nose in where it's not wanted and now, because of you, she's left.'

'I was thinking of her safety, and Christopher's. If you had any sense you'd have gone with her.'

'Well why don't *you* go now?' he snarled. 'Fuck off, and if I ever see you back here again I'll flatten you.' Crane slammed the door with an almighty crash that threatened to tear the whole jamb from the wall. Finch walked unhurriedly back towards his car, feeling too greatly relieved to be angry at Crane's behaviour.

At least his son had escaped the nightmare which looked like engulfing the whole of London.

As he started his engine a thought passed briefly through his mind.

He wondered if he would ever see Theresa or Chris again. The thought stayed with him, spinning around inside his head.

Finch drove off purposefully, knowing that there was somewhere else he had to go without delay.

As he stood waiting for the door to be opened, Finch looked around and shook his head. Flaxman Court, or at any rate the road on which the block of flats stood, was awash with reeking brown water, some of which had coagulated. There was a thick, glutinous film of scum over most of the water, and the buzzing of thousands of flies was like the low hum of an invisible generator. The insects landed gleefully on the foul-smelling muck, blissfully oblivious of the nauseating stench rising from it.

The doctor had driven along other streets in a similar condition on his journey from Kensington, some of them so badly flooded that they'd already been sealed off by the Health or Water authorities. The consequent detours had added precious time to his drive but now he stood before the door of the flat, waiting.

Lisa Foster smiled broadly when she opened the door and saw the doctor standing there.

He returned the gesture as best he could but there was no warmth in it.

'Alan, how are you?' she asked, motioning him inside.

'I should be asking *you* that question,' he said, accepting the invitation. They passed through to the sitting room.

'I'm OK now,' Lisa told him. 'I know I did everything for my mother that I could while she was alive. My conscience doesn't trouble me. I cried a lot at first, I still do sometimes, but I feel as if I'm coming to terms with her death. I just wish that it could have helped others in some way. Have there been other incidents of the disease?'

'That's what I'm here about,' he told her. 'I want to ask you a question, well, a favour more than that. Will you leave London? Now. Just pack what you need and go.'

'Is it something to do with the disease?' she said.

'It's spreading, Lisa, and no one can stop it.'

'What about a cure?'

Finch sighed.

'It's the manner in which it spreads that makes it impossible to treat.' He went on to tell her about the slugs, the cysts, the breeding and self-generation.

She listened to it all in silence, the colour slowly draining from her cheeks.

'The slugs are using human beings as food and also as . . . incubators for their eggs,' Finch said in conclusion.

167

'Then it was slugs that caused my mother's death?' Lisa asked, although it sounded more like an affirmation of the truth.

'The sewage in the streets is going to cause other health problems too,' he told her.

She seemed not to hear his last statement.

'Slugs. It doesn't seem possible.'

'I wish it weren't,' Finch said wearily.

A troubled silence descended, broken by the doctor.

'You didn't answer my question, Lisa. Will you leave London? Please. The army is being called in to evacuate this area anyway...' The words trailed off as she shook her head.

'Where am I going to go?' she asked him.

'It doesn't matter. Just leave the city. Go to one of your brothers or sisters. It's not important where you go but you have to get out.'

'Will the whole of the city be evacuated?' she wanted to know.

He shook his head.

'It's difficult to say. That isn't the plan at the moment but no one knows how events will turn out. If the slugs can't be contained in this one area then mass evacuation is the only answer.'

'You said you couldn't cure the people who catch the disease. What will happen to them?'

'The police and army have orders to shoot anyone infected.'

'Fight violence *with* violence,' she said, with obvious disapproval.

'Lisa, for God's sake, this isn't the time to be discussing the morality of the situation. People are going to die, hundreds of them, maybe even thousands, if something isn't done to stop the slugs and those they infect.' He turned away from her, lowering his voice slightly. 'I feel so helpless.' Finch laughed humourlessly. 'I'm supposed to be a doctor but I can't do a damn thing to help anyone. I couldn't even help your mother, or that young lad who was brought to me.'

'You can't blame yourself, Alan,' Lisa told him.

He turned to face her again.

'I may not be able to cure those who are already infected but at least I can try to stop some people from being killed. That's why I came here, to ask you to leave London before it's too late.'

'I haven't got anyone left now my mother's dead. The rest of my family are like strangers to me. I'm like you, Alan. We're both alone. Let me stay with you, let me help. I owe it to my mother.'

Finch shook his head almost imperceptibly, his gaze lowered. But he didn't speak.

'You're staying even though you say you can't do anything to help the victims,' Lisa continued. 'You're staying because you owe it to yourself, to your own pride. That's the reason *I* won't leave. I watched my mother die, Alan, I'm not running out now. Not when I know that others are suffering like she did.'

Finally he looked at her, seeing and hearing a strength which before he had only glimpsed. Now that strength, that fire, was on full view. During his career, Finch had learned that different people reacted to death in different ways. Lisa was showing it a defiant face, daring it to meet her head-on as it had met her mother.

He nodded, a slight smile on his lips.

'Come on,' he said, quietly. 'We've got to go. You'd better get some clothes together.'

Lisa rose and hurried off to her bedroom while Finch crossed to the sitting room window and looked out at the scum-splashed street.

An army landrover had come to a halt opposite, and as he watched, four men, automatic rifles held across their chests, jumped down from the back of the vehicle and split up, each of them making for a different door.

'Ready,' Lisa called, emerging from the bedroom with a large black hold-all. Finch turned to look at her and smiled his approval. She had changed into a pair of jeans, faded blue tennis shoes and a white T-shirt. Finch took the bag from her and they left the flat, walking close together, passing one of

169

the soldiers as they approached the doctor's car.

As he pulled away, Finch glanced across at his companion, who was busy fastening her long brown hair into a pony tail. She suddenly didn't look so vulnerable anymore. Her face, though still delicately feminine, was now set in hard lines which mirrored the determination within her.

He drove on.

Twenty-nine

Despite Sir James Hughes' insistence that the evacuation of the affected areas should be completed with as little fuss as possible, by 3.59 that Sunday afternoon television news-flashes on both the BBC and ITV networks had informed most of the country of what was happening in Soho, Bloomsbury and Piccadilly.

Those who didn't see the news on TV heard it on the radio, or by word of mouth.

The following day they would read about it in their papers. Some newspapers would even report that London was facing a plague almost on a par with 1665.

As yet, the tide of fear was rising quickly but quietly.

By morning it would have reached panic level.

Telephone switchboards were jammed as relatives and friends outside London tried to contact those in the city.

The police arrested at least a dozen people for looting evacuated houses.

Over fifty bodies were discovered in and around the area dubbed somewhat dramatically 'The Danger Zone'. Of those found, at least half had died of the disease. Most of the others had been their unfortunate victims.

A man was found with a carving knife embedded in his eye – its final resting place after his wife had used it to stab him approximately thirty-four times. She was lying in another room, dead of the contagion.

A woman and her child were found dismembered, but their killer, at the time, was nowhere to be found. He was later seen running down an alley, attempting to bury the axe he carried in the back of a policeman.

A corporal in the Coldstream Guards shot the man dead.

Four of the bodies discovered had been devoured by slugs.

The police and army had been given orders that only specially-equipped units were to remove the bodies of the dead. This they did with the utmost care, placing the corpses in transit vans so that they could be transported to the goods yard at Euston. Here massive funeral pyres had been built and the corpses were immolated under the watchful eye of members of the army medical corps.

When this particular piece of news reached the press there was a great deal of protest from the public.

The Prime Minister appeared on television that evening to assure the viewers that the situation was *under control*, the Whitehall euphemism for 'we couldn't give a fuck as long as it doesn't affect us'.

And, as yet, it didn't.

Despite the catalogue of horrors which escalated gradually through Sunday and into Monday, the deaths, the slug attacks and the disease did, indeed, remain where they had originated.

But how long this state of affairs would last no one knew.

The evacuation continued.

The house searches continued.

More bodies were found.

By 1.06 a.m. on Monday, the police and the army had effectively sealed off the 'Danger Zone'.

Deep below ground the slugs waited.

Monday – the 17th

Thirty

He hadn't slept very well the previous night, but Alan Finch still felt almost abnormally alert. His mind was so crammed with thoughts and ideas that he had found it almost impossible to rest. He could remember dozing for a couple of hours, but after the phone had rung at about six that morning he hadn't bothered settling back for another hour. He'd jumped out of bed, taken a long shower and dressed. At half past six he'd wandered downstairs and made coffee and toast. He'd sat at the kitchen table watching the breakfast TV news on the little black and white portable on the worktop as he sipped the hot black coffee.

The evacuation of dwellings in and around Bloomsbury, Piccadilly and Soho was progressing well but there were still a great many people to be moved. Many, of course, had left of their own accord after hearing what was happening from the media, but the task was by no means complete even if it was, as the newsreader put it, 'well in hand'.

The phone call which had roused Finch from his light slumber had been from the police, telling him that his surgery could not be used again until further notice because it came within the evacuation area. Finch and his colleagues and patients were to use alternative premises near Brompton Road.

The doctor finished his coffee, then got to his feet and headed for the stairs, pausing before the door of the spare room. He knocked lightly and pushed it open, peering around the white-painted partition.

Lisa was still sleeping. She lay on her back, one leg drawn

175

up slightly, the covers pushed back from her naked body.

Finch could not resist a swift glance at her supple form, but then, administering himself a swift mental rebuke, he backed out of the room. He was surprised to find that his cheeks were burning. He managed a faint smile. Was he actually embarrassed? He'd examined dozens of women in his professional capacity. He'd seen more naked bodies than most but not, he told himself, displayed in quite such a provocative fashion as now. He rubbed a hand across his face, then banged on the door loudly, coughing exaggeratedly.

'Lisa,' he called.

'Yes, OK, come in,' she murmured, her voice thick with sleep.

He waited a second, then popped his head around the door once again.

She was sitting up in bed, the sheets pulled above her breasts, her eyes heavy-lidded. He smiled at her and she smiled back sleepily.

'There's toast and coffee downstairs,' he told her.

She thanked him, asked him if she could take a shower and said she'd be down in fifteen minutes. Finch retreated from the room for the second time and returned to the kitchen, where he spooned instant coffee into another mug and replaced the kettle on the stove. As he waited for it to boil he thought about his conversation with Lisa the previous night. She had, it appeared, more or less come to terms with the death of her mother and had spoken freely about her feelings. Finch had listened with interest, his respect growing by the minute for this young woman, who when he'd first seen her less than a week ago had looked so frail and vulnerable.

Less than a week, he thought. Had all this happened so fast? So much pain and suffering in such a short time? It didn't seem possible.

Lisa entered the kitchen a moment later, dressed in the same faded blue tennis shoes but a clean pair of jeans and a sweatshirt. She sat down opposite him and sipped at her coffee. He asked if she'd slept well. She asked him what was going on with respect to the crisis.

Finch repeated what he'd heard on the news.

'One square mile doesn't sound like a very large area,' he continued. 'But there must be hundreds of people who are still in danger, and if the police and army are searching every building individually, there's no wonder it's taking time.'

'Do you think the disease will spread, Alan?' she asked him.

Finch shrugged.

'As long as the slugs continue to breed then I can't see any way of stopping it,' he told her.

'Isn't anyone working on a cure?' she wanted to know.

'There *is* no cure. Once initial contact has been made the incubation period is so short there simply isn't enough time to help the victim. I'm surprised your mother lasted so long...' He stopped in mid-sentence, lowering his gaze. 'Oh, God, I'm sorry, Lisa. I didn't mean to say that.'

She reached across the table and gently touched his hand, holding it until he faced her once more.

'I'm sorry,' he repeated. 'If I'd have been any kind of doctor she probably wouldn't have died.'

'There was nothing more you could have done,' Lisa said. 'Nothing *anyone* could have done would have saved her.'

Finch was about to say something else when there was a loud banging on his front door.

He looked up in surprise, then got to his feet and passed through the sitting room to the hall.

The banging continued until he opened the door.

A uniformed constable stood there.

'Doctor Alan Finch?' he said.

Finch nodded.

'Would you come with me please, sir?' the policeman said, taking a step back, and Finch caught sight of the red-and-white parked closeby. The driver was also looking across at him.

'What's happened?' the doctor wanted to know.

'We were told to pick you up and take you to the Yard, sir. Mr Bennett asked for you to be there. It's important.'

Finch nodded and reached for his coat, turning to see Lisa standing behind him.

'Is something wrong, Alan?' she said, seeing the policeman.

'Come on,' he said. 'You're coming with me.'

'I wasn't told about the young lady, sir,' the constable said.

'I'm not leaving her here alone.'

The uniformed man looked at Lisa, then at Finch. He nodded and headed back to the car, followed by his two charges. They all climbed into the car which, seconds later, sped off.

Thirty-one

Fuck the newspapers. Fuck the TV too, thought Keith Turner as he stood outside the Love Shop gazing at the full length, life size photograph of a naked Chinese girl with long black hair which reached her bottom. Beside this photo was another, similar one of a white girl. Both of the shots were old now, crinkled and yellowing at the edges, but the smiles of the girls as they looked back over their bare shoulders still seemed fresh and inviting to Keith.

Fuck the newspapers, he thought again, fumbling in his trouser pocket for his wallet. He didn't give a shit about any plague or whatever the hell it was they were on about. He'd been coming to the Love Shop every day for the last eight months. No matter which shift he'd worked he always found time to come and see his girls. He felt that they *were* his, he saw more of them than most men. A lot more, he thought with a chuckle. The neon sign over the door was lighted, even though it was only ten o'clock in the morning. Some of the small bulbs in the glowing sign had burned out, but he didn't need to read what it said, he knew it by heart:

Then, below that, in much smaller letters, scrawled with a felt-tip pen on a piece of cardboard and stuck on the door with Blu-Tack:

NO ONE UNDER THE AGE OF 18 ALLOWED PAST THIS POINT.
ANYONE LIKELY TO BE OFFENDED SHOULD NOT ENTER THESE PREMISES.

He pushed open the door and walked in. An unshaded light bulb hung above him, lighting his way as he descended the narrow staircase towards a curtain of beads which hung across the doorway at the bottom. He brushed through it, the beads rattling. There was a small desk immediately to his right. Behind it sat a fat, bearded man in his thirties. He was reading a newspaper and eating fish and chips, wiping his fingers on a dirty T-shirt which bore the slogan:

AIDS TURNS FRUITS INTO VEGETABLES

The smell of the food mingled with a powerful odour of damp but it was one which Keith had come to tolerate, almost welcome. He paid his money to the man, who handed back the change without looking up, his attention still on the paper.

'Any booth,' he said, motioning towards the line of closed doors which confronted Keith.

. He walked to the first booth, stepped inside and locked it behind him. The cubicle was no larger than one in a public lavatory. The walls were painted white, or what had once been white. Now they were cracked and peeling, pieces flaking off like scabrous skin. There was a single plastic seat facing what looked like a letterbox. The room smelt musky. The smell of dried perspiration and semen.

Keith seated himself and fumbled in his jacket for the coins he'd brought. There were ten fifty-pence pieces. Enough to give him at least ten minutes' viewing of the girl who, at this moment, waited behind the wall he faced. He liked it early in the morning for, more often than not, he was the only punter in the place. Others didn't start arriving until midday. Before he inserted the first 50p in the appointed slot, Keith unzipped his trousers and freed his penis which was already beginning to swell with anticipation. Smiling, he pushed in the coin and the partition rose, giving him a clear view of the area beyond.

It was about eight feet square, and he could see other peepholes for the booths on the far side. All, at the moment, closed.

There was a girl sitting naked in the middle of the tiny arena smoking a cigarette and chewing on a bacon sandwich. She looked around almost in surprise as the box opened and she found herself the subject of Keith's lecherous gaze. She took a last drag on her cigarette, then stubbed it out and pushed away the sandwich. Vicki hadn't expected any punters as early as this, in fact she hadn't expected any at all after what she'd read in the papers. Standing as it did in Lexington Street, not that far from Soho, she had expected 'Loveshop' to be closed. In fact she had even contemplated not coming to work, but she needed the money. Her kids had to be clothed and fed.

She was twenty-five, two years younger than Keith, but her face was pale and drawn and beneath the harsh lights she looked ten years older. However, almost immediately, the lights dimmed and a thunderous explosion of music filled the place. Vicki got to her feet and began dancing as provocatively as was possible at ten o'clock in the morning with her greasy breakfast slopping around inside her. She moved closer to the peep-hole through which Keith stared, rubbing her hands over her breasts, teasing her nipples in a vain attempt to make them stick out.

Keith began masturbating.

After a minute he swiftly pushed another coin into the slot as the partition began to descend, his other hand speeding up its action on his swollen organ.

Vicki continued her practised gyrations, turning away briefly when she couldn't suppress a yawn.

Keith, his ears filled with the deafening sound of the music, his eyes glued to Vicki, continued rubbing his penis, hoping that he would come before his fifty-pence pieces ran out.

Neither of them heard the screams from outside the booth.

The yells of agony uttered by the fat man as he struggled to escape the black slugs which were feeding on his ample body.

As the partition began to drop once more, Keith shoved in another coin, his breath coming in short gasps now as he watched Vicki's frenzied movements. She licked her lips, then tried to push her large breasts towards her own mouth, flicking at her nipples with her tongue. Christ, she thought, wasn't this bastard ever going to run out of money?

The music pounded away incessantly, covering the soft slurping noises made by the slugs as they eased their way effortlessly beneath the door of the booth. A black trail of them, like spilled oil, flowed from the lavatory of the club, then formed two prongs. One had engulfed the fat doorman, the other was forcing its way inside the small cubicle, like a thin finger trying to prise a path between two narrow surfaces. Even the larger slugs gained access without too much trouble.

Keith saw that he was down to just two coins so he speeded up the movement of his hand, the glorious feelings of orgasm beginning to envelop him.

He stood up, stooping slightly so that he could still see through the slit, but also wanting Vicki to see him.

She realized that he was nearly finished so, as a special treat, she moved closer to the opening, pushing her breasts towards it, allowing Keith to touch the quivering mounds with his free hand. The contact was sufficient. He grunted loudly as he climaxed, white fluid spouting from his penis in thick gouts, some of which splashed Vicki's breasts. She didn't complain, though. She merely smiled her practised smile and looked in at him, watching as he milked the last drops from his organ.

She saw the slugs gathered behind him in the cubicle.

Vicki backed off, her eyes riveted to the monstrous black horde which was moving closer to Keith. She tried to shout a warning but the music was too loud and, to her horror, she saw that the metal slat was beginning to drop once more. She banged on the wall in a last desperate attempt to alert him and then she was left with the insane vision of a man, trousers

181

around his knees and penis clutched in his hand, about to be engulfed by slugs. What a stupid way to die, she thought.

Inside the booth, Keith screamed as the first of the creatures bit into him. Blood spurted from the wounds and he fell to his knees, trying to reach the door, trying to unlock it, but the slimy mass of slugs prevented him from escaping. As they slithered over him, driving their sickle-like teeth into his flesh, he bellowed his agony. The sickly white walls of the cubicle were sprayed crimson as one of the slugs ate through his carotid artery. Keith fell forward into the seething mass.

There was a door at one end of the small arena close to where Vicki stood and she bolted for it, unconcerned about her nakedness, wanting only to escape this unspeakable horror.

The music pounded away relentlessly as she pulled at the door. The wood was swollen with dampness and it did not open easily.

Perhaps the space underneath had been too narrow for them to slide through. Or perhaps they were content to wait. Whatever the reason, the slugs outside had slithered up on top of each other against the door until they were almost at chest height.

Vicki tugged harder and the door flew open.

She had time for one scream before the ravenous wall of black death collapsed upon her.

The music continued to play, masking the obscene sounds made by the feasting slugs.

The foyer of the Regent Palace Hotel in Piccadilly was like a huge, well-decorated mausoleum. As silent as a crypt. Completely devoid of guests or staff. Five members of the Coldstream Guards had arrived an hour earlier to ensure that no one remained in the building. The manager had assured them that the place was empty but they had to be certain.

It took time, as the hotel was one of Europe's largest. Sergeant Derek Pagett and the manager, Martin Forbes, were still walking the labyrinthine corridors in search of any stray guests or staff. Both carried pass keys which would allow them entrance to any room, in the form of electronic cards which would slip the locking mechanism of the door.

Forbes was on the seventh floor. Pagett, he knew, was one floor above him. Every so often, in the unearthly silence which filled the hotel, he would hear movements from above as the sergeant passed swiftly from room to room.

Perspiration was soaking into Forbes' shirt, not all of it, he realized, the product of the scorching day. He moved quickly along the well-lit corridors, his ears alert for the slightest sound. As he reached each bend he would slow down as if expecting someone, or something, to be waiting for him around the next corner.

He pushed on, flinging open the doors which took him past the central staircase.

There were sounds close by.

Heavy footfalls.

Forbes tried to control his laboured breathing, pressing himself back into a doorway as the loud thumps drew nearer.

Pagett came striding through the door to the stairs, his automatic rifle held across his chest.

'Found anything?' he said.

Forbes shook his head gratefully, relieved that he hadn't.

'I'll go down to the sixth floor,' the sergeant said, and thudded off down the stairs.

Forbes hurried along the corridor towards the lifts, his heart thumping just that little bit faster than normal.

In a room to his left he heard a loud bang.

The manager froze, moving nearer, aware that his hands were shaking.

The sound came again.

Like wood on wood.

He reached for the pass key, inserting it into the electronic lock, pressing the slim card down until the green light above the handle flickered on. He swallowed hard and prepared to enter.

There was another bang, and the sound of breathing.

It was a second or two before he realized that the breathing was his own.

He pushed open the door and looked inside.

One of the guests had left the wardrobe door open and the breeze coming through the window had caused it to slam against the frame.

Forbes sighed, closed the door behind him and moved on.

He reached the lifts, satisfied that the seventh floor was clear. Pagett was checking the one below, so he decided to go down to five. All the lifts were on the ground floor so he jabbed the appropriate button and waited for the car to rise. The numbers lit up as it ascended.

One. Two. Three.

The manager took a handkerchief from his pocket and wiped the film of perspiration from his face.

Four. Five.

The quicker he got out of here the better.

Six.

He glanced behind him, half expecting to see one of the diseased maniacs coming at him with a knife.

The lift arrived.

There was no maniac behind him.

The doors slid open.

He stepped in. Pressing button five, he leant back against the rear wall of the car as it descended, quickly bumping to a halt at the designated floor.

Forbes took a deep breath, as if he were about to immerse his head in water, then he stepped out and hurried along the corridor to his right performing the same routine as he'd done on the other floors. As he walked, his feet thumped out a hollow rhythm on the thin carpet, but above him he could hear Pagett's progress.

The knowledge that the sergeant was also in the building brought a small amount of comfort to Forbes, although he dared not think what else might be skulking in one of the still unchecked rooms.

He turned the corner into another corridor and stopped short.

Someone had either turned out the lights or they had blown.

The corridor was in darkness.

Not the impenetrable blackness of night or of an unlit cellar, but still dark enough to send a shiver down his spine at the thought of passing along it. He clenched his fists and walked on into the gloom, his eyes darting furtively from side to side. He tried to swallow but found that his throat had constricted into a tight knot. His heart thumped against his ribs as if trying to escape the confines of his chest.

The lifts were perhaps fifty yards ahead of him.

It seemed like fifty miles.

As Forbes reached what he guessed was roughly the middle of the corridor, he stopped and listened.

There was no sound. Only the blood rushing through his veins, roaring in his ears.

No sound.

Not even that of Pagett and his heavy boots.

Silence.

Fear suddenly hit him like an invisible fist. He had never felt so alone and afraid in his life. A groan of terror escaped him as he stood motionless. He looked back over his shoulder, then ran, pounding down the darkened corridor in a desperate effort to escape the blackness. It seemed to follow him like a living thing until, finally, he emerged into the light, almost stumbling, his legs trembling.

He couldn't stand this any longer, he decided. To hell with it. Let Pagett search the rest of the building.

He didn't bother using the lift but hurtled down the stairs instead, taking them two at a time, his only concern now to be free of the stifling, threatening confines of the hotel.

As he reached the first floor landing he tripped and went sprawling, rolling over several times before crashing into the wall. The impact knocked the wind from him and he lay still for a moment gasping, but spurred on by his terror, he soon clambered to his feet and hurried down the remaining steps towards the foyer.

The stench struck him first.

Forbes slowed his pace as he reached the foyer, held back by the reeking, nauseating odour. Fighting back the urge to vomit, he felt as if he were going to faint.

At first he thought he was imagining what he saw in the foyer, that the fall he'd taken moments earlier had affected his perception in some way. But no, there was no doubt about it.

The floor of the foyer was moving.

Undulating gently as if someone were blowing air underneath it.

It was a second or two before he realized what he was seeing.

Slugs covered every square inch of the large foyer.

A living black carpet of writhing forms which slithered and oozed in their own thick mucoid secretions. The closest and largest of them were already sliding up onto the steps where Forbes swayed unsteadily.

He tried to back away but his foot slid off the edge of a step, causing him to overbalance.

Arms flailing madly, he pitched forward into the mass of slugs.

Many were crushed beneath him, their bodies bursting like overripe fruit, but hundreds more covered his body in a matter of seconds, all eager to taste his flesh.

He managed one deafening scream before a particularly large slug ate through his windpipe.

Up on the fourth floor Sergeant Pagett heard the scream and came running. Simultaneously, the men who waited outside in the Landrover crashed into the building's foyer, stopping short as they saw the slugs, many of which turned and began slithering towards them.

'Get out!' Pagett bellowed at his men as he neared the bottom of the stairs, and they needed no second warning. The sergeant himself looked down and saw that something lay amongst the slugs gathered around the foot of the staircase. An almost shapeless mass which was covered by the black abominations. He saw blood and, with horror, realized that what was beneath the slimy blanket of death was Forbes. One bloodied hand, two of the fingers already eaten to the bone, rose from the mass as if soliciting help.

Pagett gritted his teeth and backed off, raising the rifle to

186

his shoulder. He drew a bead on the point where he guessed Forbes' head to be and fired twice, the thunderous report of the FN echoing around the hotel foyer. The hand dropped and the slug-covered shape remained still. The sergeant muttered something to himself, then glanced towards the main doors of the building. He might just be able to make it across the undulating black sea of slugs, but one slip and he would end up like Forbes.

The sergeant spun round and headed back up the stairs until he reached the large, frosted-glass window at the first landing. Without hesitation he drove his rifle butt through it, shattering the glass. Moving quickly, he hauled himself up onto the ledge, cutting his hands on several jagged shards in the process.

The drop to the street below was perhaps twelve or fifteen feet. It didn't look like much of a distance, except that he would be landing on concrete.

He glanced back into the foyer at the slugs and did not hesitate any longer.

He jumped.

The impact broke both his ankles, the sound of snapping bone audible in the nearly-deserted street, and Pagett rolled over, his face a mask of pain. In a matter of seconds his men were with him, carrying him back to the waiting landrover, away from the hotel.

Away from the slugs.

Thirty-two

As they were escorted from the police car to the main entrance of New Scotland Yard, Finch wondered if this was what a

criminal felt like as he was being taken into custody. Flanked
on both sides by uniformed men, the doctor almost felt like
pulling a blanket over his head. Had the circumstances been
different he might well have found the situation amusing. As
it was, he and Lisa walked briskly into the building and
followed one of the uniformed men to a lift. It carried them to
the fifth floor, where they all stepped out into a long corridor
which looked somewhat familiar to Finch.

During the journey the doctor had attempted to discover
what was going on but the two policemen seemed to know
little more than Finch himself. Either that or they'd been
instructed not to divulge any information.

The trio stopped outside a door and the constable knocked,
leaving them alone as it was opened.

George Bennett smiled at Finch and beckoned him inside,
casting a puzzled glance at Lisa. The doctor made swift
introductions, explaining the somewhat tenuous reasons for
Lisa's presence.

'I'm sorry to hear about your mother,' said Bennett when
the doctor had finished.

Lisa smiled thinly at him and sat down in the proffered
chair.

Finch nodded greetings to the other men present. To Sir
James Hughes. To DI Grogan and a military man he hadn't
seen before.

Dressed in combat fatigues, the soldier was in his thirties,
perhaps a year or two older than Finch. On the belt round his
waist there was a holster and the doctor could see the butt of
an automatic pistol protruding from it. The man had bright
blond hair which glinted beneath the fluorescents. When he
moved, Finch saw that he dragged his left leg slightly.

The soldier looked strangely incongruous alongside the
other occupants of the room, Finch thought. And a little
menacing too.

Captain Sean Maconnell returned Finch's nod of greeting,
reserving an approving glance for Lisa. Maconnell had been
an officer in the Coldstream Guards for four years, having
risen from the ranks since first joining back in 1966. He came

188

from a family which was anything but steeped in military tradition. His father had spent most of his National Service time in the glass house, and his grandfather had been shot in 1916 as a conscientious objector. Maconnell loved the army, though, and wondered now how he would survive without it. Even after an IRA sniper's bullet had shattered his left hip six years ago, during a raid on an arms cache in the Falls Road, he had pulled through against all odds. The prospect of getting back into uniform had driven him on. For a time, doctors had thought that the Armalite bullet had succeeded in condemning him to crutches for the rest of his life. Maconnell had refused to accept their prognosis, and after months of pain and numerous operations he had managed to walk once more, albeit with a limp. But he didn't complain and only on odd occasions did it still cause him pain.

'Before we start,' Finch said. 'Could someone tell me what's going on? Why was I called?'

He was looking at Bennett but he didn't care who answered the question.

'The affected area has been cleared,' Hughes answered, scratching the scar on his chin. 'We must destroy the slugs now, before they have a chance to move on.'

'But we still don't know how to destroy them,' Finch said.

'We're sticking with the idea of cyanide,' Bennett informed him.

'But it can't be done because of the risk of poisoning,' said Finch, aghast.

Bennett ignored the doctor's protestations.

'As long as the slugs are spread through the tunnels that idea could never succeed. No matter how much cyanide we pumped down into the sewers we couldn't be sure of killing them all,' Finch added.

'If they could be gathered in one place it might just work,' Bennett said, quietly.

'There must be miles of tunnels under that area,' the doctor exclaimed. 'It's impossible.'

'Nothing is impossible,' countered Maconnell, catching Finch's gaze and holding it.

189

'What we propose to do is to drive the slugs back along the tunnels,' said the officer. 'The sewers would be sealed off one by one until all these bloody creatures were forced into one spot. Then the cyanide could be released.'

'How do you expect to "drive" them?' Finch asked.

'I'll send some engineers down there with flame throwers. Most animals retreat from fire, don't they?'

'You can't use flame throwers,' Hughes said. 'You'd blow up the entire system. We have to find another way.'

Bennett stroked his chin thoughtfully.

'Why *drive* them?' he said. 'Why not use a lure?'

The others looked at him, their expressions ranging from surprise to bewilderment.

'Let the slugs follow something instead. Lead them to the place where they're to be destroyed, don't drive them.'

'And what do we lead them with?' Grogan asked, taking another drag on his cigarette.

'They feed on human flesh, right?' the pathologist said, his tone calm and measured. 'Give them what they want.'

'My God, you're not serious,' Grogan said, gaping in astonishment. 'You want to sacrifice the lives of innocent men just so they can act as fucking bait?'

'What's a dozen or so lives compared to the number it could save?' Bennett challenged.

'There's no guarantee it would work anyway,' the DI persisted.

'I think there is,' the pathologist told him. 'The secretion left by the leading slugs, the slime trails, seems to act as a stimulant for the others. Much the same as pheromones works for ants. The stronger the secretion, the more likely the slugs are to follow it.' He paused. 'Men injected with that secretion would automatically attract the slugs.'

'But if they were injected, they'd die of the disease anyway,' Finch said.

'Not for at least six hours,' the pathologist countered. 'Six hours to clear the tunnels, that's all the time we'd need.'

'That's murder,' said Grogan. 'You're talking about murdering men in cold blood.'

'I'm talking about saving the rest of this city, millions for Christ's sake,' Bennett snapped. 'It's the only way.' He studied the faces of the others in the room. 'Don't look at me passing moral judgements, you all know I'm right.'

Commissioner Hughes turned and looked at the map of the sewer tunnels.

'How would we go about it?' he said, quietly, almost conspiratorially.

'Sir, you can't be serious,' Grogan interrupted.

The commissioner turned on him, eyes blazing.

'What choice do we have?' he snapped. 'I don't like this any more than you. I wish there *was* another way but there isn't.'

The two men regarded each other coldly for a moment then Grogan shook his head resignedly.

'The men would be put into the sewer tunnels ahead of the slugs,' Bennett said. 'They'd move in front of the hordes until they converged at a place where the cyanide could be released.'

'That gives them a great choice,' Grogan snapped. 'They either get eaten alive, poisoned or die of this fucking disease.'

'How would we seal the tunnels?' Maconnell wanted to know.

'Groups of your men could follow the slugs, at a safe distance. The tunnels could be brought down when the signal was given. The men following wouldn't be in danger as long as they kept well back. The slugs would be too intent on following the infected men.'

'So first we pinpoint where the slugs are concentrated,' Hughes said, studying the map again. He lowered his voice slightly. 'God, there must be so many of them.'

'That shouldn't be too difficult,' Maconnell said. 'Find the location of their last victims and they should be in the vicinity.'

'Where are you going to obtain the secretion in order to inject the men?' Finch wanted to know.

'From the slugs that hatched from that young boy's body,' the pathologist told him.

191

'What do we tell the men who are infected?' Grogan asked. 'That they're going to be used as food for slugs? That if the slugs don't get them they're going to die anyway?'

'We tell them nothing,' Hughes said before the pathologist could answer. He sighed. 'If any of them do make it out of the tunnels, Bennett, what happens to them then? We can't just sit around and watch them die.'

Bennett swallowed hard, then shrugged. When he spoke, his voice was low.

'They'll have to be killed. Shot, if the disease is too far advanced by the time they emerge.'

'Like rabid dogs, eh?' grunted Grogan.

An uneasy silence settled, almost as if the enormity of the proposed solution had robbed the room's occupants of the ability to speak.

Grogan lit another cigarette. Bennett sat with his hands folded on his lap, head lowered slightly.

Finch got up, went over to the map of the sewers and studied it carefully.

'The effluent will be re-cycled into drinking water,' he murmured. 'Remember what the Water Board men told us? We can't use cyanide to kill the slugs.'

'But the area where they'll be destroyed will be sealed off,' Maconnell protested.

'The slugs might not be able to get out but, short of building walls, there's no way we're going to be able to stop that poison reaching these other tunnels.' He ran his finger over the diagram. 'And, eventually, the Thames.'

'It's the only solution we have,' Hughes told him. 'We can't burn them, we can't blow them up. Poison is the only alternative.'

Finch was looking at the diagram again, narrowing his eyes as he studied several other lines, some drawn in blue, which ran parallel with the sewer tunnels.

'What are these?' he asked, indicating the lines.

'They're electricity cables,' Grogan told him.

Finch turned and looked at the others in the room, a slight smile on his face.

192

'That's how we destroy them,' he said. 'Electrocute them.'

Bennett too found that he could smile. He nodded admiringly.

'Would it work?' Hughes wanted to know.

'I don't see why not,' Bennett told him. 'A large enough current applied for long enough ought to kill them and there's no better conductor than water.'

'What sort of voltage do those cables carry?' Maconnell asked.

'We don't need to use those,' Hughes said. 'We can set up portable generators. When the slugs have been drawn into position we'll fry them.' He chuckled.

Maconnell smiled broadly.

For the first time, Lisa spoke.

'There's one thing you haven't decided,' she said, quietly. 'Who's going to be the bait? Which men go into the sewers?'

Thirty-three

At 10.28 that morning, men of the Royal Engineers succeeded in locating the first mass of slugs. They were between Dean Street and Shaftesbury Avenue in a mid-level tunnel.

Five minutes later a second group were discovered in a storm-relief sewer under Brewer Street.

A wider sweep of the area revealed the third, and largest, concentration of the creatures beneath Sherwood Street.

They appeared to be stationary, but for how long no one dared guess.

The officers in charge of each detachment of engineers relayed the information to Maconnell, who was still at New Scotland Yard, then to units of police who were also in the vicinity of Piccadilly.

Bennett lifted the last slug from the jar and deposited it in a specimen tray normally reserved for human organs. The pathologist watched the writhing black monstrosities for a moment with a mixture of fear and loathing. Some were as much as five inches long, and as thick as his index finger. He carried the tray across the lab and set it down carefully on the other workbench, his eyes never leaving the slugs, which were sliding up the sides. He knocked one back with the sharp end of a scalpel, severing one of its eye-stalks as he did. Then, opening a cupboard above him, the pathologist took out a bottle of sulphuric acid and unscrewed the stopper. He poured the lethal liquid over the slugs, watching almost gleefully as the corrosive fluid ate into their soft, slimy bodies. A choking stench rose to fill his nostrils but he continued to gaze at the creatures. The tray began to fill up with a sickly yellow mixture of pus and slime as the last of the slugs simply dissolved. Bennett emptied the glutinous contents down the sink then ran the hot tap, washing away the last vestiges of corruption. He dropped the tray in a plastic bag and sealed it, knowing that he must dispose of it as soon as possible, then he returned to the jar and peered in.

There was a thick, reeking coagulation of mucus at least two inches deep inside it.

The pathologist took the first of three syringes laid out close to him and drew off some of the slime. He then filled the rest of the receptacle with saline solution so that the fluid would flow more easily in the bloodstreams of the men to be injected.

He paused for a moment, sighing.

The plan to infect men with the disease had been his idea. An honest attempt to solve what was becoming an increasingly insoluble problem. But as he looked at the syringe and its deadly contents, he realized just how close to the truth Grogan had been.

Bennett was condemning at least a dozen men to the most agonising and horrific death imaginable.

He tried to balance that view against his own feeling that the sacrifice was necessary in order to save many more lives, but still that nagging doubt continued to surface in his mind.

Murderer.

The word flashed brightly in his mind's eye like a neon sign.

Think how many would be saved, though?

But the men who are going to die. They have families.

It's a small sacrifice.

Will their wives, girlfriends, children and parents agree with you?

Bennett stood still for a moment, resting his arms on the work top, trying to clear his mind, attempting to stop the endless self-accusations.

This *was* the only way, he told himself, filling another syringe.

As he did so, he noticed that his hands were shaking slightly.

At 10.43 six large Scania lorries arrived in Piccadilly Circus. They parked in a rough semi-circle around the Eros monument.

Detective Inspector Ray Grogan watched as troops and police opened the back doors of the lorries.

Inside each one was a KVA 1000 portable generator, fifteen feet long and as tall as a man. The machines were given a hasty check-over by the civilian engineers who maintained them.

As Grogan looked on, cables were run from the generators to the open manholes and were lowered into the gloom below until they entered the stinking water. The roar of the Scania engines was replaced by a loud hum as the machines were switched on.

They were ready.

Cables as thick as a man's arm criss-crossed Piccadilly, lying there like slumbering snakes, waiting for the power to be pumped through them.

Grogan drew another cigarette out of his rapidly dwindling packet and looked at his watch.

It was 11.04.

At 11.18 one hundred men of the First Battalion, Coldstream Guards, drew lots to decide who would descend into the sewers. They were not told the purpose of the selection. One hundred pieces of paper, twelve of them marked with an 'X', had been folded and placed in a cardboard box.

It took less than five minutes for the dozen marked scraps to be retrieved.

The men holding them were ordered out into a waiting truck, and their companions sent back to their positions around Piccadilly.

The twelve men were driven to New Scotland Yard in the truck, escorted down to the pathology lab and told to wait outside.

'I wish somebody would tell us what the bleeding hell's going on,' said Private Terry Banks, shifting his feet nervously. He scratched his chubby face and looked around at his companions.

'No doubt we just 'volunteered' for something,' Chas Granger told him.

'What kind of thing?' Banks insisted.

'If we knew that we wouldn't be standing around here with our thumbs up our arses wondering, would we?' chided Pat Morrissey.

'Shut it, will you,' snapped Simon Johnson. 'Let's see what the fucking hell they want before we start getting uptight about it.' As he was a corporal, Johnson's voice carried some authority and the men duly stopped talking.

'I wish I'd got a fag,' murmured Banks, chewing the nail on his index finger.

An acid glance from Johnson silenced him.

'Come on, corp,' said Morrissey. 'What do you reckon's going on? Why do they want us?'

'They don't necessarily want *us*,' Johnson said. 'We just happen to be the silly fuckers who drew the wrong lots.'

The men suddenly drew themselves to attention as the door of the lab was opened and they saw Captain Maconnel standing there.

'Stand easy,' he said.

The men did, but they didn't relax.

'Come inside one at a time,' Maconnell said and ushered Granger forward, closing the door behind him.

Banks tried to move to a position further down the line but Johnson shook his head.

'You're next Banks,' he said. 'You wouldn't want to miss the surprise would you?'

The private muttered something under his breath but his audible murmurings were silenced when the lab door opened again. Granger did not emerge but Banks was ordered inside.

As he entered the room he saw his companion sitting on the far side of the lab.

'Roll up your right sleeve,' said Bennett brusquely, careful to avoid looking at Banks too closely, especially at his eyes. These men he was sending to their deaths must, for him, remain faceless. He brandished the hypodermic before him, gripped Banks' wrist and then ran the needle into the pulsing fat vein in the crook of his arm, pressing down carefully on the plunger, forcing 10ml of the lethal fluid into the soldier's bloodstream. Banks winced until the needle was pulled free. Bennett pushed a swab into his free hand and told him to press it against the tiny puncture until it stopped bleeding.

Banks went and sat next to Granger and the two men watched as the same procedure was carried out, with dizzying speed, on their ten companions.

When he'd finished, Bennett washed his hands.

Would guilt wash off?

He looked at Maconnell and the officer nodded, turning towards his men.

'I'm going to keep this as short and simple as I can,' he said. 'No doubt you're all wondering what's happening.' He cleared his throat, as if to make the words come forth more easily. Finally the Captain looked away and banged the work top angrily. 'Fuck it,' he rasped. His face was set in hard lines when he turned back to look at the troops. 'You're going to enter the sewer tunnels,' he said flatly, perhaps reasoning that the lie coming next wouldn't taste so bitter if it were said quickly.

'Two of our men are down there, they've got to be found. You'll be split into three groups, four men in each. Work your way towards Piccadilly, you'll find ladders leading up from the sewer tunnels where you can get out.' He tried to swallow but his throat was as dry as chalk.

'What were the shots for, sir?' Johnson asked.

It had all been rehearsed well and Maconnell did not falter as he answered.

'As you know, the slugs pass on a disease through their slime trails. The shots will protect you against that disease.' The last few words were forced out through clenched teeth. 'Are there any questions?'

'What about the two blokes who are missing, sir?' Banks wanted to know. 'What if they've got this disease? It's incurable, isn't it?'

Maconnell nodded.

'Just find them,' he said, struggling now to retain his composure. He felt like apologizing to the men, telling them the truth. The Captain finally turned away from them. 'There's a truck waiting to take you to the designated entry points. You'll descend into the sewers there.'

The men stood as one and saluted before filing out, the last one closing the lab door behind him.

As the sound of their footsteps receded down the corridor Maconnell faced the pathologist.

'There was no other choice,' Bennett said. 'Don't you think I would have found another answer if I could?'

'Damn you, Bennett, those are my men,' hissed the Captain. 'They trust me and I've just given them a bullshit story, knowing that I'm sending them to their deaths.'

'Don't think you've got the monopoly on conscience, Maconnell,' the pathologist said, quietly.

The Captain headed for the door, pausing briefly as he reached it. 'Damn you anyway,' he snarled. 'Damn you for being right.' The door slammed and Maconnell was gone.

Bennett stood alone, the only sound in the lab the slow, steady ticking of the wall clock. He glanced at it, knowing that with or without the slugs the twelve men he'd injected would be dead in six hours.

The saline solution would cause the fluid to move more quickly through their veins, spreading the infection at maximum speed.

The small red areas around the needle marks began to itch less than fifteen minutes after the men had left the lab, and more than one of them felt a dull pain growing at the base of his skull.

The infection was already beginning to set in.

At 12.03 p.m., the first of the twelve men climbed down the metal ladder towards the black maw of the tunnel beneath Shaftesbury Avenue.

Thirty-four

Alan Finch wiped the perspiration from his face and sighed. The sun seemed even hotter today. It beat down on the city like a red-hot hammer.

Next to him, Lisa stood with her head lowered slightly, straining her ears to hear the sometimes muffled voices filtering through the army radio set up in the rear of a truck. It was parked next to one of the massive Scanias which supported a KVA 1000. The generator was still humming its tuneless refrain.

DI Grogan pushed another cigarette into his mouth and fumbled in his pocket for a match. He didn't have one.

Maconnell pulled out a lighter and lit the policeman's Marlboro for him.

A voice came from the radio again, fighting against the static.

'... no sign ... any kind of movement down here,' the voice said. '... our bloke or the slugs ... so dark ... difficult to see very far ahead even with ... torches.'

Maconnell motioned for the radio operator to hand him the microphone.

'Unit One, come in.'

The set crackled again, like someone walking on cornflakes.

'Unit One. I read ... but ... hard to hear ... signal keeps breaking up.'

'How far are you from us?' the Captain wanted to know.

'... Difficult ... reckon about three hund ... yards ... a little less.' The signal broke up completely.

'Unit One, repeat,' said Maconnell, becoming agitated.

More wild hissing. Static.

'Do you read me?'

'I hear you, sir ... just about ... we ... to a bend in the tunnel ... away to the right ...'

'Can't you do anything about this?' the officer snapped, looking angrily at the radio operator.

The man fiddled with the controls but his efforts paid little dividend.

'What if the slugs don't follow them?' said Lisa.

'They will,' Finch assured her, his voice low.

Grogan took another hefty drag on his cigarette, blowing out a long stream of smoke a moment later. He tugged on his tie, loosening it slightly.

'Unit One, to Command.'

The voice came over with momentary but startling clarity, making those nearby jump.

Maconnell snatched the microphone from the radio operator.

'This is Command. Come in,' he said.

'Sir ... there's something ... tunnel behind us. I can't see what it is ... one of the other blokes is going to check it out ... splashing about ... it could be ...'

Finch, Lisa and Grogan all turned to listen as the voice on the other end of the line rose in pitch, the sound now clearly audible between short bursts of static.

'...Jesus Christ...there's thousands of them...they're in the water...on the walls...MOVE NOW...' A scream. 'Slugs everywhere... if we can make it to the next sewer exit...where the fuck is it?...' Another scream, louder. 'Oh Jesus, Jesus...I've dropped my torch...the slugs are everywhere...where's the...'

Another voice, in pain, in agony.

'HELP ME...'

'...Captain...where's the exit...they're all over us...oh JESUS...JESUS...' Another scream, one which made the hairs on the back of Finch's neck stand up.

'...WE CAN'T GET OUT... NO... OH GOD THEY'RE ON MY FACE...MY EYES...MY EYES...'

The shrieks which issued forth could have come from hell itself.

'...MY EYES...MY EYES...'

'Turn it off,' Maconnell rasped at the wireless operator.

The man hesitated a second and the officer bellowed the order again.

The sound of the screams was cut off.

An unearthly silence descended but the echo of the shrieks seemed to hang in the air like accusations.

'Oh God,' Lisa said, softly.

Finch and Maconnell exchanged glances which seemed tinged with a mixture of guilt and sorrow.

'What about the other men?' the doctor wanted to know. 'Can you contact them?'

For long moments the officer seemed lost in thought, the screams of agony still ringing all too loudly in his ears, then he nodded, shaking himself from the great weariness which had settled over him. He told the radio operator to contact the second group of men, the unit moving along the storm-relief sewer from Brewer Street. The operator began fiddling with the controls of the machine.

Private Terry Banks held his rifle across his chest as he paddled his way through the knee-high water. The man beside him, whom he knew only as Jenkins, was holding a powerful torch in one hand and a two-way radio in the other. Behind them, Chas Granger and a tall, red-haired Scot called Lewis followed, both of them occasionally peering back over their shoulders into the almost palpable blackness. Lewis pulled the torch from his belt and flicked it on, playing the beam over the walls of the tunnel behind them. It illuminated only dark, festering green mould.

'Anything up ahead?' Lewis asked as the men waded on.

'Not yet,' Jenkins said, a note of anxiety in his voice.

'How the fuck do we know we're going in the right direction?' Lewis asked.

'Keep heading straight, they told us,' said Banks, trying to breathe through his nose to minimise the rancid stench of the effluent. 'That's right, isn't it, Chas?'

His voice echoed around the tunnel.

Granger didn't answer.

'Chas.'

'What?' he snapped, his voice low and gravelly.

'They told us to keep going straight ahead,' Banks repeated, glancing back at his companion.

Granger nodded, but as he did so, he felt the pain which had fastened itself around the base of his skull like an iron fist gripping a little tighter and he winced. His skin felt as if someone had rubbed hot ash all over it, and there was perspiration on his forehead.

On one cheek two large boils were beginning to form.

'How far to Piccadilly?' Lewis wanted to know. 'These tunnels give me the shits.'

Banks laughed, a hollow chuckle which gradually died away into the silence.

'Well, if you get the shits, there's no better place to be than down a sewer,' he said.

'Yeah, highly amusing,' Lewis said. 'How far to go?'

'I reckon about eight or nine hundred yards,' Banks told him.

They moved on, Jenkins almost slipping over in the murky river of effluent. The radio in his hand suddenly erupted into life and he raised it to his ear.

'Unit Two, come in.'

They recognized the voice as Maconnell's.

'Unit Two. We hear you, sir,' Jenkins answered. 'There's still no sign of the slugs.'

There was an uncomfortable pause, then Maconnell spoke again.

'We've lost Unit One,' he said simply.

'Oh Jesus,' Terry Banks murmured.

'Maintain your progress towards Piccadilly,' the Captain told them. 'The generators are set up.'

'Generators?' said Lewis. 'What the fuck are they going to do with generators?'

Jenkins waved a hand for the big Scot to be silent.

'Understood, sir,' he said into the two-way.

'Leave this frequency open,' Maconnell said.

Then there was silence again, broken only by the splashing of the men as they battled through the reeking water.

Granger slowed his pace, the pain at the base of his skull now spreading quickly, reaching up over the back of his head and temples until it was hammering like an out-of-control pneumatic drill. He clenched his teeth.

Another large blister had formed on his neck and, beneath his uniform he could feel others chafing against the material. He put out a hand to steady himself, touching the slimy walls. Some of the slick mould stuck to his palm but it did not seem to bother him.

He glanced across at Lewis, then forward to the men ahead of him. To Jenkins with the radio and the torch and to Banks, who still held his automatic rifle across his chest.

Granger's right hand dropped to his belt, his fingers closing around the haft of his bayonet. He began to ease it from its sheath.

'Look,' Jenkins said, shining the torch back and forth.

'Which one do we take?' Lewis asked.

The tunnel curved around to the right but there was another slightly smaller outlet to the left. Filthy water was running fairly rapidly from this other tunnel, joining the main flow. The men moved on until they were level with the second tunnel and Jenkins shone the torch inside. The beam was swallowed up by the darkness after about ten yards. What lay beyond that impenetrable wall of gloom no one knew.

'I say we stay in this tunnel,' said Banks, trying to swallow but not managing it. His mouth and throat were parched. There was a dull, insistent ache at the back of his neck which seemed to be intensifying.

'I agree,' Lewis said hurriedly, anxious to move away from the gaping black mouth and its untold secrets. Secrets which none of them cared to know.

'If we take a wrong turning we're fucked,' Banks said worriedly. 'The slugs will cut us off.'

Granger eased the bayonet free of its sheath, his eyes bulging wildly in their sockets as he studied his three companions. One of the blisters on his cheek had ruptured and he could feel thick liquid running down his skin.

'Perhaps I should check with the Captain,' Jenkins offered.

'Fuck the Captain,' snapped Banks. 'He's not down here. I say we push on.'

Something thick and heavy bumped against the private's leg and he shouted in sudden, unexpected fear, his voice reverberating around the tunnel.

The other men tensed, fearing the worst.

All except Granger who was clutching the bayonet in a talon-like grip.

Banks looked down, moving back slightly, his heart thudding madly against his ribs.

'What is it?' Jenkins said, his voice a hoarse whisper.

'It's a bloody turd, that's what it is,' Banks said, breathing a sigh of relief. He turned to look at Granger. 'What about that...'

He got no further.

The bayonet flashed forward, driven with demonic strength by Granger.

As Banks opened his mouth to protest, the blade was thrust past his lips, powering into the roof of his mouth, shattering several teeth on its passage. The vicious blade tore up through his pallet, lacerating his gums and nearly severing his bottom lip as it was torn free.

The second thrust punctured his throat just below the right ear, releasing a thick fountain of blood. Granger felt the bayonet grate on bone as he twisted it, heedless of the hot fluid which splashed him.

He turned next on Lewis, who tried to swing his rifle around in an effort to cover himself. But Granger moved with surprising agility in the knee-deep effluent. He pulled the Scot towards him, driving the bayonet into his stomach just below the navel, dragging the blade upwards until it cracked against Lewis' sternum. His stomach opened like a grinning mouth, the ragged edges of the wound stretching wide as his intestines spilled forward in a steaming tangle which made a loud splash in the filthy water. Bile, thick and green, came spilling from his slashed bladder and the Scot jerked in uncontrollable spasms as he attempted to push his innards back into the hideous rent.

With a strangled cry he fell forward, his body disappearing beneath the surface.

Jenkins took his chance and ran but the water held him back and more than once he slipped and almost fell. With the weight of water against him it was as if he were running in slow motion, every step half its normal speed. He did not look back. He did not *dare* look back but he could hear the water splashing and churning as Granger pursued him, the bayonet still in his hand.

Jenkins began to moan in terror as he heard his pursuer gaining, and in his mind's eye he could see the blade descending towards his unprotected back. He still held the torch, its light bouncing around madly as he ran.

He knew he had only one chance.

Jenkins turned and swung the heavy flashlight.

It struck Granger on the temple, causing one of the boils there to burst violently. An explosion of pus spewed from the punctured boil. The impact seemed only to stun Granger momentarily, and he kept coming.

Jenkins lashed out again. This time, his attacker ducked beneath the swing, driving the blade upwards. The point punctured Jenkins' flesh in the hollow of his armpit, tearing away some muscle as it twisted free. His arm went numb and he dropped the radio into the water. He could feel blood pouring from the wound and he backed off, holding the torch before him defiantly, its beam now illuminating Granger's bloodied, blistered face. His eyes blazed maniacally as he advanced once more.

This time Jenkins brought the torch down on Granger's shoulder but the crazed man's momentum carried him forward and both of them toppled over, the stinking brown water closing over them. A flood of filth filled Jenkins' nose and mouth and his stomach contracted violently, but before he could even try to raise himself he felt something sharp being pressed against his neck.

The bayonet sliced through muscle and veins, hacking through his carotid artery with ease.

Granger rose from beneath the water like some creature from a horror film, a swamp-bred monstrosity dripping blood and stinking water. He stood motionless for a moment, then turned and headed back towards the branch tunnel, moving quickly through the water into its enveloping blackness.

This tunnel was much narrower, and when he extended both arms he was able to touch the two sides without much difficulty. He ploughed on, blind in the darkness, moving as if by instinct. But if that instinct was correct, he should soon find what he sought.

Another two or three minutes and he was there.

The metal ladder stretched upwards towards the surface.

Towards light. Away from this stinking sewer.

Away from the slugs.

Granger was in severe pain. The steady gnawing at the base of his skull had become a raging ache. The blisters which covered his face and body throbbed and pulsed, many of them leaking pus. Nevertheless, the bayonet tucked in his belt, he began to climb. When he reached the top of the ladder he paused, sucking in deep, rasping breaths. When he coughed he tasted the foul sewer water and he hawked loudly, bringing it up, retching violently in an effort to rid himself of the effluent which he'd swallowed. He hung from the ladder a moment longer, teeth gritted against the pain. Slowly, he raised the manhole cover an inch or two.

Bright sunlight flooded into his eyes and he nearly dropped the steel lid. Peering around him after his eyes began to adjust to the brilliance, he saw that the street into which he'd emerged was deserted.

Except for the solitary army truck which was parked by the kerb.

Its driver was leaning against the cab door smoking a roll-up.

He had his back to Granger.

The private slid back the manhole cover further, cursing when it grated against the road surface, but the driver did not hear the sound. He continued puffing away at his cigarette.

Granger slid from the hole and rolled once, darting for cover in a nearby shop doorway. He looked up and spotted a street sign. There was a white arrow and one word on it:

PICCADILLY

Granger smiled crookedly, tasting something bitter which rolled from a large blister on his top lip.

He hefted the bayonet before him for a moment, then pulled the automatic rifle from his shoulder, clipping the blade to the end of the barrel. He checked the firing mechanism on the FN, ensuring that its brief spell beneath the water hadn't hampered it in any way. He ejected a shell, pleased to see that the action was as smooth as he'd hoped. He slipped the safety catch to 'OFF'.

The driver of the army truck continued smoking, oblivious to the movement behind him.

Granger guessed that there were some fifteen yards between himself and the unsuspecting driver.

Lowering the rifle, he moved forward, his eyes never leaving the driver's unprotected back.

A twisted smile spread across his ravaged face.

Thirty-five

'We've lost Number Two Unit as well, sir,' the radio operator told Maconnell, his face colouring as if he were personally to blame.

The captain slammed his fist down hard on the running board of the truck and sucked in a despairing breath.

'What now?' he said, angrily.

'Throw the switches,' Finch urged him. 'Activate the generators. If the slugs are down there it doesn't matter exactly how close they are, the electricity should kill them, anyway.'

'There are still men down there, sir,' the radio operator said.

Maconnell ignored him and turned to look at Finch.

'Give the order,' the doctor said. 'Now.'

'There's enough power here to wipe out millions of the fucking things,' Grogan added, almost excitedly.

For all he knew there *were* millions.

'Give the order,' Finch urged again, moving closer to the captain.

'But the men down there...' the radio operator protested once more.

'They're better off dead,' Maconnell whispered.

'*Then do it*,' Finch almost shouted, feeling as if he should shake the officer.

'Standby to activate the generators,' the captain roared, his powerful voice heard by everyone gathered around the now deathly-silent hub of London, Piccadilly Circus. The civilian engineers in charge of the generators waited for the final order, their machines humming like millions of angry bees. The air itself seemed to crackle with the energy waiting to be unleashed. Lisa moved closer to Finch, sensing that the time had come.

The six KVA 1000's rumbled ominously and Finch half expected to see a glow surrounding the big trucks which held them. He tried to swallow but he found that his mouth was too dry.

Grogan dropped his cigarette end and stamped on it, glancing first at Maconnell, then at the network of cables which snaked across the Circus to be swallowed up by the manhole.

Captain Maconnell exhaled almost painfully, praying that this last desperate gambit would work. He raised one arm as a signal.

'Ready,' he roared.

At that instant they all heard the screams.

For a moment no one was sure where they were coming from. Then all eyes turned towards the manhole.

The screams of agony grew louder, and for brief seconds that seemed interminable, everything and everyone froze.

Corporal Simon Johnson dragged himself from the hole and staggered a few yards, arms outstretched like a sleep-walker.

Slugs, dozens of them, clung to Johnson's face and body, eating into him as he walked.

Somehow he stayed upright on legs which had been almost eaten away by the ravenous black creatures. Blood splattered the concrete around him as he stumbled onward, trying to tug the monstrosities from his ravaged body. He had hold of one which had eaten through his left eye and, as the horrified men watched, he pulled it from the riven cavity, tugging the swollen, slimy form inch by inch from the socket as if he were drawing some huge splinter from his skin. The slug was coated with blood and vitreous liquid and it filled the empty orifice almost completely. Still screaming, despite the fact that two of the slugs were inside his mouth feasting on his tongue, Johnson tottered towards the nearest group of men,

209

his shaking hand finally pulling the other beast free from the hole in his skull. As he dropped it, he stepped on the fat shape and it burst in a shower of dark fluid.

Maconnell stepped forward, pulled the Browning from its holster and aimed. He fired once, the heavy-grain bullet taking the top of Johnson's head off. He went down in a heap, the slugs still slithering over him, some seething into the open cavity of his skull, anxious to reach the greyish-red brain now exposed by the ferocity of the bullet's exit.

Maconnell fired again, then turned away in disgust.

'Throw the switches,' he bellowed.

Finch held tightly to Lisa as the generators were activated and the first surge of power hurtled along the cables and into the sewers. There was a loud crackling which grew in pitch until it seemed to fill the air. The doctor felt his hair stand on end as electricity hissed and spluttered around him. The trucks which held the generators seemed to vibrate as the incredible power was unleashed. Over 30,000 volts was produced and more than one of the machines became hot as the power level was sustained.

In the sewers the cables danced madly in the water like the limbs of some huge over-active octopus. Slugs close by were destroyed instantly, their bodies swelling and exploding. The current whipped through the tunnels, seeking each one of them out. Their thick bodies stiffened, then collapsed, spilling reeking fluids and slime into the already rancid water.

The air inside the tunnels glowed with a dull blue light and the water itself bubbled like a geyser as it heated up. Several pockets of methane gas, ignited by the sparks, burst into flames and those watching saw tongues of fire licking briefly from the manhole. It was followed by a great brownish-white cloud of steam which covered the whole of Piccadilly Circus in an impenetrable fog. The smell of ozone was so powerful it made Finch and some of the others cough.

And still the generators roared, the cables whiplashing as the power continued to surge through them.

For a full ten minutes the electrical barrage was sustained. Then, moving from truck to truck, Maconnell gave the order for them to be shut down. Gradually, silence descended again, except for the occasional sound of coughing.

The noxious cloud of steam gradually dissipated and, once again, those in the concrete arena found themselves at the mercy of the sun.

Two soldiers near the corpse of Johnson moved forward, crushing the slugs on or near his body with their heavy boots.

'Now we wait,' the captain said, his voice low. 'Another thirty minutes and *I'll* take some men down to check the tunnels.'

'What if it hasn't worked?' asked Grogan, lighting another cigarette.

His question hung unanswered in the air, like the last vestiges of the steam.

'I just hope the other men were dead before the slugs reached them,' Maconnell said wearily. He slid the Browning back into its holster and leant on the bonnet of his Landrover.

Finch looked at his watch.

It was exactly one o'clock. In the distance, they heard the familiar chime of Big Ben, normally inaudible for anyone in Piccadilly Circus at that time of the day, but in the unusual silence the sound carried. The single strike was sounded, then died on the warm breeze which had sprung up. A wind of change, thought Finch, wondering why the thought seemed so amusing. He held Lisa close to him.

The oppressive silence was suddenly broken by the roar of a lorry engine.

Thirty-six

Taking the truck had been so easy, thought Chas Granger as

211

he stomped down on the accelerator.

The driver hadn't even heard him as he'd approached stealthily from behind. Only when the rifle had been pressed to the back of his head had he reacted, and by then, of course, it was too late. The close-range blast had ripped away most of the back and top of his skull, spraying blood, bone and fragments of brain up the side of the truck's cab. Granger had taken the keys from the dead man and started the huge vehicle up. Now, hunched over the wheel, he was travelling down Regent Street with the needle on the speedo touching seventy.

Around the next corner, he thought. Yes, sure enough, there was the first of the big Scania lorries. He could see troops scurrying around it, some even taking up firing positions, but he merely aimed the army truck at the rear of the first lorry and ducked down.

The impact when it came, was horrendous but the truck ploughed on, ripping most of the back half of the Scania away in an explosion of twisted metal. Men unwary enough to be caught in his path were flattened by the juggernaught, which roared on into the heart of Piccadilly Circus, bowling men over like skittles, crushing some of them beneath its huge wheels. Granger heard their screams and felt the almost imperceptible bumps as they were crushed to pulp beneath the truck, but with no more concern than if they had been insects.

Two shots smacked into the side window, shattering it. Glass sprayed into the cab and one of the bullets nicked his ear, tearing off the lobe. Still he drove on, aiming the lorry at a clutch of smaller vehicles parked in front of him.

Finch had seen the truck smash through the troops and lorries and now he pulled Lisa aside as it bore down on them.

Maconnell drew his Browning again, squeezing off three rounds, the second of which shattered the truck's windscreen. The glass spiderwebbed but Granger knocked a hole in it with one dripping fist, his foot still pressed firmly down on the accelerator.

He crashed into Finch's Chevette, crumpling up the car as if it had been made of paper. The doctor pulled Lisa down as a portion of the front bumper spun through the air like lethal shrapnel.

'The petrol tank,' Grogan yelled, seeing golden fluid spilling from the wreck. The DI ran for cover, seeing Finch and Lisa ahead of him.

It was a stray bullet which ignited the fuel.

There was an ear-splitting roar, followed immediately by a high-pitched scream as the petrol went up. A mushroom cloud of yellow and red flames erupted from the twisted hulk, billowing out thick black smoke. Blazing petrol spread across Piccadilly Circus like a huge fiery amoeba, reaching out to engulf anyone nearby.

The heat wave sent Lisa hurtling through the air despite Finch's efforts to hold onto her. She was blown like a leaf in an autumn wind, crashing into the side of Maconnell's Landrover with a sickening thump. A gash fully five inches wide opened across her forehead and blood spilled down her face. The doctor was catapulted into the air too, but he was more fortunate. He hit the concrete and rolled, coming to a stop with little more than a cut beneath his left eye. He immediately scrambled to his feet and rushed across to Lisa, pulling a handkerchief from his pocket. He folded it up and pressed it to the wound, cradling her head with his other hand.

DI Grogan ran to his own car and leapt behind the wheel, twisting the key hard in the ignition. He jammed the car into gear and stepped on the accelerator. The wheels spun wildly on the concrete for a second, then the Volvo shot forward as if fired from a cannon. In his rear-view mirror he caught sight of Maconnell following in the Landrover. The two vehicles sped after the fleeing truck, which was now roaring up Shaftesbury Avenue.

Just before they reached Cambridge Circus, Grogan managed to draw alongside the large truck. He could see the driver almost slumped over the wheel, his face a patchwork of boils and welts

Granger twisted the wheel of the truck and slammed it into the Volvo.

The car mounted the pavement and sideswiped a building but Grogan remained in control of the vehicle. He heard metal scrape against concrete and saw sparks flying from the side of the car as he struggled to get it back on the road. He thanked God that this part of the city had been evacuated.

As he swerved back onto the road, Maconnell drove past in the Landrover. He too drew alongside the truck, but as it turned to ram him he wrenched his own wheel and guided his vehicle out of danger. There was a scream of tyres as the two of them skidded violently but the Captain recovered first and fired two shots from his Browning.

The first hit the windowframe of the truck's cab, the second ricocheted off the wing with a loud squeal.

Cursing, Granger stuck the barrel of his rifle out of the shattered window and fired a short burst. Bullets spattered the Landrover, one of them blasting off the door handle, another blowing in part of the windscreen. A third caught Maconnell in the shoulder.

He grunted at the thudding impact, almost losing control of the Landrover as white-hot pain enveloped his arm. He felt blood running down the throbbing limb but he managed to hold onto the steering wheel, and as the lorry, the Landrover and the Volvo all roared up Charing Cross Road, they were racing level.

Grogan looked anxiously at the truck, moving away from it every so often in case the crazed driver should decide to ram him, but Granger seemed to ignore the pursuing vehicles for a moment. A wave of pain so intense he almost blacked out had swept through him, and he moaned as he felt the large pustule above his right eye burst, the sticky fluid almost blinding him. He wiped it away with the back of his hand, pressing down ever harder on the truck's accelerator as if trying to push it through the floor of the cab.

Gritting his teeth against his own pain, Maconnell aimed his automatic once more and, this time, he kept firing.

The first shot sped across the bonnet of the truck. The

second hit Granger in the side. He screamed in pain and the truck swerved, pushing the Volvo towards an oncoming bus shelter.

Grogan ducked low as his car hit the obstacle.

There was a deafening explosion of glass as the structure disintegrated, huge shards of crystal flying in all directions, some smashing through the windscreen of the policeman's car. A particularly long piece speared his left forearm, scraping the bone as it passed through, laying muscles open.

Somehow, the DI kept control of the car, aware now that they were nearing the intersection with Oxford Street.

From inside the Landrover, Maconnell squeezed off more shots.

One hit the dashboard of the truck, the next blew away part of the wing mirror.

It was the third shot the captain fired which proved to be lethal.

Moving at a speed in excess of 900 feet per second, the bullet slammed into Granger's face, ripping away most of his bottom jaw before blasting a fist-sized exit hole in the other side of his head. Blood and brain tissue exploded from the wound and coated the inside of the cab. The corpse slumped forward and, too late, Maconnell realized what was going to happen.

The big truck veered to one side, skewing into the Landrover. The bumpers of the two vehicles locked, sealing them together as surely as if they'd been welded.

The officer wrestled with the steering wheel in an effort to extricate the Landrover, but it was useless.

The wide glass doors of the Dominion Theatre loomed ahead.

Behind, Grogan stepped hard on his brakes, the Volvo spinning round in the middle of the road. He looked up in time to see the truck and its reluctant companion smash into the theatre.

They burst through the doors, ploughing on into the foyer, where seconds later they exploded. A roaring tide of fire erupted from within and Grogan ducked as his car was bombarded with lumps of debris. Pieces of glass rained down, shattering on the concrete with a series of loud crashes. The theatre's canopy, which boasted of forthcoming events, collapsed amidst a cloud of smoke and dust and there were fresh explosions as the lights inside went up. Thick, choking fumes belched from the theatre, momentarily blotting out the sun as they formed a massive dark cloud. As Grogan clambered out of his car, gripping his slashed forearm, he could feel the heat from the flames which danced and leapt around the devastated vehicles.

He heard the sound of car engines from behind him and looked round to see another Landrover and two army lorries speeding towards the scene of destruction. He noticed that there was a blue Cortina with them, and as it pulled up he saw Finch and DS Nicholson get out. Both of them looked across at the burning theatre.

'Get on the blower,' Grogan shouted to the DS. 'Get a fire engine here, quick, before the whole fucking street goes up in flames.'

'And an ambulance,' Finch called, seeing the severity of the wound on Grogan's arm.

'Is Miss Foster all right?' the policeman wanted to know.

Finch nodded.

'They've taken her to hospital. It's a bad cut but she'll be fine once they get some stitches in it.' He looked across at the flames which were still leaping from the front of the theatre. 'What about Maconnell?'

'He burned up in that lot, poor bastard.'

Finch sighed. 'Those sewer tunnels will have to be checked,' he said quietly.

Grogan nodded. He leant back against the bonnet of his car, the pain in his arm now raging.

'There could be others infected with the disease,' he said.

'The area was searched. They would have been found.'

'I hope you're right,' the DI said wearily.

Finch looked back at the burning building, at the troops who milled around it, at the glass and other debris strewn across the road.

'The newspapers will have a field day,' he said. 'What's happened in the past week should keep them going for months. Man-eating slugs.' He laughed humourlessly. 'I can't wait to see the headlines.'

He stopped staring at the fire for a moment longer and then closed his eyes, wishing he could blot out not only the sight before him but also the horrors that had gone before.

Finch knew that was not to be. What he'd seen in the last few days was burned indelibly into his memory, never to be erased.

When he opened his eyes again, Grogan had passed out.

'Where's that bloody ambulance?' the doctor yelled at Nicholson, dropping to one knee to tend to the injured DI as best he could.

High above them, like a circlet of burnished gold, the sun continued to shine.

Epilogue

Theresa Finch walked back towards the Renault, juggling an armful of soft-drink cans and food cartons, muttering to herself as hot grease from one of the hamburgers dripped onto her fingers.

A dog, shut inside a yellow Mini, barked at her as she passed. It pressed its face to one of the windows as if trying to escape the stifling confines of the car.

The car park outside the Little Chef was full of vehicles. Everything from motorbikes to eighteen-wheelers, all baking in the brilliant sunshine.

She had left London Sunday morning, after unsuccessfully trying to persuade Richard to join her and Christopher. She had driven north, towards her parents' home in Cumbria near the Scottish border, breaking the long journey with an overnight stop. It was now mid-day Monday and they would be there in an hour or two.

Perhaps her ex-husband had been right about the mysterious disease. Theresa didn't know for sure but she'd decided not to take any chances. Despite what she might think of him, Alan, she knew loved Chris more than anything else in the world.

Chris hadn't complained about the sudden departure. In fact, he'd seemed quite excited about the whole venture. As they'd continued the journey today, though, he'd become quieter and more subdued.

Now, as his mother reached the Renault, she saw him gazing listlessly out of the open side window.

'Here you are, love,' she said, handing him his Coke and

hamburger. Theresa slid into the driver's seat, fidgeting as she felt the hot plastic against her skin. She took a swig from her own can of Diet Pepsi and smiled at her son.

'Have we got far to go, Mum?' he asked her.

'Not far,' she told him, brushing some strands of blond, almost silver, hair from his forehead.

He looked up at her and smiled, a bit wanly.

Theresa noticed how red his face and arms were. The sun must be even stronger than she'd thought.

Chris ate half the hamburger and washed it down with gulps of Coke. When he finished he sat back in his seat, wishing that the pain at the base of his skull would go away.

On his right shoulder, hidden beneath his T-shirt, the first two blisters were beginning to form.